GARDEN OF SALT

GARDEN OF SALT

HUMILITY GARDEN
DELTA CITY

Felicity Savage

CONTENTS

HUMILITY
GARDEN

In the soul of every artist the murderer's ghost lives on. Some make an honoured guest of him; some chain him, and bolt the door, but know that he is not dead.

—Mary Renault

Est ubi gloria nunc Babylonia? Where are the snows of yesteryear? The earth is dancing the dance of Macabré; at times it seems to me that the Danube is crowded with ships loaded with fools going toward a dark place.

—Umberto Eco

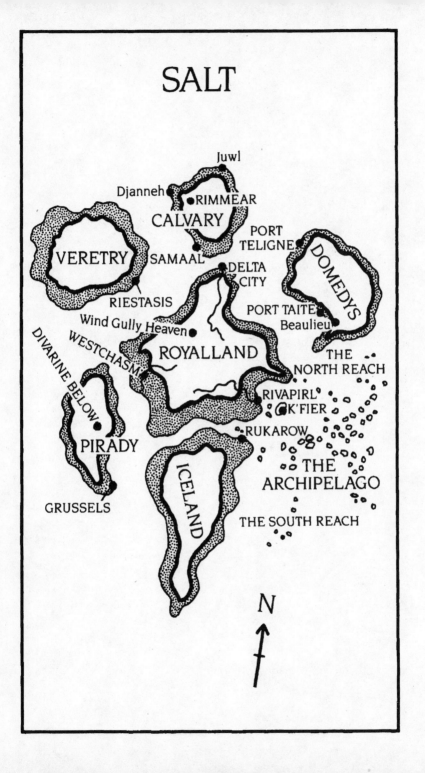

ONE

Beau knelt a little way off, smashing his head methodically into the dry-stone wall. Silky white curls tumbled over his forehead every time it hit. His lavender eyes were squeezed shut against the pain.

"It won't do any good," Humi said. She sat in the shade of a stunted oak with a torn shift in her lap. Though she'd been pretending to stitch as Beau talked and raged out his despair, at sixteen years old she wasn't callous enough to watch him hurt himself any longer. "The scars will only make you look exciting."

She got up and crossed the dell, dragging him away from the wall. The short grass scratched her legs as she pushed his hair back. There was no blood, only bruises, livid on the dark, grainy skin beneath his golden fur. He would have no scars, though she had spoken the truth: they couldn't have detracted from a beauty like his.

"I shan't go." His voice was nearly inaudible. "Humi, I won't. I won't die."

She squeezed him. It was hard not to let slip how desperately she longed that he could stay. "You've got nothing to say about it! How can you even think of disobeying the flamen?"

"I won't disobey. I'll make him take back his choice! He won't want me with a smashed face!" He pulled against her arms, but she held on. In a moment he relented. It was late summer; the sun stood midway down a sky the translucent blue of an aquamarine. The temperature was as high as it ever got in Westshine, this western province of the continent Domesdys. Humi gazed over the top of Beau's head across the low, dry valley, to a slope which had been desolate ever since time began. It was too close to the salt for anything to grow. The grass on that side was copper-colored, sparse.

Above the ridge, over an expanse of other barren ridges, a long, thin glitter sparkled. It was like the sea, but it was not the sea. It was the salt.

"You know what Mum would've given for a chance like this, Beau?" Humi said. "You know what *anyone* would give to've been born like you?"

To her, he was just Beau. Betrothed, childhood companion, worst enemy and best friend. But when he was born, the sight of him lying like a squalling, unearthly little vision next to his mother, Mercy, had driven all other expectations out of the minds of his family. They asked nothing of him beyond his face, which knew no such thing as a bad angle, and his body, which moved like fur-covered steel. They knew they would get their love's worth out of him later on.

Now that investment had been returned. The traveling flamen Godsbrother Sensuality had chosen Beau to be a ghost, a beautiful statue of himself for the gods to enjoy however they wished. In return, the Garden family would get two hundred sheep, sixty shillings' worth of metal tools, a cask of Royalland wine, and festival clothing for the whole family. All of Westshine would envy them.

It was like being told that the gleam at the bottom of your well *is* gold, as you've always hoped. There was as much laughter as tears.

That Beau was not equally overjoyed did not matter.

His ambition was to marry and have children, to be a farmer like his father and uncles. But no one suspected him of such ordinary desires. He was too beautiful. Last night, he, Humi, and their older cousins Brit and Emper had been roughhousing around the fire in the courtyard. Forgetting their grown-up dignity, Brit and Emper had teamed up to take their two smaller cousins down. Giggling hysterically, Humi had caught a sudden glimpse of Beau—his face reddish on one side from the firelight and ghostly pale on the other from the stars—and fallen silent. She did not usually notice his beauty, but right then he seemed to have become a god.

And huddled by the flames with his leman at his feet, Godsbrother Sensuality had lifted his head as if his blind, salt-encrusted eyes could see. He had stared in Beau's direction for a long moment. It was said that flamens *could* "see" the gods to bow to them. Mightn't the same be true for a beauty not quite divine, but almost? Humi had never seen a god, though one was said to have appeared to her great-grandmother. But she was sure they were as beautiful as the statuettes that her father and uncles carved. More beautiful, in their perfection.

The Divine Balance swung. Beau's life dropped down, down, down, out of sight, while his beauty was exalted to the sky.

And Humi went up into the hills to cry by herself. Without Beau she had no future here in the hamlet that her family had farmed for thousands of years. Since the time when Domesdys had been a land of stupid, heretical peasants, since before the Divinarchy came into being, the traditions had been the same. Humi would be an inferior being if she did not marry. And Beau was her only cousin anywhere near her age. Even if the others hadn't had wives or sweethearts, they would not have taken her, for she was not pretty. Her hair and face and body were all the same dirty tawny shade; her grayish-black eyes were the color of blood, her figure only passing. It had even made Beau ill-tempered about betrothing her at first, for he did have a streak of vanity, slender though it might be.

She wanted to leave Beaulieu. But where would she go? The outside world was a colorful blur of tales that the lemans of wandering flamens had told her. In it, the gem that was Delta City gleamed like a diamond. That was where the Divinarch sat and ruled over Salt. The Divinarch. God of gods. In Royalland.

Lesser gods were supposed to frequent the saltside, to appear to lonely girls tending sheep on the hills and give them strange, furless children. But those were only stories. Humi knew what she would really be when Beau was gone—old maid, work-ox, nurse for little nieces and nephews. The hamlets of the saltside strained every muscle to drag their living out of the thin earth. No one was spared. Even Beau was only worked more lightly than the others.

Humi had sunk so deep into her own misgivings that she scarcely noticed when Beau began to smash his face against the wall again. When she did see, she forestalled her impulse to grab him. Maybe that was where she'd gone wrong last time. And indeed, just when she thought she'd have to stop him before he killed himself, the sharp movements in the corner of her eye stopped. She kept her eyes down. A moment passed and another; then a heavy, painful weight came crashing down onto her feet.

"Gods' blood!" she whispered.

He stood over her, breathing shallowly. One cheek was a black mess of blood. He had dropped the stone in her lap. Wincing at the shooting pains in her ankle, she stood up. He wiped his eyes. "It's a lot harder to hurt yourself than you'd think."

"You *are* going to have a scar now, Beauty Garden."

"Made you notice, didn't I!" The leaves mottled the blue sky behind his head. The sun shone through a gap in the foliage onto his blood-smeared golden face. "Humi, you've got to come with me. I can't stand to go on my own."

Her breath jammed in her lungs. In the instant before the world turned the right way up again, her thoughts flew free of Beaulieu, out, out into a universe that was brighter and deeper than she would have dreamed possible. In Royalland, the lemans said, everything was green.

Is it true that in Delta City, the gods walk the streets every day? she wondered.

Will I ever see a god if Beau leaves me here?

What will I see?

It was agonizing to let go of those fantasies.

She had cherished hazy dreams of getting away ever since she was nine, when the outside world intruded upon the hamlet like the fanged mouth of a predator, in the form of a flamen, Godsbrother Transcendence. He had taken Humi's little sister, Thani, away to be his leman. A five-year-old chatterbox with white-blond fur, Thani had skipped away by the Godsbrother's side, leaving Humi looking after her. That was when she had first realized that it was possible to leave. And there was Humi's mother, Faith. When Humi was one year old, Faith had nearly been chosen to be a ghost to decorate the inauguration of a new Heir in Delta City. Humi knew that if her mother had been chosen, she would have gone. And Humi, growing up in someone else's care, would never have forgiven her for it.

"You've probably got chips of wall in that cut, Beau." She probed it with dexterous fingers, wiped it with a fresh oak leaf, avoiding his eyes.

Bruises were puffing his other eye shut, but he seized her shoulders without fumbling. His hands were calloused, and strong from manual labor. She couldn't writhe free. "If I have to die, I want you there with me. Come."

"Beau, you're crazy. What would I do in Delta City?" *After you die*—she could not say it.

"When the flamen told me I was chosen, he said I could take a companion. 'It is an acceptable practice, if the companion is content never to return,' he said. Now listen, why would you want to return? There's nothing for you here! Aunt would never let you farther away than Butterfly Cote to marry, and there's no one there, nor in Garden Vale. D'you want to live under her eye for the rest of your life? Working for Brit's and Emper's and Gent's families?"

His voice was rough. They were unused to expressing their emotions to one another. Her nose stung with imminent tears.

"Come with me."

The sun lay on his perfect lips. She watched them shape the words. Her fantasies fluttered round her head, blinding her. "Come with—"

"Stop! I'll ask! But she won't let me!"

"Yep," Beau said in satisfaction. "She will."

* * *

In the saltside every acre was precious. The low stone walls which marked out cultivated property stopped well short of the beginning of the salt. But sheep and goats wandered on the unclaimed brown slopes, and from time to time, parties from the hamlets ventured into the salt itself, seeking transparent berries and fruits. They wore cloths pulled over their faces. It was dangerous to go out in the salt when there were no clouds, or even at night if the stars shone brightly. The glare of every color in the rainbow at once could blind you. And even if it didn't, sooner or later a salt blizzard would come scudding over the wasteland and whip particles into your eyes, where they would take root and form crystals that grew until they filled your eye sockets.

That was how lemans became flamens, if their masters died while they were still in service, and if they rejected atheism, choosing instead to follow their masters into the flamenhood. They took pilgrimages of many days out into the salt. Returning with the salt crystals growing in their eyes, they were hailed as full-fledged Godsbrothers and Godsisters, possessed of the power to work miracles.

The salt symbolized the divine, the unknowable. The flamens' histories of the time before the Conversation Wars, when the whole world was an unmapped sprawl of barbarian kingdoms, showed that the salt had never lain farther than a few hundred leagues from the coasts of the six continents. Only the rivers of fresh water emerged from it unscathed. And it had never been explored, not even by the Wanderer, the first flamen, who had gone in sighted and come out blinded; so no one knew how large the continents really were. In terms of inhabitable country, Royalland was the largest and Domesdys the smallest, except for the Archipelago, where each island was either all salt or all soil, and people lived on fish.

The gods came from the salt. The myriad, nameless gods of wondrous appearances in the grandparents' tales—and the Delta City Incarnations, the Sage, the Mother, the Striver, the Maiden, the Heir. And the Divinarch. When they tired of living in Delta City, they returned home to Heaven, to have their places taken by others. Heaven lay in the depths of the gleaming, teeming wastelands: the abode of gods, the mecca of souls. But no one alive in 1352 had been there. Only two men had ever gone there and returned. The Wanderer, and a thousand years later a disillusioned leman, Zeniph Antiprophet. Antiprophet was devout and generous-minded, and he was so pious that when his Godsister passed away, at the age of fifty-eight, he ran crazy with grief. He swore he would seek out Heaven and reclaim her from the gods.

He didn't find her on the great barren tableau in the middle of Royalland, though he traveled up the Chrume, the great river of Royalland, and

searched the salt for so many months that his death was deemed certain.
But he did find Heaven. All children, even the most pious, knew the tales
he had spouted when he came back down the Chrume. That the beings all
Salt worshiped were not any more gods than he was. The gods themselves
had told him this, he asserted; that was nonsense, of course. Humi would
never have dreamed of falling for it. But many people did believe him.
Including many young, impressionable lemans.

When Humi's grandparents were young, there had been three flamens in
Nece town. Her great-great-grandparents had been married by a flamen
who lived in the hamlet itself, in a round stone hut that was now the silo.
Now only one flamen lived in Nece, and all the services that the others had
provided were done by wandering flamens. These Godsbrothers and Godsisters had followed the example of those who, over the past hundred and
fifty years, had uprooted themselves in an effort to tend to all the outlying
habitations that had had flamens of their own but no longer did. To wander,
they gave up their political positions of local government. The exchange
was altruistic, but it had a downside. What with this, and the increasing
frequency with which lemans relinquished the flamenhood to become lords
and ladies, the flamenhood had lost its iron grip on much of the world. Now
it had to vie undignifiedly with the atheist nobles for power. And it seemed
set to lose more still, as the Divine Cycle wound to a close and the
Divinarch grew more and more tired. A hundred and ninety was old for a
god.

Humi and Beau sat in the dell for a long time, hugging each other. When
the sun dipped toward the glittering horizon, they got up and walked home.
Though the hamlet was only a couple of miles distant, a long arm of salt lay
in the widest valley they would have to cross, and it was still too bright to
venture across. Holding hands, they followed a goat path through the furze
around its tip. Humi glanced down every now and then at the salt. Iridescent shrubs and flowers glittered red in the last of the light. Chitinous
insect wings flashed.

Beau's face was set and his hand sweated in hers. But her own compo-
sure astonished her.

She could taste the difference in the air as they crested the last ridge.
Less salty. Below, firelight flickered. The fields and outbuildings of the
hamlet were arranged so that they formed a different but equally pleasing
pattern from each hilltop: a flower, a star, a face. For centuries it had been
slowly mutating. Whenever the Garden men planted a crop, they considered its aesthetic impact on the whole valley, often hesitating for days
between, say, flat oats and the slightly darker ringers. They made frequent

trips to the ridges to judge and rejudge. Humi usually felt a tingle of appreciation when she saw it all laid out below her—aesthetics was the one topic on which she could communicate with her father and uncles. But now, in the dark, she and Beau hurried down the hill.

The hexagonal courtyard of the hamlet lay right across the road to the salt. The Garden women flurried to and fro, transferring a meal from the inside pantry onto the trestle tables that stood in an oxshoe around the fire. Six chanticleers hung spitted over the logs. Godsbrother Sensuality was ensconced in the only chair, halfway along the oxshoe. His Calvarese leman Miti sat in his lap, reporting the activity in a hushed flow of words. For a moment after Humi and Beau appeared, his voice was the only sound besides the hiss of the fire; then the women's tongues loosened again. But the tension didn't leave the air.

Beau's face drooped as he noticed it. But he said nothing. "Gent wants to settle with me about my fowls," he whispered, and strode off with his brother. Joy, Humi's youngest aunt, sent her inside with a smack to change her dirty skirt. She had to look pretty for the flamen, though he could not see her. "Inside" was the Gardens' side of the courtyard, as opposed to the oxen's side, the kitchen, or the fowl's. An unbelievably cramped four rooms. While the darkness and head-height rafters were comforting, no one could spend a day on the hillsides and not be stunned by the smell. She breathed shallowly as she fumbled her only dress on. When she came out, tugging her hair free of the neck, she went in search of her mother.

Faith was stirring a giant pot over the fire while Tici, Humi's grandmother, turned the chanticleers. Faith clung jealously to the good looks that had made her a near choice for a ghost. Her hair was like a mass of leaves, her fur chestnut brown, tinged ruby by the flames. Humi took up a position at Faith's side and locked her hands behind her back. *"My manipulative little murderess"—watch and see if she doesn't call me that,* she thought. The scathing nickname was only half fair, for Humi had never tried to manipulate anyone. But the whole world would despise her as a murderess if they knew about the Awful Thing she had done when she was nine years old. She did not want to think about that. Why had she remembered that— "Mother?"

Faith glanced up. The familiar half-annoyed, half-scared look came over her face. "What?"

"Mother, I want to go with Beau." The enormity of the thing hit her again even as she spoke the words. Her grandmother, who was deaf, turned the spit tranquilly. The fat dripped off the chanticleers; light spluttered up the far walls of the courtyard.

"You want to leave?" Faith said at last. "Why?"

It came out in lumps and spurts—the persuasive, logical reasons that she and Beau had dreamed up. Beau had convinced her, but she doubted her ability to convince Faith in turn. She twisted her fingers behind her back. "There's no one else I can marry—" It wasn't working. She knew it wasn't.

Faith drew a deep breath, stirring the stew violently, mechanically. "I bore two daughters, Humi. Neither of them was beautiful, though of course I can't say what Thani might have become. But I bore no daughter who wasn't so much greater than me that she could have lived out her life here without going mad."

"Mother? What do you mean?"

"You can go!" Faith stirred fiercely. "Now get away from me!"

Humi backed away. Eventually she bumped into a bench, where she collapsed and sat with knees drawn up, staring around at her family. Maybe they saw the look on her face, for not one of them enlisted her help for anything until the time came to sit down at table.

Faith took a seat a good way away from Humi, next to her friend Emish, a widow from Garden Vale, half a morning's walk over the hills. She was staying at Beaulieu "to help with the harvest." Humi could not look at them—she was still stunned. But she was aware of how they kept glancing at her over the fire pit.

Godsbrother Sensuality rose to his feet. Miti hopped down to stand beside him, and his voice grew suddenly audible: ". . . fresh-baked bread, chanticleers, and I think it's a vegetable stew. The table is suitably decorated with small statuettes of the Divinarch."

"That will do for now, Miti." The flamen had a deep, unsweet voice. "Brothers and sisters, the gods thank you for your faith and your hospitality toward their servants. And especially tonight, they thank you for your gift to them. The flower of your children, Beauty Garden, to be preserved forever as a ghost."

Humi realized that Beau's mother, Mercy, was crying. She sat next to Humi with tears flooding down her face. Her husband, Perance, held her tightly, but she did not take her streaming eyes off the Godsbrother.

"The councillor to whom Beauty is to be given is an atheist lady," said the flamen. He said it as casually as if he were saying Beau would be given to his spinster aunt. Not that flamens had spinster aunts, Humi thought in a flash of illogic. The Gardens sucked in their breath in horror. An opponent of the flamenhood? It was as bad as if they had been told he would not be a ghost after all.

Beau himself, whose sole consolation, Humi knew, had been that his ghost would gratify a god, looked like a caricature of shock.

"Councillor Belstem Summer—surely even here you have heard of

him?—plans to inaugurate his daughter, Aneisneida, in a seat on the Ellipse. She is replacing Godsister Purity, who died in an accident with her
leman, leaving no successor. There will be great pomp. The ceremony will
be decorated with the finest ghosts Salt can offer. Your son, Beauty, will be
an example of the virtue which we flamens can still find in Salt." Humi
couldn't believe that any of her family dared to raise their voices, but her
uncle Cand spoke, choking on his indignation. "Godsbrother, why do the
gods disgrace my nephew by giving him to one of the nobility? Why do
they smile on the atheists?"

The flamen turned his blind head toward Cand's voice. The crystals in
his eye sockets took on a fanatical gleam. "The wish of the Divinarch is that
Aneisneida be honored like any flamen who becomes a councillor. We do
the gods' will. Now be silent before I forsake your table and your hospitality, Godsman."

Cand bowed his head. The food steamed, growing colder, while no one
dared to move.

At last Godsbrother Sensuality rumbled, "May the gods take pleasure in
the food we eat," and sank into his chair. Thankfully, Cand's wife, Prudence, leaned around him to carve a chanticleer. Humi mentally heaped
the chattering voices on top of her head, waiting for her trembling to stop.

After the feast was cleared away, and the flamen established in the only
"good" room in the courtyard, Faith and Emish volunteered to watch over
the sheep. Admitting that Emish had to earn her keep if she was to stay at
Beaulieu much longer, Humi's father, Reng, let them go. They bobbed
away in the darkness, the dogs leaping around them.

Larger salt animals tended to keep away from the human country, with
one notable exception: the predators. These beasts with their rows of fangs,
their talons, and their innocent, heart-shaped faces, had no matches for
bloodthirstiness in the salt or out of it. And they had developed a taste for
humans' livestock—and whenever possible, humans themselves. "Guarding
the sheep" had two traditional implications. One was that of the most dangerous work on the farm. The other was that of a lovers' rendezvous. In this
case, the latter applied.

Hours after Faith and Emish left, Humi's eyes were still dry. She lay next
to Tici in the backmost curtained-off section of the house, on their scratchy
pallet under a feather quilt too hot for the season. Tici whuffled softly. A
few feet away on another pallet, Joy and her husband, Uth, slept deeply
after having coupled. Six-year-old Merce and their baby, Asure, breathed
more quickly.

Overhead, a predator screamed. Humi sent the gods a quick prayer for any sheep that Faith and Emish might have missed when they gathered the flock into the fold. If once the predators got a whiff of their blood, they wouldn't survive long.

But no predator could smell so delicate a scent as blood through the heavy odor of Beaulieu.

Humi knew it was the last time she would lie wrapped in this thick, stuffy darkness, surrounded by people who cared about her. She made it last for as long as possible by keeping herself awake, seeing how many fingers it took her to weave braids in the frayed edge of the quilt. But the threads were short—she couldn't get it any lower than two fingers, and those on her right hand.

TWO

The next morning, Godsbrother Sensuality worked a miracle. The wandering flamens who visited Beaulieu didn't by any means always repay their hosts with miracles: it was too taxing, not only for the flamens themselves but also for the gods.

Breakfast was cold meat and barley porridge, eaten in the courtyard. Over in the feed that Gent had scattered, the chanticleers, quails, and pigeons which were no longer Beau's responsibility sang their shrill morning music. Beau sat directly across from Humi, looking like a lamb that knows it is mutton. He kept trying to catch her eye. She stared devoutly at the statuette of the Divinarch on the table in front of her. Her body felt chilly in the breeze. The sky was the hue of a chunk of glass shivered inside; the ridges reared bleak and brown against it. Her family finished eating and stood uncomfortably around the courtyard, gazing anywhere but at the Godsbrother, who still champed at his porridge. Miti's dark eyes dared anyone to stare.

Humi mustered her courage. "Godsbrother? My name is Humility." She got the syllables of her hated full name out as quickly as possible. "Godsbrother, has my mother spoken with you about me coming with Beau to Royalland?"

A dead silence fell. It seemed that even the birds of the mountain stopped singing. "Ah, yes," the Godsbrother said, pushing himself back from the table, wiping the fur around his lips. "A young woman loyal in your attachments, who will well be able to survive on your own. Hardworking, determined, imaginative. Observant of Dividay, respectful to your elders, well able to bear children. Useful around the house."

"Humi—" Reng came up behind her and clasped her shoulders possessively. "Daughter, what is this?"

Before she had to answer, a disturbance came from behind the oxhouse.

All eyes turned toward it. Grim-faced, putting the dogs away from stained skirts, Faith and Emish came down the road from the salt.

"There's been a killing." Faith's voice carried thinly across the courtyard. "Right under our noses. Eight—*eight!*—of this year's lambs. The predators know they are tenderest, I swear, and pick them out."

Humi's father dropped his hands from her shoulders as he turned to find out the extent of the damage. She stepped back from the babble of questions, signaling Beau that they should go collect their belongings. Indoors, they wordlessly stuffed clothing into flaxen sacks. Humi listened to the splash of blood being scrubbed off hands in the dirty dishwater outside the door. Emish's soft voice described the massacre.

She looked up at Beau. "Why don't I care? I watched the lambs that're in those predators' bellies being born. Why don't I care?"

He looked as though he hadn't slept a wink—glamorously hollow-eyed, desirably vulnerable. "Dunno."

Prudence's voice rose: ". . . they're in the house. Beau! Humi!"

All the family had formed a circle on the bony earth of the road. When Humi saw Godsbrother Sensuality take the center alone, she knew what was coming. Cand said respectfully, "We're sorry to ask this, Godsbrother. But those dead lambs mean the loss of this year's generation. Of course we'll be getting the—compensation—but we may starve first. We'd been reckoning on the little ewes—"

The Godsbrother cut him off curtly. "I understand." The Gardens bent their heads in attitudes of prayer. Silence fell, as profound as if the world had stopped. Humi had watched miracles before: she didn't expect to see anything beyond the way the crystals in the Godsbrother's eye sockets bulged a little, and the sweat started out on his skull. Minutes passed. Two roosters flew at each other over by the fowl house, and Prudence peeked from behind her fingers, obviously itching to flap her skirts at them.

Finally it was done. As the larger rooster, victorious, preened his blue neckfeathers, a shrill *maa*-ing floated from the high end of the valley.

The circle broke up. Laughing, adults and children craned upward to see. Eight little flecks of white on the bleak hillside, standing out like snowballs in summer. Humi sucked in her breath as she watched them straggle downhill. Miti put his arm around Sensuality—odd to see the child half-supporting the big man—and guided him to the permanently ajar gate. "Come on then, you two!"

Faith said, "Daughter."

The three of them stood before her: her mother, her father, and Emish. There were wet splotches on Faith's dress where she'd scrubbed off the blood, but she had taken time to scrape her hair back neatly. She hugged

Humi tightly, kissing her forehead. Humi swallowed and clutched her, wanting desperately not ever to have to let go. When Reng joined the embrace, she felt that she couldn't have been happier in Heaven. "Oh, Mother, Father, I don't want . . ."

"Yes, you do. My little girl. Oh, but I love you so much!" Faith whispered. Humi couldn't name the catch in her voice—was it grief, or relief?

Reng pulled her aside. "I shall settle with your mother when you're gone. She acted out of her place. You're the only child I have left—and that means a lot to a man—and you were always a good judge of the beauty of the crops."

Those words helped Humi stay dry-eyed as her cousins and aunts and uncles and in-laws came up and embraced her. Little Asure was the only one who threatened her self-control, chuckling at Humi's solemnity. Beau, too, was running the gauntlet.

"Beauty, you couldn't have done us more honor if you'd started your own hamlet."

"You've made your aunt Faith happier than anyone else in the world could have." (That, viciously, from Reng.)

"You'll come back if you make your fortune, Humi, won't you?" said a small voice.

Humi was walking backward along the road, Beau at her side. "Goodbye!" she called, waving her arms above her head.

"Good-bye," Beau muttered. He whirled around and tramped beside her, head down. The breeze set wisps of hair dancing around Humi's face and lifted the fur on her forearms. The flamen and Miti walked so fast that she had to skip backward to keep up with them. They were talking together as if they witnessed the sundering of families every day. Her family was no more than a collage on the long, low stone wall, spots of all shades of brown, the reverse of the eight miracle-born lambs on the hill above them.

They slept on the road. Miti carried a light knapsack which held all of his and the flamen's earthly possessions; Beau and Humi's flaxen sacks seemed heavier each morning. Five hamlets later, they reached Nece town. Humi and Beau had come a-fairing here every spring and autumn ever since they could remember. Summer Fair was only three sixdays off now, and the quiet little backwater was beginning to gear itself up. Before Humi was born, not only ale but also wine had flowed at festivals, and the craftsmen's doorways had fluttered with bunting. But now the merriment had a somber edge to it. The Divine Cycle was ending. Black ribbons decorated the biceps of the children playing in the road, and the sleeves of the goodwives sweeping their steps. Black Divine Seals (little icons of the Throne) were tarred onto doors and windows. It was symbolic grief, but tinged with very real apprehension: traditionally, with the end of the Divine Cycle came upheavals. Nece citizens bobbed their heads to Sensuality and stared openly at Humi and Beau.

They departed along a country road the same afternoon. Humi and Beau craned their necks to see into the backyards of tanner, blacksmith, sculptor, cobbler, woodworker. Dust and steam puffed out from holelike doorways in the hill; on the bare ground outside, oxen switched their tails and women gossiped. They marched through the last of the mountains and into the flatcountry.

All over, the harvest was being brought in. Nevertheless, the travelers always found accommodation, for the people here were as pious as saltsiders. They tended their sheep, oxen, goats, chanticleers, bantams, pullets, harvests, and children with religious stoicism. The little ones stared at Beau; the adults said that proximity to him was remuneration enough for everyone's board. When Humi told them that they were betrothed, they looked at her with barely hidden jealousy.

They were only three months on the road.

At the beginning of winter, they neared Port Taite. The little country road merged with a highway which led from Port Taite to Port Teligne, Domesdys' capital, in the north. They walked among carts and wains along the broad, dusty road raised above fields larger than any Humi had ever seen, toward the break in the cliffs and the incredible vista of black, sparkling sea.

The city lay below.

"This is *nothing*," said Miti in one of the rare moments when he condescended to speak to Humi and Beau. "Why, the population's no more than two thousand. You should see Port Teligne, or even better, Samaal." Miti had been born in Calvary, the blazing northern continent where everyone worked the metal mines the way Domesdians worked their fields. No doubt his early memories glamorized Samaal, Humi thought dismissively. How could there ever be more houses and people gathered together than there were here? "Or you should see Delta City."

The Port Taiteans were Domesdians, with fur and hair of a thousand shades of brown, yet they weren't country folk, and they didn't gape at Beau with unashamed awe as the hamleters had done. As Miti led them into the heart of town, Beau stared up, down, and around curiously. His apparent liveliness lifted a weight from Humi's shoulders. At least a dozen times on the journey, she'd caught him trying to wreck his beauty. Once she had come on him kneeling facedown in an oxtrough, silky white curls floating.

She knew she hadn't been paying enough attention to him. She should have been with him all the time. Instead she had been talking to the hamlet folk, finding out what they thought, what they considered beautiful.

Wonders such as coffee bars, couturiers' shops, an Icelandic bathhouse, and a curiosity shop slipped past. The black ribbons of mourning hung everywhere, twisting in a little breeze. Port Taite was a pious city. It was one of those iridescent early-winter days, disconcertingly cold. The sun shone brightly on ragged clothes and unwashed heads, on gaudy pictorial signs and the frilly coats of the well-to-do atheists, on the window boxes overflowing with winter-blooming flowers.

"Hey, *saltside kids!* Get out of the *street!*" Someone grabbed both of them by their jackets and shoved them back against a shopfront, just before a huge-wheeled carriage thundered through the spot where they'd been standing. "Sorry, Beauty!" the man said, abashed, as he saw Beau. "Couldn't see your face in the sun. Sorry."

"That's all right." Beau was dazed. Dust rose between them and the oxcarts which still trundled placidly along the street. "What was that?"

"One of the young atheists. Watch, 'n'—" Another carriage hurled itself along the narrow street. This time Humi noticed the animals racing before it, attached not by a yoke but by reins that glowed red against their dark fur: draydogs, sleek hounds the size of cattle. "That's the fellow he was racing."

"Wait," said Beau, looking around in consternation. "Godsbrother Sensuality's gone."

Humi thought it a happy development. "We can find him later. Or he'll find us. He won't want to lose *you.*"

Beau turned back to their rescuer. "Godsman . . . did you see where that flamen and leman went, the ones that we were with? A heavy man with light brown fur, a Calvarese boy about so high . . ."

"Godsbrother Sensuality!" The man slapped himself on the breast. "Don't tell me you are the ghost! Why, the town's abuzz with rumors about your coming. And you are everything they say." He made a tiny bow.

"I—I—" Beau gasped.

Humi pulled his ear down. "He's not telling the truth. If everyone knew about you, you would've been spotted before now."

"The flamen is taking a room on Finilar Street. That is common knowledge. I can lead you there." The man started off along the crowded concourse. Beau beckoned Humi to follow. Annoyed, she caught up to him and whispered, "I don't trust—"

"Nonsense! He knows who Sensuality is!"

But as they hurried along, the man eyed their spindlespun clothing speculatively. "Not much farther now . . . The Silver Boat is the name of the inn Sensuality frequents. The owner puts him up for free." He led them into narrower and narrower streets, where garbage moldered outside closed back doors. Humi walked carefully, wishing she had more than one set of eyes. Two cats flurrying from a window nearly stopped her heart.

Suddenly the man halted. "Here we are!"

"The back entrance?" Humi said sarcastically as she placed herself in front of Beau. The man wheeled around and plunged toward her. The knife in his fist glinted in the sun which came down the alley.

The world slowed down, like a scene viewed through glass. Humi whirled out of the way. Beau rolled away, grunting in astonishment. Eyes darting, grinning confidently, the man turned on her. As she wrenched aside, he thrust past her and lost his balance. Catching his arm, she was on top of him in the grit, her knee crushing his throat. Broken syllables of pleading came from him; but all she knew was a terrifying desire for justice, or was it gratification?

Blood trickled and pooled. Blood bubbled like red spit out of the man's throat, soaking his collar.

The knife fell with a dull clatter. Humi stared in horror. Beau yanked her back, clamping his hand over her eyes. He muttered rhythmically as he dragged her away down the row of back doors, "You didn't mean to. He would have killed us. He thought we were helpless. He thought we had money. You didn't mean to—" over and over, till Humi shoved him away from her. They pelted on until they were exhausted. In the relative safety of a crowded thoroughfare, they examined each other for traces of the crime.

Luckily, not a drop of blood had stained their clothes or their fur, apart from Humi's hands. Those were soon cleansed with spit and polish. She glanced around. Her whole body was trembling. "It was just here we lost the Godsbrother."

Beau gazed at Humi for a long moment, and then crushed her to his chest, right there in the flow of people. His heart beat fast within his chest. "Humi, I have to thank you. That fellow would have killed me, too. Think how awful it would be to die on a pickpocket's knife when I am destined to die as a ghost in Delta City!"

"Don't speak of it! Don't say it, don't say it, don't say it—and for Heaven's sake don't *thank* me—"

By taking one life she had saved two. Of course it was worth it.

But once you start justifying taking human life, where do you stop?

A cold breeze chilled her neck.

I've killed. Again.

She was nine; her grandfather, Old Cand, was fifty-five; he knew he was dying. She couldn't see why the rest of her family wouldn't admit it. They treated death as something to tiptoe round and euphemize, while Humi sat long hours with Cand and discussed what would happen to his body when he died, and how his soul would travel from Beaulieu to Heaven-in-the-salt. Eventually the old man brought their conversation round to the topic of poisons.

She could still smell the bitter pungency of the cup she had held to his lips. He had gulped thirstily, eyes starting out of his fur. As Humi slipped away, stifling the panicky weeping which came from knowing—too late—that she had done an Awful Thing, Faith had spotted her. But by the time Faith found Cand, slumped half out of his bed, it was too late. And after that nothing was the same between mother and daughter. Now she had done it again—

A long shadow fell across their embrace. Beau pulled away. It was Godsbrother Sensuality.

"So my vagrants have found their way back. How was your outing?"

Another figure stood against the lead-paned window of the inn. As Beau stumbled through incoherent excuses, the figure swung, and Humi saw a tall, knife-faced woman in a flamen's robe. A little boy hovered by her side; sunlight glowed deep in the crystals jutting over her cheeks.

Godsbrother Sensuality said with an air of satisfaction, "This is Godsister Decisiveness. She will take charge of you from now on, Beauty."

Regardless of how they'd slept on the road, it would have been out of the question for Beau and Humi to share a bed tonight, though she'd badly wanted Beau beside her to comfort her. Instead she had Godsister Decisiveness. Before they blew out the candle, Humi saw that the flamen was flat-chested as a man, with two anomalous little flaps of fur. Thankfully, the mattress was hard enough that they didn't roll together when they lay down.

When Decisiveness's harsh breath had evened out, Humi lay awake on her back listening to the rowdiness downstairs. The wine served in an inn, Miti had informed her, was far more alcoholic than ale, and the pipes had other things in them besides tobacco.

Look what the city has done to me, she thought, *in a single afternoon.*

In the middle of the night, a nightmare of blood brought her bolt upright in bed, teeth chattering. A thin line of yellow under the door focused the blackness, turning the world the right way up. The sleepy, nightgowned silhouette of the flamen rose in front of it. Scarcely knowing where she was, Humi gave herself up to the cool hands pushing her back to the pillow. Decisiveness's fingers drew away the tormenting sights that replayed endlessly in her mind. For the rest of the night she slept dreamlessly.

* * *

They ate breakfast in the inn's dayroom, where sunlight shone dustily through leaded panes and the food tasted of silver; then they went down to the harbor. On the way, Humi noticed that Decisiveness had gained Sensuality's subtle awareness of Beau's whereabouts. The docks consisted of two quays jutting out into the bay. Since it was the windy season, dozens of ships clustered along and between them, so many abreast that in places you could have hopscotched from one quay to the other. Fishing clips rubbed shoulders with shorebound careaks and intercontinental clippers that were so top-heavy with their masts it was a wonder they didn't topple over onto the smaller vessels. Embossed luggage and crates of imported goods lay in heaps outside the holds of these tall ships. The men and women tripping down the gangplanks sported ruffles and sequins that made Humi's mouth water.

Sensuality guided his charges around the fishermen, who were unloading squirming, sharp-fanged netfuls of pickering, to a clipper whose figurehead was a mass of iron petals.

"The *Regal Flower*. Passage for four is booked. She sails with the tide."

Several fishermen, their fur stiff with salt, were bawling at men unloading baggage from the *Flower*. "Wharf's not wide enough for all of us!" Humi expected the lemans to use their unchildlike authority and reach up to touch the men, politely requesting that they lower their voices for the flamens' comfort, but Miti and little Cor merely glanced at each other and shuffled closer to the water. The wavelets knocking the sides of the ship were green-black. There was something sharp and wild about *this* salt. Overhead, terns wailed and dived.

"I shall regret you, Beauty," said Sensuality. "But when you are a ghost, I shall come visit you in the lady Aneisneida's apartments. And I shall see you with my own eyes in Heaven."

Miti's lucid dark eyes rested on Humi. Suddenly, she found herself hating the thought of his pilgrimage into the salt. If Sensuality lived till Miti was an adult, the flamen would choose a new child leman, sending Miti out into the world to make a life for himself; but if he died before the boy grew up, Miti would have the choice of flamenhood or atheism. To be a Godsbrother or a lord?

She knew which he would choose. His piety was pure and unquestioning.

"Good-bye," he said sweetly. If he knew what she'd been thinking, he didn't show it. Exemplifying the paradox of leman and child in one body, he hissed, "You'll never visit as many cities as *I* have, Humi! But just wait till you see Delta City! Then you'll know Port Taite is nothing more than a heap of rotting wood!—Come on, Godsbrother." They wound away down the pier between the thrashing silver mounds of fish.

Humi had expected nothing from the Godsbrother, but he might have been sorrier than *that* to leave Beau. After all, Beau was probably the greatest beauty he would ever come in contact with. Then she saw a thin black line of blood on Beau's cheek. And she understood. The flamen had *embraced* him—as Humi had never known a flamen to do—and one of the salt crystals had laid his cheek open.

The planks of the *Regal Flower*'s deck were interwoven like threads in a piece of fabric. They gave under Humi's feet, sending her bouncing into the air with each step. This was a Domesdian ship, all made of wood, unlike the metal-hulled and -masted Calvarese clippers berthed alongside. A bristle-faced sailor directed them belowdecks. "Here and here. At yer service, Godsister."

Decisiveness listened to Cor describe the tiny, hatchlike doors. "Only two rooms for us. Well, the ship must be crowded with Domesdian nobility. There are not usually so many lords and ladies mincing around Port Taite's wharves as Cor has described today, I assure you. We shall repeat last night's sleeping arrangements."

Humi shot a worried glance at Beau's face. Could Cor stop Beau from trying to kill himself? Would the child recognize the signs of his suicidal state of mind in time? "Very well, Godsister."

The harbor was crowded and maneuvering difficult. The crew of the *Regal Flower* wouldn't let them upstairs again till the square-rigger had passed the cliffs at the bay's mouth. But then Humi and Beau hurried up to the aft rail.

Domesdys' coast had already spread out into one long vista of cliffs, topped with tufts of winter color. Humi stood beside him in silence, just watching, as the land sank lower and lower until even the black hollow of Taite bay was lost under the glaring winter sky.

THREE

On the fifth day out, Humi lay high in the ropes, jolted by the movement of the mainmast. It was a single whippy tree trunk, and as the top lashed to and fro, shudders traveled down it, detouring through her body. A feeling of guilty freedom made her reluctant to climb down. The winter wind blew powerfully; the *Regal Flower* sheared through the foam-topped waves so fast that Humi felt the spray up in her perch.

Now that nothing was visible in any direction but a horizon where the black brine ended so sharply that it might have been cut, her own insignificance thrilled her. The moving, roaring cocoon of sails afforded her regularly spaced glimpses of that horizon. Made of common spindlespun, the sails were literally miracles: they thrummed in the wind, and Humi could see the fabric distending at every stress point. They wouldn't have lasted twenty minutes had it not been for the words which a flamen had put on them when they were made, protecting them against all storms.

She didn't hear the commotion below until one of the sailors monkeyed up the ropes to fetch her. "Young Godsie!" she read on his lips. "There's an emergency!" The look on his face told her what it was. She followed him down the ladder. The ringing in her ears did not allow her to hear his explanation, but she guessed what had happened. She felt sick.

Beau had tried to hang himself from his cabin ceiling. This was his first attempt since they had been on board, and his most serious. Cor had come on him and, being a leman, had not screamed or run but had cut the rope before any severe damage was done. Yet Beau would not or could not speak. Humi slipped down the passenger ladder and held on to it, swaying with the *Regal Flower*, rubbing the brightness out of her eyes. Finally she could see. "We've taken young Beauty in Lady Hempwaite's chamber," said the sailor worriedly. "Girl, hurry, do, he's been asking for you—"

Swallowing bile, Humi followed him to the last chamber on the corridor.

Lady Hempwaite, a Royallandic woman, went by the invented name of Zerenella: she was of that breed of nobility rich from skimming the profits off their provinces, taxes which the flamens they had replaced would never have deigned to collect. The cabin was equipped with a double bed. Tall, pale-green-furred, Lady Hempwaite stood at its foot, thin hands covering her mouth.

Beau lay in a fetal position, face toward the wall. Humi lifted the curls away from his neck, fingers trembling with care, and the awful necklace of bruises leaped out from beneath his fur at her. Each bead spread into the next, a swirl of damson and vomit. "Beau!" Her voice wobbled in and out of a whisper. "Cousin, betrothed . . . ! Why did you do this to yourself? I don't understand! Don't you care for me any longer? How could you deprive not just me, but our whole family, of your honor?"

He shifted, and the violet pools looked up at her, but they were so bloodshot she could make out no expression. "They've already got the compensation."

"Oh, Beau." She lay down next to him on the feather mattress. He strained to tighten an arm around her.

"I'm sorry." The words were slurred as if he hadn't used his voice for a sixday. "I didn't stop . . . to think . . . about *you!* Love you . . . just *forgot—*"

It was *her* fault. She'd known she wasn't spending as much time as she could with him, and since they had been on the *Regal Flower* she'd been even less attentive. "It's my fault, my fault!" she whispered. Remorse racked her. He managed to turn his face toward her. Though the smile he gave her was more than half a grimace of pain, it was so loving that Humi felt dirty. They hugged, sobbing against each other's shoulders. "You want to cheat the gods out of their due," she gasped. "You didn't care that they've already paid for you."

"Yes. It was selfish of me."

"But natural," she whispered. "So natural."

He took a deep breath, wincing. "I ought to resign myself. Even if I didn't have to be a ghost . . . no one would ever have loved me for anything except my face."

"Don't think that," she whispered, nearly crying. "*I* love you just for being Beau! And I'd marry you—and—and have your children. No flamen in the world could take that away from us. If we wanted to keep it."

There was a long, long pause. Waves crushed against the hull. "You mean, if we were to . . ."

"Escape." She said it very quietly, into his hair.

He shuddered. "It's . . . impossible."

"No! Once we get to Delta City, we could just slip away—we could have done it in Port Taite." She was scandalized at her own blasphemy. "We could live together. We could get married. Raise crops. Children."

"Gods, Humi, I—"

Zerenella Hempwaite, in front of the porthole, turned sharply on her heel. It hit Humi that her taut posture had expressed not fear for Beau, but avid interest, like someone standing outside a cage.

"Pious little saltrats," she said in her sweet singsong accent, and went to the door. "Even if he *is* to be a ghost, and sacred and all that, someone please see they get off the bed before they tear the coverlet."

She felt herself pulled up, out of Beau's arms. Her head whirled. In the salt-caked daylight from the porthole she could make out no features, but the steely grip on her arm belonged to one person—and it wasn't Lady Hempwaite's maid Wenina; it was Godsister Decisiveness. The tip of the flamen's hood bumped the cabin ceiling. She smelt faintly not of the ship but of solitary meditation, a quiet perfume like dried lavender.

"Humility."

Her voice was gentler than Humi had ever heard it.

"Godsister?"

"I must speak with young Beauty. This is not the first such incident, is it?" She clicked her tongue. "Well, I am not Godsbrother Sensuality, all heavy-handed bullishness, to let a thing like this go by the wayside in case I make it worse."

Beau whispered through his swollen throat, "Godsister?" The cracked wind instrument of his voice gave out. He raised himself painfully on one elbow.

The Godsister set Humi on her feet, straightening her as if she were a doll. But she wasn't paying attention to her anymore. Her voice resonated in the small cabin. "Beauty, I see it is urgent that I speak with you."

And Humi found herself outside the door, leaning her forehead against it, tracing the ornamentation.

She never knew what the flamen said to Beau. But one thing was certain: from that terrible gale-driven afternoon on, nothing was the same between them.

The voyage lasted three more sixdays. Every night as heartbreak pressed in on her, she lay stiffly beside Decisiveness, fists clenched. The Godsister gave sermons every Dividay: Humi forced herself to attend them, sitting among the sailors on deck to hear tales of meshed history and religion like the tale of Waywardness Flamensdaughter, who had defied her mother, a flamen councillor in Delta City, and come to a bad end. Humi was sure Decisiveness was aiming the tale at her.

After the first such sermon, she screwed herself up to speak to Beau. "You've hardly said a word to me in the past sixday. I don't understand."

He closed his eyes, tipping his face up to the blue sky as if for inspiration. "Humi, I have to be a ghost. I know it. That's what I was born for. I did . . . those things . . . because I couldn't face my destiny. But I have to. This is what Godsister Decisiveness told me: the only way people can show their appreciation of beauty like mine is to preserve it. And just think what a waste it would be . . ." He laughed wonderingly. "If I got old!"

"What has she done to you?"

He looked at her, puzzled.

Scarcely daring, Humi put out her hand to touch his face. The rough-silk sheen was the same as always. How could she have ever grown used to living with the most beautiful youth in the world? How could she ever have dreamed of having children by him?

"Please don't ask me to escape with you again," Beau said softly. She started. "I'm having a hard enough time coping with it as it is. I keep forgetting, and then wanting to deprive them of the satisfaction of having me, when I remember that one way or another I have to die."

Humi let out a harsh sob and pushed her face into his chest. He ran his hands inside her blouse collar, stroking the short fine fur on her shoulders. "I don't understand!" she muttered over and over. "I don't understand!"

He did not answer. She fancied that he had receded so far from her, inside himself, that he could not hear.

She spent a lot of time after that clinging in the tern's nest, losing herself in the giddy, rolling vista that made her feel so small. Finally the sailors allowed her to take watches alone.

It was from the height, perched above the screaming sails, that she first saw Royalland.

FOUR

Thirteen and a half centuries before, a man whose real name was soon forgotten became the first to sail the Chrume to its source. He was the Wanderer. Some said that the first miracle ever was the fact that his fragile bark completed the journey. But whether by chance, or that the gods had a hand in it, he was alive and in possession of his faculties when he reached the top of the river, having survived rapids, salt desert, and the predators who worried the Chrume like a strip of wet ribbon. He was a tenacious man. When the river vanished underground, he started up the salt mountains. But soon the slopes leveled off into a tableland, utterly barren, where not even an insect moved. The voices of the wind sang in the formations sweetly enough to make him weep for the home he would never see again. It blew salt particles into his eyes. Eventually he collapsed from exposure and starvation. It was then that the gods appeared to him, and while he slept, they bore him to Heaven.

More than a year later, he arrived back in Delta City, blinded by the salt wind but recompensed by the gods with the power to perform miracles. In the years to come, the salt crystals would not discriminate between rich and poor, half-wit and genius; they would bestow the miracle power on every leman with the dedication to seek it. But, perhaps because he was the first, the Wanderer was phenomenally strong. After his miracles failed to convince his people of the gods' existence, he persuaded a party of his friends to come to the salt to see Heaven for themselves—men and their wives and their children. They roamed long and fruitlessly, deep into the barrens. More than once they came close to mutiny. At last the gods took pity on the Wanderer's pleas, giving the party permission to enter Heaven—but only if the adults let themselves be blinded.

When they returned to their homes, the glowing tales of the children who had been their guides, combined with the power the adults now wielded, gave birth to the flamenhood. This is how women, who had been as badly off as slaves in the Wanderer's village-city on the Chrume delta, gained access to the all-powerful flamenhood. Men and women together, they spread across the world. Before the Wanderer died, he heard that an army of militant lemans had marched to the edges of the world: to the verdant forests of Veretry, to the earth-sprinkled rocks of Domesdys, to the snows of Iceland, to Calvary, whose north coast burns on the equator. The Conversion Wars were a crusade against the worship of straw dolls and underground fires, but also against ignorance and barbarism. But they should not have been called wars. Rarely did the army have to kill anyone in order to make clear the advantages of the flamenhood's arbitration. Soon the last barbarian had sworn piety, and the world became the Divinarchy. The Divinarch himself, with his Divine Guard and his five Incarnations, came to dwell in human lands.

He paved the way for fifteen successors. Over the centuries, more than one hundred and thirty gods personified the Incarnations. The Guard changed so many times that not even the flamens, each of whom memorized an entire history of religious tales as soon as his or her eyesight went, could offer an exact count. The flamens were conscientious shepherds; their miracles could right anything they believed to be a wrong. Until 1208, not one generation of their human flock veered off the path that their parents had trodden. How much the gods themselves had to do with this "dark age," no one knew. But there is a limit to the time for which any entities can hold a world frozen, once they have graced it with even such an impenetrable nugget of knowledge as the miracle power. Stability breeds influences to wreck itself from within.

And all during the centuries of the Divinarchy, there were worse contrasts between the provinces of Salt than ought to have existed. The flamens would have had it that no man live better than his neighbors, even his neighbors on the other side of the world. That was a good and fair system. But they couldn't enforce it to the letter—and that margin of human error was the source of its failure. When Zeniph Antiprophet made his revolutionary declaration that the gods were not gods at all, the gap between classes widened drastically. He showed *some* Saltish—the ex-lemans—the skills which he said he had learned from the gods. Most revolutionary was the method of inscribing speech on paper. His disciples snatched at this invention he called literacy and used it to write proclamations that they hung up in city streets where no one could read them, announcing that their "coins"—another idea Antiprophet claimed to have got from the gods—would be the new medium of transactions, that they carried more power than anything the flamens could invoke.

And it was true, as the flamenhood's numbers dwindled, so did their abilities. It was as if they drew on some pool of energy which was gradually being drained.

Also shrinking were the reserves of able, trustworthy children whose parents would let them take a leman's vows. Even these children, when their flamens died, were often enticed away by the promises of nobility—despite all they'd sworn, despite their friends' pleas. The carefree life of the city peer who let his bodyman or woman do all the work for him; the power held by the atheist who settled down to head a province; the responsibility-free roamings of an itinerant lord—all were intensely attractive.

No place glowed brighter to the new lords and ladies, in 1352, than Delta City. It sparkled in the constellation of Salt's cities like a firework. And every devotee and atheist in the city knew what an eager part the gods played in its decadence, renewing their role every evening as the sun went down.

White confections of sails had been dotting the horizon for days. Now the *Regal Flower* came into the thick of them. The vessels hailed from every country in the world. Local fishing careaks, crewed by brawny, green-furred men, tacked between the greater ships, but they were outnumbered by the transcontinental clippers. Humi could not believe the height of some of the ships crossing the *Flower*'s bow. Whenever they came close enough, she strained to see their figureheads: fish, birds, gods, flowers, women, insects.

But for size and intricacy, the city ahead topped them all.

Straight ahead, the gleaming brown highway of the Chrume swept out into the sea. This was the main channel of the river. Thousands of lesser canals had already opened off it to form a vast marshy delta, hilly with grass and rock islands of all sizes. A salty smell of fetid grass and fresh blood came to Humi's nostrils. Far, far away beyond the dank winter marsh, she saw a patchwork line of littoral.

Completely covering the rocky island they were built on, Delta City's building seemed to project sideways like barnacles over the mouth of the Chrume. As a whole, the city had a queerly agile balance, gripping the rock with its claws like a huge feathery bird.

At first it seemed as though they were headed straight for the tall, rocky cliff itself. But the river's current shunted the *Regal Flower* sideways into the lee of the island. And the *Flower* slipped farther west, caught in the sidewash of the river. By the time they actually reached the cliff, it was gone, and they were among the wharves.

"Oh, gods," Beau murmured, "make me strong."

Humi remembered that this was the city where he was going to die. A tilting forest of masts surrounded them. Flocks of gray and black gulls shrieked overhead. Deltan voices curled from quay to quay, cajoling, threatening, pleading in the names of all the gods. Waste rocked on the water. The girth of each stilt supporting the quays could have contained a small house. Men hopped frantically, very near across a gap of oily water, yelling for ropes. The sailors of the *Regal Flower* sent them whistling across the open space. There was an interminable delay while the clipper maneuvered into its berth; then the gangplank was thrust out and made secure.

The rest of the passengers had still to go below and pack their luggage, but Cor, Beau, Humi, and the Godsister carried their light sacks on their shoulders. They were the first off the ship. "Good-bye, Ollit! Bye, Rate, bye, Cidity . . ." Humi called back to the sailors as she followed Godsister Decisiveness.

From the docks, the city rose into at least six stories of wood and stone. Washing lines, and catwalks, and hanging gardens spanned the streets. Since each story overhung the street further than did the one below, they passed through many stretches of artificial darkness where the top floors had met and melded. None of the streets were more than half the width of Port Taite's, which Humi had thought oppressively narrow.

She didn't see how she could ever get used to living in a maze like this. And these were the main concourses. The roads (or tunnels) writhing away between the houses were even narrower and duskier. She hadn't imagined that her first experience of "the land where everything was green" would be like this! The only green in sight was the Deltans' fur.

Waste skidded under their shoes as they trudged along. Not one oxcart or dog carriage could be seen, though many big-wheeled sedan chairs bruised their way through the crowds. The noise was even worse than it had been at the docks. "Hold on to your bags tightly," said Decisiveness over her shoulder. As she spoke, a man slammed into her and hurried on without apologizing. None of these Deltans seemed to have any respect for the flamen. They shouted carelessly in her face as they did in everyone else's, advertising their wares or fighting or courting in slipshod, nasal accents. Humi tapped Cor's shoulder. "Shouldn't—shouldn't the city be in mourning? I don't see any black streamers—"

A shadow passed over Cor's small face, and he raised his voice to be heard. "This is Christon District. The commoners are mostly atheists. Another district, Marshtown, holds the only concentration of devotees left in the city. Maybe there the people care that their Divinarch is dying. Here no one does, or at least not openly."

Humi stumbled over a root growing out of the central gutter. Cor put out

a hand to catch her, and she smiled wanly. Smells of food drifted past her
nostrils; moisture dripped from the tunnel roof they were passing under.
She stuck out her tongue and caught it. Luckily it was only the condensation from someone's hanging garden.

"Here," murmured Cor to Decisiveness. "Here!" said the flamen over
her shoulder, and vanished up a tiny flight of stairs. Beau, whose face had
been turned despondently groundward the whole trudge, followed.

As Humi put her foot on the first tread, curiosity struck her, and she
craned back to squint at the sign over the door. It bore a crude drawing of a
bed and plate. For some reason her relief at seeing that the place was only
an inn incapacitated her. She had to wait at the door until her heart stopped
pounding. But then she looked up again, and the misshapen plate didn't
look so much like a plate. In fact, the longer she stared, the more it came to
resemble a badly drawn head.

"Humi!" came Godsister Decisiveness's voice. "Do not stay outside! It is
perilous here even during the day!"

"Coming!" She scrambled hastily up the stairs. The twisty stairwell
opened into a candlelit hall where Beau, Decisiveness, and Cor stood facing a stranger.

"Godsman Larch." Cor reached up to grasp the strange man's hand.
"This is Humility Garden, the companion of our ghost. Humi, Godsman
Larch."

"I am entrusting you and your cousin into the Godsman's care, Humi,"
Godsister Decisiveness said. "I am assured of Larch's worthiness. He is the
head of a company of beauticians who have served the flamens since the
dawn of the Divinarchy."

"You make it unnecessary for me to introduce myself, Godsister,"
Godsman Larch said with a twinkle in his eye. He bowed over Humi's
hand. "We are the House of Larch. We are just one couturier's establishment in a city which supports dozens, but there is a long-standing bond
between the House of Larch and the flamenhood. I mean that whenever
the flamens choose ghosts, they are brought here, where it is our honor to
ensure that they die in style." He chuckled at his own pun. "The house has
cleared out the rest of its customers for the duration of your stay. Godsie
Garden, I'm sure your cousin and I shall find each other stimulating."

Stimulating!? Humi thought in disbelief. She said, "I—I'm sure you
shall!"

"I am glad you have taken to each other." Decisiveness lifted her head,
and her salt crystals caught the light. "I must leave you. We will meet in
Heaven, Beauty." Like Godsbrother Sensuality before her, she enfolded

Beau in her arms. *He's going to have more scars than he could ever have given himself,* Humi thought wryly.

But then all thought fled her mind, for the Godsister's robed arms came around her, sharp edges pressing into her cheeks, and the harsh voice murmured, "I am sorry, girl. Sorry that I had to take him from you. You've survival instinct enough for two: you would have persuaded him to escape, I think. And you would have done well together. But this is the way it must be." She gave Humi a last squeeze, then departed, flapping away down the corridor like a great hunch-shouldered bird, Cor at her side.

Humi fingered her cheek. She had not felt any pain, but her fingertips came away wet, the fur slick and gleaming.

"Marked!" Godsman Larch said cheerfully. "Some say it's good luck. For your sake, I hope so!"

FIVE

The other five ghosts who had been chosen for Aneisneida had already arrived at the House of Larch. A Veretrean girl, three Royallandics, and an Icelandic who was probably the only youth in his country with a slender build (Southerners were famous for their layers of blubber). None of them could hold a candle to Beau except the Veretrean, though for the first few days they all dazzled Humi. But since exactly six had been chosen, there was no question of competition—though how the news of choices crossed oceans to reach itinerant flamens in the depths of the countrysides, Humi would have liked to know.

There was a lot she would have liked to know about the House of Larch. As the days passed away, she came to be intrigued by the sheer existence of an organization devoted to producing beauty—and the knowledge that it was but one of dozens in the city. She had nothing else to think about. She felt frustrated, secluded—wrapped in soft wool, with nothing to bump against. Beau had been given a room on the top floor, where winter light came through a window in the ceiling. Here, no one objected to their sleeping together, even in the same bed. Every day, Beau had evaluations and fittings and lessons with Godsman Larch's team of beauticians. Neither of them was permitted to go outside, so Humi came along to everything. At first the beauticians and couturiers and hairdressers ignored her, as they did the other two companions; but she slid closer along the floor until the Royallandic boy Rain moved aside to include her, and there she was, in the circle of living, breathing ghosts, the six most beautiful youths and girls in the world. She did not know why the beauticians tolerated her presence—she was only grateful that they did. Perhaps they found her amusing. Certainly she was not like the other companions, the Veretrean girl's husband and the sister of one of the Royallandic boys, both of whom sat mute and tragic in the corners of the mirror-lined rooms.

Humi loved the whole business of beautification. Along with Beau, she learned how to walk and seat herself in every kind of chair and to pose in doorways or at the head of stairs. She learned how to make an entrance. She learned all over again how to smile and frown. She learned how to flatter her face and body with clothing, how to choose it from the drawings the couturiers unrolled before them—although unlike Beau and the other ghosts, she wasn't actually given any new garments. Most important, she learned how to alter her face with dusts and shadows so that no one, looking at her, would have guessed her to be Humility. The beauticians laughed and clapped when she turned from the mirror, simpering and flashing bespangled eyes, flipping elbowfuls of skirt. After that, some of them went so far as to single her out for attention, whereas before they had simply permitted her to listen. They dallied after sessions to satisfy her greed for knowledge; they chatted with her in the corridors. On one memorable occasion, Godsie Bareed, a young Calvarese couturier, took her out to a nearby tea bar. The Christon streets hit her like a barrage of sound, smell, and sight after so many days locked in pulchritude.

The beauticians even taught her things which Beau did not learn. For example, the method of inlaying a small metal filigree into a cheek—Beau's. One shaved a small patch of fur, then administered an anesthetic. When the head rolled to one side, one began to cut with a scalpel, just deep enough to draw needle-thin lines of black blood. One worked the filigree into place in the cuts, then applied sealant. When it was peeled off some days later, the scars had been transformed into white spiked leaves radiating from behind a white iron flower.

In such a fashion the beauticians made the best of everything Beau had. Yet they didn't change him so much as they *polished* him, replacing instinct with studied elegance. He had never looked more vivaciously alive.

"If it were possible for your ghosts to be extracted from you while you lived," Godsie Bareed said, "you would not have to die. The killing is the most objectionable part of making a ghost. I shall not touch on the issue of your piety now, but I know that for one reason or another, you are all willing to die." She paused in her pacing of the circle of ghosts to crack a smile. "You all understand what conditions permitted you to be born looking this way, and the necessity of satisfying them. And none of you shirk that necessity."

Humi knew she meant, Not even the three of you—two Royallandics and the Icelandic boy—who are atheists. But Humi didn't see what difference it made, any more than it mattered whether they were going to be given to an atheist lady or a god. Being chosen as a ghost was still just as much of an honor—or tragedy—just as profitable for the family left behind.

"Now, let us make your choice of neckline for evening dress a little easier. Grace, your eyes are far apart. It is easy to place too much emphasis on them: one must at all costs avoid the heart-shaped face which will recall the visage of a predator. We are aware of the righteous distaste our gods bear for predators, and even though you are not to be given to a god, they will still see you, and might be offended . . ."

Humi listened, spellbound, storing every word in her memory.

That was a trick she had perfected by the age of twelve. When she chose to, she could relive every bite of the supper at which she had been sitting when the sixdays of practice finally fell into place, and her family's words, instead of arrowing into her ears and hanging for an instant before the next sound tumbled in and overrode them, sank into her memory as if into quicksand. It had been the fat time of autumn. Tici had cooked a great stewpot full of red beans and teajuice. There had been a clotted bottom-of-the-pot crust broken up in each helping, which Humi had relished because she thought it was oatpudding. Later the combination of excitement from her discovery and finding out that it had been blood from the ox that died had made her vomit. She could remember that too.

But the food at the House of Larch was always good. She and Beau ate alone in their room. Or Humi ate; since they had arrived, Beau had barely consumed enough to keep himself alive. It was part of the interior process which honed away every cell of excess flesh, erasing every hint of brutishness, turning the muscular farm boy into an aristocrat. The ring of cutlery was the only sound. They no longer had anything to say to each other. Beau's remarks, though obviously intended to indicate an interest in Humi's life, were so superficial that they hurt. When they finished eating, they would lie silently under the blankets until sleep shuffled over the roofs to the leaded skylight and threw itself down on them, sprawling like a wanton over their faces.

She woke at night only once during the sixdays of their residence in the House of Larch. Shouts from somewhere along the corridor penetrated her sleep. It was Rain, the ghost from Westchasm with the warm smile whose sulky sister screamed her desperation at him whenever they were alone. *That kind of companion shouldn't be allowed to come,* Humi thought. Evidently the girl had finally cracked his protective shell, and he was shouting back. He'd been looking haggard the past day or so—small wonder, if he had come to fear for his beauty—

His voice spiraled into unintelligibility. Wide awake, Humi wondered suddenly why she was so hot. The odor of sweat enveloped her. Springy curls of fur tangled her eyelashes. She was in Beau's embrace, hugged fiercely to his chest. He breathed with shuddering slowness into her hair.

The scent of two people's body smells mingled together was completely new to her. She felt dizzy. She eased his arms open and rolled to the extreme edge of the bed. The night was warm—the wool blankets were unnecessary. Her grandmother Tici, right now enduring an icy Domesdys winter, would have been glad of them. But no. The Gardens had two hundred sheep now. Tici would certainly have a warm bedjacket.

Humi folded her arms behind her head and gazed up into the stars through the skylight. Far, far above, one bluish dwarf stared down at her through the mist of the constellations.

The next morning Beau gave no indication that anything had happened. And the incident was never repeated. For as it turned out, that night was the last they ever spent together.

"It's time," said the servant who brought their breakfast. A scrub-furred young Deltan whose duties around the House of Larch were multifarious, he had often provided companionship for Humi when she could no longer stand the ghosts' silence. The tray rattled as he set it down. "Get out your finery, Beauty. You're to choose what to wear."

"I *am?*" Beau put one hand to his breast in a studied gesture which said, *Dear me, I have been longing for this chance for many sixdays, but I really don't trust my own taste, or at least I don't want you to know that I do.*

"It's a test," Quen said. "And if I was you I would eat a good breakfast. The palace banquet are *un*—" he planted a kiss on his fingers—"*un*describable—but it's all a test. Ghosts aren't allowed to eat."

Beau glanced at the tray, the steaming bowls of gruel and the tropical fruits opened out like water lilies, sitting in their own orange blood. He obviously had no intention of touching it.

Humi followed the young man out the door. "Quen. Do you have any news concerning me and the other companions?" She'd carved out a routine for herself here—and now it was over, just like that. She realized abruptly that she had not really given a thought to what would happen after this. "What am I to do when they go to the palace?"

"You're to go too, of course. And stick with Beauty till he's chosen. That's what you're here for. To look after him."

"Chosen?" Humi pounced on the crumb of information. "Again? By whom? What's the palace like? Oh, tell me!" She seized Quen's hands. The empty tray clattered to the floor. "What do the streets look like now? Is there festival, with a procession, and dancing, and food?" She was drawing on her memories of festival time in Nece.

Quen stood stock-still, looking down at her. His hair hung over his eyes in curved green bangs. "Humi," he said at last, "this isn't my place or yours."

"Oh." Mentally scolding herself, she retreated. "But tell me, please—
what are we supposed to *do?*"

He tucked his hair behind his ears. His eyes slid away from her face.
"Palace gatherings are only for palace initiates. It's not like it was in the
days of the flamens. Nobody knows anything that goes on in the palace
district now. Anybody that wants to see the new ghosts has to go on a tour.
My mum and dad took a tour when the Heir arrived here fifteen years ago,
when loads of ghosts were made. They had to wait for hours just to be
hustled through the suite where they were stood."

"But Quen, what happens to the ghosts between leaving here and—and
being stood in that suite? How are they going to die?"

"Can't tell."

"Why not?"

"Just can't. Its being secret is the most important thing about it. Hardly
anyone knows. There, I already let something slip! Every minute I've
known you, I've been scared—" Quen's fur quivered, muddying as his dark
skin became visible—"you'd ask that question, and I'd answer—"

"Why?"

"Isn't it plain? Has there ever been a companion like you?"

"You mean you were afraid you'd help me because you *like* me?"

"I never knew any ghost's companions before." Shadows moved across
his facial fur.

"Then will you help me?"

"I have to get these trays down to the kitchen! Go back to Beauty,
Humi!" And he plunged into the next bedroom as if into safety.

Humi stood in the hall while the sweat dried on her palms. Quen had
told her enough. A vague plan was forming in her mind. Beau needed
her—but for once she didn't go to him. It was only her dress sense he
would want now, and she had to have that for herself.

Hope rekindling inside her like an abnormal little flame which refuses to
be doused by water or dirt, she went downstairs.

A hush gripped the entire House of Larch. Footfalls far off in the warren
of passages creaked like the voices of the house itself, grieving for its latest
litter of children.

Humi found Ministra Bareed in the wardrobery, among racks of costumes sewn to fit long-dead youths and girls. Candlelight splashed their
racks with gold. For a moment Humi watched the couturier pace restlessly;
then she went in.

"Humility! Hasn't Eloquence ordered you to stay with Beauty?"

She hadn't known it was an order. "No, Godsie."

The couturier was a flexible woman, made of night-colored fur and bone.

She swayed edgily to and fro. "That boy must be disciplined. He is forever failing to do what we ask of him, because he believes that as a servant, it isn't his station to talk to companions and ghosts. He won't learn that in a pious establishment there's no such thing as a *servant!* Go back upstairs."

"Godsie, don't discipline Quen, please." Humi's voice sounded fragile and false even to her. "It was my fault. I asked him a lot of questions—and he wouldn't answer. Godsie, please tell me what's going to happen."

Ministra's surprise was clear. "You are a companion. I can't tell you."

"You haven't been *treating* me like a companion!"

"We haven't, have we?" She sighed. "We've never treated you as what you are, nor told you how we are failing you in not doing so. To some people it seems reckless of human life to treat a sibling or betrothed or beloved as merely the wings which bear the bird aloft, valuable during flight, to be clipped and thrown aside when the time comes for the bird to be caged. Disrupting two lives to produce one ghost seems unnecessary and even unfair."

"What do you mean—*disrupting?*"

Ministra's fingers traced the embroidery on a coat sleeve. "Look at what has already happened to you. And what is going to happen to you next is the result of being alone, penniless, and grieving in Delta City. You decide what that is."

"Do you mean you don't help me? That's not fair!"

"Whenever the question of the companions is raised, it returns to the flamenhood. And the Godsbrothers and Godsisters will always bow to tradition. It is the only thing on their side nowadays, which makes them a little hidebound. If they disregard it, they knock the ground out from under their own feet."

"Go on," said Humi in a tone designed not to stem revelations. She had perfected it over the past sixdays.

"Belstem Summer and Goquisite Ankh want to revise the entire chain of ghost choice, to make it more efficient and humane." Now Ministra's voice held passionate contempt. "They want to turn us into an *operation. They* want to select the ghosts for ceremonial occasions instead of letting the flamens do it. But we haven't yet yielded one handspan of ground."

"And I . . ."

"Tradition has never made any provision for the companions of the ghosts. Because for you, it's a voluntary thing to come here. Like suicide. There are no laws against *that.*" Her shirt rippled over bony shoulders as she shrugged. "You were told that this involved self-sacrifice on your part. It was assumed you were willing."

"I didn't know it meant being *abandoned!*" *I'd give my eyeteeth for something to hold over the cold bitch.* "I thought you were my friend, Godsie—"

Wrong move. Ministra Bareed's voice went cold. "The friendship of companion means no more to me than the friendship of a ghost. What if I denounced you for defying tradition?"

"Then I would denounce *you* to the flamens." Humi swallowed. "I would call you to account for treating me differently from the other companions, giving me false hopes of getting out of this."

"We should have treated you like them. I agree with you there. But before you denounced us—" her voice held just a faint, traitorous tremble—"I would make sure you could never say anything again."

If threats were the weapon of choice, Humi could best a hint of mutilation any day. Oddly, she felt exhilarated—at least she knew what she was dealing with. "First, I'd kill you with the scissors from your belt. I'd drive them into your throat, and watch your blood gush onto the floor. I'd . . ." She went on.

The room was silent. She could smell the other woman's horror.

"There, that's what is waiting for you if you don't help me! Well, Ministra?"

"I—I accept. Humi, you are not what I believed you to be." Humi could not believe it. She had swallowed the confabulation.

"Tell me what you want me to do for you."

SIX

The House of Larch was one of the highest buildings in Christon, commanding a view of the sky from the skylights in the penthouse. A lemon horizon in the west faded spectacularly through green into night. Godsman Larch entered from the stairs, pulling on a frockcoat. "None of you thought to turn on the lights?" he scolded the gloom-shrouded figures. "So modest! Don't you wish us to see you in your finery?"

He was the only one who laughed. Each ghost stood with a fan or purse or decorative dagger in motionless hands, close enough to the others to feel their body warmth, yet alone. Their breath whispered like an unending sigh.

Finally the last candle hissed into life. "There . . . we go!" Larch surveyed his charges, hands on hips. "Strike me down, but you all look stunning!"

His cheer was monstrous. *Is it possible to practice in the House of Larch too long?* Humi wondered.

"Line up, line up so that we can see you. Companions by the sides of your ghosts. It doesn't matter that you're wearing street clothes. No one will take offense—they'll know what you are."

No, they won't, she thought. *Gods grant me luck, and they won't!* She let her eyes drift. Only the soft, ruminative click of Larch's tongue let her know that he had realized what was wrong.

Seven ghosts. Seven ribboned, jeweled, dusted beauties, all with the same blank smile of allure—and only two drab little companions in spindlespun. Oblivious of tension, all seven ghosts gazed blindly and gracefully at nothing.

As the rest of the beauticians entered, Larch's face told them what was wrong. Frightened glances shot from man to woman. Their eyes darted along the row of ghosts. Black spots trickled across Humi's vision. She didn't know how much longer she could remain motionless.

"Well, I see nothing wrong with any of you," Larch said at last. "We should have been in the palace by nightfall. But it will do well to be fashionably late. We'll make all the better an entrance."

And the beauticians fell to chattering and laughing among themselves with an edge to their voices that was far more than relief. A decision had been made. They did not have to act. They did not have to question the premise of intrinsic beauty on which the entire ghosting process was based.

"They look superb!"

"I told you Wella would choose the violet dress—didn't I?"

"I suppose I must pay up."

"Are we going to give her a chance like this?"

"Never bet with a couturier, Godsie!"

"She deserves it. I've never seen a companion like her, and I've been here forty years this Midwinter."

"But who helped her? It must have been . . ."

"One of us. But not me."

"Not me."

"It wasn't me."

And one by one, their eyes went to Ministra Bareed, who stood by herself, gripping her arms, her face as muddy as if smeared with earth.

Beau thought, *What am I doing in this ridiculous hourglass of a coat?*

He couldn't remember. All he knew was that it was crucial to wear it with grace. On the open roof outside the penthouse, sedan chairs waited to take them away. Twisty little alleys led off the open space between the roofs. Beau was vaguely aware of lights coming from around the corners of the passages.

His keepers looked like strangers in their court regalia. Beau could not remember seeing any of them before, although he was sure he must have. They herded him and the others into the sedans like sheep into the slaughtering ring. Squashed beside a pale-furred girl whose name he had forgotten, Beau endured the bumping journey stoically. Every now and then the porters carried the sedan down another flight of stairs.

At last they settled to the real ground, not a roof or a catwalk. A porter hooked back the curtain. It was sheer luck that Beau kept his balance as he stepped down, for torchlight blazed into his eyes, disorienting him completely.

Humi glided up to him and breathed exultantly, "Don't look now, Beau! But they're admiring you!"

They were the focus of a hush spreading through the entire crowd, stopping men and women in the middle of their business, attracting every eye. Beau felt his body assuming the pose to receive adulation. After a second, Humi copied him. Her mimicry was flawless. Only a small part of his mind knew or cared what she was doing anymore, but that part saw that she had dressed herself up as a ghost and was parading around with him and the others. It was wrong—wrong! But he didn't know quite why. She was beautiful: her cheeks were flushed, her eyes sparkled. Surely she deserved as much honor as he?

He could not anchor his concentration on the question any longer. A smear of rotten fish was soiling his boot. This annoyance occupied his mind until it was thoroughly scraped off against a cobble. Then he tried to take in his surroundings. The great marketplace in which the sedans had set them down contained a sprawl of food stalls and drinking booths. Crowds of green-furred Deltans stood arrested in the middle of eating, shopping, fighting, while several pickpockets took advantage of the distraction to go roaming. The air smelled of alcohol. Torches flared everywhere, turning the sky to soot. As if in a dream, Beau heard fountains gushing, and far-flung droplets landed on his face.

"Antiprophet Square," he heard one of the couturiers say to another ghost. "Used to be the holiest place in the city. It was called Suvret Cat Square, for the first Divinarch. There were nine flamen councillors in the Ellipse, and they all lived here."

But it's not a square, it's a pentagon, Beau thought. Each side was a garden in which an ornate mansion nestled. The largest mansion of all had no garden in front, but opened straight onto the square: it resembled an overblown six-tier conch shell of gray stone. Its yawning doors looked more like a black maw the closer he came. Colored costumes seemed to flow into each other in the doorway. As Beau mounted the steps, to the stares and chatter of the crowd, his body took over. Studied poise came into play. The colors were all around him. Fingers tugged at his clothes, twitching, pulling. A voice belled out from somewhere beyond, and they withdrew, but only for a second, descending again instantly like harpies.

Behind him, there was a *clomp* of stone. The doors had shut.

It felt as though they had shut the unseasonably warm night in with them. He felt himself begin to sweat, but he knew his body was coping, smiling and bestowing kisses on cheeks, meeting no one's eyes. Dresses and tailcoats and gossamer shawls swirled. A thick stone passage created a moment of cool. Then he was standing in line with the others, Humi next to him—her breath was so quick, her eyes flashed so brilliantly, she had none of the cold, distant demeanor of a ghost! Did no one see? Maybe no one was close enough. Finery ringed them at a distance, and murmuring talk battered against the ceiling of the great room like hosts of birds. An aisle gaped slowly open between the guests, and a man and woman strolled leisurely down it. The torchlight was so brilliant that Beau could see grains of badly applied facedust in the fur around the woman's nose.

The man was hugely overweight, a Royallandic, dressed in such flagrant bad taste it could only have been intentional. "Seven."

The whole gathering was silent.

"Seven, a good number, Godsman Larch. It would have been too obvious to send six, would it not, Godsman Larch, for the number of Aneisneida's Council seat? I applaud you."

Behind the ghosts, the couturiers relaxed.

Step by step, the man led the young woman along the line, stopping her to peer over her head whenever he saw something that pleased him. "Wish we could stop them sending these little rats," he muttered when they passed Wella the Veretrean's husband. And, "That's the pick of the lot, Anei, you mark my word," as they paused before Humi.

At that unfortunate mistake, Beau realized that the man must be the atheist Belstem Summer. And the frail, pale-furred young woman must be his daughter, Aneisneida.

Beau's future owner.

Beau had no conscious wish to follow her with his eyes, but a tiny part of his mind throbbed: danger.

Don't be absurd. That feeble bundle of nerves couldn't kill a flea!

Then who would?

"A remarkable bunch!" Summer dropped his hands with offensive joviality on Beau's and another ghost's shoulders, peering between their heads. "Remarkable. Simply captivating! Gods' blood be spilled, your bunch have surpassed themselves this time, Larch!"

A ripple of pleasure ran through the beauticians grouped behind Beau. Larch emerged, bowing profoundly before the Summers. "Always my pleasure to serve you or your friends, milord," he murmured deferentially. "And especially—" he brushed his lips across her hand—"your beautiful daughter."

"Not safe to be too beautiful around here!" Summer said crudely. "You old snake, Larch! Let's be glad she isn't in any danger! Haw!"

The whole gathering broke into laughter, even Aneisneida, even Larch— even Humi, in obvious disbelief. Ice encased Beau's muscles, but he broke it to elbow her in the ribs. Summer was plainly the most dangerous man in the room. The gods only knew what would happen to Humi if she exposed herself.

Perhaps the fact that she'd sparked his attention shocked her silent. She shut her mouth and straightened her fan. When the guests surrounded them again, a crush of flounces and flutters, touching, feeling, she played the ghost admirably, keeping her dignity at the same time as she let them finger her. Beau kept one eye on her: the fear had shaken him back into himself somewhat.

At last someone exclaimed, "Why are we standing here? We should make a tour! Myrthesa, bring that dear girl along and I'll bring this one. Take her arm. Now, off we go!"

"The harpsichord salon, Selenie?"

"No, the indoor lily-pond! There's that stunning Icelandic ghost in the centre, you must remember, dear—"

Beau had never seen a ghost. So he was unprepared for the shocks that awaited him in nearly every room of the mansion. Ghosts posed clothed, naked, introspective, absorbed in obscene acts, staring arrogantly over the heads of the crowd. Each hair on their bodies was textured like diamond. So were the fashions of previous days that they wore. Visually, they had a curious impasto texture, fur and clothes and eyes alike, as if they had stepped out of paintings into three dimensions.

Surrounding each one was an aura of intense, unearthly cold which ranged from a finger's width to an armspan deep. But when Beau forced himself through it to touch a hard, perfect sleeve, expecting the diamondine to cleave to his hand like iron, it was no colder than wood. And pure, uplifting happiness dizzied him like wine.

When he touched the next one, he was gripped by a sexual climax so intense he knew he must be dying. This ghost was arched over backward, naked, one hand clutching her crotch. The next was in use as a candelabrum. Wax dribbled down his arms. From him Beau got screaming muscular pain, meant perhaps as a rather romantic reminder of what goes through the household objects we use every day. He felt sick at the thought of touching any more—but he could not tell the atheists so, and they pushed him willy-nilly into their embraces.

Now they were in a room done in typical Veretrean decor—large, with colored mosaics let into the ceiling at random places, rough-floored, chairs and tables worked in colored glass. The woman named Selenie had encircled Beau in an arm cased in so many layers of silk it might have belonged to a doll. "Of course, Aneisneida will not stand you in any of these rooms, I'm sure. She'll have you in her bedroom or her private sitting room. But isn't it nice to know your *context?* The Summers keep the ground floor for receptions. This chair set was imported from Grussels only last month—admire the scrollwork! The red coloring is, I believe, derived from boiled feathers. I have a similar set in my parlor. My husband's family holds one of the oldest lordships in Delta City. Our patriarch was a disciple of Antiprophet himself."

Humi said in a clear, disgusted voice, "Why, your family is only two hundred years old! *My* family has lived in the same valley since the barbarian years before the Wars!"

There was a brief silence. Another woman tittered, "It talks! Shed the gods' blood, but it talks!"

Missing the point altogether, a man said pugnaciously, "What does it mean by 'barbarian' times? Those were the golden days, when all the world lived free of the flamens' tyranny, and I'd have it respect this house that it's in!"

"You haven't a clue what you are talking about, Lord Moore," said the pure, bell-like voice which Beau had heard before. "Let ignorance keep quiet until it learns sense!"

In response to the voice, a glass dauphin sang a sweet, thin burr against a table. If the voice had not been scaled down to fit the room, the ornament would have broken. "Whose was the voice that slandered the flamens, my pets?" the voice asked pleasantly. As the guests fell away, Beau saw him.

His skin was pale, rainbowed in the torchlight, and furless, yet the effect was not nudity but daring. He was taller than the best man present, but preternaturally slender, light muscles defined under his shirt; his face was sharp and as perversely attractive as an undernourished child's. His eyes were enormous, one brown and one blue.

The muscles at the bases of his wings worked rhythmically; the silk edges of the slits in the back of his shirt lifted and caught in the folds of the muscle casings. The silk tightened across his chest. He scanned the knot of atheists who had taken possession of Humi, his wings caressing his shoulders like a semitransparent mantle.

This being Beau recognized from countless effigies, though they had been carved in wood, without the scintillating coloring. This was the Striver himself.

One of the Incarnations.

A god.

"Pati," someone muttered deferentially.

"I come to see what you've done for your little *sociale*, and find you insulting my people. Ah, well, you do it to our faces as well. Why should I lose sleep over it? Where's Belstem?" The Striver—*Pati?*—tapped one bare foot on the floor. Talons protruded from his heels like spurs. "Not here? Why, I thought he would have stayed to make sure none of you steal his daughter's birthday presents."

"It's not her birthday, Pati," someone said sullenly.

"Well, it ought to be, the blameless child, she deserves a birthday once in a while. Where are they? The ghosts, that is." Pati assumed a mock oratorial stance. "Too often am I misconstrued among you slow-witted humans. It is better to run the risk of overclarification than to fall into the trap of being misunderstood. Where are they?"

When the god mentioned the ghosts, Beau thought he heard a hint of emotion creep into Pati's voice. Out of the corner of an eye he saw Humi push her way to the front of the crowd, staring at the god with heedless avidity.

"I heard one speak just as I arrived," said Pati. "A ghost, giving tongue, now when they are so close to being silenced forever!"

Behind him, the air crackled and turned itself inside out. Beau had the impression that he was watching a pair of rapidly expanding sunspots. Then two gusts of hot air whooshed toward his face, and there was a smell of burning sulphur. Two more beings stood on either side of Pati.

No one screamed or fell. The Striver swung round to the newcomers with perfect aplomb. "How is business? as our friends here would say. Belstem hasn't come on the tour. I'm surprised—he likes to show off his acquisitions. And his minions quail at showing me the beauties. Can you believe their impudence!"

One of the gods was shorter than any human. She wore no garment that Beau could see, and had no wings. An abundance of dark blue hair poured to her knees, cloaking her body. Her face was an aggregate of sharp angles: she had huge, night-colored eyes. "Pati, you're tormenting them." She minced up to a Royallandic and straightened his waistcoat with elfin hands. Then she slid in among the guests, pushing her way between skirts, dropping to the floor and calling "Coo-*eeee!*" from inside wired flounces. Some women giggled nervously and danced on their toes. But no one seemed to resent her intrusion the way they did Pati's rudeness.

"What are you doing, Broken Bird?" Pati sat down on one of the glass chairs and idly picked off the scrollwork. His fingernails must have been as sharp as files. "Are you cuckolding some poor woman while she stands right next to you? I know what you get up to, and at the most inappropriate times."

One of the ladies glanced at the bits of glass on the floor and sighed. She called, "Milord Heir! Can't you make them stop? Dinner will be growing cold!"

As Beau craned, trying to see who she was speaking to, Broken Bird popped up in front of him. She had used the same trick of transportation as before, but it was not the blast of warm air which made him flinch—it was her tiny blue face pushing itself fiercely up into his. Her hair rose up to wrap his wrists, and she called piercingly, "I've got one! Patience! Charity! Here's one, and he's a lovely!" As she backed out of the crowd, keeping hold of Beau with her hair, she trod on someone's foot. Judging by the shriek, her talon had gone straight through slipper and flesh to the tiled floor. "Oh! Oh, by the Power—" she spun, hair lifting itself out of her eyes—"Lady Minnowquay, your daughter's foot! I am so sorry—"

She knelt and began gently to remove the slipper. Someone else grasped Beau by the hair and tugged him into the open.

"Oh, *yes*," his new captor breathed. "Delicious."

"Seldom if ever do I agree with you, Arity," said Pati, eyes misty behind semitransparent violet lids. "But on this we are in accord."

"Mmm . . ." The third god let Beau go. Swinging his leg over another delicate chair, he rocked to and fro, grinding his pelvis into the seat. Then he stopped and considered Beau. Beau could do nothing but smile blandly at them. "I swear that the flamens still choose the best ghosts of all."

"And you envy them in more ways than one, Arity," said Pati quickly, like a knife thrust.

Arity flinched. "I intended that as a compliment to your people, and indirectly to you. You do not deserve a clarification, and you won't get one."

"Clarification is the tool of he who harnesses the masses."

"So you see yourself as a mass, Pati? And myself as your master? I am flattered."

Pati flushed. It was a queer sight. Since he had no fur, he couldn't muddy, but his skin darkened as if blood were rushing into it, and his wings whirred. Arity smiled the tight little smile of a man who has gotten his own back, and he turned again to Beau. His skin was a muted, mossy green. It was stretched over bones less finely drawn than Pati's, and his body was stockier—more like a human's. While he had sharp cheekbones, chin, and eyebrow ridges, his face seemed more capable of human expressions than Broken Bird's or Pati's did.

Yet for all this he couldn't possibly have been taken for a Royallandic man. Besides his naked skin, his shoulder blades were long and streamlined; his bare feet were six-toed, embellished with talons that left scratches on the floor; and his finger claws could have taken Beau's eyes out with a single twist. His hair was a strange, soft purple-brown which a human would have assumed was dyed. Beau thought with a sudden flash of enlightenment: *Now I know why the gods value beauty so much. They're not beautiful themselves. That makes sense . . . doesn't it?*

"Well, Beauty," Arity said, "you certainly have style. Let me compliment you on this coat. Can I have it after you are dead?" He plucked at Beau's

sleeve. Beau already regretted choosing the ludicrous garment. The brocade was the color of unripe corn, with white lace spilling from beneath it
at cuffs and lapels. The collars, stiff as sepals, framed his face like a flower,
deepening his golden fur to ochre. He had enhanced his eyes with violet
sap. *Oh, well.* He posed, presenting Arity with the full effect.

"Oh. Oh, strike me down." The god stroked Beau's cheek. "Little boy,
will you go to bed with me? I want to fuck you and fuck you—"

Pati had recovered and was violently finishing off the chair he sat on.
"Shut up, Heirloom. Don't make the poor thing sick." He turned to Beau.
"Go away! We don't want you!" And to the rest of the gathering: "All right,
get out! Go eat your banquet, drink your wine, indulge yourselves like
hogs!"

Broken Bird tied off a bandage around the foot of the girl she had injured. "I can't *tell* you how sorry I am to spoil your evening, darling. But go
to Lady Summer and ask for proper care. Then maybe you'll be able to
dance." She smiled, brushed a kiss across the foot, and was gone in a *pouf*
of air. The girl and her mother hurried out.

Pati guffawed rudely at their backs. "Erene!" he shouted into the next
room. "I know you're there somewhere, but you've done a hell of a good
job on your face this time. I didn't spot you in all of ten minutes!—Go on,
Beauty—"

And Beau bowed, turned, and went, as fast as was graceful. "Don't break
things just to relieve your boredom, Pati," he heard Arity say. "I can do
anything I want without resorting to destruction." And he balanced on the
back of the brittle chair, making it spin round and round, graceful as a
butterfly.

Humi was waiting for Beau at the door. The lumidust on her bosom was
marked: she must have let the Deltans touch her to satisfy their curiosity, as
docile as a true ghost. She was staring with such absorption at the gods that
she hardly saw him.

"What are you waiting for?" Beau hissed. "They'll guess you're not really
a ghost!"

Her face went blank and her mouth opened. Amazing how she had made
her lips look full and pouty. But, oh, yes! He shouldn't be speaking! The
episode with the gods had jolted him completely back into his own body.

"What's that!" Pati was peering toward them keenly. "Another ghost? Is
this the one that I heard talking?"

"Don't be ridiculous, you half-winged throwback," Arity said. "Let the
poor things go! You can't get anything out of them—they're dead on their
feet."

But Beau felt the Heir's keen gaze fix them for a moment before Pati

garnered his attention with a dig which would have cracked human ribs.
That image of them stayed in Beau's head for the rest of his life: the most
revered creatures in the world perched twirling on the backs of chairs, in
an empty room with blood smears on the floor, quarreling over the meta-
physical qualities of human ghosts.

"Seafood, dear?"
Humi let her eyes drift over the plump fingers extending the fork. The
slice of flesh was white and flaky, but dense like beef. Mutely she turned to
look at the lady.
"A water porcupine. Very slow and ungainly, my dear. The young men
train dauphins to catch them. Of course, there are hardly any left in the
marshes, so this is a real rarity."
Humi shook her head slowly.
"Very well, then!" The lady—Arolette Meadowlord, her name was—
flicked the slice of porcupine onto her own plate. "But my dear, you've not
eaten much!" She gestured vexedly at Humi's plate, which was littered
with samples of this and that. Humi had in fact not eaten a bite, though she
was hungry. She realized that earlier, in the parlor, she had been inexcus-
ably reckless. Now she would have to be on her guard. Death might be in
the water porcupine or the salicornes, the sea rice or the finger rolls. She
dared not risk finding out how the atheists had chosen to kill her.
Lady Meadowlord fell to conversing with her other neighbor. Lady
Meadowlord had, it seemed, paid cash for the privilege of sitting next to
Humi, and she was angry that she couldn't make her talk.
"You coarse new nobles!" the old lord on her other side said vituperatively. "You are not acquainted with palace etiquette. You made your money
raising deer in the snow!" With their white fur and heavily built bodies, the
Meadowlords were patently Icelandic. "What does a herdsman's wife know
of ghosts? Ex-lemans such as myself know that they are not *supposed* to eat,
my dear enlightened lady, any more than they are supposed to talk. I saw
the ghosts that were chosen for Arity's inauguration. Look at her: she knows
her place, even if you don't!"
Humi had dropped her gaze to her folded hands. She'd buffed her nails
and painted little designs on them. The lumidust on her hands made her fur
look like gold-and-silver plush instead of dead stubble.
After a while she dared to look up again. The banquet hall was the largest
space she'd ever seen enclosed under a roof. Frescoes of gods and men
cavorted all over the vault above her, dim under a layer of grime. The
tapestries which ornamented the ribbed walls were stained and motheaten

with age near the top, but grew steadily richer as they descended toward the flagstones. The voices of the guests rushed like a river under the vault.

She was sure that behind his dreamy eyes, Beau, at the next table, was far more alert than he should be. And it was her fault. Why had she given him cause to worry? The chink of silver and glass filled her ears. A procession of servants carrying trays blocked her view of him. There was Wella at the next table. There were Cienci and Telli—at least she thought it was they. There was Ameli, the petite, pious Royallandic girl whom Belstem Summer seemed to have appropriated. Against all custom, he was forcing her to talk and laugh with his daughter. Aneisneida looked as though she were in worse pain than the little ghost was.

Torches flared over the exits. In the arched passage opening directly across from Humi stood a plain young Calvarese woman in a cherry-colored gown, holding Rain's hand. Her unsubtle gestures suggested that she wanted his company. *But my sister,* objected Rain with vague obstinacy, uncurling a hand toward the hall.

His sister stood like a green stain between the best tables, noticed by no one except the scurrying servants, who ducked around her. Her hands wrung her skirt. Staring around for Rain, she looked wild with fright.

Leave her, the Calvarese woman gestured impatiently. *Come on.*

Rain went. His sister scanned the guests ever more desperately. As people began to notice her, she picked up her skirts, chose an arch at random, and pelted into it. Humi shivered, clasping her empty goblet tightly. It was the skull of a salt wolverite, the gaps sealed with silver.

"Excuse me," said a voice at her shoulder. "I've been observing you with fascination, milady ghost, and I couldn't help noticing you've drunk nothing but water. There's no custom forbidding ghosts liquor. Some ladies hold that it's kindest to give them as much alcohol as they'll take; though I don't believe this, I would like to pour you some wine. May I?"

Humi turned slowly, controlling her movements right down to the eyelashes. It was her other neighbor, a young Royallandic man with a deferential, attentive manner. His hands were large and knot-muscled. She pushed her cup toward him, and he poured. "I am a merchant," he said, "born in Westchasm."

The wine eased like red oil toward the lip of the goblet. She nodded for him to stop. She thought she liked him. Where was the overfamiliarity with which atheists like Lady Meadowlord hid their curiosity? On the other hand, where was the nervous revulsion that others displayed? Until Lady Meadowlord gave up on Humi, the merchant hadn't tried to attract her attention, but he didn't seem ghoulish, like those whom she had seen star-

ing at her from corners with greedy longing. He was treating her like an
ordinary person.

"My aunt is the head of the merchants' union in Westchasm," he said.
"She sent me to negotiate a trade agreement with the lords of Delta City.
The road is dangerous, especially these days when so many people are
leaving homes that are no longer hospitable, and we needed to arrange
security for our caravans. I was eager to see the capital of the world—and it
has not disappointed me."

She nodded for him to go on. The torches burned down and were replaced. Belstem Summer's laugh roared out more and more often as he
grew drunk. A party of musicians entered the hall and, without commanding attention, began to play. Arias leaped up into the vault, echoing so that
it sounded as if fifty men rather than a dozen were playing. Bows darted
across violins, cellos, and basses; fingers walked the keys of cornets, french
horns, and saxophones. One by one, couples rose to glide between the
tables. The change in the atmosphere was magical.

"Ghosts often do not wish to dance," murmured the merchant. "But, my
dear, they are allowed other pleasures. I do not hold out much hope—but I
swear you've captured my soul."

Dishes and white cloths had been swept together from the tables. The
banqueters who had overindulged relaxed, watching the dancers drift between the tables in open spaces that seemed made for the purpose. The
merchant's hand rested lightly on Humi's sleeve.

This did not seem right somehow. But she heard her tongue betraying
her. "Yes!" Lady Meadowlord stared at them, agape, as the merchant stood
to give her an arm. He was taller than she had supposed, with the muscles
of a fisherman beneath his rust silk cutaway coat. Lace cuff brushed lace
cuff as he took her hand. They wove between the dancers toward one of the
far arches.

"The Summers' mansion is very large," the merchant whispered. "Surely
not all the rooms are occupied."

Humi laughed. She felt electricity wriggling between their joined hands.
It's the custom, she thought euphorically. *The custom!*

But not one possible retreat in the Summers' labyrinthine mansion remained empty. More often than not, the alcoves were occupied by other
couples, faces buried in each other's necks, oblivious to the world.

"I think we shall have to return to my lodgings," the Westchasm merchant whispered to Humi after they had tiptoed past the third couple engaged in actual coitus. "If you do not mind, milady?" She nodded. "I hoped
that we should not have to go outside. But it isn't far. I'm lodged in
Marshtown."

They left by a back entrance and picked their way through a brick-walled cleft in the building to the square. The merchant hailed a sedan and gave the porter a complex string of directions. Inside, in the jouncing dark, he began tentatively to kiss her. Could he tell that she had never kissed before—except Beau, once, when they were fourteen? The touch of mouth on mouth had been an unarticulated taboo between them which kept them chaste. The young merchant nibbled her lips, and his tongue licked her teeth. Abruptly, he pulled her over onto his lap.

The porter knocked on the side of the sedan, then drew back the curtain. Humi allowed herself to be led up to the front door of the house before which they had stopped. The street was a dark, canyonlike curve of shops and tall houses, all shuttered, all quiet. The porter's white livery glowed like a target where he stood by the sedan. The stars shed a misty glow over everything. When the merchant unlocked the front door, it released a dusty whiff of perfume and spices and dust.

"Up here, sweet ghost," breathed the merchant. He led her up a wide, crooked flight of stairs. At the top, she heard somebody screaming like a hare, on and on behind a closed door. The merchant grimaced and hurried her on. "The other lodgers. I shan't stay much longer—the house is not of such good repute as I thought when I came here." At the end of the hall he pushed open another door.

Two torches burned on either side of a large bed. Cascades of soft, thick lace curtained the windows, and a vase of giant speedwells stood on the floor, suffusing the room with fragrance. An empty doorway revealed further cluttered rooms.

"Oh," Humi breathed, forgetting herself, "oh, how beautiful! Milord—" she caught his hands—"Milord, I'm a virgin. Please be gentle . . ."

His throat jumped. He smiled tenderly down at her. "I'll be as gentle as I can. It will have to hurt a *little*, but I hope that if you are in enough pleasure, you will not feel the pain."

She pressed her forehead against his incongruously powerful shoulder. "Milord . . . what is your name?"

After a moment he said, "Ziniquel. My name's Ziniquel."

She whispered it time after time as he began tenderly to undress her. She shivered when her dress slid down past her breasts and then past her crotch. Thank the gods she'd taken the time to rub lumidust all over her body, not just on those parts which showed outside the dress. She thought with a thrill of pleasure that she must look like a statue in gold. Ziniquel caught his breath. "Little ghost, how corporeal you are! And how exquisite!" He pulled off coat and shirt, lace collar and boots. She could see the bulge in his silken pants, but he didn't remove them yet; smothering one of the torches with a cloth hung below it, he swept her expertly off her feet, laying her on the bed.

Later he whispered, "Here . . . hold this flower. I want to see how it goes with your fur. I see you in both bronze and gold as the torch flares—" By this time it was almost burned down. Sated, sleepy, she knew that most of the lumidust must have rubbed off. But perhaps he didn't notice in the low light. Perhaps he was no longer looking at her objectively. Her body was sore, yet more supple than she could remember ever having felt. He closed her fingers around a giant speedwell. "Hold it to your nose. No, don't . . . I see you as a wild little thing, brimming with very real violence and passion . . . fling out your arm like this. Raise your hips. Oh, for a few scratches . . ." He seemed to be talking to himself. "May I?"

Where had that little knife come from? She didn't care. She was happy to please him, and it didn't even hurt when he started slicing the skin of her chest as if preparing her for a metal filigree. He dropped his head to the slices and licked, smearing the blood artfully. "Ohhhh . . ."

And his lips were on hers again, and she hardly even noticed when he drew suddenly away from her and the air rushed between their bodies. She twisted her hips, begging wordlessly.

And he was reaching below the bed, his eyes receding into a chill, untouchable distance. In his hand was—

"*No!*" she screamed, writhing away from the snakelike jab of his hand. The speedwell's petals scattered as she threw herself off the bed. He came on, eyes like frost, all signs of desire gone.

They fooled me after all. So this is how I am to die—"I'm not a ghost! I can wash it all off!" She backed into the open doorway, casting around for water. "I never knew my disguise was *this* good! I'm not a ghost!"

Water. A sinkful, ledges littered with bottles and brushes. She snatched up a sponge and doused her face. *Why* had she rubbed the dust in so well? As Ziniquel reached her she dropped the sponge, breathing hard, fur spiked and wet. Drops turned black as they reached the blood on her chest and mingled with it. She tucked her hair behind her ears—she could do something as ungraceful as that, for she was Humility again, the illusion of beauty dispelled. "See? I'm not a ghost, am I? You can't believe it now! Look how ugly I am!"

Slowly, Ziniquel came back into his eyes. He lowered the syringe. For a moment she thought she would collapse. She grabbed a towel and scrubbed her face dry. "C-c-can I g-get dressed?"

"Yes! Yes, by the gods, put some clothes on!"

Unsuccessfully she tried to do up the falseribs of the dress and keep an eye on him at the same time. He shook his head briefly, then came and stood behind her to fasten it. He had put down the syringe, but all the same it took all her courage not to shrink away from him. "What—what was in that?" she asked.

"Oh. Salt aconite, for intense but fleeting agony." He finished the hooks and eyes, then moved away from her to light more torches. "I'll probably still have to kill you. Don't get cocky. My reputation will never survive my having been tricked like this. You're very homely; a pity you are not a little thinner, then that bone structure would show—but you'd lose your figure."

The room blazed with light. It must have been close to three in the morning. Whoever had been screaming, downstairs, had been reduced to moans. Ziniquel made a face. "Hear that? That's Mory at work. She is the cruelest of us all. I don't know that I *should* kill you—there might be a better way . . ." He cast his eyes over her.

She'd sidled away until her back was to the wall. Now she edged nearer to the vase lying on its side.

"Don't even think about it." Ziniquel sat on the end of his bed and began to dress. Not just his manner, but his voice had changed. No longer was he the gentle, romantic merchant from Westchasm. Now he was a matter-of-fact killer. No longer handsome—far more dangerous. "I could kill you with my bare hands. But I have to think about it. That was a good disguise. It had to be, to fool me. That's got to be worth something."

"I don't understand." Humi failed to keep her voice even. "You made me believe in you, and then you tried to kill me. You *did*, didn't you? It isn't all just a dream?"

"Wish it was." Ziniquel nipped shut his boot buckles. Then he looked up. "And I bet *you've* killed, yourself! Only another killer would have guessed what was coming. This has *never* happened to me before. Don't deny it!"

Humi knotted her hands, feeling her lips go dry. Was she mad to trust this man? "Murderess. That's what my mother used to call me. Manipulative little murderess."

She wondered if she had just lost her last chance to live. Survival would be enough for her right now. She'd be happy to be on the streets, where Ministra Bareed would have sent her. *Oh, gods! Pati, Broken Bird, Arity!*

Ziniquel Sevenash leaped to his feet and hugged her. Stunned, she held on as he capered around the room, cannoning into the coatstand, skidding in the dirty water. "Erene, Mory, I'm on my way now!" he crowed. "Girl, what's your name?"

"Humility—"

"Hmm. I bet they call you Humi. See, tonight we thought all but one of us would get a ghost, and then there turned out to be seven of you—

enough for us all. But praise the day that I drew the short straw! You're
going to be a ghostier."

"A . . . ?"

"There are seven of us. Each of us holds a seat on the Ellipse. Where do
you come from?"

"Domesdys—"

"Marvelous. We haven't got a Domesdian as either master ghostier or
apprentice at the moment. Oh, Humi, I'm going to show you everything!"

"You mean—you make the ghosts? *You?*"

"Isn't that obvious? Of course!"

"My cousin is a ghost. If you're telling the truth, then he has been—
chosen—by another of you." *Beau! Was that you screaming?* "I have to see
him. Take me to him."

"Erene has him," Ziniquel said annoyedly. "Do you have to?"

"Please!" she begged. "You can't *not!*"

"Oh. Oh, strike the gods." He blew out breath. "It would have to be
Erene. She and I are not the best of friends. But if you must—you are
going to be my apprentice—we should not start by disagreeing—"

He placed a hand in her back, where the falseribs cinched her waist so
small he could have circled it with two hands, and guided her into the hall.
It was still dark. They mounted two more flights of rickety stairs to a
landing where starlight came in through skylights of thick, flawed glass.
There was only one door. Ziniquel pushed it open.

Another bedroom, but far more opulent than Ziniquel's—obviously a
woman's boudoir. Feathers nodded from the torch brackets. The circular
bed was strewn with little puff pillows in jewel hues, and rugs of painted
skin covered the floor.

The door clanged shut behind them. In the adjoining room, something
fell to the floor and a woman let out a sharp exclamation. "*Hell!*" The voice
had an edge of exasperation so raw it scraped the ears. Ziniquel slid to the
doorway, quick as a snake. Humi, following, dug her fingers into his shoulder. The next room was large and messy—a workshop like Ziniquel's.
Something whitish spattered the boards next to a dropped syringe. In the
far corner Beau crouched, nude, shaking. The woman turned on Ziniquel,
furious. "What the hell?" Steel-colored hair slid from an elaborate, half-
undone coiffure. Her gray-furred face was wrathful. In one hand she
gripped another syringe. "I'll deal with you in a minute!" She began to
edge backward. The sheer, deliberate stealth of her motion made Humi's
spine crawl. Beau did not see how close she was coming until she tensed,
ready to whirl and leap on him, and—

"Beau! Ware!" Humi screamed shrilly.

Beau scurried further into the corner, letting out tiny noises of terror. The woman let the syringe fall and stood up. Her rage seemed to drop away from her like a series of husks. Underneath, she was a small woman. Her dress was crumpled off one shoulder, showing the breast. "Ziniquel, once again, what are you doing? What was the very first thing Constance taught you—could it have been never to interrupt a master at work?"

Ziniquel leaned an elbow on the doorway. "Nice job you're doing here, Erene. I can feel those waves of positive emotion coming off that ghost."

"Don't start. Just don't start. Who is this? Where's *your* ghost?"

"This is my ghost."

Humi edged out from behind him. She didn't want to get too close to the woman. Was there any way she could reach Beau?

"She doesn't look like much." The woman flicked an eye over Humi. "The flamens' standards must have dropped considerably if they chose *her*."

Ziniquel sighed resignedly. In a few well-chosen words, he told her everything Humi had told him about coming to Delta City as Beau's companion. He ended: "And I'm taking her on as apprentice. Since we're going to have a long, productive relationship, I thought I would begin by indulging her wants. This ghost is her cousin. She wanted to see him before he dies."

"You're taking her on?" the woman Erene said. "Ziniquel, is she good enough? Or is it just that you're so covetous of an apprentice that you think happenstance is providence?"

Ziniquel's moss-green fur bristled. "Erene, you don't have the right to ask me that. I'm a master ghostier, just like you. But I'll answer anyway: no matter what else I might sacrifice, I'd *never* put my art in jeopardy. You, of all people, should know that."

"All right. She's good enough. I'll trust you on that." Erene put her head on one side and gazed at him. "All the same, I don't know whether you're ready for an apprentice, Zin, especially one only two or three years younger than you. You're just too raw."

Ziniquel stared straight at Erene, challenging her. "I was as ready as anyone ever is."

She stood silent for a long minute, as if trying to remember. Finally she nodded. "Yes, you were."

It was a painful admission, Humi could see.

"But that's not what matters here. This business of apprentices is trickier than you may think." Her eyes moved to Humi.

Summoning boldness, Humi stared right back. Erene was old enough to be Humi's mother—but her soft gray fur covered any lines that might lie in her skin as smoothly as a layer of mist. Her dress was the pink of blooming roses, looped over beige underskirts. Her fingers on Humi's face felt unexpectedly gentle. "Well, girl, a murderess, huh?"

Humi nodded, gazing up into Erene's face. Nothing to be done except stick it out. No use to protest that her grandfather had wanted to die and that she hadn't meant to kill that man in Port Taite. Not good to remember that timeless moment when she had looked down and seen him lying in his blood.

"Would you like to watch me work?" Erene gestured toward Beau, in the corner. "Actually, it might add a nice edge. I was planning a masturbation scene—the implicit force in his body is extraordinary. It's not too often we get ghosts who've done physical work all their lives." She spoke now to Ziniquel. "This handsome, powerful young man, who should be able to snap his fingers and have girls come running, spending his energy touching himself alone. I had it, I was on the very edge, when you came in."

"Gods, I'm sorry!" Zin said sincerely.

"I planned him like this—" Erene arched her back, throwing out her arms.

A shared passion seemed to bloom between the two ghostiers, transcending their hostility. Ziniquel said eagerly, "But if he's gazing at her—dreaming of their being together—it will add another dimension to his emotion! The piece will have much more depth!"

"We were never lovers," Humi protested, but they paid no attention.

"I'll do it!" Erene exclaimed. "What's her name? Humi! Sit over there. On the stool by the window. Gaze at him, meet his eyes, beg, *plead* with him to come to you. Don't worry—he won't be able to." Her mouth curved. She dusted her palms on her skirts. "You say you're a murderess. Prove it."

"Hah! Nice, Errie!" Ziniquel dropped to the floor. "I have faith in you, Humi! Do it!"

Humi felt as though her heart were being shredded. Agony filled her. *Beau!*

What could she do?

Could she save them both?

No.

Could she save Beau by sacrificing herself?

Uncomprehending and wild-eyed, he had flattened himself against the wall. His teeth showed. Yet he hadn't curled around his private parts, as an animal would. He seemed to be unconsciously daring Erene to return. There was no way he would be able to pull his mind together to make an escape.

Could Humi save herself by sacrificing him?

She heard herself sob. Hardly knowing where her feet were taking her, she stumbled toward him. A strong, salty smell hit her several armspans away, but ignoring it, she collapsed at his feet. "Oh, love—"

It was clear that he didn't really recognize her. His hands buried themselves in her hair and came away, pulling strands out. His mouth vacillated, and his eyes wandered the room dazedly. The only reactions left to him were to danger and safety.

Crying, she hugged him. "I love you. I'll always love you."

She backed away from him and stumbled to the window. Hating herself, she collapsed on the stool. Like any other warm-blooded creature, she had no control over her instincts: she would do whatever was necessary to save her own skin.

SEVEN

The ghosting lasted till dawn crept under the curtains. First Erene had to bring Beau back to the peak at which she had had him before Ziniquel and Humi interrupted her. Then she merged in the new aspect of her piece, the longing for Humi. This was where Humi herself came in. She had to make herself cry, she had to kneel near Beau, extending her hands in all-too-real yearning. Ziniquel directed her in whispers. He seemed to know what Erene wanted as well as the older woman did.

Finally Beau's hand was moving steadily between his legs. His eyes held Humi's like bits of violet glass.

Erene stooped over him and ran her hands through his hair, disarraying it artfully. Ziniquel approached, watching like a predator. Erene was on her knees. She gripped her refilled syringe lightly yet firmly. "She likes robe root—it works more thoroughly," Ziniquel breathed to Humi.

"Humi!" Beau cried, speaking for the first time since she had come in. "Humi!" And his other arm curled out with the pure, fluid grace he had learned in the House of Larch, straining toward her. Ziniquel's breath sizzled. Erene's eyes did not flicker. But as Beau climaxed, head cracking back, she sprang. The needle entered his outstretched arm near the wrist. He sank to the floor, mouth opening, legs loose and apart. The stench grew worse. If Humi had looked, she too would have been sick. The catharsis held for a long moment. Then Ziniquel plunged, grabbing Beau under the elbows and backing rapidly. A brown stain followed them.

Erene did not move. Her eyes were shut tight and her whole body seemed to quiver with tension.

"Open the curtains!" Ziniquel hissed.

Stumbling over her feet, Humi obeyed. The view caught her eyes and held her there. She had forgotten that they were on the top floor. Beyond gray-tiled shoals of roofs, she could see the marshes: a vast net of canals and islands, the water pink in the first rays of light. The sun was just rising over the far-off shore, behind the grassy islands. Black flurries of birds crossed its orange disk. Their calls came peacefully over the roofs of Marshtown, harmonizing with the sounds of water and the air.

She let out her breath. Thin, cool air chilled her lungs. Below in the street, somebody called brokenly, "Wait for me, boys, wait for me! This is ghostiers' ground! Don't leave me—" She looked down and saw a brightly costumed young man throwing up in front of the townhouse. The local children, the first Marshtowners to rise, gave him a wide berth as they prodded their animals down the street. His coughs and miserable curses reached her ears clearly.

"Hello!" she called. "Did you have fun last night?"

He started and stared blearily around. Finally he looked up.

"Were you at the Summers'? I recognize you, I think. Young Lord Meadowlord, from Iceland?" She could have dropped a copper into his open mouth. "I know your mother! Give her regards from me, the ghost she sat with last night! Tell her she may see me again soon—but next time *she* will be the one in danger!" Humi laughed, an ebullient sound that careened off the windows opposite.

The young man stared for a minute longer, his horror growing. Then he picked up his coattails and ran. His first step took him skidding in a puddle of pig piss: arms flailing, he dropped his hat and left it lying as he vanished around the corner. Humi chuckled, and turned around.

"Nice," said Erene. She slumped in a leather armchair in the far corner. "You have a tongue in your head, after all." Rolling her eyes up to Ziniquel, she smiled provocatively. The other ghostier leaned in the doorway, arms folded, his face dark with battened-down fury.

Beau's body was gone. Only the various stains remained—and the smell. And the empty syringe. And the cold, radiating from the center of the floor.

Erene's voice was happy with anticipation. "Humi. Move out of the light. Now look at the middle of the floor."

Humi squinted at the spot where she could still see Beau in her mind's eye, poised as he had been at that last instant. And she *could* see him. She blinked. Like a figure blown from transparent glass, tilted over on his back so that one foot stuck stiffly into the air, like a human soap bubble. How could she have missed him for an instant? He cast a shadow on the floor, fuzzy-edged and watery but as real as her own.

She ventured toward him and touched his crystal hair. She flinched from the burning shock of cold. There was nothing else. No emotion such as there had been with the ghosts at Belstem Summer's palace. He had died exhausted, mentally burned out.

"She can see him, Zin!" Erene gloated. "Scowl all you like, it will do no good!"

Humi dragged her eyes away from the delicate figure. She looked confusedly from one ghostier to the other. "He's so cold. But I don't feel anything else. Just a sort of exhaustion. Why?"

"A new ghost is imbued with whatever emotion it felt at the moment of its death," Erene said. "Not only the paint on them, but the emotional content, is contributed by the ghostiers who make them. That's our most closely guarded secret. The world sees ghosts as shrines to the departed, whereas we see them only as art. Now that you know that, you have to stay. You can't leave."

Ziniquel's face was as dark as a rainy evening, his arms tightly folded. "What methods, Erene! Threatening her!"

"Ziniquel?" Humi appealed. "Why are you angry?"

It was Erene who answered, her voice revealing no signs of exhaustion. "Because he's still a child, and he can't help showing it. He's too young to take on an apprentice, especially one as promising as you—but *I* am in sore need of someone to carry on my craft. So I have decided to claim you. I have the right. Whatever else I may be, I am still senior ghostier, and I can claim my privileges. We will do very well together, Humi." She crooked one finger. "Come here."

Bemused, Humi circled the nexus of coldness in the center of the floor.

"Sit down."

Shrinking from Ziniquel's wrath, she obeyed.

Arthritically, as if it were a great effort, Erene stroked her head. "Save the gods. I only ever had one apprentice, and he left me. That was the worst day of my life. But this is the best, and it is only just dawning."

"Stop rubbing it in!" Ziniquel erupted. "How dare you pull this! She was *mine*, Erene!"

"It wasn't *I* who was fooled by a disguise no cleverer than one of my own! I don't think a man as naive as *that* should be allowed to have an apprentice at all, Ziniquel!"

Humi held her breath, waiting for his retort. But he flung around and stormed out of the suite. The door slammed violently.

Erene laughed like a peal of little bells. "Humi, darling—" her fingers twitched on Humi's sleeve—"I want to remember what I'm like when I have an apprentice. I want to become that woman again, because I think she's better than this one. But will you forgive me if occasionally I slide back into being the senior ghostier who no longer truly deserves her position yet clings fiercely to it?"

"Why . . . why was Ziniquel so angry?"

"I took him down a few pegs in front of you. And I confess, I haven't been exerting myself to get along with him recently. But with you I will be different."

"Wait!" Humi felt panic rising. "I haven't agreed to anything! What if I don't want . . ."

Erene's voice hardened. "Don't even *think* of leaving without my permission. Quite apart from the secret I revealed to you, there is the blood on your hands. You helped us make a ghost. And that blood never washes off. I can have you tracked down."

Humi's throat felt dry. "If you're trying to threaten me, it's no use. I've lived with blood on my hands since I was nine years old. If I wanted to leave, that wouldn't stop me."

"Ah," Erene said after a lengthy pause.

Silence fell. With a sort of gladness, Humi saw that the gray eyes were troubled. So she had managed to throw her off balance.

"Well. Are you willing to be my apprentice? Or not?"

"You're making fun of me," Humi said bitterly. "I can't refuse." She felt terribly alone, a thousand miles from Beaulieu, with no one to turn to for help. "I have nowhere else to go. I would be stupid not to stay with you. And—" perverse pride flared—"I'm not stupid. Whatever else I am."

"No," Erene said at last. "You're not."

The sunlight glinted off Beau's ghost, catching her in the eye with flashes of violet, green, orange. Humi wanted to cry. She wanted him back!

"Well, then," Erene said, and paused. Humi was silent. "I need to get out of this chair. I need some nourishment. And I expect you haven't eaten anything for at least one day. You're a country girl—I take it you can cook." Humi nodded drearily. "You'll find a fireplace, flint, tinder, and pots in the next room. Dried meat in the compartment at the bottom of the sink, oats in the closet. Why don't you make us some breakfast?"

It wasn't hard figuring out how to use the Deltan cookware and hearth. In silence Humi mixed up a hearty breakfast of oatmeal and salt pork. The food restored Erene's energy. She stood up and stretched her legs, complaining of the bruises Beau had given her. It was almost noon. The ghost of Beau glittered in the middle of the floor, easily visible in the midday light. "I suppose I must take you to meet the other ghostiers. Do change out of that dress, girl. It makes your fur look so drab."

"It looked good with gold and silver," Humi said sullenly. "And my natural fur is drab no matter what I wear." But she was glad to escape the cinch of the falseribs. The spindlespun skirt and blouse Erene offered out of the enormous wardrobe in her bedroom were much more comfortable, and they fitted well, as Erene was exactly Humi's height. Round-hipped, Erene had small breasts, and her bones showed around her waist and in her forearms. By no stretch of the imagination could she be considered beautiful, but she had a wide mouth and aggressive eyes. She was a Piradean, born of a rocky, unkind land.

"We'll have to get you some clothes of your own," she said. "And gowns for your appearances at court." She let her dress fall in a heap. Humi watched her search, naked, through the sea of garments on the floor of the bedroom. The apartment on the other side of the workshop where she had ghosted Beau comprised this bedroom, a sitting room, parlor, guest bedrooms, dining room, and bathing room. It was furnished in Piradean style, which meant a few pieces of stone-leaf furniture softened with cushions and draperies. The gorgeous boudoir that Humi and Ziniquel had first entered was simply a front, decorated for Erene's ghosts, not Erene herself. This was her sanctum. But Humi had the feeling she did not spend much time here. Several skylights in the sitting room were cracked, and a leak in the parlor ceiling had ruined a tapestry. When Humi pointed that out as they walked through the apartment, Erene had been shocked. She ran her hand over the blended colors and sagging threads like a woman noticing a wound in her body for the first time.

But at last she said that done was done, she never noticed that kind of thing until it was too late. And, complimenting Humi on her sharp eyes: "Look over the rest of the place if you want. If you like Piradean glasswork, there are some nice pieces on the dining table." But one of them had rolled to the floor and shattered to pink dust. Another had old, smelly wine lees in the bottom. Spiders scrabbled in the ceramic tub in the bathroom.

Puzzled, Humi returned to the bedroom. Erene was plucking garments haphazardly off the floor and putting them down on the wrinkled, dampish bed. "I take these to the washerwoman when I want to wear them—*if* I can find the one I want. How miserable it'll be to make this place habitable again. Perhaps I'll have to let Algia in at last—she's the only one of us who likes cleaning house. But how I hate to give in to her. Oh, well."

Fastening her dress as she went, she pushed along the wall and opened a door, revealing another landing. The hall and stairwell were cruder than Humi had noticed last night, under the influence of Ziniquel and wine. The construction looked hasty and raw—either that or very old indeed. As old as Beaulieu, so old that carpentry had been markedly more primitive. And here, unlike in Beaulieu, nobody had taken the trouble to sand or paint or limewash in a dozen centuries.

But the stairs didn't creak as Erene and Humi descended to the ground floor. Daylight shone in the cracks around the front door. They crossed a bare, dusty antechamber and stopped before the single door, whose rudely carved knob bore a patina of many fingers. Erene stooped, felt in a crack under the skirting and offered Humi a glass mug. "Here. Like this. I expect they're talking about us—we'll get the jump on them."

Humi put her ear to the bottom of the glass. She gasped. She could hear the voices inside perfectly.

"You can't blame Erene." It was a man's voice, rich and confident. "She's thirty-five. That's almost too late to start training an apprentice. Zin, you'll find another precocious little girl—maybe even another companion. Now that that trick has been thought of, more will try it. Don't sulk."

"You always defend Erene, Elicit!" Ziniquel burst out. "Last night I was tricked only because I'd never conceived such a thing could be done. Next time we'll all be on the lookout, and such a trick won't even get past the beauticians. I tell you, she's an apprentice you'd all covet!"

"Well, I wish I'd seen her disguise!" A woman laughed. "I hardly believe an untutored child could fool you, Zin!"

"She fooled even the gods. I was standing in the crowd. I saw Broken Bird pass her over."

"So when are we going to meet this extraordinary female?" The voice was so high and nasal that it rendered even that innocuous question offensive.

"How should I know, Owen?" Ziniquel asked. "You can't trust Erene. For all we know, now that she's got her hands on an apprentice—the last thing she needs us for—she'll move out altogether and leave us lying like her cast-off gowns. I wouldn't put it past her to take Humi to live with Goquisite in that frilly social crossroads of a mansion!"

"Never," the woman said instantly, and several others agreed with her. "No one has ever moved out of Tellury Crescent for any reason. Erene wouldn't go that far."

"Anyway, the strength of her position lies here." The new voice was crisp, elderly, a breath of reason. "Her Ellipse seat springs from her status as senior ghostier. She wouldn't jeopardize herself by leaving us."

"Oh, yes, she would!" Ziniquel flared. "She's screwing herself up to do it! That's why she's been so miserable these past months—all she wants is to spend all her time with Goquisite, and to hell with her political career!"

Humi realized in a flash of enlightenment that she knew who "Goquisite" was. She was Goquisite Ankh, the Ellipse councillor, commonly mentioned in the same breath as Belstem Summer.

"That isn't fair, Zin." It was a soft, husky, woman's voice, but a few words quieted the uproar which had broken out. "You're skewing things, as usual. Erene cares deeply about politics. Goquisite is only one part of her dilemma—she sees the future, and she's trying to drag us toward it. It's not her fault we're so heavy."

"What's this, Mory? Are you turning traitor too?"

"No. But I can see what Erene sees. I can sympathize with her."

The man who had spoken first—Elicit—said, "Let's not dissect poor Erene like this! We all love her—yes, even you, Zin!—and we won't turn our backs on her, no matter what she does. *That's* what the strength of her position is, if you want." He was clever, Humi thought. He meant to defuse their anger at Erene by making them feel as though she owed everything to them. "We've been looking after her since Hem left, and we won't stop now. Let's have an end to this, Zin. If she wants the apprentice, for the gods' sakes let her have her."

"But we *can't* let her have her! She was mine, and Erene simply stepped in and took her!"

"It's within her powers."

"Zin is right. She *shouldn't* use her powers like that." This must be the fourth woman ghostier. "Most of them aren't meant to be touched. They're for show, like ornamental daggers. And as for the practical ones, their use is dictated purely by decency and friendship."

"Then everything's all right!" It was the effeminate-voiced man, Owen. He sounded as though he was enjoying a last word on the affair. "Because everyone knows that Ziniquel and Erene *aren't* friends! And so they can do whatever they like to each other!"

"Gods, you'll trivialize anything to get your digs in, Owen!" Zin roared. There was silence.

Dazedly Humi opened her eyes. Erene's mouth trembled. That last exchange must have been loud enough for her to hear even without the glass.

Several dreadful moments passed.

"That's horrendous." It was a teenaged girl's voice.

"But true. Isn't it? Consider, Emni."

Some distance away a door slammed. Then another, closer by, and before Humi understood what was going on, Erene had yanked her to her feet and dragged her back from the door.

"Zin. Zin, what are you doing?"

"You can't suspect—"

When the door thudded open, they were standing side by side a respectable distance away. But Humi still had the glass in her hand. Ziniquel's eyes locked on it. He looked up at Erene, betrayal in his eyes. "I didn't think you really *were* listening. Never in a million years."

The senior ghostier breathed fast. Her hand tightened painfully on

Humi's. Ziniquel's agate eyes spoke volumes. He took a hesitant step toward Erene, as if trying a bridge.

Erene wrenched her hand from Humi's, turned on her heel, and fled.

"Damn," sobbed Ziniquel. "Oh, damn. Oh, Erene. I can't go after you anymore." He leaned against the antechamber wall, face buried in his hands, shaking.

"That's the apprentice," one of the ghostiers said from within the room. "Go speak to her."

"What's her name again?"

Humi listened, staring at the dusty reddish wood floor, not at Ziniquel. Eventually she heard him stumbling past her, up the stairs.

A knobbed finger touched her chin and eased it up. An elderly man, thin and graceful, with green Royallandic fur, stood beside her. "I'm Fra Canyonade." The old man's voice sounded crisp and assured. But his face was troubled. "That must not have sounded very well to you. It is possible that Erene and Zin could become irrevocably estranged. Erene's taking you wasn't the last straw—no, I'm sure it wasn't—but we have just been reminded that a split is possible."

"Would . . . would that be so unthinkable?" Humi asked tremulously. "It doesn't seem to me that they like each other very much, anyway . . ."

Fra guided her into the large room. It seemed like a lounge, with crude old paintings on the wall, cushioned chairs, and a great fireplace. Fifteen or so people sat around the room, some with plates neglected on their laps, staring silently at Fra and Humi.

He put his arm in hers and escorted her toward the table. He didn't move like a grandfather. If his steps were slow, they were light. "Among the ghostiers, our unity is our strength. The slightest crack in our solidarity would be unthinkable."

They stood up to greet Humi. There were Piradean, Royallandic, Calvarese, and Archipelegan faces, and one Veretrean woman, who extended a hand to Humi. She was middle-aged, with a scrubby brown apple-cheeked face and a warm smile. "Don't take it too badly, Humi. You're not the cause of the trouble, only its latest installment. Hard of Erene to do this to you, I think. I am Rita Porphyry, and this is my apprentice, Owen Phyllose." Humi didn't need to hear Owen's voice. His smile was enough to warn her that he was the cynical, soft-voiced one.

"I'm Beisa," said a plump, motherly woman in a blue dress. "And these are my apprentices Sol and Emni." They were a teenage boy and girl, with white fur and black hair identical to Beisa's. *Archipelagan,* Humi thought. Thus they didn't have to be related. All Archipelagans had the same coloring.

"I'm Mory," the Calvarese woman said. With a start, Humi recognized her . . . not in this patched skirt, but in crimson . . .

She had enticed Rain out of the banquet hall last night.

"And this is my apprentice Tris."

"Trisizim Sepal," the boy said in a precise voice. He was Calvarese too, about fourteen years of age.

"Elicit Paean," said the remaining man. His voice identified him as the man who had defended Erene. A tall, intelligent-faced Piradean, his hair was cropped as short as fur all over his scalp. "And my apprentices—" he snapped his fingers. A pale nonentity of a woman came around the table, hustling a girl of seven or eight in front of her. "Algia and Eternelipizaran." He lifted the child up into his arms and planted a kiss on her cheek. "My little prodigy!"

Wriggling out from under the kiss, Eternelipizaran complained, "I thought you'd be younger, Humi."

Everyone laughed. Elicit jogged the little girl up and down. "Maybe the next new apprentice will be your age. For now, we like Humi the way she is. Isn't that right?"

"I know we'll be friends," Humi said to the child, and there was an uncomfortable silence. She should not have spoken! She longed for Erene, or even Ziniquel, to be a buffer between her and these strangers.

"Oh, it's too bad of Erene to go off and leave the poor thing like this!" Rita burst out. "I don't think *she's* any readier to take an apprentice than Zin is!"

"Done is done, Rita." Mory, the Calvarese, squeezed the older woman's arm, keeping an eye on Humi. "All we can do is prepare her to cope with Erene's—vacillations."

"It's very easy, isn't it," Elicit said mildly, "to blame Erene for our own inefficiencies and outdated traditions?" He put Eternelipizaran down, then stepped behind Humi and gently massaged her shoulders. She wanted to wriggle out from under his touch, but she stopped herself. "Child, it's not as bad as they're making it sound! You're one of us now. We'll stand by you."

The sequence of events was too convoluted for Humi to comprehend. All she had to hang on to was Erene. Erene, at least, had expressed in no uncertain terms that she *wanted* Humi. Not that she was having her foisted on her. She twisted around to look at Elicit. "No need to take care of me. I'm Erene's apprentice, and she promised me I'll be safe with her!"

He laughed delightedly. "Oh, what a fine ghostier you'll make!"

"What a love!" Beisa said, and hugged her. The Archipelagan woman's fine perfume was incongruous with her homely dress. That inconsistency spoke of money, and plenty of it, but no self-centered vanity. The ghostiers were commoners so rich that they didn't even bother to furnish their houses. Now, as if Beisa had broken the ice, they were all crowding around, reaching to touch Humi. She was surrounded by bony, muscular, soft, hard bodies and a dozen different perfumes. It was frightening—until she relaxed: and then a wonderful sense of acceptance pervaded her. Maybe they really *did* want her, after all. Emni, Beisa's girl apprentice, hung an arm around her neck; Mory hugged her. Fra kissed her on the cheek with his old, dry lips. "If Erene ever comes back," he said, "she'll take you to see the Eftpool. It's the ritual for new apprentices."

"Imrchu," Emni said caressingly. The word was strange to Humi, but it sounded like a term of endearment. "Would you like some custard? We were just having lunch—"

EIGHT

"No outsiders are allowed to enter our houses," Emni said after lunch, when they were in a sedan, riding through Marshtown. "We don't put ourselves up on pedestals, but we have to have some indication that we're not just like the neighbors. So we have a rule that anyone who crosses our thresholds without permission incurs a dreadful punishment."

"Unless he's a god," said her brother Sol quietly. "You can't keep the gods out." The sedan jounced and jolted, curtain swayed, and outside voices discussed groceries, piglets, childbirth, theology, and a dozen other subjects, in snatches. Sol and Emni sat across from Humi in the half-dark.

"Don't nitpick," Emni admonished her twin. She turned to Humi again. "You live in Albien House with Zin, Mory, Tris, and Erene. It joins onto the Chalice, which is the ghostiers' original house. Thaumagery and Melthirr were built later. Look out the window and you'll have a good view of it as we go round the bend—you must not have had time when we were hustling you into the sedan."

Humi peered through the curtains. "Oh," she breathed in delight. The many-windowed building to which Ziniquel had brought her last night was instantly recognizable. Most townhouses tended to grow slender and crooked, even in Marshtown; the only exceptions were the mansions of the palace district. But Albien House was a pleasantly proportioned building snuggled between a glassblower's shop and the taller, equally ancient structure that was the Chalice. It had a certain immovable dignity. Humi felt proud that *she* was one of the few privileged to enter it.

"Sol and I live a little way up the street in Thaumagery House, with Beisa, Rita, and Owen," Emni said as Humi let the curtain fall and turned around. "Fra, Elicit, Eterneli, and Algia all live in Melthirr House."

"Who is Algia again?" Humi asked, trying to get them straight.

Emni glanced at her twin. Sol was a stocky boy, stingy with words, who wore his black hair shaved up the back, with long bangs. Humi had yet to see him leave Emni's side. "She *would* be the one you forget. She's the pale-furred Deltan with no chin. Officially she's Elicit's apprentice. But all she does is play mother to Eterni."

"Shush!" Sol said sharply.

Emni giggled. "And clean house for us all. One of the disadvantages of keeping our houses off limits is the dirt—we can't have servants."

"Erene's apartment is a disaster," Humi said.

"Oh, Erene. She won't let Algia, or anyone at all, apart from Elicit, inside her apartment. I don't think there's any big secret . . . I think she's just ashamed of how dirty it is. It's been more than a year since I went up there." Emni rolled her eyes. She oozed camaraderie. "She hardly goes there anymore except to work. Most nights she's away. She only sleeps at home if Goquisite is out of Delta City."

"Shut up, Em!" Sol said sharply. Emni's long black hair flew into his eyes as she twisted toward him. She buried her face in his neck.

Humi glanced dubiously from one to the other.

"All right!" The curtain was thrown back, and there was Owen, smiling unhealthily. "Here we are! Not very far after all, was it?"

The porters had stopped the sedans in the upper end of a small, steep Marshtown street. The smell of salt and reeds rotting in winter came to Humi's nostrils. On this side, the island sloped to the level of the marshes; the water could not have been more than a stone's throw away, on the other side of the buildings that lined the thoroughfare at the bottom of the hill. The parked sedan chairs spread out of the mouth of the narrow street, blocking traffic. The dull-garbed pedestrians glanced up curiously and then continued on their way, unsurprised.

Humi slid between the sedan chairs to Erene's side, where her master stood with Elicit and Rita. Elicit stopped speaking—but not before Humi caught her own name. "Shall we go in?" Rita said diplomatically.

Erene looked as though she was having a hard time battening down her anger. Without bothering to answer, she rapped hard on the plank door. It opened to reveal a plain woman with two furry babies, one on her back, one slung on a hip. "Gods' greeting, Godsie. Who . . . ?" her green face wrinkled.

Erene muddied violently.

"Oh, dear," Rita whispered.

Elicit stepped past Erene and cleared his throat.

"Ohhh! Godsman Paean!" The woman's smile lit her eyes, and she peered past Elicit into the sunlight. "Gods grant health to my children! You've brought *all* your fellows!"

"Indeed." Elicit ducked into the house and pulled the woman after him. Humi heard him muttering urgently, presumably to save Erene's face. But before he finished, Erene touched Humi's arm. "Come on," she said. "We can be the first in. When the atmosphere has only just been broken, it's really something unique."

Humi bit her lip and nodded. She followed her master straight through the house. Erene pulled her through a door, into the sunlight again, only now it was muted. Multicolored patches of light drifted over them.

"Oh! Oh, it's beautiful," Humi said involuntarily.

Erene nodded pleasedly. "It's the very repository of beauty."

The top of the dome was lower than the house, so that it would be invisible from the street, visible only from top-floor windows in the surrounding houses. Inside, metal rods branched up from the brick sidewalls to support a weight of glass that must be immense, for all that the dome looked so airy. It was a geodesic greenhouse, each triangle of glass a different brilliant color. They seemed to shift into a new pattern every time Humi looked up. Dark, fronded plants grew around the bases of the walls, drops of humidity trembling on the tips of the fronds. The air was so heavy that Humi found it hard to breathe. A pool of black water was sunk into the middle of the floor: though they had not touched it, ripples ran away from Humi's and Erene's feet.

"The atmosphere's going," Erene whispered. "The more people come in, the less it can hold out." She knelt on the brick path and reached down to the water. The reflections of the dome in the pool shook with violent queasiness. "Quick! You too."

The bricks were worn smooth as the boulders of stone walls by centuries of feet and knees. Humi's finger seemed to vanish as it entered the icy water. Something sharp and small shot past beneath the surface. The underwater gust of its passing played with her fur. She gasped.

"It touched you? Good. They're not afraid. If the efts are afraid to touch an apprentice the first time, it means that he will always be striving miserably for goals beyond his reach. Owen was one such. You have met him. My first apprentice, Hem Lakestone, didn't feel them either. But he cares nothing for a ghostier's goals now . . . Perhaps there's nothing in the superstition." Erene was silent, moving her hand in the water. "Here. Here, Telitha. This was the most beautiful ghost I was ever privileged to make. She's more than ten years old now. Telitha . . . ahhh."

Slowly, Erene lifted something out of the pool. As the surface of the water broke, Humi smelled a sudden waft of *badness*, ennui like nothing she had ever felt before—like dining rooms where meals have sat congealing for years, chambers hung with cobwebs through which ancient, obsolete men and women limp drearily, circling. The thing in Erene's hand thrashed wetly against her palm. Erene closed her fingers on it. "Hello, Telitha. How have you been?" She waited a moment, as if for a reply. "Oh, don't give me that."

For a moment Humi sensed the desperation of the invalid who tells her relatives again and again how the nurse is abusing her, and she cannot get out. Cannot get out.

She quashed her misgivings. "Can I hold her?"

"Better not. But isn't she beautiful?" Erene held the creature up to Humi's eyes. It had silver scales and a long, transparent-edged tail like a tadpole's.

It had a woman's face.

She gasped and wrenched away. Although she hadn't heard the door open and shut, the ghostiers were crowding around her. Beisa gripped her, stopping her from falling. "Throw that thing back!" she said to Erene. "It's more than a decade old, it must be starting to rot!"

"I can smell it." Mory knelt and deftly tweaked the wriggling eft out of Erene's grip. She lifted one of its scales and poked. Again Humi smelt rotting meat. "Ugh. Erene, for the gods' sake." Mory tossed the eft back into the pool. Ripples traveled back and forth, hitting the brick walls with hard *clops*.

"Quick, Humi, call your cousin," Erene said. "Beauty. Just say 'Beauty.' "

"She'll be in danger with that, won't she?" Rita said worriedly. "Gods know how many farmers call their child after his primary virtue, and how many of those have lived up to it all the way—"

"Don't be ridiculous, Rita," Erene said. "The efts will know who she means."

"Beauty, Beauty," Humi whispered. "Beau! Here!"

"That's not loud enough!" Ziniquel said in a clear, ringing voice. "You know how difficult it is to hear with your ears underwater, don't you?"

"The other day I called for a ghost of mine named Happiness," Rita said, "and you'll never guess what I got. I closed my fingers around it and brought it up into the light. I could see its *skeleton.* Its eyes dangled, yet it managed to look up at me. It must have been as old as a god."

"Rita, by the *gods*—"

"Beau!" Spray flecked Humi's face as she leaned out over the water. "Beau!"

He threw himself into her hand, alive with pent-up energy.

Their eyes met. His face and its frame of curls were stuck onto the end of the fish's body like a mask.

She was stricken with a crippling sense of guilt. "I'm sorry, Beau!" she whispered. "It was both of us, or just one! Please forgive me. It's not like it's done me any good. I don't know what I'm doing here with these people. I wanted to see the world. I wanted to live in Delta City. But I think I've got more than I bargained for." She choked tears down fruitlessly. "I want to get away."

Humi, you were born to become a ghostier. She thought she heard his voice. It sounded just as it always had, but with the added solemnity of some unguessable knowledge. *Just as I was born to be a ghost. You did right by me, betrothed.*

"What are you saying?"

You are blameless. It was my destiny.

"The Godsister did that to you!"

Destiny is destiny. Don't believe me, if you won't. I just wanted to ease your mind.

"And is this my destiny? Do I have to learn to live without you? Can't I just go—" she swallowed tears—"I want to go *home*—"

You have to live without me. Nothing can change that. And you'd be a fool to go back to Beaulieu! Even if you could get there! For a moment the voice was the old Beau's, country-inflected, making fun of her for her foolishness. *Humi, this is what you wanted all your life!* Then it went solemn again. *Are you going to throw it away now that you have it in your hand?*

"All I have in my hand is you," she whispered.

It's a game of souls. Don't you remember the thrill that ran through you when you saw my ghost in the sunlight? The feeling of power when you saw my life slip away? Don't you want more power? And more?

He flipped out of her hand like a dauphin.

"Beau!"

But he arrowed below the surface.

Destiny? Imagination? Or the Godsister's influence? Could that last beyond death?

Rita helped Humi to her feet. The air was fairly whipping around inside the dome. "Are you all right?"

"I . . ." She swallowed.

"I know, dear. It's hard."

"You don't understand." *I have to stay here. I have to stay with you.* Humi gave a sob and buried her face in Rita's scrawny, comfortable bosom.

Gently but firmly, she found herself pushed away. "Erene," Rita said, and sighed. "She's yours. Apparently you promised her you'd look after her. Well, do it." Without looking at Humi, she took her place in the ring of ghostiers around the pool. Elicit came through the door and stood beside her. The ferns lashed, the air dashed and boiled about the dome as if it were a giant arena of sky. White crests formed on the waves in the pool.

"They're going to stay to see the storm," Erene said. "Let's go." She grabbed Humi's arm and pulled her out into the corridor. The cool air flowed into her lungs like milk. A child had drawn with charcoal on this side of the door: stick figures standing in a ring, rivers of hair blowing around their heads. Humi was too dazed to speak. "Good-bye," Erene said magnanimously to the Godsie as they passed her. She was sitting in the doorway, giving suck to one of her babies. The baby's wispy fur and suction grip on the nipple reminded Humi fuzzily of her little cousin Asure. Asure, whom she would never see again. She stopped to pat its head.

"It's Elicit's." Erene laughed unkindly. "You can see it has his hair—or lack of it."

The woman muddied. "Don't speak so, Milady Gentle. Xhil will be back any minute, and he doesn't want to know about Godsman Paean and me."

"I should think he'd be happy to have all these children to raise," Humi said. "Godsie, you're very fertile."

The woman laughed. "Only this one is mine, love."

"You might as well tell her the rest, Soulf," Erene said. "Then she won't worry about getting in a fix."

The woman shifted the baby to her other breast and looked up to meet Humi's eyes. "Love, the ghostiers can't raise babies in the Crescent. And they're wise enough to know it. But just like you said, any other women would be more than happy to have extra babes. So they foster them out. I believe there are five of us foster mothers, scattered throughout Marshtown—isn't that right, Godsie Gentle?"

"Rita has two daughters. Constance had one—the girl must be nearly old enough to marry now. Beisa has a son and a daughter, and then there is Mory's son. That's right."

"And I have Ines and Virtue, Godsie Glissade's daughters, and of course your Tessen, milady. Would you like to see him?" She turned as if to call.

"No!" Erene's voice came out strained. "No, don't! He's probably at some game."

"With respect, I should think not. They all help me about the house, and so learn to spend their time profitably, milady."

Humi looked from one woman to the other. What a strange concept! What kind of woman would give away her own children? The light slanted in the front door and lit Soulf's green-gleaming breast. It was almost sunset.

They had spent hours in the Eftpool.

"We must be going," Erene said. Humi could hear the faint shrill of panes of glass vibrating in the wind. "Lady Garden and I are walking home."

Soulf nodded composedly. "As you will, Milady Gentle."

Down on the thoroughfare, the shopkeepers were rolling up their awnings for the night. Children drove animals along the street, leaving the scent of manure in their wakes. None of the passersby paid any attention to two women dressed modestly in spindlespun. As they climbed uphill, Humi asked: "Erene—who is the father? You're not married, are you?"

"Gods! No, I am not married. Tessen is Hem's. He was my first apprentice. But that was a rather gauche question, Humi."

Humi did a dance step to avoid a pile of pig dung. "I'm sorry. I thought . . . I thought I could ask you anything."

"You *can.*"

"Then—who's Goquisite? Is she Goquisite Lady Ankh?"

Erene's eyes blazed. But this time Humi stopped dead, refusing to be intimidated. Deltans pushed past them, laughing, swearing by all the gods at once. "She's Lady Ankh the councillor. And she's my friend. And to be blunt about it, Humi, she does not have a great deal of intrinsic strength, and she is standing on a razor's edge between audacity and treason. *And it's my fault.* There is a matter of business between us, that is even more important than our friendship, but I have asked the others not to tell you until I want you to know. All I can say now is that you are to be my helper. Goquisite will trust you because you're my apprentice, and maybe that will take some of the pressure off her."

Knowing she was going too far, yet unable to stop herself, Humi said: "Is *that* why you wanted me, then? Is that why you took me from Ziniquel? An extra support on which to stand this business with Goquisite?"

"You—you—" Erene stood stock-still, eyes burning with a fury beyond anything Humi could have guessed. Then she slumped. "Partly."

Humi could not believe it. She could not believe Erene had actually said that. *Well, I'll become a ghostier too,* she thought furiously. *Like you, cold and manipulative. After all, I already am, aren't I? I'll use you, just as you plan to use me.*

For you, Beau. I'll make it up to you.

NINE

Erene Gentle loved the time-consuming job of painting ghosts, especially ghosts as outstandingly handsome as Beauty Garden. Whatever other concerns might occupy her mind, this was her vocation. The seclusion with her work was like a cleansing by fire, a test of her abilities. When a ghostier over thirty years of age looked at her hand holding the paintbrush and saw that it had begun to shake, she was finished—as a ghostier, at any rate. If she had any sense, she would retire. Constance, Ziniquel's master, had loved her work so much that she had kept on and on. And it had cost her her life. But Erene hoped that she herself was years away from that yet.

Erene watched Humi like a predator for signs that the girl was weary of sitting in the corner and running errands. During this period when the master ghostiers did nothing but paint, boredom was inevitable for the apprentices. But if Humi had misgivings she hid them adroitly. It was Erene herself who felt unsure whether she had been wise to apprentice the girl. Alternately, she regretted and congratulated herself on that split-second decision made out of vindictiveness against Ziniquel.

But as Humi's patience, aesthetic taste, and self-control became apparent, Erene realized that once again chance had been kind to her.

One night, coming back from Elicit's apartments, Erene halted in the doorway, watching Humi move hesitantly across the paint-stained floor toward the ghost. She picked up Erene's palette and brush. Erene opened her mouth to stop her. The process of painting was inextricably melded with the emotional coloration of the ghost, so that no one could say where one stopped and the other began. Strictly off limits to new apprentices, both processes.

Humi knelt sucking the hogshair for a minute, forehead creased in thought. Steadying her hand on the ghost's as-yet-unpainted nose, she blocked in several more of the hard, icy curls with white. Then she made a face. Laying down the brush, she crept back to her corner, shivering with cold. She had on only a spindlespun dress, whereas Erene, like all ghostiers while they worked, wore woolens.

Erene reached behind her, slammed the outer door, and came in. "I brought you something to eat." She tossed Humi an egg-stuffed roll. Humi caught it with only a slight fumble, but when Erene looked closely, she saw that the girl's lashes shimmered like fringes of jewels around her eyes.

So she *did* feel pain. She just was not showing it to Erene. And that was good, because Erene could not hug her. Would not surrender to the maternal instincts that were growing in her every day she lived with Humi.

Erene had to set an example of hardness. She could not even congratulate Humi on her talent, although she could tell that now, now that Humi had touched it, this was going to be the best ghost Erene had made in years. The girl was a born ghostier. Her emotions flavored everything Erene had put into the ghost thus far. It might even be her best ghost since Hem left.

How long? How long was that? Erene thought. Tessen would be seven soon, wouldn't he, and it was the news of her pregnancy which had caused Hem to break with the Crescent. He had not understood why she couldn't raise their child. Or give it to him to raise. He had not understood that since they were unmarried, and she was his senior in years and rank, then it was *her* child and she would dispose of it as ghostiers always did.

So he'd stamped out of the shocked assembly of ghostiers in tears. And for two years Erene hadn't known where he was.

He had been traveling the world. Now he was back in Delta City, managing a shop that sold curiosities from the depths of the Veretrean forests, from the nomadic Icelanders, from the barbarians in the reaches of the Archipelago. On one of his voyages he'd found a wife, and they had two children. The shop was in Temeriton, the whorehouse district—a dangerous place to raise children, but subject to none of the rules of piety that bound Marshtown, for sure. Hem's clients were rich, atheistic, and increasingly seedy. He could not have removed his life farther from the Crescent if he'd moved to the wastes of Iceland.

All was forgiven and forgotten between Erene and the Lakestones, at least on the surface, and she sometimes went to visit the family, bringing presents for the children and a bottle of fine wine.

But lately she had been spending too much time in Antiprophet Square to go to Temeriton.

I must take Humi to meet Goquisite. Gods, what is Goquisite going to think? Erene was not looking forward to that confrontation. How would Goquisite take this evidence that Erene's trust in her was less than total?

Erene had sent a letter with the news that she had taken an apprentice, but had received no reply. Probably most of the atheists knew by now. Ah, well—they could not be too upset. In Ellipse, an apprentice, like a leman, was no more than an unimportant appendage of the councillor to whom he or she was attached.

They would have to revise that assumption later, after Erene had trained Humi up.

But first the girl needed quite a bit of refinement. Erene had made the appalling discovery that she didn't know how to read—didn't even have a clear idea of what writing was. But perhaps that was unsurprising. Zeniph Antiprophet had introduced the alphabet only a hundred and fifty years ago, and Humi, living in the saltside, might never have seen a book. But it should not be difficult to teach her everything she needed to know, from sightreading to social graces. Erene had only to slip a fact into a casual discussion to have it thrown back at her later. The girl was so quick to learn that Erene felt as though her child was growing by leaps and bounds, out of all control.

But though Humi seemed to have an almost unnatural appetite for learning and she was always there when Erene needed her to mix pigments or wash pans, often when Erene woke from a nap, Humi would be missing. Erene would pretend to sleep again, and a few minutes later, Humi would sneak in, breathing hard as if she had been running—or making love.

Erene suspected Ziniquel. Unscrupulous as ever, he was probably bored to death with being the one idle ghostier. He'd nearly ghosted Humi, so presumably they had already had intimate contact, even if they had not actually done the act. And she could very well envision him seducing Humi just to get his revenge on Erene.

One day she called Humi to her. Painstakingly, she explained that she didn't want Humi getting involved with any of the ghostiers. Erene herself had a long-standing relationship with Elicit, which had evolved over years—but she did not mention that. Besides, she *needed* Elicit. If it weren't for him, she would have no supporter when she needed one, no bed to crawl into when she was lonely. Humi had Erene. That should be enough.

Erene didn't disclose that, at one point or another, she had been intimate with all the adult ghostiers. She couldn't chance it that Humi might do the same. She couldn't chance it that Humi might realize that underneath their workaday exterior, all the ghostiers had an essential bond, that of *imrchim*, which was practically impermeable. (It was almost enough to make her cry, remembering how close they used to be, remembering the laughter.)

No. Erene needed the girl for herself.

So she only told her that intense relationships detracted from the energy necessary for one's work. This held true throughout a ghostier's life, but was especially important when she was first apprenticed and had so much else to cope with. Therefore, she finished, giving a little laugh to lighten the mood, squeezing Humi's hands, she really would advise against spending so much time with—whoever it was.

Humi looked at her with enormous black eyes. They had no age or emotion, only a deep, dry canniness. Erene felt suddenly uneasy. "I wasn't with anyone," Humi said.

Her hands were dry, not sweaty. "Then where do you vanish to every time I turn around?" Erene snapped.

"I've been in Marshtown. Down on the jetties. I watched the punts come back full of live eels. I watched the young men slide their dauphins out of the tanks into the marsh, and I waited with them for the dauphins to come back with water porcupines in their beaks. I sneaked out on the private jetties and watched the atheists play champions in the deep-water pens. They use every animal that can swim, and some that can't, and they bet on them all. I went back to Christon, and stood outside the House of Larch, thinking that I ought to go get my belongings. But I didn't do it. Stupid bit that I am." She grimaced at her own inadequacy. "I walked along the shopping concourses, and I went to Antiprophet Square, and I ate hot pancakes while I watched the lords and ladies go in and out of the mansions. I went up on the roof roads and talked to artists, courtesans, young atheists living rough, sculptors, and scribes. Did you know—" incredulity lit her eyes—"did you know that there are people who practice that alphabet thing you're teaching me for a *living?*"

Erene smiled, but inside she felt misgivings. Humi would have to learn that such a naïve, all-embracing outlook had no place in the life of a ghostier.

"I went down to the wharves and watched the ships unloading cargo," Humi was going on. "They're all in a tearing hurry right now, because the trade winds are going to drop off in a couple of sixdays. It makes you feel like you have to do something and go somewhere right this *minute,* just standing down there. I've been in the waterfront bars—"

Erene held up her hand. "Sweetheart. Knowing the city is essential to a ghostier's life. So is meeting people. But so is something else. What is that?"

Humi shrugged.

"Politics. The Ellipse meets every four sixdays. All of us missed the session last Sageday, so we will have to go to the next session, which is two days from now. *That* is what you ought to be thinking about."

"How can I—"

"Wait." Perhaps she should not be so harsh. "If you and I hurry, we can be finished with Beau's ghost by tomorrow and have a day to ourselves. All alone. So we should get to work right now." She cuffed the girl lightly. "I tell you, you are never going to want to see blue again after you have mixed me the exact color of your cousin's eyes."

Humi said, "If the efts didn't turn silver, we could go make a comparison."

"Mix that pigment!" More danger—"You are not even to *think* about going back to the Eftpool until you have made a ghost of your own. It's forbidden."

Humi bent into the cupboard to get a mortar. Her tawny hair fell forward, almost hiding the muddy color of her face.

"You have been going, haven't you?"

Humi straightened up, standing with her back to the sink, small and sturdy as a carving of blond wood in her paint-stained dress. She held her head high, but there was a tremor in her voice as she said, "What if I have?"

"Oh, child," Erene laughed sadly. "Child, I went too, when I was Molatio Ash's apprentice."

Humi said nothing.

What can you expect? Erene asked herself. *You killed her betrothed. You haven't exactly created a friendly environment for her. You haven't trusted her enough to tell her very much of the truth at all. What kind of caretaker are you?*

No kind of caretaker. A master.

A little more truth, she thought angrily to herself.

"Do you know why I took you away from Ziniquel? I told you back then, but you probably don't remember. I am getting old, and I must have an apprentice for the sake of my art. That is the first and foremost reason. That is the *only* reason."

Humi tossed her head. "You told me that wasn't all."

Erene could not bring herself to say the rest: "For you, too." She could hear Humi silently pleading for it, but she could not say it.

Hem's desertion had left such deep scars. She had not even realized—

"Give me that mortar," she said. "Now! And I need chalk, white, and lake pigments, and a dab of moss essence—"

When Erene took Humi to collect her flaxen sack of belongings from the House of Larch the next day, she discovered that Humi had made her first enemy. The ties between the House of Larch and the Crescent were old and hoary, steeped in the conviction that each institution had the other to thank for its existence but dared not acknowledge it. Favors tended to be repaid in full, and grudges lived long, mischievous lives. Erene was friendly enough with Ministra Bareed; it was shocking to see the way Ministra and Humi circled each other like cats.

As they walked back through Christon, Humi explained with rare effusiveness, "I outbluffed her when I was persuading her to help me put one over on you. She realizes that now, and she's seething."

"The House of Larch are the best of their kind," Erene said. "Everyone who was anyone used to patronize them, up until about fifteen years ago. Now there are hardly any rich devotees left in the city, and they have a shortage of customers. They're terrified that they'll have to either revise their precious traditions—in which case they would lose the flamens' business—or close down." She thought with pity of all the beauticians living their lives on tiptoe in that dark, rickety townhouse, living for those moments of glory before the court, one every fifteen years or so. She looked sidelong at Humi. "They're just drudges, trapped in tradition. There are really no similarities between them and us at all."

"They see beauty flower under their hands, like us. That would make up for anything," Humi argued. "I would be a beautician, if I wasn't going to be a ghostier."

"Yes!" Erene laughed, relieved that Humi had passed her impromptu test. It was almost a miracle how the girl surpassed every standard Erene set her. "I believe," Erene said, "in the irresistible lure of beauty. I think if two rival ladies could be given a ghost to work over, they would be fast friends afterward. And both ghostiers and beauticians have more sense than ladies. The ghosts will always unite us." But thinking of scheming fools like the Ladies Nearecloud, Gulley, Crane, and others left her with the unsettling thought of one particular lady, shrewd as a barnyard hen, with delicate bones and soft black hair. *Goquisite.* A greater lure even than beauty united the two of them. Freedom. Freedom from the crushing, stifling weight of piety.

She asked abruptly, "Who was your first enemy, Humi?"

Taken off balance, Humi gaped for a moment. Then her eyes went flat. "My mother."

"Oh, love." And Erene embraced her right there in the street, between wafts of fishmongery and the hot, raunchy scent of a leatherworker's shop. "You'll do. Yes, you'll do." Incredibly, Humi let herself be held. The crowds pushed around them. Erene was astonished to find that the fur below her eyes was wet. This was the moment of commitment. This was when she brought herself to say, "Humi, the Erene Gentle who deserved her name and position is coming back. And it's all due to you. I've needed your presence for longer than I've known. I think—" She swallowed. "I think I could love you as if you were my own child."

Humi shifted uncomfortably. "I don't need a mother! Didn't you hear what I just said? I need a friend and a teacher. But not any more mothers."

Erene's head whirled. As the daughter of a Grussels merchant, she had rebelled against the idea of children, but it was so long since she'd been that cosseted, overeducated girl. So long since she'd shed fierce tears over the fate from which she could see no escape—marriage to a stranger, children, a life lived in an old rut. So long since the ghostier Molatio Ash had arrived one day to buy some gold lichen pigment and visit with her father—those were the days when ghostiers could travel, when they didn't have all they could do to keep abreast of events in Delta City—since, magically, he and thirteen-year-old Erene had each known that the other was the one they had been searching for.

Ignoring Erene's father's anger, Molatio had spirited her away.

Erene had been naïve, precocious; Molatio had been like a second father to her. For a long time now she had harbored a secret dream to play mother to another child. She wanted to teach that child all she knew—not just ghosting, but how to cook for a hungry man, and old wives' tales, and how to embroider cloth and write beautiful calligraphy. It was a treasured fantasy.

But Humi was not that child.

Humi, Erene saw now, would chafe against any relationship that implied the existence of an adult and a child.

"Very well, my—apprentice," she said softly. "No mothering." A gang of young men pushed past. In the lingering whiffs of their perfume she let go of Humi. "But that doesn't mean you will be unloved."

Humi looked down, smiling tremulously, and touched her cheek as if flicking off an itch. "It won't be difficult for you to love me more than *my* mother did."

Erene was struck by a pang of adoration. "Oh, by the gods. You poor thing." She hugged her again. Humi quivered like a bird in her arms. She had long lashes, for all they were so pale. Long, graceful lashes. Erene laid her face against hers, just holding her, until the fishmonger stamped out of his shop and told them they were making a spectacle in front of his window.

TEN

Strangers thronged Tellury Crescent. The locals lounged in their upstairs windows, commenting loudly on the visitors, dropping pipe ash on their heads. "Court business," Erene had warned Humi, "always takes place at night." To her, the Crescent felt like a river of embers, a glow of lantern-light shadowed with eddying bodies, hot and pungent. She held Erene's hand tightly, shuffling by her side wherever the crowd carried them. The lantern light hung so bright in the air that she could see the bluish clouds of smoke sinking from the Marshtowners' pipes. One by one, the ghostiers carried the ghosts downstairs and posed them outside Thaumagery, Albien, and Melthirr Houses, and in the shallow, railinged strip of yard before the Chalice. This was the only time the public would be able to see them, so socialites condescended to rub shoulders with merchants and commoners. Little Eterneli marched before each ghost to clear the way, blossoming under the attention she received, flirting with the strangers who tousled her heavy green curls. "Algia was like that too, once," Erene said quietly to Humi. "But she's been here a long time now. She has lost her stomach for everything except Elicit. He overwhelmed her with love. And he will do the same thing to Eterneli eventually. But he can't help it—he expects so much of them."

At least his safety is assured, Humi thought. *Maybe he's just canny. Maybe he doesn't want to end up dead. Like Constance, Ziniquel's master.*

They drifted with the flow of the crowd. There was Wella the Veretrean, standing on the threshold of Melthirr House, her mint-pale fur glowing in the dark doorway. She clasped an armful of flowers to her breast. Diamond tears sparkled on her cheeks; but through them, she was smiling. Elicit had let her die in happiness.

Rain was another matter. His rib cage had been opened up like a shell-fish, and he had been tortured until only his beautiful, pain-racked face remained human. Humi remembered Mory leading him into darkness, demure in her cerise dress . . . his sister running, crazed with terror and bewilderment . . .

The last ghost in the line was Beau. Lanterns nodded like the bolls of bog-cotton above his head. Voices muttered and hummed, pointing out details. Sweat prickled over Humi's body in hot and cold waves. There he sat on the ground, manipulating himself in front of all these people, degrading himself and her and all the Gardens for years to come. Unwashed bodies hemmed her in so tightly she couldn't escape. She stood stiff, fists clenched, ears ringing.

But before she had to break, a man in the white-and-gold Summer livery elbowed her aside. "Milady Gentle?" He bowed before Erene. Behind him, several teams of draydogs were forcing a path through the crowd. "Lord Summer. The ghosts."

"Show's over," someone muttered. The crowd began to disperse.

Erene looked the man up and down with cool disdain. "Give my greetings to your master. You will find one of those carts unnecessary."

"Pardon?"

"Are you deaf? You'll need only six carts."

"Milady." One by one, the other retainers were loading the ghosts onto the carts and draping them with sheets. "Dammit, you're right!" The head retainer regarded the last cart. Humi had a sudden, awful fear that they would pick her up and sling her bodily onto it. But he shook his head and called out to the others to move. The carts creaked to the mouth of Tellury Crescent, their drivers blowing on fingers that were numb from touching the ghosts.

As the crowd drained, Humi breathed a sigh of relief. All day the ghostiers had been irritable with weariness, yet unable to rest because their task was not yet over, and now their spirits seemed to rise like hot air balloons. They joked and roughhoused, caring nothing for the gaping stragglers. The Marshtowners chuckled tolerantly as they closed their upstairs windows. The ghostiers were *their* children, though precocious and wayward.

And then sedan chairs rattled up to the Chalice. Five—six—seven. As Ziniquel tickled her, Humi stopped laughing, dismayed. One after another, the preposterously liveried porters fell to a halt, turning out their calves and stiffening their spines. The leader stuffed a hat on his sweat-damp hair, only to sweep it off again. "Greetings from the Divinarch, miladies and milords!"

Erene smiled unpleasantly. "You almost arrived in time to see our ghosts, Merisand. Belstem's retainers have taken them to the palace now."

The other ghostiers held their breath. But the man's expression remained implacable. "The Divinarch hopes he was correct to assume you would appreciate the use of his sedans."

"We appreciate it greatly," Elicit interjected quickly.

Erene sighed. "Come then, Humi. The night is not over yet. Though I had not expected the Divinarch to be quite so prompt in calling Ellipse. The sun has only just set."

Obediently, Humi followed her into the sedan and sat back in the sumptuous cushions. On the curved wall, a candle burned behind a faceted-glass shield. The sedan started to rattle over the cobblestones. Erene gestured ahead. "Humi, the man who is pulling this sedan is Afet Merisand, the head porter at the Old Palace. He is one of the few humans the Divinarch will speak with face to face. He's also one of far too many humans who know about our conspiracy."

"What—what conspiracy?" Humi's heart dropped sickeningly.

Erene sighed. "I'm reluctant to tell you . . . somehow, it feels as though our holiday together is ending." She touched Humi's knee, letting her hand linger. "But you won't understand anything at Ellipse tonight unless you know about the undercurrents. The fact is that Goquisite and I are conspiring to bring down the Divinarch."

Oh, gods. Conspiracy. Against—against the gods?

"We want to win freedom from their rule. All the Ellipse councillors know what we are doing, and all of the ghostiers have had to acknowledge it, however reluctantly. So I think it is time that you know, too. And I want you to understand. We are not fools. We are deadly serious. And we are the product of an ethos which has been fermenting as long as there has been atheism."

"You—you're an atheist?" *I thought she had told me everything!* Humi thought wildly. *How much more is there?*

"I have been an atheist for some years," Erene nodded. "It is quite difficult to remain pious when one interacts with the gods face to face, day by day. A flamen's piety is—*blind*—and the rest of the ghostiers . . ." She shook her head. "I don't know how they do it. They are some of the most intractably pious men and women in Delta City. They don't see that the gods' rule is over and that it is time for mortals to rule themselves. The flamens' arbitration has degenerated into positive injustice—if it was ever fair—and Goquisite and I have bound ourselves to oust the Divinarch, and all the gods in the Ellipse along with him."

She sprawled on her elbows in the cushions, relaxed now that she had hit her stride. Humi heard Reason in her voice—Reason, that persuasive devil who has brought down monarchs before and would not hesitate to stoop to a senior ghostier. But her mind rebelled against it. The Divinarch was *divine!* What kind of temerity did it take to dream, much less actually plan, to oust him?

"We won't make our move for quite a while yet, of course," Erene said. "The Divinarch is surrounded night and day by the Divine Guard. All we can do is test the waters around potential accomplices and, when we're sure of them, enlist them in the cause. Belstem is our strongest ally—in fact, many people think he is the ringleader. Our moment will come just after the Divinarch's death, before the Heir assumes the Throne. While the world mourns, we will strike. The Throne will never have another occupant. It was built for gods, not humans, and our world has no use for another dictator." Erene clasped her knees, and her eyes shone. "The Ellipse will take on the power of arbitration. Our votes will become law all over the Divinarchy. The disparity between rich and poor is growing, and that alone should give us more to do than any Divinarch has had for centuries. But that is as it should be. The Conversion Wars can't cast their shadow down all of time. We are finally emerging from that blackness."

The hubbub of the palace district swirled in blips around the sedan. Merisand's leather-shod feet thudded outside the shell.

For some reason, a memory of home kept running through Humi's mind. Every Dividay, if a wandering flamen was not there to preach, the Garden family took a statuette of the Divinarch and stood it on a wood pedestal on the middle of the courtyard. Then they knelt in a circle and prayed. Humi remembered her uncle Cand's rough, reverent voice rising out of the courtyard, floating to the ridges. *Bring us rain, but not too much . . . let lambs be born, but not too many . . . send us a flamen, and soon, to heal the canker on Mercy's thigh . . .*

"Erene, what will people do without the Divinarch? Who will they pray to?"

With an annoyed expression, Erene leaned forward and rapped a complex rhythm on the paneling. Merisand's footsteps slowed for a moment, as if in response, then picked up again. "Soon even the saltsiders will be atheists. That problem will not exist."

"But if the Divinarch and the Incarnations are gone, people will pray to their new rulers. To believe in rulers," Humi said, suddenly sure of herself, "people have to think they're superior to themselves. Before you know it, Erene, *you'll* be a god, along with the other councillors. Do you think you're better than the rest of us?" Erene opened her mouth to reply, but Humi rushed on. "And you know what else you're leaving out? Miracles. If the flamens go, miracles will go with them. I'm a saltsider; I know how one miracle makes the difference between a good year and a year when your middle sticks to your spine in the winter and you wonder if living on salt rabbits, will allow you to see spring. In Calvary and Iceland, the weather is so harsh that people couldn't live at all if not for miracles."

"The lords of those provinces will provide for their people," Erene said firmly.

"The flamens will resist."

"But they'll lose. Because they're too decent to kill. And if *we* have to, then we are ready."

"Not more wars," Humi said.

"Gods' blood, no!" Erene shook her head. "One clean strike, like an amputation—cutting down only those who are determined to die for the Divinarch—and the new regime will slide easily into place."

"Who's going to do the killing?"

Erene shook her head.

"Is it the other ghostiers? Are they part of this too?" The prospect seemed horrible. She had always known there was something different about Erene—but if the other ghostiers turned out to be atheists, that would undermine Humi's whole world—

"Gods, no!" Erene seemed shocked. "I told you they're pious! I have no illusions that they will ever join the cause. Most of them refuse to know even as much as I have told you. And let me warn you that you should not try to make them understand. It will only drive a wedge between you. I know how difficult it is not to share things with them—it can be the most difficult thing in all the world. But now you understand why I told you not to get too close to any of them. We are on different sides."

Humi twisted her fingers together. It seemed so strange that she had lived with them for a month, and gotten to know them so well, and never known that they were on different sides. It was quite clear to her where her loyalty lay—but it saddened her. Trust had come so hard between her and Erene. She could not ruin it over this. She would not. "All right," she said. "I'll keep it to myself."

Erene kissed her cheek. "That's a darling. It's not even a matter of secrecy, really, just etiquette. The Divinarch himself, and the rest of the gods, know everything, and they must have told the flamens, so that everything we plan is known to the whole Ellipse. Nobody can keep anything from the gods—there could be one of them hidden away in even the most secluded meeting room, listening. They can come and go at will. You've seen that. They are powerful in and of themselves. Goquisite and I often ask ourselves what they are going to do when they decide we are a real danger."

Humi's bowels froze. She failed to see where there was any question. *Surely they'll crush you, take away all your privileges and exile you to the farthest island of the Archipelago—if they don't kill you!* "But—but what are they doing now, if *they* know everything?"

"Nothing." Erene's breath puffed out in frustration. "The Divinarch takes no action to stop the eroding of his power. In fact, he takes no action at all. *And we do not know why,* unless it is just that he is old and half-mad. I am sure some of the Incarnations would act against us if he let them, but they can do nothing without his consent!"

The sedan swung hard left. A new surface resounded beneath the wheels. Erene uncrumpled her skirts, reached out and twitched Humi's neck ribbons straight. "We are here." The sedan stopped. Erene scrambled out, tucking wisps of hair behind her ears. Humi followed.

The sight of the Old Palace crowded her confusion out of her mind.

Afet Merisand had set the sedan down inside the gate of an enormous courtyard. Oases of fountains and greenery dotted the cobbles. Outlandishly costumed humans crossed the open space; household animals snorted and played. The other sedans stood empty by the gate. Flocks of night birds held raucous court on the surrounding roofs. Humi could hear the sea, somewhere below, it sounded like. The tang of brine in the air overpowered more normal smells of dung and food and fuel, but she could detect quite a powerful smell of burning sulphur.

The seaward side of the courtyard sprang up into the night like a fountain of wood, a fantastic edifice bearing torchlit balconies like cups of flowers. Far away, a pair of enormous, three-man-high oaken doors stood ajar.

"Farewell," Erene smiled to Merisand. "Propel not thy chariot into mischance, you sly old fop." She started to walk across the courtyard. Belatedly Humi realized that she was seeing as many gods as humans. *Members of the Divine Guard.* The strange faces. Each god's body seemed cast in a different, unique form. She was too dazzled by their strangeness to tell their genders. Their intense, pure voices rang out louder than the mortals', louder than the birds, effortlessly, like melodies over the sound of the sea.

A sharp fingernail meandered down her spine. She yelped and spun.

"Hello, Humility," Arity, Heir to the Divinarchy, said. "You were the ghost that spoke, weren't you?" There had been no whiff of sulphur; he must have arrived the ordinary way, by coming up behind her. His face glowed a smooth green in the light from the lanterns in the nearby oasis. He turned to Erene. "You're late. The entire Ellipse is milling around, waiting for you. Where have you been?"

"I had a thing to talk over with my apprentice," Erene said smoothly. "I told the porter to take us by a longer route." Humi marveled at her demeanor. Arity might have been a friend Erene had just met in the street—never mind that he was a god. Never mind that seconds earlier, Erene had been plotting to deprive him of his throne. "What is the Heir to the Divinarch doing out in the courtyard," she asked, "when assassins may lurk around every corner?"

"Picking dandelions," Arity said shortly. He began to walk towards the palace, his heel talons clicking on the cobbles. Then he shot a glance back at Humi. "What do you think, little ghost?"

"It's—it's beautiful—"

"There used not to be any humans living here." They passed into the racket of the lobby. "That was before the Ellipse passed an edict stating that human servants had to come and clean every two sixdays, because it was dangerous to the Divinarch's health. And now there are many humans living in the Divinarch's household. But there used to be stalactites of tallow below the torches, and stalagmites dripping to meet them. Hundreds of years old at the bases, I should think. And a smell of soot, mixed with the perfumes of generations of Divine Guards."

Arity himself was wearing perfume. Humi sniffed. It reminded her of the salt near her home.

"It was quite repulsive," Erene said.

"If you do not like to breathe the past."

"It still looks rather dirty," Humi ventured, trying to make peace. They mounted a wide stairway. Cobwebs hung from the ceiling of the stairwell, and dust obscured the features of the ghosts which stood in niches in the banister.

Arity stopped and looked at her with a half-smile. "I seconded the edict."

She blinked. "Milord—"

"*Gods,*" Erene spat angrily. "Can you not make sense for *once,* Arity!" She seized Humi's arm and hurried up the stairs, leaving Arity behind.

"I do, only not to you, Milady Gentle!" he called after them. The flow of humans and mortals eddied around him, giving him a wide berth. As Humi looked over her shoulder, he winked out of existence.

I will understand, Humi thought, shaking her head to rid her eyes of the blind spot. *I have to understand.*

Erene left her apprentice at the door of the Elliptical Chamber, directing her to one of the little alcoves from which, like the other apprentices, she could watch the session through a peephole. Apprentices could not enter the chamber. Only councillors, lemans, and the Divine Guards that accompanied the Divinarch. It was at the Old Palace's heart, buried like the yolk of an egg in concentric ellipses of rooms: an enormous bare room with a ceiling black-dappled above the chandeliers and wooden panels gleaming with age. No skylights or windows. But it was only ever used at night anyhow. The gods slept during the day, and it would be unthinkable for Ellipse to meet without the gods—at least, officially. In actual fact, most of the Ellipse's decisions were made in Antiprophet Square, in Goquisite's or Belstem's parlor.

It was near impossible to accomplish anything in session these days, what with the schisms between the councillors and the Divinarch's increasing reluctance to attend. The twenty-first seat always stood empty, as a reminder that no Divine Seals would be given out. Erene herself, as the most powerful councillor, had come to shoulder the task of arbitration to some degree; but the pious councillors, and the Incarnations, did not accept her authority.

Everyone seemed to be present, talking in groups clearly divided along political lines: nobles, ghostiers, flamens, gods. Heads turned to acknowledge her arrival, and they began to drift toward their seats. Goquisite broke off her conversation with Marasthizinith Crane and hurried over to Erene. Her round dark eyes lit up. "A pleasure to see you, my friend." Her voice overflowed with warmth.

With a laugh, Erene gave her a swift embrace. "It's been too long!"

"What is this that I hear about a new apprentice? I thought that when Hem left, that was the end of that nonsense."

"Goq," Erene said. "You hardly *knew* me before Hem left. And right afterward, it was natural for me to be disenchanted with the very idea of apprenticeship. But I *have* to have an apprentice. Ghosting is the be all and end all of me." She wished she was still as sure of that now, in the chamber, in Goquisite's presence, as she had been while she painted Beauty Garden's ghost. "Without it, I wouldn't *be* here in Delta City." That was the truth. "I wouldn't be on the Ellipse."

Goquisite's round arms went around her neck. Erene shut her eyes, praying that Goquisite would accept that easy explanation. Goquisite awakened protective urges in her like those that Humi did, only subtly different. *Please believe me. I just want to spare you.*

"Will you partake of late supper at my house?" Goquisite asked. "I think it's time—" She whispered, her voice giggly with secrecy, "I think it's time that we work on Marasthizinith."

Oh, gods. Erene had planned to take Humi back to Tellury Crescent tonight and go over the Ellipse session, laying out whatever important arguments had cropped up, telling her what she should take seriously and what she should not. Nuance of voice and face, especially with the gods, would often prove vital. She had planned for them to share a cold supper, with wine, and then sleep as long as they both wished in the bedroom that Algia had rendered so clean.

"Of course I'll come," she said. "I'll bring Humi. She won't be any trouble."

Goquisite pouted. "I suppose I ought to meet her."

"Shall we begin?" Erene said loudly to the assembly. She walked around the council table to her seat, number 20, taking care not to catch Goquisite's eye as Goquisite sank into seat number 4. They could not be seen to favor each other once the Ellipse changed from a social gathering to a political machine. Erene was glad she was wearing a fine violet dress with a low-cut back—that frivolity might decrease suspicions that they had been talking of the conspiracy. She took her time gathering up her skirts and arranging them over the chair before she sat down. "We will wait for the Divinarch. Patience please, everyone. And—" she let a note of sarcasm creep into her voice—"let us maintain a respectful silence."

"Pfuh." In seat number 14, Belstem Summer sat like a sack of wheat, uncouth in a bright yellow tailcoat and hose. The other nobles' seats were all in the low numbers: Aneisneida Summer's was 6. On either side of Belstem sat the ghostiers, and between Fra, in seat 13, and Erene sat all five Incarnations: Pati the Striver, the Maiden Hope, Broken Bird, the Sage Bronze Water, and Arity the Heir. Broken Bird and Hope were actually numbers 1 and 2, but they had brought their chairs around so that they could converse privately with the others. The five of them whispered together like bosom friends, controlling their voices so as not to make Erene lose face by openly disobeying her request for silence. No one would have guessed that they belonged to two bitterly opposed factions.

The division within their ranks was even commoner knowledge than Erene, Goquisite, and Belstem's conspiracy was. If not for the Divinarch's refusal to react to the atheists' growing power, and presumably to let the others react, Erene thought, she would have had real rivals in Pati and Hope. Broken Bird and Bronze Water were no threat—as far as she could see, they agreed with the Divinarch's philosophy of inaction. But Pati and Hope were different. Together with most of the Divine Guard, they had proclaimed themselves warriors in a battle against all things atheistic. Outside the Elliptical Chamber, they were as harmless as the others—Erene supposed she had the Divinarch to thank for that—but when the gods lost the confrontation which they knew full well was coming, would Pati step down from his post with grace? Or would he stage a recoup, a debacle which even Erene, ghostier and sometime torturer, could not imagine?

She did not know.

Beside her, Arity sat with his elbows on the table, absently braiding three fat, wormlike strands of Broken Bird's hair. If there was one being in Delta City who disquieted her more than Pati did, it was Arity. As the main beneficiary of Pati's crusade to keep power in the hands of the gods, the Heir ought to have backed the Striver all the way. But every stand he took in Ellipse contradicted the one before. And no other god would dream of putting himself out to palliate a situation rather than to worsen it. When the other Incarnations faced off, two against two, as inevitably happened, Arity was the peacemaker.

If *only* Erene knew what was going through his mind.

A purplish-limned patch in the air—

The whoosh of heat made Erene blink. When she opened her eyes, one sunspot had become two realities, standing on the table beneath the chandelier.

"The Divinarch!" announced the tall young Divine Guard, his hair rising of its own accord. The Divinarch of Royalland, Calvary, Veretry, Pirady, Iceland, the Archipelago, and Domesdys, et al., straightened up. He was no taller than a ten-year-old child. His bones showed through folds of naked, gray-pink skin like sculptures draped with a silk curtain. His blond curls were now no more than white wisps on his skull. The living mustaches which had once reached his waist had shriveled: they twitched constantly, like snakes hung by their tails. His once clear blue eyes were cloudy. He was 191 years old.

He looks worse than last time, Erene thought with pity. Presumptuous to feel sorry for him. But who could help it when they saw this?

"Greetings to the Ellipse." His voice was still strong, and he did not bother to moderate it. "Tonight's topic is the inauguration of Aneisneida Summer, and what it means not only to our Ellipse but to our whole world." He coughed. Erene moved her hand away from the spatters of white blood that landed on the table before her. "The precedent in question is, Should it become customary for Ellipse seats to be hereditary, or should we name Aneisneida an exception and devise a method for choosing the successors of councillors who are to be succeeded by neither lemans nor apprentices? I beg you to discount the fact that Aneisneida's predecessor was a flamen, for as we all know Godsister Purity and her leman died together, caught in a fire, leaving the seat open to the most appropriate candidate." The Divinarch caught Belstem's eye with his cloudy one, and Erene saw Lord Summer flinch slightly. "I am unwell. I shall not stay. I await your decision, and at the end of the session I shall pass a verdict—or maybe I shall not. Sunrise, my friend, let us go."

The Guard shut his eyes for a minute, mustering his strength, and then they went.

"What's the point?" Ziniquel sighed from the seat number 12 in the aftermath of their departure. "We all know there'll be no verdict. We're just going through the motions—"

"Order!" Erene said sharply. Ziniquel muddied, but she did not look at him. "I announce this session open!"

"Should we revise the laws of succession, you will hold the unenviable position of precedent, Aneisneida," Godsbrother Puritanism said immediately. "I should like to hear your position." Aneisneida was pale—not unusual for her—but her hands gripped the table, trembling. Puritanism's leman, Auspi, murmured in his ear. Puritanism pursed his lips. Where the salt crystals grew in his eyes, they flooded out of the sockets onto his forehead and cheeks. It gave him a fearsome look, as if his eyes were flaming with white fire. "Aneisneida?" he said.

Her eyes darted to her father's in a wild plea for aid. Erene mentally commended Belstem for his silence. He must be going through anguish right now, keeping himself from jumping in to help her.

The Maiden, Hope, said in a voice like a length of satin falling to the floor, "Go on, Councillor Summer. We're listening."

Aneisneida rose shakily to her feet. Erene ground her teeth as she heard snickers. "Councillors," Aneisneida said, "I am the first mortal councillor ever to accede to the Ellipse without passing through either lemanhood or Tellury Crescent. I feel that I am the first in what should be a long tradition of noble councillors. As the youngest councillor, I hope before I die to see a full eight seats around this table occupied by men and women like me."

Puritanism went rigid. "Summer! Why have you put this inflammatory nonsense into the mouth of your child?"

Belstem protested self-righteously, "She composed every word of her speech herself!"

"May I go on?" Aneisneida's voice trembled.

"We shall have words!" said Puritanism. "We shall have words, Summer!"

"I am Summer too," Aneisneida said, more strongly. "And the winter is over." ("How precious," Pati muttered sardonically.) "The tradition of passing seats from master to apprentice, or flamen to leman, is outdated. A master and apprentice come together late in life as compared to a parent and child. They may be of such different temperaments that the focus of the seat is changed when it is passed from one to the other, and thus the balance of the entire council disturbed. There can never be a really close relationship between two people who will consider murdering each other for personal gain." That was a direct jab at the ghostiers. "The younger can never fully understand the older, nor respect his position.

"I speak of all crafts, all positions. Children are chosen as apprentices by craftsmen who are no relation to them. They are taken as cabin boys on ships. They are apprenticed to traders who travel up and down the country with the seasons. Separating lines of succession from bloodlines ignores one of the most valuable treasures we humans possess: our racial differences. The combination of a master from one continent and an apprentice from another cancels out the unique perspective which each of them brings to the craft. Over the hundreds of years since the Conversion Wars, this practice has wiped out the indigenous languages of each continent, each province, so that we all speak more or less the same tongue. Many people do not even know that there used to be many languages.

"There is also a problem with our lack of records. Even in Delta City, most of the important families have come into being in the last two centuries. They are cut off from their ancient history by the severance of their founding member, usually an ex-leman, from his or her family. They know nothing of their heritage. Families are the natural warp of history. By chopping them up to make one child a leman, another a ghostier's apprentice, a third a cabin boy, we destroy the sense of nuclear *community* which each province, each town, and each household ought to hold dear above all else.

"I propose a law detailing changes in these objectionable customs. It would be foolish to try to correct centuries of wrongheadedness at a stroke, but it is high time we councillors gave birth to a beginning. I believe that I am she."

There was dead silence as her chair scraped again.

Far below, the sea lapped against the cliff.

Belstem tipped back in his chair, laced his hands on his stomach, and began almost inaudibly to hum.

"*You* composed this speech, Belstem," Erene said icily, breaking the silence, "because it's what you've been wanting to say for a long time—and you thought we would not be as hard on Anei as we would on you." Her mind boiled coldly. When she did not admire Belstem, she despised him. Right now she could have ground him under her heel. *No truly close relationship between two people who will consider murdering each other . . . No?* Some detached part of her mind was whispering, *Humi, Humi.*

"The peace within and between the continents is the flamenhood's greatest accomplishment. I acknowledge that freely. Their custom of choosing lemans in one place and setting them down in another is a vital ingredient of that peace. Do you want to upset everything that centuries have proved to be wholesome, just to consolidate your triumph over the flamenhood?" Elicit's voice cracked as he said, "How high have you set your sights, man? Are you *insane?*" Words appeared to fail him.

But words never failed Pati the Striver. "You spineless worm, Belstem," he said silkily, "you slithering, crawling ground thing that harbors longings to be greater than the *gods.* Your arrogance comes dangerously near to treason, and I'll see you recant or I'll see you thrown out of Ellipse."

But by the end of the session, that goal was not realized. Belstem held the floor alone against Pati, Broken Bird, Bronze Water, Hope, and all the ghostiers, including Erene. Usually she backed Belstem, but this time she knew he had gone too far. Pietimazar Seaade and Marasthizinith Crane had swung back and forth, not wanting to alienate themselves from anyone. Erene hadn't let herself hope that Goquisite would not back Belstem, no matter how preposterous his scheme might be; when Lady Ankh first voiced her disagreement with him, Erene had hardly been able to keep from rushing around the table to hug her.

It was a measure of Belstem's phenomenal powers of argument that by the time everyone else in the Chamber was exhausted, and Erene finally called a halt, he hadn't yet been put at a disadvantage. Next session they would end him, Erene thought as the councillors straggled toward the door. Goquisite took her arm, saying that she had told her porters to wait at the Ferien entrance. Erene's mind still lingered on the session. *Surprise was on his side tonight, but we'll prepare an argument for next time and finish this madness.*

She would not let herself wonder whether, once the conspiracy succeeded, Belstem might swing permanently to this extreme end of the spectrum.

We'll make him see sense.

ELEVEN

Alone in the juddering sedan after the session, on the way to pay a visit to Goquisite Ankh's mansion that she had not anticipated and did not want, Humi struggled to understand the thing that had happened to her during Ellipse.

Spark and clash, her memories flowed, fusing with each other like pieces of a divine jigsaw.

The first: the Eftpool.

The second: Several days ago, as she wandered alone along the roof roads, a terribly drunk young man staggered up to her. He grabbed her collars and breathed alcoholically into her face: "*I see . . . I see . . .*" Then in a voice which might have belonged to a different person, "Godsie, if you don't stop me I'm going to be taken with prophecy. It's happened once already, and I'm afraid, deathly afraid. Slap me, hit me, please—"

He winced and let go of her, his arms jerking like windmill blades. More out of fright than anything else, she hit him hard across the face. He blinked—spasmed—heaved a shuddering sigh.

"Thank you . . . Can you take me over there? I would be obliged . . ." The discreet wooden sign, swinging in the breeze, denoted a hard-liquor daylight bar. Wrinkling her nose at the smell blowing from the door, Humi half-supported him to the threshold. "Won't you have a . . . a . . . a glass of wine?" he asked. "A glass with me? I'm a leman. I'm perfectly safe—"

Drunkenness didn't attract her, not in others or in herself. Since he was a leman, that made it even less excusable.

The whole episode frightened her. She excused herself with the truth, saying that she had to get back before her master woke up. It worked like a charm. She had never seen him again.

The third memory: She sat in a soft, musty-smelling armchair in an alcove outside the Elliptical Chamber. She had long since forgotten the sweetmeats that had been left for her refreshment. She pressed her nose to the glass of the peephole, captivated, as Pati leapt up on the table, commanding the Chamber. Belstem, on his feet, tried to shout him down. The glass reduced their voices to squeaking, but if Humi strained her ears she could make out the words—

A soft *thump*, and a gust of warm air hit the back of her neck, bumping her forehead against the glass. She smelled burning sulphur.

The Divinarch stood by the chair, his presence too intense for the tiny room. A tall, crop-haired Guard held him with one arm. The Guard sneezed, looked over what was left of the sweetmeats, and took a piece of marchpane.

The Divinarch's voice threatened to drive the air from Humi's eardrums. "Mortal girl Humility. As misnamed as my *firchresi* Patience."

"Y-yes, Milord God?" Determined not to be at a disadvantage, Humi got to her feet. She towered over the Divinarch.

But he turned his face up toward her, and the papery skin slid back from his nose and the clustered fangs in his mouth. "Of late the land has been riddled with prophecy. The lemans who are taken by it spout all kinds of ominous sayings, which are most often taken to prognosticate the end of my reign. The like of which prophecies I do not need." He laughed. Instantly the Guard handed him a square of linen bleached so white that the new blood he coughed up was nearly invisible. "Most recently taken," the Divinarch continued when he got his breath, "was Lexi Treeborn, leman of the councillor Godsbrother Joyfulness. Whether he is to be believed or not . . . that is up to you. These were his words to you, and he called you by name, though afterward he remembered it not.

"*You lean out the window with the ghost of your childhood companion behind you, and look towards the sunrise. And your body longs to follow the birds across the marshes. You shall follow them, yea, and to Heaven. You shall receive the highest honor the world can bestow upon you. Yet you shall live a life of deception. Your heart shall be heavy as a rock veined with iron. And the truth is ineffable. Not even the gods know it. You cannot know it. You must learn to face it. It is ineffable.*

"Tell me, child, what am I to make of this?"

And of course, Humi had already met Lexi. And he had nearly prophesied again.

In the sedan, Humi shivered. Brilliant, frightening pyrotechnics ignited in her mind. She wondered that they didn't shine through her skull and light up the dark. Brilliance: she caught glimpses of the meaning of the prophecy. But she could not understand it, any more than Lexi had.

* * *

"I don't know," Marasthizinith said. "Honestly—I couldn't commit myself to anything so—so—"

"Dangerous as openly affiliating yourself with us?" Goquisite suggested sweetly.

"No, no!" Marasthizinith's eyes were wild. "No—it's just—that I am timid, you know that, and a delicate character! How can I successfully engage in—in—subversive activities?"

Erene leaned back into the luxury of the overstuffed loveseat, wine cup suspended between thumb and forefinger. She enjoyed these exercises in persuasion. "Pieti has given us his allegiance. Did you know that?" She was anticipating an event which had not actually happened, but which she knew would soon. "I assure you nothing undue will be required of you. You're the only councillor left whose allegiance we are not sure of. You must join us—or . . ." She lifted her cup to her lips and with delicate lasciviousness sucked the dark red liquid.

"Or," Goquisite picked up her cue, "we shall have to . . . reconsider. One suspects you of piety, Maras. Is this justified? Or are you just scared?" She slid a glance full of secret laughter to Erene, and her hand stole out across the arm of the loveseat. Hooking little fingers with her, Erene luxuriated in contentment. (She refused to remember Humi, who sat alone not twenty feet away, in the unlit corner of the sitting room.) Maras couldn't possibly hold out against both of them. No matter what their weaknesses, together Erene and Goquisite formed an inquisition machine that could reduce far more sturdy prey than Marasthizinith Crane to quivering pudding.

"I—I don't know . . ." With a shaking hand, Maras poured herself more wine. When she put down the decanter the one-legged side table rocked and nearly toppled. "What would I have to do?"

"I told you. Nothing," Goquisite said patiently. "Except refrain from betraying who is at the center of the conspiracy."

"You and Erene." Myopic brown eyes skittered from one to the other. "I thought it was Belstem."

"So do most people. And so do those abroad who guess that something of this sort is afoot. But this way, if by some mischance Belstem should *not* outlive the Divinarch, all would not be lost." Erene hoped she managed to keep spite out of her voice. When pressed, Belstem had confessed to writing Aneisneida's speech. But he had demonstrated no penitence.

"We are enlarging our network of supporters all the time," Goquisite said. "But you won't have to worry about that, Maras—it's Erene and I who probe the allegiances of the lesser nobles, who search out the accounts of the Wars that will help us mount our coup."

"Perhaps that is where *I* could be of help," Maras burst out eagerly. "I daresay I am the most knowledgeable among us on the subject of history. For a long time, I have taken an interest—"

Erene suppressed a smile and sipped her wine. They had her now. It was only a matter of careful reeling in.

All right. They've got her. Humi sat in the corner, arms folded, glowering at the candlelit circle of sofas and lounge chairs. She wasn't tired—the tea she'd drunk when they came in had seen to that—but she was sick of Goquisite and her befrilled parlor and the thousands of meticulously dusted figurines on shelves. She was weary of Erene's making cow eyes at the woman. She was so obvious! The motion of her head above the back of the loveseat betrayed a slight but perceptible tension. Humi took a vindictive pleasure in that. Maybe Erene thought she'd put Humi out of sight and mind; maybe she thought that as soon as they left here, she'd be able to hold out her arms and Humi would come running. But it wasn't as easy as that. Humi could already tell that she would never like Goquisite. The inattentive way Lady Ankh had looked her over when they were intro-duced—she had been talking to Erene and twirling a wineglass at the same time—had made her feel like an animal, a poodle or a salt cat, a pet.

The far door swept open. The three in the candlelight started. A figure clad in a dark cloak strode in, shaking out his moss-green hair. Drops flew. A candle hissed. "Milady Ankh, Milady Crane, a pleasure. Erene, I've come for Humi. Do you know it's three in the morning? She's a ghostier, not a hired servant! She ought to be at home in Tellury Crescent, in bed."

Humi levered her stiff body up and hurried toward Ziniquel. "Here I am!" she called with a relief that she'd meant to conceal.

"*Imrchu*, I wouldn't dream of letting you sit in a corner all night," Zini-quel said. As he brushed past Erene and Goquisite to meet her, his drip-ping cloak slapped Erene's face. She remained silent. Ziniquel ignored her tacit plea for peace. "I have a cloak for you, Humi. Here. We're walking. I couldn't get a sedan at this ungodly hour."

"It's perfectly possible," Erene said. "Goquisite has three porters regu-larly detailed for the night shift, and more on call."

Ziniquel guided Humi toward the door. He spoke without turning. "I don't think it's wise for a porter in Ankh livery to be seen bringing *anyone* home to Tellury Crescent at this hour of the night." His tone gave the last phrase a meaning unsuitable for polite company. Erene's face went muddy gray.

Ziniquel's rudeness emboldened Humi. Her irritation boiled to the surface. "Good night, Erene! If I see you at home, until then. If not, until tomorrow!"

Ziniquel shut the door on a ringing silence. "I wonder how they'll smooth *that* over." He chuckled. "Goquisite is not very deft at dealing with situations once she loses control."

Now that she was alone with him, Humi felt suddenly shy. The last time they had seen each other privately, she had been dressed as a ghost. It made her muddy to remember what had happened that night. But he seemed to feel no awkwardness.

The angular spiral stairwell was lined with ghosts. "Goquisite is an avid collector, especially of ghosts canted towards the darker end of the spectrum. She admires your cousin's ghost greatly. Erene has dedicated several of her works to her."

Footmen struggled to conceal their surprise as Ziniquel and Humi passed between them, out into the night. Icy rain roared like a sea on the tropical garden which rambled around Goquisite's mansion and up its walls. The scents of bruised greenery rose around them as they ducked under broad magnolia and rhododendron leaves. Antiprophet Square glistened. An occasional light reflected on the cobbles, but as they left the palace district behind, these petered out, and the muffled sounds of carousing gave way to barking dogs and snuffling pigs. Marshtown laid itself silent, bare, to the rain.

"We're home," Ziniquel said abruptly.

Humi had not even recognized Tellury Crescent. Albien House looked more forbidding than usual, heavier, a scarecrow-roofed shadow against the night. The door was unlocked, as always. A single light burned in the hall that the Chalice and Albien House shared. It was as bare of furnishings as ever, but right now it seemed to Humi that it would be a crime to place anything here besides their feet. "Talk about *wet!*" Ziniquel said. "Humi, do you want a hot drink?"

Caught in the middle of wringing out her hair, she nodded. "I'd—I'd be glad."

Their wet footprints followed them up the stairs. "How about chocolate?"

"What's that?"

"You don't—gods! Your manners are so sophisticated, sometimes I forget you're just a saltsider!" He grinned at her. "It'll be a rare treat to introduce you to chocolate. Cacao bean, no honey."

Humi hadn't been inside his workshop since she had posed as a ghost. The lace-curtained bedchamber awakened disturbing memories. Shivers ran up her spine. In the middle of the workshop floor, cross-legged in the midst of scattered palettes, pigment pots, and brushes, sat another ghost.

It was Wella's husband.

Humi sprang back halfway to the door. "Gods! What—why didn't you send it with the others?"

"What?" Ziniquel followed her eyes. "It's just a ghost."

"I was a companion alo- along with him." Her teeth chattered in the cold as she sidled forward. "He was Elicit's ghost's husband." The Veretrean boy looked peacefully absorbed in a book. She couldn't believe his silky sheet of hair was diamondine until she brought herself to touch it. Cold—cold, and hard. So were the pages of the book. So were his lips, whose dark-sheened flesh looked so tender, caught up by one pearly tooth. When she touched the diamondine, she felt no despair or desolation, only the steady, peaceful zest for life of one who is studying what he loves. None of the other ghosts she'd seen tonight compared to this one for technical excellence. But she knew that he came of tree-farmer folk, like his wife, and that he could never have felt such an emotion in his life.

The ghost's spell dissipated.

"What are you going to do with it?"

"I don't know yet." Ziniquel stood watching her. "Probably give it to one of the flamens. Joyfulness, perhaps. He loves books—he gets Lexi to read to him, even though it's an atheist thing."

"But it would be wasted on him. A flamen can't see."

"The art of ghosting was conceived for blind men. He can *feel.* And he won't cache the ghost away in his home, as the Summers have done with the commissioned ones—he'll put it in a tavern or public place, so that common people can feel it. Maybe he'll even send it abroad. That's why I give my ghosts to the flamenhood. I want them to be used, not coveted." He stopped, then shrugged, seeming a little abashed at his own passion.

"Then most of the ghosts that you make—they *aren't* commissioned?"

Ziniquel snorted. "The last time anyone commissioned ghosts was for Arity's inauguration. Fifteen years ago. If we only worked once every fifteen years, we would soon lose our credibility in the Ellipse."

"So how do we find our ghosts? How did you get hold of this one?"

"Usually—well, usually, we seduce them. That's another talent ghostiers have to have."

Humi remembered Mory leading Rain out of the hall . . . Erene with her dress torn off one shoulder . . . She would *never* be able to do that! "Not me!"

"I wouldn't have thought you had any potential as an apprentice if I hadn't seen that you could," Ziniquel said. "It's not as hard as it sounds. All

I do is sit in my favorite haunts—in disguise, of course—and the ghosts find *me*. And I hear from Emni that you're already learning the technique." Humi flushed. Did her explorations through the city count as practice for ghost-hunting expeditions then? "All the runaways in the world come to Delta City. A good many of them are penniless when they get here, and those are generally the youngest and most beautiful. Here's the manifesto." He recited, "*Ghosts must represent every part of Salt. They must be young. They must be beautiful, which means that they must be instantly and constantly pleasing to the eye. And unless they be extremely exceptional, their beauty must conform to some degree with fashion as dictated by the present court. The ghostier's eye having fallen upon a young man or woman conforming to these standards, it is up to him to judge whether the decay of his or her beauty is exigence sufficient to weigh heavier than his or her life in the Divine Balance.*"

"Oh," Humi said. "Erene hasn't told me any of this."

Ziniquel laughed unpleasantly. "She hasn't told you much, has she?"

"She hasn't exactly had leisure to teach me lately." Humi rose to Erene's defense. "She's had other things to worry about."

"Oh? What could be more important than the tutoring of an apprentice?" Ziniquel's eyes were hard as green ice.

"Court business," Humi spat, "that wouldn't be difficult for her to accomplish at all if it weren't for the rest of you sitting in her way like *stones*—"

"Humi! You're not responsible for her. You don't have to defend her to me. And I—" He stepped forward and closed his hands on her shoulders. "I shouldn't shift my anger onto you. The rift is between Erene and myself. I apologize."

Humi found herself trembling.

"I don't think you understand. Do you understand?" Gently, he lifted her chin with one hand.

Horrifying herself, Humi burst into tears. "She's my master. I depend on her goodwill! I'm on her *side!*"

Ziniquel shook his head disbelievingly. He pulled her close and held her to his chest, rocking back and forth. "What has she been telling you? Your talent depends on us—*all* of us! You can be on her side and ours both at once. The rules of ghosting aren't like those of other crafts. If she died or moved out of the Crescent, you'd have the choice of staying in the Crescent and being taught by one of the other masters. She knows that, and it probably influences her decisions. So in a way, *you* have power over *her.*"

"But that's not the point."

His cloak smelled of rain. Steadied in his arms, she began to relax.

"What I mean is that—" he paused, as if searching for words to describe something he took for granted—"there are thirteen people who would make you welcome if you crawled into their beds late at night. You will never want for someone to care for you, to love you. There isn't *just* Erene. We are all your family. In the language of the gods, there are no words for father, mother, brother, sister—but there are a hundred different words for *friend,* and one of them applies specifically to ghostiers." He moved her away a little and looked into her face. "The gods don't like people to know that they have their own language. Or that they created a word especially for us. So we only use it among ourselves."

"Tell me," Humi said, fascinated, her tears slowing.

"We are *imrchim.* You are my *imrchu.* I am your *imrchi.*"

The word was redolent of embraces and whispers. Humi felt a sense of awe. *The language of the gods . . .*

"Our companionship is essential to our art. You must remember that. Never reject your *imrchim,* or your talent will fade away too."

"What about Erene?"

"I didn't say anything about her," Ziniquel said brusquely, and moved away. Humi hugged herself, suddenly cold in her wet clothes. "How about that chocolate?"

His apartment was as higgledy-piggledy as Erene's, but in a friendlier, lived-in way. Hearth fires smoldered in every room. The furniture was dark with age. The small kitchen held a far wider array of foods than Erene's did (even now that Algia had put it in good repair). Humi watched as Ziniquel prepared the chocolate; then he led her into the living room. "It's so home-like," she said sincerely.

He shrugged. "The others use their apartments to remind themselves of their origins. So do I, and I'm Deltan."

"But these must—" She stopped. Then she said, "These must have been Constance Searidge's rooms before they were yours."

"She was Icelandic. I changed them completely."

The fire had died to embers, its heat intensified by the humidity in the room. The windows dripped condensation. The imported pine wood logs released a sharp scent of resin. Ziniquel stared into the fire.

"Will you tell me about her?" Humi said softly.

"You must have heard by now. It's only one of our stories."

She shook her head.

"Gods . . . Why is it falling to me to tell you all our secrets? I'm not your master." He sank back on the fleece rug. "Sorry. I didn't mean that the way it sounded. Really, I'm happy to speak for the *imrchim.* And I suppose I'm a good spokesman, because I'm not ashamed of anything I've done." He stared up at her, hands behind his head.

It seemed impossible that this hot-tempered, cold-blooded creature, dangerous as an unsheathed knife, would talk to her. Impossible that he trusted her with his secrets. But then, she was his *imrchu.* "Tell me," she said.

The story of Constance Searidge's death was a drama which the ghostiers reenacted many times per generation. In fact, only two of the current master ghostiers had got where they now were by their own masters' natural deaths or resignations. He wouldn't tell Humi which they were. One had to respect the fact, he said, that some of them were secretly ashamed of their deeds, and of the hunger for power, an essential component of the ghostier's character, that had brought them to commit those deeds. Ordinary people would have been dogged by guilt all their days. The ghostiers' talent lay in their ability to shrug off almost all of it. The more, the better the ghostier.

Ziniquel's murder of Constance Searidge had hinged on her refusal to acknowledge that she was old and her heart weak, on her confidence that Ziniquel would compensate for her weakness and ask nothing in return, and on the bodies of several infants. Ziniquel hadn't killed them. Babies died by the dozen every day in Delta City, victims of disease and poverty. While Constance was out, he turned the room into the scene of a massacre. It had been furnished all in white, with textural paintings and fleeces. The blood stood out as if something had been savaged on the snow. "It was too much for her to take, murderess though she was. Ghostiers aren't hardhearted, you know—we're just able to direct our compassion where it matters. We do have our vulnerabilities. And I knew Constance's."

So ridiculously easy. Humi closed her eyes.

"She looked much older after she died."

"What did you do with the body?"

"I locked the door on the whole ugly mess and left it. There was an Ellipse meeting that night. I invented an excuse to come into the Chamber, and I claimed Constance's seat. I was safe then. I brought the others here and showed them what I had done."

Humi shivered. Her imagination provided color for the scene, most of it red. "All that for an old chair with '12' carved on the back. It seems so pointless."

"Haven't you felt it yet?" Ziniquel's voice was quiet, but it made Humi shiver. "Ghosting *is* power. Our god-given license to kill extends to *anyone,* Humi, anyone at all, provided that we can make a beautiful enough ghost out of them to swing the Divine Balance. That's where we get our seats in

Ellipse. Because right back at the beginning of civilization, the gods made us the most powerful people in the Divinarchy."

"Is power that important? I thought art was the key—"

"Oh, no. *Oh,* no." Zin smiled mirthlessly. "Power is all-important. And for many of us it doesn't stop with ghosting. It doesn't even stop with the Ellipse. Many of us, throughout the ages, have been consumed by ambition. They've let the ice into their hearts. Erene is one of those, I think."

"Are you?"

"Not me." He gestured around the room. "I'm content. I wouldn't even miss the Ellipse, were you to take it away from me, as long as I could still ghost."

She felt the heat of the fire, imbuing the air with its sweet pine scent. But the ice was there. It was outside in the rain, waiting. She felt something else too, like a current running invisibly between her and Ziniquel. The near-obscene things which he had done to her sixdays ago, in that lace-hung chamber.

She slipped down to the rug and snuggled against his side. "Ziniquel."

"Mmm?" He stroked her arm, smiling down at her.

"Do—do *imrchim* make love to each other?"

"They do indeed." A log crashed in the fire. His hand picked at the nubs in her sleeve. "But not you and me."

She pressed her face into his shoulder, unspeakably embarrassed. His bones were prominent under the linen tunic, his flesh hot from the fire.

"Wait," he said, laughter in his voice. "Let me explain. You're a virgin, right?"

She nodded.

"And you're only sixteen! You're not ready for that."

"Erene told me not to," she said into his shirt. "But I thought you said you loved me."

"I do. *Making* love is different. I think Erene was right this time, much as I hate to admit it—it's too early for you. You want to find your feet among all of us, not get hopelessly attached to one person. Specially not me." He squeezed her. Disappointment washed through her like a tide. She had a feeling of a giant, irrevocable step taken—a crossroads left behind. It had to do with more than just Ziniquel. It had to do with Erene. Obeying her. Loving her. The business Humi had promised to help her with. The things the Divinarch had said to her, for her ears alone. But she did not want power or recognition; she only wanted someone to hold her and kiss her tenderly. She wanted this man.

"Who were your other lovers?" she asked.

"Erene. Mory. Elicit. Owen. No one right now. But I suppose you can tell I have my eye on Emni. If it wasn't for her attachment to Sol, she and I would be lovers. I'm pretty sure of that."

"You were *Owen's* lover?"

"Yes, I'm a lover-of-men at times." He looked down at her face. "Is that taboo in Domesdys?"

"What—no, that's not what I meant! Oh, Zin." She snuggled against him. "I don't want anything more from you than love."

"You've got that." He sounded vaguely puzzled. She was reminded, with a sudden feeling of age and wisdom, that he was just nineteen, and that this was the only life he'd ever known. "From all the others too. Never doubt it. You are our *imrchu.*"

She fell asleep there, lying with her head on his shoulder.

She dreamed of Beau, and efts circling in clouds of bloody water, and Constance Searidge lying dead with her head in Ziniquel's lap. Ziniquel howled silent grief. The Divinarch's mouthful of fangs grinned solemnly in his pinkish-gray child's face. *Curiosity is our worst flaw,* he said to Humi. *As a race, we gods have always been victim to it. Now our decline falls upon us soft as snow, because we delved too far and uncovered the Great Irony which we never should have known. Stunned by it, we let ourselves drift. And the current of time carries us downward.*

Follow the birds, Humility.

Gold streamed in the window. Outside, sparrows and starlings swooped and fluttered, darting across a strip of bright azure sky. For a moment their warbling tore at her heart. But then all was hidden beneath the bright reality of waking.

Her cheek rested on a feather pillow. A multicolored blanket snuggled her in warmth. The fire crackled cheerfully.

"Good morning!" Zin called, opening the back door of the apartment. "I've brought breakfast!"

She could smell apple pastries and hot chicory.

"Fresh from Frivalley's bakery! How did you sleep?"

TWELVE

That day, over the lunch dishes, Humi talked to Owen. In the afternoon she spoke long and earnestly with Emni. And gradually the ghostiers' complicated shorthand of affection and death opened up to her.

The spice of constant danger raised their companionship above the mundane. These men and women whose vocation was so closely tied into death were spoiled for anything else, like sugar addicts whose palates find all other foods dull. The possibility of the hidden syringe lay in each embrace: and so apparent betrayals were really fair victories. And what looked to an outsider like murder was only a lapse of wariness on the part of the victim.

Keeping this in mind, Humi saw that it was impossible for them to be merely fellow craftsmen. They became *imrchim.*

Rita was living in the shadow of the axe, just as Constance had. But *she* was canny enough to be aware of it. That was the reason she took such joy in life. Her every day was borrowed from Owen. "I'm just taking my time. Soon that seat is going to be *mine*," Owen boasted to Humi. But later, Emni told Humi that he had already made several attempts which Rita had sidestepped.

Every master was in danger from him, for the ghostiers' law of succession was nonrestrictive—but Rita made the easiest target, since she and Owen shared living quarters. She held seat number 11 in the Ellipse— inferior only to Fra's, Ziniquel's, and Erene's among those held by the ghostiers.

Emni and Humi sat on the lip of the twins' big, sunken bed in their white-walled bedroom. This apartment was a model specimen of what Humi doubted she and Erene would ever have: a family home. The walls were scattered with the Archipelagan ink paintings for which the twins and Beisa shared a talent. Bubbly as always, Emni seemed happy to gossip. "Algia's twenty-seven. That's almost *too* old to become a master. Elicit thinks he's safe from her—and I agree." She laughed. "She's just too wa-tery. Any potential she *had* is all gone."

Privately, Humi thought Elicit had displayed a keen eye for apprentice material when he picked Algia. Several times, she had surprised a sneaking look of red danger in the woman's eyes.

"Me and Sol aren't fully trained yet, of course," Emni said. "We've only been here four years. And Beisa teaches thoroughly and slowly. Seven years is the minimum which makes a master ghostier—we'll likely take longer. Zin did it in just under six, but he shouldn't have. His accession was fair but not really welcome among the rest of us. Even if Constance was past her prime, she was as astute a councillor and as brave a friend as anyone."

"Isn't that rather the point?" Humi asked. "She was past her prime as a ghostier, so she had to go."

Emni grimaced. "Yes. You're catching on fast. That's what Ziniquel said. But I thought he was just making excuses for his own ambition—he's very unscrupulous."

"Do you like him?"

Emni looked at her, puzzled. "Of course. I love him."

Do you know he's attracted to you, though? "Em, I'd like to know about you and Sol. You grew up together, didn't you?"

"Yes."

Humi waited. Emni poured both of them more watered wine. As she relidded the pitcher, she said carefully, "Sol and I are complete opposites. Beisa has told us both, privately, that only one of us has the potential to be a master ghostier. But she wouldn't say which. And I don't suppose we'll ever know, not until she starts to fail, or until one of us gets impatient. *Then* we'll see which of us stood up in the womb and which lay curled around his or her ankles."

"What a horrible thought to live with," Humi said sincerely.

"We manage." Emni gulped wine. "Don't tell anybody that, Humi. I—I never told anyone before. And I know Sol hasn't either. He wouldn't like it if he knew I'd told you." Humi nodded sympathetically. "It'd be easier," Emni said with a trace of anger, "if we only knew whether Beisa took him along as company for me—or me for him. And only later started treating us equally. But she won't tell."

"Maybe she doesn't—"

"Supper, Em!" Sol put his head around the door. "Oh, hello, Humi." Grinning, he seemed perfectly friendly. "Erene's been back for a while. She was looking for you. But now she's helping Rita serve up." He paused. "You'll find them in the Chalice kitchen."

Humi recognized a hint when she heard one. "See you in a bit, Em," she said, and levering herself to her feet, she went out into the hall. When she heard the door close behind her, she came back and put her ear to the crack.

"What did you tell her?" Sol's voice was harsh.

"Nothing you wouldn't have told her yourself." Emni's self-righteousness quailed into defensiveness. "Don't worry, Sol! She's sweet! I love her! I want her to be our friend!"

Sol said bitterly, "She'll split us apart. She can't possibly understand how it is between you and me."

"We're brother and sister. She could *never* split us apart! Besides, she has other things to worry about. What's it going to be like for her as Erene's apprentice?"

"See! Your mind's already full of her concerns!" There were rustles, and a little gasp. Sol said roughly, "It's just that I couldn't stand to lose you, Em. Do you see? I couldn't stand it."

"I love you too!" To Humi's horror, Emni began to weep. "I promise I won't talk to her anymore!"

Silence. Or nearly.

Humi felt a loneliness open up inside her. Intellectually she did not envy their closeness. But for some reason she wanted to cry. She hurried through the apartment. Beisa was sitting in the last of the light, sketching two Marshtown youngsters squatting in the window opposite, sharing a pipe. As Humi passed, she looked up and smiled, the smile of a sorely tried mother who is glad that her children are making other friends at last.

THIRTEEN

Erene got the summons from the Divinarch that morning, by courier dove, as she tried to dress in the cramped bedroom without waking Humi. It said to come alone. Erene did not know why she had asked Elicit. Maybe she needed to share something with him. She felt they were not so close as they had been. Once, they had been two Piradean ghostiers, bound by trade and ethnicity, so similar in their likes and dislikes that they could finish each other's sentences. When they lay together in bed, she had the strangest feeling that they were one complete person, that she could not move without moving Elicit's body, too. That kinship had started the day Erene arrived in Delta City, young and bursting with life; it had weathered Hem, Erene's atheism, and even Erene's friendship with Goquisite. But it seemed as though it might not weather Erene's snatching Humi from Ziniquel.

So she had brought him today, to show him that she trusted him.

They swept to the end of the hall, where a queue of vacant-eyed Deltans ended before a pair of oaken doors. "We have a prior appointment," she said kindly to the first woman in line, and they entered the Throne Room. The guard pulled the doors shut behind them. Jeweled chandeliers shook sprinkles of colored light over the walls. The vastness of the hall made the Throne look diminutive. Human-made, it was a thousand-year-old tribute to the first Divinarch, less a chair than an enormous, elaborate setting for the Divinarch's tiny body, trimmed with age-blackened bits and bobs and fetishes from every corner of the six continents and the Archipelago. On a dozen pedestals built into it stood Divine Guards, Arity, Pati, Hope, Broken Bird, and Bronze Water among them. *Even Incarnations have to do whatever duty the old idiot feels like assigning them!* Erene thought disgustedly.

She squeezed Elicit's hand as they bowed to the Throne. "I am sorry we are late, Divinarch. Several streets in Christon were blocked by beggars.

They had overturned produce carts to loot them. It is disgraceful how many paupers there are this year."

"It is the same from Samaal to Rukarow," the Divinarch said. Unlike most gods, he made no attempt to moderate his voice for the sake of human ears. "Many, many of my subjects have sunk to destitution who before were able to eat."

He yawned tremendously, stretching his little body until it quivered, and leaped down from the Throne, a wizened pink monkey child with enormous fangs and eyes. His mustaches jerked spastically. He appeared to be having a good day. "You may all go now," he said, looking around at the gods on the pedestals. "All of you."

The gods' voices sparkled like fireworks.

"Milord!"

"And leave you alone with a ghostier and an insurgent? We're not going anywhere, Old One!"

"Er-serbalu, iye fash graumir?"

"Yes, I am going to make you leave! Go away. Go on. Even you, Pati!"

"Do you think he's cracked, Errie?" Elicit whispered.

"He's not mad," Pati answered from the Throne, his white face glassy, his wings thrumming. Gods had sharp ears. "Just deluded. I don't know what he's planning. Both of you had better be on your guard." He vanished.

One by one, shooting distrustful glances at Erene and Elicit, the other gods followed. Erene blinked to clear the spots from her eyes.

"Good," the Divinarch said, rubbing his hands. "I can still make them do my bidding. When I get too old for *that*, it will truly be time to die . . . ! Lady Gentle, I have been wanting to talk to you alone for a long time. And you, Godsman Paean, you might as well hear too. The *firim* would make such a to-do if they heard what I am going to tell you." He perched on the base of the Throne, drawing his knees up. "So, Lady Gentle, why do you think there are so many beggars in the streets this autumn?"

"It is the taxes," Erene said cautiously. "Belstem Lord Summer has raised them again."

"And why did he raise them last year . . . and again this year?"

"To improve the economy, Divinarch." Why did he want to hear this? He must know already. "To put power in the hands of those who have the capital and therefore the influence to use it effectively. To give the lower classes an incentive to better themselves."

"Glib!" The Divinarch steepled his fingers. "Answer me. Why do you and Belstem want the common classes to better themselves?"

"Everyone should desire to better themselves."

"Aha. Now we come to the rub. The flamens believe that all mortals should be equal, and equally content. Whereas, if I hear you right, Belstem does not believe in contentment. He thinks that mortal society should have a dynamic, preferably an upward dynamic, though as in the case of the beggars, it can so easily be a downward one. He believes in constant movement between the social strata. I seem to recall that his word for this change is 'progress'."

"With all due respect, Divinarch, you know the atheistic position as well as I do." Erene bobbed her head. "You're leading up to something. What is it?"

"Watch out!" Elicit breathed in agony.

The Divinarch's voice rang with satisfaction. "In my opinion, Lady Gentle, Godsman Paean, Lord Summer is right to raise the taxes."

Elicit gasped.

"It *is* time for mortal society to *progress*, to outgrow the constraints imposed on it by the flamenhood. We the gods are no longer relevant to you. We can share in this progress, or not, as humanity dictates. Erene, you and Belstem are geniuses, pioneers, as great as the Wanderer and the Antiprophet. I salute you."

Oh, gods, Erene thought. *No. He's joking, but this is it, this is the end with Elicit. He'll never trust me again. He'll think I set him up to hear this.*

And, sure enough, Elicit thrust himself to his feet and stepped forward, staring at the Divinarch, his hands clenching into fists. "Lord god, that's not possible. You and Erene are enemies! You know perfectly well that she wants to prevent Arity from taking the Throne when you return to Heaven!" His voice cracked as he begged, "You want to stop her!"

"Wrong!" the Divinarch sat up, claws on knees. "I do *not* want to stop her! Of course, in order to keep the peace, I cannot act to help her either. But she need not fear my retribution. In fact, she has my blessing, whatever that is worth." He laughed. *Perhaps he is not joking.* Erene scarcely dared to think it. Blood spattered his trousers, mingling with the gemlike bits of light from the chandeliers on the white cloth. "Lady Gentle, I have undermined the peace my ancestors maintained for generations. I have made a philosophy of my deeds. I am supreme among bunglers!"

"He's mad," Elicit muttered. "He must be."

"No. I am not." Erene shivered at the tone of relentless cheer in the Divinarch's voice. "*This* is what I pride myself on: all my life, I have made my own choices. Alone among gods, I have followed my whims instead of the traditions set up for me by others. A hundred and fifty years ago, when I lived in Heaven, I found a lost, half-dead human. I took him in. While he healed, he explored Heaven—and unlike the Wanderer, thirteen hundred years ago, he understood Heaven for what it was. He absorbed our secrets, learning everything he needed to bring mortal society neck and neck with ours. And he developed the concept of equality that he called atheism." The Divinarch chortled. "I sent him back to the world of mortals. I did it! I was the instrument of your receiving those secrets that helped you to understand that we are no more gods than you are!"

"No," Elicit whispered. "I don't believe a word of it."

Erene's heart bled for him. At the same time, she listened, hypnotized. "Go on, Divinarch," she breathed.

"But even I was not expecting the rapidity with which atheism spread." The Divinarch sighed. "Our race was only ever superior to yours because we had existed for so much longer. But our civilization hasn't changed since time before time. And once we gave you humans a hand out of the bog of barbarity, you drew equal with us in what is, compared to the length of our history, no more than a day and a night. In a few minutes, you will draw ahead." He shook his head.

"Yes?" Erene breathed after a long pause.

Bronze Water reappeared suddenly, standing on the Throne above the Divinarch. "We *should* have expected it," the Incarnation said. "We should have known, from our experience with the Wanderer, what one lone human could do to the gods. Even before the Wanderer—when we watched primitive ghostiers at work, and for the first time fell in love with something human—we should have understood. Ghosting is the only craft you invented that we did not. It illustrates what is human: the ability to bring something out of nothing with only faith and heart for tools. Like the miracle power."

"Divinarch," she said helplessly, her heart overflowing. "Bronze Water— I want to thank you—you have justified everything I believe in—"

Elicit was shaking, his face hidden in his hands. She could see him struggling to make excuses for the gods within his mind. She suppressed her own pity.

"I thank you, and I think I understand. You believe we are due to take precedence over you. Broken Bird is of your persuasion, I would guess. But the younger generation have reacted to your signing away their birthright, asserting that they are superior to humans and have the right to rule over us."

The Divinarch and Bronze Water stared at her, two sets of unreadable god eyes. "I really think that we have explained ourselves," he said gently. "I think you should go now." He slid down off the Throne and began to hobble away. Bronze Water followed, like a burly father going after a child. The Divinarch's mustaches bounced like springs, but his gait was arthritic.

The windowless hall felt huge, yet unsafe, as if the sea were trembling at the doors, waiting to roar in. What was she to do with this? This license to revolution? The Divinarch had given her an edge not only over enemies but over friends as well. He had as good as picked her over Belstem to head the regime that would replace the Divinarchy after his death. She could now state her own position in so many words, both in Ellipse and in social situations, without fearing punishment. No one would understand her daring, and so they would respect it.

But she could not share the knowledge, not even with Goquisite. To tell Goquisite would be to tell Delta City. The masses would not understand: anarchy loomed, a fulminating specter.

Lucky the Divinarch had picked *her* to hear his stand, instead of some noble with a loose tongue!

Lucky she had brought no one besides Elicit, who would die rather than remember what the Divinarch had said, much less pass it on!

The whites of his eyes were blood-veined. She looked at him, unable to speak, unable to tell him how much she needed him, that she would not have hurt him for the world—"You don't actually believe him, do you?" His voice was ragged. "He's mad. Or he's playing with your mind. Gods are intellectual demons. He could trick you as easily as snapping his fingers."

For a moment doubt gripped her, but then she shook her head. All the Divinarch had stated was his personal beliefs. And she was sure that everything he said, he believed.

I did the deed! I sent Antiprophet back! he had said.

And what other explanation could there possibly be for the gods' inactivity but that they were all obeying him?

"Let's go home," she said almost inaudibly. "Please, Elicit. Let's go. Let's not fight again."

He started to move, then stopped. So tall and gray, like a rock showered by water as the bits of light from the chandeliers danced on his fur. "We used to be more than *imrchim*, Erene. Not even Hem came between us. And you know I never cared for Algia or Eterneli or Soulf one-tenth as much as I care for you."

Oh, Elicit! "I—I love you—"

His face hardened. "I used to paint your likeness on my ghosts. You never saw, but they were all you. I used to dream about you even on the nights when we slept in each other's arms."

She imagined throwing herself at him. She imagined it so vividly that she smelled the camphor on his seldom-used court clothes. "Can't you just love me?" she whispered. "Does it have to be this that comes between us? Does this have to be the last thing?"

"Erene, it wasn't you who was forsaken for a clique of fashionable mon-

keys spouting blasphemy. I can't sacrifice my integrity. Not even for you."
She could tell he was very near tears.

"*Next!*" a god's voice howled faintly from outside, and a draught from the
waiting hall blew in as the great doors swung open. Erene saw the sentinel's confusion as he registered on two lone mortals and an empty Throne.

"Don't let the petitioners see, Orange Bracken!" The air exploded in a
spot of color. Pati appeared between Erene and the Divine Guard. His
wings churned as he began to shove one door shut. Elicit took Erene's
hand in a rough grip that could have been anything except intimate, pulling
her toward the doors.

"Thank you, Striver. Just let us out . . . We're finished here. Yes, quite
finished."

For several nights in a row, Humi had slept alone at the top of Albien
House. Last night her pillow had been wet with tears. Erene appeared to
have left the Crescent. Humi would have given a year of her life to take
back her rudeness the night of the Ellipse. Since then, her relations with
Erene had been normal. But now there was this. What else had she done
wrong? Who else could have caused this disappearance?

The other ghostiers looked at her sorrowfully. Though she knew she
could have gone to any of them for comfort, she would not. She wanted
Erene. She had not known it was possible to miss someone so much whom
she had known for only such a short time.

Finally Erene returned for dinner. After the meal, the *imrchim* left Humi
alone with her in the Chalice. *Now or never,* Humi thought, and gripping
her goblet of mulled wine tightly, she asked Erene where she had been
going every night.

The senior ghostier remained silent a moment, tracing the raised silver
design on her cup with her thumb. "I have my own room in Goquisite's
mansion," she said at last. "A canopied feather-mattressed bed, a girl ghost
that my master Molatio made in a niche, a pet piglet with its own basket by
the fire, and Goquisite's room just down the hall. Every morning, we meet
in her room and cuddle up under the comforters to order breakfast. It is
convenient for me to stay there, because I conduct a good deal of my
business at court late at night."

"But what about me?" Humi said. "Where do I fit into that?"

Erene drained her cup. "Get me some more wine."

Humi pattered down into the kitchen, poured more from the saucepan
on the range, and silently tendered Erene the refilled cup.

"I told you I would be a good master," Erene said. "And I meant to stick to that. I still mean to. But I have been slipping. I know where my priorities lie. And I have been avoiding it."

"Where is it?"

Erene hesitated. "I've been a coward. I waited to tell you. And everyone. They aren't going to like it. But it can't be helped."

"What is it?" Humi asked with a sense of dread.

"You and I—we're moving out. We're going to establish ourselves at Goquisite's. Goq and I have arranged for an entire wing of her mansion to be decorated as a separate household. The only thing we won't have there is a workshop—and of course we will be coming back here to work."

But when are you going to find time to teach me? I have to learn to ghost. She felt the need like a hunger pang. *I have to.* For a fleeting moment, she thought about asking if she could remain in the Crescent and take lessons from Ziniquel or Fra. But she remembered how much she had missed Erene. And she remembered, as if it had been a lifetime ago, the promises they had made as they stood in a bustling Christon street.

Erene wanted this to work so badly. Humi could see it in her eyes. Probably to her it looked like the perfect solution.

And Humi had the power to *make* it that. *If you don't have time for me, I'll teach myself,* she vowed silently. *You won't know anything is wrong. I'll stand up for you.* "It sounds wonderful, Erene," she said. "Let's tell everyone tonight."

"Oh, darling," Erene said, and hugged her with the wine cup still in her hand, hard. Wine sloshed onto Humi's shoulder. "I knew I could depend on you, sweetheart. I knew I could trust you."

FOURTEEN

Thani and Godsbrother Transcendence lay in the small stone hut which the village kept furnished for wandering flamens. Night outside: a herb-scented candle burned in a sconce. In Calvarese style, the bed was made up of a heap of felted throws on the floor, soft and snuggly, but Thani chose to pillow her head on Transcendence's bony arm. Her whole body felt shaky with the aftermath of tears. Transcendence's fingers moved through her hair, soothing her. "Sssh. Sssh. I have to tell you your prophecy."

"I don't want to know," she whispered. If she could have undone the whole day, she would have. Prophecy killed lemans if it took them too often, she knew that, and she was afraid: even though this was her first time, she had never experienced worse pain. It had started with a few twinges while she led Transcendence through the village this morning. They had just arrived at the oasis at dawn, after a night of hard walking, and so they had not yet seen any of the Calvarese sick who awaited their help; somehow Transcendence had managed to do three miracles on no sleep and a breakfast of black chicory. Thani longed for his selfless endurance. She herself had thought she might fall down at any minute.

Perhaps her exhaustion had made her an easy target for the prophecy. (She thought of it as a dark little cloud of foreknowledge drifting through the air, looking for a leman in whom to spend its malice.) It had felt as if all her limbs were being torn apart. Unbearable stresses racked her joints, and nearby villagers ran to her as she fell to the ground, arms splayed, teeth clenched. As clearly as a judgment, she saw the sun blazing in the middle of a circle of dark faces before it went out.

She had come to right here, in this hut. A Calvarese woman old enough to be her grandmother was bathing her face. Thani could not remember her own grandmother: had her name been . . . Tici? The woman cooed gently to her. Thani knew she could not afford to be perceived as vulnerable. She pushed the woman away and screamed for Transcendence.

Now she shuddered and sniffled, snuggling into the hard, angular curve of his body. When adolescence had first started to usurp her body, she had hated it, for flamen and leman moved from oasis to oasis too quickly for her to become comfortable enough with any other woman to ask her what these changes meant. But now, at thirteen, she was comfortable with herself. This way, she could be close to Transcendence as never before. "Tell me, then," she whispered, marshaling her courage.

"You said: *We must go to Royalland. To Delta City. There is a thing to do. Danger to the Divinarch. Danger to the Divinarchy itself. There is a traitor to kill, a figurehead of piety who has turned. I must obey the dictates of the gods.*" Transcendence paused. Thani held her breath, dreading a name. "The rest was gibberish."

"It was incomplete, then!" she cried in relief. "We can't obey it!" The very thought of going back to Royalland made her queasy. Like most lemans, she had been to Delta City once, right after Transcendence chose her, to learn her duties, and that was enough. She loved Calvary. She loved the sun on sand and crags, the skeletal towers of gears which lowered men down the mines, the way they reared black against the brazen sky. She loved eating the spicy, soupy messes that set your mouth on fire, just so that you shouldn't forget, in the evening, how hot the blazing sun was that would rise to greet you on the morrow.

"Leman," Transcendence said sternly, "did I hear you suggest that we disobey the prophecy?"

With difficulty Thani swallowed tears, hiding her face in the pelt of white on his chest. "No! I meant only that—we can't! Until we receive clearer guidance from the gods. I mean, how are we to know who we have to kill, unless—" she hated to say it, but she had to—"unless I prophesy again? Surely the duty that we *know* is more important? I mean, we're expected at Firoun next sixday—and after that, Samadh—we can't deprive them of the miracles we would do there—"

"Child," Transcendence said, "we go on. For now. Rest assured that the gods will tell us what we must do. Prophecy is their least ambiguous voice, but I also know their bidding in my heart, when it is imperative."

"Do you know it now?" she asked.

He sighed. "No. But it will come to me, or else to you. We have been chosen for this deed, Thani. It is a test of our faith. Somehow they will let us know how we may do their bidding—and until then we will watch."

She nodded, hardly registering the words, hearing only that for now, they would not go to Royalland. He would not be able to see it if she nodded, so she gave the rote obeisance that to her was anything but a platitude: "Yes, master. I obey you, and through you, I obey the gods."

Outside, one of the oasis hounds barked. High overhead, the scream of a predator trailed thinly down the night wind. Transcendence held her close, as if any noise which evoked the existence of a world outside the little hut threatened their togetherness. When all fell quiet, he rolled her gently onto her back. His fingers traced paths from her collarbone to her pubis, circling each nipple. A tingling warmth grew inside her.

He was her life. And he knew what she looked like only through touching her.

Strange to think he'd never seen her face. She could itemize his in every detail. He had stridden into her babyhood home along the road to the salt, like any other wandering flamen, hood thrown back so that he could enjoy the mild Domesdys rain. Even then his hair had been white. He was alone: his first leman, a girl then nineteen, had gotten married the sixday before, to a boy who lived in Nece. This he told Thani's sister, who was feeding the poultry in the courtyard. Humi ran out to the cornfield, where Thani was helping Mother glean the last stalks, and called out that a flamen had come alone. Not joyfully—Humi had not, Thani remembered dimly, been a joyful child—but with a face like stone.

Thani pushed her face into Transcendence's mop of white hair. She caught his stark-tendoned wrists and pulled him down on top of her, entwining her legs with his. Heat grew between their bodies. "I love you," she said passionately as he caressed her. He smelled of salt and sand and cumin, of the desert.

FIFTEEN

Mell slumped on the tavern stool, weary but satisfied, paying no attention to the sailors from Westchasm wrangling as they pushed in out of the rain. It had taken him months to get here from Calvary, sleeping his way from ship to ship (and he'd had a *hard* time of it before he learned to pick out which sailors were lovers-of-men at first sight) but finally he had arrived. Delta City. He'd longed to come here ever since he could remember. Now he felt a warm sense of lassitude—and he was sweetly conscious of the attention he was already receiving. The boys at home had been right. Ragged clothing *couldn't* disguise beauty. The woman in the expensive cloak, in the corner, had been staring at him for fifteen minutes. She seemed like his best prospect at the moment. Mell felt more comfortable with men, but he would sleep with a woman if it paid well, especially one as pretty as this one. You got introduced to both sexes rough and early in the bronze mines, and you learned to appreciate whatever came your way.

A snaky-looking fellow by the bar eyed Mell too. Mell suspected that *he* had very different intentions. A pickpocket, maybe, who kept his eyes open for tenderfeet fresh from the country. Or a cruising pimp. Plumped in the middle of a stinking marsh the way Delta City was, everyone had to arrive via the docks, whether they came from overseas or upriver, and many of them hadn't a clue what they were in for. Many greenies would fall victim to that fellow. Even now he was straightening his collar, popping a sprig of basil into his mouth to sweeten his breath, and preparing to mince over to Mell's corner.

Not a chance, friend. Mell swallowed the last of his beer and got up. Donning his best smile, he wove gracefully between the tables to the woman in the cloak. "Milady," he purred, "it's raining very heavily, and I am fresh out of lodgings. How would you say to a trade? Me, in exchange for the sharing of your bed tonight?"

She stood up and held out a hand to him. The candle over her head flared green. It smelled pungently of sap. "Indeed, you may share my bed," she said. "Indeed."

Familiar now, the darkness of her room, once the damp bedroom in Erene's apartment at Tellury Crescent. Erene did not mind her sleeping here instead of at Antiprophet Square every once in a while—so she knew she was not missed. And there had been no question of sneaking Mell into Goquisite's mansion, for gods-knew-who might have seen her and stopped her. Or at least let him know what he was in for.

Familiar the pillow-scattered bed. Familiar its scent, the floral perfume she had picked for a signature mixed with the smell of ink from the treatises on beauty she read at bedtime. Intoxicating, the slim body in her arms, his accomplished kisses. She hoped he couldn't tell how inexperienced she was—as a lover, but also as a ghostier. Solo ghosting was forbidden to apprentices. But somehow she knew she was ready. Since she grew confident of her place at Tellury Crescent, and knew that they would not throw her out no matter what they caught her doing, she had been itching to break a few rules.

She had decided to leave it up to chance—go to a dockside tavern and see what happened. And Mell Cujegrass had happened. He was handsome as only a Calvarese could be, his sultry good looks sizzling with sexuality. He wore his hair long, with a miner's forelock. One of his temples bore a shiny burn. When she saw him across the tavern, that tiny imperfection had struck into her eyes like a knife.

Ziniquel had been right, when he said that all she had to do was wait and the ghosts would come.

Panting, momentarily spent, Mell rolled away. "Do I satisfy you? Are you pleased with your choice? Many courtesans can be found on the docks, you know, milady. But I warrant I am the best."

"You . . . hh . . . you are . . ." She knew he was not in fact a courtesan, but fresh off the boat. So proud. So young. So fiery. And doomed to die. She *knew* that, were it allowable for her to tell him what came next, he would accept no compensation such as the flamens had paid the Garden family. He would give himself to her, welcoming the glory of having his beauty admired for ages to come.

It was just that this way it felt like cheating. She closed her hands on his arms, pulling him toward her. "The cold's getting under the covers. Come here."

"Mmm . . . ahhh, that tickles."

"You sound so surprised when you laugh."

"I grew up in the bronze mines. There's not much to laugh at there."

She traced his collarbone with her teeth. The fur in the hollows of his neck still tasted of metal. "You're superb."

"Let *me* taste *you*." He dragged her away from his throat as roughly as if she were a small animal. "Come here, little one—" He drove his lips against her mouth and his arousal between her thighs. Then he penetrated her. Caught up in her dreams of ghosting, Humi had practically forgotten her virginity. Pain shot through her like a dart. She wondered if he could tell that he was her first lover.

Four in the morning, and it was all over, and Humi felt nauseous. The mirror in the bathroom showed her tousled hair and a face the color of gravemud. An hour ago, she had woken up and realized that she would die if she did not replenish her body. Single-mindedly, she had dragged herself to the pantry cupboard and wolfed down everything in sight.

Before that . . .

The beginning of the night—after Mell had pulled away from her, looking down at her face with the first stirrings of doubt, and she had realized that *now*, now she had to do it—swam back into her mind like a nightmare.

She remembered patching together the clues that Erene had dropped over the months. Finally understanding that infuriating vagueness at the heart of everything Erene said.

Ghosting was indescribable.

Death was the flight of a soul from the material plane. As Humi drove the knife into Mell's ribs, she had understood the sheer, staggering psychic force one had to employ to block that flight. At last, she had felt the sickening slackness as the soul despaired of ever getting away and dropped sideways, slipping out of her grasp like a fish. She wondered why she had ever wanted to do this. She was alone in the apartment with scores of candles blazing and she wanted to die. How could she have done it? How could she ever have let herself be beguiled into a profession that required her to kill human beings?

He had trusted her. That was the worst of it.

I killed him. I killed him. Oh, by the gods.

The basin's china rim was cold and sharp. It left red trenches in her palms. A little pinkish water remained in the bottom. She splashed her face, toweled her fur with the sleeve of her blouse. Two rooms away, the body sprawled beside its ghost, slack and foul. She could not even remember how she had posed the ghost. She dreaded to go and see whether it had come out well. "If it's a mess, I'm damned in the eyes of the gods. It has to be beautiful enough to weigh more than Mell's life in the Balance. Why did

I do it before I was sure I could do it well?" She sat on the hard marble floor, whining softly. "Overconfidence! Damn!" The legs of the basin stand rose to a dizzying height above her. She had committed a crime worthy of a predator. No excuse—no escape. No going back. No excuse—

The bathroom door opened, footsteps circled her, and a hand touched her shoulder. She yelped and wrenched away, scrambling to her feet. Only belatedly did she realize the touch had been gentle.

The Heir to the Divinarchy stood in the doorway, slim, barefoot, clothed in black.

"That is an inspired ghost you have made."

His purplish-brown hair blazed like a fire of dead leaves.

Humi shivered. She was too wretched even to be surprised at his appearance. "Milord Heir, don't say things you don't mean! Do you realize what a crime I've committed?"

Arity hitched himself up on the basin and swung his feet. It bore him without breaking. He must be lighter than he looked. "All the usual qualms." Humi could not take her eyes off his face. She had not seen him at close quarters since that first evening at the Old Palace. She had forgotten how beautiful he was. His eyes were abnormally large, but unlike those of the other Incarnations, they held compassion that Humi could only label human. "From what I can make out," he said in a clear, textureless voice scaled down so as not to destroy the bathroom, "you think you have killed for no purpose. You cannot imagine what possessed you. You hate yourself for your heedless arrogance." He shook his head and laughed. "By the Power, girl! If you want to feel guilty, visit the Eftpool! The eft will tell you that it wants its life back, or that it thinks its death was justified, whatever impulse comes out on top. But does it really matter?"

"He wanted to live," she whispered. "There was that vitality in him. Not like Beau."

"It doesn't matter! By the ghostiers' standards, you have pulled off a coup! Here, let me show you." Beckoning with his chin, he led her to the bedroom.

She looked down.

He sprawled on his back on the white fluffy carpet, mouth open. Blood filled his mouth and trickled down his dark cheek to the ear. His hands clawed, frozen, at the stab wound under his ribs. The body had taken some time to die after the spirit fled.

The ghost stood erect, contraposto, beside her bed, the fingers of one hand in his mouth as if he were licking them. His eyes crinkled in surprise and wonder. She had caught him just as he was beginning to laugh. That streak of childlike innocence showed plainly.

Arity took her arm and ushered her into the brightly lit living room. He sat her down on the cold stone floor by the dead hearth, then leaned forward and shoved the embers with the heel of his hand. They sputtered into flame. "You made your ghost reflect the subject you drew it from. None of the other ghostiers do that. They construct artificial works of art out of their own imaginations. You, because you chose an incredible subject, have made one of the most powerful ghosts I have ever experienced. And it's not even painted yet!"

"But—but I didn't even know what I was—" She could not keep her eyes from filling with tears. Then she sobbed and sagged forward into his arms. He caught her and held her, supporting her weight with the kind of gentleness that is born of great strength. His chest felt like an unbreakable stone shell. His body heat was twice that of a human. Sobbing, scandalized at herself, Humi thought wildly: *He's a god! A god!*

But he had made it all right for her to go on living.

"Thank you, thank you, milord—"

"My pleasure," he said gently. Then his voice hardened. "But don't speak to me that way. If you love me, don't."

She pulled away and looked at him.

He shook his head slightly. "Don't use the word *god*, if you want to please me. That's all."

Fear moved in her. "Why shouldn't I call you a god? That's what you *are*—" He sighed sadly. "I'm sorry. Milord." She ducked her head, the shorthand of worship coming back to her. "It's not my place to ask questions. I won't call you a god anymore."

"Damn! By the Power, you mortals are impossible!" It exploded from him. She brought her eyes up. "Impossible!" Then he took a deep breath, his shoulders quivering. She could see that his smile was forced. "All right, Humility. I would not force you. Call me whatever you want." And he vanished.

Later that night Humi watched stolidly as Erene circled the ghost, her court slippers tapping on the workshop floor. She reached out and fingered a transparent eyelash. Her face was cold, gray, unreadable. Humi hitched one hip on the windowsill. Outside in the Crescent, the sky drizzled with dawn. Of course Humi wanted Erene's approval—but it did not seem to matter as intensely as it had when Erene was the only person who *ever* saw anything she did. A feeling of weightlessness buoyed her up. Now that Arity the Heir, the ultimate authority on beauty, had approved of her ghost, Erene could not destroy her happiness.

"You are not a master ghostier," Erene said finally.

"How could I be?"

"If anyone were to know about this ghost, you would be severely censured."

Humi shook her head. "Erene, they wouldn't."

"Don't get clever with me, girl! I don't mean the ghostiers!" Erene turned on her. "I mean the nobles, especially Goquisite! Be sure that they have all learned the rules of ghosting, so that they can use them on us. And I hope it comes as no surprise that Goquisite would count it as a victory to have you disgraced."

Humi swallowed. Maybe she had been stupider than she thought.

"So, how is this? We will say he is mine." Erene touched the ghost again, her fingers lingering on his diamondine chest. "I'll present him to the Divinarch. That is always a graceful gesture on the part of a ghostier. And this time, I have a special debt to the Divinarch that I have not been able to think how to repay."

"But—" The memory of ghosting tingled in Humi's fingers. Like plunging your hands in a basket of knives, holding on to the soul until it slipped down into the Eftpool. She had put so much pain into this ghost. She wanted the credit for it! Ashamed of her own selfishness, she turned and said to the street, "I would have liked to give him to Arity."

"What?"

Humi turned back to the room. "Nothing. But—but Erene, what if I make another one? What will we do about that?"

Erene's brows drew together. "Haven't I made it clear how much trouble *this* one could cause? Are you seeking to jeopardize us both? For the gods' sake, Humi! It's against the rules!"

She swallowed. How could she put it without seeming rude? The muddy, salty scent of the drizzle invaded the room. "We've already broken so many rules, you and me, Erene. Does this really matter? Don't you want me to be the best ghostier I can be? And besides—" She remembered the feeling of power. The knowledge that she could create beauty that weighed even more than life in the Divine Balance. "I'd be a liar if I told you I would never do it again."

Erene rubbed her face. When she took her hands away, the palms were silver, and dark gray patches stood out on her cheeks. "Humi—" she cracked a smile—"I seem to have forgotten to tell you how proud I am of you. It is a marvelous ghost. Any one of the *imrchim* would be proud of it."

Humi let out a shaky breath she had not known she was holding.

"You must just understand how hard things are for me right now. Belstem will not give ground over the wheat levies from Royalland." An edge entered Erene's voice. "Did you ever hear such a thing? I do not know what he means to do with the money, but he insists that the Summer establishment must get a double share, now that there are two councillors in the family . . ." Her voice slowed down. "Anyhow, obviously I didn't make a ghost last night. And you did."

"It'll be years before I'm as good as you are now," Humi said loyally, because she felt the current of death pull between them. The air of the room shivered like moving water. The undertow tugged at her. Mentally, she slapped it away, terrified.

Erene seemed not to notice the tension. "All in all, you exceed my wildest hopes, darling." She held out her arms.

Humi hung back, glancing from Erene's peach-colored dress and silver-dusted breast to her own paint-stained skirt and blouse. "I'll muss your—"

"Silly girl." Erene laughed tenderly. "It's time I took it all off anyhow. I've been up all night at court. We'll celebrate your first ghost by sleeping here today."

Thankfully, Humi stepped forward and laid her cheek on the senior ghostier's shoulder. The metallic tang of Erene's facedust cut her nostrils. She thought, *I didn't even care about Beau as much as I care about Erene. I lied—I would have given up ghosting if she had asked me to.*

And she could not help remembering how Arity the Heir had felt in her arms: hot, hollow, unbreakable as stone.

SIXTEEN

Months stretched into years. Summers and winters soaked Delta City with the flavor of the sea. Humi found that she was spreading herself thinner and thinner in the attempt to strike a balance between Tellury Crescent and Antiprophet Square. At first she retreated back into the ghostiers' shelter as often as she could, but it was very difficult to resist the pull of court society. Goquisite, Erene, Marasthizinith, Belstem, Aneisneida, and Pietimazar, and their backstabbing, glittering circle of acquaintances sucked her in almost unstoppably. They did not want her in particular—she was only an apprentice—but they would have her anyway. Attend one *sociale,* and she would find six invitations on her pillow, all of whose senders would be offended if she did not appear.

Her solution was to gradually drop out of sight. All ghostiers disguised themselves from time to time, for their forays into the city demanded anonymity, but by the time Humi turned nineteen, she disguised herself so often that Humility Garden scarcely ever showed her face at the Ankh mansion. She had become a recluse, devoted to her art.

Meanwhile Humi went about court in facedust, hairdust, eyepaint, and full costume, as any one of a dozen different personas. What with the height spurt Humi put on in her eighteenth year, Goquisite often took her for a stranger when she was herself. Her tawny fur had got a green tinge from her wearing facedust so much of the time. When Goquisite *did* recognize her, she treated her like one of the guests who dropped in and out of the mansion at all hours—polite, friendly, bestowing confidences and kisses that were no more sincere than her glowing, all-purpose smile.

Humi perpetually failed to understand how this shallow woman could provide adequate companionship for Erene. She reminded herself that Goquisite had been a leman when she was a child, like all the first-generation nobles: there must be some keen edge, some perceptive capacity, hidden under the satin ruffles and soft flesh. But she still could not fathom their friendship. All she could do was watch in wonder as they took down their opposition like predators taking down sheep. For Erene's part, Humi knew that her commitment to Goquisite was extraordinary. When Humi and Erene were alone, Humi often felt that her master was talking not to Humi but to a semblance of Goquisite that sat in Humi's place. She tolerated the indignity in silence. She knew how much Erene depended on her.

When they returned to the Crescent, Erene relied on Humi to shield her from the other ghostiers' tacit disapproval. (Ziniquel did not bother to hide his contempt. He would not even sit in the same room with Erene any more. Humi dreaded the day when he would not be able to restrict his dislike to Erene.)

She tried to convince Erene not to upbraid herself over the loss of their confidence, but to accept it as a fair exchange for her freedom to move about the court. For that was essentially what it was. But at the same time Humi understood that no ghostier could let this loss pass without rage and grief. For without her *imrchim,* a ghostier simply was not. Moreover, the ghostiers' political clout sprang from their unity: and even as the nobles' conspiracy extended its tentacles into the provinces of Royalland and overseas, Erene was jeopardizing the base of her power at home, in Ellipse. At the moment, all the ghostiers still voted with her—but how long could that last?

Humi felt the fabric of their life stretching, stretching, fraying at the edges.

Thus, Erene certainly had no time to consider Humi's tender feelings. She had no time to wonder if Humi might have developed political motives beyond loyalty to her, and put them into play. (Humi had not, but she knew Erene was foolish not to take the possibility into account. For that was what apprentices were supposed to do.)

Apprentices were not supposed to ghost. But Humi needed ghosting the way addicts needed their opiates. At the end of each day she spent encased in lace and facedust, helping Erene take care of her business in the salons of the city, she went hunting or she escaped in a sedan to Tellury Crescent. She ran upstairs, tore off her gown, dropped a sweaty, loose old dress over her head, and threw herself into the aesthetic dilemmas of her latest ghost as if into sweet oblivion.

And energy that she could never access any other time, not even when she needed it, welled up like clotted urgent speech in her fingers.

She guessed that it was partly the sexual links between her and her ghosts that provided this energy. But that was forbidden. When it came down to the act, ghostiers were supposed to keep themselves apart. That way, they did not completely lose themselves in their art. But Humi had started by breaking that rule, and now she could not stop. The other ghost-iers knew, of course; they shook their heads at her but did not stop her. And there was one thing they did not know—the reason she never became lovers with any of them. The illicit air of the lovemaking made her tense with a wild ecstasy she knew none of her *imrchim* could duplicate. The ghost boys' and girls' caresses licked her body like whips. And painting them, afterward, fulfilled the need that that generated. It was a vicious circle.

When she finally collapsed in her boudoir, Arity would come.

After that first ghost, he visited her regularly. She soon stopped trying to guess why—he was a god, and therefore his actions were impossible to analyze. He would *teth* into her room on the top floor of Albien House, and they would sample cold delicacies which she filched from the Chalice kitchen. He devoured them hungrily, sitting with her in the soft, feminine boudoir that she had constructed out of Erene's old living room. Here, she both brought her ghosts and slept herself on the nights that she spent painting.

Her early conversations with Arity seemed stilted to her, more awkward than anything else. Hopeless of his favor, she wondered why he kept com-ing. But then, about a year into their friendship, while comparing garments, she made an accidental discovery. All over his body, talons grew in clusters. Thick, brown cat-claws like those on his hands and feet, bursting painfully from green skin. He reacted with outrage when she dared to ask him about them, and she did not see him for several sixdays; but when he returned, their friendship seemed to have deepened immeasurably. He trimmed them regularly, he said, so that generally there were only flat brown circles on his flesh. Just sometimes, he missed some. She was enchanted. It was as if he no longer felt he needed to keep up his godlike, insouciant front before her. They could now sit in silence without his having to make witty, pointless remarks. Sometimes he came to her in blind furies which drove him stamping and hissing the length of the room, and she cowered from him until it blew over. Then he would sink down with his head in her lap, and smile.

In return for this new trust he placed in her, she started to volunteer her own worries. Her fear that people would discover Erene was not making her own ghosts; her fear that Belstem was getting too extremist to be tolerated. And other, small day-to-day things.

And Arity seemed genuinely to care. He listened with furrowed brow and gave advice which, though occasionally facetious, was generally well meant. If he saw that she was exhausted and fretful, he would become solicitous, humoring her mood until she started to laugh.

She found herself telling him all her woes. Once in a while she would make herself cry with worry, and he would pull her into his arms and hold her the way he had the first time she ever cried in front of him. The sheer strangeness of his heat, and his muscles sliding like butter over his rib cage, stopped her tears, like a blow to the face. She was reminded just how different they were: that Arity was, after all, preternatural.

No matter how often he came, she knew nothing about him. He never told her where he went when he vanished into his sunspot. She never saw him except in her apartment. In public, he behaved like a bawd and spoke in ciphers, like all the other gods; she wondered if this could really be the same person who lay with his head in her lap, talking of aesthetics and fashion. In Ellipse, he seemed possessed of an ability to bring about resolutions when it seemed the Incarnations would not ever agree, though often these made for short-term peace rather than long-term efficiency. Sometimes, as she watched through the peephole, her gaze resting on his slim back, she wondered whether he was consciously preparing himself for the role of Divinarch. Was that why he sometimes acted so distant?

The Divinarch. The Old One. *Er-serbali aes hymannin.*

Though he did not know it, in dropped words and phrases, Arity was teaching her the language of the gods.

"I am so tired," he said, leaning against the headboard of Humi's big white bed. "I fell asleep in Ellipse last night. I don't know what to do about it."

Humi lounged on a pile of cushions at the other end of the bed, her legs curled up in the chenille pool of her evening gown. Her hair was red and her fur gold: she was young Lady Fellwren, who lived a couple of days' journey up the Chrume. She had returned from a midnight *sociale* at Marasthizinith Crane's and was just mustering her energy to change, when Arity arrived. "Perhaps it is because the flamens of the city are doing so many miracles this summer," she said. "Perhaps they are draining you. Have you been to Shimorning yet? Or Temeriton? The heat is worst there. Flies everywhere, and such a smell of the sewers. Belstem and his famous police force, of course, do nothing to help." She heard her voice go acerbic. "The flamens have all they can do to keep the people alive."

"That wouldn't have any effect on me, Humi," Arity said.

She yawned again. "Whatever you say, milord." Though she had propped all the windows in the apartment wide, letting in the fetid stink of the marsh that no perfumes could disguise, the boudoir was hot. This summer was sopping with humidity. Foul water had brought disease to the city, and shortages provoked crime, inspiring Belstem to place rewards on the heads of the underworld crime lords like Gold Dagger and the Hangman, who headed rob-and-resell operations. The famine on the mainland had brought the predators swooping as far as Marshtown at night. "I think each summer has been hotter than the one before as long as I can remember," Humi said, at the exact moment when a predator screamed long and thin overhead.

Arity cocked his head, listening. Then he looked back at her. "You know, Humi, I think you should be able to see by now that I'm not a god."

"Oh, don't be silly," she said, quenching a spark of fear. She always dreaded his bringing this up. "If you're not a god, what are you?"

He sat still, legs crossed, green ankles bare, his gold earrings glimmering in the dusky tangle of his hair. "We're not divine. I can tell you that. Among ourselves, we speak your language as much as we do ours, but we don't call ourselves gods. We call ourselves *auchresh*." She had never heard the word before. It had a hideous sonority. "In your language, that would be *exotics*."

"Exotics? *Auchresh*?"

"Yes. And our language is *auchraug*. The flamenhood made us into gods seventeen generations ago, with little or no encouragement." He rocked forward and said with a strange intensity, "Some of us are ready to step down. But we cannot. Partly because so many mortals base their lives on worshiping us and partly because some of us still won't give up the privileges that come with being gods."

"Shut up," Humi said. "I don't want to hear."

"I never thought of you as willfully ignorant."

There was no answer to that that would let her off easily. She swallowed a lump of apprehension.

"I want you to understand." He glanced down at his ankles. "I want you to know why I am the way I am."

He *never* mentioned the talons that sprouted randomly all over his body. Not even by implication. Suddenly the room seemed darker. The mechanical clock on the wall of the boudoir struck two.

"Do you want to know the truth?" Arity said carefully. "I'll show it to you. Can you take it?"

She could not reply. Fear crippled her. How humbling, to have the scared little devotee inside her exposed! She'd thought that she had left that little girl behind in Domesdys. How naïve, to suppose she could escape her childhood so easily.

She stared at her hands. On each nail was painted a little crown, the symbol of the Throne. Goquisite had started the trend, and a woman like

Lady Fellwren followed every trend that came along. But the crowns were chipping off. Humi needed to repaint them before tomorrow. She needed to select a gown for the lace-knitting *sociale* at Lady Haricot's. Erene needed Humi to work on Lady Haricot . . . "I have so much to do, Arity," she said. "Is this really the right night for a grand revelation?"

His face darkened like water before a squall. One hand flew out in frustration, the thumbnail catching her cheek. She feared he was going to erupt into one of his unpredictable rages. "Is there *ever* a right time for truth? Truth isn't a welcome guest in this city! One has to force it in wherever it will fit!" But then he must have caught sight of the blood oozing through her fur. He enveloped her in his arms and rocked her fiercely, subliminating the violence. She felt his tongue licking her cheek, rough like a cat's. The heat of his body scalded her through her falseribs and her gown. "I'm sorry!" he hissed. "I'm sorry!" Her blood smelled salty on his breath. "Hang on!"

And she felt nothing. His arms vanished from around her. She was neither hot nor cold, submerged in a boundless currentless ocean the temperature of blood—

And then—

Starlight.

On her other side, bright panels like windows.

Her eyes hurt as the pupils expanded. No, it wasn't just her eyes, it was her whole body, and by the gods it hurt! She was expanding from a superdense speck to her proper size and by the gods it *hurt*—

Warm wind washed over her. She staggered, and caught onto a balustrade. It was still dark. Stars danced in sparkling mists overhead, and away before her spread another immense glittering.

A man's voice came close by. The world snapped into focus. That glittering was the sea in starlight, so far below that Humi might as well have been standing on a cliff. No, not a cliff, a balcony, with a solid house at her back, and Arity standing a few steps behind her. She could see nothing of the city. This was the high, rocky, southern prow of the island, beneath which the Chrume slithered like a great, gleaming lizard of water.

"Arity!" she called in panic, pushing her hair out of her eyes as she spun around.

"I haven't betrayed you, Humi." He was right there, squinting against the wind. "This is Hope's house. You didn't know we had houses in the city, did you? Those slatted windows behind you lead to the rooftop dining room."

"How did we get here?" But she knew before he said it.

"That was *teth˝tach ching.*"

Her tiredness had vanished, extracted from her by the wind like a string of scarves from an illusionist's sleeve. The rumble of the tide colliding with the river came faintly to her ears. "All right, then, Arity. What are you? Not a god. Not a mortal. What?"

"An *auchresh*."

"But what's that?"

"I knew you wouldn't believe it from me. That's why we're here. Hope!" he called. "Come upstairs! I've brought you a visitor!"

Footsteps inside the house. One of the slatted blinds rattled up, and a winged silhouette, her skirt swirling about her ankles, stepped into the window. "Pati! Is it you?"

Humi caught her breath. Not even Arity, in his most unguarded moments, had ever sounded as *human* as this. Certainly she had never heard the Maiden, who epitomized feminine timidity and modesty, sound so nakedly *yearning*.

Hope must have seen Humi the minute she stepped out through the window. Her face went closed. Her wings snapped open behind her like upside-down, ragged fans. "What the fuck, Arity!" She dropped into the language of the gods—*auchraug*—speaking too fast for Humi to follow. Arity listened, arms folded. When Hope stopped for breath, he asked a quiet question. Silence held for a moment. Then Hope spat strings of gutteral syllables at him. Humi blinked, gazing from one god to the other, the fact that they were arguing over her growing less and less relevant.

Finally Arity turned to her and said, "It'll be all right, Humi! I'll be back soon! Trust me—" He turned to the window and ducked inside under the blind. His shadow dwindled on the bright slats.

Hope took a measured pace forward into the starlight, her mouth a thin line. Even with her golden hair loose around her face, wearing a shapeless gored dress that hid her figure, she was transcendently lovely. Humi stood feet apart, arms folded, staring at her.

"Well," Hope said at length, "Arity says you are Erene Gentle's apprentice. But I don't think I've ever seen you before."

Humi raised one hand and dragged it across her face. She teased the front locks of her hair clean.

"Ahhh. All right. I've seen you among the *imrchim*."

False confidence was the only way to bluff this out. "I would hardly have recognized you like this, either."

"Ah, yes." Hope rubbed the flawed silk of her sleeve between thumb and forefinger. "I was expecting another visitor, one who does not judge me on my wardrobe . . . I do not know what Arity thinks I am! He expects me to tell you something that we do not even mention among ourselves!"

"Don't, then."

"But I am curious now. Can the barrier between *auchresh* and *hymannim* be abolished? Arity thinks so." *I thought we already had abolished it,* Humi thought. But Hope was continuing, "Pati would say that the barrier is sacred. But surely not even he would object to finding out if it is possible." What was her relationship with Pati? Humi wondered. Before, she had sounded like an expectant lover. But it had never occurred to Humi that two gods might be sexually involved with each other. Like two mortals. Hope raised a thin golden hand to her mouth and spoke through her fingers. "Why did Arity choose *you* to hear this?"

"Why not?"

Hope shook her head. "You *hymannim!*" That meant mortals, humans. "You think so differently."

"Would one of you automatically think you were unworthy, then?" Humi frowned. "Arity never seemed—"

Hope laughed. "Arity is the most discontented of us all! But Pati and I are proud of our race." She drew herself up in her loose dress. "We are determined to make a future for ourselves, though the world has united to deny us our place."

"What about Arity, then?"

"Arity . . . poor Arity. If he had his life to do over he would choose to be mortal."

A queer, potent disappointment washed through Humi. *There, then.* She stared at the far-down river. *There's the attraction I hold for him. So there is nothing else.*

Hope was pacing to and fro along the balcony, wing edges fluttering behind her. From the clawed elbows above her head, the wings fell to her knees, like a golden carapace, and her skirt swirled under their trailing edges. "We believe in the Power that is all around us," she said. "It is greater than any of us. It carries us along like a tide. And I think it means me to speak truth tonight, even though the words burn my tongue." She looked straight at Humi. "We are predators."

"What?"

Hope nodded.

"Predators." Humi felt the world going black.

"All of us. Everyone."

Predators. All my life I have worshiped predators.

Then common sense kicked in.

"No, you're not. You can't possibly be. Predators have more sense than animals but less than humans. They just scream and hunt and kill. And you're coolheaded, sane, intelligent beings, whether you have souls or not!

You don't live on fresh meat! You can't fly! You don't . . . come from the salt . . ." Her voice trailed off.

"But we do," Hope said. "We're the reject predators. The deformed—"

"Hope, I'm—Hope?" A tall, thin figure materialized in the shadows. His eyes gleamed like metal as he glided out into the starlight. "Hope, it's a mortal! What is it doing here?" Humi cringed, but he did not turn on her. She herself seemed no more important than a stray dog. "What have you been telling it?"

Hope's beautiful face was white with horror and her hands clamped onto each other like vises. She spilled out a stream of *auchraug*.

"You haven't," Pati said. "Oh, by the *Power*, Hope!" His voice hardened. "This is some scheme of Arity's, isn't it?"

"I knew I shouldn't have let him persuade me!" Hope moaned.

"Did she believe you, Hope?" There was a gust of sulphur, and Arity balanced on the balustrade, feet wide. "Well, well. Pati." His hair blew around his face. "Throwback."

"No," Humi whispered desperately.

The gods had voices greater than any human's, and hearing like bats. Pati swung toward her. "Mortal!" His voice dripped contempt. "You can't possibly understand what it means! So lose your mind denying it! We're beasts, dangerous beasts with nothing godly about us. Just like our parents! Hideous, fanged monsters!"

"But we're *not* like our parents," Arity said. "They cast us out at birth. In the salt there is no creature who can kill a predator—so they have to control their own numbers. Each litter contains one strong, able, flighted predator, and the exotics. The flightless, weak *auchresh*. They roll us out of their lairs and drop us down the crags. Baby *auchresh* die on the salt, in the sun. But just like their flighted brothers and sisters, they can move and cry and put food in their mouths. Most die, but some crawl off the smelly mountains and survive. Eventually they find their older siblings in the Heavens."

"I don't understand," Humi said desperately. *I don't want to understand.*

Hope pushed around Pati. Her face was set. "The reason why there are so few women among us is because any species needs more females than it does males, and so fewer of us are born deformed. And we are weaker than the males, so we die in greater numbers. Ugly facts. I do not know why you want to hear them."

"Every one of us is sterile," Arity said. "We depend on the predators for our existence."

"But our brains have conquered the world," Pati said. "There's justice for you, mortal! What did you weaklings do with your ability to reproduce?

Nothing except roll around in the grass like pigs, until we came and organized you!"

Humi could not stand it any longer. Their faces, their strangeness, their shouting. *My family worships predators.* She scrambled up on the balustrade, kicking at Hope's hands, leaning on the warm pillow of the wind. Swaying dangerously.

"You are the first human to learn this since Antiprophet!" Pati shouted. "What are you going to do with it?"

Antiprophet! Her ears hurt from their unmodulated voices. Arity tried to take her in his arms. She fought him. "Don't touch me! What did you ever befriend me for? Why are you putting me through this?"

His voice hissed. "We cannot fly. Instead, we have this."

And he stepped off the balcony.

The glittering turmoil of tide and river spun upward. They were weightless. Nothing pulled them down, they weren't falling, but the water was zooming up to meet her. Black waves, silver, a roaring in Humi's ears—terror—

Nothingness.

Warmth, and comfort, and well-being.

She lurched to the surface, and found herself lying beside Erene in bed. The gray walls of the Gentle suite, with their rippled pattern, seemed to hang at a distance like sheets of cloud. Sunlight fluttered in rectangles on the floor. Insensible to conventional decorating tactics, Erene had tacked linen curtains over the skylights at the start of summer and let them fill with crisped insects. She said she liked the patterns.

Groggily, Humi rolled over. Erene breathed with trancelike slowness, her dark hair a coarse tangle over her face. Tenderly Humi parted it and dropped a kiss on the ghostier's ear. Erene did not move. *She must be exhausted,* Humi thought. *When did we get back last night?*

Then she remembered.

She thrust herself up, her heart beating so fast that black spots danced across her vision.

And a piece of parchment slipped to the floor. She leaned over the edge of the bed, scooped it up and read the flawless script in a glance. "Sundown, tonight. Your boudoir." And the little hieroglyph which meant "Charity, Heir to the Divinarchy."

The door cracked open. "Erene?" Goquisite's head came in. "Oh, Humi! I thought you spent the night at the Crescent."

"Erene's sleeping. Perhaps you could come back later."

Goquisite padded into the room. "Actually, Humi, I have been wanting to see you." She wore a petal-pink camisole that bared her shoulders and ballooning harem pants, with a gauzy robe over the whole ensemble. "Oooh, these tiles are so cold!"

"That is my favorite touch in this suite," Humi said, watching Goquisite pick her way from rug to rug. "It reminds me that my feet are on the ground." Lady Ankh's gaze dropped to Humi's chest as she came to stand beside the bed.

"May I ask why you're wearing your evening gown?"

Humi had not even realized that she was still fully clothed. *Thank you, Arity,* she thought angrily, *for making me look like an uncouth idiot in front of her!* "I—I was too tired to change. What did you want to ask me?"

"Actually, it was about Erene." Goquisite appeared to study each detail of Humi's gown with interest, but Humi sensed she was trying to put her concern into words. Finally she looked up. Humi was shocked by the worry in the small black eyes. "Humi, she is terribly unhappy. Maybe you have not noticed."

Humi closed her eyes for a second, trying to swallow a lump in her throat. "I've noticed."

"And I think I know what is wrong with her. She hasn't made a ghost in a year and a half. Because she passes yours off as hers, no one knows that she has let months and months go by without making any of her own." Goquisite wrung her hands distressedly. "I have to help her!"

Humi had never let down her guard in front of Goquisite, and she would not now. But the urge to relinquish the burden of responsibility was undeniably powerful. She had known for too long that something had to be done about Erene's dry spell. And she had done nothing. She had not even gotten around to asking anyone else's advice, as Goquisite had.

But now danger threatened. If Goquisite had made the connection between Erene's failure to ghost and her depression, who else, knowing the symptom, might suspect the cause? The linen curtains over the skylights shook as a breeze blew. The dead flies rolled and bounced. The rectangles of light on the bed jumped, and for a moment Humi had the impression that the ceiling was breaking apart like a dying flower, that the life she and Erene and Goquisite had constructed so carefully on a foundation of deceit and disguise would come sliding down on their heads.

"You surprise me, Goquisite," she said in a low voice. "I did not think you would understand."

"I understand Erene," Goquisite said. "And it's breaking my heart to see her like this. You have to do something, Humi. Help her."

I? I have to?

But in matters of ghosting, Goquisite would be worse than useless. It was to her credit that she understood that.

Humi heaved a sigh that made her ribs hurt inside her falseribs. "What do you suggest?"

"I . . ." Goquisite looked at her, puzzled. "I thought you would know what to do, once I brought the matter to your attention."

If I knew what to do, I would have done it a long time ago! "But of course I do!" Humi said. "I was just testing you. Of course I . . ." Then it came to her.

Who else knows her as well as I do?

Her old apprentice.

"I think it would be better for you not to know," she said, confident now.

Goquisite glanced down at the stone-leaf night table. "What's this?" She picked up the parchment. "Meeting a secret lover, Humi?"

"No!" Humi snatched the parchment and folded it small, tucking it into the bodice of her gown. She took the opportunity to dash two tears from her eyes. Something had to give way; something had to go. She could not be at Tellury Crescent at sundown. Not with this new concern. She could not allow a minor part of her life to usurp center stage, not when Erene was dying in the footlights. She hoped, swallowing hard, that Arity would not think she had betrayed him—or, gods forbid, that she was *frightened* of what he had revealed to her—

But if he wanted her full attention, he should have picked someone whose time hung heavy on her hands!

He just used me to test his theories about hymannin, she thought to herself. *When I started to unload my worries on him, gods know why he didn't find someone else! Well, Ari, maybe now you'll stay away from us! We* hymannim *are pale creatures compared to you, and predictable in our loyalties.*

She swung her legs out of bed. The weight of the chenille hem dropped around her ankles like a circle of chain. She bent and started to unhook the dress at the back. "I will arrange things today, Goquisite."

Goquisite smiled with unmistakable relief and obvious, childlike confidence in Humi's abilities. She turned to go. "Send Erene over to me when she wakes, will you, Humi? We have guests for breakfast."

"Certainly."

The door closed. Humi hung doubled over, unmoving. Under the coverlet, Erene slept on.

SEVENTEEN

Delta City broiled in a thick, smelly, diseased soup of heat that afternoon. Scarcely anyone was abroad in the Lockreed Concourse, though it was the main concourse of Temeriton, the district that lay behind the docks at the northernmost end of the island. Stepping from her sedan into the shade of an awning, Humi took pity on her porter. "You may go. Return for me in . . . oh, shall we say a couple of hours?"

"Yes . . . Milady Garden. Good to serve you once again, Milady Garden." He rested in the traces for a moment, head hanging, then shambled away to turn in at the first pub he passed.

The awning announced, "Delights and Diversions." All along the concourse, decrepits clotted the shade. A beggar with a gangrenous leg who dozed beside the shop door looked blearily up at her, sticking out his bowl.

Humi tossed a copper into the bowl and bent to adjust her hat in the window. The dull green-tawny hue of her fur made her wince. Every time she saw her own hands today, she panicked, thinking that she had somehow forgotten to disguise herself before coming out. She felt uncomfortably vulnerable. But she guessed that it was better not to deceive Hem in any way.

"You and I have never met, milady," said a low, rumbling voice. "But I take it that you are Humility."

An immense man with a mane of black curls stood in the doorway of Delights and Diversions, nearly filling it. His eyes were the yellow of the sunlight on the cobbled concourse.

"A fine young lady. Dressed fit to *be* a ghost rather than make them. How old are you—twenty-two, twenty-three?"

"Nineteen." Humi found her voice. "And that's old enough. If I were still in Domesdys, I'd already be a mother twice over."

"I'm sure you would," Hem said implacably. "I'm sure you would. Well, I expect you have come about Erene." She gaped. "Come in."

She followed him into the waft of cool air. The door shut with a jingle. When her eyes adjusted, she saw a small, dim room lined floor to ceiling with books, knickknacks, effigies, statuettes, dried butterflies and salt flowers, and so forth. Racks laden with more stuff stood on the floor. Mobiles and wreaths turned slowly from the ceiling. Behind a counter sat a Veretrean woman with fur the same green as old copper. A small child curled on her lap, languidly mouthing the woman's black braid. A hint of pride crept into Hem's voice as he said, "Humility, this is my wife, Pleasantry Lakestone. Leasa, this is Humility, Lady Garden. Erene's new apprentice."

"Call me Humi, please, Godsie."

Leasa smiled. "We knew Erene had taken another apprentice, of course, but none of the merchants' wives from whom I get gossip are quite sure of who's who in Antiprophet Square, so we did not know your name. Or whether you were old or young, Calvarese or Icelandic." She held up the child. "Humi, this is my daughter Sensitivity . . . Ensi."

Humi put down her hat to shake the child's chubby hand. Ensi smiled at her, a sudden, heart-stopping beam of toothlessness, and tightened her fingers. Humi couldn't remember how long it had been since she last touched a child. She'd never gotten into the habit of visiting the ghostiers' children in Marshtown as the other women did, mainly because Erene had no real relationship with her son, Tessen. But she had never before regretted that oversight.

She turned to face Hem. "Godsman Lakestone, it is hard for me to admit this—" she dimpled—"but I need help." She had to get it out. "Erene has stopped making ghosts."

Hem visibly flinched.

"I—I don't know what to do. Should I confront her? Should I ignore her pain? I can't do that. Is there any precedent?"

"Why didn't you go to Tellury Crescent?" Hem was recovering. "This is a matter for the ghostiers, not for a shopkeeper!"

"The ghostiers would use the information to persuade the Ellipse that Erene is not fit to hold the twentieth seat," Humi said simply.

"So it is that bad," Hem said at length.

The door jingled. A Deltan woman in smeared yellow facedust puffed in, with a sweating lackey waving a fan over her head. "Leasa!" she cooed. "How are you today?"

Hem pulled a quick face at Humi. "Greetings, Milady Catgut . . . Humi, shall we go within? Ensi!" He hurried them around the counter and through a door. In the narrow back room, which was furnished with a sofa and a low table, a few toys lay on the floor. Small, high windows showed the other side of a back alley. Hem delved into a cold-closet in the wall and produced a bottle of red wine and a dish of water-gateaux. Ensi climbed on the bench next to Humi, murmuring quietly to her doll. Hem poured the wine. It was chilled, delicious. Sunlight from the alley made a long, narrow grid on the wall above Humi's head.

"I know very little of palace affairs," Hem said. "Only hearsay. I knew I was leaving it all behind when I opened Delights. Our customers are avid socialites, and as atheistic as any, but since none of them have the palace entrée, they have no information to speak of. And Leasa and I are not in the habit of scrounging for gossip on the streets."

"Then this will be a long story," Humi said.

"She has knotted a real cat's cradle this time, hasn't she?" Hem said when Humi finished.

The sun had gone down. The wine bottle had grown sweaty.

"What advice have you for me?" she said.

He pursed his lips. "Believe me when I say that for five years, I loved Erene just as much as you seem to. She was my sun and moon. I think it is in no way a disadvantage to be able to give one's heart completely, as you and I can—rather, if we give it into safe hands, we can become the happiest men and women alive." A smile tweaked his lips as he looked down at his little girl, who had gone to sleep with her head in Humi's lap. "But if I learned one important thing from my life with the ghostiers, it was this: Nobody can live more than one life. You cannot manage anyone's affairs other than your own—mine, the affairs of Hemlock Lakestone; yours, those of Humility Garden. That is the danger of disguising oneself. One risks taking on more responsibility than any of us can handle—which is surprisingly little if one wants to live a good life."

"Nonsense!" Humi sat forward, momentarily forgetting about Ensi. "That is patently untrue. What are the greatest leaders of men but those who take responsibility for thousands of lives?"

"Those are the men and women who die young. Just think: ghosts, in their beauty, exemplify the aesthetic excellence of our whole race. And they must die for it. Already, by making ghosts for Erene, you are living for her. Stop now, here! Let her correct her own negligence, or die her own death!" His wineglass squealed as he turned it in his powerful hands.

"How can you say that?" Humi asked. "You know I love her the way you loved her. I cannot possibly untangle my life from hers." Humi looked down at the little girl in her lap. She fingered the soft green down around

Ensi's ear. Ensi's pink lips were mushed against Humi's skirt, and she breathed in little snorts.

And the Balance swung. Humi took a deep breath. "Shall I take her up to bed for you?"

Hem looked annoyed at the change of subject. Humi wormed her arms under the rumple-furred child, picked her up, and carried her out. On the staircase, she met a boy of ten or so, stinking of sweat and dust from walking in the heat. He didn't ask who she was, just stared at her. Depositing Ensi in the bedroom, Humi smoothed her hair and dropped a kiss on her forehead. The room was cool, being crushed against the second story of another house and therefore windowless. Looking down at the child, Humi thought, *Erene just needs a little push in the right direction. Something slightly different. Something that will get her applause from the people whose approval she cherishes.*

Her instincts screamed out against such a thing, but her loyalty overruled it.

Ensi would be perfect.

Coming downstairs, she stood in the doorway of the back room and said, "Sell her to me."

Hem froze. The boy was kneeling beside him. He grinned in delight. "Father! She gonna take Ens away?"

"Shut up, Meri," Hem said coldly. "Humi—I will overlook that thing you just said."

"I knew I had to come here," Humi said. "And now I know why. I never thought of you before, but this morning it was clear in my mind. How much do you want?" Twin impulses made her smile meanly at him: the desire to coerce him into selling Ensi, and her inner disgust at what she was doing. "You cannot possibly be making enough from the shop to be living comfortably. How much? I am generous."

Hem surged to his feet and seized her shoulders, pushing her back against the doorjamb. In the twilight he seemed even bigger than he was, his eyes like yellow suns. "Do not endanger your soul like this! Gods, Humi, *leave* the ghostiers if this is what they are doing to you! I do not even know you, but I know that you have a *soul! Stop it!*"

"You couldn't *take* Tellury Crescent!" Humi twisted away and fled up the first few stairs, whirling to scold him. "The ghostiers were too much for you! You couldn't bear the intimacy! You never understood the bond that makes us die for each other!"

"Mother! Moth—Hoo—hoomi—" Ensi sat down hard on the step behind Humi, banging her head on the banister. One little hand went up to the bump, and the corners of her mouth fell, and she began to cry loudly.

Humi twisted around. The baby stretched out her arms and let herself fall against Humi's skirts. Humi scooped her up, pressing kisses over the button nose and wet green cheeks. "There. It's all right. Let me feel—"

She stopped.

Hem stared up at her from the bottom of the stairs. "So," he said measuredly. "So. A true killer."

Ensi kept on blubbering. Belatedly, Humi said, "It's just a little hurt!"

As Leasa bustled through from the shop, her face creased with worry, Humi delivered the girl into her arms. "She's all right, Leasa! I'm sorry, but I think I must say good-bye—I have—I have to get back—"

Hem escorted her to the door in silence. Outside, the twilight was sullen, the sky red-fleeced, black roofs looming against the sunset like predators in silhouette. The owners of brothels and taverns stepped out of doors to poke flaming brands up into their door lanterns. Gaudy signs leered brightly in the lantern light as the street lit up for the second time that day. More beggars than ever appeared to take advantage of the strollers who frequented Temeriton for its nighttime offerings.

Hem stood in the doorway, arms folded. "This is not a good place to raise children. But what can we do? Leasa and I are not rich. There is, as you so correctly observed, a limit to the amount of money one can make from selling knickknacks."

Humi's porter pulled her sedan up to the door. She lifted the curtain aside, gathered her skirt in one hand, and turned back. "Hem—I'm sorry."

"You realized what you were doing in time. They have not completely sophisticated you yet." Hem shook his head. "I can hardly believe that I once lived where such obscene displays are commonplace."

Humi looked at him with curiosity. "Do you still believe in ghosting, then?"

"What do you mean? I am a believer in the gods. And in destiny."

She smiled. "I wish I'd got to know you better. We spent all afternoon talking about Erene."

"That was as much my fault as yours. I suppose it has been too long since I spoke of her to anyone. It accumulates, like a need. She used to come and visit, bringing perfume and laughter and presents for Ensi and Meri . . . I can still tell you the flavor of her scent. Bitter cocoa and honeysuckle." He laughed shortly.

"Yes. She loves that scent, though I don't particularly like it." Humi glanced up at the dark windows. The odor of rotting flesh from the beggar at the doorway drifted past her nostrils. Shuddering, she stepped into the sedan. "Good-bye, Hem. Thank you."

Ensi toddled out and wrapped one arm around her father's leg, waving good-bye as the porter started at a run down the street.

Once they had turned the corner and Humi's feeling of warmth and virtue died down, she bit her knuckles and thought: *What am I going to do? I can't go back empty-handed! What am I going to do?*

As the sedan rattled through Shimorning, the porter cursed and swerved. Humi poked her head out of the curtains and saw a crowd of beggar children. One, a girl of about twelve, carried a toddler on her back that seemed untouched by the dirt on its sister and its sling. Its leaf-green fur glistened with health. It laughed gurglingly at Humi.

She stopped the sedan and got out. "How much will you take for it?" she said, pointing.

It crawled all over the sedan as they rode back to Antiprophet Square. Humi was glad that it was an annoying baby, not particularly endearing. It also helped that she had refused to let its sister tell her its name, age, or sex. She carried it inside under her cloak and left it chewing on the canopy of Erene's bed, with an artfully scrawled note pinned to its garment that said, "This baby's parents died. Take it, milady. It's yours."

When she returned from dinner at the Summers', now disguised as Lady Bonnevine, a Deltan native, Goquisite met her in the hall and enfolded her in an embrace. Her voice was squeaky with emotion as she said, "Erene has gone to Tellury Crescent. She left word that she will not be back for at least two sixdays."

Humi disengaged herself and blinked, hard. Goquisite beamed. Tears stood in her eyes. "Thank you."

"I'll go tonight. To help her with the ghost." Her mind raced. While Erene ghosted, in the total seclusion that was traditional, how would Humi manage? She would have to assist Erene by night and employ a persona whom Erene would believably trust with her business during the day. Lady Falippe Greenbranch might do. Falippe was an heiress and a third-generation noble from Veretry who dwelt in lodgings in the city that (Humi had heard the ladies conjecture) she kept secret because they weren't as opulent as she would have liked.

Yes, Erene would trust her. It was just a pity she wasn't a more pleasant person. Humi had already had to play her often enough to keep her credible; it was going to be an ordeal to act her for several straight sixdays.

And Arity, she thought. *There isn't a chance that I'll get to explain. But what is there to explain?*

She crossed her arms over her chest. She felt painfully empty.

EIGHTEEN

"So she came back after all," Ziniquel said, looking sidewise at Elicit.

Elicit did not answer. He scraped hard, angrily, at the little ghost of a rat that he was whittling down to nothing. Apprentice ghostiers often made tiny animals for practice; this was one of Algia's that had turned out ridiculously posed. No use for it. He shoved the blade hard with his thumb and made the diamondine squeal.

"You didn't expect her to, did you?"

Elicit turned on the younger man. "Shut up. You don't know what you're talking about."

Ziniquel fell silent. Below their swinging feet, a side channel of the Chrume washed around the stilts of the jetty, creating a brown-and-black-marbled pattern that one part of Elicit's mind noted and stored away for future use. Somewhere amid the waving grasses of the marsh islands were hidden the boats that had set off from Marshtown at dawn. Though the heat of the day had diminished, they had not come back yet; the jetties that jutted out side by side by side all along the marshfront were not crowded. Old men talked, smoked, nodded over their fishing lines. A few women mended nets and clothes. Children dashed around, ostensibly in the care of their grandfathers, their shrill voices rising into the summer sky like smoke.

"I keep thinking of Tessen," Elicit said abruptly. "How could she do such a thing when she has a child herself?"

"It's not exactly an innovation," Ziniquel said. "Maybe for a ghostier who is a mother. But certainly child ghosts are nothing new."

"It ought to be different for a woman," Elicit said helplessly. His gorge rose every time he thought of Tessen—active, alive Tessen, fostered with Soulf Freebird, whose lover he had been for a time when Erene first started to draw away from him. He would have acted as a father to Tessen had Erene not expressly requested that he stay away from the boy. She wanted him to have an ordinary life. You had to give her credit for that. And atheist though she was, she had given him a proper name.

"Emni said that if the child was a born ghost, she would do it." Ziniquel shrugged, leaning back on his hands, his fine-furred throat bared to the sun. Again, the ghostier part of Elicit noted his pose—easy, unconcerned—and stored it away for future use. Zin was far from carefree, of course—none of the *imrchim* had that luxury—but his lithe body managed to give the impression of ease. Conversely, Elicit had heard himself described (by Mory, but it could have been any objective observer) as a knotted bundle of gray ropes.

It had seemed funny at the time. But somehow he had not been able to shake that image of himself as a stooped, careworn old man. Age *did* sit heavy on his shoulders. The conundrum of Algia and Eterneli weighed on his mind. Neither of them was a fit successor to him, not artistically or politically. And he knew it was his own fault. He had made Algia the pale creature she was and had stunted vivid Eterneli's independence until now she took his every word as scripture and dared not go out alone without an older ghostier.

Elicit winced every time he mentally compared her with Mory's dark, passionate Tris or the Southwind twins.

And he knew why he had done it. Subconsciously, he had been afraid of dying. Afraid of being superseded.

Afraid of aging out of his talent and his virility alike. The two things were a good deal the same, after all.

Most of the time he lived each day as it unfurled before him, rejoicing, as Rita did, in the physical things of life. If you looked at it right, each moment was diamondine.

But sometimes (like today), he could not help resenting the young, radiant ghostiers like Ziniquel.

The young, radiant ghostier sneezed. He opened his eyes and darted a sideways look at Elicit. "You still love her."

"What bullshit," Elicit said solidly. "She betrayed me."

"You love her." Ziniquel's hand slid out over the sunwarped boards of the jetty, stopped a moment, then curled around Elicit's thigh. Bony fingers that had touched him far more intimately than this kneaded the great muscle on the inside of Elicit's thigh until Elicit closed his hand over Ziniquel's, stopping him.

"You can't lie to me, Godsman Paean," Ziniquel said. "You know you never stopped loving her."

Tidal waters surged choppily around the foot of the jetty. Elicit stared down at the brown-and-black foam. He always thought that the grief had

died. But then he saw Erene with this baby ghost and he felt a desperate
need to protect her from the damage she was doing to herself. The need
was corrosive, unending. Sometimes at night he could not bear it, and he
crept in the dark to Algia, hating himself every moment.

Humi sat cross-legged on her bed, drinking hot wine. It was nearly
midnight. The workshop was silent. Erene had dragged out the process of
ghosting intolerably, taking frequent breaks to sit and do nothing or to
sleep. It was as if she had slumped down on a soft patch of grass by the
wayside and could not bring herself to get up again. And at the beginning
she had tortured that baby as no warm-blooded creature should be tortured, simply for the sake of prolonging it.

Humi was racked by a sense of guilt. But had she the child to buy over
again, or Erene to let drown in inadequacy, she knew she would make the
same choice.

Putting down the mug, she padded through the apartment. The workshop door screeched as she opened it—but the heap of silk skirts and fur
that was Erene didn't stir. Beside the armchair sat the baby ghost, blocked
in with the subtle washes Erene liked. These light colors had stood untouched for months, while the front of the cupboard became a jumble of
Humi's richer pigments. The baby's arms circled above its head, and it rose
on its bottom a little, grinning. Too close! How could Erene have let herself
fall asleep within the aura of its cold? Already her fur was tipped with frost.
How could she have forgotten?

Steeling herself against the chill, Humi closed her arms round the ghost,
lifted it and carried it to a safe distance. So light. *You betrayed me*, it cried
wordlessly. *You nipped my life out. You, Humi, you!*

*Ugh. I hope Erene will provide some good strong emotion to block that
out.*

The torches were sputtering. Rubbing her bare arms, Humi circled the
workshop, replacing them. She gathered up the remnants of the meal she'd
brought Erene earlier in the evening. By the gods, it felt strange to play the
servant again! Strange, but good. She dropped a kiss on the stubbornly
creased gray brow. The senior ghostier shuddered but did not wake. Humi
stood for a moment, biting her lip, then slid into the chair next to Erene.
She cuddled up with her, laying her cheek on Erene's breast, melting the
frost with her own body heat.

NINETEEN

Black shrouds draped every door lintel in Samaal. Everyone wore black somewhere, often in bands tying up their black hair. The sight comforted Thani. Playing truant while Transcendence slept, drifting along crushed in the crowd, she felt for a moment that she was again the girl she'd been before she prophesied. It was three years; she was sixteen now, and it did not seem likely she would ever prophesy again, the interval had been so long. But that single, garbled flood of words, three years ago, had altered both her and Transcendence's lives. It had inspired in both of them a deep-seated dissatisfaction.

Through her, Transcendence had glimpsed the salty glimmer of Heaven. In her darkest moments, she wondered if he *wanted* her to prophesy again, whether he would give anything to focus the dimly seen door into greatness.

Sometimes she even wanted it herself, so that he'd be happy with her.

Her eighteenth birthday was not so far off now. And she did not know what would happen to her after Transcendence cast her off. Growing up was doing strange things to her. But now their grand circuit had brought them to Samaal. Maybe she would find an answer here.

She leaned on the seawall, looking out over the docks. Almost all the ships had metal hulls and masts. The sun flashed blindingly on them. Piles of rope lay coiled at the base of the seawall. The sea that spread to the horizon was an upside-down night sky, silver constellations swimming as the sun turned on tiny waves. This street, lined behind her with bars and shady, shuttered establishments, was the bottommost of dozens of tiers that lined a natural harbor in the barren coast. Calvary encouraged its people to use stone and metal in building: standing at the top of the whole tin-roofed cascade of Samaal, just as the sun breasted the eastern rim, was enough to blind you for a day.

Thani heaved a shuddering sigh and rested her chin on her hand. She breathed deeply of the racy reek of the crowd: bodies cleansed only by the chafe of the sand in their clothing. "Pardon me, Godsie," a pleasant voice said next to her. "You're not Calvarese? You wouldn't be Domesdian, would you?"

Thani turned. A young, tawny-furred sailor, hair hacked off short, had spoken.

"I can't tell you how good it is to see a pale face so far from home!" he said. "The sun's got to your fur and hair—or are you Icelandic?"

"No," she said, "I'm from Westshine province."

"Gods! I don't believe it! I'm from Ruche!" Ruche was the next province to Westshine. His delight was infectious. Cautiously, Thani smiled. "Will you sit down and have a glass?" he asked. "It'd be so good to talk of home—"

He doesn't know I'm a leman, Thani thought. *But then, how should he? There are dozens of other reasons for a foreigner to be in the capital.*

She thought of Transcendence, napping in their lodgings on the seventh tier.

She smiled and let the crowd push her closer against the young man.

He took her to a stone-flagged, relatively quiet bar, where sailors from all over the Divinarchy and immodestly dressed Calvarese women sat on stools at small, high tables. A bargirl put shots of sand liquor in front of them. The sailor showed Thani how to empty the glass at one gulp. He laughed when she made a face. "Not used to drinking? How old are you?"

She could have told him then. But she did not. "Oh," she said, "twenty . . . one . . . My father is a merchant. We moved to Samaal three years ago." She felt her face going muddy. She was terrible at lying.

But he did not pursue the subject. He was too eager to talk about his home and family. He was the youngest of thirteen cousins in a saltside hamlet, and there had really been no option but for him to go to sea. But he missed the saltside. Sometimes on deck, he said, he would look up from mending the ropes and think the sea was the salt, glittering. The *yeep* of flying fish sounded like sheep. The afternoon wore away as he rambled on, his voice throbbing with longing and increasing drunkenness. Thani might have been bored, but she was not. A strange, muted excitement pulsed through her: she knew she, too, was drunk, and she did not care. When, downing his sixth shot, the sailor draped a perfunctory arm over her shoulders, she snuggled against him. "Careful," he winced. "I've two cracked ribs, and they're not healin'—"

"Why don't you go see a flamen?"

He shrugged. "They've more 'portant things to take care of than a fellow

who can 'eal on 'is own. Don' hurt bad 'nuff, anyhow, for me to go botherin'
. . . I've . . . other things t' do . . ." He kissed her face sloppily. A pang
of excitement went through her. "You're a swee' girl," he said.

But her training would not let her leave it there. She insisted stupidly,
"You should go to a flamen! My flamen, Godsbrother Transcendence, would
work a miracle for you—"

"Hold u . . ." He pulled away. Careful not to slur his words, he said,
"*Your* flamen?"

"Yes! He'd be happy—"

"You're—you're a leman." He stood up, heedless of the table, which
crashed to the floor, smashing the dozen or so glasses they had emptied
between them. "You're a leman . . . And you were . . . Gods!" He blun-
dered backward, his pleasant face a mask of revulsion. The customers
stared. "I was . . . Get *out* of here!"

Thani did not need to be told twice. Her hands locked over her mouth,
she turned and ran out into the last of the afternoon. Her drunkenness
made her feel as if she were wading through the air like water. Tears
blinded her as she ran up metal-roofed stairway after stairway, until the last
vestiges of crowds vanished and she doubled over, panting, alone in a
sunbathed, silent street. Over the roofs, the golden orb of the sun was about
to immerse itself in the welter of red dust on the western rim. Fine sand
drifted lazily in the air. Dogs lay flat on doorsteps, their jowls flapping with
their breath.

Thani pulled her jacket about herself. Tears streamed down her cheeks.
How could she have gone along with him? Why had she thought she
wanted it? Why had she thought she could get away with it, in a pious city
like Samaal?

She knew of only one cure for misery like this. One she had always
known.

She pushed through the lacy metal door. "Transcendence, it's me," she
blurted. "I'm sorry I was out so long. I'll never do it again. Never. I'm so
sorry . . ." He did not stir. He sat asleep in the only chair, snoring a little,
his head pillowed on the stone table, on which stood a half full crate of
cactusfruit. They had been grateful when the owner of this house had given
them free lodgings, and Transcendence made sure that Thani did not temper her gratitude with even one whit of reproach when they learned that
the lodgings were made up of a single room and no bed. Thani dropped to
her knees on the floor, burying her head in his robed lap. He stirred and,
half asleep, stroked her head.

Gradually the room stopped spinning. She could see under the table,
through the pierce-holes in the door to the street. Cobbles and metal doors.

All so rigid. She wanted the mutable forms of sand dunes. She wanted freedom. She knew she would never be able to tell Transcendence about her transgression, now that the first flush of self-disgust was gone. Perhaps in the future, when she acted extra pious to make up for it, he would praise her for her renewed fervor. And she would writhe. "Oh, gods," she whispered, "take me back to the desert." The young sailor's kiss burned like a swelling on her cheek. "Take me back where I am safe."

TWENTY

Half-sensible, Humi rose on Dividay, threw the curtains wide, and stumbled through her toilette. She was late for brunch at the Summer mansion, but she could not summon a servant to assist her. No one must know that Falippe Greenbranch and Humility were the same person. Blinking, she powdered her face gold, re-dyed her hair deep red, and curled it.

Her mind was truly numb with tiredness. But she did not realize just how numb it was until she was at the Summers', lounging on a sofa, nibbling on quail eggs and seed-toast, and she remembered: *Dividay services.*

"And the conspiracy has a new ally, my dear Lady Greenbranch," Belstem said portentously. "Not being from the city, I don't expect you will have heard. He is a recent acquaintance of mine and Lady Gentle's. Hrrmp!" It was almost midday, and she did not have time to change back to herself if she wanted to catch any of the services at all. Her dress was light violet taffeta, ruffle-skirted in the new style: Marshtowners would think she was an atheist lady come to poke fun; but there was no help for it. She cut Belstem off in midsentence, excused herself, and slipped out of the mansion by a side door. She fled across the square and flagged down one of the porters who lounged around the Ankh mansion's gates, waiting to work.

"Where to, milady?" he asked.

"Circle through Marshtown until you find Godsbrother Joyfulness' congregation." Damn! she could almost hear him raising his eyebrows. As they entered Marshtown, the familiar scents of rotting grass, fish, pig dung, and incense seeped into the sedan. Humi breathed deeply as the wheels bumped over the cobbles. She knew this district so well that her mind supplied a street name every time the sedan swung around a corner. She had come to services here every single sixday since she had arrived in Tellury Crescent. The ghostiers always came to Marshtown; wandering flamens preached in the streets throughout the city, causing blockages in a traffic that did not stop for the day of worship, but the flamen councillors in Marshtown drew the largest congregations, and for the ghostiers, demonstrating their loyalty to the councillors was as strategically important as their piety itself.

"We must stand together!" she heard from outside the sedan. "Above all, we devotees must stand together. Those with a little to spare must aid those who have nothing."

The sedan slowed to a stop. The porter let the poles bump softly to the cobbles.

"There has been discontent in the countryside, and all of you have seen the restlessness in the slums of our own city. Crying at the gates of the nobility does no one any good, because the food has all been shipped off for profit. So we flamens must feed the poor, the weak, and the young. We are draining the gods' resources. We cannot save the world all on our own! It is up to you. You must prove that devotees still have more compassion than blasphemers. You must keep the old ways . . ."

The porter poked his face through the curtains. "This 's as close as I can get, milady—"

"Wait for me here," Humi whispered, and got out. Gathering her pink skirt in one arm, she picked her way between the seated Marshtowners. Godsbrother Joyfulness stood on a podium made of fish crates, declaiming with grand gestures. He was telling the parable of Bravery Godgifted's argument with the Third Divinarch: he acted different parts magnificently, and the salt crystals seemed to leap about in his eye sockets, glinting in the sun. He was a big Royallandic man in his thirties, handsome, with fur dappled like sunlight on the leaves of a beech tree.

Humi sank to her knees by the corner of a ramshackle townhouse. Beside the podium, Joyfulness' leman Flexibility gazed up worshipfully at him. Lexi was a nineteen-year-old Archipelagan, thin and intense. He was Joyfulness' first leman, and in their case everything scurrilously implied about the flamen-leman relationship was true. The sight of him made Humi uneasy. She could not forget the prophecy that the Divinarch had divulged to her three years ago. *You shall receive the highest honor the world can bestow upon you. Yet you shall live a life of deception. Your heart shall be heavy as a rock veined with iron. And the truth is ineffable. The truth is ineffable—*

It had cast a shadow over her future that dimmed, but never went away—a shadow as long as the shadow of a predator standing with folded wings at sunset, with edges as bright as broken glass. It kept receding from her days.

"And so—in the end—we will all become one people again!" Joyfulness smacked his fists together. There was an incredible power in his voice, as if he were drawing on Lexi's adoration, the adoration of all the crowd. He sounded almost godlike as he boomed, "Devotees—blasphemers—all one under the sun, praising the gods, living in peace!" And a murmuring broke out, surging along below the eaves where the sun lay in needles on the thatch. The crowd pressed around Joyfulness in a tradition as old as the flamenhood, each man, woman, and child pushing to touch him once for luck and health. Humi stayed kneeling on the dusty cobbles, her head leaning against a drainpipe made of bundles of dry reeds. She felt as light as if her blood had turned to bubbles. This was the first service she had attended since Arity revealed the true nature of the *auchresh* to her. That night she had, willy-nilly, become an atheist. She had feared that with her childhood illusions about the gods shattered, the flamens' teachings would no longer have the power to move her; but Joyfulness' sermon had pierced her, both stilling her and raising her soul to a silent, clear peak from which she could see for leagues.

At last she rose and crossed the street. In her soft-soled court slippers, she felt as if she were floating. The crowd around Joyfulness had thinned enough that the ghostiers saw her immediately. They always recognized her, no matter what she wore, and they gathered around her, enfolding her in quick, sincere hugs. She envied them their freedom to wear sleeveless summer garments. Nothing marked them out from the run of Marshtowners except the disturbing depths in their eyes, those little shadowy death's heads for which she always looked in the mirror when she was Humility Garden again. Lexi's voice rippled in the background, smooth and ceaseless, as they embraced her: Ziniquel, Rita, Mory, Beisa, Sol, Emni. "I *am* going to come visit you in the square," Emni said. She giggled. "Beisa says just for one day it won't corrupt me. Won't that be marvelous!"

"Wonderful!" Humi said honestly. "I'll show you all around—"

Algia, Eterneli, Trizisim, Owen. "What is that you're *wearing*, Humi?" Owen asked. "Who are you supposed to *be?*" She did not answer. Elicit. As always, his hug seemed a little restrained. "Are you coming back with us for lunch?" he asked distractedly.

"I can't." Ruefully she straightened her hair ribbon. "I have to leave before I am recognized. I shouldn't be here dressed like this. I must just pay my respects to the Godsbrother, then I—"

The cracking, sighing hiss of Lexi's voice came right in her ear. "I see . . ."

Humi twisted. Lexi's features were rigid, eyes peeled so wide the whites were visible, and his hands opened and closed jerkily by his sides.

"Flexibility?" the Godsbrother said. Clumsily, he floundered toward Lexi, pawing the air. "Are you all right?"

A tiny popping noise came from Lexi's lips. His head cracked back, and as he went suddenly limp Humi caught him. "Godsbrother!" Hot and cold sweats washed over her body. "We're over here!"

Joyfulness plunged toward the sound of her voice. He swept Lexi into his arms. "Flexibility! I fear for him, Godsies and Godsmen. This is the seventh time—"

Seventh? Humi thought incredulously, at the same time as a nearby Marshtown woman burst out, "Seven prophetic fits? Godsbrother, how— how is it that he's still alive?"

Unnatural tremors ran through Lexi's body. Joyfulness' head came up, gazing blindly, proudly, around the crowd. "I must ask you all to leave. Now. Some prophecies are too dangerous to be heard by the laity—"

Lexi's mouth snapped open. He began, jerkily and in jarring accents, to speak. "*I see . . .*" Rising in Joyfulness' arms, he looked straight into Humi's eyes. She felt her face muddying as all the eyes turned to her. "*She shall not die for many long years. And before she does, she shall receive the highest honor the world can bestow upon mortal or god. Yet she will count it a curse. For she will meet her end alone, forsaken by family, friends, gods, and mortals, in agony.* You will perish in agony!" he shouted at her. "You will perish by your own hand!"

And he went limp. A faint grating sound came from his chest. "*I . . . sss . . .*" White spittle bubbled up between his lips.

"Lexi! Lexi!" Joyfulness roared. He shook the boy frantically. "Gods—"

"He's dead, Godsbrother," Rita said, reaching to hold him back. "He's dead!" The big man went rigid, then sagged, sobbing, his face pressed to Lexi's thin chest.

"Oh, gods." Humi hugged herself. "Oh, shed the gods' blood." She felt the eyes of Marshtowners and ghostiers on her. Her face was dark under Falippe's yellow facedust. Ziniquel came toward her, hands outstretched, and she retreated, stumbling over the gutter in the center of the street. He had to see—she mustn't be recognized as herself: Red curls bobbed about her cheeks, she had yellow-green fur the color of autumn apples, and her features were pinched but full of sex appeal. As far as the courtiers and socialites and flamens would ever know, Lexi had directed his prophecy at Falippe Greenbranch.

"Humi—" Zin said, quite loudly.

Shut up! She whirled away from him. Desperate, she snapped her fingers at the porter. "I'm ready to leave!" He had to *see*—"I think I have heard enough to tell a fine anecdote this evening at Lady Crane's!"

"Slummers!" a local man with beetling brows said loudly as she passed. She climbed into the sedan and, sinking back against the hard teak seat, discovered that she was shaking. The curtains kept the sun out, but when she wiped her forehead, her fingers came away covered with a slime of facedust and sweat. She grabbed a handful of her skirt and scrubbed her cheeks, her neck, her bosom, frenziedly cleaning off Falippe, cleaning off everything that could link her to this street corner in Marshtown, to this prophecy. Nothing to do with her, Humi! She did not believe in destiny. If she could shift it off onto an imaginary character this easily—*this* easily— where was its power? Nowhere! That was where!

"Where to, milady?" the porter called back respectfully.

The Eftpool? No. Beau is obsessed with destiny. I don't need to hear any more obscure pronouncements today. Have to get away. Where?

Hobnailed footsteps tramped past. The cremators' men, coming for Lexi. It could not have been more than ten minutes since he died, but Humi wasn't surprised. On occasions like this, when a flamen or leman's dignity was at stake, the flamens' all-pervading influence over Marshtown showed like the scheme of a salt-ant colony seen through glass salt.

Humi finished cleaning her face, ripped her dress down the front, and kicked it into the bottom of the sedan. The bodice held her shape, like the discarded husk of a cricket. Air circulated coolly under her slip. "To the Old Palace!" *I'm not going to see Arity. I'm going to see if everything he and Hope and Pati told me is true. I'm not going to see Arity.* "The Quelide entrance. Where no one will see me go in."

The door banged against the wall. Reflex brought Hope's head up. No one ever used doors in the Divine Guards' quarters: like the ghostiers, they let no outsiders enter their domain—a labyrinth of traps and tunnels and cavernous lairs that took up the top five floors of the Old Palace—and besides, *auchresh* who could *teth*" had small need of doors. Most of the corridors were full of junk, and so dirty that one could see one's footprints on the floor.

Besides, it was midday. Everyone should be here, if not sleeping, then making the most of these daylight hours when the humans thought they were sleeping.

"It's just Arity making a theatrical entrance, as usual," Pati muttered, pulling Hope back down. "He can't get over how important he is now that he's filling in for the Divinarch. Goes out during the day. Sleeps like a human—*wrchrethri!* Keep on."

Hope caressed him for a moment, then she raised herself on one elbow.

"Wait, Pati. It's a mortal. Oh, by the Power. Her hair's full of cobwebs. She must have found her way up the stairs."

Pati peered through the murk. "Can't be—but it is! Silver Rat, Sepia, Val, everyone, look at that!" In one leap he was off the bed. "How dare it!"

The girl stood in the doorway, small and fragile in a violet slip. Hope's heart sank as she recognized Humility Garden, the ghostier's apprentice. She had done her best to forget that night on her balcony when Pati and Arity had, as usual, lost control of themselves and turned a civilized exchange into a disastrous contest as to who could act most undecorously in the fight to cut the other one down. The difference was that they did not usually go all out at each other in front of a mortal. When Arity appeared alone, morose and snappish, the night after the debacle, Hope had thought the thing was finished. But apparently, it had made a deep impression on the Garden girl. Now she thought, *We've unblocked a hole of saltworms. How long are the vermin going to keep crawling out?*

Fury radiated off Pati like sparks. He *teth¨d* across the floor, leaving a sulphuric vacuum at Hope's side. "Milady *Garden*."

The girl's hands flew to her ears at his voice, though it did not sound especially loud to Hope.

"How pleasant to see you. Might it be too much to ask you to explain this honor?"

The *auchresh* in the sunken pool, the *auchresh* arguing philosophy over in the lamplight, the *auchresh* couples in the darkest corners, all stopped what they were doing. Slowly, on the far side of the room where he had been playing Conversion with Evel and River Grass, Arity stood up. "Have a care, Pati."

"How much of a fool can you be, Arity?" Pati gazed at Humi. "How much will it take to convince you that this was idiocy?"

"I didn't bring her here!" Arity reappeared right behind Humi.

"Damn it, Arity," Hope whispered. "For the Power's sake, don't touch her!" If Arity felt anything for the girl, he would be a lunatic to let Pati know it. She rolled around Silver Rat and stood up, her wings snapping open.

Luckily, Arity had seen that, too. He stood stiffly behind Humi, arms at his sides. Humi glanced back at him and moved a step or two away. "I don't know what she's doing here," Arity said.

"However she got here, take her out *now*." This time Pati moderated his voice, but Hope could see anger crackling around him. He was the only *auchresh* she knew who could combine wrath and nudity without losing his dignity. "You were the inspiration for her coming here, if nothing else. Mortals are no use, not to play with or question or nibble on. She's Lady

Gentle's nurse-chick, and it doesn't say much for you that that's all you can attract. I should have set my sights on Goquisite Ankh, at least, if I were you."

Arity did not move. "She's nothing to do with me."

"You befriended her."

"She's not my responsibility."

The girl shuffled a little farther away from him. Hope sat down on the edge of the bed platform and let her head fall against Silver Rat's thigh. He stroked her hair without taking his eyes off Humi. The girl looked small and lost, like a rat cowering between two peacocks. But her black eyes were holes in her furry face. Hope could tell she was drinking up every detail of the Divine Guards' private quarters—from the marble floor, scarred as a fisherman's arms, to the ceiling black with incense smoke, and all the *auchresh*-crafted furniture which no human had ever laid eyes on, not since the Old Palace was built.

"I don't need your protection, Arity," the girl said in decent *auchraug*. Every *auchresh* in the room, including Pati and Arity, gaped. "Striver, I did not come as a ghostier's apprentice. Nor as an atheist, nor as a devotee. I came by myself." Implied was, *And I can look after myself.*

"Oh, ho, a fighting chick," Pati jeered. Then his voice went dry and he dropped into the dissonance of harshness and melody that was *auchraug,* speaking fast so that the girl would not understand. "She's seen too much. And she speaks our tongue. Get her out. Now."

"I had no idea that she knew *auchraug.* And I am *not* responsible for her."

"Where could she have learned it but from you? You wouldn't have done that for anyone but a *ghauthiju.* She must be your *ghauthiju.* What I want to know, Ari, is how you found time to have a human *ghauthiju* between your *teth¨s* back to Wind Gully Heaven and your bouts of smoking and fucking and arguing with us. We are your *elpechim.* You'd do well to remember that. You are part of *lesh kervayim*—" the cabal—"and you owe loyalty to no one but us."

He meant, *To me.* Hope's heart sank. The tension between Arity and Pati arose from their having spent their Foundlinghoods in the same Heaven, Wind Gully Heaven in the salt of Royalland. As a rule, the Heir had the highest status among the Incarnations, but when Arity arrived fifteen years ago, Pati had already gotten used to lording it over docile old Autumn Rain. Not much had changed since then, except that Arity chafed worse against Pati's control.

Now his voice was steely as a blade. "I owe nothing to you or any of your

pigheaded reactionaries. I am Heir, law unto myself, and if I choose to have
a visitor then I shall have one."

"My dear Charity, you may have her. You may do whatever you like with
her. But she certainly cannot leave."

"Pati!" Hope heard the cry of pain and knew that Arity had backed down.
Once again, the king was victorious. "Can you never let down your guard?
Never? I saw you just now. You were intertwined with Hope and Silver and
Val. They were making love to you. You lay there like a great drone while
they worked on your mouth and your nipples and your penis. Yet all the
time you had one eye open. I remember you before you went off to Delta
City. I was a Foundling, learning to talk, and you were the first *mainraui* of
Wind Gully Heaven. I thought your wings were the proof of your maleness,
not the signs of a throwback. You taught me how to read and write, how to
dance and shoot, how to make love. In those days *you* would make love to
me. Remember that? You would tell me just to lie there in the starlight
falling on the brocade coverlet in your room, and you—" His voice broke.

Through a blur, Hope thought, *Thank the Power the human couldn't
understand* that. *She's heard enough secrets already.* Hope had grown up in
Divaring Below, in Fewarauw—Pirady. She had not met Pati until she
came to Delta City. But then he had been only five years on the job, and
still unjaded. Still the noble, compassionate *mainraui* Arity described. That
was when she had fallen so deeply in love with him.

Bitter tears stung the inside of her nose. She could hear tears in Arity's
voice, too, as he demanded, "Don't you remember? Can't you just ease up
now and then?"

"With every word you speak," and Pati's eyes glittered, "you lay another
seal on the girl's death."

"They're going to tear each other apart again." Glass Mountain's voice
came soft by Hope's ear. He was the oldest of *lesh kervayim,* Divine Guard
but not Incarnation. He wouldn't interfere. She knew whose job it was to
interfere—and she dreaded it like stepping into a blizzard.

She stood up, fanning her wings. Sheets of veined, leathery gold with
claws at each elbow, they weren't just vestiges like Pati's, but genuine
wings that could do everything except fly. The inability to fly was the lowest
common denominator of the *auchresh* race. And if the cut-off mark had
been just a little bit higher—some deviance in the size of the wings, some
human roundness in the face, some mutation like Arity's body talons or
Val's extra fingers—then Hope would not have been *auchresh*. She would
have been kicked out of any Heaven that Found her, expelled as a predator
baby. Ever since she was Found she had been painfully aware of this. And
since she was such a bad representative of *auchresh iuim,* she would never

have become the Maiden had any other young women been at liberty to go: but she had been the only one in the whole world. She and Broken Bird were two of perhaps three hundred female *auchresh* all over the Divinarchy. And the rest were wanted at home.

It was different here in Delta City. The cabal listened to her, but they did not automatically obey her, not unless she joined forces with Pati. That was part of why she allied herself with him, of course. How could it not be? But her relationship with him was not a subject for casual contemplation. It was like her gender, something which she hated and cherished. Like her useless, resplendent wings. Put together, those three things granted her a certain invulnerability.

Naked, she *teth¨d* between Pati and Arity. The Garden girl cast her a beseeching gaze. Hope gave the girl a tiny smile, pushed her away, and said in *auchraug* to Pati, "Let me settle this."

"The Maiden has nothing to do with a quarrel between Striver and Heir. Go away, Hope." Pati had a supercilious smile on his face, but his spine was as rigid as an iron rod, and his gaze locked with Arity's.

"I'm not being the Maiden. I'm a neutral observer who refuses to let you savage each other. This is a quarrel between the Striver and *Arity,* not the Heir. Arity spoke as himself, not the Heir, just now, because his being the Heir takes you both into the realm of safety, away from the bone, where you can hurt each other as much as you like and it doesn't count for anything. That's why you're still insisting on being the Striver, isn't it? You don't want to get hurt."

"Don't be absurd, Hope."

"You're no more a god than I am. But you think you are—and that is the danger. You are starting to think that you can do whatever you like." Inspiration was coming to her, as it sometimes did in these situations. She pushed Humi and Arity away behind her as she faced Pati. "Arity wants to see whether you can overcome the barrier between *auchresh* and *hymannim.* Whether we all can. It's a test, Pati, and you're failing, because of your oh-so-godly stubbornness."

He was a tall white flame in the gloom. His mismatched eyes bored into her. Incense combined sickly with the steam from the pool on whose tiled lip half the Divine Guard sat listening. "Pati, this *does* come down to politics," she said. "You think the way to win our fight, yours and mine against Erene Gentle, is by battling secrecy with secrecy, aggression with aggression. Because we are limited beings, that is the only way we know how to fight. But that is letting her fight on her own ground. And therefore she'll triumph through sheer weight of numbers. We don't need to match her every step. We need our own, innovative politics."

Exactly what the *auchresh*, as a race, had never been able to come up with to save their lives.

So—

They needed humans.

Hope couldn't believe her own cleverness.

She seized Pati's hands. "We'll make this girl part of *lesh kervayim*. We won't protect her from them. We'll see if she can handle it. If she can— then just think! A ghostier's apprentice fighting for us! Her position is unique. She could recruit other humans, atheists and devotees alike, to our cause. It would cut the ground out from under Erene Gentle's feet!"

"She's Erene Gentle's apprentice."

That slowed Hope for a minute. Then she shook her head impatiently. "It doesn't matter. Humans are good at duplicity. You didn't think Arity worked for *lesh kervayim?* Never underestimate him, Pati. This could mean the Throne."

For a moment Pati was still, staring down at her. Then he swaggered round her, grinning at Arity with the infectious charm that the Striver could summon at will, clapping the younger *auchresh* on the back. "Arity, I apologize! I'm truly sorry! I was hotheaded and unforgivably rude!" He swung to Hope. "It's a flawless plan!" And to the human, with impeccable courtliness, as if he really believed her his equal: "Milady Garden, I welcome you to the Divine Guards' private quarters."

Her eyes were like black swamp-holes, uncomprehending. Of course, her head must be buzzing from all the shouting. And even if she spoke a little *auchraug*, she could have no idea of what had just been planned. "Striver." She bobbed her head.

"Call me Pati." A show of teeth. "Would you like introductions to everyone? Or would you prefer to merge in naturally, as it were?"

"Pati," Arity said wearily. "That'll do." He glanced around. "Don't let them ride her too hard, will you?" And he vanished.

Hope coughed as the draft of sulphur hit her face. "What horrible manners!" She smiled at the human.

"Well, well!" Pati turned to Humi. She was peering wildly into the shadows of the room, probably feeling as if she had been deserted in the predators' den, her shoulders hunched in desperation. Again she reminded Hope of a rat in a corner. "He's gone off in a huff," Pati said slowly so that she would be able to understand. "I shouldn't count on him too heavily, if I were you. He's terribly self-absorbed." They moved toward the bed platform, where the *auchresh* who had been playing with Hope and Pati waited, half-hidden in a high sea of coverlets. Some of them had used the time to put on clothes. "This is Glass Mountain." Pati pointed. "This is

Silver Rat. This is Val, short for Valor . . . this is Voli, for Frivolity. . . . We use mortal names in the Heavens now, you see. Almost all *auchresh* of my generation or younger are named for virtues." He laughed pleasantly. "My full name is Patience."

Someone was bashing Humi's temples in with a shovel. Gods only knew why: the smoke in the Divine Guards' quarters was no worse than in most human taverns. All the *auchresh* smoked pipes, even gentle, feminine Hope, but their tobacco was only the mild weed that Marshtowners liked of an evening. She had never seen most of these gods before, or else she had never paid attention to them because they were only sentinels. Some of their strange bodily characteristics were enough to make her hair stand on end. Like Arity (Arity who had gone and left her here alone), they were slender as rapiers. Like Arity, they wore earrings.

And they treated each other with a licentiousness that would have made the most extroverted atheist go muddy. Humi was glad of the gloom which obscured her own face. She had thought the night gatherings at Pietimazar's and Belstem's were bad enough—but the *auchresh* had *no* shame! And in between caressing each other, they dropped off to sleep like cats in the sun. And over each other's slumbering bodies, they talked on and on, half in guttural *auchraug*, half in mortal. What she could understand of their conversation, she found fascinating: biting, perceptive, and unfailingly witty, halfway between the impenetrably circular nonsense that the Incarnations spouted in public and the deep tranquility she shared with Arity.

Had shared with Arity. She gazed blearily at Pati and Hope, who were french-kissing while the rest of the circle discussed something with frequent shouts of laughter. Despairing, she thought, *How can I ever hope to treat them as they treat each other?* She felt like a child at a grown-ups' party. In one night, she'd learned more secrets than she had in three years of slinking around Antiprophet Square under the cloaks of her various personas. But she would never be able to use *these* secrets. She would simply be disbelieved.

"Do you know what? I think we ought to pierce Humi's ears." Val was heavily built for an *auchresh*, foppish in an eerie, intense way. His hands each had eight fingers. He reached over and toyed with her earlobe. "To show she's one of us now."

Someone else said approvingly, "She has such beautiful earrings, but they're just clamps."

They were Falippe's. Humi would have torn them off earlier, had she remembered.

"I think we *should* do it." Val signaled an *auchresh*. "Misty, we're going to give her *wrillim!* You still have the equipment, don't you?"

"*Wrillim*—is that the *auchraug* word for earrings?" Humi asked. "Will they hurt?"

Val looked at her in surprise. "No, no, not a bit. Hope—Pati—everyone! Who has some pretty *wrillim* for her?"

The gods volunteered various metal loops, studs, and porcelain ornaments. Humi the socialite bobbed up: she chose the simplest and most striking, a pair of gold hoops as large as the circle of her thumb and forefinger.

"Those are mine," Hope said. "I should be delighted for you to have them."

Val used his steely fingers to close them through her flesh, slowly. She tried not to wince—first at his touch, then at the pain.

"There!" He closed Falippe's earclasps in her sweating palm. "Here are the old ones. They're pretty, but Hope's suit you much better."

She nodded and tried to smile. Nothing suited *her,* ugly little greenish-furred human that she was, couldn't he see that? The smell of the smoke was nauseating. Why did she notice it suddenly? Was it because her head was hurting so much? She would not throw up in public. She would not. The hoops bumped gently against her neck. She would not throw up—

"In the name of the Power," Hope said suddenly, disgustedly. "Look at her! Just look! Can't you see this is all too much? I *know* it was my idea, but she's only a human, and you've been treating her like a Foundling! I'm taking her home." She scrambled to her feet and folded Humi in her arms, pushing one knee between her legs, her breath hot on Humi's cheek. Humi felt herself go limp as a mouse in a cat's paws, cloudily aware of Pati's voice sneering at Hope for her softness. Then the room blinked into nothingness, the color of shut eyes. She could not breathe. But this time she did not black out. She thought, *This—is—teth "tach ching*—and held on to those words like a talisman. *Teth "tach ching.*

Her feet hit the floor. Something crunched under her slippers like broken glass, and she was in the workshop in Tellury Crescent. Impossibly, it was still afternoon, and Hope stood facing her, looking diminished in the sunlight, like a skinny, jaundiced teenager. Her wings reached from wall to wall of the long room. She was still naked. But it was her eyes, not her private parts, that she hid with her hands, squinting at Humi in the sunlight from the row of windows. "Ouch, this is bright!"

Humi shook her head wordlessly. She could not assimilate the experiences of the afternoon as rapidly as *lesh kervayim* seemed to have assimilated her. She could not find words for the mixture of exhaustion, nausea, and exhilaration she felt.

"We've accepted you, you know."

"But on what terms? You can't be *rewarding* me for barging in like that! What am I paying for my audacity?"

"Ah." Hope smiled uncomfortably. "You're sharp. But I think I'll leave it up to Pati to tell you. After all, it's his Power-cursed cause."

It sounded suspiciously as if Hope felt ashamed. Humi said nervously, "What is it?"

"Tomorrow. Or rather, tonight. You'll find out tonight." The *auchresh iu* forced a smile. "It's not as bad as all that." She yawned. "It's about four in the morning for me now. When I see you next, it will be four in the morning for *you.*"

"But how am I to get there? I can't traipse up all those stairways again—"

"One of the *kervayim* will come. Be here." And Hope turned into a purple-edged spot on the air that dwindled and vanished.

Humi rubbed her aching temples. Her *wrillim* bumped gently against her jaw. *There's no question of ducking out on* lesh kervayim *the way I ducked out on Arity,* she thought. *And anyway, there's no point now. This is far more serious. Gods, what have I got myself into? What do they want of me?*

The workshop smelled of chocolate and chalk. Familiar, good smells. But Humi could not forget Arity, Arity saying in the mortal tongue, *Don't let them ride her too hard,* as if he *meant* the innuendo, as if he thought some of the gods would *want* her, as if any *auchresh* would *ever* condescend to such a thing—

She remembered Arity, looking at her with troubled, unreadable eyes, looking at her for one moment and then *teth"ing,* leaving her alone—

Her breath came fast. She whirled. The baby ghost lay scattered in smithereens on the floor of the workshop: a chubby arm here, a button nose there, diamondine slivers in the cracks of the floorboards. Erene was nowhere to be seen.

TWENTY-ONE

In the corner of the bar, a yellow bitch dog danced on her hind legs. Her grizzled trainer gripped her front paws, crooning lovingly to her, displaying broken teeth as he grinned slyly at the crowd. Shimorning was by and large an atheistic district: the working men yelled blasphemies for praise as they tossed coppers. The dog moaned, and her trainer dealt her a blow that contacted her muzzle with a bony smack. "Keeps gettin' above 'erself!" he told the audience. "Gotta keep 'er in line!"

Erene grimaced with distaste. She brought her attention back to the corner table where she, Belstem, and their new allies Gold Dagger and the Hangman huddled. So sordid, this bar, exemplifying the very worst aspects of atheistic culture. But it was all she had now. When Belstem's courier arrived at the Crescent, she had been sitting staring helplessly at her ghost. She had finished the pigment painting, down to the last brushstroke, but somehow the emotion painting had not happened. The baby still wailed with the uncomprehending pain of betrayal every time she touched it. Ghosting was an intuitive craft: Erene had not known how she did it when she could still do it. Now that it had gone, she did not know how to get it back. She had been sitting there, openmouthed with horror, when the call came from the street.

She had greeted the courier as if he were her angel of deliverance. On the pretense of going to get her cloak, she had pushed the ghost onto the floor. Watching it fly into fragments felt good. Childish, but good.

Only now she thought, *Was this how it felt for Molatio? Constance? Is this how it feels for everyone when the end is in sight?*

I'm thirty-eight. That's not old.

Far more dreadful than encroaching age loomed the possibility that perhaps she was rusty. That her talent had vanished through neglect. That she had not lost the ability to ghost but had forgotten how.

The part of her that did not care, the atheistic part, gazed steadily from one crime lord to the other. "Are we agreed, then?"

Gold Dagger had smeared his blobby features with grime, as he always did when he came out in public. The bright hilt at his belt, winking in the light of the candle that swung over the table, gave the only clue to his identity: Belstem had placed a price on his head which might have persuaded even the Shimorning commoners who benefited from his rob-and-resell trade to betray him. Belstem had promised to cancel the price now that they were allied, but Erene did not blame Gold Dagger for his continued cynicism.

The Hangman sat with his face hidden in a black cowl, hands joined inside voluminous sleeves. "Let me see if I have this clear, milady," he said in a light, ironic voice. "When the Divinarch dies, you want to rid the city of its key devotees: anyone, in other words, who might make trouble for you later on. Prominent merchants, shipowners, and bureaucrats. You do not fear the flamens—but you want to wipe out the entire secular government of Marshtown, and the undesirable elements of the other districts' governments. Yes?"

Erene nodded. Paintpots and brushes, rags and turpentine, waltzed distractingly across her mind. "It has been obvious to me for some time that when we act, it cannot be the clean coup d'état to which we thought we could limit ourselves."

"Other words, you come up with a plan, we come up with the muscle to carry it out," Gold Dagger said.

"Do not be so hasty to commit yourself," the Hangman said warningly. "She needs us."

"And you need us." Erene did not miss a beat. "You know you cannot stay ahead of Belstem's price much longer, Gold Dagger. And Hangman, what's to stop him from persecuting you too?" She paused. "And quite apart from that, think what it will mean, after the revolution, to be the heroes who helped us implement the change."

"Oh, we are with you," the Hangman said, and laughed. "Never fear."

" 'Ow's this?" Gold Dagger leaned across the table, his piggy eyes cold. "Two hundred strong men, immigrants and Deltans both, and twenty women for lightweight jobs. Me and Hangman'll work out the split. Two hundred's enough t' take the Old Palace, easy. The day the Divinarch pops off, they'll all down tools and gather in the streets surroundin' the Palace. It'll be up to you from there."

"Their weapons?" Erene croaked.

"Knives, bows, rapiers."

"Slingshots, cuirasses, blowpipes," the Hangman added.

She folded her hands on the table, nodding, and for a moment she feared she would not be able to stop, that her head would keep dipping and dipping lower, like a mechanical thing. "What do you think, Belstem?"

Belstem had hitched his chair around so he could watch the stage. He laughed richly, clapping his fat hands, as a puppy was coaxed out on stage and sniffed worriedly at its mother's hindquarters. "Make them fuck!" he roared, and hurled a gold crown onto the stage.

"Yes, milady," the Hangman said. "I think you do need us."

This time Erene knew she could hear laughter in his high-pitched voice. She nodded dully, acknowledging his point. His eyes gleamed inside the black hood like smears of poison. She thought of the smashed ghost back in Tellury Crescent, hoping to work up enough energy with self-hatred that she could push herself on for the next few minutes; but the thought of her failure inspired neither exigency nor guilt. The ice was dripping.

In the old days, the flamen councillors of the Ellipse had inhabited five magnificent, plain stone mansions in Suvret Cat Square. The mansions had been on a kind of permanent loan to them from the people of Delta City. Free men and women who would have scorned the name of "servant" had come from the rest of the city to keep them clean and well fed. The entire district had been so quiet you could hear leman choirs singing.

Those were the days before the market was installed in the square, before coffeehouses and classy brothels sprang up on every corner of the palace district, before Godsbrother Puritanism, the last of the old guard, withdrew from the square and the atheists went wild, planting gardens and carving the mansions into gargoyles and lacework.

But Pietimazar Seaade topped all the rest. He had torn down a thousand-year-old mansion, leaving only the stone skeleton, and filled in the gaps with windows to build his folly. He employed teams of servants whose sole duty was to keep candles burning in every room. The mansion would have lit the whole square at night, if it had not crouched like a paranoid beetle trying to see out of the top of its head in the middle of his topiary garden. The stark shapes of the trees meant nothing to anybody except Pieti and his little adopted daughter; the pair of them spent a good deal of their time among the statues and hedges, ignoring the trimmers and waterers who kept the garden as green, in its austere way, as Goquisite's tropical paradise, even in the height of summer.

But inside, it looked much like any other house. And the same denizens of Antiprophet Square attended Pietimazar's salons as anyone else's. Wine flowed freely. So did money. Pieti approved of gambling, though Goquisite and several other ladies had chosen to frown on it as dissolute. The room was smoky, dimmer than outside; nevertheless everyone was dressed to the nines, and Erene was no exception. Covertly, she checked the other ladies' garb.

"Errie, *relax*," Goquisite said. "You don't seem able to sit still this evening. What is wrong with you?"

Erene leaned her head against a pillar. "It has been a long day." Desolately, she hoped Goquisite would be content with that platitude.

"Your ghost is finished, isn't it? That sweet little orphan? When can we see it?"

The horror was that she did accept that platitude. "Soon."

Goquisite pursed her lips and laid a hand on Erene's skirt. "Something is *wrong*, Errie."

Erene closed her eyes for a second. "I didn't want to tell you before, for fear you would worry. Earlier this evening I met with Gold Dagger."

Goquisite yelped. "Errie, that man is *dangerous!* Dear Heaven, what were you doing?"

Erene looked tiredly over at the round, worried little face. "Belstem was there, too. We were talking of popular support. The news is favorable: atheism is more popular among the lower classes than ever before. And we were talking of hired knives and cudgels." Goquisite's nose wrinkled. "I know it is distasteful, but we have to consider these things. The Divinarch cannot last much longer. It's six months since he came to Ellipse, and three since any human has seen him. We need to solidify our support."

Goquisite shivered. Her change of subject was so blatant as to be rude if it had not been pertinent. "You're wrong in one thing, dear. Afet Merisand is here. Haven't you spoken to him? He says *he* is in communication with the Divinarch." Her eyes widened. "The Divinarch wants to see you as soon as possible."

A shiver of dread ran through Erene.

Her last audience, which had given her the boldness to make so many of her latter-day promises and alliances and miscomputations, came back to her every day. The Divinarch had assured her in language as plain as any god ever used that she was his golden child. But she had not heard a word to confirm or condemn that since. What did he want with her now? Her mind conjured up a host of dreadful possibilities. At the same time, those possibilities were strangely seductive.

She rose and swung sharply toward the door. Her dress, a puff of sapphire taffeta, frothed around her calves.

"Errie, wait!" Goquisite called.

Erene could not wait. She had to find Humi. Only Humi—who had grown into such a striking girl, tall and long-lashed, sporting a different figure and face every day—could accompany her to this dread audience, could bear her up no matter what happened. Erene needed the lone star by which she navigated this treacherous, uncharted sea.

She saw Falippe Greenbranch perching at one of the gambling tables, laughing, flirting, tossing the dice high in the air. Most men liked nothing better than to win at meaningless sports; the order was simpering losses, then wine, then promises of an even greater surrender. Humi was an expert. Her face was haggard, her fur staring, but no one else seemed to notice. Yet no amount of careful makeup could disguise her exhaustion from someone who, in her deepest heart, still thought of herself as a mother.

Erene caught her eye. Then she excused herself to Pieti and his tiny, ridiculously dressed daughter, and swept out into the night. She stepped between the topiary hedges and waited just out of the light from the arched windows. Five minutes later, Humi emerged, an expectant smile on her face, skirt gathered in one hand as she peered around, still in character. "Psst," Erene whispered.

Humi dropped her skirts and fled to her, hugging her. "Oh, Erene! Where were you this afternoon? The ghost is broken. I was longing to come to you all evening. But Falippe wouldn't look twice at an overdressed, middle-aged ghostier when there are *men* in sight!" She scrubbed her face with her hands, and a cloud of gold facedust puffed out, twinkling in the gleam from the bay windows. She sneezed, and it was as if she slipped out from under a Falippe-shaped piece of stained glass. Her face was bleak, her bosom flat, shoulders slumped.

"Falippe can't be an easy persona to wear," Erene said sympathetically.

Humi shuddered. "This morning—never mind, you'll hear about it soon enough. Gods' blood, I hate her!" Weakly she began to laugh. "I'm going to spread the rumor that she got pregnant and found it necessary to go home incognito. You mustn't ever tell anyone that she was me. Anyone. Ever. All right?"

"I'm so flattered that you are doing this for me," Erene said softly.

Humi clicked her tongue as if to say, *Nonsense. Of course I do it for you.* Erene cast a glance around the clearing. Typically, Pieti hadn't seen fit to spoil the minimalism of his topiary with benches, so Erene knelt on the lush, short grass and pulled Humi down next to her. "There, child. It's all right. I love you. I love you—"

"Gods, Erene!" Humi pulled away. "Where do you think we are?"

Erene took a deep breath, consciously avoiding disagreement. "The Divinarch has summoned me," she said. "I need you to come with me to the Old Palace, tonight." She glanced up at the stars. "Now, in fact."

"Oh, gods." Humi blinked, and seemed to rock on her knees, catching

Erene's shoulder for balance. "I'm sorry. I have—I have other obligations—"

"What do you mean?" Erene strove to keep her tone reasonable. "Your only obligation is to me. You just admitted it."

"I know. But this is something different. If I don't keep this commitment, I will be in danger of my life, I think."

Humi wiped her sleeve across her face. It came away yellow across the shirring, cleaning her cheeks but leaving her eye sockets golden. "I would if I could, Erene!"

"Then tell me the truth! Don't speak in ciphers." Erene grimaced. "You look like a raccoon."

Humi glanced upward, as if in an anguished plea to the gods. "I can't! I'm sorry!" She stood up. "I have to go—I have to meet them at the Crescent—"

"Then go." The words choked Erene like mouthfuls of flour. "Go."

"Gods! Don't do this, Erene—"

"Go!" Erene rose to her feet, pointing. "Not another word! Go! And don't think to foist yourself on me again, with your half-truths and your—your fair-weather loyalty!"

Humi gave a wordless, disbelieving wail and darted away through the topiary, her skirts flapping palely after her like banners. A crow *craaked* as she startled it. Erene stood still, breathing hard. Love and honesty. The two things went hand in hand. Her eyes burned. Giving in to the storm of desolation within her, she turned her head and spat viciously on the spot where Humi had stood.

Then as fast as it had blown up, the storm died. She sagged, face in her hands, melting, melting.

"All this space discomforts me," the Divinarch said. "Now that I am shrunken, I like smaller rooms. Follow me, milady. I expect you will want to be sitting down anyhow, when you hear what I have to tell you." He laughed. Sliding painfully down from the Throne, he padded toward the back of the great hall. Erene followed him. Silently, like a procession of outlandish ducklings, all the Divine Guards who had been standing on the Throne jumped down and came after her.

The Divinarch reached up to twist a near-invisible wooden doorknob in the wall and waved Erene in. "What ghouls you are. Go away," he said to the Guards and shut the door in their faces. Smiling broadly, he gestured around. "Do have a seat!"

Erene obeyed. A merry fire burned in the hearth. Two armchairs stood on a little rug, the skin of some dappled beast she had never seen. A one-

legged table, on which a game of Conversion was arrayed, was made of the
nacreous shell of some water-going creature balanced on a white tusk as
thick as her thigh. Precious jewels formed the Conversion pieces: rubies for
one player, peridots for the other. The room felt as if it might mean home
and hospitality to someone so different from Erene that she could not even
imagine the way his mind worked.

The Divinarch produced two cups of a cold greenish beverage. It
smoked and bubbled in Erene's throat, and the minty taste evaporated fast
off her tongue. *"Khath,"* he said. "An Uarechi beverage." Erene did not ask
where Uarech was. She looked down at the gameboard and moved a leman
piece two squares ahead, the traditional opening move.

He smiled. "Very well. Let us play."

Before they had made ten moves Erene was losing badly. She could not
bring herself to care about the game, though she knew that in some incomprehensible way, it was probably significant. Her thoughts flew insolently
here and there like a flock of butterflies. Tellury Crescent, Goquisite, Humi,
wherever she might be. Humi, whom she had lost. Lost. Lost. She watched
as her hand moved a flamen and laid what was left of her position in rubble.

"I think these pieces are damaging your morale, milady," the Divinarch
said. With a sweep of one skinny arm, he cleared the board. The pieces fell
rattling, glinting like little hot coals on the carpet. "This game is very old. I
think we must revise its symbolism." He kicked his Divinarch piece
straight into the fire. "There! Much better!"

Erene stared at him.

"I saw only the traditional figures," the Divinarch explained. "A set of
Incarnations for each player, a pair of flamens, an army of lemans, and the
Divinarch piece." His pinkish-gray mustaches leaped spastically as he
talked. He reached under his chair and brought up a double handful of new
pieces. "Here. What do you think of these."

The peridot Divinarch piece, a tall, regal woman, had Erene's own face.
Unmistakable. The other one did too. She turned them both in her fingers,
tracing the faceted features.

"And here are Goquisite and Belstem to stand in for the flamens, and a
ghostier or two for good measure. Here is your army of sycophants. Here is
mine. Let us play."

"Milord Divinarch," she said, "please don't tease me like this. Tell me
what you have brought me here for and let me go."

He frowned. "What do you expect of me? Have I failed to amuse you?
Oh, very well. So much for symbols, then." He stood up and tipped the
table over. Erene stifled a scream of disproportionate panic as the pieces
cascaded over her lap, stinging her legs with sharp little crowns and dag-

gers and syringes. They mixed with the first set on the floor so that the hearth seemed thick with shattered glass. The Divinarch stood erect, breathing hard. The fire seemed to crouch down in the hearth like a frightened animal. Shadows bloomed in the corners.

Erene got slowly to her feet. The shadows seemed to leap up behind the Divinarch, lending him stature so that they were of equal height.

"When a battle starts," he said, "all other rules than the One Rule of combat become obsolete. Councillors must become generals. Voting stones must become whetstones. Or both will be crushed under the battle wagon. I have chosen you, Erene Gentle, because you are a ghostier, because you can kill."

Emptily, she thought, *not any more*. There was a time when this charge would have made her heart race. But she had lost Humi. *Not anymore*.

"I am dying. There will be war after I am gone. So I choose you to be my successor, because you will be able to cut it off short. You will be able to control the conflict and bring the Divinarchy safely into human rule like a ship into harbor. Your hand will be firm on the tiller. For I sense that of all the atheists on the Ellipse, you have both the hunger for power and the ability to keep it."

She shook her head. "Thank you, Divinarch, but no."

"*What?*" The Divinarch's eyes bulged.

"There was a time when I would have rejoiced to be named your successor. Not any more. I'm thirty-eight." She plucked at her dress, showing him where she had laced her falseribs tighter over her hollow stomach, leaving the front panel slack. "I've lost the ability to make ghosts. I've lost my edge." She drew a shuddering breath. "I've lost my *imrchim*. I think that I've lost the ability to feel."

His mustaches stuck straight out, quivering with fury. "You will be Heir! I have chosen you, and you will do as I order!"

She had to laugh at the irony. "Isn't the idea rather that I would make a good Heir because in the past I have dared to disobey you? The moment you attempt to orchestrate your downfall, Divinarch, you are defeating your own purpose." She no longer cared how she talked to him.

"I will be known as the Divinarch who ended the rule of the gods!" His voice boomed like a cracked bell. She winced but did not bother to cover her ears. "You will *not* disrupt my plan like this!"

"But Divinarch, I'm not even a good choice. The ghostiers don't trust me any longer. The atheists resent me for doing too much of their work for them. The flamens have not respected me since I moved out of Tellury Crescent. If I tried to assert myself as Heir, my support would crumble like a sand castle."

His grin was mad. "But you have no choice, milady. I have had my sycophants spread the rumors. By the time you return to Antiprophet Square, all the atheists in Delta City will have heard the news. Lady Ankh will already have started to arrange the celebration."

Whirling, dizzying blackness. Erene grabbed the chair for balance. She clung to the light of the fire, that feeble flickering which was the eye of the howling darkness that threatened to engulf her.

Now she knew the truth. This room with its weightless burden floated, like the whole of Delta City, on a spider thread above the howling abyss. It dinned in her ears, tore at her mind. She was sinking through the floor.

Darkness . . .

What else was left for her?

She smiled brilliantly. She must play the game just a little longer. "I can hardly wait. If you would order my sedan, I should be getting back. As you say, Lady Ankh must be impatient to congratulate me."

TWENTY-TWO

Light gleamed on dark swamp water. Reflections of cut-glass lanterns rippled into fragments as the rafts swayed, rising and falling to the thump of dancing feet. There must have been upward of three dozen railinged flatboats, spreading into the channels as if someone had dumped them off the Marshtown jetties like dye. Each raft was a completely different marvel of decoration. Justifiably proud of her accomplishment, Goquisite had invited what seemed like five hundred Deltans and foreigners to the ball. The central rafts held what she called a "buffet" supper; half the assembly thought that eating without sitting down was barbaric, the rest that it was a delightful novelty. At least twenty ghosts watched over the buffet tables, projecting a cold that took the breath away (and kept the hors d'oeuvres nicely chilled).

To the Marshtowners, Shimorningers, and Westpointers who sat in the marshfront taverns, the boats looked like bubbles of light: floating musicboxes where tiny figures circled and glittered to far-off, tinkling tunes. Ostensibly, Goquisite Lady Ankh had thrown this party for the Midsummer festival. Rumor whispered that the nobles were celebrating on a promise of something far greater. But the denizens of the taverns, well versed in cynicism where their lords and ladies were concerned, took neither explanation at face value. "What folly!" the Marshtowners said angrily. "To claim that the Divinarch has willingly relinquished the Throne. Blasphemy!"

"Lucky fuckin' bitch," grumbled the working stiffs in Shimorning, burying their noses in pints of cheap beer. "Just because she useter be pious, an' changed her mind. Coulda been you 'r me."

"Don't know and don't care, but bet your ass there'll be some loot worth picking up come morning," the fishermen-smugglers in Westpoint sniffed.

To Erene, on the rafts, Delta City looked like a long, low strip of glitter, rising at one end to a dark prow. It might as well have been as far away as

her long-lost childhood. She recognized everyone she saw. That was a sign
of how far from her roots in Marshtown she had risen. Outlandishly dressed
nobles streamed onto the rafts as if Delta City were the boat, and sinking.
The other ghostiers were the only people she knew who had not come. And
what kind of sign was that? Actually, she felt glad they had not come. Glad.
Disguised or not, they would embarrass her. They were anachronisms,
country bumpkins, outmoded. Marshtown clung to them like a smell.

Lady Ankh had taken umbrage at Erene's refusal to confirm the rumors
of her honor, and had not spoken to her in a sixday. She was holding court
on another raft in a childish bid to prove that she was more popular than
Erene. She had always been childish: Erene saw that now. Still a leman in
many respects, she was devious in her leeching of love and protection from
those onto whom her instincts made her latch.

Humi was the one Erene longed for. She hoped the grief wouldn't be too
hard on her apprentice. It would not be fair to drag her, too, down into the
blackness. *Humi* had not overreached herself; Humi had not committed the
unforgivable sin of estranging her *imrchim*. In a real sense, this long night
had started when Elicit ended their years of love, that day in the Throne
Room, with one word. She missed him so much . . .

Not being a ghostier, Erene Gentle was nothing.

Amazing how that nothingness didn't show.

Lady Nearecloud was looking at her inquisitively. She shook herself. "I
agree. Absolutely." The lady smiled satisfiedly and began to prattle again.
The lanterns lit the raft as bright as day. The new gowns, which sported a
ruffle every finger-length from the hips to the floor, glided and jostled, the
women's upper bodies in nipped-in bodices rising like reeds from a tumbled stream. The necklines were so low they revealed the women's armpits.
Erene's shoulders had become better as she grew older, and her fur was
glossy. Well made up, she was one of the most attractive women here. *Well,*
she thought wryly, *the very least I can do is go out in style.* The men wore
breeches so tight they looked like smooth, furless skin; their coattails had as
many ruffles as their wives' dresses. All except Belstem's. He wore an
ancient green boatman's coat and a pair of egregiously flowered jodhpurs.
"Well, Erene!" He waddled up to her, massive and imposing. Lady
Nearecloud melted respectfully away. "Where's Goquisite, then?"

Erene bent just enough to clasp him in a half-embrace. "She's somewhere over there, I fancy, making the country nobility feel at home. She
has a flair for putting people at their ease."

"Doesn't she, though!" Belstem hacked impressively into a lace nothing
of a handkerchief, stared at it, wiped his hand on his jodhpurs. "Bloody
useless scrap. It's Anei's fault. She tells me I have to wear these new ruffles,

even on my hankies. I told her, wear 'em yourself! The girl honestly thought I meant to make her wear a man's coat. Haw!"

"How old is Aneisneida now?" Erene asked. "She must be twenty-five or -six—"

"Older than that!" Belstem snorted. "Came to ask you about this rumor, Erene. Not a grain of truth in it, eh? We're making fools of ourselves with this party?" His eyes were piggy. Erene knew he was clever enough to understand that there was a good deal of truth in the rumor and that he was wondering whether he should take umbrage at Erene for having super-seded him in the Divinarch's esteem.

"Shouldn't Anei be thinking about marriage?" Erene persisted. "It would be good for her to get out from under your wing—"

"Couldn't allow *that!*" The worshipers who had gathered around them tittered, but Erene knew Belstem had not meant it as a joke.

"What would you say to Soderingal Nearecloud as a son-in-law? His mother was telling me just this minute that he is in need of a wife's calming influence. And I notice that they seem to enjoy each other's company." She glanced across the raft. As if on strings, the heads of the worshipers turned to see. In a little alcove decorated with a pair of ghosts and floating on an outrigger, a pale-furred woman sat, talking animatedly with a saturnine young man. "He is a year or two younger than she, but that should pose no obstacles—"

"Fat fucking chance!" Belstem growled. "Everyone knows he's Gold Dagger's bastard by Halliet!" The worshipers gasped. "If I let her marry *him,* I'd be letting Gold Dagger get his foot in the door of the Ellipse Chamber! The beginning of the end! Swarmed by the commoners! Only us ex-lemans are the *real* nobility!" He turned a complete circle, slowly. "And you lot 'ud better remember it!" Spittle flecked his chin. The lesser nobles were not tittering any longer.

"Belstem," one of them ventured, "shall we go see what Goquisite has provided for supper?"

"No," Erene said sweetly. She flashed a smile, keeping her eyes hard to remind Belstem that he must not reveal his alliance with Gold Dagger. "Belstem, you really must face the fact that the way you use your daughter is intolerable. I like you; that is why I want you to see what you are doing to her. Aneisneida deserves to live." She cocked her head, smiling as he splut-tered a rebuttal.

This was a relatively good moment. There would not be many more. She was paddling fiercely to keep herself on top of the whirling, dizzying black-ness, but she did not know how much longer she could stay afloat alone.

* * *

Dressed as herself, tawny hair gilded just a little to catch the light, Humi glided from raft to raft, dodging burdened servants and musicians, bobbing curtseys to the nobles. They looked straight through her. Not one of them recognized her, and she was profoundly grateful for it. A buzzing nexus of conversation on the middle raft told her where Goquisite was. But where was Erene? This evening was nothing but a tangle of unanswered questions. *I've been lax,* Humi thought desperately. *Too lax. The ghost was broken. I should have made her tell me what happened. I shouldn't have let it slide. Where is she?*

Since their argument in Pietimazar's garden, they had not spoken. Every time Humi had called at the Ankh mansion, Erene had been out (though Humi saw her personal sedan by the gate). Eventually Humi had stopped trying. And every night, of course, she had been busy. It seemed that she had been living two lives forever. One at night in the Divine Guards' quarters, learning the ways of the *auchresh,* mastering their speech and gradually understanding what they wanted from her; one during the day, her usual calendar of obligations. She could not have said when she had last got more than two straight hours of sleep. But tonight the unpredictable seesaw of fatigue lifted her high on caffeine and wine and worry.

She wasn't so sure about helping Pati to oppose the conspiracy. But she had no choice. And anyhow, Pati had not asked her actually to do anything for him yet. He had just grown friendlier. His ironic wit stimulated her like wine. By comparison, Hope's standoffishness had blossomed into a warmth that seemed to surprise her as much as it surprised Humi. And there were Glass, Moon, Val, Sepia, Silver, and the other Divine Guards she'd come to know. The affinity she felt with them all astonished her.

Not Arity. Once, when Hope *teth˝d* into the Divine Guards' quarters with Humi, he had been there, talking earnestly with Pati, tracing an absent pattern on his leg as he listened to what the Striver had to say. He had looked up, and his eyes had met Humi's through acres of smoke and steam. And she had said something that was lost forever under the din of the Divine Guards' speech. And his face closed and he *teth˝d.* His friendship had been a constant presence in her life ever since she made her first ghost. The way she missed him frightened her.

Even worse was the yearning that ran through her whenever she caught sight of him here and there on her search through the rafts. Leaping up and down on an outrigger to see if he could puncture it with his heel talons; cavorting with Broken Bird or Pati while a crowd of humans goggled; gobbling hors d'oeuvres under the silent censure of the buffet ghosts; kissing Bronze Water on top of one of the flower-arched bridges.

Humi found Erene on the second raft of the northwest chain, engaged in conversation with Belstem, surrounded by a circle of sycophants.

She sidled closer. Horror washed through her.

Erene seemed lively, striking, clearly the soul of the party, and she was charming her admirers no end. But it was not Erene. To Humi, it was painfully clear that the senior ghostier had locked her body on automatic pilot while she went away. Gods knew where.

It kept popping into Humi's mind that the senior ghostier was in the grip of a waking nightmare.

She is sitting cross-legged, hands over her ears, trying to figure out how to keep on going when she comes back.

If she comes back.

Can that rumor be true? *But then why isn't she rejoicing with everyone else?*

Unconsciously, Humi had been twisting the red velvet of her skirt in her hands. A sizzling rip brought her back to the present.

Of course the Divinarch hasn't chosen her for Heir. Pati or Hope would have told me.

Would they? How much do they really trust me?

Water lapped on either side of her where she stood in the corner, as if it were trying to pinch her off from the crowd of nobles, to set her afloat on her own little raft. She rose on tiptoe and stared straight at Erene. And met her eyes. Even at this distance, Erene's eyes were whirling, dizzying vortexes. Everything Humi had ever shared with her—the laughter and kisses, the ghosts, the bitter cocoa and honeysuckle perfume, the dresses, the anger, the lessons in ghosting and in life—reeled faster than light across her mind.

Humi choked as if she were drowning. Erene smiled, sadly, and turned her head a little. While she held Humi's eyes, her voice had not stopped bouncing like a bright ball over the music from the next raft. A splinter stabbed into Humi's hand as she fell against the railing. The black water underneath and the night above her seemed to crush her, as if she were a beetle pinned between two sheets of iron.

She pushed forward between the onlookers, gibbering.

"Who is this strange little person?" Erene asked the group, smiling. "Does anyone know?"

"Just an intruder, milady. I'll get rid of her." A minor lord grabbed Humi and tossed her backward.

She slumped against the flower-hung bridge, sobbing, dry-eyed. Arity stretched over from his perch on the rail and touched her with a talon.

"Are you all right, milady?"

* * *

The unwritten code which governed the gods' behavior around humans said that Arity had to *teth*ˮ here and there without warning, perch on the railings chatting snidely with the Incarnations and off-duty Divine Guards, flatten the atheists with sudden displays of wit. Wherever he went he must evoke adulation.

The others complied with the rules more or less freely. But Humi thought that had Arity had his choice, he would have liked nothing better than to tug on a ruffled frock coat and tight breeches and blend urbanely with the human crowd.

Now for the first time in the evening she found him alone.

"Where have you *been?*" she blurted, looking up at him. "You haven't come to see me in sixdays!" How quickly it all welled to the surface. Tears prickled her nose. "You never cared for me! I mean less to you than a rat in a cage might—"

"*Oh.*" He clamped his arms over his stomach, rocking as if he were hurt, hazel eyes blind. "What did you think I meant when I asked you to come to the Divine Guards' quarters? Why didn't you *come?*"

"I had to be with Erene! Couldn't you tell that?"

"Did you know the risk I ran telling you what we are? Do you know what the others thought when you didn't show up that night? *Traitor*—soft-hearted throwback—"

"And I *did* come! And you were there. And—" now came the worst grievance of all—"you said, *I have nothing to do with her, She's not my responsibility*—"

"Should I have given them a way to get at me through you?" Arity's voice rose. "And you through me? I was keeping us both safe! Pati suspects already!"

"You're afraid of him."

"*You're* afraid of him."

The world seemed to have shrunk to the little ramshackle bower on the bridge, with the two of them, mortal and god, spilling equally rank, boiling pain out in front of each other.

"You're afraid of us all. Even me. You keep coming because you're afraid of what will happen to you if you don't. You want nothing more than to get out of the whole affair, never to see us again."

Humi took a deep breath. "At first that was true. Gods know I had other things to do with my nights. Like sleep." She paused. "But right now, I would keep going back even if they didn't come to fetch me. Nothing else stimulates me like their talk. I don't feel mortal when I'm around them—I feel unique. Because I'm the only mortal they've ever known, I mean *known*, I am in control of the way they see me. I can be whatever I want. Best of all, I can be Humi. And every night"—she swallowed—"every night, I hope I'll see you there. And every night I feel sick to my stomach when you are not there."

He rocked to and fro, short, violent movements. After a minute he jumped down from the railing. She cringed, but then she saw anger flicker in his eyes, and she straightened her back and stood up, countering his intensity with courage.

"Milady," he said in a caressing voice, "dance with me."

Her heart skipped a beat. "Not—not here."

"What do you mean?" He reached for her hand.

"Not here. Somewhere that people can see us."

For a second his eyes went blue. She had never seen that before. But it was only a trick of the lantern light. His shoulders twitched as if, had he wings, they would be whirring.

"Come on, then." His fingers dug into her shoulder as he guided her to the largest raft. The other dancers murmured at the sight of the oddly matched couple, but by this time many of the lesser socialites had left, and the palace initiates were accustomed to the sight of gods mingling with mortals, even if not quite like this. The other Incarnations appeared to have left too. Images of black water, the shores of grassy islands, and once a nightsharque fin imprinted themselves on Humi's eyes as he twirled her to a fast waltz. She felt so disoriented . . . it was almost like *teth ¨tach ching*. The swamp reeked of mud so ancient and slimy it should never have seen air. In this heat, the water levels were half normal. She fixed her eyes on the blur of other couples spinning past beyond their clasped hands. Their perfumes filled her nose. But Arity's perfume was the strongest. His natural body scent, salt and flowers. She was wearing bitter cocoa and honeysuckle.

"Earlier," she said, "something happened while everyone else was watching Hope and Pati make a spectacle of themselves off the eastern raft."

Arity barked a laugh, and at the startled glances they received, shut his mouth sharply. "They went too far. There are nightsharques everywhere this summer! And it's extremely difficult to *teth ¨* out of water! No one dares scold Pati, but I daresay Broken Bird will dress Hope down pretty roundly. You were saying?"

Humi remembered the blackness. She remembered the terrifying feeling of inadequacy that swallowed her when she looked into her master's eyes. She felt the tug of the past.

"Never mind."

With a fanfare, the waltz closed. Panting, the dancers dropped to a halt. A scatter of clapping rose into the night air. "Lords and ladies, in a moment we will play you our final suite of the night," shouted a spokesman for the orchestra.

The couples began breathlessly to chat. Black-clothed servants slipped discreetly between them, relighting the lanterns that had gone out. Humi looked at Arity. He was staring bleakly past her at lord and lady, merchant and merchantees, mortal men and women from every country in the world, with a sprinkling of Divine Guards from the salt who embodied the authority, if not the actuality, of otherworldliness. "Let's get out of here," he said.

Make a ghost. They expected it of her tonight. *Tonight!* The new regime would certainly be well decorated. Ghosts continued to top the list of status symbols among atheists. Didn't they see how ironic it was that as forward-looking, progressive, trend-setting as they styled themselves, they allowed their tastes in such a basic thing as beauty to be dictated by the gods?

Well, Erene wouldn't put it past Goquisite, for one, not even to *know* that it was the first Divinarch, in his infatuation with the only human-created art form, who had raised ghostiers to the Ellipse and turned ghosts into a near-sacred commodity. After all, Goquisite certainly knew the ghostiers' custom of disguising themselves, and she did not care that Erene wasn't disguised.

She couldn't ghost as herself—that was the last, forbidden surrender of the self to which almost no one could stand up. Did they think she could do anything? Did they think normal rules did not apply to her? Well, no matter. She could just catch some little person whose awe of the senior ghostier, twentieth councillor, favorite of the Divinarch, et cetera paralyzed him. She would wrap him in her web of glamour and take him back to Tellury Crescent and kill him and stuff his body under the bed. Then it would be over.

Most of the lesser socialites had left. Too bad. They would have made the best candidates—

"Lady Gentle," the man beside her whispered, "your slip is showing."

She turned on him in anger. Then she stopped. He was a young, smooth-furred Piradean, all silvery fur and eyes that flashed like turned hematites. "You'll do," she said.

"She's drunk," someone whispered.

"You haven't been drinking, have you?" the young man said. "Oh, mi-lady, that would not be wise—"

What right had he to ask her something like that? She hadn't drunk a drop of wine. That was the awful thing. She was stone cold sober and most of the lanterns had gone out and the orchestra was dripping with sweat, playing an endless waltz for the few entwined couples who rocked in each other's arms, and broken glasses and crushed bits of food littered the boards. The lords and ladies stood watching her, silent, the women's hands resting possessively on their partners' elbows, lips pursed.

Deliberately, Erene staggered.

The young Piradean caught her arm. "Ease up, easy," he whispered. "You're as rigid as a ghost. Do you remember when you took an apprentice who was a talking ghost, remember that—what do you remember? Anything?"

"Who are you?" she said. The young man began to lead her away. "Good night, Goquisite!" she shouted.

"Good night," Goquisite trilled. And Erene heard her saying to a nearby lord, in a low, worried voice, "Once she gets him home she will take control, never fear. She's just putting on an act. It is—it is like being disguised, only with words—"

A sedan waited for them on the jetty. "The Ankh mansion, Gentle wing!" Erene called automatically. She only realized her mistake as the porter swung north instead of south. She ought to have taken her ghost to Tellury Crescent. *Well, what the hell does it matter?* The wheels juddered up and down like a drum roll on the Marshtown cobbles. She gripped the young man's arm to keep from being thrown about. His flesh was ropy, the bones prominent; he wasn't that young after all. She looked up at his face. He turned that spellbinding smile on her, and though she could scarcely see the gleam of his teeth, her limbs liquefied.

"Gods," she whispered. "What are you doing here?" Then she wrenched away from him, drove the heel of her hand into her eyes. "No, of course not. I'm sorry. You weren't even there. None of the *imrchim* were—they have better taste than to indulge in expensive displays of bad taste like that—"

"So do you," he said. "Usually. My love."

And he pulled her to him and kissed her deeply, pushing her backward with an arm around her shoulders, pushing her down on the seat. First she struggled. But she knew his kiss. She knew the angles of this body. She reached up and pushed off the curly dark wig, and ran her hand over short hard fuzz. She knew him: they had once been a soul in two bodies, a creative impulse split in half, the twin-chambered heart of the new cadre of ghostiers.

"Porter!" She started out of his arms and poked her head between the curtains, into the rush of starlight. "Change of orders! Take us to Tellury Crescent!"

"Don't be a little fool!" Elicit said. He stuck his head out. "Porter! Ignore that! The Ankh mansion!" Then he sank down beside Erene again, pulling her over onto his lap, clutching her close, kissing her every other word. "It's important to spend our last night there. To change the way you will remember it in your mind. For your sake. And besides, the last thing we want is for the ghostiers to come back and find us."

"Come back from where?"

"We all had bad enough taste to attend that expensive debacle." His voice laughed for a moment; it turned bitter again. "Except for Eterneli and Algia."

"You went in disguise."

"Those of us who went, yes."

She hadn't recognized them. She had not so much as known them. The blackness roared up under the sedan, and juddering became floating, dangerously smooth—

Frenziedly, she curled in Elicit's lap, pulling his arms around her. "Tear this dress off me, 'Lici," she muttered. "Rub my facedust off. Rip the earclasps off. Pull the necklace off my throat. Strangle me with it. Change me, erase me, take me, lose me, change me—"

"Gods!" He bent over her, closing her between his knees and chest, holding her so tight she could scarcely breathe. "What have they done to you!" His mouth locked on hers, and he bore down as if he would press hard enough that they blended into one being.

In her bedroom in Antiprophet Square on the great silk-sheeted bed, under the starlight billowing in the canvas, they did much more than kiss. After her second climax, Erene lost count. The dark tantalized her with glimpses of sweat-sheened fur, gleaming teeth, a long thigh. Never had there been a more skilled lover than Elicit. Never had there been any lover but Elicit. Hem was a dim memory. She could not even remember the names of the others she had had while she lived in Antiprophet Square, the one-night comforters. Elicit was as considerate as an aged man and as rawly passionate as a boy. How long had it been since she was satisfied?

The room smelled edible. She wanted to lick the air to taste the faint scent of bitter cocoa and honeysuckle. For the first time in years, she remembered why she loved that scent. Pirady in late spring, Grussels city, her father's garden paved with reddish flower beds; a vine climbing up a brick wall; young Erene lying with her hands behind her head staring up at

a blue blue sky across which flew a cloud of green buds dipping and dancing on the ash tree.

The bed was a rumpled sea of sheets. Elicit stroked her back, warm,
satiated. She burrowed her head into his armpit and wept desperately, nails
piercing his arms as she clung to him.

TWENTY-THREE

Arity and Humi stood alone on the roof of Broken Bird's teetering tower of an eyrie. From Hope's townhouse a couple of streets away came loud *auchresh* voices and the thump of a *beleth* drum. The Divine Guards were holding their own post-celebration ball.

"I ought to be with the Old One." Arity leaned stiff-armed on the balustrade. Far below, the Chrume rolled past with an immense, slow rumbling. "He's bedridden most of the time now, so he likes me to report to him every night, telling him about political developments. He told me to come to him after this ball."

"Ari." Humi leaned beside him. "Is there any truth in the rumor that he has chosen Erene as his successor?"

Arity was silent for a minute. Then he said, "I don't know. He met with her about four sixdays ago. I don't know what he told her."

"Would you care if it were true? Pati cares. Of course, he would fight to put you on the Throne no matter what the Divinarch wanted, but if Erene was the legal successor, she could carry a good many of his supporters."

"To tell the truth, Humi, I don't really care," Arity said. He smiled tiredly at her. "Listen how politics pervades our conversation. Was there a time when you thought intrigues would never usurp your heart? When you thought friendship was the only thing worth having? And listen to us now."

"You never think of the Throne, do you?" she said. "After all, you're only the one destined to sit on it."

A muscle twitched in Arity's jaw as he stared down at the Chrume. Humi began to regret what she had said. But speaking again seemed impossibly risky. Finally she leaned against his side.

It seemed that he started. Then, slowly, he put his arm around her. He'd done so a thousand times before, yet this time she was acutely aware of it.

The stars shone brilliantly. Right overhead, Skyheart burned a hole in the heavens.

"People were staring at us tonight." He released her. A current of misery swept through her.

"They're not staring now." She picked up his arm and placed it around her waist again. Though she could hardly feel his fingers through the perpetual ache of her falseribs, she knew they had tightened over her stomach.

"Yes. No one can see us now, can they?" He slowly turned her around till they were face to face. In the hollow of his neck, a huddle of claw-tips shone, about to break through the skin. The starlight permitted only the faintest tinge of green in his face. Brown-mauve curls lay limp on his forehead.

Humi remembered. "But they saw us leave together. You know what they will think. Could there be a juicier—"

"By the Power!" Roughly, he pulled her forward into his arms. "Do we *care?* Do we care if the whole world knows?"

She laid her head on his breast. "That . . ."

He stopped speaking as sharply as if he had been stabbed. His breath against her cheek came fast and shallow; she had an idea that he was clutching her rigidly. Damn this dress! She didn't dare lift her face from his shirt. The silk was so thin she could have bruised her cheek on his collarbone, singed it on the heat of his skin.

"Arity, I can't stand this," she whispered.

"What?"

"That I love you."

Moments passed. He shuddered, a long sigh that dizzied her with its fragrance. "How long have you known that?"

"About three hours." She ventured to kiss his neck. Salt sweat sprang out in a nervous reaction wherever her lips touched. Pungent, not rancid. Hot and sweet. Could salt be sweet? "Since I realized why I had been missing you so much. Why my whole body tingled every time I thought of you."

"You humans are less continent than we," he whispered, half jesting, half admiring. "I think now that I have known—for sure—for months. Ever since Pati threw it in my face as an insult. After you came, that first time, he and I had an argument."

"What had that to do with me?"

"We were arguing about you. My relationship with you."

Oh. Humi shivered. "And he said?"

"He insulted me. He accused me of treason to the *auchresh* as a race and *lesh kervayim* in particular. But his evidence wouldn't have been terrible at all if he had put it in other terms. The only reason it hit me so hard was that

. . . well, that it was true." Wonderingly, his lips brushed her hair. Then she felt fingernails in the tender flesh under her jaw, lifting her face. Just before their lips met, he shot a wry glance at her.

She burst into giggles, very quickly losing her breath. "Don't *look* at me like that!"

He loosed one arm to run fingers through her hair, lips curving. "Forgive me. It just came to me that I had never looked at you before. No, I don't mean that! I mean that I'd never seen how beautiful you are. Undisguised. Aroused."

"There's never been anyone else. No one but you."

"Not for me, either. Not since Pati, in Wind Gully Heaven." He corrected himself. "*Never*. Never has there been anyone like you."

She wrapped her arms around his neck and kissed him.

He responded with skill that was somewhat shocking.

She'd burn. No, she'd melt like frost brought into a hot room.

She couldn't stand such ecstasy longer than a second or two at a time. All other worries were forgotten. Time slowed as they stood on the balcony of the spiral-staired steeple high over the Chrume, joined at the mouth by these darting, gulping little kisses. She could not tell which of their hearts was beating harder. Her legs were the last parts of her to melt; as they crumpled, she caught herself on Arity with a gasp. The wicker floor creaked. "Are we allowed to do this?" she whispered. "*Auchresh* and mortal?"

"Is it possible? Is it allowed?" Arity mimicked, kindly. "That's what I have been wondering for two of the most hellish months of my life. We *are* doing it. What better proof?"

"But we haven't given it the ultimate test." Humi attempted to leer. Arity burst out laughing so loudly she had to cover her ears. When he managed to stop, he suggested a shockingly lewd remedy for that situation.

Then he paused.

It came to Humi that he was waiting for her consent.

She kissed him again. Fire and ice bubbled in her veins. "God or not, *auchresh* or not, there is nothing I would like better than to—"

Teth ˮ.

She *felt* the expanse of night around them contract, the wicker catwalk become a lumpy, glassy floor, the sky shrink to an irregular oblong.

"I used to come here when I was a new Foundling," Arity said, "when I wanted to get away from the overwhelming weight that was civilization. Later, Pati and I used it as a trysting place." His voice echoed spookily, as if the room were very high. "I'm sorry. I didn't mean it that way."

She clung to his arm. "Where are we?"

"In the salt. Your eyes will adjust in a moment." But of course he could see in the dark. With sure steps, he led her to a thing like a large, feather-soft carpet. "It's still here. Good. We are completely safe."

"I hate the thought of you and Pati making love," she murmured. Chills ravished her body as he unhooked her dress and slid it down her arms.

"Because we are both male? *Auchresh* don't have much choice about that, you know."

"No, no, no—it's because—well." She did not know whether to admit that although the Striver was exciting to be with, she strongly disliked him. She was still not sure whether he and Arity were friends. "Was your relationship anything like his and Hope's?"

"Yes." The first falserib, then one by one the others, gave way under Arity's fingers. Humi breathed deeply. "He treated me like a plaything. I see that now. I was in love with him. But he wasn't with me. Or maybe he found it very easy to fall out of love. When he had to go to Delta City and leave me behind, he took *ghauthiji* after *ghauthiji*, and when Hope came along he swooped her up with no qualms at all over me. He'd always wanted a woman lover—for the prestige which would come to him in the Heavens with being her *irissi*, as much as anything else."

She sighed. "Oh, that feels better . . . Ari, I was used to the idea of men lying with men before I ever came among *lesh kervayim*. My mother, you know, was a lover-of-women—a *kiru iu*. And I think Erene is too—or would like to be. Or she is attracted to both." She shivered as he began the row of infinitesimal pearl buttons down her underdress.

He knelt before her, fingers flashing down the curve of her belly. She could see his face now, frowning in concentration, but not at the buttons. "My Humi," he said in *auchraug*. "She has pushed you so far. Placed such a strain on your loyalty."

She shut her eyes and said in the same language, "I will follow her to the death."

"But there is a conflict of interests. And I'm sure you've seen where it lies." Arity lifted each foot in turn to peel away its stocking, laying them neatly aside. "There is your link with *lesh kervayim*. And if you link yourself with me, it can do nothing but cement that. How can you forward the conspiracy against the Divinarch—against *us*—at the same time as you support us?"

The stark phrases brought the impossibility of it home to her like a knife grating on bone. For the past month she had been pursuing just those interests that Arity described as conflicting. But she had felt as if she were going to melt with fatigue.

"Dear heart," he said quickly, reaching up to caress her cheek. "It's just

that if you are involved with me, everything will have more ramifications."
He hugged her, tenderly prying her fingers away, drying her trickling eyes.
"I was giving you a last chance to say no."

"While you undress me!" Her head jerked up; she stared at him in
amazement. "From any other *auchresh*, that would be a cruel joke. But you
really meant it." She searched his face. "You really are concerned that I
choose you of my own free will." *Because what you fear above all is acting
toward me as you think a god would.*

The way he avoided her gaze told her she was right.

A red-hot surge of love suffused her.

"Oh, Arity, I choose you with all my heart," and she pulled him unresist-
ing to her, curly brown head bowed, and unbuttoned his shirt. Outside, a
salt bird called, its cry diminishing as it darted over the top of the chimney
to the next night flower.

He smelt of flowers. His nipples were hard as stones. Humi gasped, then
bent her head to them, licking first one, then the other, darting her tongue
over the aureolae. He shuddered with desire, arching his back, rigid in her
grasp. Then he opened his eyes—such enormous eyes—and smiled stiffly.

She saw her own body gleam in the starlight, the best light by which to
make love. The pelt of heavier fur at her groin was wet. She felt it slippery
as though she were dripping down there. Arity was trembling, no longer
really seeing her, she thought, as he covered her face with kisses. She could
not breathe. His member was a hot hard lump. She was on her back, he
pinning her to the carpet, kissing her so greedily she couldn't tell when one
kiss stopped and the next began. The air felt like a cold wind on her sex.
She craved him. "I want you. Oh, god, I want you."

He satisfied her craving.

It is unnatural for *auchresh* to sleep at night. Humi woke before dawn to
feel Arity slipping her stockings onto her feet. In the rosy gray light, she
could see that they had slept in a large cavern at the bottom of a chimney
with a narrow, high-up mouth. The air was mild, not chilly but pleasant.
Woody salt debris lay in the corners as if swept there by rain; a warren of
saltmice had set up housekeeping in the far edge of the feather carpet from
where she and Arity had slept. Tiny transparent-furred squeakers, they
watched her from a distance, peeping. "Where are we, anyway?" she asked,
yawning, just before Arity caught her in his arms and *teth¨d* them up onto
the rim of the chimney.

He kissed her neck, turning her so she could see the whole vista. "Deep
in *Kithrilindu*."

"Royalland?"

"Not really. No human has ever set foot here."

Humi freed herself and walked a small circle, skirt swishing around bare feet. "Now one has."

The chimney was set like a socket into a brushy, rock-strewn hillside, its dark mouth insignificant in the grand sweep of the slope. Far behind them reared a ridge on which jagged formations branched against a still-dark sky. The formations grew smoother and more rounded as they sank toward a flat, glassy plain, the floor of a sea so large that it spread over the horizon.

The spectacle was the no-color, all-colors of salt, its opacity ranging from dirt-dark formations to the transparent, glacially quiet plain. Humi could imagine the dazzle that would blaze from that vast mirror when the sun rose.

"The Sea of Storms." Respect hushed Arity's voice. "*Writh aes Haraules.* Yes, it looks innocent; you've come upon it at one of its good times. Do you see how nothing is moving down there—not even an insect? Now look all around you." She obeyed—and smiled in delight. Everywhere flickers of movement caught her eye: the saltplants rustling, the myriad little salt animals that dwelt in the brush going to ground to wait out the day. Only insects braved the sun in the salt. The acid scent of growing things fragranced the breeze. "In the Sea, blizzards can boil up in ten minutes. When they come up this coast, the Sea looks like an endless, seething cauldron. And the storms froth up the Wind Gully like uphill flash floods, white with particles scoured off the Sea, carrying whatever has got in their way. We used to fish for treasure-trove out of the windows."

Humi breathed: "From where?"

"Heaven. I lived here for twenty years." He pointed around the bowl at what she'd thought was a grove of formations, branching and corkscrewing up for fifty armspans, and as she looked, they became Heaven: a fairy-tale castle with spires, crenellations, towers, and a keep the size of a small hill. The turrets were aquamarine-blue, just barely distinguishable from the hillside round about. Now that she knew what to listen for, she could hear *auchresh* voices like bells and trumpets, the words incomprehensible with distance.

She turned impulsively to Arity. "*Teth* us there!"

"Not so fast! Just having been around *lesh kervayim* doesn't mean you understand *auchresh* who have never seen a mortal."

"Tell me the difference, then."

"There is one important thing you should know. At some point in history, we *auchresh* developed a status system." He took her hands. "It has been getting stricter all through the centuries, even as our knowing how mortals lived changed other things in our society. The system is not inflexible, like the castes of pre-Divinarchy Calvary. Rather, one's status changes as one enters into and leaves relationships. You and I used to be *elpechim.* Good friends who are not lovers. Now we're *irissim.*" He squeezed her. It was delicious to feel the bone of his hip and the hard curve of his thigh so close, under the fabric, and to remember how the green skin had looked naked.

"What's *irissim?*"

"Two who are bound together as closely as possible. Lovers. Friends. I cannot say it in mortal. It is too deep."

She shivered, resting her head on his shoulder. "Zin told me that the gods have a hundred words for 'friend.' Like *imrchim.* Are all of those status words, then?"

"Yes. But everything in *auchraug* is a status word in one way or another. And the 'friendship' words don't always convey significant amounts of status, and it's not all changeable—in a Heaven like Wind Gully, there is free flow depending on who is in the good books of whom, who is looking after a Foundling, who has become a *mainraui,* and so on. Certain things never change. For example, women automatically have high status. But in a larger Heaven, there will be a limit to the status any particular *auchresh* can gain, depending on who took him in when he was a Foundling. However, if any group of *auchresh,* be they *kervayim, irissim, saduim,* plain *ruthyalim,* or something else, take in enough Foundlings, they move up a little."

"Whew."

"But you don't need to worry about most of that in Wind Gully. Just assume that being a woman, you can say whatever you want to most people. I'll warn you if there's an exception. Oh, yes, just make sure they know you are a woman right away—you are *tith*ˉ*ahu.* Technically, since you are apprentice to the senior ghostier in Delta City, you are *perich*ˉ*hu,* superior to them, but I daren't go that far."

"Ari, you're worried. You don't have to take me if you don't . . ."

Nothingness.

". . . want to . . ."

Wind Gully Heaven leaped and gushed over them like some fantastic, frozen fountain. Carved pinnacles spiked the dawn. Loud, sweet *auchresh* voices, speaking pure *auchraug,* spiraled from window to high-arched window.

Humi gulped and clung to Arity. They waited; two small figures hidden in the tree-height formations which grew against the walls of the keep, until at last they were seen. One voice after another dropped into stunned silence. Someone called out, "Is it the *mainrauim?* Is someone hurt?"

"It's Charity!" *Auchresh* streamed out of a dozen different doors and windows. A bulky, bald male with green-dappled skin came in front. At the sight of Arity, his face lit up.

"Wrought Leaf!" Arity held out his hands, but the man ignored them, hugging him close in the testing fashion men have. When he was released, Arity waved vigorously at the growing crowd. "*Ruthyalim!* It's been so long since I've seen you!"

"Wonderful to have you back!" the dappled *auchresh* Wrought Leaf rumbled. "We began to wonder whether you had forgotten that we were still here! But—*ahh*—who is this?"

Arity took Humi by the hand and drew her forward. "My *irissu.*"

Thank you for not being ashamed of me. She gave the *auchresh* her best social smile. They weren't bestial, as she'd half feared they would be, ugly relations kept locked away in the salt for fear they would scare the humans. Yes, a few grotesque mutations bobbed above the crowd—but if she focused her eyes just halfway she could pretend they were all human. They stared and whispered like any saltside hamleters would if an atheist lord were to drive into the courtyard and ask for hospitality. But they wore elaborately tattered and slitted garments that no hamleter would dream of donning, and their only ornaments besides their *wrillim* were their bodies within. Most had rudimentary wings. She had to keep reminding herself that they were all males, *kerim:* several smaller ones whom Humi supposed to be adolescents wriggled between them, blinking at Humi from the safety of their "parents'" arms. Foundlings.

"Greetings," she said in her smoothest *auchraug.* "My name is Humility. It is a human virtue-name." *Volunteer your status*—"I'm *tith¨ahu.* You are Wrought Leaf, *tith¨ahi?*" She stepped forward, trusting instinct when she opened her arms rather than offering a hand. For a second the big *auchresh* looked astonished, but then he stooped to clasp her shoulders in a ritual embrace. When the creaking of her bones reached everyone's ears, he let her go, abashed.

"Excuse me, *tith¨ahu.*"

Thank the gods—ah, the Power. That hurt. Unobtrusively, Humi flexed her shoulders to make sure they weren't broken. Lavender . . . cilantro and dill . . . "*Tith¨ahi*, would I be correct in guessing that you are an herbalist?"

He looked pleased. The thick, twiggy *uurthricim*—living mustaches— that half hid his mouth jostled. "How do you know? Yes, I am pharmacist of Wind Gully Heaven, as well as *o-serbali.* Some say I am a master of the craft. But I daresay Arity has told you all about me, and the others." Several other *auchresh* moved forward between the tree-holes. "The other *o-serbalim.*"

Apologizing for her ignorance, Humi shot Arity a quelling look. She did not even know the word that Wrought Leaf had used.

Serbali? "Leader of the people," Arity approximated in her ear, voice strained. "The *o-serbalim* counsel the *serbali,* or in Wind Gully's case, the *serbalu,* Sweet Mouse-eater, an *iu.*"

"Meet the *o-serbalim, tith"ahu.*" Leaf clapped each man on the back hard enough to knock him down, had he been human. "Blizzard Dancer. Red Rat. Curved Steeple. Writhing Snake. We do not have many virtue names here—"

"*Lesh mainrauim!*" a Foundling caroled suddenly, dashing out of the trees. "They return! With good eatings!"

Writhing Snake, an old, shaggy *auchresh,* smiled shyly at Humi. "Excuse the Foundling's loudness, *irissu ae Arity—*"

These young men *could* have been gods.

Lithe and muscular, wing-mantled each in his own way, they loped through the trees from the scrubby hillside, skin glowing with exertion. Sweat dripped down their necks. Their fangs showed in pearly grins of delight.

If one of *these* appeared to her on a deserted hillside in Westshine—

The stories of god-begotten children might be true.

Six of them, stripped to the waist, carried poles on which they had slung a number of scaly, antlered beasts whose fish-eyes bulged glassily. Others bore sacks of what looked like transparent broccoli. Still others carried hunting paraphernalia. "Magnificent deer!" The *auchresh* pressed deferentially around. "Did you find the winkleaf plants for me?"—"I'll go tell Calm Shore you're back, so he can get ready to butcher the escorets—"

Arity pinched her arm. Here amid these rough-carved people, he looked almost human in face and form. (The *mainrauim* weren't human—they were more. They were the Divine Guard before dissolution, orgies, and vice had gotten to them.) "Wind Gully's only claim to fame is that it has somehow managed to produce two Incarnations," he said sourly. He glanced at the *mainrauim.* The exultation of their return had worn off; now as the Wind Gully Heaveners swarmed about them, they stared curiously at Humi. "And Pati and I only occurred because near here—so near that the *mainrauim* must *teth"* to reach safe hunting grounds—is one of the filthiest predator lairs in Kithrilindu. Wind Gully picks and chooses its Foundlings. They adopt only the most intelligent, unlike some Heavens in more remote places, which take whatever they can find."

Humi laughed. "Ari, I believe you're jealous!"

"Of course I'm jealous! These louts have seen exactly two women in all their misbegotten lives, neither of whom can compare to you!"

"Louts or not, they are marvelous specimens . . ." Humi flirted her eyelashes at the nearest one.

Arity growled wordlessly and seized her by the arms and fastened his mouth over hers.

Her spine melted.

At last he broke away, shaking his hair back, throat jumping. "By the Power, I love you, Humility!"

"Don't call me that." Between the silver-leafed branches of the trees, the sky was rosy. The breeze licked through her fur, warm as running blood, warm as a tongue. It would be another sweltering day. She pressed her head against his chest, trying to breast the swell of adoration. "I love you."

Wrought Leaf cleared his throat deferentially. "Arity, would you and your *irissu* care to take supper with the *mainrauim?* We have but to butcher the escorets, and then it will be ready—"

"The *iu* is pleased to accept your offer," Arity said formally. The edge that had vanished when he spoke to her was back.

In the inner fastnesses of the Heaven, they met Wind Gully's own women: Sweet Mouse-eater and Flowering Crevice, the first the Heaven's imperious old *serbalu,* the other a heavily mutated creature with slab lips and four hands' worth of fingers. She and Wrought Leaf (who, were it not for his piebald skin, could have passed for a blacksmith in any Domesdys village) kissed like lovers. "He has higher status than the rest of the *o-serbalim* right now because he's her *ghauthiji,*" Arity whispered. "But she already has her eye on one of the *mainraui,* Running Fox. Wrought Leaf accepts that he will soon fall from favor. When one has so many years and so few lovers to choose among, one ends up trying them all."

"But the Divine Guard aren't like that!" Humi said as the Wind Gully Heaveners began to butcher the deer. Their kitchen was a dark salt cavern. Down one wall burbled a freshet. "There is true love among them, Arity! I know how Crooked Moon and Unani feel about each other, and they are just one example—"

"People say that living among humans has corrupted them." Arity gazed at the sprightly Foundling boys, their elbows and bare feet callused horn-hard, who were sweeping the blood from the butchering into the freshet. "I do not know. But I do know that the larger Heavens are structured much like human cities. And *that* is corruption! We can rest assured that a thousand years ago our Heavens weren't like Delta City! Here in Wind Gully, I think our civilization is very much as it must have been when the *auchresh* people first cohered out of scattered groups of outcast predators. It feels as if we've been here forever. And yet on the level of the individual—as

everywhere in the salt—there is a transcience, a weightlessness in the air.
Do you feel it?"

"I feel it." She shivered. Over eons, the freshet had worn a spreading
stain of diamondine in the wall. She pushed her finger along it, releasing a
high-pitched ringing sound. The nearest Foundling took fright and splattered her with water. "Eeeow!" it yelped, and bared its fangs in terror,
mumbling incoherent apologies.

"It's all right, Luc!" Arity sidled toward the boy. "He can't talk properly
yet,—he's very newFound—here, Luc, Luc . . ."

Trembling, the Foundling let himself be won over. Arity cuddled him.
Humi found the picture fascinating: an adolescent with a man's voice who
needed to be reassured like a toddler. "It's only a human," Arity whispered.
"A human girl. See, she has fur. Not like you. Those things on her feet are
shoes . . ." Humi let Luc stroke her cheek and touch her slippers. Then
he tried to kiss her on the mouth.

Hiding her shock, she repulsed him as gently as she knew how.

"I'm afraid my Lucidity has a long way to go." The *serbalu* Sweet Mouse-
eater stood over them, supporting herself on a twisted transparent-wood
walker. She smelled of blood; it splattered the front of her shirt and
breeches, and the wrinkled breasts exposed through peepholes. Her skin
and hair were as iridescent as Pati's, her eyes pink. "It will be another
decade before he is civilized, I daresay, and I don't know that I'll see that
many more years . . . Are you two coming to supper, then?"

"It'll take a *decade* to civilize that child?" Humi hissed as they followed
her halting steps out of the cavern.

Arity's voice was sullen. "We are not human. We do not meet our children until they are too old to be shaped like children. You have no idea
what it is to try to tame a youth who has been feral for fifteen years or more!
You have no conception of how lucky you are to be able to have babies!"

Humi blinked and pressed close to him.

In a lace-walled tower where the breeze from the hillside blew across the
tables, they ate a hearty breakfast (or supper) of venison cutlets, fried at
table. For dessert there were vegetables (or fruit) which looked like broccoli
but tasted like mangoes. Humi didn't wonder if she could stomach salt food
until the meal was over, but she felt no immediate ill effects. And anyway,
hadn't they always harvested berries from the salt near Beaulieu, and
hunted there when times got lean? The tablecloths were splattered with
grease from the frying, but no one seemed to mind the mess. Easy laughter
greeted Luc's breakage of an entire set of glassware. *Easy come, easy go,
but we will always be here.*

The *mainrauim* clearly held the highest status within the Heaven. While several older men cleared the tables, the younger hunters sat back and talked with Humi and Arity, drinking hot *gherry* (a thick, dark red, bitter beverage), lifting their feet off the tables only long enough for the men to slide the tablecloths out. They thought it hilarious the way they had to lower their voices so Humi wouldn't go deaf when they spoke. In fact, they knew nothing whatsoever about humanity: they wanted her to enlighten them. As long as they remembered to keep their voices down, she was in her element. They asked intelligent questions about Delta City, often out-stripping her ability to describe it in *auchraug,* but Arity refused to trans-late. *Something is wrong with him,* Humi thought. *He's not just jealous. It's more than that.*

It was clear from the way the *mainrauim* treated him that they envied, idolized, and took pride in him. Could that be why he seemed so ill at ease?

Then without warning, visible through the lacy walls of the dining room, the rim of the sun peeked in a fury of gold and red over the *Writh aes Haraules.* The salt sea exploded with brilliance. Humi broke off in the middle of a sentence and scrambled under the table. *Mainrauim* arms came around her, sheltering her face. She felt herself being lifted and carried along. The *mainrauim* ignored Arity's desperate shouts to put her down.

"She's very tender, isn't she? We may not *like* the sun, but we can *tolerate* it."

"But don't you adore how she's furry, like a mouse?" Yellow Twilight fingered her calf.

"Claws off!" yelled Arity.

They set her down in the cool, torchlit stair that spiraled down the middle of the tower. "Do you need us to carry you any farther?" Running Fox asked hopefully.

"Sorry, we have to be going, *ruthyalim!*" Arity grabbed Humi against him. "We'll just give our farewells to the *serbalu.*"

Sweet Mouse-eater's bedchamber would not have seemed out of place in Goquisite's mansion, except that the brocades and tapestries that Humi fingered all had the slithery feel of salt fiber. Since time out of mind, Arity had told her, the *auchresh* had been masters of the handcrafts which made this Heaven so beautiful. Treatments for different consistencies of salt, from the granite-hard stonesalt to the cheesy stuff the Foundlings gathered from its hollows; treatments for the tough, fibrous roots of the formations so that they could be woven; for their substance so they could be worked like metal or wood; treatments to reveal one color over another: the *auchresh* were masters of them all. It was not much harder to eke out a living in the salt than in human country, if one was born to it.

Propped on cushions on her bed, Sweet Mouse-eater caressed Wrought Leaf's and Flowering Crevice's heads. "So you are leaving already?"

"Yes," Arity said flatly.

A fluffy salt cat sharpened claws on the rug. Wrought Leaf followed Humi's gaze. "Milky has gotten used to our society, but he's rare," the *o-serbali* said wistfully. "Every human family has domestic animals, so Arity tells us. We are not blessed like that. Animals have an instinct for— *erhmmm*. Our lineage."

"If we didn't always meet in mansions, where one encounters only the occasional poodle to yip and cringe," Arity said, "you would have noticed their reactions to me too, Humi."

"I should like to see those mansions." Wrought Leaf lay flat on his back, one hand linked with Flowering Crevice's over a splash of dried blood on Sweet Mouse-eater's shirt. It was clear they were going to spend the day together. Humi had a sudden, chilling glimpse of something much deeper than she had seen yet in Wind Gully, much deeper than Arity had implied in his flippant dismissal of relationships here. After all, he had said: There is no mortal word deep enough to describe the concept of *irissim* . . . She wondered about the *mainrauim*. Would they go to bed with whoever happened to be nearest? And the other *auchresh* with whom she'd spoken— older, younger, and lesser? What about them?

He's wrong about Wrought Leaf falling from favor, she thought. *It's impossible that life be no more than an endless game of musical beds. There has to be love.*

There has to be love.

What good is any honor if there is nothing to sweeten it? What was my life, before I knew Ari as an irissi?

"But the glories of the human world are not for me. Return some time, *tith˜ahu.*" Wrought Leaf's pupils rolled, indicating that he couldn't see her properly. She stepped closer. "Come when there is a storm. Strangers to the Heaven find the blizzards an amazing sight."

"Arity!" Sweet Mouse-eater's voice was querulous and worried. "Can you *teth˜* all the way back to human country from here?"

"Of course I can! Many thanks for your hospitality, *ruthyalu*. Humi, hold on—"

And her feet hit hard cobbles. She staggered, having great difficulty in reorienting herself. It felt as if all the cares she had left behind were settling back onto her shoulders like a flock of lead pigeons. Mora, the daughter of Frivalley the baker, waved cheerfully at her through the steamy shop window. Then her mouth dropped open as she saw Arity. *What does it matter?* Humi thought, a touch wildly. *Everyone will know soon enough.*

All she cared about was that she loved him, loved him, *loved him* with every nerve and muscle. The sounds of humans and animals waking up came to their ears. She could smell the bread in Frivalley's ovens. She was hardly ever up early enough for that. The sky was strangely dark, with a few bright white clouds scattered overhead. Of course, Wind Gully Heaven lay to the east, farther back along the path of the sun. Just the two of them standing in the Crescent, with nothing between them except a thin, cold wind.

He gripped her hands tightly. "Well, that was my home."

"Arity, what's *wrong?*"

"I'd no idea how they would take you! I was afraid of so many things—I was ready to *teth*˝ you away at any moment. But I didn't have to be." Her hands were tingly-numb where he gripped them. "There is hope for our races after all. Oh, Humi, I love you for the woman, not the mortal, that you are, and that I am free to do so is—"

Tears clogged his voice. Humi hugged him roughly, pulling his head onto her shoulder. He let himself be held, trembling. *If I knew half of what he was afraid of, it'd probably be* me *collapsing all over* him. "I love you." It was all she could say, and it was inadequate.

Lifting his head, he smiled, hazel eyes crinkling. "Sundown, tonight. Your boudoir."

She answered with all her heart, in the affirmative this time. "I'll be there."

He brushed fingers tenderly down her cheek, and vanished. The wind swirled away the white-powder footprints he had left on the cobbles.

The hem of Humi's gown was tattered from catching on the salt formations. Letting it drag on the cobbles, she walked slowly toward the Chalice and went in.

Elicit roused Erene at dawn with a soft, insistent shaking. Servants, maids, friends—gods knew who she had gathered about her in this elegant purgatory. Anyone might come in. "Erene, get dressed. We're leaving."

"What . . . ?" She raised herself on one elbow. In the light of a new day, squinting with tiredness, she was even more beautiful than he remembered. Elicit's heart nearly stopped before he could get his wits about him, pull her up, and kiss her. She wriggled away, laughing.

"Did you sleep well?"

Outside, the sky was shell-pink, paling to light blue near the top of the great window. The air had cooled off during the night. Elicit watched her pull open chests and closets, clicking her tongue in quiet disbelief at the feathered fripperies that dripped out. Finally she found a plain beige dress.

She tied a headscarf around her hair that deepened her gray fur to charcoal and made her eyes snap. "Where are we going?" she asked.

"Not to Marshtown."

Shutting her eyes for a moment, she nodded.

"To the docks. I know it's not the windy season, but there should be at least one ship leaving for Pirady. We'll go to Grussels and then work our way along the coast. There are rocky bays where no one goes. I grew up in one. We won't need money there."

"My father used to take me along the coast on holidays. I know the area you mean."

Elicit could almost taste the salt spray. "White waves . . . gray rocks . . . trees thick on the tops of the cliffs, spreading inland . . . seagulls in the air like bits of foam. We'll build a house in the woods."

She unlatched the window and stepped out onto a wrought-iron balcony. Elicit followed. They stood looking down on a tropical garden walled in by gray stone buildings. Beyond the roots of these buildings, far away, water glinted: the Chrume. *I've had it with rivers,* Elicit thought. *I've spent too much of my life on the edge of a marsh.*

Erene leaned on the rail. Dew darkened the elbows of her dress. "Perhaps we won't have to be quite alone. Do you think I'm too old to have another child?"

He kissed the side of her face.

"I mean, really, I should like to take Tessen with us, but—"

"*No,*" Elicit said, surprising himself with his own harshness. "For the boy's sake, no! He doesn't deserve to be saddled with us."

"I was about to say that once I would have swooped down on Soulf and carried him off without a second thought. Now I never would, though."

"Sorry," Elicit said. "Forgive me." He had meant to flirt, but even to him it did not sound flirtatious.

The sun was coming up.

"You're forgiven," she said in a voice free of laughter.

He took her arm. "Let's go."

The bedroom was larger than he had guessed it would be—he had never been upstairs in the Gentle Wing—and strewn with personal bits and pieces. But as they passed through, Erene didn't touch or pick up a single object. Shushing each other's giggles, they crept downstairs. A breath of cold made the fur on Elicit's arms stand up. He glanced around, and saw the ghost of a naked Calvarese girl standing in a baroque-painted alcove. He shuddered. The morbidity of it shocked him. There were no ghosts in Tellury Crescent, nor had ever been. What kind of ghostier decorated her home this way? What kind of pain had she willingly subjected herself to every time she climbed these stairs, when the cold reminded her what part of her life had died?

He turned to her with the questions on his lips. Then he saw her eyes squeezed shut against tears, and her mouth trembling.

He dug her with an elbow. "Race you to the entrance, Erene. Without waking anyone up!"

The loser by two seconds, she fetched up in his arms against the ornate front door, pliant and merry again. The long hall with its checkered floor was empty, daylit by arrow-slit windows. A torch or two still guttered in brackets. Outside, the air was cool and moist; leaves brushed their faces as they walked down the drive. The market square was still silent, the stalls shuttered. A pig snuffled under a grocer's cart for rotten pomegranates.

"All right," Elicit said, drawing a deep breath. "The docks."

"Do we want everyone to know? We could walk. Or take a sedan."

For a second Elicit's mind rebelled. *You're mad, man! Your career! Algia and Eterneli! Your ghosts, your Ellipse seat, your* imrchim!

Damn me, he thought. *I've never been saner in my life.*

"We'd better walk," he said. "And take the back streets, not the concourses."

Erene turned to glance back at the mansion in the garden. "I wish I had said good-bye to Goquisite. No, I don't! What am I thinking?" She turned in his arms, scrutinizing each of the five mansions which surrounded the square. Their palatial weight oppressed Elicit. "But there is someone I do have to say good-bye to. You know who I mean."

"You still *have* someone to say good-bye to. I envy you."

"Oh, don't," Erene cuffed him gently. "Were she anyone else, we would be on our way to the docks now. But unlike the others, she will understand if we wake her up just to say good-bye."

The dawn came in through the windows of the seldom-used library in the back of the Chalice. It crept palely around the bookcases and woke Humi. She swam slowly toward wakefulness, aching from having slept with her head on one arm of a leather armchair and her legs draped over the other arm. Her facial fur was stiff with tears. After Arity left her, she had sat down in the one place in Tellury Crescent where she knew no one would hear her, buried her face in her hands, and cried her eyes out. Only after the sobs abated had it occurred to her that she had been crying with happiness.

A hand gripped the forearm where her head rested. Gray-furred fingers flattened the silvery puff sleeve, inches from her face: knotted, familiar fingers. Awareness flooded through her; she sat up, rubbing her eyes. Elicit stood over her, smiling kindly. Erene floated near-weightless on his arm.

"Elicit . . . ?" Her head spun.

"Don't ask any questions, darling," Erene said. "We've come to say goodbye."

"Gods, Erene!" Humi caught Erene's hand and pressed it to her lips. "Last night you looked so—unnatural—I was so afraid something was wrong."

"Something was wrong. And for hours I thought it had finished me."

"If something had happened to you while I was with him, I would have killed myself—"

"Who was he?"

She could hardly keep from smiling as she said his name. "Arity."

"Gods!" Elicit flinched back. "Humi, watch your step!"

She nodded as the smile drained fast from her face.

"My poor apprentice," Erene said. "I'm leaving you the twentieth seat. It's not a gift. You'll have to fight for it, and then fight to keep it. If you're crafty, sly, murderous, and underhanded, you could be the most powerful ghostier of this generation."

"What? You're—"

"I'm also leaving you the conspiracy. I'm leaving you the atheists, and I'm leaving you Gold Dagger and the Hangman—Belstem will tell you what we have with them."

"Erene, you're not *leaving* me—"

"Sssh." Erene embraced her, kissing her on the lips. The senior ghostier's heart pounded wildly against Humi's breast, convincing her that she was not dreaming. When Erene let go, Elicit hugged Humi. He squeezed her twice, quickly, and it felt as if some silent understanding passed between them. In three years, she had never understood him as well as she did now. He loved Erene. Just that. He loved her.

"Look after her for me, 'Lici," she whispered in his ear. "The most important thing in the world is for her to be happy." *Can you really say that?* she asked herself. *Whether you mean it, or not?*

If one woman's happiness isn't the most important thing in the world, what is?

Dizzy from the scent of his fur, she accompanied them to the bay windows.

"We'll have to leave this way," Elicit said. "The Crescent's awake now, and we would rather not be recognized."

"The gate to Reedmill Street should be unlocked," Humi said. "Go between the houses—you know the way. Watch out for the pig droppings."

"Now to the docks?" she heard Erene say as Elicit squeezed after her through a break in the fence that enclosed the Chalice's tiny backyard.

"Yes. Let me hold that up for you—"

Humi shut the bay window and rested her forehand on it, undecided as to whether to laugh or cry. As clearly as she had ever felt anything, she felt the drumming of Erene's heart under her hands, like a freed bird's wings. Her palms throbbed against the cold glass of the window. The sun rose for the second time that morning, flooding the sky with white, striking her eyes full of gold.

TWENTY-FOUR

The ghostiers' tales of triumph are not like anyone else's. One apprentice slept in the Ellipse chamber for a sixday in order to be there to claim his seat; another gave her master a grain of arsenic every day for a year; another bribed his master with gold to retire. Ziniquel Sevenash's cleverly evoked cardiac arrest also made legend. But unlike other things Humi was to do that year, her capture of the twentieth seat was simple and unremarkable.

All the following sixday, Goquisite assumed that Erene was holed up in her workshop in Tellury Crescent, ghosting the stunning young Piradean man with whom she had left the ball. Only the ghostiers knew what had really happened. Ghostiers rarely abdicated; murder was far more common. The discovery that Elicit had been so discontented with life in Tellury Crescent that he had chosen Erene over ghosting, over his own apprentices, over political power, unsettled older ghostiers like Rita and Beisa. It threatened their monopoly on each other's love and death; even though both of the escapees were *imrchim*, they had been able to leave the rest of the *imrchim* without qualms.

To reassert their solidarity, the ghostiers had to reach a consensus. After a wracking discussion, they accorded Elicit's seat to Trisizim, Mory's apprentice. He was eighteen now, unusually talented, his only drawback his extreme introversion. But he would simply have to learn politics by doing. Biting his lip, he agreed in a mumble, his black bangs falling over his eyes.

Owen was not fit to take on the responsibilities that came with the twentieth seat, so by a series of deceptions, Erene's and Elicit's elopement was kept from him. It was kept from Algia, too. No one should have the seat but Humi.

For once she had no doubts of her own worth. The fire of Arity's love burned them out of her. She had never felt so confident of her own ability to keep all of Erene's irons in the fire, and her own, too, floating through the days when Erene was still supposed to be in Delta City with a serenity that made people look twice at her and smile.

She spent her nights with the *auchresh*. She seemed to have stopped needing more than a couple of hours of sleep. Arity both nourished and refreshed her.

He worried for her, too. He was the only Incarnation who knew Erene was gone. They had agreed, with the rest of the ghostiers, that it should be kept from the others, lest they tell the atheists. If Belstem knew that Erene was not dead, he would overturn heaven and earth to get her back. Humi was loath to have it widely supposed that she had killed Erene, but she could see that it was unavoidable.

On one of these waiting days, when the city seemed suspended in amber, Humi got a letter from Elicit. The courier dove flew into her hands as she leaned out the window at dawn. She untied the little parcel from its leg and let the bird go. "This is the last time you will hear from us," she read in tiny script. "We have taken passage on a fast clipper to Grussels. The first day out, we were married by a flamen. We think that Erene is pregnant. Tell Algia to look after Eterneli. Luck go with you, *imrchu.*"

The Ellipse session was Dividay night. Humi got to the Chamber before anyone else and lowered herself into Erene's seat. On either side of her, Marasthizinith and Puritanism's leman Auspi looked daggers at her. Everyone else pretended to ignore her presence. She waited, the certainty of success cooling her blood, until Arity had officially opened the council "in lieu of the Divinarch, whose poor health deprives us yet again of his company." Then he nodded briefly at her.

She stood up, gripping the table. The torches flared; soot drifted over the table of refreshments beside the door. "I should like to make a proclamation. Serenity Gentle is dead. I, Humility Garden, her apprentice, claim her seat and her status as senior ghostier by virtue of three years' training in her workshop."

There was a dead silence.

She caught Ziniquel's eye. He glowed with pride. *Three years to master,* he mouthed. *Nobody has ever done it.*

And through the soundproofed glass of Owen's alcove, she felt his glare of sheer murder.

Then Tris rose to his feet. "And I, Trisizim Sepal, apprentice of Mory Carmine, claim the seat and the status of Felicitous Paean by virtue of seven years' training in Mory Carmine's workshop." He kept his head up, his bangs tucked behind his ears, staring proudly around the Chamber. "Are there any challengers?"

There were not. Humi had the feeling that Tris's claim had been more of an aftershock; everyone was still reeling from her own pronouncement. Silence filled the Chamber.

Her triumph rang like a thousand little bells in her ears.

After the session—an absurdly mundane discussion of the laws which had to be introduced to limit free copying of books, yet another of the trivial things which Erene and Goquisite had dreamed up to fritter away the time of the Divinarch's illness—she stayed alone in the Chamber, resting her head on the table. The wooden surface was smooth and black from generations of fingers. The seat of her chair was smooth and black from generations of behinds.

She reached under the table and fingered the "20" carved on her very own voting stone in its little niche. *In three years, you too can become the most powerful human in the Divinarchy,* she thought wryly. *In three years.*

She caught her breath, struck dumb by the sheer odds against it.

At last she stumbled out of the Chamber into the silence of the Old Palace's innards. Down the infinite length of the corridor torches flared, one after another until the bright spots fuzzed into a single yellow glow. Here in the very nexus of the human world, she could not smell the sea, though it was so close. Only soot.

She lay with Arity in the Divine Guards' quarters. The great room was nearly deserted, as it was early morning for the Guards, and most of them had to be elsewhere, watching for civil reactions to Humi's pronouncement. "Did you see Pati's face when you stood up?" Arity asked.

She lay flat on her back, staring at the shadowed ceiling.

"He was delighted. He expects your full support—something that he never had from Erene." Arity's voice was low, troubled. "How are you going to manage? Belstem Summer will expect you to dedicate yourself to him, the way Erene did. And now you are senior ghostier, so you will have to dedicate yourself to the ghostiers or lose them as Erene did. Why did you take the seat, my Humi?"

She made her voice bright. "Come on! Do you think I am mad, to turn it down? Or even worse, to let Owen or Algia get it? I think you think Owen could handle it better than I could. Don't you? Huh?"

"I would rather see him die than you—"

She hissed at him, "I had no choice!" Then, embarrassed by her admission, she wrapped her arms around his neck and pulled him down. They lay naked on the big circular bed platform. She smelled tobacco smoke ingrained in his skin. "But as long as I have you," she whispered, "I can do anything."

"You will always have me. I'm not so sure about the other." He sighed, and stroked her thigh. On the other side of the room, someone was quietly practicing the *ouzal*, the lutelike instrument of Kithrilindu. "No one ever said that it's impossible to sit on a fence, darling. I just wish it weren't you who had to do it. That's all." He lowered his mouth to hers, and they made love in silence, for once unwatched.

The Sky Cock tavern seethed with angry voices. Hope perched in the shadows of the rafters, looking down at the calm ghostiers and furious atheists. She supposed the atheists' violent reaction was justified: after all, Humi had killed Erene, who had been both their leader and their prodigy. Not even Hope had expected such a thing from her. But she supposed it was the ghostiers' way. Certainly, *they* seemed calm enough as they watched the fracas. Quailing before his eminent guests, the innkeeper hadn't dared even to offer them drinks. "Wine, you disrespectful slug!" Belstem snarled. "And plenty of it!"

Goquisite paced the room, dark cloak and hair flying as she swung about. "We cannot allow it. It is unthinkable! She must be displaced!"

Pieti gave her a pitying look. "It is the way of the ghostiers, Goquisite. You resent her merely because she murdered your friend." He leaned back in the straw-stuffed chair, cuddling his little daughter, who (long inured to bickering councillors) stood solid as a little ghost against his leg. "In terms of the conspiracy, is there any real reason we need Erene rather than Humi? Is not the fact that we have the senior ghostier on our side the most important thing?"

"*I* think so," the little girl said. To Hope, she was more interesting than all her quarreling elders. The Maiden watched closely as the ghostier girl Eternelipizaran—whose face was still tear-streaked from Elicit's death—smiled at her. It was obviously a tentative offer of communication, despite the fact that Eternelipizaran was a good five years older, but Pieti's daughter instantly quailed, hiding her head in her "father's" lap. Hope's heart ached for both girls. One stunted by the crush of Elicit Paean's expectations, the other pressed transparent by Councillor Seaade's gold-encrusted upbringing. *But if I had a child,* she thought, *not a Foundling, a real child— it would grow up just as warped as either of these little girls, here among the* wrchrethrim. *Who am I to criticize?* And the old familiar pang shot through her heart. For of course it was impossible.

No, Hope, you can't really have a baby, that was just a story your *breideii* was telling you. The female equipment in your body is fundamentally impaired. That's why the predators cast you out. You wouldn't even be a woman, mentally speaking, if you hadn't learned it from the humans. The *iuim* of the isolated heavens are not "feminine." They don't wear dresses or submit to masculine power. They don't manipulate their men with smiles and words. They don't bear children. But it doesn't matter. Mortals are so puny that reproduction has to be the raison d'être of each of their lives, while *we* can devote our time to philosophy and art and having fun. Why should you waste your life tending brats?

Yet the longing for children was something all *auchresh* (and especially, Hope maintained, females) knew intimately, like an inner emptiness.

The room snapped back into focus in her eyes as Goquisite paused directly beneath her perch to glare at Pieti. "Do you dare to call Erene my *friend?* She was the sister of my heart." Her voice shook. "We would have spent our old age together—"

"Don't be cloying," Pieti barked. "You're putting it on. Erene was acting so strangely in those last days that you're as glad as not she's gone. Because she was embarrassing you. Isn't that right?"

"*Oh!*" Goquisite hid her face in her hands.

"Dear, *I* understand." Maras got up and tried to put a consoling arm around Goquisite's shoulders. No one could accuse Maras of piety these days: she was a dedicated member of the conspiracy, and she revered Goquisite, striving to emulate her poise and urbanity. She dressed to the nines. In gatherings of lesser socialites, Hope had seen her shine—but beside Goquisite, she was revealed to be in horse-faced middle age, her veneer of sophistication crumpled. Goquisite flinched from her embrace. Maras had to settle for an anxious gaze into the councillor's eyes. "We understand your sorrow and sympathize with your anger—"

"You do *not* understand!" Goquisite's voice burned. "You are a pretentious featherhead! But at least you agree that Humility must go! It is ridiculous to suppose that an untried girl can cope with everything Errie did! She has severely overstepped herself—"

"I think she has not." Fra's voice came like cool wind. "It would be wise for you to take into account that after Humi killed Erene, we discussed her among ourselves, and we decided that her abilities qualify her. She has been making ghosts for three years. That is more qualification than any of *us* had when we acceded to Ellipse."

"Don't tell them about the ghosts!" Rita hissed.

"It has to come out sometime." Emni's voice was light and strong. "All those ghosts you believed were Erene's—they were Humi's. Did your fur stand on end to feel their emotions? It was Humi who reached into your soul. Did you clamor to be the next to receive one of her masterpieces? In private, Erene and Humi laughed at you."

The atheists were still, thunderstruck. Hope shifted her knee off a splinter. She had known about the ghosts, of course—but of those below, only Goquisite seemed to have shared the secret.

"In other words," said Fra drily into the silence, "Humi is fully worthy of her position. She has already proved herself to you, even if you did not know it. And there is nothing, miladies and milords, that you can do about it."

Silence.

"Well, maybe," Marasthizinith Crane said timidly. "She might be the start of an infusion of young blood . . . this might not be *all* bad!"

"I back the girl," Belstem said unexpectedly. "You ghostiers are all getting old. It's been far too long since any of you killed each other. Unhealthy, as far as my readings into your history show." Leaning on the mantelpiece, warming his haunches, he spoke into his glass of wine. "Pity Erene and Elicit had to be the first to go. Good councillors. On the other hand, the Calvarese kid seems bright, and as for Humi, she looks like the best choice anyone could have made to replace Erene. If she's been making all those ghosts she's gotta be competent." Unspoken was, *I think we've traded a faltering ally for a fresh one.* "Put that in your pipes and smoke it." He turned back to the fire.

But she's not on your side, Summer, Hope thought. *She's on ours.*

Goquisite stepped with brittle grace to an easy chair and sank down. A smell of mustiness rose; she waved it away. Hope stifled a sneeze. "Well, you have made your position clear, Belstem. That being the case, we should perhaps plan Erene's funeral in such a manner that it can double as Humi's inauguration ball." Her sarcasm was heavy. "That is what the ghostiers would do, is it not?"

"You are well versed in our customs, milady," Ziniquel said. He straddled his chair, long legs sticking out, ignoring her sarcasm. "And if you offered to host the affair, I'm sure Humi would be most obliged."

"I have offered, I believe." Hope leaned dangerously far out of the shadows to see Goquisite's eyes. They were dead as rotten wood. "Does tomorrow night suit?" Goquisite brushed away Maras's objections. "I assure you, I am used to organizing *sociales* on such short notice." She laughed humorlessly.

Hope knew where Arity and Humi were. She shut her eyes, visualizing the scarred wood floor, the empty air in the Divine Guards' quarters. She hoped not too many *auchresh* were there. Ugly accidents could happen when one *teth*'d into crowds. She dropped off the rafter, wings snapping open with a *thump* that brought the humans' heads up, and for the barest fraction of a second she was flying.

TWENTY-FIVE

Humi was so deeply in love that for many sixdays she could overlook small things. For instance, the fact that the other two-thirds of the conspiracy did not trust her. Goquisite hated her for (so she thought) killing Erene. Belstem would not divulge his reasons for treating her like an enemy, to be tolerated and used but not trusted. Humi guessed that part of his irritability stemmed from the fact that Aneisneida and Soderingal Nearecloud, Gold Dagger's bastard, were now seen everywhere together, boating, dancing, shopping. They were engaged. But that made Belstem's willfulness no less trying. It was a strange change from the days of her apprenticehood, when, under the guise of various personas, she had enjoyed acceptance and even popularity in Antiprophet Square. But now she had killed off most of them. Sometimes she forgot that Humility Garden was not supposed to be a socialite, a practiced dissembler, but a raw, pious young ghostier, clay for the conspiracy to mold. But she had never been that. When had acting so many characters turned her real self into a persona?

Only alone with Arity could she be what she thought might be her *real* self.

They gave in to wild impulses together. She had never felt so free as when, in the middle of one of Belstem's dinners, Arity caught her eye. She reached under the table and closed her fingers around his hand. "Let's get out of here," he mouthed. "Somewhere wet."

One after the other, they excused themselves, and in the gilded washroom Arity put his arms around her and she felt herself dissolve and they were in the middle of a wide green plain with a thunderstorm rumbling overhead. Rain always pounded Veretry, even when Delta City was cracked and dry. They rolled naked in the grass. The storm needled her bare back, stimulating her to a height far above any place her ghosts' caresses had taken her, in the days when she made hungry love to them rather than coldheartedly seducing them. They lay locked together on the soaked grass, feeding from each other's mouths, she grabbing his buttocks, pulling him deeper and deeper inside her, as if she could fuse them into one being.

The whole city knew about them. From what the *imrchim* told her, they were a scandal in Marshtown, and only the ghostiers' efforts kept the flamens from publicly denouncing her. As it was the flamens were making strange, impenetrable statements about Arity. It would be unthinkable for them to condemn a god—but prophecy obeyed no such rules. And gossip said that several recent prophecies, both in Delta City and elsewhere, had mentioned Arity's name.

Humi had little time to listen to gossip. Since she was the youngest, Goquisite and Belstem unloaded most of the conspiracy's donkey-work on her. This meant numerous visits to Gold Dagger and his peers—men either puffy or sharkish from too much drink, jingling with money. She detested them.

Gradually, the murderous heat of summer boiled away, leaving the city at the mercy of a dry, brown autumn. Humi envied Arity's fatalistic disregard for politics. Each day, she seemed to find herself deeper embroiled in all her connections. Bronze Water and Broken Bird were the saving of her. She had not really known them before, but now, for some reason ("They want to steal you from Pati," Arity said cynically), they decided that she was worth cultivating. Seasoned diplomats both, they gave unstintingly of their expertise. If not for them, she couldn't have figured out how to play Pati off against Belstem in Ellipse. Certainly she couldn't have prevented the councillors from realizing just who instigated the showdowns that left nearly every session in a shambles. Maybe the tactics were destructive. But Humi could see no other way to avoid being torn in half—if not in thirds, so many people had claims on her, or quarters.

And it seemed to be working, keeping the Ellipse just off the boil, even though floors and floors away, the Divinarch complained through the Guards of being waked up by the shouting. He had deteriorated so much that now he slept at night, like a mortal.

One packed-sand street made up the northernmost town in the world: Juwl, on the coast of Calvary. Juwl's beach kissed the equator. Here the men worked barren fields, not mines. Here there was no mining machinery, nor markets, nor traders. Leather doors flapped in a wind that never stopped. In the evenings, the women walked to the stony strip of beach and called their sea hens. And the hens came flying in flocks, the roosters leading, like flames in their blue metallic feathers, over the black waves that rolled to the end of the earth.

Transcendence stood in the middle of a small herb patch behind one of the huts, staring blindly at the streaked evening sky, his white hair tangled down his back. His weathered throat jumped. His bare feet crushed a pungent scent of thyme from the herbs.

Thani knelt in the back door of the hut, hands clasped in a posture of supplication. Her whole body screamed for her to relax. The stresses of her prophetic fit this afternoon had racked her beyond any pain that she remembered, beyond any pain she had thought possible. She had to regain Transcendence's trust. Behind her, the children of the town shuffled and whispered. *If only the brats would go away!* She checked herself. *Gods, Thani, haven't you blasphemed enough today?*

At that reminder, tears spilled down her cheeks. "Transcendence, I take it back!" she called. "I can be pious again for you, if you'll just let me try!"

"You cannot expect to blaspheme against prophecy and escape twice, leman. When you were fourteen, I excused you because of your youth. This time, the offense is unpardonable." His voice was old, cracked. She winced to hear it. But at least she had got him talking.

"I believe in my prophecy! I believe in the guidance of the gods." If she could only get him to relent—"I'll go to Delta City! I'll do what I said had to be done! You don't even have to come with me, I'll do it by my—"

"Do you really believe, leman, that I would let you go alone?" His voice was cold. "You have already proven yourself untrustworthy."

"Oh, Godsbrother!" She was sobbing uncontrollably. The wind blew hot on her back. She fell face first to the ground, digging her fingers into the dry, sandy earth, breathing in lemon-scented gulps of air. "Please— please—"

She felt him step farther away. His voice throbbed. "Why? Gods, why must it be thus?" She knew he was speaking in the direction of the salt, which lay so close to the sea here that one could see it from the tops of the hills behind the town. "Not only for my leman to be given to prophecy, but for her to blaspheme against her own words! She was once so dear to me. Why must she constantly deny your will? Why can she not acquiesce to the prophecy, which is nothing less than your voices?"

Because it sounds so improbable! Because I'm not yet salt-eyed, and so I can't be sure! For the first time in her life, the salt pilgrimage she might have to make loomed ahead of her like a salvation, not a doom. *I want to understand. I want to so badly.*

She stared into the darkness enclosed by her arms on the earth.

Transcendence bent and touched her back with an arthritic finger. There was no gentleness in that poke. "Leman, we will obey the prophecy. He has fallen from godhood. He must die."

"I told you I would—"

"But you are a blasphemer. You will fulfill the prophecy because I tell you to: I will not have you to try to ingratiate yourself with me."

Giving in to the anguish of her body, she flopped flat, rolling onto her back, and wept. The tears ran down her cheeks into her hair. Overhead the clouds ran away from the salt like water into the sky. The black-brown faces of the children intruded into her sight, in a circle like the mouth of a well high above her, asking her in their high, guttural voices if she was all right.

And out of the kissing, as if out of a forge, had emerged a chain whose red-hot links bound Humi and Arity together so powerfully that, Humi thought, looking down at herself as if from a distance as she lay in his arms on the long afternoons when she should have been going about the business of the Ellipse, nothing, she thought, *nothing* could ever separate them. Had Erene and Elicit felt this way? Frightening thought. Could she escape even if she wanted to?

But she did not want to. She hated the thought even of moving enough to be reminded that they possessed two separate bodies. So she did not know if it was possible to get away. Dusty skewers of sunlight pierced between the black drapes with which she had hung the walls of her Tellury Crescent boudoir, blocking out all the sounds from the street, so that it felt as if the room hung in nothingness, suspended on the tips of a dozen swords like a powdery black gourd.

And at night Arity took her harvesting with the *mainrauim* of Wind Gully Heaven. By starlight the salt forest in Kithrilindu looked much like the Chrumecountry around Delta City: fruits like transparent organs strung trees and bushes, and animals crashed away through the undergrowth, and owls' eyes caught the starlight as the caroling voices of the *mainrauim* startled them from their roosts. Humi and Arity fell behind, holding hands, eyes filled with starlight.

"Should we have let so many people know about us?" she asked finally. "Sometimes I feel as if this is too good to last."

Arity pulled a friccas fruit off a bush and sank his fangs into it. He offered her some.

"By the Power, I envy you, Ari!"

His voice was grave as he pulled her close. "It's not that I don't worry. I do. But I don't see any reason to let them spoil our time together. This is all we have in the world, when you come down to it. The amount of time we can spend together before we die." Tossing the friccas fruit into the shadows, he took hold of her face and lifted her on her toes to kiss her. She tasted the tangy juice. "What is the Throne?" he said into her lips. "A hunk of wood and metal. It doesn't deserve so much of your worry."

"When I'm with you, I know you're right. But as soon as we're apart— Power, I should be at Belstem's right now."

"You shouldn't be anywhere but here." They stopped walking. The voices of the *mainrauim* receded into the distance. The air was pleasantly cool and dewy.

"It's all right for you," she said. "You don't *care*. People look at me on the streets and I hear them whispering, *There goes the councillor who fucks a god*." Her voice trembled with bitterness.

"Do you really care what they say?"

"Yes! I do! I can't stand being this vulnerable!" Around them the forest swayed and whispered. Starlight filtered down through the trees, and Humi dropped her face into her hands. "I wish—I wish I had my personas back—"

Instantly Arity pulled her close, caressing her as if her misery were dirt to be smoothed out of her fur. "Humi! Tell me. Tell me now."

"I'm afraid." Tears choked her. She had to get it out. "I love you too much."

"Oh, Power," he said distractedly. "I love you too much, too! But do you know how lucky we are to be able to say that? This is the single best thing that could have happened to either of us."

She knew. Oh, she knew. And the knowledge dried the tears in her eyes like a blast of hot wind.

"You can't control this kind of thing."

"No." She let her head fall back on his shoulder, standing there in his arms. A new cluster of talons on his neck pricked her ear as she gazed up through the foliage of the salt trees to the stars. "You can't, can you?" Constellations: Skyheart. The Wheel.

"They're too close," Pati said, standing at Hope's side by the wall of the Rimmear tavern. "Too close by far." His tone suggested that Arity and Humi had ventured too near one of the flaming spots on the stretches of fire salt to be found in the middle of Uarech. But they were only laughing and betting with their neighbors by the night-colored arches of the windows, where tables and chairs had been pushed back so that the patrons of the tavern could hold mouse races. "It can't last."

"Five says it can," Hope said. "They're *irissim*. Can't you tell?"

"A god and a mortal, *irissim*? Ha! Arity's infatuated. I can see that. And infatuations at this level are dangerous." He clicked his tongue.

"Pati," Hope said with a sinking of the heart. "What are you thinking?"

He smiled at her with all his teeth.

She quivered her wings in the limited space between her back and the wall. She did not like Rimmear. The heat made her tired. The *auchresh* here talked too much, too fast, and one had to *pay* for a glass of tea or a pipe of tobacco. *Pay*, for the Power's sake! With money! She returned to the salt to get *away* from the ugly, mercenary aspects of Delta City! She wanted to be in Divaring Below right now, splashing through the shallows of the lake under the open stars. She resented Pati for making her come all the way to Calvary on this petty spying trip.

"Arity should be careful," Pati said. "It's quite possible she means to take advantage of him."

"Can't you stop suspecting anyone for one moment? It looks perfectly simple to me. They're in love."

A Foundling passed in front of them. Except for a flapping apron, it was stark naked. It tugged Pati's shirt and pointed to a vacant table. Pati nodded to the Foundling, seized Hope by the wrist and swooped between the patrons to release her over one of the amber saltwood chairs so that she floated down like a piece of silk. She put her thin elbows onto the table and rested her chin in her hands.

"Poor Hope. She knows all about unfair advantages." Pati smiled, the white skin around his eyes crinkling with affection and pity.

"I came of my own free will," she snapped, not moving her head. She didn't know why she kept on trying to hold her own. Some innate fear of being totally dissolved in his will. Ridiculous: he already knew all about her, everything she could think of, except maybe her secret desire to have a child, and *no one* knew that. Apart from that cavity in the middle of her body, she was his creature.

He signaled the Foundling. "A glass of *khath* for the *iu!*" It wrinkled its nose, as if to say that *iuim* got no special treatment here in Rimmear, thank you, but it brought the *khath* anyhow. Pati tossed it a coin. Hope gulped gratefully at the clear liquid.

"I think we have to pry them apart somehow." Pati watched her drink. "Neither of them is as effective in Ellipse as they both were before this foolishness started. And I don't like the way they have got out of my control."

She blinked at him, that he would sit there and say that. "Your arrogance defies belief."

"Whenever he comes to the quarters, he brings her. They're inseparable. It could have something to do with Councillor Gentle's death—Humility needs someone to latch on to, if you see what I mean—but I wouldn't bet on that. No, it's just foolishness, such as Ari has always been prone to."

Hope turned her head and looked through the fog of smoke. Humi had just placed a winning bet. The group of Uarechians with whom they were racing mice erupted in loud *auchresh* laughter, showing broken teeth in mutated mouths. Arity pinned Humi against one of the arches and planted a victory kiss on her lips. Her closed eyelids trembled, purple with a frighteningly disproportionate ecstasy. Hope hugged herself. Even across the tavern, the sight singed some tender thing in her. Being excluded inspired both relief and sadness that she would never be part of something similar. She was too old now.

"They're doing what should not be done." Pati's face was a pinched white beak. He stared past her, unconsciously gripping the edge of the table so hard that his nails were purple. "*Irissim.* It's blasphemy."

"Stop it. 'Gods'! This would be a better world if that word had never been invented." She glanced around. "Look at this Heaven. Pimps, beggars, *ghauthi keres*, look at that man slapping the Foundling's buttocks, the poor little thing has so many bruises—if your precious flamens *did* come here after they died, what would they think? They'd die again, of shock!"

"It should not be. It cannot be. But they are doing it." He reached out and grabbed her *khath*, drained it in a sucking gulp. "He is Heir. We cannot let him open himself up to scorn and censure this way. The gods must remain ineffable." She heard something crack in his hand; startled, he looked down. A piece of the edge of the perforated stone table lay in his palm, blood welling up around it from a ragged gash. Hope watched curiously as a flush came over his face and he closed his fist around the splinter.

"You understand nothing about human emotions, do you, Pati?" she said.

"Why should I?" A spasm of pain crossed his face. He clasped his good hand around the injured one. "I'm not human."

She felt tiny feet scurry over her toes. Looking down, she saw an escaped racing mouse sitting under the table, lapping the drops of blood that fell regularly to the floor. "We have to remove this distraction, Hope," he said. And she heard that thing she had never thought to hear in his voice again as he said, "We can't let Ari make himself this vulnerable." A tiny transparent creature, the mouse grew solid as it consumed the viscous white blood, as if it were coming into existence. *Power*, Hope thought, *I am weak.*

TWENTY-SIX

"You and Arity make a nice couple," Rita said to Humi one night, "but don't get a swelled head."

"What would I do without you, Rita?" Humi said sincerely.

She knew the older ghostier was right. So the first day that Arity had to go alone into the salt, she disguised herself as her first persona of all: Rosi, who had been Erene's personal maid. Dabbing green facedust on her nose, she grinned at herself in the mirror. *I can still do this! Remember those days . . .*

The sun poured in like honey through the windows. The frills she had had put up all over the room, to make it as different as possible from the black *auchresh* nest of her Tellury Crescent boudoir, hung immobile like the petals of flowers when there is no wind. Sitting here disguising herself reminded her of Erene. Dressing to go out at night, nudging each other for space before the mirror . . . lazily nibbling chunks of melon for breakfast, those mornings when Goquisite was away . . . her sitting at Erene's feet before the hearth, a beauty treatise splayed face-down on her lap, telling her master the irritations of her day . . .

Though she had not admitted it to herself as long as Erene "lived," Humi's apprentice status had helped her preserve certain traits of childhood. Now she really had left those things behind. She could no longer hide behind Erene. She had to take whatever Delta City threw at her full in the face, as Humility Garden.

But not today.

She slipped on houseshoes and wandered through the familiar, soothing luxury of the suite to the door that she had had knocked into the back staircase. Male and female domestics passed up and down all day.

"Hey, Rosi! Ain't seen you in months!"

"Where you been? Goin' down to the kitchen? I'll come see you when I finish these fly-papers."

"Ain't seen you about, Rosi—where you been?"

Humi grinned at the last speaker, Goquisite's room valet. "Sick."

He shifted the hot-water buckets he carried. "Pity 'bout Milady Erene, ain't it? Never would've thought that quiet little apprentice of hers 'ud do her in."

Humi winced. "Yeah, well, the apprentice's taken me on now. I ain't complainin'."

"Hah! Nor'd I, if I was you!" He shrugged to readjust the buckets and went on his way. Humi continued down to the back kitchen, where the servants gathered when their duties permitted. "Hey, Rosi!" greeted her when she entered. Grinning, she accepted a seat by the enormous cookfire, where a spit of chihuahuas sizzled for the dinner party she would attend as herself that evening. She felt good. A different kind of good. The denizens of the kitchen were so unlike the atheistic councillors, all of whom had spent their childhoods in similar circumstances before being chosen as lemans. Strange how these commoners weren't resentful of the children of their class who had created a new, elite society around themselves. Rather, they were proud of them. There wasn't a one of these men and women who didn't speak of Goquisite as if she were his or her own daughter or cousin.

Smiling, Humi listened to the story of somebody's sister's wedding. One of the new atheistic ceremonies, held indoors. It sounded as though it had actually been beautiful.

"Hey, Rosi!" It was Deservi, one of the undercooks. "Didja meet God-sister Philanthropy?"

The flamen sat at the big, crudely built kitchen table, drinking a mug of broth. She was a woman of heavy build with turquoise fur, in a linen robe, her leman a butter-braided girl of twelve. It amazed Humi how the kitchen workers bobbed their heads whenever they passed her chair, even though they were mostly atheists. Childhood values were slow to die. "Greetin's, Godsister," she said respectfully.

"It's a long morning we've had," the leman said. "Many miracles. There's a sight of suffering in this city."

From her accent and her pale fur, Humi guessed the girl to be Icelandic. Humi's ignorance of Iceland—and in fact, most of the Divinarchy—was a severe drawback to her as a politician. None of the other councillors was any better off, but almost unconsciously she decided to take this opportunity to learn more. "Godsister? How long've you been in the city?"

"Several weeks." The flamen raised her head. "Cook, have you anything stronger than broth?"

"Wine? Surely. Rosi, you want some too?" Deservi swooped two cups out of the stone sluice where a boy was washing dishes and poured from a stone bottle. The wine was a full-bodied red, light in color, sweet-smelling. As Deservi handed it to her, Humi blinked. The point of contact between her fingers and the mug seemed to have flashed purple. But of course it had only been her eyes. She should stop skimping on sleep. "Cheers, God-sister," she said, and raised the glass and drained it.

Why had everyone in the kitchen gone silent?

She twisted on her stool, trying to speak, staring at their faces. It was as if a cylinder of glass had been dropped around her, thickening by the second.

Darker . . .

Dark, opaque glass . . .

Silence. As if her ears were clogged with wool.

The most curious feeling.

She stirred a little.

A prickling . . . a tingling . . . As if something as thin and bubbly as champagne is running in my veins. I wonder if I should open my eyes? Hmm . . . an interesting challenge. Yes, I think I will.

The heavy-jawed, homely face of Deservi peered at her, green eyes filled with worry.

Humi blinked and said, "Deservi, there's an odd taste in my mouth. I don't think that wine can have been very good."

The cook's face lit up, and she flew out of Humi's field of vision. "She's awright! Talkin' a bit funny, but awright! C'mere everyone, gimme a hand—"

"That's quite all right." But Humi's limbs were shaky. She used Deservi's arms to pull herself upright. She was sitting on the grimy cushions in the chimney-nook. She rubbed her hands, breathing in the familiar scents of roast meat and chopped greens. "What on earth happened?"

"It were the Godsister as saved you." The dish-washer boy pointed reverently to the kitchen table. The robed shape sat slumped, head on arms, with the lamen bending anxiously over her. "Me dad says they're nought but frauds, but I'd never seen one of 'em work 'er tricks before. I swear I'll nivver chuck rotten fruits at 'em agin, Rosi. She saved ya."

Scandalizing that any child should reach adolescence without having seen a miracle! Yet for all her saltside birth, and her deep though deeply altered piety, Humi felt awed and a little frightened that a miracle had finally been worked on *her.* She'd been a healthy child; this was the first time in her life. So *that* had been the sensation. A tickly flood of bubbles surrounding her, flowing through her mouth and nose into her blood, cleansing it. She dropped to her knees to look up into the flamen's face. "Are you all right, Godsister?" To the leman—"Is she exhausted?"

"Aye, she's so. She was already tired but she couldna let you die. You was poisoned, know that?"

Gods! She turned back to the room. "Where did that wine come from?"

"I dunno," Deservi said. "Why? It couldn't of been that. We've been drinkin' it for days."

It could have been nothing else. That flash—

Someone had changed the cup that Deservi extended for the cup that reached Humi's hand. But that person must have been able to *teth*˝. And if they had been here, however briefly, they had seen the flamen. They had known that Humi would be saved. The fire flickered, sizzling with lard dripping from the chihuahuas. Humi needed Arity. She needed his arms around her.

She shut her eyes and clenched her teeth. *Don't wreck your disguise!* As it was, they might put two and two together.

"Aaah . . ." The flamen lifted her head. The salt crystals glowed white against the rare, south-Veretrean turquoise color of her fur. Once, Godsister Philanthropy had been very beautiful. "My child, stand up." Humi got to her feet. "Do you know who would have wanted to do such a thing, and to you, of all people?" She shook her head. The Godsister wrapped her arm around her leman, who helped her to her feet. "I shall leave now, my friends. You have been good to me. I swear, I shall remember the feel of that poison for the rest of my life. It would have taken you like a numbing sleep, kindly, but none the less deadly."

"What was it?" Humi whispered. As a ghostier she knew every poison that could be swallowed, injected, or applied to the body. But many had no taste or smell.

"I would not know it by name," Philanthropy began, but the leman interjected, "A salt poison, Godsister. Those be the worst. Almond-flower."

The flamen smiled. "Why, Ragran, I did not know you were such an expert on poisons!"

"I'd an uncle that was an atheist pharmacist," the girl said as they moved toward the door.

Deservi smiled. "You just sit right back down, Godsister, till you feel better, an' you can have a share of our evenin' meal." She turned to the head cook, fat, elderly Alour. "Can't she, ma'm?"

"O' course." Alour lifted her pine-green jowls. "We always 'elp them what 'elps ours, and Rosi's one of ours. O' course the Godsister can stay."

But Humi clutched herself, thinking, *Almond-flower. What if it had been salt aconite, which kills in a third of a second flat? What then?*

*   *   *

But she never even told Arity about the incident. It was knocked out of her mind by the happenings of the next day. On a clear jewel of a morning with sharp edges, when the sky over Delta City looked like strong tea and the air tasted of smoke (for some of the fields on the mainland were so dry that spontaneous combustion was occurring), Owen murdered Rita.

It was past two in the afternoon. Nearly everyone in the city was outside—Humi had gone with the other ghostiers to bathe off the Marshtown jetties—when it happened. Owen told them exactly what he had done, afterward, in salacious detail. He came up behind Rita as she sat reading on the roof of Thaumagery House, the book a handspan from her nose, skirts rucked to her thighs so that her withered old legs could feel the sun, and stabbed her in the heart. Straightforward, cold-blooded, and so easy it was almost like cheating.

When he showed off the corpse, washed and dried, it was such a shock to discover Rita had had gray hair that no one could speak.

He claimed the seat—number 12—that very evening. Not a single councillor, neither atheist nor flamen nor ghostier nor god, greeted his claim with applause. Only, perhaps, Eterneli in her alcove, who had started sleeping with him though she was only thirteen. Rita had been a staunch supporter of the flamenhood, and therefore an enemy of the atheists, but not even they could deny that she had seen the fair side of every debate and had had many years of wisdom in the ways of the Ellipse.

Humi felt her loss like a hard blow to the ribs. If it had been within her power, she would have barred Owen from taking the seat and put one of the twins in his place. Preferably Sol. He was chafing to attain master status, and she thought he was getting dangerous. But it ws not within her power, and Owen clearly could not care less whether anyone approved or not. He sat all evening with his arms folded, saying nothing, grinning like a cat which has gotten the cream after ten years of trying to knock it off the shelf.

Soon after, the weather broke. With the Divine Guards, Humi and Arity went to dance in the rain, high in Kithrilindu where the skies opened over mountains that had been worn to lace by years of cloudbursts. They somersaulted over the smooth, wet, white formations and slid down chutes, laughing. The whole day was remarkably free of tension between *auchresh*, and between Humi and the *auchresh*. For the first time since Rita's death, she felt that everything might still be all right.

But when she got home, fluffy-furred and lethargic, wearing someone else's silk uniform, she found the ghostiers crying in each other's arms. Sol had murdered Beisa and Emni.

And I knew, she thought, horror-stricken. *I knew he was becoming dangerous and I did nothing.*

Nothing I could have done.

Oh, Emni!

He sat amid them in the Chalice, elbows on knees, scowling from under his heavy white brows at anyone who seemed to be approaching. Thaumagery House was now empty but for him and Owen. "I wish them joy of each other!" Mory snarled, her nose running as she wept. "He had no need to kill Em too! Not her!"

"She was my friend." Humi hid her face in her arms. *I suppose Emni lay curled around his feet in the womb, after all.*

"You're missing the point," Ziniquel said miserably. "To kill not just the master, but the competition? It's not done."

The breakdown of tradition. Humi knew that that was half the crisis. After all, murder was the ghostiers' bosom friend; they never blanched when it poked its head up in their midst. This was their way of life. But seldom in living history had there been so few ghostiers as there were now. The *imrchim* were used to having numbers to cushion their interactions. Yet the thinning out of Tellury Crescent had a streamlining effect on their vote in Ellipse. Humi's leadership seemed less questionable to Sol, Owen, and Trisizim than it did to Mory and Ziniquel, who had served through Erene's term, or Fra, who had seen Molatio Ash inaugurated. And her reputation for shrewdness fooled Owen and Sol entirely. So they remained loyal.

Their old masters had the last laugh, though it echoed hollowly out of the grave.

And Emni, who was *not* dead, laughed unpleasantly between her teeth. Sol's poison had nearly killed her, but he'd skimped on the dose. That stinginess would be the death of him someday, Humi read in his sister's flashing eyes. Gentle Emni, laughing Emni, nursed secretly back to health by Fra in Melthirr House, wanted nothing more than to kill her brother.

But she would settle for an Ellipse seat.

Preferably a better seat than Sol's.

Perhaps Fra saw what was coming, and took the safe way out. Perhaps Emni, who still had a trace of softheartedness in her, presented him with an ultimatum. At any rate, at the first Ellipse session of winter, when sleet glittered in the torchlight and in wet tracks on the floor, Fra Canyonade abdicated in favor of Emni Southwind. As the Archipelagan woman stepped into the Chamber, demure in a yellow dress, she gave Sol a look of detestation that froze Humi all the way up at the top of the table.

"I could feel it in my bones," Humi said that night. She lay in Arity's arms, in the black-draped, salt-scented nest that was the only place she could get to sleep now. "Ari, I can't have this kind of enmity between them. They're worse than Erene and Zin ever were."

Absently Arity stroked her stomach. "They're beyond your control, love."

She pushed his hand away. "Perhaps. But Arity, if I could only hold them all in the hollow of my palm!"

The room whirled as he pulled her on top of him, clamping her face between his hands. His natural perfume stung her nostrils, rancid with fear. "Don't talk like that! Sometimes I *worry* about you!"

"All right." She lay still. "I won't. Let me go."

It seemed as though these months lasted for years. Humi scolded herself every time she did something reckless. *None of us is invulnerable! And who should know better than you, senior ghostier?* Locked away in a dark closet of her mind: the suspicious incidents, starting with the poisoned wine in Goquisite's kitchen and recurring at more or less regular intervals. The Divine Guard's pipe that had been too strong for her, the fish that hadn't been fresh enough, the syringe that had sprung a hairline crack. The ghost who had tried to retaliate. And a host of lesser things.

But she hadn't time for anyone who wanted her dead. She scarcely had time to be careful. All she could do was ride the crest of the wave as autumn bleached into winter. The icy weather wore on, and on. The stink of refuse hung sharp in the clear, cold air.

Ziniquel and Emni started a passionate love affair. Humi knew that he had always been fond of Emni, but because of her bond with Sol it had been impractical for him to reveal his feelings. Just as the twins had sworn, their bond was unbreakable—but now it was transformed from love into hatred. This was the moment for Zin to declare his love, and Humi didn't blame him for taking advantage of it. The pair became oblivious to the outside world, just as Humi and Arity had. Humi could look at them and smile, even as she wondered uncomfortably just how far she and Arity had come from that state.

Soon after Midwinter, while everyone in the city and the surrounding country was sleeping off their excesses, Algia got out of her narrow bed and crept through the wet Crescent to Thaumagery House. She climbed the stairs to Owen's room. Tears running down her face, she stabbed him in the throat fifteen times, so that his blood soaked the sheet and dripped onto the floor. Then she collapsed on his body, mingling her tears with his blood, weeping fit to wake the dead.

Humi had the story from Eterneli, who'd stood frozen in the door, watching everything. Algia hadn't thought to look around, though she had known that Eterni was sleeping with Owen, and it made perfect sense that she should be there.

Humi hated nothing worse than funerals. Especially when she did not want to admit to herself that she was not sorry for Owen's death. Not sorry to the point that she had had him buried in the pious tradition—easiest to do without making waves—though he had been an atheist.

The Godsbrother droned dolorously on; a Godsister waited nearby to take his place when his voice wore out. It would be hours yet until the coffin was laid in the ground of the great cemetery on the bank of the Chrume. A tree wept droplets down the neck of Humi's black mourning dress. Rowans and willows and hazels crowded among the grave statues, stretching away in the endless disorder of an abandoned statuary yard.

Fissures of self-doubt were beginning to creep over her golden bubble. She was unable to comfort Eterni. It was to Mory that the thirteen-year-old had first fled, weeping for her lover. Only then had Mory sought Humi. When her tears were exhausted, Eterneli went back to Algia in Melthirr House. Now they refused to leave one another. The illogic of it was stunning, but Humi supposed they recognized each other's grief. Algia said she was going to take Eterneli as apprentice.

Well, what difference did one more broken tradition make now? Humi, Emni, Mory, and Ziniquel had agreed that Algia had had to become a master, or else drop out of Tellury Crescent as Hem had done, or go insane. She was thirty-five. "I'm only twenty-eight," Mory said, "yet I'm the most experienced of us all now. It seems only yesterday that I was a new master, struggling to assert myself in Ellipse."

"I remember when you killed Isen. I was apprentice to Constance then." Ziniquel shook his head. "It doesn't seem natural. Five of us, one after another. Who would have said, Humi, that you would be the only one of us to gain the Ellipse without committing a murder?"

"You're forgetting Fra," Humi said forlornly. "He tells me he's very happy in his little house beside the Chrume . . ."

"Keeping bees!" Ziniquel looked as though he would burst with indignation. "How could anyone keep *bees* after having been a ghostier?"

"You're still young, Zin," Emni said tolerantly, breezily ignoring the fact that she herself was not yet twenty. "Maybe you'll understand why Fra made the choice he did, when it's *your* turn to get out while the going's good." She kissed him. He lifted his eyebrows but reciprocated the kiss. Gradually she pushed him deeper into the sofa, shifting onto his lap. Their affair was still at the stage where passion can attack without warning, irresistibly.

Mory caught Humi's eye, wryly amused. *He* is *still young.*

And Humi felt the panic of a toddler taking its first shaky steps, who looks for its parents and sees them turn once to wave before vanishing into a deep, black, impenetrable cave.

Of what kind of rabble am I senior ghostier now? Where are the wise, kind imrchim *among whom I found myself four years ago? Is it my fault everything has changed?*

"In Heaven!" finished the flamen to renewed wails from the gathering. Rain blotted Eterneli's headscarf and trickled down her cheeks, pasting her fur flat. She looked like a grown woman, with her bones showing. "All those whom we have ever lost, we shall meet in Heaven!"

My gods, Humi thought wryly. *I hope not.*

TWENTY-SEVEN

"Ari," Humi said, "I met my sister last night."

"Who?"

"Thankfulness. My little sister. She's in Delta City."

"What's she doing here?"

"She's a leman. She's here with her flamen."

"I'd like to meet her." He gazed through the flawed glass of a window in the Chalice, playing with the lace of his open-neck shirt, barefoot as always. His green ankles were dusty. The lead between the windowpanes dented his forehead. Behind them, the ghostiers read and talked quietly; a fire crackled in the hearth under the rudely carved mantel. "Perhaps when it stops raining, we can pay them a visit. Where are they—" he yawned— "where are they staying?"

"Ari," she said in vexation, "I wish you'd go to sleep!"

He looked quizzically at her.

"Pati hates it when you don't sleep with them!"

"Pati can go fuck himself. It makes sense for me to sleep on the same schedule as you. Otherwise, you *don't* sleep. And I can't stand it when you don't get enough rest."

She did not want to say that she was afraid Pati might be much angrier than Arity gave him credit for. "Your eyes look funny in the daylight," she said unhappily.

"Well, your eyes look funny *all* the time." She leaned her head on his knee. He tousled her hair.

"Don't," she said. "I gilded it fresh to go to Goquisite's tonight—"

"So now I can't even touch you?" But his voice was jesting. She pulled his hand down and kissed the clawed fingertips.

Earlier that afternoon—

She was wandering along the Lockreed Concourse, disguised once again as the Deltan maid Rosi, taking a much-needed break from the long-winded, beforehand discussions of the new regime that Belstem insisted on conducting. Delicious scents wafted to her nose from shopfronts and beverage vendors. She bought a cup of mutton broth. These days, she never ate at dinners or banquets, or even at tea parties: one could not know what had happened between the kitchen and one's mouth. But here, she saw the man chuck the meat into the cauldron, stir it, dip the pottery mug in, and put it steaming into her hands. The heat drove the winter chill out of her body. The taste brought Beaulieu back in a rush of memory. And she looked up and saw the flamen and leman standing on the corner of Lockreed and Bowery Crescent, the leman an unusually great distance ahead of the flamen, a sullen, sunbleached blond girl, very thin. She couldn't have looked less Domesdian. But Humi would have sworn—

No. It can't be.

She gulped her broth, keeping her head down. "You seen that white-headed flamen, there, before, friend?" she asked the customer on her left.

He pulled his lower lip, thinking. "Yeah. 'E's new around here. Stayin' someplace Godsbrother Puritanism put him up, from what I hear . . . don't know what he's doing in Christon. Name of Transubstantiation or Tranquillity, sump'n like that."

"Transcendence!" Humi yelped, and dropped her broth cup. The canyonlike, terraced buildings channeled the city's voices into a tapestry of sound, woven with scents—cooked meat, fish, toasted bulrushes, offal, ammonia, molten metal—through which she slipped on her way to the corner. She circled a boy carrying a huge stack of dried sandfish and touched the blond leman's shoulder.

The girl spun, brows drawn together. Then her mouth fell open.

The concourse shrank to one small bubble of silence.

"Excuse me, dear." Humi's social voice grated on the stillness. Wrong! Wrong voice—wrong persona—"I couldn't help noticing that you rather resemble—" She scrubbed an arm across her face. *"Thani?"*

"You've changed." Thani's voice was hard, defending against recognition. "You look Royallandic."

"It's only dust!" Humi raised her arm again, then stopped. "But you recognize my face—don't you? Don't you?"

"I . . . think so." Thani reached out and rubbed one finger across Humi's cheek, staring at the tawny smudge. "Yes. Gods! I thought you were long dead."

"So did I. So did I you."

She opened her arms to embrace the girl, but Thani stepped neatly away, leaving her standing there looking foolish. "Humi?" Thani glanced at the

Godsbrother. His white brows drew down over the salt crystals as he turned in the direction of their voices, and his mouth fumbled around displeasure. "Can we go somewhere to talk?"

"Surely. Surely. Gods, where do we *start?* But you can't leave him, can you?"

"*Him?* He doesn't care about me. Fuck him." Thani's voice was bleak. She sounded much older than—Sixteen? Seventeen? A mere child. "Can we go?"

"Ye-yes." *He'll wait here, I suppose.* Putting her hand through Thani's arm, Humi led her down Bowery Crescent, where the carpet vendors kept shop. Tapestry fringes swayed as they passed under the nearest doorway. The cool draft of the passage enveloped them. Smells of wool and leather laced the dark; voices haggled over prices, leisurely, prepared to take all afternoon. They passed on, out into the long, shallow yard where the vendors kept their stock before they cataloged it. Hundreds of rolls leaned against each other and against a few long-suffering trees; secondhand carpets hung over lines, being aired. They created roofless enclosures. Humi led Thani inside one of these plush "rooms" and sank down on the ground, facing her.

"How is it you can come back here?" Thani asked distrustfully.

"Oh, I could walk off with a carpet if I wanted to," Humi said without thinking. "If they recognized me, they'd have been bowing and scraping." She bit her tongue.

"Oh, really? Are you a lady? Are you married to a Royallandic lord?" Thani's face said that that would explain everything neatly but drearily, for if Humi was an atheistic lady then Thani would have to hate her for it.

"I'm . . ." *Discretion above everything!* warned Erene, whose disregard of her own advice had brought her to be outcast by her own *imrchim.* Humi closed her mouth. Finally she said, "I'm a ghostier." That meant nothing to Thani, of course: she was safe.

"You don't look like a . . . whatever that is. You look . . ." A shadow crossed Thani's face. "Twenty-five. Beautiful."

Humi shut her eyes for a second, restraining tears. Why did that blunt assessment mean so much to her? "And you?" she blurted. "You look older too. Grown up. Your hair's so light. Have you been in the sun?"

Thani grimaced guilelessly. She dragged her fingers through her hair, and the coarsely scissored crop stood on end. "Oh, Humi. Yes. We've been wandering. Westshine, at first . . . we stayed a long time at each hamlet. I suppose it was so I could get used to the life. Then we went to Delta City, and I learned all the secrets of being a leman. It's not just describing what you see. I hated the city, but I don't remember its being like this, before—

not so uncaring and closed-in, nor so smelly. Last time nobody tried to pick our pockets. Last time nobody said she needed a miracle, then when we entered her dirty little apartment, held out a bag of farthings and asked, 'Can you change these into crowns for me?' "

Humi winced. She knew she seldom saw the real underside of Delta City.

"After that we went to Calvary. We've been wandering for about seven years."

"Do you like it?" *Gods, I sound inane!*

"Transcendence says his life's work is Calvary. So is mine. I'd . . . I'd do anything to go back."

"Why don't you?"

Thani rubbed her face. "I—I don't think he's going to take me."

"Whyever shouldn't he?"

"We—we have a task to do here. And I'm afraid that he is only keeping me until that task is accomplished. Then he'll claim that I am too old to be a leman and that he came here to find a Deltan child to be his next one." She had, Humi saw, been trying very hard to keep her face impassive. Now, suddenly, she doubled over and hid her face in her rough green skirt, shaking. Her rough-cut hair slid slowly off her neck. Humi wanted to comfort her, but she did not dare. What was it like to have no one in the world except your flamen, to be bound to him by this devastating dignity that wouldn't allow anyone to see the frailty behind it? All the lemans she had known were so serene, full of inner tranquillity, even poor dead Lexi, who had made no attempt to hide his passion for Joyfulness. The others sublimated it into serenity. But perhaps their flamens' love for them was not a result of this equilibrium, as she'd believed, but the very linchpin of their existence. Would all of them fall apart like this if it were taken away?

How can you just sit here and watch her break? She's your sister! "My dear, I'm so sorry—" Humi tried to take Thani in her arms.

The girl wrenched away, flattening herself against the side of the carpet. It ballooned dangerously behind her. Dust puffed into the air, stinging Humi's nose. "Leave me alone! You're a lady!" So that was what Thani chose to believe. Well, it was Humi's own fault for not being honest with her. "All I want from you is help!" Her eyes grew bleak, cunning. "I'm your *sister*. You have to help me."

"You are my sister," Humi said.

"Do you know any Ellipse councillors? Any important flamens? Anyone you could ask? I know I can't force Transcendence to love me again, but if I could just be with him. That's all I ask, to be with him. Then maybe he would come around."

Humi took a deep breath. She leaned forward, slowly, so as not to present any threat of contact to Thani. The thin ruffles of her servant's dress puffed to fill the space between their knees. "Tell me exactly what it is that you want. I'll see what I can do."

She did not tell any of this to Arity. She did not have time. For a knocking rattled the window, and Arity leaped back. Afet Merisand's face was pressed against the panes among the raindrops, round and frightening as a moonfish. "Me?" Humi pointed to herself.

The porter nodded and gestured.

"What does he want?" Emni came up and closed her hands on Humi's shoulders. "I wouldn't ride ten feet in that man's sedan if I were you, Humi."

"He's the Divinarch's favorite, Emni," Arity said. He turned to Humi. "Whatever it is, we'd better go."

Gratitude flooded her, quieting the fears that had sprung up to choke rationality as springtime weeds choked crops. He would come with her. He would look after her. But when they got outside, he squinting against the daylight, she clutching an openwork shawl that Algia had thrown around her shoulders, Afet shook his head. He panted, smoking like a draydog in the rain, and he smelled like one too. "Just—Milady Garden."

Arity loomed over the muscular Deltan. Ordinarily slight for an *auchresh,* he seemed truly godly as he boomed, "I am the Heir! And I do not need your pathetic conveyance to go wherever I want!"

"True," Afet said. "But the Divinarch wants to see Milady Garden alone."

Ziniquel gasped, "Gods, Humi—"

"Not a word!" she ordered. Even to her, her voice sounded unusually harsh. "Ari—" she stretched a hand out to him—"I think I'd better go—"

"I shan't let you." He placed a possessive hand on her arm.

She shook it off and got into the sedan. Deferentially, Afet hooked the curtain closed. From outside she heard, "Humi!" Then, "He's gone—"

Then this would be proving to herself that she did not *depend* on him. That she loved him, but did not need him in order to be effective. "Let's go," she said, her voice steely.

Gods, the city smelled pungent today! It was this cold weather. Voices carried on the breeze, too.

But soon they were thudding up the wooden ramp into the courtyard of the Old Palace, and Merisand slowed to a walk. *Where are we going?* Humi wondered, and she poked her head out of the curtain. Darkness surrounded them. Something thudded by in the other direction, brushing her hair with a gust of wind, and she knew it could have taken her head off. The sedan stopped; Merisand helped her out. The floor was of earth, and lumpy. "We are in the stables. Since it is raining. I hope you do not mind, milady."

"It would hardly behoove me to object."

Slowly her eyes adjusted to the darkness. It was a vast, low barn lined with stalls, booming with porters' flying feet. They wove among the incoming and outgoing sedans to a little door tucked between two stalls and passed into a corridor.

"I must guide you myself, milady."

"All right, all right! And stop calling me milady!" She looked sidewise at him. "I think we know too much about each other for that."

"Ah . . . and what knowledge would that be, mi . . . ah, Lady Garden?"

She laughed. Except for a couple of human servants, the hall down which they were walking was deserted. The torches hadn't been replaced. "Oh, things such as that you were the go-between for Aneisneida and Soderingal during the months Belstem tried to stop them from communicating. That you arranged their trysts."

"That's not true!" He darted a glance at her, and tried again. "I was acting on the Divinarch's orders!"

"Mmm." They turned into a lesser corridor. Afet was muddy with anger from collar to hatbrim. "Belstem has called their engagement the beginning of the end," Humi said. "He says that it takes the Ellipse down another rung, from domination by flamens past domination by nobles to domination by commoners. Why on earth would the Divinarch encourage something like that?"

"I do not know my monarch's motives!"

She allowed him that. "Well," she said soberly, "I suppose I have come to find them out, haven't I? I suppose that is why he wants me."

They climbed a shallow spiral stair. Merisand stopped before a plain door. "This is the stateroom. I do not enter unless I am summoned."

Humi pushed the crystal bar and went in.

This room was as large as the Chalice—larger. Checkered tiles covered the floor. Abstract frescoes in a light, rich palette swam in the corners of her eyes, forming fleeting pictures. A few pieces of *auchresh* furniture stood here and there. A high wind surged throughout the room. One entire wall was a pane of glass, a foot thick, with segments swung open, and outside on a wooden balcony a great, wheeled bed stood, its canopies flying like banners.

Humi looked around once more to see if she had missed anything, then ventured outside.

The wind took her breath away, but it was not unbearable. The wide wooden balcony ran the length of the whole sea-front of the Old Palace: the bed was the only thing on it. Vessels of all sizes and descriptions cluttered the ridged green sea, maneuvering in and out of the wharves with the constancy of ants trooping into a hole.

In the bed lay the Divinarch of Royalland, Calvary, Veretry, Pirady, Iceland, the sundry isles of the Archipelago, and Domesdys, et al., dead.

Humi screamed. She scrambled up and kneeled on the coverlet, grabbing the Divinarch's shriveled wrist. "Milord! Oh, gods . . ."

He opened one eye. "Ehhh? What the hell?"

She hugged herself. Gods. Gods. His eyes were protruberant orbs of red-laced milk. Cold urgency took over: she slid off the foot of the bed and began to shove it inside. "Are you all right, Divinarch?" she shouted in *auchraug.*

"I am dying," he croaked in mortal. He appeared to find nothing strange about her speaking his language, although she had never used it in his hearing before. Maybe he didn't realize she was not an *auchresh.* But he must know—he had sent for her. Difficult to imagine this shriveled being in the bed doing such a strenuous thing. He raised himself from the pillows, peering down, his ancient visage contorted with effort. "Aaagh! Do not shut the doors." He was still speaking mortal. "I am fond of the wind—it tastes of salt, and I am homesickly. You—you are Humility? Arity's *irissu?"*

"Yes." She looked at him questioningly.

"I sent for you. I am old . . . I cannot constantly be tiptoeing around other people's homes. Not like the young ones. I do not know much of what is happening, except that which Arity and Pati tell me. And of course their reports disagree, so that I am at a loss until Bird and Bronze come and tell me yet another version. My *firchresim* . . . such a pity that they are *auchresh.* They are both good men." His speech was punctuated with wheezes.

Humi frowned. "Why is it a pity that they are *auchresh,* milord?"

"Aaah. Human, come sit by me."

Careful not to jolt him, Humi climbed back up onto the bed and sat cross-legged on the slick salt-brocade. His limbs were like sticks beneath the coverlet. His skin looked grubby against the white salt-fiber pillow. She twisted her fingers together. "Divinarch? Why would you regret that Arity and Pati are *auchresh?"*

"Ah . . . I know nothing." He wheezed. "I cannot remember."

"Then why send for me?" Surprising herself with her daring, she leaned forward. "Let's be honest. You remember more than you say, Divinarch. Age hasn't diminished you that much."

He laughed. Humi winced and blocked her ears. She had grown used to Arity's modulating his voice. "Tee-hee! Hee! Hee! Ghostier girl, I *am* clever!" Sparks of fun danced in the cataract-filled depths of his eyes. "But can you tell me why I should not have made you work to learn that?"

"No." The wind skirled through the room. *And I can see you're going to make me work for everything else you tell me, too.* She meant to say, *Have you chosen me to be Heir?* But at the last moment she did not dare. She settled for, "Divinarch, that time you sent for Erene, six months ago . . . what did you tell her?"

"We played a game of Conversion. Human, my handkerchief!"

She found the blood-stiff square and stuffed it into his hand. He coughed into it, the force bringing him up off the pillow, but he only flopped back down again. Humi winced. The sound was like metal scraping metal inside his lungs.

"You are . . . an intelligent . . . human," he said when he finally managed to stop. "There are a great many prophecies including your name. Move closer . . . no, put your arm around me. I do not disgust you, do I?"

She settled next to him. The degree of his illness was evident in the cool sponginess of his skin. "No." Then she used the secret weapon Arity had given her, so long ago she could not remember when: "Golden Antelope."

"Eeaaahh!" He spasmed. "I have not been called by that name in a century or more!"

"I'm sorry." She looked out at the sea vista. "Golden Antelope."

For a time he was silent, each breath a victory over frailty and phlegm. The wind carried away the smell of the blood which from time to time he coughed up. "I have not been Golden Antelope since I was young, in Anemone Channel Heaven." Now he was speaking *auchraug*. He seemed not to have noticed the transition. A shiver wriggled between Humi's shoulder blades. "A hamlet, you would call it. On a tributary of the Chrume, deep in Kithrilindu. Back then I was Antelope, *mainraui*. To the first human I ever knew, a young man calling himself Zeniph, I was Gold.

"I will not bore you by telling the story of how I befriended him and was punished by being made to live out my days here in Delta City. The *serbalim* thought that perhaps if I became Divinarch, I could repair the damage I did. They were wrong."

Humi was quiet. The wind seemed almost warm. Perhaps she was getting used to it. At last she extracted her arm and slid down, curling up next to Golden Antelope like a child. Kicking off her slippers, she snuggled carefully under the heavy brocade. "Divinarch? Tell me tales." She rolled onto her back. "Tell me about when you were young. Not about Antiprophet. Anything except him. How did you and the other Foundlings amuse yourselves before he entered your life?"

"We were foolish."

"All children are foolish."

"And because of that, they are carefree." The Divinarch coughed. Then, slowly, he related tales of his life in Anemone Channel Heaven to her. "It was an era when everyone lived for the moment, perceiving the beauty in each other, treating their own existence as a thing to worship and at the same time to laugh at."

Humi was inspired to interrupt, "Being a ghostier is turning that sense of wonder to one's own ends. I suppose we humans were never quite as innocent as you were."

"Oh, no. Never. Because, you see, you have always had children. Without that responsibility, one is free to indulge in a great deal of silly introspection and sheer fun. When I was young, the Heavens still deserved their name . . ."

And he told her of his first lover, his first hunt as a *mainraui*, and the moment when he was summoned before the *serbalim*, when they told him that he was the Heir. Humi got up to shut the portals, and lay back down. Gradually the afternoon dimmed. The ships on the sea ran out lanterns at bow and stern which seemed to toss independently of each other, like fireflies on the dark sea.

"I have failed as Divinarch. But I take pride in my failure." The old *auchresh*'s voice rang out commandingly. "Not everyone can claim the single-handed destruction of a religion *and* of an empire. I think the Wanderer is my only competitor in all of history. You modern councillors do not concern yourself with affairs overseas, other than to make sure your representatives obey you." Humi winced. "But I can tell you, Humility, that when I die, if I am not immediately replaced with another figure of power, there will be war. Calvary will break way to form a state of its own. Iceland and Pirady will band together. Domesdys and Veretry will splinter. The Archipelago will slide back into anarchy.

"Yes . . . I think I have earned myself a place in the histories. My name should loom larger even than Antiprophet's. Do you hear that, Zeniph?" he shouted suddenly.

Humi swallowed fear. "Golden Antelope, do you *want* all this to happen? Is that why you are encouraging the degradation of the Ellipse?"

After a pause, he said, "I want to avoid it at all costs!" He paused again. "That is why I have taken it on me to name a Heir who can represent every part of the Divinarchy."

Oh no, Humi thought with a sinking of her heart.

But he was still talking. "The last century has proved what I always believed—that your race is equal or superior to mine. I have changed this city from a quiet, pious town where commoners bowed low before the gods to a brawling, crime-ridden metropolis where the gods cover their faces and walk unseen. I wish to see the transformation completed. And so I chose to remain here until the end."

Humi could not speak.

"The Last Divinarch. I should like to be called that."

"It's a good title."

"I do not want flattery from you. If I sicken you," and with a tremendous effort he turned his head, "then by all means admit it."

"*Er-serbali?*" She had to know something. "That game of Conversion you said you played with Erene—who won?"

The Divinarch was silent for several minutes. His breath labored. "I did."

She sat up, pulling her knees to her chest.

"It had to be, Humility. She was the sacrifice. The cat's paw."

"What do you mean?" Erene had been strong—she had been anything *but* a cat's paw—

"I named her Heir for that very reason. I knew that the first human I named would die of it, and if it were Councillor Gentle, it would make sense to the populace that her title pass down to you. I did not know it would be *you* who killed her—" he laughed—"but things like that happen."

Humi gasped. Out of sheer spite, she longed to tell him the truth behind Erene's disappearance. How could he have plotted so cold-bloodedly? Had she—had she drastically misunderstood his motives?

"You have been my choice all along," he said. "The Divinarchy is yours to keep or destroy. Because in the end, what have we to follow except prophecies? And the prophecies name you."

"Divinarch, the prophecies also say I will be forsaken by all gods and mortals!" she burst out. "And I don't see *that* happening anytime soon! They're contradictory! How can you believe in them?" So much frustration and anxiety growing like white grass in the shadows of those prophecies, tangling up over the years—"They're nothing but the spewings of crazy lemans!" So black, so *insubstantial*—

In a flash of sulphur, Pati appeared beside the bed and backhanded Humi against the headboard. "So you *are* here! Arity was right!" He stared down at the Divinarch. "Old one, what have you told her?"

"Ahhhh. *Firchresi*, meet Humility." The Divinarch grinned, his eyes shut, revealing loose, rotted fangs. "My new Heir."

"Heir." Pati's face darkened and his wings trembled, but he controlled himself. It came to Humi that he had been expecting this. "What about Arity?"

"They are *irissim*. They can make up their differences."

"*Er-serbali*, this isn't about *irissim!* This is about godhead."

Golden Antelope's eyes closed. A trickle of white blood issued from his mouth.

Pati erupted into motion, rolling him over, bending his face to his chest. "Oh, no," he hissed, blinked out and reappeared squatting on the bed, a long-legged spider in breeches and jacket. He chafed the Divinarch's wrists while Humi coughed the sulphur out of her lungs. "If you've let him slip away, I'll kill you—"

The Divinarch's eyes opened. With a wheeze he breathed in. "No—I am not quite slipped yet." Out . . . Sea fog gusted into the room with the wind, curling down Humi's neck. She rubbed bare arms, teeth chattering. "I am glad you are here," the Divinarch said with difficulty.

Pati swallowed. "*Breideii.*" He let go of the thin wrists and bowed his head, his iridescent bangs brushing the Divinarch's face.

"My most wayward *firchresi*, and most beloved. Not many revere my name."

"I do," Humi whispered, moved by the first display of real emotion she had ever seen from Pati. "You're a great man, Divinarch."

"That is well." The Divinarch's eyes shone. "And you will make me greater yet."

"But no," Pati said. "My *breideii*, you cannot."

"She is better suited to lead this world than you, or Arity, or any of the others, Pati."

A nimbus of barely controlled anger shimmered around Pati. "She is a human on the foolish side of twenty!"

"Does that disqualify her?" The Divinarch lay still and small in the twilight, eyes closed. "It is prophesied," he croaked.

"A pox on prophecy. Prophecies cannot fulfill themselves."

Cold terror knotted in Humi's stomach. Prophecy or no prophecy, no one could change the Old One's mind for him. Not even Pati. So why had the Divinarch told Pati? He *wanted* this reaction. He *meant* to create a schism between the two of them.

All at once, as if a dark pane of glass shattered, letting her see clearly, she understood his plan. And caught her breath with horror. It depended on her own reluctance and her conviction that she was unfit to be Heir. It had so nearly succeeded! To use Pati like that—to use *her* like that—and Erene—over dozens of years—

"What a note to go out on!" The Divinarch was laughing. Each chuckle cost him a fortune in blood. It smelled rancid, as liquid from deep inside a body nearly two centuries old well might. "What a—note—" A look of alarm crossed his face. "By the Power—"

Concern chased everything else from Pati's voice. "Old One?"

"It . . . is . . ."

"Divinarch, don't go!"

"*Quiet!*"

"Change your mind, Divinarch! I don't want the Throne! Stay, keep it—"

The Divinarch's face took on a beatific expression. It was clear he had not heard a word she said. "Such a tintinnabulation," he said in lucid *auchraug*. "Like the music of the celestial spheres, heard through a wall of water. Listen!"

The sharp reek of blood pervaded the air.

Humi and Pati raised their heads and stared at each other.

They were alone in the rapidly darkening room.

All over the world, the mismatched machinery of the Divinarchy geared and meshed and clanked, working as it always had. But in the cold, dark stateroom of the Old Palace, its helm swung free.

The world doesn't know it has stopped, and so it keeps on going.

Pati strode up and down. Minutes ticked by. Humi guessed he was wrestling with jealousy, loyalty, grief, and greed. She feared that if she moved, he would leap at her and strangle her.

The Divinarch wanted war. What else could assure him as long a chapter in the history books? He had said that he'd named her Heir because she would satisfy all the warring factions; but in fact he had named her because he knew she could not do so, knew she knew that, and would back out, as in fact she had planned to do. That would leave Arity, who did not want to be Heir either, firmly in Pati's grip. In that situation, the atheists could not do other than rebel. And the Divinarchy would not just be dissolved, it would be torn apart.

All because of Golden Antelope.

A little, innocent, pinkish-gray corpse. She had to thwart him somehow. "Where is Arity!" she heard Pati mutter, and, "I cannot leave her alone!" She could see where he was only by the flash of his iridescent hair and the screech of his talons on the floor as he swung about. The *auchresh*-built chair she sat in was far from comfortable, but it was the furthest from the dark hulk of the bed. In its tall canopied ornamentation, she saw now that it looked a great deal like the Throne.

And three bright *auchresh* shapes appeared by the window. Heel talons clacked on the floor. Humi started to her feet. Broken Bird, Hope, Bronze Water; and the door crashed open, letting in a wedge of torchlight. It looked like all of the ghostier councillors, with Arity at their head, and Goquisite and Belstem bringing up the rear, the latter puffing heavily— and, gods, the flamen councillors too, and *Transcendence?* What was he doing here? And *Thani?* And why did no one seem to notice them?

"I'm sorry, Pati!" Arity called. "It took me so long to find them all—"

"He's dead," Pati said.

Everyone had been about to speak, but Pati's words fell on the plane of imminent speech and shattered it like glass. Each human and *auchresh* started violently, then fell still. Even the lemans seemed tongue-tied. All of them stood separate, leaderless, like shadows on the pale whirling forms of the frescoes.

"And he has left you—" Pati came forward smoothly, the brightest figure in the room as the door swung closed—"your Heir, Ar—"

Humi drew a deep breath. "Me," she said clearly, making them all turn to look at her. "I am the Heir."

Pati came at her. Spidery hands closed on her chin and nape, no doubt ready to break her neck, and she shrieked, "It's not what it sounds like!"

Somebody grabbed Pati from behind, but his hands remained where they were. "If you had just remained *silent,*" he hissed, "then we could have ignored his senile idiocies—"

But it was Pati who had not been thinking straight. *Thank gods,* she thought in a blur, *that he reacted so violently. This way everyone knows I was telling the truth*—"He named—" she was breathing hard, as if each inhalation would be her last—"he named—me Heir—to produce—just this effect, Pati!"

"Let go of her, Pati!" Humi recognized Hope's voice. Her vision was beginning to turn black.

"No violence!" Bronze Water warned loudly.

Pati let go. Slowly, dusting his palms off on his clothes, he stepped back.

Humi turned to face the councillors (*what was Thani doing here?*) and gingerly felt her neck. "The Divinarch gloried in his failure. I thought at first that he just wanted to put me on the seat of power to consolidate his defeat. Then I understood that he wanted more than that. He *meant* for me to back down. And when Arity took the Throne, the existence of the con- spiracy—let's not look shocked, we all know about it—would cause a war. A war that would make the Conversion Wars look like a street brawl."

As she stood there in her white slippers and everyday dress, in the gloomy fog with the briny reek of the sea coming in, she had them all in the palm of her hand. Just what she had always wanted. She took a deep breath and used her most persuasive Ellipse tone. "Are we going to give it to him? Or are we going to fashion ourselves a new peace?"

"War . . ." Pati hissed, smiling. "Perhaps that is what is needed."

Panicking, Humi sought Arity with her eyes. Their gazes met across the room in a near-perfect understanding. "Hmm," he said easily, canting his weight to one side. The lemans' voices murmured softly, describing his magnificence. "Let me see how this would unfold. If I took the Throne . . ."

"Then we would fight you!" Belstem cut in, breathing fast with excitement. "We would fight you in the streets, in the countryside, and in the salt! Humi has been named Heir!"

"You prove my point, Belstem," Humi said bleakly. "There would be war. And even if we took Delta City, it would continue. Wouldn't it, Pati?" His face said everything. "Then we would have the power and the police forces, but you would have the common people. We would be even. World-wide civil war. Can you imagine it? Any of you?" She wished she could see their faces. The dark frustrated her. "There's only one way to avoid this disaster." She took a deep breath. "You must accept me as Divinarch."

And voices broke out, arguing spasmodically in the dark. *Yes—She is the one—don't you see, we can avoid the dying*—The balance swung wildly. The wind had dropped. There was nothing to influence it. It trembled. Then, with a decisive clink of weights, it came down—and doubtful, increasingly cowed, the voices said—*We can't let her—this liberty—this blasphemy—*

"Yes, it is blasphemy," a girl's voice said quietly. Humi did not think any one heard. "But it is ordained. All the prophecies connect with each other." The voice was soft, almost wondering. "It is ordained."

And Arity said in an unmodulated, effortless voice, "It is the only way! We must agree. We must all enforce Humi's right to take the Throne. Then, and only then, are we safe from anarchy!"

Gods, Ari, if it weren't for you—

"The prophecies are nonsense," Pati said flatly. "Get out, all of you. Now."

Argument erupted again, but this time the voices were uncontrolled, violent, and colored with fear. "We will not tolerate this blasphemy," shouted Godsbrother Puritanism, and Auspi dragged him at a run to the Striver's side. Joyfulness followed him. The ghostiers wavered, their voices low but passionate, and then with a terrible sinking of the heart Humi saw Sol and Algia edging toward Pati—*losing faith in her, no faith—*

"Wait!" Arity danced back to frown at Pati. The Striver shone like a candle flame in the fog. The room had gotten very cold. "Striver, speak for

yourself! *You* will not permit it? You're not the Heir. I say, for all the
auchresh, for the whole Divinarchy"—he flung a heedless arm to the
room—"we accept her!"

"But it *can't* be ordained," Humi heard the same female voice say
fumblingly. Now she recognized it. It was Thani. "If they reject her after
all—then how can it be?"

"Shut up, Arity," Pati said in *auchraug*. His voice was deadly. "She's the
head of the conspiracy! This would mean the end of our race as we know
it!"

"The prophecies are not yet complete, because we have not completed
them." Transcendence. Humi turned her head and saw him and Thani on
the edge of the loose group of ghostiers, two dark shapes facing each other.
Transcendence's voice came low and fierce like a sword. *"Complete them."*

"The end of our race as we know it is already upon us!" Arity shouted.
More ghostiers shuffled toward Pati. "If you think you can stem the tide,
Pati, you're wrong! All we can do is cut our losses!"

"For you, Godsbrother," Humi heard Thani say—and her hand flashed
out of her blouse with a long shining dirk, and she went for Arity. Everyone
in the room it seemed saw her at once, and moved slowly to converge on
her, but Arity, oblivious, stepped out to confront Pati, and Humi shouted,
finally freeing her tongue, "Thani, don't be a fool!" And Arity's stride carried him directly into the range of Thani's thrust and he halted there,
turning to Humi to see what was wrong. And Thani's knife caught him in
the neck. Blood gouted from the wound and Arity executed a half-circle
and collapsed. Thani stooped over him like a rapidly pecking bird, stabbing
and stabbing again, sawing the knife in the wounds she made all over his
torso.

It was unbelievable how quickly his blood covered the floor.

Humi did not even know that she moved, but she was on her knees in
the pool of it, torn between touching him and injuring him further. *"Irissi."*
His blood had the fresh metallic smell which comes straight from the heart.
She *saw* his heart fighting to beat in the jagged pulp that was his rib cage,
pumping his life away.

"I think I'm dying."

She *saw* a shredded lung fluttering, garbling the words.

"I love you."

"Irissi—"

"No," Pati sobbed. "I don't believe it. It can't be. I shan't let it! Out of
the way, mortal!" And he shoved her onto her back in the blood, and
slipping and sliding, he and Bronze and Broken Bird somehow got all their
hands under Arity without letting his heart and guts fall out of his body.

Arity's eyelids were drooping, his face bleaching. "I shan't let it happen, not to you! Hope, pull yourself together, we need help!" Sobbing, Hope fluttered to the ground, her wings trembling stiff and wide like a screen behind them. To Humi, struggling to get up in the slippery blood, a white light seemed to emanate from Arity's ruined body, uniting all of the Incarnations with the tears dripping freely from their faces. *"Three—"*

The overlapping shapes of black light faded from the air.

The smell of sulphur dispersed in the fog.

Far below, the sea thumped against solid rock, and the wind keened on the balcony.

Arity's blood trickled slowly into the cracks between the tiles.

A buzzing filled Humi's ears and the night held her like a fly in honey.

Mory had pinned Thani's arms behind her. Sol and Trisizim together had caught Transcendence. Thani's rhythmic, useless struggles, like those of a fly caught in a web, were the only part of the dreadful tableau that was still moving.

Someone touched her shoulder, then quickly withdrew. With an enormous effort, she looked around and saw Ziniquel and Belstem, standing side by side for what must have been the first time in their lives.

Ziniquel said gently, "He's gone. They're all gone. There can be no question of who is Heir now."

"No," Belstem rumbled. "No question."

She stumbled to her feet. As they raised her on their shoulders, the blood on her clothes slicking their fur, she covered her mouth with her hand, digging fingernails into her cheek to keep from vomiting. The other councillors, flamens and ghostiers, went ahead of them, and Sol flung open the door of the stateroom.

Torchlight streamed in. The corridor was packed solid with Old Palace domestics, their faces seamed with worry, and here or there a flamen or a noble.

"The Divinarch is dead," Sol said. "The Divine Cycle is over."

A moan swelled. He quieted it by beckoning Ziniquel and Belstem forward. They displayed Humi over their heads like a prize boar on a platter, the centerpiece of a banquet. *In a moment,* she thought, *they will drive knives into me.*

"Long live the Divinarch!" Sol shouted.

After five stunned seconds, they began to cheer.

TWENTY-EIGHT

Far away in Beaulieu, they creak back home after the Midwinter festival in Nece. The carts bump over the stony road to the salt. Merce, and Asure, and Gent's new wife's baby all nod off to sleep in the hay-smelling dark under the stretched cloths that keep the rain off their heads.

Far away in Pirady, Erene is kneading bread on a dark, gnarled table, putting her weight behind each movement. She can see out the window to the roiling gray sea. A storm is blowing up. Elicit sits under the window, carving a leg for the birthing stool that the local midwife has told him to make. Erene stops kneading for a minute to massage her back. Elicit looks up. "It's all right," she says, and smiles. "I just felt . . ."

News from Delta City never reaches them until months after the fact, here in this isolated Shikorn bay.

Far away in Calvary, in the hot, clanking depths of a twenty-four-hour bronze mine, a young man steals a moment to rest on the handle of his pick. *I have to leave this place,* he thinks, watching the bovine profile of his crewmate in the red gleam of slow fire from below. *I have to get out.*

And back in Royalland, the predator's wings flap more slowly as it nears home, winging over the brown expanse of the Chrume that gleams in the starlight as it rolls into the sea.

"I have the girl and the flamen under lock and key." Humi took a deep, slow breath, gazing around the half-empty Ellipse Chamber. Only four councillors were missing—but because they were gods, their absence was as outstanding as if they had been ten. Fifteen people in the room, including Humi herself. When she came in, she had sat down one seat to the left, in the chair which had been empty as long as she remembered. It felt almost like sacrilege. She kept having panic attacks. Everyone looked scruffy and bleary-faced, hair uncoiffed, cravats tied wrong. "The question before the Ellipse is, What is to be done with them? At present they are confined in the lodgings in Christon that Godsbrother Puritanism, so I hear, procured for them."

And guarded by Gold Dagger's and the Hangman's men, who will choose death over failure.

"Kill them," Pati said in a frozen voice. "Never was death better deserved."

As far as anyone knew, the Striver—now Humi's Heir—was the only god left in Delta City. He had arrived back the night after Arity's death. He would speak to no one, not even Humi, and she could not manage to get him alone. He sat apart from the other councillors, knees drawn up to his ears, wrapped in his wings, voice tolling out of the leathery cowl. "Kill them."

"I agree." Belstem had lost weight since the accident. Yellow sleep clotted the corners of his eyes. "They have proved themselves a danger. Their long exposure to the Calvary sun must have damaged their minds."

"No," Puritanism boomed at Humi's shoulder. "I move unconditional death for the leman who struck the blow, for her crime of divinicide. But not for Godsbrother Transcendence. Let him go where he will. He acted according to a prophecy that that very leman made. And painful as it sounds, that prophecy was congruous with a number of others. At first, we did not believe the prophecies because they were so shocking. But nevertheless, Joyfulness and I assisted the pair in following their mandate, and now all comes clear. Charity was a renegade to the gods: he loved human ways, valuing them over his divine remove. He had to die. The tragedy is that his death has only made way for an even greater outrage." His head swung in Humi's direction.

"This was prophesied too," someone protested.

"That is the tragedy," Joyfulness said quietly.

Humi gripped the edge of the table to stop herself shaking. "I can see there is no need to vote. The leman shall die. But how?" At the same time as she hated Puritanism for having enabled Thani to fulfill her prophecy, Humi felt a bleak gratitude to him: she could not have made the decision. Emotionally razed, she could not possibly have given the word to kill her sister, any more than she could have pardoned her.

Ziniquel stood. "Divinarch, the ghostiers have a suggestion." She blinked. Difficult to remember that she was not a ghostier any more, not allowed to ghost, that when she moved to the left her very identity had changed. "We recommend that she be given to us. We will bear her crime in mind—" pious anger darkened his face—"and ghost her in commensurate fashion."

"It is fitting," Goquisite said.

Belstem belched, got up and went to pour himself more wine. He had been drinking steadily.

I cannot do it, Humi thought, panicky. "Shall we vote on that, then?" she said.

"What? What are we doing?" The heights of the Chamber caught Belstem's whisper, amplifying it to an embarrassing volume. He sat down heavily. Wine sloshed onto the table.

Aneisneida touched her father's hand. She glowed with health: her fur was tinted silver so that it looked attractively fair rather than pale, and the torchlight brought out the gold in her eyes. Her wedding with Soderingal Nearecloud was, as far as Humi knew, still scheduled for next Dividay, despite the catastrophe that had thrown everything else in the capital on hold. "Father, we're approving the ghostiers' claim on the leman who murdered Arity."

"Approving? Good. One can never trust lemans—slippery creatures. I should know. I was one. You weren't, girl—you'll never know what it really means to be an atheist, with fire in your belly and Antiprophet's words in your head—"

"No, Father." Aneisneida put Belstem's voting stone in his hand, then opened the plump fingers over the "yes" channel under the cornice of the table.

Humi listened to the subtle rattle-plop as the stones skated through the passageways. The voting system worked by an ancient, mysterious system of holes and slides; each stone was a slightly different size, and the interior of the ancient table conducted them through the channels to two little drawers at Humi's fingertips, one for "yes" and one for "no." The consensus would be unquestioned. A good thing; she hadn't the head to do sums right now. She was well rested, and probably she had eaten something this evening—Mory or Emni or Zin would have seen to that, they still looked after her even though technically speaking she was no longer an *imrchu*— but she felt as exhausted as ever she had at the height of her power as twentieth councillor. Her skull throbbed. She could not concentrate, or rather she could concentrate perfectly, it was just that it wasn't *her*, Humi, doing it. The woman sitting in the Divinarch's seat, the twenty-first councillor, was the Divinarch, a ruler who had lost her Heir, not a woman who had lost her *irissi*. Some of them saw her grief under the shell, no doubt: they would all be poking and prying for it. But she didn't care. Her heart wasn't in the pretense.

Where *was* her heart?

Yesterday she had gone to Gold Dagger's new mansion in Shimorning—

without a price on his head, he was easier to find these days than when they were first acquainted—and told him to call off those two hundred men and women with their rapiers, knives, blow-darts, garrotes, and so on. Yes, of course he and the Hangman would still be honored as favorites of the Throne, but their aid would not be needed. The conspiracy had succeeded, the revolution was over. Even if no one seemed to have noticed that yet.

And all the sixday since the catastrophe she had felt as though she were walking in a dream. Accepting that Arity had ceased to exist would be the first, hardest part of waking up to her new role; and she had not even gotten there yet. The worst part of it was that she had no lust for revenge. Not revenge against Thani. Especially if her cruel, ascetic Godsbrother went free, leaving Thani to take the ghostiers' syringes for him.

Puritanism's leman Auspi touched her on the shoulder. Humi startled. To her horror, the girl recoiled as if in fear. "What?" Humi asked as gently as she could.

"Count the vote," Auspi mouthed nervously.

She knocked the heel of a hand against her head. "Oh, yes!" Yanking the little drawers open in haste to cover up her fault, she only just saved the lefthand "No" drawer from falling on the floor.

But it would not have mattered. It was empty.

At first light, as the winter-gray clouds brightened and the sea birds keened around the turrets of the Old Palace, she woke and knew that she had to salvage at least some of her integrity.

She breakfasted on papaya-fried goose in the lacy-walled *auchresh* dining room where no humans had ever come during the Old One's reign. Her roster of noble guests praised the beauty of the architecture and passed the butter. The goose, a hot, filling breakfast suitable for a winter's day, nauseated her. She excused herself.

By eleven o'clock she was in Trebank Road.

It was a twisty, tunnel-roofed alley in Christon where Puritanism had apparently seen fit to lodge Thani and Transcendence. "Good to see you, Divinarch," grinned the gap-toothed guard at the top of the dark little staircase. "She's a bad one, she is! Gonna ghost 'er?"

At his insolence, the bodyguards Belstem had assigned Humi stirred. She stared at the guard distastefully and swept into the apartment. One room, it contained a stained mattress, a window, and a chamberpot. Thani sat slumped on the windowsill, eyes shut, head falling to one side. Tear-tracks marred her grimy fur. At Humi's entrance, she looked up. Her eyes flickered only dully with recognition. "What are *you* here for?"

Humi reached behind her and closed the door. "Do you want to go free?"

Thani stiffened. Then tears welled up in her eyes again. "Humi, don't tease me. They let Transcendence go. But not me. I begged and cried and hung on to him, but they kicked me back in here. They're going to kill me."

Humi's throat filled with pity. She fingered the tallow-crusted candlestick on the wall.

"Why are they killing me?" Thani asked. "Godsbrother Puritanism let us into the Old Palace. He gave us his word that we would be protected—"

Humi clenched her fists at the thought of Puritanism leaning back in his chair, handing down sentence so righteously. *Oh, little sister, did you never hear of a scapegoat?* "I shan't let them kill you," she said. "I'm taking you out of here."

"Oh, Humi—" Thani swung her legs off the windowsill clumsily, as if she had been sitting there all night. She floundered over to Humi and hugged her. Tears flooded from her eyes, but now she was laughing through them and wiping her nose, her body all soft with joy. "I can't believe it."

Between them Humi thought she felt the tension of the terrible deed Thani had done.

"Transcendence told me he would book passage out of the city on Maidensday for two, in case I could get out somehow, but neither of us really thought they would let me go—" Not Arity. Something quite different was weighing on her sister's mind.

"But wait," Humi said. "I thought Transcendence didn't want you anymore."

"Everything's all right now. We didn't want to die hating one another. He said that I had completed the prophecy well, and that he could do nothing other than admire me. We were going to die in each other's arms. Nothing else mattered to us. But then they let him go. He didn't want to go without me, but they dragged him out cursing them—and I can't think how he is faring, blind as he is, alone on the docks—"

Humi had expected Thani to be resigned to death, to need coaxing back to life. She had expected her to have forgotten her childish dependence on Transcendence, to have discarded it like a useless ornament in the face of death. She had thought that anyone who killed a god would be charred to a shell by the experience itself. But Thani seemed to have come out of it relatively unscathed, even healed. Even having lost sight of the deed that she had done, in the greater horror of her separation from Transcendence. She smiled, and wept, and kissed Humi on the cheek. The room smelled of urine. Humi's head spun. The floor rocked under her feet.

On the way back in the sedan, Thani shivered in her thin Calvarese blouse. Humi offered her her mantle, but the leman shook her head, smiling. She looked beautiful with her fur standing up from her goosebumps, showing smooth, dark skin. Fur like frozen streaked light. In the few days of her imprisonment, her cheekbones had gained definition, as had the tendons of her neck. Her tangled crop of hair pleased the eye in its very messiness. Humi the ghostier had no trouble seeing the ghost in her; somebody would have had a field day. But she did not change her mind.

She took the back stairs up to her apartment so that she didn't have to lead Thani through the clutter of syringes, bottles, and pigment pots which was her workshop. No point in frightening her with the fate she had so narrowly avoided. "Do you want something to eat before you go?"

"Yes!" Thani turned and beamed at her quite suddenly, as if she were half submerged in a delicious dream. "I'd better, hadn't I? They didn't give me anything while I was in there . . ."

The scent of porridge still permeated the apartment an hour later, as Humi sat Thani down before the mirror in her dressing room. Hearty porridge, thick enough to stand a spoon up in, with diced ham, and dried pears on the side. While she prepared it, Humi had found herself checking the oats for moths; it seemed years since she had last come here. Lifetimes since she had spent her last night in the boudoir with Arity, just the two of them in the blackness. She had made sure the door to the boudoir was securely shut. She would not take Thani in there. A sixday ago, only a sixday ago, they had made love until the day was half over, and then come downstairs and had sandfish fritters for lunch, and sat together in the window of the Chalice, that fated afternoon—

"I'm going to disguise you so that you can leave the city in safety," Humi said. Thani had a thin, hard body with full breasts. Touching her nearly made Humi vomit, but that had nothing to do with *her*, so she forced herself to relax as she worked darker and darker brown dusts into the girl's bosom. "I'm disguising you as a Calvarese. It *is* Calvary you have to reach, right?"

"I don't know." Thani was smiling. "And I don't care, just so long as I'm going with Transcendence. I thought my life was Calvary. It isn't. It's him."

Why? Why does she care so much? The mirror, a heart-shaped thing that Humi had gotten as a gift from some Icelandic noble, was tall enough to frame both of them against the soft pastel collage of the room. Humi made herself smile into it. Why had she picked colors that would show dust so easily? she asked herself, to take her mind off her jealousy. From time to time, she might want to come back and touch the curtains, and pick up the ornaments, and lie down in the boudoir in the salty sea of black sheets—

Thani grabbed her hand. Thani's was a cold little paw, all bones and

calluses. "I could never understand why you ladies want to look at yourselves all the time . . . but see here!"

Humi saw. And nearly dropped the facedust brush. Two faces, one below
the other: one framed with messy blond layers, one with a tawny puff of
hair; one belonging to a fast-blooming adolescent, one to a willowy woman.
But the features were the same. Small, slightly pouted lips, long-lashed
eyes, intelligent foreheads. And their expressions identical, to the very self-
mocking quirk at the mouth.

"You see . . . ?" Thani let go of Humi's hand, smiling up at her.

Humi drove her fingers into Thani's cheeks, forcing away the smile,
dampening her radiance with brown facedust. "Don't worry if it comes off a
little on your fingers," she said. "It only has to last until you get out of the
city." As she worked sepia through Thani's fur, the likeness vanished. The
girl sitting under her hands became a docile dark stranger. "Pick a ship
which caters not to nobility but to ordinary people. I'll give you commoner's clothes, and the money to choose your vessel. Keep it hidden."

"You're very generous," Thani said sadly.

Later Humi saw her to the doorway, unrecognizable in some of Mory's
oldest clothes. Thani stood in the street, twisting her brown fingers together. "Humi . . . why? Why did you do this for me?"

Humi shrugged, and without thinking, mentioned the thing neither of
them had mentioned. "Arity's gone. You're still alive. What good would it
have done to let you die, too?"

Thani took a step back. She looked almost horrified. "You'd never have
said that the last time I met you. That about its not doing any good. It's
done something to you. Oh, gods, if I'd known—" She shivered. "If I'd
known—"

Bile boiled up in Humi's throat. For a moment she could not speak. *The
effect on me? How much more can we trivialize it?* "Done is done," she said.
She leaned her head on the doorjamb. "Now get out of here."

"I wish . . . oh, gods, Humi!" Her radiance was shining through the
brown facedust. The Crescent was alive with passersby. People looked
curiously at her—perhaps Humi had made her *too* striking: it was unheard
of for anyone other than a ghostier to *leave* Albien House, and Thani was
definitely not a ghostier—Humi cut her off hastily. "I don't care what you
wish! Get out of here!"

"But—"

"Good-bye!"

Thani stayed there for a moment, indecisive. Then, hooking Mory's
jacket about her shoulders, she vanished into the crowd. Humi stayed lean-

ing at the door for she had no idea how long, scarcely feeling the cold, wondering what there was left worth living for.

Pati came to her that night. She was having the Divinarch's suite redecorated to her own, more forgiving tastes as fast as the workers could go, but Palace law prohibited them from working at night, even though there were no more gods to roam the halls, no more forbidden glimpses of *auchresh* life to be caught. She sat alone in the dark, rocking on a wicker chair Emni had sent from Tellury Crescent, her eyes wide and dry as she stared at the mastlights on the sea. The small kindnesses the ghostiers did her reduced her to tears if she dwelt on them. *Trade goes on,* she told herself absurdly.

Pati slipped his arms around her neck from behind and kissed her, his lips dry and hot, the tip of his tongue wetting her fur.

She wrenched away without speaking.

"We almost made a mistake!" He came around in front of her, a narrow silhouette on the fleecy night sky. "What a concept! War as triumph! Golden Antelope meant to drag as many people down with him as possible, didn't he? That's what gave him pleasure. And it took you to fathom it in time."

"Stop it, Pati," she said, too tired to react to his flattery.

He looked hurt. "I'm only trying to maintain a facade of courtesy."

"In that case, you should not slander the Divinarch."

"*You* are Divinarch. Golden Antelope is dead." Pat squatted down in front of her, his white face screwed up, almost human with earnesty. She smelled salt perfume. He must have just come from the salt. "All he cared about was how he'd look in the histories. He only wanted war so that he should be remembered as the one who started it. But he is defeated at last—though not on such a grand scale, maybe, as he planned."

"There is that," she admitted grudgingly. They had peace. That incredible state of affairs, which she had not dreamed possible before the Divinarch named her Heir, shone like the sole bright spot in her personal night. "I think that even without the Incarnations, I can hold things together. I do think it is possible to start a new Divine Cycle with me as Divinarch—after all, the common people never see the gods anyway, it doesn't matter to *them* whether the gods are in Delta City or not, whether a god sits on the Throne or not, just so long as they are there to be worshiped. We are making as little fuss over this reallocation of power as possible."

"Humi," Pati said, "I decided several days ago not to play games with you. I think it only fair to let you know that I don't plan to lose by this."

She felt herself turning the color of mud.

"I wouldn't want to gratify the Old One after all."

She mustered her wits. "What—what do you expect of me?"

"Oh, no more than when you first gained the Ellipse. Your full support. Shall I say that I intend to be the power behind the Throne? Yes, why not? But listen well. This time around, I don't want you playing me off against Belstem. I don't want slander-fights. I want motions. Votes. And Divine Seals."

Erene! Elicit! Beisa! Fra! Rita! Arity!

"Why don't you just put your hands around my neck and kill me right now?" she said in a dry whisper. "Then you'd have everything you want."

For a moment he did not breathe. His face distorted like an illusion in the wind, the flame of him brightening and brightening, swaying toward her. She flinched back. His body burned with energy. She could actually feel his heat on her legs.

Then he rocked back on his thin haunches. "Are we agreed?"

Far below, she heard a rising sea slapping against the face of the island. Voices yelled orders as the sidewash from the Chrume carried ships close to the cliff below the Palace. Sea pigeons cooed from their nests in the turrets.

"I have no choice, have I?" she said bitterly. "We have an agreement."

TWENTY-NINE

The heavy, wet rain of the last days of winter plopped heavily on the roofs of Marshtown. Humi did not bother to open her parasol as she got out of her sedan and greeted Soulf Freebird. She didn't remember half this many lines on Soulf's face. But of course the woman believed Elicit had died. Strange to think that it was only six months ago that he and Erene had made their escape from Tellury Crescent and Antiprophet Square.

The strongholds of piety and atheism might be named for shapes with corners, Humi thought, but in reality they were knotted circles one had to cut in order to escape. Neither Erene nor Elicit had ever made a wiser decision than to cut them, but they had injured people in their going. Love as powerful as theirs always burned those in the vicinity. Humi should know, for she had once burned the world. And been burned by her sister's even less conventional love for Godsbrother Transcendence. Gods knew where her sister was now. Humi had not heard from her since she and the flamen left the city, months ago.

Soulf's children cowered warily in the door, as though they were used to ducking out of their mother's way. Soulf's husband, Xhil, glowered out of a window, clenching his pipe in his teeth.

"Divinarch." Slowly, painfully, Soulf bowed to the ground. She glanced behind Humi. "Do you wish to bring your retainers in as well?"

"I would not even have brought them this far did they not insist on accompanying me," Humi said. "Believe me, it goes against the grain even to let them know that I come here."

"They're dressed like the gods used to!" piped one of the children sud-denly—Mory's younger daughter, a Calvarese-Deltan halfbreed, now seven. Humi essayed a smile at the girl, then winced as she glanced behind her at her guards. They lounged uncomfortably up and down the little

street, getting wetter and wetter, cringing under the scrutiny of the locals
who had gathered at the mouth of the street to stare and mutter.

"I've changed my mind," she said. "I'm going in alone. Let them amuse
themselves here." She bent to the little girl. "See that reddish-furred one in
the yellow silk? He might have some sweetmeats if you ask nicely." She
turned back to Soulf. "Half of them are Marshtowners born and bred."

"Truth, Milady Divinarch?"

"Absolutely. One atheist Guard is at home today because one pious
Guard has winterfever. We go to such lengths to preserve the balance."
Failing to bring a smile to the woman's stolid face, Humi sighed and
brushed past her into the house. She supposed it should not come as a
surprise that Soulf did not trust her. Even if Soulf had liked Humi, the
ghostier's apprentice, that ghostier's apprentice was long gone now. So was
the master ghostier who had replaced her. Humi had not made a ghost
since she became Divinarch. She was not allowed to. And she had not had
the time or energy to revise the rules. They provided a convenient excuse.

A Marshtowner like Soulf ought to trust Humi simply because she was
Divinarch. But how could you have faith in a Divinarch who supported you
in Ellipse, laid the Divine Seal on all manner of bylaws to protect your
rights as a devotee, lived as a Divinarch ought in the Palace—yet whose
very humanity flouted all your beliefs and traditions? You couldn't. You had
to hold back, and mutter with your friends that the yoke she laid on your
neck was past bearing.

Reverse those conditions, and one saw why the atheists didn't trust her
either. Oh, they acclaimed her in public. They had to. She was the embodiment of their successful revolution, and (publicly) they praised her for
warding off the bloodshed which everyone had feared was inevitable. (But
secretly, perhaps, they had anticipated it with relish. Humi knew that Gold
Dagger, for one, was disgruntled at not having his men made the heroes of
the revolution.) And even Belstem and Goquisite, Humi knew, were wondering how much longer it was going to be before the new regime really
came in. The very position of Divinarch ought to be abolished, they said, in
favor of the rule of the Ellipse. That was what they had planned long ago
with Erene. Nothing would have made Humi happier; but there was Pati.

As for the flamens, from oldest to youngest, highest to lowest, they
openly reviled her.

"Sooner or later, one of them is going to catch me off guard," she whispered aloud as she walked down the passage inside Soulf's house. "Like
yesterday. I don't have time to feel sorry for myself. I shouldn't be here."
She slipped through the fleece-lined door of the Eftpool and shut it tightly.
Steamy warmth enveloped her. Multicolored lights poured over the

fronded plants and the pool. Today, because of the rain streaming down the half-globe roof, the light wavered as though the whole room were under water. Humidity enveloped her, moistening her upper lip and the backs of her knees. There was a metallic tang of green. Dropping to her knees, she lowered one hand into the black water.

The efts were active today, rushing agitatedly round and round. One bit her finger. As the atmosphere began to deteriorate, the light seemed to fade, and the air stirred like a great beast waking. A presagement of the storm disturbed the ribbons at her throat. Even on this leisure jaunt, Humi was dressed as the Divinarch ought to be, in a tight-bodiced couturier's creation. "Mell?" she whispered.

He rubbed with naive arrogance against her wrist. *I know you're going to pick me up.* "No, not today! Send me Beau."

With a peevish flick of his tail, he departed. She waited, wondering if her cousin would come. As he wasn't one of her own ghosts, he didn't always oblige. But she needed him. She had come to see him often when she was an apprentice, but only once or twice after she attained master status; however, now that she lived in the Palace, she was resigned to having a fish for her best friend. "Beau . . . Beau . . . Here, Beauty!"

With all his old vigor, Beau threw himself at her hand. She thrust her other arm down and scooped him up. Eftpool water soaked her sleeve and splattered her lap, *wetter* somehow than any other water, dark black until the moment it hit. The dress would never be the same, but she didn't care. "Beau! How are you?" She was so glad to see him that she scarcely noticed the smell of decay which accompanied him into the air. He thrashed, giving her a lively glare.

"I'm glad. Oh, Beau—" she caught her breath against losing control— "someone tried to kill me yesterday—"

Who?

"Who wants me dead? An *auchresh.* One of the decorators in the great hall downstairs hurled his glass-cutting wheel at me. One of my bodyguards took it in the face. The decorator said the wheel was pulled out of his hand by something like another, invisible hand."

Beau's face took on an expression of alarm. Minute lips worked. She nearly dropped him. "They wouldn't do that!" *Belstem and Goquisite, Maras and Pieti—betray me? Set up the whole series of attempts on my life to convince me they were perpetrated by an* auchresh? "No. That would be divinicide! It's unthinkable."

His silver gaze penetrated her. *It wouldn't be divinicide. No one thinks you're a god. And anyway, that taboo has already been broken once.*

"They wouldn't have had any reason to kill me before they saw that I wasn't going to do what they wanted! And this is the first attempt since I took the Throne."

His eyebrows capered wildly.

"Well—" Humi felt her mouth trembling. "Maybe it's not, actually." She sat down heavily on the bricks, clutching him to her breast. "Oh, Beau," she sobbed. "I liked being an Ellipse councillor. It was like standing in a high, high place day and night, wondering whether to jump. But this is different. Being second in the world is so different from being first. I wish I'd never loved Arity! It made everything so perfect for such a short time. And now that he is gone I can't stop thinking about him, and I can't function without him—"

Don't think about him, Humi. It makes it worse. What about the others?

"I wish I'd never known what it is to be an *imrchu* either!" Terrible thought! Yet she did not regret it. She didn't *want* to be *imrchu* of the ragtag company that was the ghostiers now. No one had stepped into her spot on Ellipse, because there simply was no one qualified. Ziniquel had taken over the nominal duties of senior ghostier. But the twentieth seat remained empty! They justified it by saying that since four Incarnations were gone, the number of seats had to stay even. But it flouted all tradition. What was Tellury Crescent coming to? All the ghostiers had taken new apprentices. She could not remember the names of the children. "None of them are my friends anymore except Zin, Mory, and Emni. And not even *they* really trust me—there are too many people giving me unworkable advice, and they can't depend on me. When I talk to them, I feel that we are holding different conversations." She sobbed. "You're the only confidant I have left. And you're an eft!"

Don't blame me for that, his stillness said mournfully.

"But what am I to do? If you're right that I'm in danger from the atheists, it must be because they have guessed that I'm Pati's puppet." She scoured her eyes with her wet sleeve. "I'm keeping the peace. I count that as my greatest achievement. But I don't know how long I can hold on. It could be the flamens attempting my life: It was they who killed Arity—that would explain why the attempts are so inept. They don't have access to my private life. But if it is them, I have no hope of changing their minds. *They're* going to hate me whatever I do, just for being mortal."

Beau flicked his tail at the heavy signet on her forefinger.

"No, Beau. That isn't an option."

Flick.

"I know, I've got myself caught! Tied between a wild dog, a sharquette, and a predator! Where can I go without making everything worse? The city is holding its breath." She chuckled bitterly through her tears. "The only people that I *know* are still supporting me are Gold Dagger and the Hangman. They keep their promises to me, because I pay them. But what use is that, when what I need is a miracle—and all the flamens in the world would die rather than give me one!"

The wind pulled locks of hair out of her jeweled hairclasp. *It's appalling,* she thought blurrily. The Divinarch of Royalland, Calvary, Veretry, Pirady, Iceland, the sundry isles of the Archipelago, and Domesdys, et al., sitting sniveling on the Eftpool floor, hugging a fish. *What would my subjects say if they could see me? They'd be justified in casting me to the predators!*

At that she sat up on her heels. Pride straightened her spine. She marshaled her strength, caressing the filigreed flower on Beau's silver cheek. The wind was getting louder, the water splashing choppily. Beau wriggled, then lay still. Eyes carved of solid silver flesh met hers. Four years in the Eftpool had taught him both humor and wisdom: no longer a raw saltsider, absorbed in the conundrum of his own beauty, with no attention to spare for her troubles, he lived only to hear her troubles. *Follow your heart, Humi,* he said.

"I think I have no heart to follow."

He lay still. Struck by the recurrence of an old fear, she hooked hair out of her eyes, examined his flutter-tailed body.

Beneath one delicate fin she found it. A gray-green eyesore of mold.

"Beau, it can't be."

I didn't want you to know!

"Not you! You're only four years old!"

You've made a lot of use of me. You came to see me even before Erene told you to stay away, and many times afterward. She *came too, many times—*

He gave a buck, a twist, and rocketed out of her grip, arrowing gracefully beneath the surface.

"Beau!" How long would that grace last? How long until he wasted to a skeleton hung with tattered flesh? For a moment, despair threatened. Then she straightened her back.

She was Divinarch.

My last friend. She forced her way through the storm to the door. She paused outside, smoothing hair and skirts. *My last friend.* The Divinarch must look impeccable at all times. In the sudden quiet of the corridor, angry voices came faintly to her ears. Local reactionaries, probably, who had seen her retinue outside and demanded an audience. *My last friend.*

Well, she existed to serve her subjects.

Soulf's children scurried out of her way as she swept toward the street.

THIRTY

When Arity was dying, Hope *teth"d* with him to Rimmear. She knew that
for some reason, he had liked Uarech, where the night sky looked like the
inside of a hammered steel bowl, perforated with stars. It bounced her cries
for mercy right back down. Arity tossed and turned like a feverish child
when the Striver tried to enfold him in his wings. (And fever set in.) Pati
strode out, hurt, and did not return.

But Arity clutched at Hope's dress. So she stayed. She installed him
anonymously, with a staff of young *keres,* in a townhouse where he could
see the sky through the network of bridges over the chasm. Not that he
knew the sky, she thought some nights when she left the sickroom, slump-
ing against the wall, too exhausted and miserable to weep. In the first few
days, when delirium made him writhe against the white bandages that
stiffened his torso to a sausage, he called for Humi until Hope feared he
would do himself an injury. So she climbed between the sheets with him
and let him cover her with feverish kisses. He scratched her face and
breasts painfully with his talons as he tried to caress her.

When he came back to himself again, he seemed to forget these epi-
sodes. Desperation gave way to rancor and second-guessing. It was as if the
old Arity had been only a two-dimensional precursor of this bitter, mature
kere. Hope spent hours lying in the sickroom, holding him to her breast,
watching fuzzy shadows creep across the floor as the blazing Uarech sun
moved across the curtains. He pinned everything on Pati. She suspected
that it was not direct blame for the attack that had so nearly killed him, but
a thousand old, fermented resentments boiling to the surface. Pati had
bested Arity in everything they'd ever done. And it wasn't that Arity didn't
have the authority to order Pati out of his sight. As Heir, his authority had
been secondary only to that of the Divinarch. Hope had always wondered
at his fundamental inability to defy Pati. Over the course of these days, she

learned that his apparent disregard for politics was an outgrowth of that inability, not the other way around. Maybe it was somehow a result of the years they had spent together in that tiny Heaven in Kithrilindu. But she could not guess at anything beyond the jumbled reminiscences.

When he recovered as far as he ever would, he clammed up. His talons had grown out all over his body, so that he looked like a crippled humanoid rosebush with brown thorns. He refused to visit anyone he had known in Uarech. In fact, he moved to lodgings on a lower tier, sinking himself in total anonymity. Sadly, Hope saw he did not want or need her any more; so she went home.

Divaring Below was the largest Heaven in Fewarauw, a veritable city of *auchresh* on the shore of a lake nestled among spiky mountains. On Hope's return, Divaring's *serbalim* presented her with a house by the lakeshore, complete with servants who represented the whole ladder of social status, so that by speaking to her top *o-serbali* she could contact anyone in the city. However, she found that she did not want to. She walked on the shores of the lake at twilight; she attended the social functions put on by Divaring Below's circle of high-status *auchresh;* she suffered herself to be surrounded by a swarm of *keres*. From time to time she took a *ghauthiji*. She even made an *iu* friend or two, and revisited her Foundlinghood haunts with them.

But it was all paralyzingly dull. She missed Arity. She missed Pati. *Lesh kervayim* had scattered all over the world. Despite her misgivings regarding their activities, their visits were the highlights to which she looked forward for days in advance.

And of course Pati's visits were the best of all. Whenever he *teth¨d* to Fewarauw to see her, Hope met him in a disreputable tavern named the Skeldive, where the revolution-minded young *auchresh* of Divaring Below whiled away their spare time. No one knew her here. Under a male name, she had leased a permanent room to which Pati could *teth¨* in safety and rest in afterward. Since her return from Delta City, Hope had discovered that she did many things which were unheard of for *iuim*—or in some cases anyone of high status—or in some cases any *auchresh*. She often had to stop her mouth before she shocked her honorable elders pink. She was one of *lesh wrchrethrim:* the corrupted. The human-influenced. The ancients used it as a derogatory term, but the young thought it fashionable, at the same time as they embraced the ideas that *lesh kervayim* sprinkled anonymously in their midst, the concepts of hatred and contempt for humanity.

They sat downstairs at a little table, sipping *skri*. The multi-arched common room was foggy with smoke as well as the sulphuric stink of arrivals and departures. The human vice of pipe smoking, popularized by the Divine Guard, had recently become all the rage in Divaring Below. The salt herb which low-status *auchresh* substituted for tobacco reeked—it was a variety of catnip—but the anonymity that smoking it afforded her was worth the discomfort. When she had a pipe in her hand and *kere* clothes on, nobody looked twice at her. Pati had an aura of electric wide-awakeness. When he *teth˝d* into the leased room, he had exclaimed, "I've done it! I've done it!" She had had no idea what he was talking about, but she hadn't had time to ask before he pulled her into his arms, devouring her with kisses. Throwing her facedown on the foot of the bed, he had taken her with a violence that was almost rape. Troubled by his urgency, she had lain awake beside him afterward while he slept like a log.

"So what have you been doing with yourself, Hopie?" he said brightly. He looked as though he were going to divulge some delicious secret to her and just wanted to enjoy the wait for a few minutes. "Who have you told about my coming?"

"Nobody."

"Of course not."

"Pati, if I had," she said tiredly, "you would be surrounded by adulators right now. The youngsters down here are all as proud as peacocks. They all speak *auchraug,* they haven't any of those silly conceits about human ascendancy espoused by their *perich˝him,* and they worship your name. They would come to take back Delta City by force of arms if you needed them."

His smile faded. He played with his glass. "Mmm. I didn't know feelings were running that high."

"I myself have tried to explain to the *serbalim* that they may have an insurrection on their hands if they continue to prohibit all *auchresh* from going to the human lands. But I have no influence next to Broken Bird and Bronze Water. The *serbalim* are all listening to them."

"What? What about Broken Bird and Bronze?"

"You didn't know?"

He shook his head. "Hopie, honestly, I've had all I can do to keep my finger on the pulse of Delta City. This is why I need you."

She told him. "Your name may be all over the streets, but the Mother and the Sage are speaking into the ears that count. They're going the rounds of the major Heavens, preaching Golden Antelope's philosophy. And they're gaining followers among the *serbalim*—the *auchresh* that count. Many people think we ought to break off contact with the human lands altogether— that it's done both peoples enough harm already."

Pati swallowed his *skri* at a gulp. His pupils shrank, then expanded, fluttering, as his body assimilated the alcohol. "What can we do about it?"

"*We* don't need to. *Lesh kervayim* are."

"They haven't been reporting to me—"

"They can't, Pati. They told me it worries them that they're acting without your approval, but they dare not break the prohibition on *teth"ing* into human lands, because the penalty is expulsion from Heaven. So I told them that you would approve of anything they do in your name."

"Within *reason!*" Pati's nails flurried an angry rhythm on the table, denting the saltwood. "But Broken Bird and Bronze are the highest-status *auchresh* in the world now that Golden Antelope's gone. The cabal can't defy *them!*"

"Not openly, maybe." Hope glanced around. At a nearby table sat a prominent young Divaring Below reactionary, surrounded by friends and disciples. Others threaded their way between the tables, stopping to laugh out loud or plant a kiss on a friend's lips. They wore bright silk shirts and breeches, not traditional Fewarauwan gray. One intimation that Pati was here, and the Skeldive would go wild. "*Lesh kervayim* are going amongst the *auchresh* of the small Heavens," Hope said. "They are telling the story of Arity's death, and the stasis which has gripped the Ellipse since Humi became Divinarch. I know what happened in the stateroom the night the Old One died: I know the story is a string of extenuating circumstances; but as *lesh kervayim* tell it, the flamens have joined up with the atheists, and Humi was in league with all of them all along, plotting to seize power. Fewarauw is cooking like a lidded pot, Pati. If you wanted an army, you'd have one in five minutes."

He laid his hands flat on the table, turning them as if admiring imperfect works of art. Hope saw the scar he had given himself in Rimmear trailing around the side of his left hand, a purple crease between the bony thumb and index finger. For the first time, his voice betrayed weariness. "This shows how much I rely on you, Hope. I didn't know a whisper of this. Delta City is hermetically sealed." She was quiet. Finally he looked up. "What can you tell me about the other continents?"

"Val and Sepi were reticent, to say the least." Hope recalled their guarded speech and traditional clothes, their broad-brimmed hats, the way they slipped to her door in the middle of the day. "But I gather that things are much the same everywhere, allowing for differences in temperament."

"I could strangle those idiots. Hope, what on earth did you go authorizing them for?"

His displeasure shocked Hope. "What do you mean? They're fighting for *you!* Pati, it seems odd that *I* have to be the one to say this, but maybe you're too closely involved in affairs in Delta City to see that this stasis can't last much longer. The atheists are going to get angry with Humi very soon. Things are going to erupt. And what are you going to do about it? At least *lesh kervayim* are making some preparations!" She felt compelled to add, "Even if I don't agree with their methods. It's foolhardy to inflame the *firim.*"

Pati sat back in his chair, gazing at her out of his different-colored eyes. "But here is what you don't know, Hope. I have made preparations. And perhaps I can even make use of these *firim.*" He jumped to his feet. "I shouldn't have come here now—I might miss the action. I wanted to fetch you to guard my back; I was about to tell you when you started prattling about our idiot *kervayim.*" He glanced around the room. *Auchresh* stared at him, drawing suspiciously on their pipes. The prominent reactionary leaned over to a henchman and muttered something in his ear.

"Do you think," Pati asked, looking down at her, his wings fluttering, "that I really could raise an extempore army?"

Draped over the back of her chair, Hope's wings lifted in an instinctive reaction to danger. With an effort, she stilled them. "Why don't you," she said slowly, "explain why you would want to do that."

"I've arranged for the Divinarch's demise. She's been warned: she's fair game. She knows that I am behind the warnings, for she went so far as to offer me her life. And I should be getting back to make sure that it goes off all right. It's several hours later in Delta City than it is here, but the little ceremony which I plan to disrupt is not scheduled for any particular time. It's a private gathering at Godsbrother Puritanism's, hosted by the ghost-iers, for both atheists and devotees."

Hope scarcely heard. Because she had never heard of any attempts on Humi's health or position, she had assumed that Pati had not been serious when he talked about removing distractions. But he had not just been serious; he had been talking life and death. Humi must have kept these warnings quiet, either out of stupid pride or because she really did not know who was trying to kill her. "I never thought you meant it!" she gasped.

"Of course I meant it." Pati's eyes darkened. "And it was going perfectly smoothly, until . . . until . . . the thing with Arity. So I am going to use the groundwork that I laid to achieve a different end."

She hardly dared to say it, in case she was wrong. "To make yourself Divinarch."

"Hope, I have to." His eyes pleaded with her. "You must see that."

"Arity will hate you for this," she said through stiff lips.

"Arity already hates me. If he feels anything, any more."

"I shan't let you do it!" She bounced to her feet on half-opened wings. "Pati, you can't resort to such underhandedness. It's bad enough in Val and

Sepia and Silver, but for all our sakes, never mind Humi's, I can't allow it in you."

"Do you think you can stop it? Her death is prophesied!"

"Not necessarily! Prophecies don't come true until someone fulfills them!" Hope felt herself losing the stately bearing which had been her trademark since she came back to Divaring Below. Her voice scaled up, up—now all the *auchresh* in the Skeldive would know she was an *iu*—"I love you, Pati, but I can't let you get away with this—"

He smiled, agonizingly slowly. "Hope, I never knew you to wax so sentimental about a mortal. And it's not as though I didn't give her a chance. After she became Divinarch, I allowed half a year to see whether she could succeed on the Throne. She could not. She vacillates intolerably. Balancing acts are one thing; indecisiveness is another. Her idea of strategy is to degrade the Ellipse into a mud-slinging fight, so that nothing is accomplished. Exactly the same as when she was twentieth councillor. But now that she is the ruler of the human lands, it is unacceptable. In Delta City, Samaal, Rivapirl, Westchasm, K'Fier, Port Teligne, Rukarow, and the other cities, the silent struggle of atheists against devotees has come to a head. You are quite right when you think that soon things are going to erupt."

"Just as the Old One wanted," Hope said with dry lips.

"Just so. I am taking over in a last-ditch attempt to prevent war."

"Pati. I know you. You won't stop there—"

With one foot, he shoved the table with the half-empty glasses away. He stood facing her, arms folded, perfectly relaxed—but it was the relaxation of a predator on the wing. "Be quiet," he said through his teeth. "Come with me."

"Pati?" came a voice from a nearby table. "Pati? *Serbali?* Is that really—"

Pati turned and grinned at the *kere* with all his teeth. "Hello there! What's your name? Want to help me take Delta City?"

"I'm going," Hope said. "Where is she? Tellury Crescent?"

Someone in a far corner dropped a glass. A clamor of voices reverberated through the Skeldive, and the *auchresh* crowded around Hope and Pati's table, touching Pati as if he were a lucky statue. None of them had ever seen their vaunted leader, of course, but no one else would have had the nerve to impersonate him. He smiled past her at them. "My *cujalim!*" Charisma radiated off him like heat.

Hope felt sick. "I'm going," she said, feeling futile.

His brows drew together, just slightly. "She's not at—"

"Your love for me is your weakness, Pati." She kissed him by way of thanks. His lips were stiff. The *auchresh* cheered her; someone pulled off her cap, letting her hair slither down. The tavernmaster jumped on a table,

shouting, adding to the clamor as he tried to quiet the chaos. Some Divar-
ingians bawled joyously at Pati, and others brandished their weapons, cres-
cent-knives and projectile throwers. Fewarauwan culture still revolved
around its hunters. They were prepared.

"Hope, no one is at Tellury Crescent!" Pati shouted. "I never said they
were!"

But she had already *teth"d.*

THIRTY-ONE

"Good evening. Many thanks for your hospitality." Humi smiled with frozen lips at Auspi as she glided into Godsbrother Puritanism's parlor on Dore Street. A few ghosts on pedestals relieved the formal grouping of chairs and tables. She recognized some of her own. That should have been pleasant, but all she felt was the irony of it: there was Simmel, a Calvarese girl, one of her favorites, sitting smoking on a plinth, proud and self-willed—unable to reach or help Humi, as she felt herself fading like a shadow when clouds thicken over the sun.

She knew the signs for what they were. None of the ghostiers had come near her in days, and though the atheists wouldn't have spoken to her in any case, they'd been avoiding her more assiduously than usual.

But perhaps she had lost track of time. It stretched like elastic. Just when she wasn't expecting it, she would look up and find that a sixday had gone by. At her very lowest guess, it had been several sixdays since she'd had a conversation with another human being: her evenings spent sitting in the rooms of state, alone, or with guests whose puerile small talk grated like gravel on her ears, felt like purgatory. Oh, yes; the Hangman had come to visit her on Sageday. They had talked of Domesdys. The Hangman was really a woman. She had run away from Port Teligne at the age of eleven; for five years she had lived in Delta City as a boy, and then one day she woke up and realized that she was a criminal. After that, she had concealed her gender on purpose. The conversation had served only to remind Humi that other places existed beside the arid garden she had made of the Palace and that she could not go there. She had sent the Hangman off sharply.

Such a wide gap between the political and the personal, though the amount of contact one sustained with a person might remain the same! So strange to remember that many, if not all, of the people sitting in this parlor had once been her friends!

She chose a seat in the center of the room. She felt no irritation when the human Guards arrayed themselves in concentric rings around her, closing off her view of all but a portion of the room. She'd finally accepted the Guards' dogged companionship; the other day, driven by desperation, she had even tried to strike up a conversation with a couple of them. They had remained silent, martyred expressions creeping onto their handsome faces. Belstem must have told them to let nothing slip. But it would have been foolish to talk to them, at any rate. They reported every word she spoke to Belstem and Aneisneida.

She became aware that the whole Ellipse was here, watching her. She disposed of her gracious smile. The lemans, too, and the multicolored gaggle of children and teenagers who were the ghostiers' new apprentices. Even some garden-variety flamens and socialites! My, Puritanism had taken his nose down out of the air! What were they doing here?

No one was speaking. Hadn't they been, a minute ago? She looked around confusedly.

"Divinarch?" Goquisite gazed coldly at her. "We asked you a question. Why have you ceased to make ghosts? It is disturbing to us all."

"You see, you are so very talented," Algia said sweetly. She wore a ridiculously furbelowed dress. "Tellury Crescent feels the loss of your creations."

"I am no longer a ghostier," Humi fumbled, taken off balance. "I am Divinarch. Why would you want me to make ghosts? That would require me to neglect my other duties."

"Do you not see? Your position requires you both to make ghosts and to govern the land. You are still senior ghostier," Sol said reasonably. "It is not legal for you to stop making ghosts. After all, that is the offense Erene died for."

"Is it my fault that there is no one qualified to take my place as senior ghostier?" Humi asked. Why had she let them put her on the defensive? "I should think that is your fault, as much as anyone else's!"

"Oh, well struck!" Soderingal Summer Nearecloud muttered piercingly.

Gold Dagger was here too, the spring mud from the streets still on his boots, those boots resting on Simmel's veneered plinth. He winked at Humi. The signal of comradeship was like a sip of water to a woman lost in the desert. "It is my own business what I may choose to do and not to do," she said. "I am the Divinarch. And I would thank you all not to question my choices."

"She must've promised the Heir she wouldn't make ghosts any more," piped a young voice. "She does everything he says."

"I perceive," Humi's ringing tones quavered only slightly, "that the pur-

pose of this salon is not to discuss what I do with my spare time. Milady
Ankh, could we introduce the topic of the gathering?"

"She thinks everything has to do with politics," said the same high-
pitched voice. It was Eternelipizaran.

"Could someone shut that child up!" Goquisite hissed, then cleared her
throat. "Yes. Milady Divinarch, we wish to broach a delicate subject: your
stand on atheism as a political code. Asking your venerable pardons, Puritanism, Joyfulness. Especially asking your pardon as our host, Puritanism."

Humi grasped the arms of her chair. "My stand on atheism is the same as
it has always been. It must coexist with piety: neither doctrine must become militant. I strive to preserve this balance in my arbitration over the
Ellipse. Is this not self-evident?"

Belstem coughed. Goquisite tried to suppress a smile. "Milady, I fear it
is all too evident."

"Thank you! I favor neither atheism nor piety. I vote predominantly for
neither one nor the other. I bestow equal numbers of Divine Seals on
each."

"Milady!" Belstem objected. "You may not favor either doctrine, but that
is not wise! You have not bestowed a Divine Seal in almost four months.
The scrolls recording the proposals on which you have not yet decided fill
half my study!"

Sol said insinuatingly, "Is it not significant that Lord Summer must be
the one to file the Ellipse's decisions?"

"*I* haven't time!" Immediately Humi saw she had been wrong to defend
herself against a comment which had been meant as a subliminal reinforce-
ment of the mood. Significant looks passed among the guests.

"Divine Seals aside," amended Goquisite. "What is your personal opinion of atheism, milady? That's what we *really* wish to find out."

"Well!" said a local socialite. Apparently her rulebook of etiquette had
been breached. *Milady, you'll see a good deal more than that before they're
through,* Humi thought.

"I don't think I am at liberty to express a personal opinion," she said.
"The Divinarch must be impartial. I cannot admit to a bias which would
offend some of you gathered here today, and I wonder at you for demanding it of me, Milady Ankh."

A couple of the other flamens nodded approvingly. Humi gathered she'd
scored a point. But Goquisite made a swift comeback. "The Divinarch may
always have been impartial. But never before has he had to deal with more
than one significant faction. He has always been pious, because that was his
only choice. In order for you to follow in the footsteps of your predecessors,
you too must declare for one party and one alone."

"But what about my immediate predecessor!" Humi felt herself losing her grip. Her chair in the middle of the room suddenly seemed less isolated. The faces of the councillors pressed in around her, while Goquisite smiled sweetly from an intrusive proximity. "*He* had to deal with the same conditions I face!"

"And his strategy?" Ziniquel said in the clear voice he reserved for public statements. She could not believe he was speaking. Not against her. "*Laissez-faire!* That is not acceptable any longer! Things have come to a head, Humi. You've got to declare!"

With growing horror, she realized that she was not going to be able to speak for the next few minutes. She shook her head mutely.

The whispers increased in volume until Goquisite said, "I see that the Divinarch is overcome by the gravity of her dilemma. Perhaps we should refresh ourselves while she collects her mind."

The less callous guests greeted her suggestion with gratitude. Puritanism rumbled an order to Auspi, who pattered out of the room along with two of the apprentices to fetch refreshments. The flamen councillors kept no servants.

At last Humi looked up. A ray of weak sun pierced through a window, dispelling the gray drizzle which had persisted all day. It was spring. Back in Beaulieu, her uncles and her father would be deciding which crops to plant to produce the best aesthetic impact from the hilltops. Gossip about the new, human Divinarch must have filtered through the hills to the saltside. Did they have any idea who the gossip referred to? She wished most of it weren't so slanderous. Simmel sat on her plinth, her dark hair glowing auburn in the sun. Humi had gotten her as she was telling her her life story. What a sordid little tale it had been! But Humi had always been attracted to Calvarese ghosts; maybe it was because somewhere deep inside, in some symbolic way which she had not the energy to figure out now, she identified with their rough-and-tumble existence. Raised the third of four children in the bronze town of Hijjaro, in northwestern Calvary, Simmel had gone hungry every day. Sorting ore at three years old, raped by her father at eight, first lover at twelve. How could Humi identify with that?

Time slowed and zoomed, slowed and zoomed. Her ears rang with a tintinnabulation like thousands of tiny bells. Only after a long while (as it seemed to her) did a voice penetrate her trance.

"Gateaux?" Auspi extended a tray of small cakes, each one a masterpiece of the cake decorator's art. "A gateau, milady?"

She must have been repeating the question for some minutes. All the eyes in the room were fixed upon them, and a muddy flush was creeping up the girl's neck. "A gateau, milady?"

"Yes." The word did not come out. Humi tried again. "Yes, thank you." She took the nearest one and bit into it. It was delicious, she was sure, but it tasted like wood pulp. "They are very good gateaux, Godsbrother Puritanism. I compliment whoever gave them to you."

At her words, the councillors relaxed and began to chat again. What had they expected? she wondered. That she would vomit on the floor? She forced herself to finish the cake. "Is there any wine?"

"Wine, Auspi!" Puritanism ordered.

Auspi left the room. The ray of sun wavered and vanished, the drizzle commencing again. Goquisite said, "Milady, have you given any thought to the matter?"

Was there something I needed to give thought to? "I . . ."

"I have an idea! Why don't we put it to the vote?" Maras said brightly, a little too late.

You missed your cue, Humi thought as the last few minutes returned to her. *You need to brush up on your timing, Milady Crane!*

"Put *what* to the vote, do I hear you ask?" Maras continued. "Why, the Divinarch's stance. She seems unwilling to declare for either faction present, and it really is time that she does declare. So if she is impartial, surely that's the best way to decide where she stands."

"An excellent idea," Goquisite said irritably. "The whole Ellipse is present except for the Heir. Belstem, shall we?"

Clearing his throat impressively, rinsing his teeth with his tongue, Belstem stood up and rested his weight on a small secretaire. It seemed liable to give way at any moment. "Since you ask my advice, I feel obliged to give it." He was a worse actor even than Maras. "Our city is in disarray. My police are in constant demand to quell riots before they swamp whole districts. So are the other councillors' men."

Gold Dagger laughed out loud, then caught himself. He transferred his feet to an embroidered sofa and twiddled his thumbs.

Belstem ignored him. "Now, there are two causes for these riots." He looked at Joyfulness. Joyfulness' new leman, a little blond boy named, Humi remembered, Tine, nudged the flamen in the ribs. Joyfulness wrapped Tine's little hand in his.

"One cause," he said, "is that there are more immigrants in Delta City than ever before, and they vie with our indigent poor, so that large numbers of people have no food or work or shelter. And there are not enough flamens to ease their need. Many of them are here in the first place because their homes are uninhabitable: that is, the flamens who have always made their living conditions bearable with miracles are gone. This argues for a return to piety, and a push for more lemans to join the flamenhood."

"Sounds reasonable to me," Humi said.

Belstem glared at her. "*However*, the other, more pressing cause of discontent—and this goes for the Divinarchy as a whole—is that many atheists are disappointed in their Divinarch. The revolution against the old regime has been successful. But where is the new regime? We are caught in limbo. We have not yet been permitted to put economic reforms into effect. We have not yet been permitted to help the starving people to help themselves. Our hands are tied."

"We hold that instead of simply asking a flamen to fulfill one's need, one should work for one's daily bread," Trisizim clarified. Since when, Humi wondered, had *he* been an atheist?

"I could not have put it better myself," Belstem growled. "Now the origin of this problem lies with the Divinarch, who has not permitted—"

Humi stood up. "I think I should be allowed to defend—"

Her guards surrounded her, pushing her back down. Her elbow banged painfully against the arm of her chair. "Jerithu? Skimmeren? Hafi?" she said. They avoided her eyes.

"The fault," Belstem repeated guiltily, "obviously lies with the Divinarch. I propose—in short—a change of Divinarch. Erhmm. The Ellipse—erhmm—has the Ellipse got any suggestions?"

The guards moved aside so that Humi could see him glance ostentatiously around the parlor. Goquisite's lips moved: she must have been suggesting that Belstem himself would make an admirable Divinarch. Humi couldn't hear a word, nor his demurral, the pretty phrases Goquisite used to persuade him, his suspiciously rapid consent. The ringing was back in her ears.

"Who supports Belstem for Divinarch!"

The applause was polite yet deafening.

"Shall we put it to the vote?"

Ziniquel was beginning to look uncomfortable. Straddling a chair, he grimaced and blurted, "Yes!"

Humi watched as with much unnecessary talk, they improvised a system of silent voting, dropping scraps of paper into a basket which Pieti's adopted daughter carried around to each councillor. The voices of the lemans sounded troubled (a near-impossibility); the lesser socialites looked on, round-eyed. Goquisite took the basket from the girl, stood up and smoothed her skirts. She started to pick through the papers, turning each one over, pursing her lips and noting it on a tablet. "This is a farce," Humi said. Goquisite started, and dropped the basket. "I'm sure there is no need to count the votes. Why don't you just get on with . . ." What was she saying again? The room swam. "With . . ." She shook her head angrily. "With . . . with it."

Goquisite could not look Humi in the eye. That felt like a triumph. "I—I feel that after all, we have no need to count the votes," Goquisite said. "The Ellipse chooses Belstem Summer for Divinarch. All that remains is for you to bestow the Divine Seal on the decision, Divinarch. There can be no appeal. The vote was unanimous."

In the dead silence that ensued, Auspi pattered into the room. She hurried over to Humi with silver tray, wineglass, and bottle. "Sorry," she apologized. "I couldn't find the wine. A godsman in the cellars gave me some—"

In that instant, Humi knew exactly what was in the transparent liquid streaming from the mouth of the bottle into the goblet. They had planned everything, even down to this, reinforcing their plot so many times that everything else became unnecessary. Why had they bothered with the elaborate setup, if all along, they planned to resort to this? *When bloodshed starts, laws turn obsolete,* Golden Antelope had said. He had forgotten to mention *absurd.* Humi wanted to laugh.

Then, without transition, she had no desire to laugh at all. The ray of sun reappeared through the window, slanting between Auspi's thin, black-clad arm and body, illuminating the goblet like a giant diamond.

Perfectly clear. She hoped it would be tasteless.

"Thank you, Auspi." She lifted the glass out of the sun. "To your health, my *imrchim*—lords and ladies—Godsisters and Godsbrothers."

She drank.

Her throat seizes up. Numbness races from her fingers and toes toward her heart, constricting it. She cannot feel her body. She cannot see through her eyes.

A door slams against a wall, and there is a smell of sulphur. *"No!* Damn him!"

It must be an *auchresh* voice, to penetrate this blackness that is getting deeper by the millisecond.

"She is dying! That was poison, salt aconite, stupid humans, lethal in less than a minute, *do something—*"

"We didn't do it!" A woman is screaming. Humi can just hear the words. "We didn't want to kill her, just to make her abdicate, we didn't—"

"It was you who killed her, with poison or without! *Godsbrother!* Quickly! Help her!"

She tumbles endlessly into blackness. It is opaque and soft as wool. Cold as a snowy night.

THIRTY-TWO

A man is crying.

Horrendous sound.

Racking sobs.

A woman tries to comfort him.

He keeps weeping.

"Pull yourselves together, idiots!"

No woman has a voice this loud. It is like a faraway gong.

Humi is in darkness. Her mind is working very slowly: she has only just figured out that she is sitting with her head on someone's shoulder, her limbs sprawled out on cushions. She can feel her body, though she cannot move, and the pain is still far away, for which she is grateful. Her eyes hurt the worst. As if they are filled with sand.

She would like to pass out again, but the voices rattle like gravel on her ears, keeping her in the black land on the edge of unconsciousness.

"We killed—let the blaspheming atheists kill her—"

"She is not dead. And they did *not* kill her. Pati did. How else do you think he knew to appear when the confusion was at its height? He got you all into his control masterfully, did he not? Was it not reassuring to see those gods appear with their knives and their crossbows? Weren't you grateful when they started to give orders?"

The man gulps. "We—"

"Zin! Zin! It's all right, love! You knew her best—where can we take her?"

Where has Humi heard this voice before?

"H-h . . . Emni, I can't think. All those dead bodies . . . Maras-thizinith . . . Pieti . . . even his little *daughter*, for the gods' sake! All dead!"

What has happened? Who is dead? Humi is not. She knows that, although just now she doesn't know much else.

"Never mind!" The woman is near tears herself, but she insists, "Just try to think, Zin!"

With a massive effort, the man controls his grief. "Hem. His name is Hem. He runs a curiosity shop in Temeriton. He used to be Erene's apprentice . . . It's all I can think of!"

"Anywhere will do, as long as Pati is not likely to run across her there." The loud voice is cold, irritable. Why does Humi think it should be sweet? "He would be extremely vexed to find out she is alive. I would not put it past him to take steps."

"I hardly see the Divinarch frequenting the worst part of the whorehouse district in the near future!" the woman says.

"Quite right. He will be too busy. Now remember, Ziniquel, and you, Solemnity, keep your mouths shut about this. Only we three, and of course Godsbrother Joyfulness, know that she is not nailed in that coffin in Joyfulness' parlor, too contorted from the effects of the poison to be displayed to the public. We must keep it that way."

"Agreed, Maiden. Gods! Agreed."

The blackness lifts with a bump, and reorientates many times, up, down, and swinging. She recognizes the familiar motion of a sedan. Now and then the voices intrude on the blackness again, but she doesn't try to understand them. She has no sense of direction or time.

There is a jolt. She feels herself topple sideways as the person on whom she is leaning starts up, rapping on the side of the sedan to get the porter's attention. Ziniquel's voice calls, "Stop here."

DELTA
CITY

This is for all my people who've respected me doing my thing—or who've tried to interfere, thus producing an equal but opposite reaction! Props also to everyone who showed support on the 16th. It meant a lot. In chronological order: James, Margaret, Matthew; Donald Alec, Donald Allen, Ian, Rachel, Roddy, Sharon; Hannah, Saffy, & The Little School in general; Diane; Andrea, Andrew, Ari, Ashish, Brent, Chong, Chris, Cory, Dayone, Ethan, Gary × 2, Greg, Jamil, Jen, (my special rid), John, Julian, Julio, Justin, Kara, Kiet, Lawrence, Malik, Matt, Mike, Mina, Miriam, Nathan, Oleg, Ravi & The Rest, Sandhya, Sarah; Joe; and everybody I've left out either accidentally or on purpose.

CONTENTS

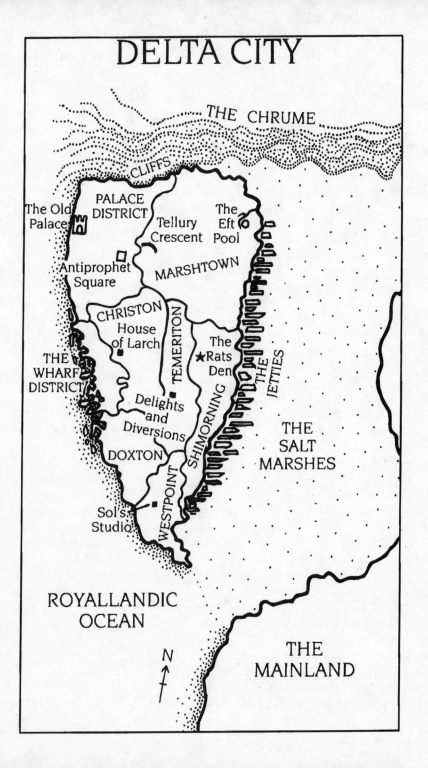

"Miracles are according to the ignorance wherein we are by nature, and not according to nature's essence . . ."

—Montaigne, *Essays*

THE REDHEAD

Gete and his father returned to Sarberra behind the rest of the fleet. The sun was half-sunk in the ruby glitter of the sea. They tied their boat to its crag, slung the catch on their backs, and started up the path that wound between hillocks of gorse and heather.

Gannelets winged their way home. High overhead, Gete saw the batlike shadow of an early-rising predator. The village clung to the eastern slope of the island. Its stone huts glowed pink in the sunset. Dusk was a relief to eyes that had squinted at the black sparkle of the sea all day, searching for the little disturbances that indicated shoals of surface-feeding swordfish. As they entered the village, Gete and Da avoided waddling geese, bone-thin cats, and dirty, sleepy toddlers. Something was not as usual . . . Gete had it! An evening as still and sweet-smelling as this, anyone with a minute to call his own should be taking the air, puffing on heather-stem pipes, mending clothes, repairing friendships.

"Da," he started, but before his weary brain could find the right words, Da had gone ahead down the dark gangway between their home and the Silverfins'.

Gete closed his mouth, plunked the net of barely moving fish he carried in the cold-box out back, and went into the kitchen.

A fug of smoke filled the room. Women and children swarmed, twittering. Gete sensed an air of macabre excitement at someone else's misfortune. But everyone who mattered was here; who could that be? The men sat around the hearth, discoursing with slighly more animation than usual. Heavy boots, heavy smocks, heavy faces.

Nights, Gete generally took his place on the edge of the circle—it wasn't worth offending his elders by going off on his own, might give them the wrong impression, what with him being a redhead and all they'd be quick to think he had a chip on his shoulder; didn't make sense, but that was the

way of the world. Amazing to think it wasn't that long ago he'd been drool-
ing with happiness, *one of the men at last!*, drop-jawed like an idiot as he
swiveled his face from speaker to speaker.

He'd heard all the conversations there were to have, now—four-hands
times each, maybe five-hands. Now while the men talked, his thoughts
went to Heaven. It lay on the nearby salt island of Faraxa. He had never
been there. But everything Desti said about it made it sound more fascinating. Desti said he'd take Gete there as soon as his *serbalim* gave him
permission. Nebulous, cranky beings! Desti wouldn't dream of going
against their orders, even though he resented them. They did not like his
coming to Sarberra, although they had not expressly forbidden it. Could
they really be as sagacious as he painted them?

Desti himself was so ordinary. Smiling and equable, always ready to help
caulk a hull or quiet a crying child. Gete's mother insisted on mending his
tattered tunic and breeches for him, not seeing that the holes were *decoration,* like the fish and birds she embroidered on her own family's festival
smocks.

But back when Desti first started visiting Sarberra, he had been much
stranger than he was now, more violent. It had taken him several months
just to get used to working in sunlight.

What kind of village could Heaven be, to support such impractical behavior? Gete wondered. Or was it so inhospitable that the gods *had* to
indulge in impracticalities, just to keep their heads straight?

Gete wondered so much about Heaven that he knew it could not be good
for him. Like right now. Standing here with his mouth open, letting his
thoughts drift! Anchor out, boy!

He sidled through the gathering and located Da just as he pushed between two younger fishermen and plopped himself down in the circle. His
stool screeched at its misfortune. The smell of sea salt hung around the men
like smoke: it permeated their coarse white fur and their hair. Gete
breathed deeply, gripping Da's fish-scale-splotched shoulders. He winked
at Tience and Rag and Imp and Tim, who all stood behind their own
fathers. "I should na say he'll last the night," Godsman Stickleback pronounced with certainty. "Did ye na see the fella's face? He looked ninety
and he could not be more than sixty."

"Na," Old Godsman Flamefish interrupted, with the privilege of age.
Power gleamed in his cataract-filled eyes. "Na sixty at all, not at all. Old,
that man is! Old! Eighty is more like it . . ."

"Na," Godsman Sharquetooth said. "He is not more than fifty-five. Fifty-
eight at the outside!"

Gete could feel the tension in his father's shoulders. Da was physically restraining himself from interrupting the exchange. Not even the pigments and gaudy rags he donned for the children's amusement at festival time could make Teous Gullfeather a figure of fun. At times Gete had tried hard, inside his own head, to make Da look pompous; but he just could not do it.

Da cut in respectfully, "Who is this man? What has passed?"

"Eh?" Old Flamefish turned their way, head poking out like a sea turtle's. "Ah, Teous Gullfeather! Tis a flamen who has come! Gods-brother . . ."

"Transcendence," someone supplied.

"Tis so. Has the summer fever, he do, and he's dying. Divinarch preserve us. His leman rowed him from Letherra all by herself. She's na so old, neither, poor little scrap, and does he die, she must take his place here and now . . . we will be responsible . . ."

Gete kissed the top of Da's head, then turned away to see what there was to eat. A flamen was a flamen—even if it seemed strange, almost blasphemous, for one to be doing such an ordinary thing as dying. You'd think he would rejuvenate himself with a miracle. But everything flamens and lemans did was strange—they were far harder to understand than the one god that Gete knew. Wasn't that odd! Gete caught his mother's eye. She disengaged herself from the chattering flock of women and he hugged her in greeting. Her body felt small in his arms; his chin touched the top of her head. He pointed at the cooking hearth. "Eh?"

"How is it ye're so skinny, my son, when all ye think of is food?" She pulled his head down so that she could kiss his cheek. "It'd be disrespectful to lay things out till the flamen's gone, poor man, but ye might as well have some stew. No telling how long he'll cling to this world, and 'twont be as tasty tomorrow. Desti's watching it."

Desti was not only stirring the big turtle-shell pot but minding several babies. His silvery-white wings, as tattered as his shirt, buzzed behind his shoulders, so fast that Gete was worried. Once, Desti had opened his wings too suddenly and taken a small child's finger off. After that he had been more careful. This absentmindedness meant he was really upset. "What's wrong wit ye?" Gete asked in between mouthfuls of stew that he gulped without chewing.

"He keeps asking to see me. Your Mother Brownfern hasn't let anyone know. But I can hear him through the wall."

Gete couldn't hear anything over the noise of voices and spattering flames, but he knew Desti had faculties that were more than human.

"I've never seen one of *them* before." Desti cursed in his own language and yanked a little Sharquetooth girl out of the hearth. "*Haugthirre* child!

How does he know I'm here? I stayed out of sight! Should I go in to see him, or would that just be throwing oil on a fire? He won't lie *still!*"

Gete served himself seconds and began to eat. *So* good. Salt and fresh fish. Coriander and other herbs from his mother's garden. Autumn was the best time for herbs. He wished all the world would clear out; after a hard day on the water, a man deserved peace and quiet—

"You stupid *haugthirre hymanni!* Mannerless!" Desti cuffed Gete on the back of the head, so hard that Gete dropped the bowl on a child, who squealed. Gete's teeth knocked together on the spoon and he swallowed a chip, the shock made him lose his balance. His head smashed into the stone wall. Stars exploded between his temples. Growling, he struggled back, ready to fetch Desti a proper one, when the god grabbed his wrists with one hand and his shoulder with the other, holding him immobile. "I'm sorry! I always *forget!*" And Desti was kissing him, on his forehead, his cheeks, he was always so contrite—

"And you *oughter* be!" Gete struggled away. "Gods' blood, what's the *matter* with you?"

Before the god could answer, the door to the inner room swung open and everyone in the kitchen turned. A half-naked, scraggy, white-headed apparition staggered out on the arm of a blond-furred girl. His head swung ponderously. All the noise in the room drained into silence as he stumbled toward Desti, muttering. Desti sprang to his feet and flattened himself against the wall, fingers seeking the cracks as if he were trying to find a door handle. The girl—the leman—had tear paths on the fur of her cheeks. "Lord . . ." the flamen sighed, coming on. "Lord god . . ."

Mother Brownfern burst out of the inner room. "Godsbrother!" At once reverent and righteously scandalized at her patient's behavior, she grabbed the flamen's arm and dug her heels in.

"Please, Transcendence!" The leman had a thin, young voice. "Please lie down. There's no god here." Fiercely, she gestured at Desti to get out. The translucent lids of Desti's huge silvery eyes flickered up and down. He didn't move.

"How dare you lie to me, leman!" the flamen shouted. His voice boomed like a horn. "I feel him! You cannot know how I feel him! He is like a shining sun on my blindness!" *Gods,* Gete thought.

Belatedly, a couple of women jumped up to help maneuver the flamen backwards. The men hitched themselves around on their stools, mouths dropping open, heads swiveling. After a painfully undignified struggle, the Godsbrother was hauled back once more into the inner room.

Desti's fingers closed on Gete's wrist in an unbreakable grip. "I have to see him." Gete cringed under the eyes of everyone in the room as Desti pulled him toward the inner door. "He can't possibly see me. It's a myth. I must find out. We are not gods, we never have been! That is what the *serbalim* say!" He pulled Gete through the rude plank door of the bedroom, and as it closed behind them, hot smoky firelight gave way to steamy darkness, and the smell of smoke and stew gave way to the pungent smell of boiled herbs. Gamesfoot, to draw out the fever. It didn't seem to be working. Gete's nostrils flared as he detected the smell of death. The leman and Mother Brownfern were kneeling on either side of the pallet, holding the Godsbrother down: they seemed frozen in place, their pale faces turned toward Gete and Desti.

"Lord," muttered the Godsbrother, and he shook them off like unwanted garments. Struggling to his knees, he lowered his forehead to the goatskin coverlet. "My lord god, instruct me. Am I obeying your wishes by continuing in the Archipelago? Or must I return to Delta City? The Divinarch has issued a call to all of us to return. But I feel that I am needed here. But I no longer hear you so clearly in my heart as I did." He stopped, breathing heavily. "On this island alone, two children lie sick. There is a blight on the mountain flax. These rocks were never meant to support humanity! I am *needed* here! Lord god, what must I do?"

"I'm not a *serbali*," Desti said. "I'm not even a *mainraui*. I'm inferior. I'm *wrchrethre*. Why are you asking me?" His wings quivered. His voice rose. "All I know is Fresh Spring Heaven and Sarberra! I know nothing of you and your cities and Divinarches!"

The leman sobbed. Gete staggered back out of reach of Desti's wings. "Lord god!" the flamen begged. "Please . . ." He had been sinking deeper and deeper into his prostration as he spoke. Now his head turned so that all his weight rested on one cheek. He let out a whuffling sigh.

Panic gripped Gete. How much worse luck could there be than to see a flamen dying? He reached for Desti's arm. "Let's get out of here. Mother Brownfern'll say you did it. Anything to shift the blame. Dry old bitch—"

Desti swung around. Pale furless face, strained unseeing silver eyes. Then he pulled away and vanished into thin air.

It hurt Thani almost more than his actual death that when the Sarberrans laid his corpse out, Transcendence's mouth settled slowly into a smile. The heat in the inner room of the hut made him stiffen fast, and as rictus set in, his smile became more pronounced. He had been gaunt when he died, and now the skin of the corpse tightened over the skull so that it looked almost as though he were laughing; gloating cruelly over the desolation in which he had abandoned her.

Grief numbed her to the core, so that she fumbled for words to thank the islanders for their hospitality. Gone. He was gone. Out of determination to complete her duties as a leman—not out of any sense of obligation to the cadaver—she watched over him all night, resisting the Archipelagans' efforts to coax her away, refusing their offers to take her place. What did they know about her flamen? Transcendence had hated these islands. You'd never have known it, watching him bend his white head to listen to the fishermen's wives and children, spend energy he didn't have to work miracles for them; but then again, he had had nothing against the Archipelagans themselves. They were just a procession of hungry mouths, injured limbs, and blighted crops, like any other people. What Transcendence hated was the dazzling heat, the everlasting smell of fish, the hours they spent sailing from island to island, the breeze that never let up so that after a while it felt like a sandstorm in your face; no, it couldn't have been more different from their beloved Calvarese deserts!

Calvary. At night as they walked the vast empty spaces, stars glittered like the gods' embroidery on the black sky, and Thani scuffed trails in the sand with her feet, and Transcendence's tolling voice instructed her in the stories and religious parables which she would eventually need to pursue their calling.

After their nightmarish stay in Delta City, she had been sure Transcendence would take her back to Calvary. She had done her duty—hadn't she? What more did he want?

But her prophecy had changed the direction of both their lives as utterly as a bend in the bank of a stream. Now that Thani had killed a god (although it hadn't felt as if *she* were doing it: it wasn't *her* bringing the knife down, stabbing him again and again, cutting him to bits where he lay in his pool of white innocent blood . . . Now that she had done *that*, even were they to go back to Calvary, it would not be the same. That was what Transcendence had said, closing the subject forever, as they stood on the deck of *K'Fier Diamondback*, while Thani watched Delta City vanish over the horizon.

Three years, and she had shrugged off her bitterness. The decisions and responsibilities of itinerancy left no time for it. She pleaded with Transcendence to go slower, to spare himself. But he obeyed the guidance in his heart, even to the extent of ignoring the call for all flamens to return to Delta City and make obeisance to their new Divinarch—a god who had replaced Thani's very own sister (killed her, they said). Humi, that ambitious and exotic sibling from whom Thani had felt so alienated the last time they met. Even when they were children Thani had not loved her sister, but Humi's memory was disproportionately prominent in her thoughts as she and Transcendence sailed deeper and deeper into the North Reach.

The seas grew stranger: fully half the islands revealed themselves as monumental jewels set in the water, glittering, warning the traveler not to approach any closer if he valued his eyes. Salt islands. Heavens. As they passed them, the sea seemed to rise and fall without moving, like black dunes.

The North Reach islanders clucked at Thani for doing "man's" work; they used Transcendence as a glorified midwife. Most of them had only seen a flamen once, perhaps twice before. Some of them did not even know that the Old One, the seventeenth Divinarch, had died! They had never heard of Thani's sister, or the new Divinarch, the master of the Hands.

Transcendence's body had weakened. His mind, lucid as ever, had chafed against the limitations of the husk that housed it.

Thani rubbed the heels of her hands into her eyes. The candle sputtered. Surely the night must end!

Overtaxed, summer fever, susceptible—

But the fever had not killed him. Wretchedly, she knew *she* had killed him. Four years ago, when she prophesied. That day, they were caught. From then on, their decline had been as inevitable as if they were caught in a river pouring into a gorge and over a cliff.

The murder of a god. It had changed the whole world. Thani's sister had saved Thani and Transcendence from execution for their crime; still, as Delta City shrank in the distance, Thani had been violently on edge, expecting to be killed at any moment, the way she had killed the Heir to the Divinarchy.

But the gods had known they did not have to lift a finger. The Archipelago would do their work for them.

Sails swelled whitely, grew, billowing across the North Reach. Darkness pulsed. She was in a hot, smelly room in a little hut on an island, but it felt like Purgatory. Every time the seal's-fat candle flickered, the corpse's face looked more like a skull. And Thani had a better view of the life ahead of her: a life as limited as death.

She leaned back, resting her head against the wall. Scent of rancid fat and raw-tanned leather. For once, her fair, short hair was tangle-free; the stones caught it up in little fans, as if she were underwater. Her scalp ached as if it were sewn together patchwork with a dozen seams. She stared into the kinetic shadows of the roof.

Harrima was too small to support predators—a mere peak of salt rising out of the water. Godsman Gullfeather and his redheaded son ferried Thani there in their stinking fishing boat, with that inexplicable god perching on the bowsprit to watch out for a cove. The Gullfeathers young and old had to

tie rags over their eyes and she had to squint through her lashes, but the
god's eyes could tolerate the rainbow glare of the salt with ease.

She felt like crying. She wiped her nose on her sleeve.

There was *Faith*, her and Transcendence's sailboat. Another boy of the
village had brought it to Harrima. He stood waiting on the shore. In silence, the Gullfeathers helped Thani out. The god looked at her with distrust not unmixed with fear. She refused to meet his eyes as she climbed to
the shore. The other boy took her place in the Gullfeathers' boat and the
redhead cast off. Soon they were gone.

Faith bobbed on the swell, a little brown shell tied to a formation that
overhung the cove.

She hated that boat!

Her eyes were already starting to hurt. It was time.

She turned on her heel and started up the mountain. She no longer
bothered to squint. Soon she found a flat place where she could rest and
wait.

The delirium took her after two days without food or water.

*Sand ridges gleam rosy in the dawn. A small tent is pitched in the gray
shadows, in a dry valley between dunes. The child crouches behind a pile of
rocks above it, on the western slope. She has risen early to watch the kanga-
roo rats drinking dew off the cacti. They lick and hop and lick as the line of
day sinks down the hill, hastening to get their fill before the sun burns the
desert to bone.*

Garment by garment, Thani shucked her clothes. They were nothing but
a nuisance to her now. Her fur was darker on her torso and legs, which had
seldom seen the Calvarese sun; her breasts were the tawny brown hue
she'd been all over as a child.

When she surfaced from another whirlpool of dreams, she knew taking
off her clothes had done no good. If there was one thing the Archipelago
shared with Calvary, it was heat. In Delta City it was hot too, she remembered confusedly as the sun hammered her into the salt. Royalland's was a
sticky heat, soupy with the reek of the marshes. Calvary was dry. Here, the
sun was merciless, like a cudgel embedded with broken glass. It came
through the formations just as it would through dirty windows, so that there
was no shade anywhere. It burned her to lie down, but she could not even
think about standing up. She lay in the open, breathing, just breathing. She
could not smell anything. The inside of her nose was baked. Would the
wind never rise? Was it true she had once *dreaded* the storm that would
take her vision?

*Another morning, another resting place, and wild juniper bushes scramble
up the hill. A clear spring runs down into the olive green hollow. Here,*

beehive huts cluster, stone soap bubbles which have not burst or multiplied for two thousand years. Black-furred children rush outdoors, tweeting to each other. Another child stands with her father lover Godsbrother on top of one of the surrounding hills, looking down at the oasis then smiling up at him: she is pleased with herself. She timed their approach so that they should arrive here just at dawn. But of course he cannot see it—

A cool breath of wind touched her. Memory ripped to shreds and blew away, like a sail tearing loose from its shrouds. She groaned. As the sun sank beneath the sea, the formations began to creak in the rising wind, and the dusk gave her strength. She struggled to her feet and began to climb the slope.

Particles of salt borne in the whirling gusts scoured her body. Salt briars cut her feet. Branches snagged her naked limbs. Her fur was sticky with blood when she finally reached the top of the mountain.

The blizzard raced so thickly over the bald crest that she could see nothing. Sobbing, laughing, bleeding, lightheaded, she danced. She stumbled, fell, got up again, a pale embodiment of the storm, battering herself farther and farther toward numbness. When the pain reached a certain intensity, she stepped to one side and looked at herself. A black-splotched piebald spector with jerking limbs, making herself a fool for no one to see.

Horrendous! said that self, who had stepped aside. *You look as though you're having a seizure!*

Then the pain got worse again and dragged her back to herself. Particles invaded her eye sockets, like swarms of angry bees. Tears spilled down her cheeks. The wind howled in delight.

Another gust swirled into her eyes. She winced, in the way one does when stubbing a toe that has gone to sleep. She could not feel anything.

Later she went even farther away.

DIVARING BELOW

"*Delighted* that you could come!"

Serbalu Sugar Bird stood on tiptoe to look into Hope's face, beaming. "Everyone has been asking after you! You never come home anymore!"

Sugar Bird wore no face paint, to show off her porcelain-smooth, coral-colored skin. But her panniered gown, the latest Rimmear fashion, crushed her figure into an hourglass, forcing her chest up into the semblance of a bosom.

Hope embraced her, then complimented her on her fetching choker of white stones.

"Straight from the jewel shops of Veretry!" Sugar Bird said proudly. "Moonstones! I'm disappointed that my dear little Uali has gone over into the service of the dictator, of course, but since he has chosen to waste his potential in human country, it is just as well that he has the wherewithal to send me souvenirs."

Broken Bird and Bronze Water would not look too kindly if they heard that. "It's stunning, Sugar!"

It was almost certainly quartz not moonstones. Behind Hope the receiving line lengthened, *serbalim* chattering louder in an attempt to broadcast their impatience, fluttering their fans. Hope stepped past Sugar Bird, her tulle skirts bouncing around her ankles. "Shall we sit together at dinner, Sugar?" It was rude even to ask, considering that Sugar was hostess, but Hope was the celebrity here, more so than Broken Bird and Bronze Water (*if* they had come). She might as well make the best of it.

Sugar Bird clicked her tongue with mock impatience. "I have already placed you on my left hand, darling! Naturally!"

"You're such a dear!" Hope kept her voice light as she said, "You'll have to tell me all about your new little Foundling."

"You have never even *seen* him?" Sugar Bird made a glittery moue at the next *auchresh* in line. "We should make the Maiden promise to attend at least one ball a month, shouldn't we? One is in danger of forgetting that she is a Divaringian at all!"

Bronze and Broken Bird traveled all year, *teth¨ing* from Heaven to Heaven with scarcely a holdover; they had started to become something of a fixture. Hope had heard it said (in a whisper, of course) that before you missed them, there they were again. It was affectionate chaffing—the *auchresh* world trusted and respected Bird and Bronze—but Hope was a novelty. She hardly ever, as Sugar had observed, found time to return to the salt anymore. She was more *wrchrethre* than any *iu* had ever been. Even Bird and Bronze's sincerest supporters fell silent when she entered a room—not on purpose, just to stare at her. It was wearying.

There was no longer a prohibition on venturing into human country. But while the political impasse of Pati's fiery dictatorship and Broken Bird and Bronze Water's disarmingly coolheaded influence over the *serbalim* lasted, none was needed. Hope *lived* in human country. But unlike Pati and his Hands, she was welcome back in Heaven whenever she wanted to come. (No *serbali* could refuse to receive the Divinarch when he made his infrequent sallies into the salt; but those visits, replete with marching musicians and corps of Hands, were looked upon more as traveling freak shows than honest efforts to improve diplomatic relations.)

They still called her the Maiden. They still looked at her out of the sides of their eyes. Now she knew how the Incarnations had used to feel in Delta City, in the old days.

She stood between two rows of blank-faced, white-tuniced *triccilim*. She took a deep breath and moved in among the circulating *auchresh*. Everyone greeted her as a familiar. Her cheeks were covered with kisses. Garishly made-up *keres* beamed at her, exaggerating every nod so that their *wrillim* jangled loudly enough to be heard over the roar of conversation. *Iuim*, few in number, pushed their way through their entourages of males to hug and squeal over Hope. Some of the males, too, were cynosures of attention: garbed in the mesh hose with floor-length coattails that had become all the rage, they affected a remote, blasé manner. She felt most kindly toward these.

Auchresh society had started to originate its own fashions. It had to. There were no human fashions anymore. But the *auchresh* styles were no more practical than those the Deltan couture houses had used to come up with, and Hope did not think them very flattering.

Two *keres* were waiting for her to notice them. Power! What were their names—"Wonderful to see you again, Pink Claw!" she exclaimed. "Honored, Stami!"

They bobbed their heads and retreated. She looked around for the next wave. There was none. She must have greeted just about everyone who was someone. The lower-status guests—mostly *keres* her own age—stood nervously at a distance, clattering their jewelry. Somewhere a fountain played. Voices thundered through the hall. The musicians were sawing away with all their might to make themselves heard.

One strove so hard for delicacy here, didn't one? But delicacy was a thing of daylight. Detailed embroidery. Landscaped gardens with bees buzzing over rosebushes. Night blunted all fine points, it blurred filigreed whorls of meaning, it blended multiple layers of tact. Night evoked vivid colors, exaggerated forms, outré behavior.

Yet one strove . . . with a determination which was, itself, essentially *auchresh* . . . for delicacy.

The gong boomed hollowly. Hope envisioned supper. Waiters clad in white to the chin—fearfully impractical. Dishes hidden by smoky glass covers, so that one must guess at what one was going to have to stomach. Witty small talk with strangers.

And no one to hold responsible for the whole hilarious satire. No one at all.

Except, perhaps, Bronze Water and Broken Bird.

She quelled a surge of anger.

They had better be able to explain themselves!

They had better have come!

One of Pati's more foppish personal Hands, Eyrie, had sworn they were going to be at Sugar Bird's tonight. But Hope had not seen nor heard a whisper of them. And if Eyrie had been wrong she would not know, because she could not ask. She was not officially in communication with the *er-serbalim*, and she had no contacts in Divaring Below to do legwork for her. Even here, she was sealed off from the salt.

The tide of *auchresh* surged slowly in the direction of the dining hall. Claws, hands, *urthriccim* caught her sleeves. "Maiden! I heard that Sugar Bird has roast salt quails for the first course!"

She curved her lips into an urbane smile and worked her way across the flow to the edge of the foyer. Ribbed, transparent walls soared up into a geodesic vault. From the outside, she remembered, the mansion resembled a bloated water porcupine rising from the lake. But on the inside, the ridges provided welcome excuses for little alcoves tucked between them. She chose one swathed in pale blue curtains. Mercifully, it was empty. She sank down with a sigh of relief on the frugetsfur cushions, and lit a pipe. The *serbalim*, influenced by Bird and Bronze, frowned on tobacco as a human vice. As she smoked, her wings trembled behind the cushioned seat.

Why did I ever build the Folly?
No! For pity's sake don't start on that now!

She rubbed a scratchy lace sleeve across her eyes. She had to go sit on Sugar Bird's left hand and catch up on the gossip. If she didn't, Sugar would think she had left the ball without warning, and she would have to do exactly that because otherwise things would be so awkward. And when would she have her next chance to talk to Broken and Bronze? She could not foresee any time when their paths might cross again.

The blue frugetsfur was seductively soft.

Never before in her long life had she stood alone in the world's eye, without someone whom she could love and look to for direction. Once it had been Pati. Even while they were parted, in the last days of Humi's Divine Cycle, while Hope tried vainly to graft herself back onto the world of Divaring Below, it had been Pati. Right up until he seized the Throne.

But she could no longer tolerate him. All she had now was the Folly. And her secrets. She was chained with secrets. Promises she had made, and the principles she could not discard in order to break those promises. Chains.

If only she could take these brittle costume balls seriously, it would be some small release! Then maybe she could relearn the art of the essential, sweaty socializing that followed. Maybe she could raise a . . .

She could plainly hear the fountain tinkling. The music had stopped.

With the tip of one golden finger, she ground out her pipe. The hot ash sent waves of pain up her arm. She got up, left the alcove, and went to find the dining hall. When she got there, their voices crashed over her like a wave. They had not yet started the soup.

"I *hope* you have something to say for yourselves!" She rested her hip on the back of a chair and dug her toe talons into the rug. "You're not helping relations between Pati and the *serbalim!* As long as our people are persuaded that humans are inferior creatures we cannot gain by associating with, they won't take anything the *kere* who has proclaimed himself Divinarch over human country says seriously. They refuse even to listen to him. He is humiliated. If he breaks his ties with the salt altogether, it will be all your fault."

"A breakdown in communications is inevitable, I am afraid, Hope." Broken Bird's voice was gentle. "Pati's extremism has placed him on one side of a gulf which I am afraid we must recognize, for better or worse."

Hope sighed in exasperation. Broken Bird perched on the rim of the gold tub in which Bronze Water reclined, massaging the loose skin of his scalp. A scent of peonies rose in the steam. The parlor was chaotic with *teth˜ing* boxes that disgorged outfits suitable for every Heaven, from a rural

Eithilindre "family" to cosmopolitan Rimmear. The luxury of this guest
suite infuriated Hope. Eyrie's information was good, as she had discovered
by systematically exploring the mansion (all the other guests had either
fallen asleep, *teth*"d home, or reeled off in pairs and threes to continue
their reveals in private; as far as Sugar Bird knew, Hope had gone home
too) but hardly anyone in the household knew the *er-serbalim* were here.
This was a rest stop for them, courtesy of Sugar Bird's *irissi* Tree Seed, a
man as reserved as Sugar was gregarious, who took no part in her balls and
sociales. Hope felt she might like Tree Seed, if she ever talked to him.

"Why haven't you contacted me, at least?" she said to Broken Bird. "That
would have done *something* toward repairing the breakdown of communications! And surely, quite apart from that, I had a right to know that you
planned to foment unrest in the Heavens."

"Unrest?" Bronze twisted up to see her, frowning through the steam.
"The Heavens are far calmer than they were before Pati's coup."

"*Schism*, then. Young *keres* are slipping off in droves to follow Pati. Your
rationales don't satisfy them. Before long the *serbalim* will have to react to
the loss of their *triccilim* and Foundlings. They can't turn a blind eye forever."

Broken Bird gripped the rim of the tub with her feet and said in a bright,
mean voice, "It will never reach that point, because Pati can't last. When
the humans vanquish him, peace will return."

"*If* the humans ever controlled human country—which I think impossible—that still wouldn't be real peace! It would be only a facsimile!" Hope
moderated her voice with difficulty. Daylight crept around the edges of the
heavy tapestry drapes over the window. She was on a human schedule, like
the Hands, and right now she had been awake for twenty-four hours, not
counting the hours gained in her *teth*" to Divaring Below. Tiredness and
frustration shortened her temper. "In telling the *auchresh* to maroon ourselves in the salt, the way we were before the Wanderer, you're ignoring
the last fourteen centuries of history! You claim the word *god* no longer
applies to us. You tell *auchresh* not to think of themselves as gods because
the word springs from our relations with humanity. But you *must* see that
in advocating the pure, uncorrupted *auchresh* way of life, you're assuming
that there *is* an *auchresh* way of life. And what I've seen tonight persuades
me finally that there is not."

She had them both watching her now.

"You say our race has stopped developing." Broken Bird opened her
mouth, but Hope hurried on. "I know, that has been the conventional
wisdom for thousands of years. And we do have our biological limitations.
But we take pride in our intelligence, and rightly, for once one of us is

civilized, he can learn anything. And we've been soaking up changes from humanity for thirteen centuries. Even as we gave them knowledge, they gave us it back, altered. We're *not* a static race, just differently structured from the humans, and if you call the way of life we have here in Divaring Below ecstatic and eternal, then you're wrong. It's no more than a parody of Deltan society before the fall, enacted in darkness."

Bronze rose out of the water like a mountain draped in satin. Broken Bird sprang off his shoulders, flying through the air to land on her feet. She picked up the wet hem of her dress and scrutinized it. "Oh, Hope," she murmured, gazing sadly at the broderie verenaise, "are you trying to say the conclusions Golden Antelope drew about our race were *wrong?*"

"I am! He was a madman!"

"I quite agree. He believed we were inferior to the humans. Bronze and I take the far better considered view that we are *superior.*" She pulled her dress off over her head and minced toward Hope, presenting her back to her. Bronze Water toweled himself, his back to the women. Hope helped Broken Bird out of her false-ribs and the moss-green petticoat underneath. The small *iu* walked over to a trunk, stopping on the way to pat Bronze on the back, and pulled a loose salt-flax dress over her head.

"*This* must have come from human country," Hope said, holding up the beribboned petticoat.

"It was a present from little Humility Garden." Broken Bird leaned against Bronze Water. He caressed her with fat, sheeny fingers. Hope tried to recall if they had used to express affection so openly. "We used to like her, didn't we, Bronze? We helped her find her feet. Of all the lords and ladies Pati put an end to, she is the only one I would bring back from the dead, if I could. So you see I do not like to throw the petticoat away."

Hope wondered what Broken Bird would say if she knew Humi was not dead. She would probably be scandalized, and see that matters were put to rights immediately. "Hypocrisy is an easy trap to fall into," she said pointedly.

"You are too impatient, Hope!" Bronze said. "You were ever so." He had dressed in breeches and a dark purple tunic that disguised his paunch. The paunch had enlarged significantly since the last time she saw him; yet he was still not laughable, he possessed a kind of dynamism that gave her the idea that unlike Broken Bird, he meant everything he said. "Nonetheless I have a soft spot for you, Maiden. Let us untangle this tangle." He indicated a scroll-armed couch and quirked an eyebrow at her. Warily, Hope perched on its arm. Bronze Water climbed heavily onto the couch and squatted up so that their eyes were on a level. "Golden Antelope," he enunciated, "was a madman."

"I'm glad we agree on something."

"He glorified in failure. He was ready to sacrifice both human and *auchresh* lives indiscriminately to attain his goal. His goal *was* the wanton sacrifice of lives. Thank the Power, the Divine Balance swung in our favor, not his, and now I feel there is no danger of upheaval within the salt. I cannot say the same for human country."

"Pati has it well under control."

"But the balance between the races is still delicate. That is what we must work on. We must actively craft a peace that can devolve into an isolationism agreed to by both *auchresh* and humans. That's what Broken Bird and I are doing."

"Lulling us into complacency?" Hope muttered. She sat up straight and said more loudly, "But you deal only with the *serbalim*. What an incentive to schism! Aren't you *aware* of the lower classes of *auchresh*?"

"One has status," Bronze said. "One must speak to ears attuned to one's voice."

"And that's not even the point." She stood up. Daylight came in strongly around the drapes, washing the taper flames out. Soon the sun would rise. As she paced, anger pumped through her veins. "The point is that you are *wrong*. There must be change. It can come peacefully, or violently, but we can't return to what we were! Oh, Power, I can't go over it again. I can't make you understand." She slumped against the wall. Daylight flooded along it into her eyes. She was momentarily blind. And they were touching her, their arms slipping around her in that uniquely innocent *auchresh* gesture of comfort. Their body heat warmed her. She felt she had come to a place of safety. She knew that was not the case. "Dear," Broken Bird murmured, "don't you understand? Pati does not represent humanity! There is no *need* for us to deal with him!"

And Bronze, gently: "Hope, sweetheart, are you *really* an unbiased observer? Think. Pati was your *irissi*. Then your *elpechi*. Now—I don't know what you are to each other. But however things stand, you are not so close as you were. You don't have to tell us. We can see it. It seems to me as if you must feel some . . . bitterness. Might *that* not be what's making you obsessed with his role in this?"

He was right. She was a female. And weak. And Pati had been all in all to her.

"No!" She thrust them away. "How much lower can you sink without admitting it to yourselves? We are all *wrechrethre*. Pati is an *auchresh* of our times—an example even *you* will end up following whether you like it or not."

"Hope."

The scent of peonies was cloying. She stepped back against the curtains. "I don't know when we'll meet again. If you want to find me—have someone describe the Folly. Nobody will notice if you come. Status doesn't show on the outside, you know. Not in the city."

She *teth¨d* away from their protests.

The thrum of Delta City soaked into her skin. Her forearm fell over her face. She lay crumpled on the floor as if there were nothing inside her clothes. It was later in the day in Delta City, of course, a golden midsummer morning. Sun came hotly through the glass. This was her cupola. It gave the Folly a faintly ludicrous silhouette: an upward-thrusting fountain topped by a pimple. None of her servants were allowed up here, even to clean.

Her forearm cast a welcome weight of shade over her eyes. She stared into the deep ocher color, the honeycomb pattern of fine lines. Her skin seemed to ripple like the surface of a stream.

She would sleep for a while. Perhaps later she would go visit Humi. It was always good to be reminded that there was someone in a worse fix than yourself. She could tell Humi for certain, this time, that Broken Bird and Bronze Water thought she was dead. And as usual, she would have to refrain from mentioning Arity. The temptation was always there. But Hope knew better than to say anything, now that Humi seemed to be getting over him. Hope had felt such a rush of relief when Humi finally raised the question of a recoup. Not least because it proved she was consigning her love to the past, focusing on other things. It was better that she forget Arity. They could never meet. And Arity was no longer the *auchresh* he had been. The last time Hope had seen him, he had slung his arm around the ugly young *kere* beside him and told her to go away.

The ceiling rippled. She stood up, gasping in the cool shadows of the roof.

A SLOW NIGHT IN HEAVEN

"Eights," Sual said to the hustler, grinning with stained fangs. His right hand drifted over the knife at his thigh. "Saw it come up eights. You can't cheat me, *hymanni*-fucker. I got friends."

Arity hoped Su wasn't relying on him to prove that claim. He had no heart for a fight. The stars glowed brilliantly over the chasm, shining on the broad stone windowsills of the lamplit tavern. Sitting in the eastern window, his bad leg dangling into the chasm, Arity could not help thinking. As a rule, he tried to avoid that activity. *Khath* helped. Transparent distilled *ruiks*blood, it numbed the brain and ruined the body—much the same thing alcohol did for humans. But tonight the glass felt so heavy he thought it might fall from his fingers.

He took a swig and glanced at the stage. The entertainment had not got any better since he and Su came in. A young *ghauthi kere* was making overtures to a chained predator, trying to arouse its sheathed penis. Later on the *auchresh* and the animal would couple, the *haugthule* raking the boy's shoulders with clipped talons, the boy screaming with pain as he was split in this self-abasing acknowledgment of his parentage.

It held the audience spellbound. It had shocked Arity too, the first few times he saw it, but that was a couple of years ago. Nothing had changed since, except the sizes and shapes of the participants. This was a small *haugthule,* no more than Foundling-size, snapping dispiritedly at its handler. The sickly green hue of its wings was probably due to its having been kept out of fresh air too long. Its cupid's-bow mouth drooped at the corner, and as the long lashes fluttered Arity swore he saw tears in its eyes.

But predators did not cry, or at least that was the common wisdom, and Arity would rather not get close enough to find out the truth.

He felt restless tonight. News had filtered down to this honeycomb of streets, this cesspit he called home, where the dregs of Rimmear washed to and fro: news of a new predator in Rimmear, this one a man. The Divinarch was coming. With pomp and splendor and free *khath* for all of Heaven's hungry poor, he was coming to discuss some matter or other of failed communications with the *serbalim*. It was quite a momentous occasion. Peach Branch, a fat fuzzy-headed *serbali* whom Arity had seen once from a distance, had issued a proclamation. Moreover, the Divinarch was bringing a fully fledged retinue of Hands: to the *auchresh* among whom Arity drifted, *they* were the most interesting part. Even low status *firim* had heard tales of the *wrchrethrim*. They spoke of them with mixed awe and contempt.

But Arity himself could not stop thinking about the Divinarch.

A shard of his other life, the life he did not think about. Poking painfully through.

(Sometimes Delta City and all in it seemed only to have been figments of an encroaching insanity which had rushed near and enswarmed him in a dripping cloud, while he was injured maybe, tormenting him with false tastes of happiness before he woke to the unsubtle world.)

On the stage the *haugthule* yowled, a long shriek of misery. The boy scrambled backward, terrified out of his pretense of boredom. Laughter rippled from nearby tables.

Arity gulped the rest of his drink, grateful to have his thoughts interrupted. He touched Sual's yellow hair. "Let's get out of here."

Su did not hear. Su was gambling with heart and soul and complete concentration. Su, or Unusual Day, was the best distraction Arity had found from memories, with his laughing eyes and his darting tongue and childish questions. Did Arity really love him? Was the roof of the chasm made of glass, or was the sky a picture painted on it? Sual had never tried to climb higher in the city than the highest bridge. But ignorance breeds a superficial worldliness that impresses the overly refined, and when Arity was new and naked from his illness, he had been completely taken in. Now he knew the truth, it was too much bother to redefine their relationship. Not that it ever had been defined, in words. Su was a good lover: he found Arity's scars erotic. Also the thorns.

Arity slid down and pressed his face against Su's shoulder. "Hustlers be a Power-damned sight stupider at the Blue Skybird," he said to Su, by way of an opening, and also to flatter this hustler, who was looking dangerous on the other side of the table. "Let's go." He had discovered that he badly wanted to leave before the show started in earnest.

"*Haugthirre* hasn't said I don't owe him no *denear* yet." Under his ragged, billowy shirt, Su was as rigid as the back of his chair. Eyes locked, he and the hustler stared each other down. Rudimentary wings poked high behind their heads, like hackles, like—memories tweaked at Arity's mind. Cats in an alley—

"I said, I want to *go,*" he said loudly, jerking Su up.

Caught off guard, Su stumbled out of his chair, twisting and fighting to keep his eyes locked with the hustler's. After a minute he gave a hiss of despair and threw himself ahead of Arity. Arity staggered on his bad leg. "Damn *idiot* cripple boy." Su reached around and shoved him in the back, right where he must know the worst scar was, because several thorns grew out of it, poking holes in the weave of Arity's shirt. "Find us somewhere that *haughthirre* cheat won't find *me,* then!"

"Is it that serious?" Arity's heart sank: Su was a tricky business proposition at the best of times. Given even partial access to Arity's supply of *denear,* he went wild.

Su laughed. "All I'm sayin' is, the dear old Skybird won't save us this time. We're too hot. Less get over to other side an lay hands on Nifi and Red Sedge. Safety in numbers, an that."

They passed through a curtain of swinging himmisfur strips into a chilly, smoke-free passage. Servingmen, naked like overgrown versions of the Foundlings employed by taverns on the top tier, hurried along with pots of *khath.* The passage hiccuped Arity and Su out into the street. Starlight swam down between the eaves of the buildings that teetered over the street. No one was about. Arity thought he heard a disturbance behind in the tavern and wheeled, awkwardly.

Su plucked at him. "Less go. I mean it: I swore em too damn much. I was sure I had that last roll cornered."

"I got it downtier if you want to pay," Arity said. He might as well use Hope's money, if she was determined to give it to him. Better that than get murdered when some *kuiros* found out about his riches.

"Nah. We'll lose em, come on."

They took off uphill at a lope. All of Rimmear's streets sloped upward to the bridges. The Laughing Haugthule Tavern received starlight only because it was on the edge of the chasm; the rest of the tier was buried black under a league and a half of city. Arity felt Rimmear looming like a cliff behind him, humming.

Footsteps echoed on the slick salt in a side alley.

Su glanced sideways and said "Shit." He grabbed Arity's arm, pulling him faster. Sweat broke out on Arity's temples. The thorns stopped him from wiping at it.

Behind them there was a shattering crash. This time Arity could not help spinning in Su's grip. He could see nothing around the corner, but he heard shouts trumpeting like bugles. Most of those with dirty work to do

here did it as cleanly as possible, in private: this gave the streets a spe-
ciously safe, quiet feel, when in fact anyone who looked like a country boy
would not last three corners. Only occasionally did violence spill into the
open. Arity cursed the noise for giving the footsteps a chance to work their
way around ahead. "Leave me here—" he panted, as much out of a need to
stop running as anything else. "You'll outdistance em."

"He'll take it outta you."

"We're only *ghauthijim.*"

"But he's a *haugthule.* Come on—"

Ahead of them, the bridge swooped upward like a pale ribbon. They
dashed out onto the rusty, ringing expanse. One decrepit guardrail stood up
from the edge like a row of spines. The smelly wind of the chasm gusted
dangerously from all the points of the compass. The other bridges, above
and below, crisscrossing, joining, curved around this bridge in a celestial
network that might aeons ago have been crafted to replace the constellations with something better designed. All the bridges were close to empty.
Slow night.

But here you could tell nothing from the looks of things, just as you could
tell everything from the way things looked.

At an intersection, a fat blue-skinned *auchresh* welled up in front of
them.

"Shit!" Su yelped.

An ancient, stinking *iu* and her escort of *keres* was waddling along behind Su and Arity. Su nearly knocked them off the bridge as he dashed
back the way they had come. Arity muttered an apology to the old woman
as he followed. The scars in his sides were cutting him in half. He could not
keep up.

"*Ailoa* . . . *!*" a voice hailed them from the bridge above. " 'Ello, nameless low-status! Impoverished cheat! I take it out o your *skin!*" The hustler
from the Laughing Haugthule swung over the guardrail of the bridge some
thirty feet above and plummeted down to their bridge. The flexible metal
dropped when he hit, them snapped back, tossing Arity into the air. The
old *iu,* who by now had reached the downslope, gave a croaking screech.
Arity struggled to get to his feet. As the blue-skinned *kuiros* pelted past
him, almost casually he brought a fist the size of a small dog into the back of
Arity's head. "Cripple," Arity heard him say, and then the world cascaded
slowly apart in a waterfall of white.

There was a fire on the east side of the chasm. The Laughing Haugthule
Tavern was burning. The flammable salt insulation under its tiles flared
yellow and blue. People were screaming and climbing out on the window-

306 GARDEN OF SALT

sills. Somebody dropped off, down, down, writhing like a spider. Arity thought groggily that he should really go do something about the deaths. Help. Something. Yes.

That was the kind of thing that had got him half-killed in Delta City, wasn't it? His scruples. A heart, an actual heart! Sin for an *auchresh!* In Delta City, the only thing that had saved his face was the Heir's arrogance, which had kept him aloof and incomprehensible, as much to himself as to others. Now his scruples were negated by his powerlessness. Almost always, but not quite often enough.

So he'd reshaped the Heir's arrogance. Remade the cage into armor. Dull, patchwork stuff, let him blend in nicely while keeping him clean and dry inside, like a snail in a garbage heap.

Hadn't done him much good against the *kuiros's* fist though, had it?

One of his legs was hanging off the edge of the bridge. With an effort, he locked an elbow around the stump of a guardrail and pulled himself to safety. He flopped back, shuddering with the effort. Stars filled his eyes. Stars pooled in his brain. An old *auchresh* plodded past, grumbling to himself about corpses on his bridge again. Undoubtedly he had a knife. Arity held still until the muttering died away. Then he steeled himself to get up.

And above him wings flapped, leathery, tired. The wind died around him, blocked off. Claws chinked on metal.

Auchresh could not fly.

It was a predator. Possibly the one from the Laughing Haugthule. It squatted in front of him, running the chain through its wicked little claws, wondering whether Arity was good to eat. It picked its nose. It cocked its head on one side like a winged green Foundling.

Arity shrank back, weaker even than when the leman's knife had bit into his body, when he had felt his blood rushing out of him. This was the living ghost of his ancestors. This was shame alive. He reached carefully for his knife.

Yet there was the fascination that brought countless *auchresh* back to the Laughing Haugthule and taverns like it night after night after night, to turn glasses of *khath* in their hands and stare at the stage, and it held him immobile.

The predator darted its head at him and bit him on the shoulder.

He yelled and struck out with his knife.

It flinched back, snorted through its nostrils, and lifted into the night.

On the edge of the chasm, the tavern subsided into white-hot ashes.

* * *

After painstakingly knotting his tunic around his bitten shoulder, Arity got up and shuffled down the bridge. He smelled Sual before he reached him. The hustler and his friends had emptied their bladders on his body. Also they had done worse things. No doubt these particular mutilations were their signature, and they meant the body to stand as some sort of monument to their prowess. Mutilation was a new trend that the *kuirim* had picked up from tales of Delta City which were only just now reaching them. Arity thought it hubristic, and he hated it as he hated all things that reminded him of the city. And for once, he could do something about it. Panting, he heaved the body into the chasm. Let it choke the river along with the rest of Rimmear's waste.

He supposed he would be sorrier for Sual. But they had only been *ghauthijim.* He stretched, feeling each puckered scar on his torso bite deep. How marvelous that he was not compelled to grieve.

He dragged himself home.

Home was a rickety building on the bottommost tier. The skylights were splattered with muck thrown down from the city, but at least there *were* skylights. He paid enough for them. The curtains that one hooked over them during the day were rolled up, thick with salt dust. He never unrolled them. He laid clean clothes on the bed, then stripped off the soiled ones in a method perfected by time and practice, ignoring the ache in his shoulder, eyes shut so that he would not have to see himself before he got the other garments on.

The dawn brightened overhead as he cooked supper. The sunlight in the salt was so remorseless that it would cook your food for you, especially when it came through the flawed panes of glass salt that passed for windows here, but Arity was used to his little stove. Su had won it from the proprietor of a cookhouse for him. He felt a pang only when, unthinking, he laid two plates on the floor.

He finished the food in a daze. Then he lay on his bed, watching the square of cloudy sunlight creep across the floor. The room looked as bright and flat as a chord on an out-of-tune *farader,* but uglier. Every time he drifted partway into sleep, his heart would thud, and he struggled to open his eyes, desperate to escape the images of bat wings and mindless gold eyes, and clawed hands playing with a broken chain.

When he finally did sleep, of course, there was Pati.

HEIR

Because Gete's mother had taken the dying flamen in, his leman had become the responsibility of the Gullfeather family.

"Better go get her today!" Godsman Stickleback said to Gete's father. Four dawns had passed since they left the girl on Harrima salt. A breeze ruffled the sea. The eastern sky glowed pink, but night's dark skirts trailed behind Sarberra peak. At the rock harbor, the troop of men and boys separated to their boats.

Gete's father wheeled around. "Why ent *you* get her, Godsman Stickleback?" All along the crags, faces blank with sleep turned toward him, then away, uninterested. Kin Stickleback was the only man ever awake enough to talk in the mornings, and he would as a matter of habit rattle on and on, whether the others listened or not. "We have our dinners to catch!" Gete's Da said. "And my wife owes the hag Brownfern a passel of fish for her help wi' the Godsbrother. Ye go."

"Ye want the girl to die? 'Twill be on yer head, yerself an yer fine redhead son."

"Her own boat is on the island!"

"An let me put my hands on the woodhead whose idea 'twas to take it!" Godsman Stickleback knew it had been Old Flamefish's idea, and that Gete's father would say nothing against the old man. He rested one foot on the prow of his boat and opening his mouth peculiarly wide, cocked his head on one side. Gete's father stamped down into the boat and said, "Let's go." Hypnotized, Gete neglected to let down the centerboard before he untied the boat. They skidded across the wavelets toward Godsman Stickleback's boat, and Gete scrambled to give her a keel. They darted away, reaching across the breeze. Gete's father staggered, caught the tiller, and threw back his head and laughed.

"Right then, boy! We'll go see does that girl still live, and does she, I do guarantee we'll get ourselves a little miracle by way of thanks!" Da's laugh was infectious. Gete joined in.

The sun rose. Red spangled wine curled away from the side of the boat. Gete pulled the jib in tight, then wrapped the ropes around his fist and leaned back. Sometimes, on a long reach, you got to thinking that the world had ground to a stop, that everything in the whole vast machine was hanging there quivering, waiting for you to break the note and go about.

But not today. He couldn't stop thinking of Desti. Since the incident with the flamen, when the old Domesdean man had sensed Desti through the wall of the kitchen and called on him for guidance which Desti could not or would not give, the god had been away from Sarberra. When he came back, he was rude and uncompanionable. And loath though Gete was to admit it, that left him at loose ends. When he was small, he had been good friends with the other boys, but since they got older, Tience and Rag and the others had learned that Gete's red hair marked him out as an object of suspicion. Whenever a goat died or a net was lost, people looked askance at the redhead. So with increasing frequency, he fell back on Desti's friendship.

And that marked him out as an object of suspicion, too.

Desti, you turtle, he thought as the sails belled sweetly, tugging on the ropes. His father sat at the tiller, brows furrowed; he was probably wondering where the swordfish shoals were likeliest to be today, and how long they would have to look for them after picking up the leman. *Desti, you stupid sea-pig.*

She sat on a salt tree stump, her feet dangling over the water. Gete saw through the rag he had tied over his eyes that she was not clothed. He was grateful they weren't close enough for her to see him go muddy: since his fur was white to transparent, even whiter than most Archipelagans', when it stood on end, his dark skin *showed.*

But after all, she could not see anything. Her eyes were gray and milky like the sky before rain. Behind her, the salt brush rustled with a deceptively wet sound. She held onto a transparent sapling and pulled herself upright. Scabs marred her body from head to toe; one of her large dark nipples was sliced half off. "By the gods," Gete's father muttered, and brushed a hand over his heart. "Divinarch in heaven."

Gete just sat with his mouth open, caught between looking at her and showing her disrespect.

"Well, get on with ye!" his father said sharply. "Help her aboard!"

Gete climbed out onto the salt and extended a hand. She shied back like a wild beast. She was horribly thin. As he stood helplessly, she wrinkled her brows, opened her mouth, then closed it, and put her head on one side, appearing to *search* him with cloudy eyes.

His father swore in exasperation. "Dammit, boy, go fetch the little boat. *I'll* see to her!"

Gratefully, Gete obeyed, scrambling away to where *Faith* bobbed against the rocks. To take his mind off the leman's disconcerting behavior, he thought how very hot the salt was. He had never come here before this episode. Twigs, rocks, all burned his bare feet as if he were standing on the hot hearth on a winter's night. He climbed into *Faith* and let down the sail, aware that his father was gentling the girl into their boat. "What's yer name, sweetheart? Ye can tell me. Ye're safe, now." Da's voice carried clearly across the salt.

"Tha—aah," he heard, in a croak that at first he did not identify as a human voice. He ducked under *Faith*'s boom and saw the leman's cropped blond hair flying as she shook her head. Gete's father had given her his shirt to wear, and she clutched it about her throat as she said doubtfully, "Not Thani. Not . . . anymore. Godsister Thankfulness."

Gete's throat closed. Untying the painter, he twisted *Faith*'s tiller and she leaped off over the waves.

Several women were waiting by Sarberra bay. They greeted him first with cries of concern and then with disappointment when they realized the flamen wasn't aboard. "Poor little thing." Godsie Tiler squinted out over the waves, brushing fingers over the knot of her head scarf. "She's but a young girl . . ."

They meant to mother her! Gete could not stop himself from smiling as he tied *Faith* to a crag. How long would their good intentions last when they were confronted with that imperious, confused girl whose eyes one could not even meet? No longer than a stone could float!

But when Da sailed up with the girl, she docilely permitted herself to be led off, submitting to criticism of her thinness and plans to feed her up. Gete watched the blond head bob away up the hill amid the dark ones. It struck him that she was not a woman in the usual sense of the word. She had probably been a very good leman.

"There's na one for you to be moonin' over!" his father said, reaching up from the boat to slap Gete's ankle affectionately. "She's a Godsister. And Domesdean to boot, eh? Move yerself. We've got the rest of the day to find us a shoal."

Godsie Gullfeather declared supper communal. So many of her friends had already invited themselves to gape at the newmade flamen that Gete understood she could not turn the rest of the islanders away. Communal meant that everyone brought food; Gete gorged himself on a lip-licking variety of dishes. Afterward the women set to work clearing up, and Da trudged off to a gathering at Old Flamefish's hearth. Men only. No boys. Gete played with his little sisters in front of the cook-hearth, not wanting to think about the fact that since Desti was not here, and wherever the other boys were they would not welcome his joining them, he had nothing to do.

While the little girls were absorbed in a picture puzzle he had drawn them with a stick of charcoal, the flamen emerged from the inner room. She stood in her bare feet, in a robe the women had whipped up for her. Precious salt-flax cloth. How could she repay them? That was a blasphemous thought. He squashed it.

"Regretfulness," she said.

Gete opened his mouth but said nothing. Her cloudy eyes seemed to look straight into him. Had she really lost all her sight? Or was it fading slowly, like a sigh going out from the lungs of a corpse?

"I want you to be my leman," she said. She sat down beside his sisters and wrapped her arms around her knees. "Will you?"

He could not speak. She was a creature straight out of witch stories. Her milky eyes and her sun-bleached fur with its dark roots repulsed him.

"Answer me!" Her colorless brows drew together. "Are you there?"

"Do—do I have a choice?"

His sisters watched, round-eyed. One was three, the other six. His mother was watching too, hands on hips, frowning.

"Yes," the flamen said testily. "You are old enough to choose."

"Then—then no!"

And the door swung back and the room was full of men. Tience and Rag and Imp and Tim came behind their fathers, looking scared yet excited. They had fooled him. Da came forward with a smile on his face, his arms held out, and an expression in his eyes that told Gete his heart was breaking. "Blessings of the gods, my son!" He folded Gete in his arms. "I pray you'll be happy," he muttered, "I do so—"

Gete wrenched away. He could not think of how to put his refusal so as not to slight the Godsister, but his face must have said it well enough. They were all staring at him. "I can't," he said miserably. "Much too old. Don't know why she wants me. Sorry!" If he stayed in here a moment longer, the very weight of their gazes would squash him into acquiescence. "Sorry!" he yelped.

He swung around and dashed out the yard door, out into the night. The windows of the village winked out one by one as he threw himself up the mountain. Gorse snagged his shirt, depositing prickles in his fur, and more than once he sank a foot in one of the little bog holes that never dried up even in summer. Sweat soaked his body. The nippy breeze chilled him. The stars shone faintly behind scudding clouds. Their glow showed him nothing except the heavy pyramidic blackness of the peak. "Desti!" he shouted. "Desti!"

He clambered higher, up the steep rock faces and knolls.

"Desti! Goddamn you!" The wind wuthered in the rocks, bringing a faint perfume of gorse blossoms. *"Desti!"*

The mountain had never felt so inhospitable. It shrugged under him, and he slipped and put his hand in a fresh pile of goat droppings. Cursing, he staggered upward, up to the summit.

In what could have been one hour, or many, he was weeping on his hands and knees. "Gods damn you, I need your help, offal-brain pig god! I have to get away from here! They've tricked me!"

Silence.

"Desti!"

Some way down the hill, there was the scuffle of a fox making a kill. A rabbit's shriek.

The truth hit him like a sharp knife, taking his breath away.

Desti was a god. He ought to be able to hear Gete's prayers. Maybe he could hear. But even so, he was not coming to answer them.

Beaten, Gete dragged himself home. He washed off in the hen trough and came dripping into the kitchen. It felt very late. The flamen sat alone by the fire, her chin in her hands, staring at the scattering of embers in the banked fire.

She raised her head when he entered. Her face wore an expression of blank exhaustion. It made her look young and vulnerable.

" 'S me. *Sorry.* I acted like a child." He advanced. Then he heaved a sigh and stopped to speak to her. "I'll come with you, so."

She took his hand and pressed it to her cheek. It was an awkward moment. Gete felt a drop of hotness on his hand. Quickly, he withdrew.

"Come," he said. "Let's find you a pallet to sleep on."

They left next morning before the fishermen. Gete said his good-byes to his family with a strange sense that they were making a to-do about nothing. He kept forgetting that he was not going out to the shoals with Da, and that he would not return with him at sunset.

The entire population of Sarberra, even Godsman Sharquetooth's crippled son Arden, carried in his mother's arms, came sleepy-eyed to see them off. *Faith* wallowed under the weight of so many provisions that Gete finally had to call a halt to the gifts, for it was clear that the Godsister was not going to. When somebody lowered a basket into the boat, she just moved her feet to make room for it, smiling vaguely. "All set! We're wanting to drop anchor at Riethella tonight an make Taramia tomorrow. This's all we need."

Brave words, but he had never even been to Taramia. His heart was pounding. For the first time in years, his friends threw their arms around him. Even the girls of the village, who as a rule would not let a boy anywhere near them, hugged him. It came to him that they were all looking at him with awe. Bitter triumph. Strangely enough, when he embraced his parents and sisters he did not feel the crippling emotion he had expected.

The only thing that reached deep inside and twisted his heart was the knowledge that now his father had no sons. There was no excuse for that betrayal: not even Da's avowal of pride. "Do well, me son. Wear your name as if it fits you." Da squeezed Gete tightly and let go. Gete could not meet his eyes. He swallowed. Redhead or not, he was Da's only heir . . .

Better not think on that! He stood up to cast off.

But the Godsister was getting to her feet. *Faith* rocked. The Godsister had no feel for the sea, though she held ropes better than any other girl he knew. "I have to—"

"What?" he snarled softly.

"I've to pay them back. It's a rule. If I don't do it now"—she was standing precariously in the stern of the boat; people gaped at her—"I'll never—"

Abruptly time seemed to grind to a halt. The sea stopped lapping against the rocks. A crying baby fell silent, or rather it was still crying, but the sound hung protracted in the frozen air. *Like being on a reach,* Gete thought, or tried to think. *That feeling*—but his brain had gone as heavy as wet sand. Moments did not exist in this heightened, brightened, hardened version of the world. But if they had, the phenomenon would have lasted a moment, just long enough for everyone to recognize it for what it was and *twitch*—

the sun bounced up as if it were on a spring. Pink gold rays arrowed over the sea.

Everyone's limbs seemed to loosen, laughter broke forth as if some danger had passed, and above their voices, Gete heard little Arden's shriek: *"Mum!* Lemme down!"

He scrambled to the ground and jumped up and down, screaming with joy.

Well, well, Maybe the girl had no timing—but she was the real thing. Gete could not help grinning. Then he struck his forehead with the heel of his hand: this was their chance. Quickly, he cast off and brought *Faith* about. "Sit now," he hissed at Thankfulness, and she collapsed into the stern. He swung the boat's nose away from the wind. "Good-bye!" he shouted to the crowd. Her voice echoed his thinly. "Good-bye . . . good-bye . . ."

Before *Faith* rounded the point, he saw the fishing fleet scattering out from the coast, their patched sails puffing in the wind.

Thankfulness laughed. She ran out of breath fast, and held her side. "I forgot the circle. Damn, I forgot everything. I've helped Transcendence with it a thousand times, too."

Gete was rather taken aback by her sudden familiarity. He said stiffly, "Only natural. Yer first time, an all."

"Ah, but it wasn't my first time. I had to work a miracle on myself to keep myself alive, on that island."

"Thought you couldn't work miracles on yourself," Gete said.

"Never again."

"Why? Is't a rule or somethin?"

"Yes. There are a great many rules. Nothing arcane, for that comes naturally: but the dictates of proper conduct." Now she was speaking formally. "You will learn them all in Delta City."

"That's where we're going?"

"Yes. As fast as we may."

"To the Divinarch?"

"At his behest."

Gete nodded. He did not know exactly what she meant, but he got the gist. A traitorous excitement was surging through him. He had consented to leave his home in a fit of fatalism, when he had felt sure that there were no such things as honesty or loyalty in the world. Now, all at once, he realized that there were, and that he was leaving them behind. Instead he was taking on a kind of bondage, a loyalty he did not feel. That ought to weigh like a stone around his neck.

But he had seldom felt so exhilarated. *Faith*'s prow sliced the waves into dancing white curls.

Delta City!

If only he could tell Desti!

AN ENDLESS NIGHT IN THE
WHOREHOUSE DISTRICT

Summer was over. Humi could feel it in the wind coming through the high windows of Hem's living room. Now came cold, and the children would fret because they could not go outside, and the foxglove on her windowsill would die. Her eyes might not be good for anything else anymore, but they could still fill with tears, and did so at the slightest provocation. *You can't cry now!* she told herself, as she always did. *You have sewing to do!*

And Ensi was pulling at her. "Auntie Humi, play with me! I'm bored!"

Five years old, and not allowed outside, it was small wonder the child was bored. In fact, her patience had lasted an amazingly long time. Humi just wished she had been able to amuse herself until Godsie Woodlock's petticoat was finished.

"Please!" Ensi's hard little head butted against Humi's thigh. "Please please please—"

"Just a few more minutes. Try to hold out." Stab, stab, stab, tiny whip-stitches. This was the only way she could even partially repay Hem and Leasa for their kindness. It was a good thing she was already blind, she thought with black humor, because if she wasn't she would have lost her sight from doing fine work. There were few jobs to be had in a city where hundreds of women who had once prided themselves on their idleness must now work to help keep their families. Apart from prostitution, to which she had not sunk, and would not, sewing was the only employment open to a blind woman who had still not learned to think of the world in terms of sounds and smells and sharp corners, whose eyes they told her were still as black as ever.

A woman who had been Divinarch.

She should not even *think* along those lines, in case the Hands could somehow—she smiled at her foolishness—read her thoughts.

But they were so good at sniffing out anyone who had been an atheist. Anyone they disliked for any reason at all. Most of the atheists she had known in the old days were gone now, saving only those whom Pati had spared for his own, unfathomable purposes. The merchants were calling themselves *Godsie* and *Godsman* now. But quick reconversions seldom fooled the Hands. They said they took those they arrested to Purgatory, but as they said it they laughed nastily, and Humi knew better than anyone else in the city that *Purgatory* was no more than a code word made up by Pati for the thing that most people called Heaven.

So she must not make a single move that might draw attention to the house of a humble Temeriton shopkeeper.

And she *must* get this petticoat finished.

Swoop and stab and measure the distance to the edge of the cloth by feel. "All right, En. All done!"

Working at her own speed, pretending not to hear the little girl's joyous cries, she folded the dress and put it in the basket. Then she slid off the sofa to the floor, patting the air. Her hands encountered nothing. "You'd better stay still, you know . . . I can hear you if you move so much as a hair . . ." She concentrated on picking Ensi's excited breath out of the weave of background noise. The ting of the shop bell, Leasa's gentle voice talking to a customer, a drunkard reeling up the alley, his smell overpowering the autumn scent on the wind, the rattle of sedan wheels in the concourse . . . *Ah.* Humi flattened herself to the floor like a stalking beast, curling her lip for the benefit of the child whom she knew was watching, hypnotized like a bird before a snake. *"Gotcha!"*

But Ensi had darted out of her hands. Humi heard high, hysterical laughter and the patter of little feet on the stairs.

She sat back on her heels. "You're getting bratty."

"I'm coming down," Ensi answered, but stayed on the stairs.

Humi pushed her hair out of her eyes. Now that she no longer dyed it, it had returned to its natural texture, so nappy it would not stay in a braid. Probably as good a disguise as anything that Humility Garden, ghostier, had ever come up with. The Divinarch, she remembered, had used to have an immaculately arranged coiffure.

"Here I come, Auntie!" With a squeak of varnished wood, En catapulted off the banister into Humi's lap. Taken off guard, Humi toppled backward and banged her elbow on the low table.

"You brat!" Pain blurred her judgment. She slapped at Ensi and felt her palm connect.

"Aaaaah!" Ensi blubbered. "Me going to Mama—"

Humi caught her as she staggered to her feet. *"No. We have to let Mama alone. She's very busy." And right now, one customer could make the difference between covering costs and borrowing to pay the rent.* Hope had not visited the Lakestones' house since the very beginning of the summer, and so the money they counted on from her had left a gaping hole in *Delights and Diversions'* finances. In these times of tightened belts, it was impossible, Hem had explained, to make such a venture as a curiosity shop show a profit. Yet it would be too risky to branch out in a new direction. They might lose everything.

Humi knew, though Hem did not say it, that the danger was not of losing money, but of Humi's being uncovered. The family were like rabbits frozen in an open field, unable to move an ear in case the circling predators spotted them.

She felt wretched, yet there was nothing she could do except silently try to show her gratitude.

Ensi was still crying. Frenziedly, Humi rocked her in her arms, wrung by the peculiar desperation to comfort her which came of that occasion, more than four years ago, when she had almost sacrificed Ensi to Erene. The family had probably forgotten the incident, but Humi still felt as if she had to make up for her lapse of feeling. She felt as if they were looking over her shoulder every minute to make sure she wasn't doing uncouth ghostier things to the child. "Let's go out to the alley and play with the kitties!" she suggested. Never mind the chills: if she could only get Ensi to quiet down—

"I dowanna!"

"I think Sharque's sitting on the back doorstep waiting for you. I think he's thinking, 'Where could Ensi be today?'" Inwardly, she winced. But Ensi wiped her face. Humi could hear her scrubbing her fur.

"All right."

Thanking the gods, Humi led her out to the hall and fumbled for the latch of the back door. Ensi pushed her aside, muttered "Lemme," and catapulted outside.

Cold wind licked Humi's fur. Cats, dogs, pigs, peacocks, and other semidomestic beasts could always be found combing Temeriton's back alleys in search of food. They were Ensi's only playmates, at least since the Whitehills, the last neighboring family with small children, had moved to the mainland. "Better starve than be arrested and have my sons thrown into the gutter," Servat Whitehill had asserted. There were not enough ferries to carry all Delta City's would-be émigrés to the mainland, and not enough work to keep them alive once they got there. The Hands had finally declared that to cross the Chrume or board any ship bound for another Royal-land port, one needed a passport costing fifty shillings. People had started fleeing overseas instead, but they were dribbling away more slowly.

Ensi had finally got the cat she called Sharque to stay still. She struck up a one-sided conversation with it. From the high, frantic tone of her voice, it was clear that she was getting sick. *I'm a bad caretaker,* Humi thought. "Stay away from that old man!" she called, remembering the drunkard, who usually spent his days in the alley, dozing. Ensi made an absent yes noise.

Humi lowered herself to the doorstep. The smells of boiling lentils and mangy cat and drunk beggar did not bother her. She imagined the pale gray expanses of sky visible between the roofs. She tasted the salt in the wind that washed past her face. It gave her a sensation of freedom other-wise lacking in her days: a sensation of delicious danger. Perhaps it would rain.

Rain was one of the good things about autumn, especially after a summer such as they had had, sixday after sixday of dust and parched throats. If it *did* rain, she would go out and stand in the middle of the alley. She would get soaked, like the cats, like the squawking seagulls. Leasa would scold her when she came inside—for risking illness, for risking being seen—but she would not repent. She would not care if she got ill.

It did not rain.

When eight o'clock came and Leasa locked up the shop and Hem came back from the junk merchants, and the wind coming in the windows was still dry, Humi made up her mind not to be disappointed. It was a small thing, after all. But at the dinner table, she was struck by an uncontrollable wave of misery. Unable to hold it back, she fled upstairs to the tiny room Hem had partitioned off from the children's bedroom for her, and soaked both her sleeves with bitter tears.

She recovered in time to say good night to Hem and Leasa. *Sorry, sorry, sorry,* she thought helplessly. The softness in Leasa's voice told her that her face betrayed her. But they all knew about her crying fits. How could they not?

When they were asleep, she had the run of the house. She poured herself a glass of cheap Riestasis and entered the shop. She paced between the racks, noting Hem's new purchase of some little brass prayer bells, brush-ing her fingers over the statuettes of Hands that lined the shelves. Wood, with limbs defined by their drapery. These were selling faster than any-thing except the paintings of Pati. She pressed her face to the door, listen-ing to the outside. Lockreed Concourse was not what it had been before the fall, of course—but it was still the first place Deltans came to forget their troubles. And people had enough of *those* to keep any number of watering places and women's establishments in business. Doors thunked, releasing bursts of noise. Sedans tinkled up and down the street.

Humi sighed, dunked her wineglass in the kitchen washbucket, and wandered upstairs.

She had a secret.

The box under her bed overflowed with brushes and pigments. Ziniquel and Emni had brought them to her. She did not know why they had bothered; wasn't it obvious to them that a blind woman could not paint? But when she realized what she *could* do, the first ray of hope had penetrated the blackness in which she lived.

She stood her latest ghost on her bed and unwrapped it, sucking her fingers from time to time to warm them. A seagull: Meri, the Lakestones' son, had caught it for her. Any apprentice would muddy with shame to practice on such a creature. But she was not *painting* it, as an apprentice would have. Rather, she was coloring it with more emotion than she had used on some humans in her days as senior ghostier, but the only pigment she had used was a matte white wash. She was *carving* it with the ghostier's chisels, all different sizes, with which one traditionally chipped at ghosts to make a hand hold a book, or define locks of hair from a mass. She had *willed* the legendary blind man's sensitivity into her fingers—as she had done for the cat and the pigeon and the rat ghosts under her bed. She had carved its feathers into an exaggerated sheath of knives. She had made its tail a spiked, inlaid fan with different textures telling the picutre story of a lovers' tryst. She was shaping its face into what she hoped was a realistic human scowl.

Meri told her it was a realistic scowl.

She awaited the judgment of a more sophisticated audience.

Would her crude, wood-chiseler's approach work as well as paint? Would the textures she had created seize the eye and pull the viewer into the seagull's cold, to touch it and experience its all too human frustration with its imprisonment in this body?

Did such a sophisticated audience still exist?

Would she ever have the chance to show it to them, or was she torturing herself with false hope?

She rubbed her eyes with her fingers.

Outside, a cat was being eaten alive by a pig, or possibly a predator.

On the other side of the partition, Meri and Ensi breathed heavily.

She raised her face in the dark, teeth bared, shivering.

* * *

At first she had thought that Hem and Leasa kept the shutters closed for fear the sunlight would hurt her. She had railed at them to open the windows in the name of the gods, in the name of the Divinarch, on pain of torture.

They had closed the door and left her.

It was the wisest thing they could have done. Alone, she had to come face-to-face, so to speak, with the horrifying truth inside her head.

The blackness around her was neither the result of closed windows nor a side-effect of Pati's poison, soon to wear off. The rushed, impromptu nature of the miracle Godsbrother Joyfulness had worked on her had left her alive, but blind.

At first it had been like living in a safe box, locked away from all human contact. Hem and Leasa tiptoed around her as if she were a wounded predator. Ensi and Meri had been frightened to stay in the same room with her. Then she had realized that *she* had to hold out her hand first. Little by little, they reciprocated her overtures, and the four rooms behind the shop became habitable again. At the same time, figures from her old life started to seep into her new one. The débacle at Godsbrother Puritanism's had left few survivors, and those who remained were only voices (footsteps, rustling hems, annoyingly audible little habits that she'd never noticed before).

They would not tell her anything they thought might offend her. It was startling, and funny, to realize most of them were still afraid of her.

But—she reasoned—if Aneisneida and Soderingal Nearecloud, Gold Dagger, and the Hangman still feared her, then she must still bear *some* resemblance to the woman she had been.

One night as she lay in bed weak with holding back the tears for him, exhausted with trying not to sleep so that she might not dream of him, she came face to face with the implication of her own continuing survival. It burned like a fire, lighting up her mind. In later months, it would prove a freedom wheel such as children lit at midwinter. It spun off possibilities like sparks, and each spark died. But that first night, she only felt it as a burning, consuming thing, like a new infatuation, a chimera that took her mind off her tears.

Revenge.

She was still Humility Garden, Divinarch of Royalland, Calvary, Veretry, Pirady, Iceland, the sundry isles of the Archipelago, and Domesdys et al. Nothing had changed. Pati's coup had wreaked havoc on the world, and damaged her badly. She was not a fool, to deny that. But his poison had broadened her vision even as it ruined it.

It had been an incident. One that had passed.

It was her bounden duty and heart's desire to repair the damage it had done.

Revenge.

Someday, she would have her realm back or die in the trying. And until then she would carve seagulls.

THE FREEDOM WHEEL

Arity missed Sual more than he had expected to. He wondered, when a large enough dose of *khath* opened some of the closed doors in his mind, whether the year in Delta City might not have rendered him *incapable* of that utterly superficial passion that was central to *auchresh* nature. Or maybe he had been born like this. There had not been anyone before Pati, had there? No. And there had not been anyone in the years between Pati and *her*. (Not even numb with *khath* did he allow himself to think her name.) No one except for a few of *lesh kervayim* who had practically thrust themselves down his throat, not to put too fine a point on it. After he rejected them as *ghauthijim*, the consensus had gone around that the Heir was cold and a little strange. Uppity, but too weak to back up his dramatics.

That was what they had thought of him.

On the first count, at least, they had been wrong.

Weak.

He shuffled up the creaking stairs of his building, gripping the saltwood banister. His head felt disconnected from his feet. The night was only half over, but he was sick of the taverns. Down here, there seemed always to be a kind of alcoholic slop washing around the floors, as if the river had overflowed its crumbling banks. (The river. Ridiculous that after living here more than two years, he still did not know that river's name, or if it had one.) Down here, the ancient servingboys grinned with blackened fangs and pressed themselves against you when they poured your *khath*. They were serving two drinks for the *denear* of one in honor of the Divinarch's arrival, and Arity had foolishly taken advantage of the offer. *You revolt me,* he thought to himself. Extraordinary what a falloff in quality there was between the tier where Sual had lived, where the Laughing Haughthule had stood, and the bottommost tier of all, where he lived.

He reached the landing and hung over the newel post. He vomited into the stairwell, great retches that left him sagging over the post, his eyes watering, listening to his puke splatter on the floor of the hall far below. If the thorns had grown on his stomach, the spot pressures might have injured something inside him; but like a porcupine's prickles, they grew only on his back and throat, through his hair, and on the backs of his arms, with a few scattered on his chest.

The lingering effects of the *khath* allowed him to think about them, too.

His head was much clearer now. He would sleep for a while, and then go out again.

Down here, just as on the topmost tiers where the *serbalim* lived, some bars stayed open even through the day. It was considered fashionable. The hypocrisy.

His door sagged open on its one hinge. "Charity"—he murmured in mortal, to which he reverted when he was alone—"your brain is rotting. Even if the lock doesn't work, you could *close* the *door.*"

Shaking his head, he went in.

Pati sat on the bed. He was a pale shade in the starlight drifting from the skylights. His eyes burned with an inner light, one blue and one brown.

Just as he had sat waiting in his suite in Wind Gully Heaven, those first nights when terrified, yet honored beyond speech, Arity had crept through the passages to receive the mainraui's *favor.*

Dumb with terror, Arity stumbled back against the doorway, clutching his throat as if he could somehow enable himself to speak.

"Oh, in the name of the Power." Pati spoke in mortal. He got up and pulled Arity bodily into the room, then kicked the door shut. "Collect yourself, man! I'm not a shade. You're not hallucinating."

How long since Arity had heard someone else speak in this language?

"I didn't think I was hallucinating."

Pati did not notice that he had been insulted. "I thought it would be best to wait for you. I know where you spend every moment of your wretched existence: I could have come and grabbed you out of one of your repulsive little haunts. But I didn't want to embarrass you by recognizing you down there." He narrowed his eyes. "Ari, you look terrible."

Arity gestured around the bare little room. "Why do you think I don't have any tapers? If you want to admire my thorns, you should come back during the day."

"Are you inviting me?" Pati licked his lips, grinning wickedly.

"Pah." Arity turned away. "I'm not quite that desperate. I've heard things. You and all the Hands live like humans. You even live with humans. A case of the ruler and subject pigging in together. Your most trusted servants are flamens and lemans."

"Just who have you been talking to? I was not aware such slander was on the streets."

"Hope." Then Arity cursed himself as Pati's face darkened and he swore in *auchraug*.

"Damned *iu!* She works against me every opportunity she gets!"

Arity smiled, this time in pure pleasure. He could get one up on Pati and at the same time give him a filthier, more correct picture of the man he himself had become. "What makes you think those things prejudiced me *against* you?"

There was a pause. Then Pati grinned, showing his white fangs. Closing his hand on Arity's wrist, he dragged Arity over to the bed and sat him down. "So you *do* miss Delta City."

"I wouldn't go back there for the world."

"That doesn't mean you don't miss it."

"Not the place. Just the people."

"Oh? Who?"

Damn! He must still be drunk. He was falling into all of Pati's traps. "Never you mind."

Pati arched a pale eyebrow. "Are you sure?" He paused. *"Irissi . . ."*

Irissi! The memories were rushing back. He could not fend them off. *The door creaks and he turns. The muscles in his neck ripple. I am mute with awe, waiting for him to laugh and order me out because I have not brought the* gherry *he requested. But instead, after a minute, he smiles. His smile is like the sun that is creeping around the curtains of his room.*

My fear is a valid memory, the nervousness of a boy going to his first lover, but the cruelty and vanity in that smile were superimposed by later years. This Pati *isn't the Striver. He's young and sincere. He gets up, tilts his head, and kisses me.*

Arity shook his head. Fear thrilled through him. "Get out of my room!"

"You don't want to remember, do you?"

"Remember *what?*"

"There's nothing like reprising an experience to bring it back."

"Leave me alone!"

Pati settled more comfortably on the bed. Arity became aware that the Divinarch smelled of expensive perfume, and a second later, he realized he had thought of Pati for the first time in his official capacity. Like dunking his head in cold water, he remembered who Pati was. Such a gap. He was speaking to the *Divinarch*. The man's first blow had found a chink in his armor and cut all the way to the bone. But it was not too late to undo the damage. All he had to do was invoke reality.

He retreated, on his feet. "They'll be looking for you. You must have been missed."

"Oh, not to worry. I scheduled this in." Pati glanced up at the skylight. "I have another couple of hours yet."

For some reason this cut deeper than anything else. Arity heard his voice rising like a child's. "You fitted me into your *schedule* as if I was any *serbali?*"

"What else could I have done? I am Divinarch! All of those common *serbalim*, as you call them, have claims on me."

"And you rank me with them. You grubbing, sycophantic diplomat. Your memory is shorter than a Foundling's cock. Why are you in Rimmear then?" Arity did not know why he felt cheated. "A matter of failed communication?"

"In a manner of speaking."

"If I were to *teth¨* right now, you would never see me again. *There's* a failure of communication for you." His mind was made up now. He glanced at his cookstove, his clothes chest, his dusty curtains, mentally saying goodbye to them. The Ugly Iu Tavern? Or the Sadui's Rest? Which was likeliest to be empty at this hour?

"Ah." Pati laughed. "But you are not *going* to *teth¨*, are you?"

The moment stretched.

Arity lifted his hands, palms out. The city throbbed outside, softly, like blood in his ears. "What do you want of me?" His voice sounded strange to him.

"I want you to come back to Delta City."

"For my health? The air here may smell bad, but I am assured it is an excellent physic for weariness." *Of life.*

"You will die before long if you keep on like this. One cannot expect to consume enough *khath* every night to fill the Chrume and survive. But that is hardly the point. I want you for *my* sake, not yours."

Arity folded his arms. "At least you're honest."

"I owe you nothing Ari, whereas you owe *me* your life."

So *that* was it! Arity waggled a finger in the air, grinning. All was solved. So cold-blooded! "You think you had anything to do with it, *ruthyali?* I owe my life to Hope. She nursed me back to health. And I've thanked her many times, I believe. Now get out."

"The last time she came to visit, you had some ugly yellow-haired *ghauthi kere* in your arms. You turned her away."

"She *told* you that?"

Pati's mouth twisted. "*There's* an *iu* who ought to watch her step. She feeds me crumbs of information from time to time. You ought to be careful with her. But to her credit, she would never tell me something she believed important to you."

It would not have been important before Sual died. None of this would have been important before Sual died. "His name was Unusual Day," he told Pati, shrugging. "I loved him."

Pati sat forward. "Was?" he prodded.

"I killed him. I gave him more *denear* than he could handle. He went wild."

"What did you expect him to do? You're lucky you haven't yet been killed yourself, if you're running around throwing money at every *kere* with sex appeal. You weren't made to live in Rimmear."

Arity laughed. He flung around the room, kicking the cookstove, shoving the pillows off the bed, slamming the door. Splintery dents appeared in the walls where he punched them. His scars stung unbearably. Breathing hard, he rammed both hands up against the skylight, almost cracking it. The city towered on one side, like a giant curtain caught in the act of sweeping across the stars. "Shut up, damn your eyes! Shut up! I love it here!"

"Forever," Pati whispered obscurely. His arms went around Arity from behind. Arity's hands broke apart. A knife entered his bitten shoulder but he hardly noticed. Pati was kissing his neck, mouthing one of the thorns. The soft rings of flesh at the bases were exquisitely sensitive. Arity froze.

"Do it again," Sual hissed. They stood in a curve of the corridor at the Green Jewel Saloon, pressed against each other in the shadows. "Do it, damn you, cripple—"

Arity obliged. He didn't know how he had ever had the courage to come on to Sual. The kere's *breath was redolent of spices and his hair shone like the sun. He touched several of Arity's thorns, working them back and forth, laughing when he felt Arity stiffen. "Power, these're funny! Never seen em before! You can feel that, uh? Oh, cripple boy—"*

His hands were buried in the dusty salt-fabric folds of the curtains. Pati moved closer, rubbing against his back, almost dancing against him. The thorns on Arity's shoulder blades were piercing both their shirts, drawing blood from Pati's torso. Pati's breath came shallowly. Arity felt his erection hot against his buttocks. He almost lost control then, but memories were still cascading through his mind. By that thin skin of abstraction, his armor held.

"You're scarcely more than a Foundling, aren't you?" Pati held Arity off to look at him. Arity shivered and tried to bury his head in Pati's armpit. "Whose were you?"

"Win-Winding Stream's—"

"He's raised you to be a beautiful auchresh." *Pati kissed him.*

"*I love you,* mainraui," *Arity whispered.*

"*Pati. My name is Pati. I have a virtue name, just like you.*"

A few minutes later Pati guided the boy toward the bed. The braced platform gave a little when Arity flopped back on it. The sunlight coming around the edges of the curtains lit up the colors in the coverlet. "*Don't hold on to me,*" *Pati scolded.* "*I want to show you the best of this, and I can only do that if you trust me enough to lie still.*"

But overtaken by boldness, Arity pulled him down on top of him. He kissed him again and again, his eyes wide. A white strip of sunlight twisted across Pati's shoulders as he writhed, plucking at the laces of Arity's breeches. "*Ah—you wicked little Foundling—*"

And starlight poured down over them as Arity turned and kissed Pati. He brushed his tongue over Pati's lips, and at the threat of intimacy, in an automatic reflex, the armor drew tighter around him, stifling him for a moment, like a second, impermeable skin. He panicked.

And then it was gone. He was free: sensuously free. Yet he was protected. The armor had melded with his own skin. He could no longer feel it. It *was* his skin, *was* his scars.

He did not trust Pati. That was . . . a given . . .

But it would be a crime, a weakness, to stay away from him merely because he feared him. A crime likewise to kiss this way, to run his hands down the perfumed body of the Divinarch, but who cared? Sual was dead. And no one cared. Not even Arity. For with this surrender to the past, he escaped Sual's death, escaped the misery and boredom of his existence. And he made up for leaving Sual alone by giving himself body and soul to Death itself, in the form of an *auchresh* with bicolored eyes and iridescent wings.

The foxglove on the windowsill was dead. Its leaves stuck to the fur of Humi's leg, when she sat there above the alley. Cold air licked around her, inside her nightgown. Autumn rode on it: the stink of the decaying marshes. She knew it was as dark outside her head as it was inside, but that made no difference.

Knot and pull, split the thread, stitch stitch stitch.

She had finished her ghost of the seagull. Now she expected to stay up the whole night sewing. Since her days as twentieth councillor, when she had kept a double schedule, socializing with the Antiprophet Square set in the daytime and the *auchresh* after sundown, she had needed less than no sleep.

Behind her, she felt a hot gust of sulfur. Someone stumbled over the seagull that Humi had left on the floor, and hissed a curse.

Humi twisted around. "Hope?"

"What's this on the floor?" Humi recognized Hope's voice, though the *auchresh* moderated it down to a whisper. "It's not a ghost, is it?"

Humi muddied violently. She prayed Hope could not see well enough in the dark to make out the hue of her face.

"It *is!* I thought you couldn't—"

"I can't. It's not a real ghost." She swallowed, and qualified, "It's a technique I invented. Different from painting."

"A-a-ahhh." Hope must be clutching the seagull to her breast. Humi slid off the windowsill and sat down on her bed, biting her lip. She heard Hope's heel talons clicking on the floor. "Humi, this is . . . it's . . . So . . . so much *grief* . . ."

"Give it to me!"

Hope laid the ghost on the coverlet. Humi located it by its aura of cold, scooped it up, and stowed it under the bed.

"Why haven't you shown it to Ziniquel and Emni? Or Mory and Tris? We could probably find those two if we tried."

"It's too much of me."

"That never used to worry you."

Humi would have been delighted that Hope had come, if she would only leave it alone! Tears were gathering in her nose. Oh, gods. "I . . ." Unable to help it, she sniffed loudly.

"*Oh.*" The *auchresh* hopped up on the bed, careful not to make the planks creak, and hugged Humi. She rocked her back and forth, crooning. "I'm sorry . . . I'm sorry . . . it's my fault . . ." The heat of her body was magic. Almost involuntarily, curled there, Humi relaxed. Hope smelled of soot and sea breeze. She must have come straight from the Old Palace.

Why had she come at this hour?

Had she discovered something?

The instinct awoke in Humi, questing.

She pushed the *auchresh* away and sat up. She wiped her face. "I am just so glad to see you." Her voice still trembled. "I was convinced you weren't coming again."

"Humi, the day I don't crave sight of you is the day I am dead." Hope folded her wings with a disturbingly loud rustle. She touched Humi's nightgowned knee. "But it's not safe for me to be here. And I am so hellishly busy. I have been promising myself that I would come since the middle of the summer. But it hasn't happened. I'm sorry."

"Has *anything* happened?" Humi held her breath.

"Talk." Hope sighed. "A great deal of talk. It is something. The subject is out in the open, at least. I have tested the waters in the Nearecloud mansion and in the Crescent. Aneisneida, Soderingal, Zin, and Emni all say they would support you in a recoup."

"Anyone in his right mind would support anyone other than Pati!"

"Have you forgotten that you are Humility Garden? The city remembers you. The first and last human Divinarch. A sort of mystique hangs around your memory. Even those few who know you are alive speak of you with reverence."

"But not one of them will risk his skin for me."

"Can *I* help it if they are afraid? Can you blame them for *being* afraid?"

Humi sighed. "The city is a Freedom wheel," she said. "Giving off sparks. But none of them ever catch. So much wet, dead wood." She paused, and said ironically, "But there is always this. If we give Pati enough rope, perhaps he will hang himself."

Hope made a curious little sound. "And strangle the whole city in the process! He's clever! And he has charisma! It won't happen. He has got the flamens—and not just the flamens, either—dancing at his fingertips. He's got the whole world in his fist."

"Well, then, what can we do against him?"

Hope's wings fluttered, snapping. Humi felt their gusts in her face. "Sometimes I think we can do nothing."

"Stop it. You'll wake the children."

"And the secrets. Humi, I am cursed with secrets."

She stiffened. "What are you keeping from me?"

"I cannot tell you! I am sorry!"

In the alley, a herd of feral pigs grunted, scraping through the garbage with their trotters.

Pati held up a set of Hand's clothes—shirt and breeches of fawn silk. "This?" The torch in the closet flickered, casting his hooknosed shadow onto the wall. "Or this?" A mortal man's clothes. "Or this?" *Auchresh* clothes, with a Kithrilindic look to the cutouts. "You can't continue in those rags, anyhow. It would reflect badly on me."

How quickly he had asserted control! Arity's first instinct was to reach for the human clothes. But as his hand went out, he thought better of it and took the Hand's outfit. A smile creased Pati's face. "Good. You haven't forgotten how humans' minds work after all, have you?"

Arity turned his back, stripped, and pulled on the new clothes.

"You'll have to start clipping your thorns again, too." Pati's voice came unhurriedly, as casual as the blow the blue-skinned *kuiros* had dealt Arity on the head. "There's nothing to be done about your scars. But really, you can't live as a member of the ruling class of Delta City while you look like a hedgehog."

"I do *not* look like a hedgehog."

"A rosebush, then."

Arity turned around, tugging the shirt down. It had caught on a thorn in back, and he felt it rip. "You brought me back here to stand beside the Throne looking exactly the way you want me to, so that everyone knows I have succumbed to you. This is what I want to know. Do you want me—or do you want my head on a pike?"

Pati stood in the door of the closet. The torchlight blackened the room behind him. "I want *you.* To alter yourself as much as I ask you to. I want to adorn you, beautiful one. Won't you let me?" His voice took on a cajoling tone. "Don't you remember Wind Gully Heaven, how you would steal one of my garments, and roll it up and pin it to your sleeve, so everyone knew we were lovers?" His voice was seductive as sweet cream.

"*Power.*" Arity could not bear it. What had he gotten into? Snatching the torch off its bracket, ignoring Pati's cry, he dashed it into one of the racks of clothes. They were salt-fiber fabric, so flameproof. The flame sputtered and went out.

In the other room, there was the creak of a door opening. A sleepy *auchresh* voice called, "Pati? Are you back?"

Pati spun. "Melin! Go away!"

"*Cujali!* I knew it was you! You just cried out, didn't you?" Footsteps. "Is something wrong?"

"No!" Pati lifted on tiptoe and shouted. "*Hands!*" His voice boomed as if his lungs were a pair of brazen bells. Even Arity clapped his hands to his ears. "*Hands!* Take him! Take him to Westpoint!" He strode forward and pulled Arity's hands down. A brief struggle erupted in the other room. Pati held Arity close. The Divinarch's heart was pounding. When all was quiet, he let go.

"Who was that? Your lover?" Arity had not realized that Pati's physical strength was superior to his own. His eyes watered. "And you're throwing him over for me. Well, well, well. All right. I'll cut my thorns. I'll hold my head high. Anything for you, Divinarch. I am your servant."

"Then stand at the right hand of my throne, Arity. Be my Heir."

"No!"

"You said you would do anything."

"Anything but that!"

"Be a Hand, then. My Inviolate One." Pati wrapped his arms around Arity. Endearments tumbled from his lips. Far below, the sea crashed against the cliffs. Pati kissed the tears out of Arity's eyes.

"Who was that I saw as we *teth*¨*d* in?" Arity whispered. "Not your *cujali*. Before that. A small, winged one. He *teth*¨*d*."

Pati gripped him tighter. "No one knows we are here. The city believes the Palace to be empty but for a few servants and Hands. But when we return *next* from Uarech, everyone will see you, for you shall stand on my Throne. Heir or no Heir. All my Hands attend me from time to time. And if you will have it that way, you shall be no exception."

"Yes," Arity whispered. "That's all I ask, milord Divinarch. That's all I have ever asked."

Downstairs, Humi prepared bitter chocolate and poured it into two pottery cuplets. They stood in the shop to drink it, talking desultorily of trade and Deltans they both knew: who had been arrested, who had left the city. Presumably, Hope was watching the last of the nightlife dribbling along the street. Humi watched the blackness inside her head. The mobiles hanging from the ceiling tinkled every time Hope shifted her wings.

Aneisneida's baby Fiamorina had just celebrated her second birthday. "When I look at her, it seems to have been a hundred years since the fall," Hope said. "One realizes how little politics matter, in the grand scheme of things."

Humi laughed. "How beautiful, Hope. But politics matter more than anything. Without politics, there wouldn't be a world for Fiamorina to grow up in."

Hope did not answer. Humi hated that the *auchresh* kept secrets from her. She supposed Hope had a good reason; yet it saddened her. Would they drink chocolate and talk of nothing forever, while the city atrophied in Pati's iron grip?

But Humi could not risk alienating the only real friend she had. No matter how useless Hope believed it was, she would keep on proselytizing on Humi's behalf. That would not change. Hope was loyal. Unlike Zin and Emni, Aneisneida and Soderingal. They had all disappointed Humi. She had not seen any of them in more than a year.

Hope stretched, setting the mobiles jangling, and said, "I must go." Humi accepted her empty chocolate cup and a kiss on each cheek. "Oh," Hope said, "I almost forgot this." She took Humi's hand and closed it around a lumpy weight.

Humi felt the shapes of coins inside a leather bag. "Oh, you don't have to," she said automatically, but the words stuck in her throat. In order for *Delights and Diversions* to survive, Hope did have to. And Hope knew that. "We'll pay you back as soon as the shop starts making a profit," she said awkwardly. "Hem hates taking loans."

"Tell him to consider it a gift," Hope said firmly. "As always."

Humi bounced the little bag in her palm. At least five hundred shillings, if it was silver. She swallowed. "Hope, do you have any idea when I shall see you—"

Sulfur gusted around her face. She choked on the second half of her sentence.

Once again she was alone in the shop.

The air seemed colder now the *auchresh* was gone. Humi breathed deeply, once, twice, sticking her fingers in the corners of her eyes, and went back behind the counter.

Power, Hope thought as her feet hit the floor of her bedroom. *Why couldn't I tell her? Why couldn't I?* "She must have thought it odd beyond comprehension!" She flopped back onto her sumptuous bed. The springs accommodated her wings. She lay still, feeling the tension drain out of her great shoulder muscles. *If Ari is returning to the city, she will have to know sometime, and better that she find out from me—* "Why on earth would I come in the middle of the night, rattle on about her ghost for several minutes, and then talk of nothing, unless I was cracked?"

"Milady Hope?" A candle appeared around the door at the far end of the long room, casting a yellow glow on the polished floor and the elaborately carved oak bureaus on either side of the door. Above it hung the wrinkled face of Hope's favorite human servant, Godsie Grenworth. "Is all well, milady?"

"Yes, Godsie. Go to bed. No need to send Shari—I can undress by myself."

"Ah, yes. Not as if you was one of them ladies as used to be, any'ow, with dozens of different buttons . . ." The old woman withdrew. Hope valued her, though she was sometimes overbearing. It was hard enough to get any servants: few Deltans, be they pious or atheistic, would agree to serve Hope as if she were just anybody. Harder yet to get them to call her *Milady,* though she thought it the most innocuous title out of those she had to choose from. Certainly, she could no longer style herself a god. That would lump her along with the Hands.

She laced her hands behind her head. Drawing her feet up onto the bed, she stared at the midnight sky she had had painted on the ceiling. *Power, Arity,* she thought, *have you no self-respect? None at all?*

DIVINE INTERVENTION

Qalma was twice as large an island as Sarberra. A stone town straggled uphill from the docks, vanishing around a ridge that was scattered with trees. Gete could not keep from staring as he jumped out of *Faith* and made her fast. He had never seen a tree before, except on salt Harrima, and those hadn't been real.

He stooped, found Thankfulness's hand, and jerked her up onto the dock. Without reproaching him for his clumsiness, she straightened, turning her head as if she could still see, biting her lip. She stared with salt-crystalled eyes toward the town, the brown bundles sitting in the sun, the doll-sized figures working on the terraces to the east, the blue cone of the peak above. Gete grabbed the rucksack that held their possessions from her and hefted it over his shoulder.

"Gete . . ." she said in that trailing way she had.

"Godsister."

"This place feels god touched."

He said nothing. Over the six days of their traveling, he had learned to keep his mouth shut. It was less frustrating than receiving such answers as, "Because the gods will it so." Or that penetrating, milky stare of hers. Impossible to tell what was passing through the mind behind those blind eyes with their glitter-studded irises. She just stared, and said nothing, and Gete cringed like a bird being eyed by a cat.

"What is this place called?" she asked abruptly.

"Qalma, Godsister."

"Ah, yes. I was here with Transcendence once, I believe. 'Heavy Water'—I think that is what that word meant, in the beginning of time, before the Archipelagan language was melded with the outside tongues. I think Transcendence told me so." She started to blink, then stopped. Gete remembered she had said that blinking scratched the insides of her eyelids to blood. Eventually the lids would grow back into the orbital hollows, making room for the crystals. "The eighth house on the left. I think that is where we will find him."

"Who?"

She stared at him as if she could not believe he had to ask. Finally, she said, "The god."

Faith bobbed alongside the granite pier. All the other boats must be out at sea. Gete hoped he hadn't tied up in anyone's prized berth. But even if he *had*—well, a leman could commandeer anything his flamen needed, couldn't he? Thankfulness's foot slipped on old fish scales, and she grabbed his arm for balance. Woodenly, correctly, he set her on her feet.

"Ah . . . aaaah. Hold on to me, leman . . . please."

He did as he was commanded. Slowly, they progressed along the pier and started up the broad bedrock slope of the road. Gete looked back and saw evenly spaced splotches on the pier shining in the afternoon glare. The marks of fish piling. In parts of the Reach where the nets did not lure swordfish, but the bigger, poison-tailed coelakates, you could not carry the catch up from the boat—it would twist around and sting you. Coelakates could stay alive out of water for hours, and their stings had caused deaths even on Sarberra, which was really too far north for their shoals. So Mid-Reach fishermen must leave their catch on the dock overnight to die.

Thankfulness drew a sharp breath, and stumbled.

"What's wrong, Godsister?"

"No . . ."—she was breathing hard—". . . thing. It is just the heat. You remember that . . . I was not very well yesterday."

It seemed that with her, unwellness was perpetual. Maybe it had to do with the salt crystals' throbbing incipience, or her incomplete recovery from her ordeal on Harrima. She was still thin. In the shadows of her cowl, her collarbone stuck up, razor-sharp as a ridge of rock sticking out of a hillside. But then again, maybe all flamens were like her. He hadn't encountered many of them, had he? And that wasn't just because Sarberra was so far out of the way of the world—it had to do with the new Divinarch, and the fact that many flamens (Thani had told Gete) were forsaking his service. Maybe, as a result, the remaining ones had to draw more on the strength of their own bodies. Thankfulness constantly complained of headaches and weakness. And although guilt whispered at him, Gete could not help resenting her for it.

The mirage of Delta City had receded far into the future, superseded by the specter of his loyalty to her. For the gods' sakes, it was like being *married!* Except he didn't even *like* her!

She shuffled beside him toward the eighth house. Her shoes were falling apart. In the few weeks they had known each other, he had already had to get her one pair of new shoes and two new robes; he had no idea how she managed to wear things out so fast.

"'Tis an old man sitting by the door," he said. "And a little babe asleep with him."

"I know."

"You—what?"

"I—I—" She made an anguished little sound. "Gods' greeting, venerable Godsman!" she sputtered. "I am Godsister Thankfulness! I am only just come from . . ." "Shettara," Gete murmured. "From Shettara! Would I be correct in assuming that you harbor a god in your home? I should like to do him honor—"

"God? Easter? Ah, he's out to the fishing." The old man squinted at Thankfulness and Gete. "Gods' greeting to ye, flamen. He'll na be back for 'nother few hours, does the sunshine hold. But ye—ye must be sent from the Divinarch himself. We have sore need of ye in this house." He stood up, laying the baby on the bench, and bowed his gray head to Thankfulness. "Me only son is dying."

The god Easter was an unhuman looking creature with ragged scraps of wings on his shoulders and muscle-bound arms that reached nearly to the ground. Nothing like slim, handsome Desti. The lines on his face made him look about Gete's father's age, but Gete knew he was probably much older. His full name was Warm Easterly. Gete did not get a chance to speak to him before supper, nor did Thankfulness get a chance to make her obeisances to him. In fact, Gete wondered if she even *knew* the god had arrived back in Qalma with the rest of the men: in order to find out whether she really could sense these things, he had not told her.

He looked out the door of the Finspine house and saw the god gutting yesterday's catch with the other fishermen, on the scale-covered stones around the well at the top of Qalma town. They must have carried the catch up the hill early this morning.

On Sarberra, gutting would be women's work. But here, the women had not yet got back from the terrace gardens, and so the men finished with the coelakates and dispersed to their houses to cook up the supper their wives had prepared in the morning, affectionately chaffing each other in a way that made Gete's heart ache.

All except Hasti Finspine. He lay ill in an inner room with only his old mother to tend him. Some days ago he had been stung in the face by a coelakate: his fever had developed complications and he breathed painfully, with a bubbling deep in his lungs. The room smelled of the noxious fluid he coughed up. A purple blister had cracked one cheek open like an over-cooked loaf of bread.

Eventually Godsie Finspine returned from the terraces with her four children, all of them covered in dirt. The bustle of the family dinner was subdued. Thankfulness startled when Gete finally described Easter's entrance, but she said nothing. Perhaps she was saving herself for the work she had to do later on.

It was imperative that Hasti Finspine return to health. Qalma might look prosperous, but in truth, Godsie Finspine whispered, standing by Gete as Thankfulness knelt at Hasti's head, their margin of survival was as thin as a starved cat. Gete knew the story. He'd grown up with it! As he hauled his first net out of the water at age six, in the spring sunshine, the winter gales had howled in the back of his mind. He'd seen the storms behind the approval in his father's eyes. All Archipelagans had eyes the color of night. (Except Gete, whose were blue.) The loss of one able body could diminish the season's returns enough that not all the islanders would live through the winter. Of course Warm Easterly could take the Finspines' boat out, Godsie Finspine said, but one god could not do *everything!* Could he?

She asked Gete this last question as if Warm Easterly were a volatile, unknown quantity, a cause for dire apprehension. It served only to remind Gete that this was *her husband* lying on the pallet.

"I will heal him." Under her fur, Thankfulness's face bore lines of strain. "Owing to the conditions, I must dispense with the ritual, but I *will* have silence. Out, all of you." She nodded stiffly to Warm Easterly. "Even you, milord god."

Obediently, the gathered islanders, and one god, shuffled toward the door. At that moment, there was a flash in the shadows. Gete smelled brimstone, and he saw a slight yellow-clad figure—silver wings—owlish eyes—

Desti saw him, too, and knocked Qalmans out of the way as he dived for the door. Gete went after him. Warm Easterly tried to intervene, shouting in that incredibly loud voice that Desti had sometimes lapsed into, too. But the children were in the way, and Thankfulness cried piercingly, "Leman! Leman . . . ! What is it? *Where are you?*" Her voice was panicky.

The tail of Desti's tunic whisked around the outer door. Gete plunged after him. A noisy rain was falling from the twilight sky. Rivers streamed down the street. Gete sneezed water out of his nose as he pursued Desti up the street, across the open square with the well, and onto the ridge. The ground was much lumpier than it had looked from a distance. He had trouble keeping the god in sight as they clambered over hummocks and little ravines. Why didn't Desti vanish? Gete wondered blurrily. Then Gete would have no chance of catching him! But again and again he glimpsed the yellow tunic. Grass flattened to mud under his feet. He slipped and cursed, pushing wet hair out of his eyes.

Ahead, Desti vanished through a line of trees. Gete arrived panting at the rustling, wet barrier. For some absurd reason he hesitated. Then he shut his eyes and pushed through, half-jumping, half-falling over a stone wall into a muddy ditch sheltered from the rain.

Goats sniggered in alarm and scrambled away.

Desti stood barefoot in the mud, his wings bedraggled, both palms up in a gesture of surrender such as children make to end a game of tag.

"Why didn't you vanish?" Gete panted. "I never woulda caught you!"

"I would have lost you if I wanted to."

"You feared of anyone seeing us talking? You want me to say I never found you?"

Desti looked at his feet. Water droplets flew off one wing as it snapped out, then folded in again.

"Well, if that's how tis, you damn well better have something worth sayin' to say," Gete said viciously. He scuffled a clear place in the goats' droppings on the side of the ditch, sat down, and glared at Desti.

After a moment the god came and sat down beside him, leaning against the stone wall, his feet drawn up. The rain thundered on the leaves overhead. Now and then, a fat drop splatted on the earth. For a long time neither of them spoke. A stealthy sense of lassitude crept over Gete. He remembered the Dividay afternoons they had spent on the mountain, taking advantage of the holy day to eat wild bayberries and watch the clouds go by. Sometimes cloudbursts made them shelter under crags. Leaning against each other's backs—Desti's wings were surprisingly comfortable—they would stare at the raindrops plummeting past the mouth of the little cave. They seldom needed to talk.

Now, sitting in the mud on Qalma, Gete did not want to talk to Desti any more than he had back then. But he *had* to. He had to know why Desti had scarcely returned to Sarberra after Godsbrother Transcendence's arrival.

That probably meant asking about Heaven and the *serbalim*. The part of Desti's life which had nothing to do with Gete—which evidently included Qalma. The thought of reducing Desti's comfortable mystery to cold reality saddened Gete. Nonetheless, he said, "Have you been back to Sarberra since?"

Desti shook his head. The god's hands, twisting between his knees, were longer and slimmer than Gete had ever noticed before. The nails were shaped like chicken claws, clipped off short at the ends of his fingers. "My *serbalim* forbade me to go back."

"You and your *serbalim*."

"They said they would banish me from Heaven if I ever visited human country again."

"So what are you doing here?"

"I'm coming to that." Desti looked at Gete. "They never liked me visiting Sarberra in the first place. You know that. And then, sea-pig that I am, I let them find out about the flamen's recognizing me. That was enough for Briar Finger and Sweet Tornmouth. They said I was violating *er-serbali* law. Easter tells me they were lying—the *er-serbalim* haven't prohibited us from going into human country. But since we're so far away from anywhere, Briar and Sweet Tornmouth can do whatever they like."

"But what're you doing here *now*?"

Desti licked his lips. "I came to see Easter."

"What's he doing here? Is he from your Heaven, too?"

"He's been expelled. He wouldn't obey the *serbalim*, and they took away his *ruthyali* status. He lives here. I think—I think I have been expelled, too."

The rain hissed down on the leaves. Gete swallowed. His grudge against Desti suddenly seemed to have lost all its meaning. "You and me're in the same boat, then," he said. "Me elders told me to shove off. I'm not living on Sarberra now."

"What? Why are you—then what are *you* here for? I thought it was a fishing trip or something—"

Gete laughed. "Haven't cast a net in ten sixdays." As briefly as possible, he told the story of his having been press-ganged into lemanhood.

"Oh." Desti shuddered. "I'm sorry."

"I am, too!"

"It isn't that bad, is it?"

Gete did not answer. Some goats ventured back into the ditch and chomped at the leaves on the top of the wall, bringing a shower of rain-drops down on Gete and Desti. After a time Gete said, "But it was *your* fault, as much as 'twas anyone's."

"What?" Desti twisted around and looked at him. "What did *I* do?"

"Ye didn't answer my prayers. I thought you were a god like the flamen said ye were. And I wanted you to come take me away, or change their minds—or something!"

"I can't hear prayers! You *know* that!"

"Yeah. I know now. Now it's too late!"

The goats tossed their heads and climbed back up into the rain. The water in the bottom of the ditch was becoming a small river. Desti slid his foot down and splashed in it. "Power . . . I really do owe you one!"

"You don't owe me anything. Don't give me any easy rides."

"Well, I want to tell you anyway." Desti splashed harder in the water. "First of all, my people have a name which isn't gods. We call ourselves *auchresh.*"

"What? *What*-esh?"

"We're predators, really. Predators' children. Our Heavens are built near predator lairs, so we can keep our numbers up. There's a lair on salt Fulima—that's where I was born. It came time for my *breideii* White Oakenroot to take a Foundling, so he *teth¨d* over to Fulima and found me living on the water's edge, on raw fish, trying to keep myself hidden from the predators. They would've eaten me, even though one of them gave birth to me. I was about your age, I think. I don't remember, but that's how Oak says it was. He brought me back to Faraxa—"

"Wait," Gete said. "Predators gave *birth* to you?"

"Haven't I just told you so?"

Predators? The winged, fanged beasts that lived on salt islands and flew across the seas at night to prey on humans' homes and holdings? They were *animals!* Imagination could conjure up no creatures bloodier or more cunning. What could predators have to do with the gods?

Desti seemed to be saying that the gods weren't gods at all, but *descendants* of those beasts. But—but if he was telling the truth—if there were no real gods—then what of Transcendence's vision?

Gete asked a question at random out of the dozens filling his mind. "Your brei—whatever—he's your father? He adopted you? Then you're just like us?"

"Yes." Desti bit his lip. "Yes and no . . ." He stopped speaking. His head came up. "Oh, Power. Curses." A half-guilty, half-frightened look came over his face, as if he had been caught nicking someone else's catch. Gete followed his stare to the place where the stone wall curved into the night. There did not seem to be anything wrong. But Desti had those faculties, that extraordinarily powerful hearing—*not* human—ears like a predator's—

"Thank the Power I've found you!" Warm Easterly hurried along the ditch, knocking down a rain shower of droplets with his massive head and shoulders. "Desti, what have you been telling the boy?"

"Nothing." Desti's wings whirred. "Nothing."

"You have. I can see it on his face."

"Gete, I'm sorry! It was all lies!" Desti flickered, and vanished.

Easter shouted something unintelligible, in an impossibly loud voice, and grabbed vainly at the shrinking hole in the air.

Gete flattened himself against the wall. Divine retribution appeared to be visiting itself on him for having entertained the notion that Desti's people might possibly be something other than gods. *Please go away—it wasn't me—*

Easter squatted down in the bottom of the ditch. "Desti didn't handle that very well! Don't blame him for it. He's young. He doesn't know how to manage relations with your people yet."

Gete knuckled his eyes. "But was it—was it *true?* All that about"—he gulped—"predators?"

Easter's big fists rested on the ground, like those of the Veretrean apes Gete had once seen painted on a plate that had come all the way from K'Fier. This god was not handsome. Not like Desti, whom some of the girls had sighed over. *If only 'tweren't for his wings—*

"Desti is forty." Easter's eyes crinkled. His skin was pale in the dark. "By our standards, he is scarcely into his teens. Younger than you."

Gete gripped a wet, licheny stone that protruded from the wall. "I don't understand."

"You don't need to. Just forgive him. You'll probably never see him again. There's nothing to be gained by *not* forgiving him."

"But—but—" *But what should I forgive him for?* In the turmoil of his incomprehension, Gete had lost sight of the reason he had been angry with Desti in the first place.

"I won't punish him. Don't worry about that. But there's a lesson it is high time for him to learn; one that *firim* all over the world have learned: your people find it easier not to understand things. Since you are comfortable living with paradoxes, why should we make things more complicated by explaining them to you?" Easter's face became grave. "And of course, there is the danger of the Hands for those who know too much. And the disapproval of the *serbalim.* Both for you and for us. In light of *that,* it may be a long time before we can share all of the truth as we understand it with you." Easter rocked to and fro on his heels. "For now, it is enough that we share meat and hard work."

He looked straight at Gete. The rain was coming down harder, plopping through the trees. "Why aren't you with your Godsister?"

Thankfulness.

Oh, no.

Guilt drove everything else out of Gete's head. He sprang to his feet. "Oh, gods!" For the last couple of hours, he had forgotten her as completely as you can forget anyone. *What kind of leman am I?* "Oh, gods—"

"Your best move is to get back to her quickly, I think." Easter boosted himself to his feet and wrapped those long arms around Gete. He was drenched with rain, yet he still smelled of salt, the way Desti had whenever he arrived on Sarberra. But *this* was the salt of the sea, of nets and sun and sails, not the flowery vaguely good-to-eat scent of the transparent islands—

Blackness cut off Gete's breath. His pulse. His nerves. All his links to himself. Panic came in a flood. But since he had no body, it seemed queerly distant from him. *Did he knife me? Am I dying?*

His brain flopped like a fish out of water as his feet hit the wet rock of the village street. Silver piles of coelakates gleamed way down on the quay. Rain roared. Gete's teeth chattered. "What did ye *do?*"

The god laughed. He stood a little way uphill, with his hand on the door of another house. "Go to your flamen, boy. Do your duty."

"What about you?"

"I have more than one house here." Easter smiled again, lifted the latch, and went in.

In the ordinary way.

Gete's eyeballs hurt. So did his whole body, in subtle, unfamiliar places. His spine and the roots of his hair ached. Grown boy though he was, his eyes stung with tears. His hands shook as he lifted the latch and went inside.

She was not there. The hearth at the end of the room glowed sullenly. The room was filled with trembling shadows. All the supper pans hung neatly on the walls. The table was pushed against the downhill wall. Barrels and packages of foodstuffs lined the wall between the table and the hearth.

Gete wiped his eyes. He put his ear to the inner door and then opened it a crack, letting a wedge of dim firelight into the inner room. He counted the figures on the various pallets. The four Finspine children. Hasti's younger brother, Refu Finspine, and his wife. Their three children. The grandparents. On the farthest pallet, Nali and Hasti Finspine lay curled together, although the atmosphere in the room was warm to stifling. Godsie Finspine's round arm clasped her husband's shoulders. Her fur shone pale in the darkness.

The room smelled of burned herbs. Gete recognized the reek of fumigation.

So Thani had done her miracle.

Gods, gods, and I wasn't here!

He might not like her very much, but his failure to do his duty stung him into an agony. He closed the door carefully and rested his head on the planks. What kind of leman was he? What kind of man failed at the only task life had given him?

He was no more use than a fish on dry land. Flapping around ineffectually like one of those damn coelakates. Helpless as a girl in a boat.

But there was *one* girl who could handle a boat.

He would not have acted like this back on Sarberra!

But then, back on Sarberra, he had never had his entire religion infused with doubt in the course of a single evening. Back on Sarberra, he had never had decisions like this to make. He had never had to be so strong, the sole crutch of this sickly, frail girl who was nonetheless so heavy to bear up—

"Gete," she said in a voice like a feather drifting across the floor.

He started upright, dashing the tears away. *"Godsister?"*

In the shadows of the barrels, in a nook beside the hearth, her eyes shone like opaque red jewels. She must have been sleeping. Her breath was so faint he could not hear it over the whisper of the rain outside.

He rushed to kneel at her side. "Can you forgive me? I'll try harder, I'll do better by you—"

"I—I'm all right. Really."

Her hair was matted. Tenderly he lifted her up, laying her head on his knees so that he could comb out the tangles. "Tell me if it pulls." Each sleeve of her robe hung in two pieces, and the seam around the hood was frayed, too, trailing threads over her shoulders. " 'S *that* how you wear out your clothes so fast? The miracles?"

"I think so. I don't know why, though." Her voice was so soft he could hardly hear her. "Regretfulness, I am so tired. I don't think I am doing this right. It shouldn't be so hard to work miracles—and I can't think of any possible reason why they should spill over into my *hair* and my *clothes.*"

"Things're different than they were," Gete reminded her.

"They are! They are! Sometimes, when I work a miracle I feel as if I am balancing the whole world on my shoulders, and taking a terrible risk with it—that I am only just holding it, and that if I drop it the Divine Balance itself will shatter—"

Gete shivered. "Idle dreams," he said firmly.

"All our lives are idle dreams." Her chuckle was fainter even than her voice. Gete worked at a tangle on her nape, lifting her a little to reach it. The knobs of her spine protruded, all the way up to the base of her neck. She was naked under the disintegrating robe, having taken off the shift dress she wore under it during the day. He laid her back on his knees and massaged her forehead. "That feels good." A spasm of pain made her clench her teeth, but she knotted her jaw. "Go on," she said.

She was stoic and brave. Bending down, Gete dropped a kiss on her forehead. Then he came to his senses and straightened up. "Sorry!" he whispered, and yanked at the tangles.

She had gone very still. Now she frowned. "You're hurting me, Gete."

"I'm sorry. I said I was sorry." Was that a sparkle on her lashes? Could she still cry?

"I mean you're hurting me in . . . hurting me. If you hate me, then just tell me so, don't pull my hair like that. I'll put you away from me and take another leman right here on Qalma."

"Godsister, how can you say such a thing?"

"You put a good face on it, but I can tell. I made the wrong choice. Well, none of us is infallible. I'll just choose again." She shrugged, her eyes still closed.

He did not know how to reassure her. Frantically, he scooped her up in his arms. She was as light as a small child. How did you tell a girl you had suddenly realized that you loved her? Was this normal? Or was it like incest? No—everyone knew that flamens and lemans—it was all right!

He kissed her. Messily, because he had started crying again. "Godsister, don't put me away. I'll stay with you as long as you'll have me. I beg of you. Keep me by you."

Tears spilled from her eyes. She wrapped her arms around his neck and pressed her lips to his mouth. She had small, crooked teeth. How could someone so thin and ill-kempt be so pretty? He didn't know. He only knew she *was* pretty, even beautiful, with her milky globes of eyelids and the blood trickling out from under them onto her cheeks. His hands moved not of his own will, but according to some deeper instinct (it *must* be instinct, for he certainly did not know what to do with a girl) as he stripped the robe away. She had big joints and wide angular hips. He remembered his first sight of her, before flamenhood set in. She had been a sturdy girl. *And will be again. She will be again!*

Her face contorted in anguish when he finally penetrated her. There was no resistance, only a torrent of pleasure that swept him away faster than he had expected. Her thin fingers gripped his back and she hissed between her teeth, wordlessly, as his thrusts shook her.

It culminated.

A moment afterward, catching him completely off guard, came the wash of tenderness.

"I talked to Desti tonight," he whispered.

"Don't want to know." She snuggled her head into his armpit.

"What happened?" Gete said.

"Whah?"

"You useta be as cold as a raw fish. Now you're all cuddly."

A whisper of laughter. "I suppose . . . I made the right choice, after all."

"How can you tell, just from . . . that? From what we did?" Funny, ironic, that he should be the one doubting their bond, after that violent joining!

"If we were another man and woman, what we did wouldn't mean much," she said. "You of all people should know that." Her milky, granulated orbs were red in the dying firelight, like a dead fish's. "But since we are flamen and leman . . . well, I believe it's triggered something."

"What?"

"The flamen-leman bond. Don't you feel it?"

The rain pattered on the roof. Gete shut his eyes and tried to find his way deep inside himself. He could not find anything mystical, or any new thing at all apart from his desire for her. He said so.

She gave a relieved peal of laughter.

"Oh!" He shut his mouth.

"But it's broader than that, too. There's a . . . responsibility that you will come to feel, the way I felt responsible for Transcendence. Almost as if I was the adult and he the child. It's like looking back through a flawed window, but I can remember. Your task is to safeguard the world, by safeguarding me. If that doesn't rest lightly on your shoulders, well, it *shouldn't!* But as long as you accept the responsibility, we'll do well."

He shivered. Then he pulled her over and kissed her. "I accept *you.*"

She whispered wonderingly into his mouth, "I always did wonder what it felt like from the other side."

"Thankfulness . . . Thani?"

"Mmm. I was almost asleep."

The fire had nearly gone out. Strings of vegetables hung from the ceiling, undulating in the shadows, like vines dangling from the tree cover of a forest Gete had never seen. That primeval Veretrean forest, perhaps, where apes like Warm Easterly swung from limb to limb of gargantuan celery stalks.

"Why did you choose me in the first place? I was so useless, for so long. Why didn't you choose someone . . . easier? Younger?"

Thani sighed. She sounded wide-awake now as she said, "It's not like picking the prime billy out of the flock, Gete. I chose you because I didn't think you were born to live on Sarberra. If *I* hadn't been a leman, I would have been perfectly happy growing up in the Domesdys saltside, marrying one of my cousins, working the fields, bearing babies. I wouldn't want to do to another child what was done to me. The pain of separation from one's destiny is intense, although short-lived. But wherever *your* destiny lies, I was, and am, pretty sure it's not on Sarberra."

"But how could you tell . . . how did you know . . ." A shudder passed over Gete's scalp as he remembered salt Harrima. She had stared at him. It had almost been as if she had recognized him, without being able to see him.

"I knew it when I saw you."

"Could you still *see*? After your ordeal?"

She chuckled. "In a way. I was half delirious. I knew my sight was going to go soon, and I had already lost my ability to distinguish shapes. The salt undergrowth was a blur. But when you stepped out of the boat, I saw your hair, and I knew it would be a long time before I lost my ability to see *that*. It's like carrots—I don't suppose you have those in the Archipelago."

Gete extracted a lock of his hair from under her head and stared at it. "Nope."

"Or like those flowers your people plant in front of your houses. Witch's wands. I was absolutely terrified of not being able to see my own leman, and for that reason, I decided to choose you. Later, as I listened to your mother and the other Sarberrans talking, I realized my instincts had been right. You were different. So I told your father I wanted you. And he said they would meet to decide whether they could spare you."

"But . . ." This seemed to fly in the face of everything she had said before. "Was it completely random, then? If I had black hair, you'd never have noticed me, and I'd still be on Sarberra?"

"It's all tied up. Your beauty, your destiny. The surface is inseparable from the essence. The surface *is* the essence."

She paused.

"No one makes ghosts anymore. I had a sister who was a ghostier—a maker of ghosts. She's dead. Maybe her friends still ply their trade, but the flamens no longer choose ghosts from the continents. The Divinarch chooses his own now, without asking our advice, and there are no beauticians, no presentations, no viewings in Delta City. But if there *were*, I'm convinced you would already have been chosen. You are so lovely."

Gete had never been called lovely before. He did not know whether to take her seriously.

"Your path leads to Delta City. It would have led you there whether I came to Sarberra or not. But thank the gods, I was right when I perceived qualities in you beyond mere beauty, that would be useful to me now, in a different age, when different things are required of us."

Gete silently thanked the gods in his turn that times had changed. He did not want to die as a ghost. He wanted to live. Delta City seemed unimportant now, no more than a crystallization of his future with Thani.

"How much can you see now?" he asked. "Can you still see my hair?"

She shook her head. "Everything is blurred into a kind of eternal twilight. In the sun, there are rainbows. I can see movement, if it's fast."

He winced.

She must have felt his distaste. Her voice rang suddenly clear. "And I pray, leman, for the day when even those remaining impurities vanish from my perception, when I will thank the gods that I no longer need to falsify myself to my people!"

"*Sorry!*" Gete pulled her close, trying to restore the sense of ease between them. He could not stop forgetting this other side of her, the side that made him doubt everything Desti had told him about the gods. But it seemed that only one or the other, could exist at a time in her bony, overworked frame.

IN THE GOLDEN EGG

Leaves and branches filtered out the noise of Rimmear. Limping as fast as he could in the middle of a column of Hands, beside an Eithilindrian who grinned all the time, along a tunnel of salt trees pruned to concavity, Arity's sense of displacement was heightened. He felt as if he were back in human country, in one of the gardens on the Royallandic mainland that she had shown him, when they had *teth¨d* after—

Best not to think.

Rose Eye, *serbali* of Rimmear, lived high on this landscaped hillside above the chasm. None of the edifices up here, pastiches of Delta City's Antiprophet Square mansions for the most part, were more than a couple of hundred years old. Mazelike gardens showcased them to advantage. Each seemed cocooned from the next, propounding an illusion of rambling parklands on what was actually a steep mountainside. Here, deep in Rose Eye's quiet garden, Arity was acutely aware of the multitudes of shades that made Rimmear's atmosphere so stifling. Their whispers crept down his back like fingers.

Rimmear, like most Heavens, traced its roots back to the dawn of *auchresh* civilization, to the time before Heavens were called Heavens. Delta City was nowhere near as old. When Arity and Pati returned to Rimmear after their flying visit to Delta City, the weight of the city's history had dropped on him like a stone. He had actually cried out, and Pati had put his arms around him.

Best not to think!

Rimmear's legendarians asserted that the city had taken root on the banks of the river of the chasm. It had been a tiny, prehistoric Heaven of houses built to look like the spiky *treikos* formations that prevailed in the bottomlands. Most of those ancient dwellings were now taverns, walled in by gimcrack salt-wood buildings. Arity remembered getting drunk in one of

them, staggering away, puking as he ran, from a would-be *ghauthiji* who
had got him trapped between two of the spikes sticking out around the
back door. The ancient *auchresh* had armored their homes not just for
camouflage, but to protect them from attacks by the predators who had
regularly, so the legends said, besieged Heaven. Back then, they had been
an active menace to Rimmear, as well as the source of its children. Not
chained pets whose lust voyeurs used to arouse their sagging penises.

Down in the depths where there are no Foundlings.

The lower tiers got their children from the upper tiers. Everyone in
Rimmear cycled slowly downward. It was a law of nature. A law of status.
Of course, some *wrchrethre* souls whose status outweighed that of everyone
else in Rimmear deliberately buried themselves on the bottom tiers, to
meld themselves to the honeycomb structure of the city in a final act of self-
abnegation.

But Pati had rescued him.

This visit to Rose Eye was the last of Pati's diplomatic missions that the
Divinarch, in his unscheduled dalliance with Arity, had postponed.

The Hands tramped along between curving salt hedgerows that Rose
Eye had had imported from Recharabhy.

"Just a courtesy visit," Pati said yesterday as they lay in sunshine in the
diplomatic hotel. "Half an hour. Can't *not* visit any of the *serbalim*, they'd
put their noses in the air and then spread rumors about me. Which I do *not*
need! Most of them only have status because their *breideii* was a *serbali*:
they haven't done anything to merit it, and they do nothing with it besides
throw parties. Huneyash, Green Feather, and Dessica mainly control Rimmear. And I've failed to make any impact on *them* this time round. We
might as well go home." He had thought for a minute, playing with Arity's
hair. "Rose Eye is not completely to be disregarded, though."

Hearing a new note in his voice, Arity looked around. His heart sank.
"He's more of a blusterer than anything else, but he's highly unpredictable.
And because he has the favor of those thrice damned *er-serbalim* who were
once your and my *saduim*, ashamed though I am to remember it . . . he
has some influence. In fact, I think the *er-serbalim* may even be in Rimmear now. They don't advertise their travels much anymore. But then
again, I had that from Blushing Cat, and she is notorious for spreading
gossip."

Above the trees a perfect golden egg rose, standing on end, glittering in
the night. It was Rose Eye's mansion. The hedges gave way to a steep
slope, scattered with trees, and out of these a high fence of laced-together
salt beeches rose around the egg, enclosing an inner lawn. Under an arch

that passed for a gateway in the fence, Foundlings stood sentinel in a yellow glare of torchlight.

The Eithilindrian Hand beside Arity, a lanky green spider of a fellow (they had been paired off by skin tone), gaped unselfconsciously at the mansion beyond. He dug Arity in the ribs. "Eh. See those shines? Them're *windows!*"

Arity's eyes widened. The edifice was monstrous, and farther off than he had thought.

The Hands started to move again. Arity saw that they were leaving half the column behind. The banner bearers and "Way!" criers sprawled under the trees, already engaged in their off-hours pastimes of teasing the Foundlings and digging their toes into the grass.

Everything about serving the Divinarch seemed to be tedious, dangerous, pointless, or some combination of the three. Arity's post since they had returned from Delta City had been at the inmost door of Pati's lodgings. He was, as he had requested, in the regular rotation.

The mansion was a vast chunk of rock salt hauled somehow from the tumbled crest of the mountain, shoddily carved. Up close, the egg shape was vastly imperfect. Arity reached out to touch the salt as they filed into a dark opening at the bottom. The rock was splintery.

The passage led into a hacked-out vault filled with the lazy rumble of *auchresh* voices. A huge bonfire shone at either end. The hands broke formation and milled around, greeting Rose Eye's servants, swaggering, patently aware of their superiority to these *salthirre* folk. Blue Kestrel, the only real friend Arity had managed to make among the Hands, told him that Pati taught the Hands that status was a bad guide to value. Pati did not allow them to turn up their noses at mixing with lower-status *auchresh*. But most, particularly the *ex-mainrauim* and *ex-serbalim*, could not be broken of lifelong habits.

A knot of Hands bore down on Arity like a heavy beast charging its prey. Before he could move, he was absorbed. "Couldn't face this without *you*," Pati said, grinning, wrapping pale fingers around his arm. "Cheer up! Why so gloomy? Not enough intellectual stimulation among the rank and file? That's what *I'm* good for—"

Shoddily decorated staircases and halls and corridors passed around them like illusions.

They must have ascended very high in the egg by the time they finally stopped. The Hands ushered Arity and Pati toward a lacquered door. Pati had Arity's wrist securely in his grip. A servant in a ribboned bonnet snapped to attention. "The Divinarch!" he trumpeted.

"Shut up, Boli!" someone bellowed from within. "He's not coming until dawn! Tell whoever it is to go away! I'm busy!"

Pati shoved the *kere* aside. "This could be interesting." He thrust the door open. The room was an antechamber with one wall completely made of windows and the others draped with tapestries. Rose Eye sat blobbily on a pile of cushions, mouth open in shock. Broken Bird and Bronze Water— they *were* here?—sat on an overstuffed loveseat. A small, miserable-looking *auchresh* in Uarechi clothing stood in the middle of the room, wringing his hands.

The door slammed. Broken Bird and Bronze Water stared at Pati, not bothering to hide their astonishment, as he lowered himself deliberately into a high-backed chair. Arity took up his stance behind it.

"Oh, Heir," Bronze Water said. His face went slowly soft with pain. Arity had been wrong: the *er-serbalim* were not astonished to see Pati, but *him*. "Has he caught you, too?"

Broken Bird elbowed him. "In the Power's *name!* We are conducting business! Please go outside and wait, both of you. Pati, it was too bad of you to bring him here," she added in a lower voice. She turned her head away. A sea of wrinkles lapped around her neck. Arity's heart twisted. He looked away from her, at the spectacular view of the chasm which filled the wall like a mural. Lights winked all the way down the west side of the ravine, giving the impression of a waterfall sliding downward more slowly than any water could. Above the ridge, the sky was the charcoal gray of waves on a cloudy day.

Pati stirred, and Arity knew he was itching to remind Broken Bird that he was not to be ordered around like some Foundling. He said smoothly, "My dear Rose Eye, I believe there has been a misunderstanding. I do apologize. This is the hour we agreed on. But finish your business; I shall not disturb you."

As if suddenly unfrozen, the little *kere* in country clothes whirled around, dropped at Pati's feet, and said in a rush, "Please, Divinarch, grant me lenience! The *serbali* Rose Eye, grace guard his step, won't. Please. I've *teth*"d all the way from the eastern saltside in skips and hops. I know my *serbalim* back in Heaven will pardon me if *you* tell them—"

"What is this?" Pati said, at the same time as Rose Eye said, "Shush, *khrithi!*"

Pati pressed on, "Why do you need my lenience? Have you killed someone? I do not pardon wanton violence—"

The little man laughed bitterly. "No, most respected Divinarch, I haven't killed a *kere* in my life, for all I was *mainraui* when I was younger! All I did was pay a few visits to a human Heaven." He said the word in mortal, sending a thrill through Arity. "A *village*. In the Uarechi saltside—Ruhaab is its name—"

"The scum is lying," Bronze Water broke in. "He has moved out of his Heaven. He *lives* in this human village. We have it on authority from his *serbalu*."

"Faint Starbreath has recently become enamored of the honored *er-serbalim* Bronze Water and Broken Bird's thinking," the *auchresh* said. "She declared in front of all of us that it was no longer permissible to leave the salt. Then she expelled me from Heaven. My question is, must I suffer for something she has decided? Divinarch, I beg you—"

Broken Bird laughed derisively. "Hear him lie outright now, Pati! The truth is that he first visited this human hole, this Ruhaab, *after* the *serbalu* made her decision. We have this on authority from his accomplices in crime. Several of them, after they heard our teachings from the *serbalu*, became curious about the human lands. They walked to the edge of the salt, and there encountered their first humans. Bronze and I take full responsibility for this." Her voice hardened. "But it is upon this *kere's* own head that he flaunted his misdeeds until his *serbalu* had no choice but to banish him from Heaven. He is trying to have the best of both worlds."

The little *auchresh's* gaze flickered from one of them to the other. Arity saw that he was not stupid, but that he was at his wits' end. He had cast his stone, made his appeal to Pati, and been caught out in his lie. Now he could only await his fate.

But Pati's eyes gleamed maliciously, and Arity knew what he was going to say before he said it. "I believe him. The *serbalu* must have lied to bolster her reputation." He turned to the *kere*. "I grant you lenience."

Rose Eye hissed.

"Pati," Bronze Water said in mortal, "beware! Your relationships in Uarech have never been better than shaky. You cannot afford to have it noised about that you slandered a *serbalu*, even one as obscure as this fat fool."

"But Divinarch, it's plain that the fellow is lying!" Rose Eye exploded. Arity saw that he was too dense to understand that Bronze Water had been speaking another language, or that he himself was dancing to Pati's tune. He positively bubbled with vitriol. "Not only has he lied to your face, but he has cast dust on the teachings of the *er-serbalim* themselves!" He made a devoted obeisance to Broken Bird and Bronze Water's couch. "What other evidence do you need? You must deny him lenience!"

Pati smiled imperturbably down at the little *kere*. "Go out and tell my Hands that I have revoked your punishment. They will issue you a Divine Seal, which you can take home to your *serbalu*."

"This is *my* affair!" Rose Eye frothed. "This is my *khrithi*. Divinarch, I am sorry to inform you that in the salt, and particularly in Uarech, your Divine Seals are worth no more than the stone they are made of!"

Pati leaned back in his chair and steepled his fingers. Arity saw that lethal glitter in his eyes which appeared when he was at his most dangerous and his most vulnerable. But people were always too busy being afraid of him to take advantage of his weakness. Arity himself was no exception. Pati said in a calm tone calculated to provoke, "But I am Divinarch all over the world, my dear *tith˝ahi*. I may do what I like." Broken Bird and Bronze Water expostulated in horror. Rose Eye let loose a landslide of objections. Pati ignored them. He leaned forward and said to the little *kere*, "Go home, my friend. Just *teth˝*. I'll send one of my Hands after you. Oh, and don't forget to tell the Ruhaab humans that it is by the grace of the Divinarch you are still free to visit them."

The *kere* scrambled to his feet, face shining. Arity felt sick. To him, each outburst seemed like a badly penned step in a rather plodding stage play. Pati was the playwright, a ruthless manipulator who did not care if his situations were predictable, or ugly, as long as the actors went through the motions.

"Don't get carried away, Rose Eye," Broken Bird wailed. "He's using you to wipe his feet."

Pati sat up and bared his teeth.

But Rose Eye shouted at the little *kere*, "You will not leave this room without my permission!" When the other tried it anyway, Rose Eye plunged on him, preventing him from vanishing, and bore him to the floor. Fangs flashed. The door burst open: the Hands poured in like a pack of silken-coated hounds. The trumpeter added his voice to the confusion.

Arity stepped farther back. Pati pulled his feet up out of the way and sat cross-legged, watching avidly.

Arity turned to stare out of the window. The chalky dawn sat heavily on the glimmering city. All of the lights were still slipping downward, or so it appeared to Arity's eyes, one by one by one.

The furor quieted. As it became manageable to the senses, it twanged back into his consciousness. The smell of fresh blood stung his nostrils. A pair of Fists bundled the nameless *kere* efficiently into a salt-fiber sack. Of course the one who did not count had died. His death meant nothing in the grand circles where Pati, Broken Bird, and Bronze Water trod. Just another light winking out.

And he had been a liar and an opportunist, anyway.

All the extra people who had rushed in stood about awkwardly while Rose Eye cleaned his hands in a basin someone held. Pati folded his mouth into a severe line. Broken Bird threw him a furious glance, then shook her skirts out over the white splotch on the carpet. "Are you, perhaps, going to offer us *morothe*, Rose Eye dear?" she asked sweetly. But her eyes flicked to Arity. "I *am* fond of a small sip of something when the night wears on and on like this."

Arity had no chance to flee to the servants' cavern. He found himself lining up with the other Hands along one wall of the *morothe* cavern. The interminable conventions of the courtesy call set in, like winter. Even such a one as Pati, who had fastened an empire together with blood, was neutralized by etiquette. In accordance with the Uarechi *morothe* tradition, the big, high-windowed cavern was empty but for a stone table and chairs. Pati sat across from Rose Eye, feet up, gulping his fifth glass of cool green liquid, discussing local politics. They did not touch on anything dangerous. All hatred must be veiled, all social gaffes smoothed over. The outbreak of animosity that had caused the death of the little *kere* had to be forgotten for the sake of peace in the salt.

But Arity guessed he would hear more of the incident from Pati. The incident was an outrageous crystallization of a rumor that had recently filtered down to the bottom tiers: the fertilization of mortal properties with *auchresh* ingenuity. When he first heard the rumors, he had thought them too outrageous to be true. *Auchresh* living in saltside villages in Calvary, Pirady, Veretry, Domesdys, Iceland? On human-inhabited islands of the Archipelago? In Royalland? *Auchresh* finding *acceptance* among humans? That was impossible!

And yet tonight he had seen it confirmed or at least asserted.

Broken Bird and Bronze Water got up from the table. They stood by the arched windows that looked out over the torch-lit lawn. At last they put down their glasses and drifted behind the line of Hands. Arity steeled himself. Right on cue, he felt a touch on his shoulder. He spun around, facing the two *er-serbalim*. Hopefully, Rose Eye and Pati were too busy smiling and despising each other to notice. "Come away!" Broken Bird moderated her voice to a whisper. Her little blue face puckered. "Please don't let yourself get caught up in this! Just come with us, Arity—we'll take you somewhere safe! We have friends in every continent—"

Sooner or later, the Hands would have to know who he had been. He spoke in clear, articulate mortal without worrying what they would think. He could shrug off the structures of *auchraug* as easily as he had shrugged off the false slum accent that he had affected in the lower tiers. "Bird, I have no wish to become involved in your cause instead of Pati's."

"We have no cause," Bronze Water said in *auchraug*. "Causes are un-*auchresh*. We only preach sanity."

They believed that, he thought. "I need no one's help. Leave me alone."

"Where did he find you?" Bronze Water said. "Have you been in Rimmear all this time? Hope would not tell us."

Broken Bird raised herself on tiptoe, peering into Arity's face. She was so close that he could feel her body heat and smell the dry, salty scent of age. "What did he *do*? How did he catch you like this?"

"I chose to come here. I was sick of spending my nights drunk and my days dreaming."

"You chose . . . this?" Bird waved her hand at the line of Hands: exotic mutates polished and uniformed like shiny toys.

"Bird, you don't know anything about making choices. And that is because you don't know what free will is. You have always worked as the agent of past traditions; you know no other way to operate. The only difference is that now, the traditions are twisted to your purposes, instead of the other way round."

Her face screwed up like a rag. "That is what you would say," she hissed. "*Hymanni* lover."

Don't—no—don't remember—

"Pati is bound by tradition too, Arity," Bronze Water said. "Do you think you are the banner-bearer of some new, free-thinking breed of *auchresh*? We are *all* the tools of tradition."

"Pati only propounds certain of our traditions because he *believes* in them," Arity said. "That is the mystery of Pati: how devoutly, under all the flair and egotism, he believes. I don't know exactly. I don't think anyone knows. But I'm not talking about Pati. I'm talking about me. I think I am the only person in this room who knows what free will really is."

Broken Bird's nose wrinkled cynically.

Arity's heart beat fast. He hissed in a low voice, "Free will is not pretentious cause flaunting. It is being one of the masses. Being absorbed. Being willing to do whatever you are told, and *liking* it that way. *Not caring. That* is free will."

Broken Bird looked frightened. "Being a slave?"

"If you will!"

Bronze Water, staring at Arity, pulled her away. She held onto his arms, her claws sewing his sleeves. Arity felt like shouting. He had won. He was free now to do exactly what he wanted. "Come away," Bronze Water muttered. "There's nothing we can do for him. Maybe after the glamour has worn off—"

"But he's in love with him," Broken Bird said, picking holes in Bronze

Water's sleeve. "He always has been. *That's* why he sees this as—as a *noble surrender*. What a monster, what a *haugthirre,* what a throwback—" Methodically, she continued stringing insults together, switching to mortal when she ran out of *auchraug* epithets for Pati.

Arity spun on one heel talon and faced front again. His neighbors poked him in the ribs. One of them unbent so far as to hiss, "What was *that* about? Didn't know you'd learned mortal already!"

"Tell you later," he murmured.

Better if he told them himself. Several of the Hands back in Delta City had been *lesh kervayim,* and he could not avoid them forever. Quite apart from them, there must be others left in the city who would recognize him. He would just have to trust his new peers not to revile him.

At the table, Pati and Rose Eye roared with false jocosity over some anecdote Pati had related. In the shadows, Broken Bird continued her whispered defamation of Pati's sexuality, private habits, and ancestry. Arity had not known there were so many foul words in the two tongues. The sun was about to rise from behind the ridge, striking through the salt trees, turning trunks and leaves transparent. Already the gardens were bleaching to the gray that preceded clarity.

THE DEATH OF COMELINESS

Sol Southwind leaned out the window of his lodgings, thinking about his twin sister. Beneath, a brace of porkers snuffled about on the tunnel roof of Dock Street. Someone had thrown them a bucket of waste. Amazing how although there were no guardrails, the pigs slithered about the roofs on their trotters, snorting up the slops, and managed not to fall off. It was the middle of the day. A hazy chill day. Westpoint was no less damp than Marshtown in autumn, even though it was higher above the marshes.

All the way across the city, he could feel her.

He closed his eyes. What would she be doing at this time of day? Gliding to and fro in the stone kitchen of the Chalice, tying an apron over the outmoded gown that was the only outward sign of her nostalgia for the old days, helping Algia and Eterneli wash up after lunch? No, that didn't quite work. Was she in Melthirr House, with her family? Emni, Zin, and their baby were the core of the decimated *imrchim*. It had been a dark day for the ghostiers when they were reduced to a family! Or perhaps Emni was in the workshop they had made out of Erene and Humi's old apartment, instructing one of her new apprentices. *But what will they do with their craft, Em?* Sol thought with a flash of anger. Why are you bothering? The image dissolved as frustration overtook him. Why were she and Ziniquel troubling themselves to train a new generation of ghostiers? He wondered for the thousandth time. The apprentices would never have a venue for their art, unless they allied themselves with the Marshtown devotees—and all of *those*, just because of where they lived, had apostatic leanings. An alliance with Marshtown might well be the thing that would resolve the Divinarch to bring his thumb down on Tellury Crescent.

Emni and Zin insisted their imperative was to keep the *imrchim* together. They said they wanted to preserve the traditions. Chalice, Eftpool, excursions every Dividay to hear sermons, and so forth and so on. Sol could have—and on the day he moved out of Tellury Crescent, *had*—told them they had already failed. Who was left? Mory and Tris were gone. Algia remained. Eterneli. Zin. Emni. The baby, Lighte. The apprentices Emni and Zin had recruited—Tan, Suret, and Yste. Tan was a flamboyant youth from Christon with a tendency toward old-fashioned atheism, who relied on ghostier immunity to keep him safe from the Hands. Zin had found Suret on a visit to Riestasis in Veretry. She was dark and compact, with smoldering eyes that belied her gentle nature. Yste was a Calvarese-Deltan boy, about twelve years old, the most talented of the three, but odious.

And *Sol* was the only one the Divinarch patronized. That left the others stranded. Had they realized before, how heavily they had come to depend on the noble court? Humi and Erene had systematically cut the *imrchim's* ties to the Divinarchy. Now they were foundering.

Emni and Ziniquel had two options. Apostasy, or the Divinarch-worship Sol had chosen, which he would be the first to admit was superficial nonsense. The Divinarch's pet flamens called Pati the Only God, Practitioner of Divine Power. The Hands were his Inviolate Servants. No one with a mind of his own could believe such stuff. Sol could not explain how the flamens did. But had anyone ever understood the flamens? They sang Pati's praises, and he starved the city by arresting its nobles, merchants, craftsmen, and shipwrights on charges of atheism. Then there were the murders. Whenever Sol left his lodgings, he came across bodies lying ostracized in the streets, or bundled into corners, splotched with their own black blood, daymoths buzzing around their orifices. People attended sermons these days because they knew that the murder victims had mostly shown symptoms of atheism. And Deltans, wisely, valued survival over integrity.

At the beginning of the tyranny, the imrchim Mory and Tris had rushed off into Marshtown to follow the apostates—those few flamens who had refused to swear allegiance to a cruel, unjust, and possibly mad god. The last Sol had heard, there were prices on their heads. Emni and Zin were too cowardly to follow them—though they reviled Sol to his face for truckling to Pati.

Sol had his own reasons for staying in the Divinarch's good books. Emni would thank him in the end.

And anyhow, he entertained real doubts about the apostates. From time to time, Mory and Tris's ghosts surfaced in the Westpoint markets. Powerful pieces painted in dark colors, they were contorted with the cruelty inherent in Mory's work, which she had passed on to Tris. Sol had bought a few because of their curiosity value, but had had to put them away in closets. Even he, who was not deluded as to the value of ruthlessness, was sickened by them.

Ruthlessness had its uses. It had helped him kill Beisa. And it would have helped him kill Emni, too, if his resolve had not been weakened by that streak of softheartedness he despised in both her and himself, which caused him to level off the spoonful of green amaranth. He had left the thing to chance rather than making it certain. And that had ruined his chances at the post of senior ghostier.

When he held the tenth seat on the Ellipse, he'd been a better ghostier than any of the others would admit. And his ruthlessness was also the reason Pati patronized him. None of the others would do the work he did. It was necessary for him to keep cruelty to the fore. The boys and girls he ghosted on his own initiative, now that he had all day and all night to work, were dreadfully beautiful—but the subjects the Divinarch commissioned were transcendent. He dreaded making them. After he finished each one, he sent it to the Palace as quickly as possible.

Over *those* emotions (wild dogs straining at their chains, tussling whirl-winds) he needed only to paint a gloss of his own interpretation. Over those flamboyant colors, which lingered even after being turned into diamondine, he needed only to paint a gloss of pigment.

He shook himself in the cold air. Something ran over his feet. He started back with an oath. Would those damn rats never leave him alone! It leaped on his bed and clashed its teeth at him. His hand closed on a silver mirror that hung by the window, and he hurled it, smashing the rat against the wall. It kicked feebly on the counterpane.

He would throw it to the pigs. They were used to such largesse. He plucked at his shirt, trying to circulate air into his fur. His lodgings still had an atmosphere of having been closed up for decades. He had shifted all the furniture into this room in order to empty out the workshop, so it was crammed to the ceiling with modish, shoddy statuary and ornaments that Sol's landlord had appropriated when some minor atheist was arrested, but which he had never found a buyer for. Ingrained dirt colored the walls a medium shade of sewage. Sol sometimes wondered how he had borne this place for two and a half years. The view was the only part he liked. Since this was one of the tallest buildings on the "stern" of the island—and the waist of the city dipped lower before the ground started to rise again at the end of the wharves—on a clear day, one could see straight over the slums of Westpoint and Temeriton, over the ridged acres of roofs that were Doxton, over the domes and peaks of Christon, to the edge of Marshtown, which sprawled toward him down the slope of the island. At this distance, the roofs blurred into a slate-colored haze.

Today, the cold sepia haze obscured everything beyond the first few streets.

Yet he could feel her.

Emni.

I know where you are.

But he could not find her. He had tried the Chalice and Albien House; he tried again. She was not there.

A sharp, rotten stench of sulfur hit his nose. He wheeled. A Hand stood at the door, his delicate yellow nostrils flared.

"Greetings, Godsman Southwind, master ghostier," he said in a dull voice. "I bring a message from the Divinarch. Are you occupied?"

Another one.

Gods. I had thought there wouldn't be another. It's been so long since the last. Six months?

Remembering himself, he bowed. "I am the Divinarch's servant, revered one. I am never occupied when he needs me."

No wings sprouted from the Hand's shoulders. He was almost human-looking—like most of the messengers the Divinarch sent Sol—but plain to the point of ugliness, with that snub nose and sunflower-yellow skin. He had been crying, and made no effort to hide it. Sol tried not to look at the puffy eyelids as he waited to hear the familiar message.

But standing at the door, twisting his head like a bird looking around a new cage, the Hand said, "I see no ghosts. Do you really live here, Godsman?"

Sol concealed his surprise. All the others had come out and told him why they were here, and then had spoken no more. The first time, Sol had been nervous to the point of embarrassing both himself and the Hand. Gods never reached that point where they were beyond embarrassment. But by now, he had enough confidence to bend and twist their limbs as if they were mannequins with rotating joints. They were astonishingly obedient. Or maybe they didn't feel pain the same way mortals did. There was no way to know.

"Would the Inviolate One like to see my workshop?"

The Hand pulled a face, then nodded. He followed Sol between the bureaus, and harpsichord stools, and reclining chairs, and empty picture frames, and ghost pedestals, to the kitchen door. "Are these things your . . . props?" he asked, eyeing a giant set of needlepoint fire tongs.

Sol laughed. He kicked a pile of gold-leaf hatboxes. "Gods, no! I've been trying to make the landlord take the whole lot away for two years. I think pretty soon, I'll just chuck it all out of the window."

The Hand was not paying any attention. On his face was a curious, sour look as though he were trying to absorb himself in Sol's speech—trying so hard that he was absorbed in the trying.

Sol led the Hand down the tiny, gallery-like kitchen and into the workshop. It was blessedly bare. Had he not been afraid of spoiling the atmosphere, he would have spent all day here. Chisels and paintbrushes stood beside the sink at the far end of the room. The partly finished ghost of a five-year-old Deltan girl stood under the window.

The Hand looked up, down, and around, pale eyelashes beating. "Is everything you need to make a ghost in here?"

Sol's head came up proudly. "I could make a ghost with my bare hands."

"But of course." The Hand essayed a smile. Then it twisted into something else. "Like Pati, you need no tool but yourself. I did not realize."

"Our faith is our tool, Inviolate One."

The Hand shook his head in annoyance. "What is your name, ghostier? I mean, what do your friends call you?"

The empty floor lay between them. The Hand shone like a piece cut out from an Archipelagan summer. Bright, breezy days in the South Reach . . . out in the boat with Dadda . . . thousands upon thousands of silver wrigglers in the net. Honeyfish. He and Emni had both grown strong on that sweet, floury flesh.

"I have no friends, revered one. But when I did have one—she called me Sol."

The Hand nodded sharply. More and more, despite his pug face, he reminded Sol of a bird. "And my name is Melin. That was not always my name, though. I started my civilized life as Flying Warbler, in a small Heaven in Carelastre named Rainbow Gorge. When the Divinarch started to take an interest in me, he renamed me for what he perceived as my primary virtue."

"Comeliness."

"How did you know?"

"It's a common name, Inviolate One."

"Yes . . . I suppose so. But as common as that . . ." The Hand rubbed the bridge of his nose. "I thought I was more than a *ghauthiji* to him. I knew there were *ghauthijim* before me; I knew there would be *ghauthijim* after me. But I didn't think he would bring a new boy to our suite so soon! Power grant that the new one sees his true nature faster than I did!" He smiled lopsidedly. "I'm a wastrel by nature, Sol. A stupid wastrel. That's why I left Rainbow Gorge. I was no good to anyone, not being strong enough for a *mainraui*, nor talented at any craft, nor especially interested in stories—except when they had humans in them. So I left. My *breideim* wept that they would never see me again. How was I to know they would be right? Must one always listen to warnings? And if one does—what then of life?"

Sol had already heard more than he wanted. He sensed that whether he responded or not, Melin was going to go on. "Sometimes I wish someone had warned *me.*"

The Hand laughed. He rolled up a sleeve. "This is what I got for not listening." It was a half-healed burn, deep and meandering. "And this." He shook hair back from his neck, revealing deeply bruised tooth marks. Sol flashed back to his worst days with Emni. "But the worst marks are *here.*" Melin tapped his temple. "I did the arm myself, when I could get away, and I smuggled in a friend to do the neck. There's worse under my breeches."

Sol would have to do it quickly now. Before he lost his nerve. He looked past the Hand, at the wall cupboard that held the syringes and poisons. "Your ghost will be different from the others," he said. "I shan't be able to help putting this into my interpretation." *It will be like a threat*—"Pati will know what you've said to me."

"Good! Let him know! Let him worry that the whole city is whispering about his private life!"

"I shan't tell anyone." Sol rubbed his eyes. "How do you think I've survived this long? By spreading rumors? But what if he decides I am a danger to him? I think I shall have to make you so beautiful"—*exaggerate* the threatening aspect, burlesque it to make it harmless, but dignify it with a touch of the tragic—"that I become indispensable to him. I can do that—"

The Hand's face went suddenly kind. "Don't worry. There are thousands of rumors. They don't hurt him. He's vulnerable, but not where you'd think."

And there was that touch of the tragic in the living flesh. Sol would hardly have to work at all.

"And *you're* not in any danger until you find out where that vulnerability is. As I did. Don't ever flatter yourself that you're indispensable! He won *my* allegiance from a thousand miles off without knowing I was alive. He can do the same with anyone he chooses. He doesn't need you."

Sol inhaled sharply. Now it was undeniable. He had always known, in the back of his mind, why all the subjects the Divinarch commissioned looked alike. The apostates said one thing of him; the flamens whose services Sol attended said another. Now he *knew.* There could be no more doubts about the nature of the thing he served.

Yet he could not stop serving. And *that* was the bond that let him and this Hand understand each other, which would allow him to paint his ghost with stunning verisimilitude, although their lives had touched only as two precipices crunch together over a chasm.

From beneath the window of the workshop, far down in the side alley, came the regular hiss of air. It was the bellows of the Hasper brothers' forge, which they only operated at night in the summer and autumn months. Muted hammers beat a tattoo on stone. The smell of burning metal curled up.

Sol was used to both the noise and the smell. It took the scream of a predator, swooping in over Westpoint, to wake him. By the time he swam up into a swooning, drifting consciousness, he had forgotten what startled him out of sleep.

Humid air filled his lungs like wool. In the starlight, he could see the ghost of Melin standing, faintly luminescent, in the middle of the floor. Drowsy pride suffused him. *Isn't it a miracle,* he thought, *how death can redeem not just the ugly—for ugliness is nothing but a matter of viewpoint, after all—but the indifferent?* This god was indifferent, if anyone ever was.

He had stuffed the indifferent out the window to the pigs. Most of it should be gone by now.

Abruptly he was wide awake. The thought of Melin scattered half eaten over the roofs turned his stomach. The hunger pangs waking in his belly seemed a cruel grace note to his nausea.

A *toothy* noise came from the direction of the front room. Chewing? Of course not. His imagination had been working overtime, and now it was creating something from nothing—child's play, after creating something from a material as hard to grasp as death.

He sat up.

There was the hunger of the body, and then there was the hunger of the soul.

It seemed that Dividay mornings had always been sunny and breezy. Pockets of cloud clung in the hollows of the land as all the inhabitants of Gelska climbed to the flat, open summit of the island and knelt in a circle. Even the toddlers knew not to speak. The horizon of the sea was at once a perfect circle and a straight line, encompassing the world. The solid blue block of the sky, pricked by the peaks of distant islands, held down the sea.

Gelska's own flamen, Godsister Honesty, stood tall in the center of the circle. Beside Sol, Emni fidgeted, skinny as a foam sprite, moving her mouth silently while the rest of the islanders lifted their voices in harmonized devotions. For once in his childish life, Sol was not aware of her. He thrust his small, earnest voice up, thanking the gods for blueness, and summer, and honeyfish for breakfast, and the knowledge that everything would stay the same forever.

Fuzzy memories were the storms in the Eftpool, and the steam-bath warmth on a winter's afternoon, and on a summer's day, his breath frosting under the dome. Silver ripples on the circle of black water. The swimmy kaleidoscope of colors in which a hundred generations of ghostiers had read something—or nothing.

He had not visited the Eftpool since he made his first ghost of a god. He was terrified of what he might find. Nothing—or *something?* Each ghostier's efts came only to that ghostier's call. So his secret was safe, as long as he stayed away.

The end justifies the means. The end justifies the means. *The end*—

Someday he would have Tellury Crescent for his own. Only Emni stood in his way—and Zin, to a lesser extent, because Sol had no scruples about offing *him* if it became politic to do so. When Pati finally decided to bring them down, Sol would be there. He would be their chosen successor. He *knew* it. He would bring in new apprentices, revitalize the whole organization, reshaping it for this age in which Emni and Zin's traditions simply were not viable. He would ask for pardons for Mory and Tris, and in gratitude they would come back and help him. Their temperaments would not prevent them from allying themselves with a traitor. And Pati would be so impressed that he'd return all of their Ellipse seats, and then—and *then*—Sol would be well on his way to making the ghostiers a power such as they had been for thirteen centuries.

Such as they would be again.

The end justifies—

"Gods," he said aloud.

He got to his feet. His muscles were as stiff as knots in wood.

That was *definitely* the noise of champing coming from the other room.

He slipped silently through the kitchen. Detecting no movement in the maze of furniture, he skirted the room and approached the window from one side.

There it was, perched on the roof of the street tunnel below. Folded wings shielded its back. It had a child's body, toes gripping the ridgepole, knees up on either side of its ears. Its face was small, human, heart-shaped. It stuffed pieces of Melin's carcass into its mouth with dreadful speed. Its fangs glittered in the starlight.

Sol choked off a noise of disgust.

Fair curls flopped in the starlight as the predator scooped another fistful of meat out of the corpse's face.

Gods, Em. I need you! Need you . . . ! Remember how we used to come together after one of us made a ghost? I know I sometimes pushed you away—just to prove that you would come back—but all the time, I loved you for caring—

And intuition leaped, death-defying, earth-repudiating, across the city, and found her. She had been in Thaumagery House all along. Now her lover and baby lay with her, sleeping in the great, sunken bed. *Why did she go to Thaumagery? To be alone. Why must they come and plague her?*

Sol had hated living alone in that dusty bat cave after Owen died. Emni went there now mostly, he thought, to make him feel guilty. On one of his visits to the Crescent, she had told him it brought back memories of Beisa.

I do not need to be reminded of *you*, she said, which keeps me from making proper use of the place. You come here far too often. What do you want of me? Do you expect me to tell you where Humi lives?

Gods' blood. She covered her mouth.

"Oh, sweetheart," Ziniquel said, shaking his head, "that's torn it."

Now in Thaumagery House, Zin snored faintly, one arm thrown over her stomach. The sheet lapped like white water to the edges of the bed. Emni stared up into the darkness, playing with her long black braid.

I haven't been well Sol felt her think. *But I can't afford to be unwell. The* imrchim *need me. Zin says I got up too soon after having Lighte. Or could it be Sol doing it to me poisoning me again?* Hatred flared briefly, like an ember bursting into flame. *I would suspect him if he were on the other side of the world not just in Westpoint. But I'll kill him first I'll kill him before he takes me away from them.*

Sol wrenched away. Breaking his hands off the windowsill, he crouched down low, shuddering.

IMPATIENCE

"Can you not quiet her?" Aneisneida did not want to think about how nervous she felt. It was absurd! She was only going to see the Divinarch. Her father would have been ashamed of her.

But he had always been ashamed of her anyhow.

She frowned at the scared young nurse who was jogging Fiamorina up and down. The smell of wet commoners thickened the air. Apart from Fiamorina's crying, the hall was silent. Aneisneida had been the only supplicant with the temerity to bring a fractious toddler to an audience with the Divinarch. But she had not planned to queue behind hundreds of nobodies! She had assumed that she would receive special treatment, as she had every previous time Pati summoned her to his presence.

Instead she found herself turned away from the great oaken doors, back to the end of the line. At Pati's pleasure, she supposed. To keep her on her toes. Anger bubbled. She would dress him down properly for that! She would . . . she would . . .

If only she dared!

This time she would speak to him the way her father would have, whether Pati was sitting on the Throne or a wooden bench: not as a god, but as an equal.

"Do you think I employ you to hold her while she cries?" she snapped at the nurse. "I employ you to make her fit to be my daughter—or at least look like it in public. People are *watching.*"

"She's hungry, milady," the nurse said. "Shhhh, love. Where is Milord, Lady Nearecloud?"

"I believe he went to find refreshments." *A mug of ale,* Aneisneida thought with rising frustration, *at some unspeakable Marshtown tavern, where he will be as happy as a cockle in the mud, swapping smut with the regulars.*

She glanced ahead. "We're almost there."

Only five or so drab petitioners waited ahead of them. Two Hands stood tall at the great doors, smooth-skinned and impassive. Twisty horns grew from the temples of one; crimson wings jutted behind the shoulders of the other. In the old days they would have been called Divine Guards. Pati's main change when he took over had been to instruct the Hands not to expel troublemakers, but just to knife them.

This new practice made for distinctly quieter queues.

With a throb of longing that was almost pain, Aneisneida remembered the old days. As a child she had occasionally glimpsed the petitioners as her father hustled her to the Throne Room to take up some issue with the Divinarch which he had not resolved to his satisfaction in Ellipse. Once— *once*—they had had to wait outside. Aneisneida had been about ten. A little girl accompanying her parents—mossy-furred commoners, all three of them—had stared at her. Aneisneida stared right back. Something was strange: *she* had fixed her gaze on the other's snubby face, but the girl kept looking a little lower, no matter how Aneisneida wriggled out from under her gaze. At last the girl put out her hand and fingered the embroidery on Aneisneida's bodice.

Aneisneida squealed and scrambled around Belstem. From behind the safety of her father's bulk, she hissed vituperatively at the other girl.

For all she knew, that girl could be standing behind her now, fallen on hard times, silently criticizing Aneisneida's ability to keep her child quiet. Aneisneida wanted to sink into the floor.

"Can you not—" she started to say to the nurse.

But at that moment a rank hessian smell blew into her face, and a gaggle of Deltans pushed around her as they emerged from the Throne Room. Without noticing, she had reached the head of the line. The Hands nodded, simultaneously—*they must practice that*, she thought—and desperately, *Where is Soderingal?*

Gathering up nurse and child, she swept in.

Now she faces her lord, small and daunted as a pale-furred mouse, fascinated.

Where are you, Soderingal?

The chandeliers in the Throne Room are not lit, probably to conserve tallow. Her lord has forced economies on the people and the Palace alike which are oddly conceived, to say the least. Aneisneida's father would have laughed in the face of anyone who suggested that perhaps it was not necessary to keep all the rooms in the Summer mansion lit, all night. Aneisneida's father believed in the good life. She no longer dares to live anything approxi-

mating the good life. Aneisneida's father did not believe in the gods. He would have sneezed, sans handkerchief, at anyone who suggested he bow down to one of them. Aneisneida does not dare not to bow down to them.

Especially this one.

The only illumination in the room comes from him. His pale hands and pale face shine like more jewels on the Throne—that massive conglomeration of trinkets, glued together with black age. His stillness is hypnotic. Aneisneida feels her heart slowing. Even Fiamorina, at the back of the Throne Room, has stopped crying. It is as if time has ground to a halt.

"Report," he says, in his unmoderated divine voice, and the word vibrates through her bones. Her back straightens. All her limbs dangle inside the silk casings of her court dress, her fine atheistic dress, like the limbs of a marionette whose strings are wound around the puppeteer's finger. Words bubble in her throat. Everything she knows . . . even about Humi . . .

And then another voice exclaims from the Throne, "Name of the Power. That's the Summer girl! Pati, I thought—Hope told me—they were all dead!"

Pati growls with annoyance.

Aneisneida shakes her head.

"I keep this one alive," Pati says. "For my pleasure." The voice is loud as ten trumpets, but Aneisneida can bear it. It is no longer divine.

She takes a breath of relief. Father, I haven't let you down—

The doors swing open, screeching faintly. They never used to screech. Oil must be another of Pati's ludicrous economies. Soderingal comes in past the sentinels, striding easily, just drunk enough to tip his feathered hat insolently to the Divinarch. His court clothes are soaked black with rain. Aneisneida rushes to him, weak, wanting support.

But as usual, she ended up supporting him, holding him up as his initial show of confidence gave way to drunken staggering. She felt furious with him for leaving her in the lurch. But she recognized that he had saved her. She had been on the brink of blacking out. It had happened before, and it was hard to forget afterward, very hard to dismiss the whole thing as a dizzy spell, because afterward Hands would come and taunt her with things she had told Pati. Just little things. She was usually able to break the spell before she revealed anything important, by thinking hard about her father, but there was always the possibility that she would not be able to. And so she was abjectly grateful to Soder.

"How many have you had?" she whispered.

"Where's Fia?" Shaking his hair like a wet dog, he wiped the rain from his brows, and searched the Throne Room with narrowed eyes. "Eh, Anei? Where's me peridot doll baby?"

Aneisneida pointed at the nurse, who had retreated into a corner. But Soderingal did not follow her indication. His mouth had dropped open. He was staring at the throne. "Suck me," he whispered with his habitual crudeness. "If that ain't the 'Eir. *Look!*"

She looked.

And gasped.

Smaller than the other Hands in the twilight, he stood in a niche halfway around the lefthand crag of the Throne. It was unquestionably Arity. Smaller? No, just hunched. His hair was clipped close to his head. His expression was withdrawn, distant.

Feeling their stares, he seemed to wince and shrink into himself.

"Look 'ow 'e stands all lopsided," Soderingal whispered. "There's something wrong with 'im."

"I'm not surprised." Aneisneida kept her voice steady by an act of will. "Don't you remember what that leman *did* to him?"

"Wasn't there. But I 'eard. By all rights 'e ought to be dead."

"No one could have survived so much damage! But of course he lives because he is a god, and immortal." The easy answer that issued from her lips horrified her. One picked up doctrine so quickly when one was forced to socialize with the pious, for lack of anyone better.

The troulbe was that she had never quite understood that part of her father's lessons. If they were not gods, what were they?

All she knew was that she must be obedient to the letter of her own, faithless faith. "I suppose . . . I suppose they recuperate faster than we do. Or their bodies are different."

"It's a miracle," Soderingal whispered, staring.

"There are no miracles! The flamens are shams!"

Soderingal shook his head mutely. Aneisneida whirled. The Divinarch leaned forward in his seat, chin on hand, watching them confer with an amused smile in his face.

Soder sidled back from the Throne.

The dog, Aneisneida thought.

"Milord!" She dipped her head gracefully. With an effort, she put Arity to the back of her mind. She would deal with him when she had time to think. Obviously, Humi had to know he was alive. Like Pati, Humi could convince you of anything she chose—for instance, that a recoup was possible. But when you left her presence, the fire went out of your belly. For fear of having a longer-lasting conviction instilled in her, Aneisneida had avoided Temeriton for a good year. Now she would have to go back. Humi had to know about *this*.

But she should not think about Humi now. In Humi's archenemy's presence, that was somehow, obscurely, dangerous.

In the corner, Soderingal cooed to Fiamorina. Aneisneida ground her teeth and curtseyed to the Throne. "I do apologize for our rudeness!" She dimpled. "Family troubles!"

"I quite see. Is it not delightful to live in proximity to those who are dear to you?" the Divinarch said ironically.

Aneisneida tittered obligingly.

"I know I enjoy it." He smiled. His eyes flickered sideways. Then he beckoned, and Arity clambered around, stepping on the projecting bits of the Throne, and laid his head on Pati's shoulder. Pati wrapped his arm about Arity's waist and kissed the cropped brown hair, smiling over his head at Aneisneida the whole time. Aneisneida gaped. Pati let go and Arity returned to his pedestal, his fingers drifting over the places Pati had touched: a faint smile hovered on his mouth. Aneisneida felt certain they were lovers.

But why was Arity standing on the wrong side of the Throne? He was the Heir!

She let her confusion show on her face. At least a year ago, she had realized that the best way to keep the life which Pati had so inexplicably granted her (out of contempt? pity? awareness that she was powerless?) was to let everything show. Fear, eagerness to please, revulsion. In short, she acted like a monkey. She was not sure if the capacity for keeping secrets she had discovered in herself shortly afterward was a result of her deliberately exaggerated vapidity—a new layer of personality growing underneath, so to speak, as the old rose to the surface and molted—or if it had been there all along, and only now showed itself. Sometimes she thought that she had not come alive until after her father died.

Sometimes she castigated herself for entertaining such thoughts for a minute.

The Divinarch was watching her, bicolored eyes narrowed, fingers steepled. Belatedly, she realized he could see her thinking.

She turned a cartwheel and threw a few balls into the air. "I am afraid not much of note has passed since we last spoke, milord. Godsie Shafteel, the wife of Pie Shafteel, the pious governor of Christon, you know, has a gorgeous new evening dress. I know there is no longer any call for us to wear such things . . . but . . . I am thinking of having one made to a similar pattern. Would you allow me such an indulgence?"

He was smiling. "What pattern is it?"

She illustrated with her hands. "Big satiny panniers. *And* a bustle. Underneath, lace skirts, ruched up to show a colorful underskirt of some heavier fabric." The dress she wore now was of Veretrean silk, in the style that compressed one's torso to a slender stem. Aneisneida prided herself on her figure, especially after having borne a child, which was why she had worn this gown rather than any of the dozens of others she had no occasion to put on anymore. Its ruffles cascaded from a dropped yoke to the floor. It was more than three years old. The seams were starting to weaken. Aneisneida's mouth watered as she described Inali Shafteel's gown. "I believe she dreamed the design up herself. She is most awfully clever in that way."

"No doubt." The Divinarch nodded. "I give you permission to have it made."

"Thank you!" Quick, before he changed his mind, what else was there to tell? "Oh, yes, and Essne Stockold has given birth to an adorable little son—"

But he had leaned back. He was shaking his head, fingers in front of his mouth hiding a smile like a pale V in the dark. "Now, Aneisneida. You are cleverer than this. You know I don't really wish to hear about dresses. Who has turned apostate, who has died, who has fled abroad, who has gone to the mainland? You are my most reliable informant." The smile vanished. "How is the city holding?"

She drew a deep, shaky breath. Now she dared not do anything other than tell the truth. He had multitudes of other human informants whose reports he would trust over hers at the drop of a feather.

"No one has vanished in the last weeks except those you know of." That was the most delicate way of saying *those whom the Hands have abducted.* "And there are not so many of those anymore, because"—how to put it?— "there are very few atheists left in government and business. Very few. Soderingal and I are the only ones who used to move in high society." She could not help reaffirming, "And you give us permission to keep our titles, don't you, Divinarch?"

"I do, indeed."

"And as for the secular governments of the districts, they have reached a concentration of pious men and women that the city has not seen since before Antiprophet's days." She decided she ought to qualify that poetic statement. "I don't think."

The Divinarch laughed out loud. "Go on."

"The council of Temeriton, for example, used to be entirely atheistic, but now it has no members left from before. Many of the merchants who have gained seats are newly pious—but one bends where the wind is blowing. Does one not?" Quickly, she qualified that, too. "They worship your name."

He keeps me for my atheism. She must not lapse into the pious idiom. "Unlike me. But then, I am not a councillor, not anymore, milord. No disrespect, milord."

She gabbled on, playing her part. When her report was over, she retreated to Soderingal and the nurse, her mouth empty and tasteless from talking too much. What was this drag in her step? She was *limping!* Twisted, like Arity on the Throne, by her own ignoble role—

Nonsense. She dismissed those fancies.

A sudden rush of blood to her temples reminded her that she had not had anything to eat since morning. Taverns served black bread and fish. Vile stuff. But she would stomach it in the service of her *real* Divinarch. Humi. Aneisneida hated Pati with her blood and bones! And whatever Humi's shortcomings, Aneisneida felt proud to serve her. Visiting her made Aneisneida feel a little better about toadying to a god.

She straightened her back inside her corset.

And it would be delightful to have a resurrection, rather than a death, to report. Even if the resurrected party was the Heir—a god whose ambivalence had always confused Aneisneida at best, and intimidated her at worst. Humi had to know. He had been her lover. She would *have* to do something, now that Arity seemed to belong to Pati. Such an unheard-of alliance simply could not last.

"Take Fia home," Aneisneida said to the nurse. "Our sedans are waiting at the Fewpole Gate. You can find your way back there." She turned to Soder, smiling brightly. "Dearest, how near is the tavern where you got that ale?"

In the middle of a fisherman's plea for money to repair his shark-ravaged boat, Pati let loose a jaw-splitting yawn. "Audiences are over!" He stretched his arms in the air, smiling like a cat. "Clear the room, my *firim.*"

Several Hands leaped eagerly off the Throne, grabbed the old man, and marched him to the doors. When he quavered in protest, they punched him in the face. Black blood trailed across the floor. When the doors slammed behind them, Arity heard their loud, glad voices echoing down the hall: "Go home! You've missed your chance, all of you! Come back next sixday! Go home! Go home!" And several thin screams.

"Get out of here," Pati said to the Hands that were left. "Cut it."

Iole blurted, "But, *perich¨hi*—" and bit it off.

"What? Get out!" Pati half-turned to look at Arity. With a different note in his voice, he said, "Not you!"

"Very well, *perich¨hi,*" Arity said.

One by one, the Hands *teth¨d,* glancing at him. They knew he was the favored one. They did not envy him; rather, they were glad that Pati finally had someone whom he would not tire of. Arity was grateful to them for understanding that he did not want special treatment, even if he was not sure he wanted to learn the details of Pati's liaisons with Melin and other favored Hands, which they had promised to reveal to him.

He gripped a protruberance on the Throne to keep from swaying. He did not have the endurance of the others, and standing immobile all day had taken a toll on him. Perhaps if he moved, his blood would start flowing again. He jumped clumsily to the ground and began to pace. Now that the room was empty, he did not try to disguise his ugly, rolling gait; he swung his arms over his head, and blood rushed into tense muscles. Outside, night had fallen. Indoors, it had been twilight all day. The *auchresh* could see perfectly. The petitioners had been at a distinct disadvantage. Arity had seen Aneisneida Summer blink and move her hands about in front of her face long before she or her husband saw him.

Aneisneida. That was that, now, of course. Rumors would fly throughout the city. Not that it mattered: the city Arity had loved, which he would never have let see him in this condition, was dead. (What did Aneisneida *do* with herself all day?)

Today, Arity had seen what Delta City had been reduced to. Pati *must* realize how his tyranny had impoverished and cowed the people! Petitioners . . . endless petitioners who asked no more than food.

"How can you justify it?" he said aloud. "How can anyone justify such a miserable mess?"

Pati slumped low in the Throne, wings hunched up behind his ears. "The purge is part of the cure. We should turn the corner in a matter of months."

"I saw no signs of that today."

"Didn't you hear Aneisneida? Atheism is almost eradicated."

Arity said impatiently, "It seems to me that the city was a good deal more prosperous when the nobles were in control."

"But we were decaying inside. That's why I keep Aneisneida and Soderingal around—they're specimens of a vanishing species. Every time I see them, they remind me why I did away with the others of their kind. They embody everything that sickens me. An absence of understanding. Self-serving frivolity. *You* saw it. And people like them were engulfing the world."

The lifestyle of the nobles might have been self-serving. But weren't humans at heart self-serving? The small indulgences one had permitted oneself in such an atmosphere, the freedom to love whom one wanted and laugh at the others, the silly innocent giddiness of Delta City society in those days had compensated—hadn't it?—for the stupid individuals one did sometimes encounter.

Pati said, "If I hadn't done something about it, I would have been shirking my responsibility."

Arity's heart sank. "You're not still talking about *divine responsibility*, are you?"

"Divinity exists," said Pati, hooding his head with his wings.

Arity coughed disgustedly. "The humans have seen us fall on our faces too often now to believe in us. Piety is just a behavior. I'll tell you what they do believe: that the flamens hold the key to their survival, and they know you control the flamens; that the Hands will kill anyone who gets out of line, and you control the Hands. That's power! Why can't you settle for that?"

"My being able to kill people doesn't justify what you saw today." Pati's voice was cold, withdrawn. "After all, your little human *irissu* used to control the flamens, and the crime lords, which was more or less the same thing. If that were all, I could have left things in *her* hands."

The swell of grief at hearing *your little human* irissu was delayed, but inevitable. Arity shut his teeth and waited for it to pass. "Then—why—didn't you?"

"She was incompetent. But that's not the point." Pati leaned forward in the Throne. His face and hands glowed in the twilight. "There is nothing respect-worthy or even properly thought out in atheism. It's flawed in its conception. Humans are incapable of understanding us as their equals—supposing that we *were* their equals—and to me, their inability to understand proves they are our inferiors. I've seen it time and time again. They cannot *help* worshipping us." Contempt hardened his voice. "They used to say openly that they didn't believe we were divine, yet even in those days, none of them could ever speak to us without quivering."

"And you wanted to make sure it stayed that way." Arity hated Pati's reasoned, intractable self-delusion. He hated it because *he* could not understand it. A hard, grainy crystal of misery lodged in his lungs. "You love people to be afraid of you. That's why you have all the flamens in the world come and swear vows to you. If you didn't have to spend your time making sure of the flamens, you could hold more audiences, but no. You love seeing them grovel before you. Concern for the human race!" He swore in *auchraug*, reusing some of the expletives he had heard Broken Bird employ in Rimmear. "You want them securely in your fist. There's no more to it than that."

"Isn't there?"

Arity had been staring blurrily at the base of the Throne, his eyes dark with tears. The new note in Pati's voice brought his head up. Pati was standing in the Throne. His wings fanned out behind his head. High over his head, the prisms in the chandeliers tinkled as the wind from his wings knocked them together. He seemed larger than natural. His voice split into thousands of echoes. "Isn't there?"

"*Power*, Pati. Stop showing off!"

Like a paper figure folding, Pati collapsed into the Throne. He grinned impishly.

"Why the hell?"

"Now do you see why I am convinced the humans are stupid?" His eyes still burned palely, but he was the right size again. His wings were folded at his back, his arms curled lazily along the ornate arms of his seat. "Go on! Argue with me, Wind Gully Foundling!"

Rainbows drifted around Arity's head. He hated to admit it, but Pati's tricks were not completely wasted on him. He should have saved the whole business for later—kept it inside his head, to ponder when Pati slept and Arity lay on his back beside him, drifting through multicolored layers of insomnia. He should never have spoken, rather than have to go through the pain and humiliation of dropping the issue now.

"Did I frighten it, then?" Pati jumped off the Throne and kissed Arity's nose. "Ohhh."

"Power, Pati." Arity moved away. "I'm close to eighty years old. Not a Foundling. I'm civilized. Leave it."

But Pati hugged him from behind, kissing the back of his neck. "Can't leave you. Can't do without you, *irissi*. Not again. Not anymore." All the laughter was gone from his voice.

Thrills ran through Arity like ripples of sound from the fingers of a *farader* maestro. He was malleable in Pati's hands and he thought, *I'm losing my pride. Have to lose something, I suppose, to be free.* Divine, *auchresh*, predator, human, what did it matter? This was Pati. Arity could touch him and be touched by him, unencumbered by the armor which had sealed him off from Sual. He turned and kissed him.

"Let's go to bed." Pati's thin hot body folded around Arity's. Nothingness abolished them simultaneously. Arity's sense of proportion vanished, redly, with the dark Throne Room, dissolving in preparation to change into something else altogether.

GOSSIP

It proved unnecessary for Aneisneida to sacrifice her gastric sensibilities. Soderingal reminded her that it would be suicide to visit *Delights and Diversions* wearing her court dress. She had to go home first and change into commoner's clothes. Hateful garments! The skirt and blouse rubbed her fur the wrong way wherever they touched her. But it was unreasonable not to have a plate of cold supper while she was at home. She ate in the brightly lit dining room at one end of the table, watched by a bevy of flaking ghosts, while upstairs Fia screamed as the nurse put her to bed. Then the steward, Sailoner, informed Aneisneida that she had promised to visit Godsie Stockold—she of the newborn son. Essne had to be put off by courier, and Aneisneida's whole calendar—a humbler roster of names than it had once been, but still crowded, for she was the greatest lady in the city—rearranged.

It was the middle of the night before she and Soderingal reached Temeriton.

They left their sedan on the Lockreed Concourse. Revelers of all descriptions swaggered and sidled past. All the doors on the street stood open, spilling torchlight and women's husky laughter. Aneisneida knew that if she stayed long enough, she would see most of her male acquaintances, and possibly some of the female ones; she had already glimpsed a pair of Hands entering the Silver Fountain brothel. Their taste for human whores was well-documented.

But for all the merriment, an air of dreary timelessness hung over the street. Every foot of cobbles had been trod before. A lady did not linger here, if she valued her reputation.

Soderingal's head was bobbing to the pipe music trickling from the nearest open door: a slow, breathy melody that meandered up and down, up and down, as if it could go on forever.

Aneisneida dragged him away. Not for the first time, she reflected that their marriage had started as that favorite scenario of farceurs—the swash-buckling social climber and the gullible heiress. But it had changed slowly but drastically until she did not know what a playwright would make of it now. A tragicomedy? Just tragedy?

She had to drag him about to get him to accomplish anything. And he was pigheaded about the most ridiculous little things. But had he always been like this? Or had he once been sensitive and flattering? Had he always drunk too much? Or had it gotten worse since the coup? She could not remember properly, because like all the foolish girls in the farces, she had been blindly in love with him. She sometimes wondered whether he had ever loved her, or only the mug and bottle, and her father's money.

If *that* were the truth, what a horrible shock it must have been when Pati's Hands killed Belstem and stripped Aneisneida of nine-tenths of her newly inherited estate!

Soder had coped rather well, she thought. There was still something admirable there, under the unkempt mien and the perpetual stink of booze. If only she could lay her finger on it.

The street gleamed with the rain that had passed. They left the torchlight as they stepped into the back alley. Clouds hid the stars in the narrow slit of sky overhead. Soderingal caught Aneisneida's arm, preventing her from treading on a hideously alive heap of rags. He knocked on the door.

Humi opened it, hovering in the shadows, one finger to her lips. She frowned uncomprehendingly. "Hello . . . ?"

"It's me, Humi," Aneisneida said. "And Soder."

"Oh . . . Oh, gods! What are you doing here? I—I mean, I'm delighted to see you! I knew you must come soon. We have much to talk of. My plans are progressing beautifully. Sssh. Don't wake the family." She smiled beau-tifully with her mouth and stood aside. She wore plain green, like pious but not desperately poor women. Her hair was twisted into a Rivapirl coil, with only one big wave that she had missed hanging loose in the back. *As if,* Aneisneida thought, *she really* was *expecting us.*

Or maybe she never sleeps.

She shivered.

"It has been a long time. Why, if I may come to the point, do I have the pleasure of seeing you at such an unusual hour?"

"Oh—oh, well, actually . . ." Aneisneida trailed off. Somehow she could not deliver her news. It would be as if she had come to poke sticks at the caged lionet. Cruel.

"Well," Humi said after a pause. "At any rate, I am looking forward to hearing how you have progressed with gathering public support for us. I am so isolated here! But Hope tells me that the city chafes under Pati, and that any rumor of a recoup is well received." She led them into the small, sparsely furnished living room and showed them to the sofa. She fumbled with the candle bracket by the door for a moment, and turned back to them, her smile self-mocking. "Soderingal, could I trouble you to light the candles? I *cannot* master that task."

Soderingal looked her up and down appreciatively as he took the flint and steel. "Amazing 'ow you look after yourself, all things considered."

"Thank you."

"But I'm afraid I 'aven't got much news from the public-support province. Can't do nothing without mentioning your name. Still set on keeping it secret?"

"I think it would be most unwise to reveal myself at this point." Carefully, Humi suggested, "The Summer name would do."

"Oh, no," Soderingal said instantly. "Not come hell an' high water. We're only *alive* on suff'rance from Pati—sorry, milady Divinarch! We're Nearecloud now, an' even *speaking* the Summer name ud be the death of us—"

He sounded impassioned. Yet all the time he spoke, he was staring at Humi's undusted, sleek bosom. Aneisneida broke in. "The heart of the matter is that we need to rouse the people's hearts. They are cowed. And unless, Humi, you are willing to let it be noised that you are still alive, I do not see how we are to manage it."

"Because not one of you," Humi said gently, "not you nor Soderingal nor any of the ghostiers, is willing to risk his own name for the cause of liberty for the world."

"Well," Soderingal protested, "that doesn't seem 'xactly *fair* when it's *your*—"

"I know. I know. It is my throne at stake. The last thing I wish is to strain your loyalty, my friends!" She sighed. "I think eventually I shall leave this house and travel the city, perhaps even the continent, drumming up support. Numbers are essential. We must crush Pati as he crushed us, with force of arms."

The obstacle to that course of action was salient. Reflections of the candle flames lay on Humi's eyes like appliqués. Neither Aneisneida nor Soderingal spoke.

"Yet perhaps there is a better course of action. Perhaps we will see it after we have a glass to drink." She crouched down, displaying the tawny down on her nape and the gentle slope of her shoulders, to burrow in a wall cupboard.

"Everything goes better with a swallow of wine," Soderingal said approvingly.

Humi rose to her feet, holding a half-empty bottle of second-grade rye liquor. Even in the wavering candlelight, Aneisneida could see how muddy her face was.

Trust Soder! Aneisneida leaped into the breach. "My *favorite!* Do pour out, Humi! Or would you rather that I—"

"I can do *this* quite well." Humi's head turned blindly, seemingly at random, as she knelt by the low table and uncorked the bottle. "But thank you." Whenever her stare swung across Aneisneida's gaze, her features looked momentarily, frighteningly, expressionless. She seemed to be concentrating on something within herself. Perhaps her humiliating blindness. Perhaps her poverty. Her name, Aneisneida thought, had finally become appropriate.

She put that thought out of her mind. The idea of seeing Humi at a disadvantage frightened her so deep inside that she could not even identify the thing that made her think to herself, defiantly, *What if she is blind? She is still Humi. The recoup will go forward. And maybe—now here's an idea—maybe she will even win Arity over, so that we have an agent in the Palace! I think that is quite a wonderful thought!*

The liquid in Soderingal's goblet rose to within a finger's width of the rim. Humi righted the bottle and asked Aneisneida whether she too would partake.

"Of course," Aneisneida said warmly.

"She 'ad her pinky finger crooked over the rim all the time, so she could feel the wine rising," Soderingal murmured under his breath. "Not so clever as all that, eh?" He chuckled.

"How has little Fiamorina been since we talked last?" Humi asked composedly as she tipped the bottle for the second time.

"Oh! Her fur's thickening like grass in spring." Soder grinned, diverted. "She's a real beauty. Pale green. Like that."

He pointed at Humi's dress. Humi looked blank.

Gods! Aneisneida took a deep breath. "Humi, we came because we have some news for you. Someone is alive whom we thought was dead. I'm sure you will be delighted to hear that Arity is living." She paused. Humi did not seem to have understood the significance of the statement. Aneisneida elaborated. "You must recall. Charity. The Heir. A god. He is unchanged—well, almost—he appears to have a limp, and he has cut his hair—and he is living as the Divinarch's lover. At least that is what Soderingal and I think. We saw them embrace, in the Throne Room. We did not speak to him—"

Something splashed her knee. She jerked back, and gasped. Rye liquor flooded the table, gleaming in the candlelight, dripping onto the floor. Humi knelt stiff and still as one of her ghosts. Her arm appeared to be frozen, tilting the bottle over the glass. The last of the liquor flowed out with a series of glugs. "Oh, gods," Aneisneida gasped, and clung to Soderingal.

"Think p'r'aps we'd better be going, Divinarch." Soderingal pulled Aneisneida to her feet. He reached down, rescued the brimming glass, and took a swig. "Nice t' see you—"

"Oh, come *on*," Aneisneida whispered. "Come *on!*" Soderingal paused in the door of the living room, chewing his lip. *I am going to cry,* she thought, appalled at herself. She felt like an indulged child whose father has slapped her.

The bottle dropped out of Humi's hand, chinked on the floorboards, rolled under the settee. Then Humi lifted the corners of her mouth. "I agree, Lord Nearecloud," she said, wheezing a little. "This is one visit perhaps better cut short." Like an afterthought, she added, "You *were* telling the truth—just now—weren't you? He is alive? He is Pati's lover again?"

Again? Aneisneida thought. *What?*

Soderingal's grip tightened on Aneisneida's arm. "We was telling true. And 'ow I wish we 'adn't been."

Humi gave a laugh, like the bark of a dog. "So do I."

Soderingal pulled Aneisneida stumbling out into the little dark hall. The back door took an age to open: the latch was cranky. But Humi was there, pushing them aside, working the latch. Her face was blank. But the hand that rested on Aneisneida's arm shook like a rickety house in a gale.

The Neareclouds could not escape over the threshold fast enough. The door closed behind them and the latch dropped. They stumbled down the alley. It had started raining again—but not heavily. Aneisneida would not be able to disguise it if she cried. She took a shuddering breath.

The Lockreed Concourse had gone quiet. The only doors still open lay closer to the center of town, where they had left their sedan. The glistening street, humped like a snake so that the water ran off into the side gutters, was nearly deserted. The lanterns over the brothel signs glowed red. Soderingal crossed the street, pulling Aneisneida from pool to pool of light. Then she heard a faint sound braided into the city's hum.

The chink of heel talons on cobbles.

A Hand.

No.

And she *recognized* the smaller of the two approaching figures, *recog-*

nized the slim, incongruously breeched silhouette. Recognized the one god
in Delta City who had such high-set, sweeping wings.

They came face to face.

In the dark, it would have been possible to mutter "Excuse me," and
pass on. Aneisneida had done it before. Hope's companion was a Veretrean
in the prime of life: a sailor, from the cut of his clothes. From the smell of
him he was also as drunk as a bat in daylight. He grinned at them, showing
perfect teeth. He did not realize the situation. Did not realize that he *was*
the situation.

It was still possible to make the best of things. Aneisneida lowered her
face and made to go around the pair.

"What in the merry hell you doin 'ere, Hope?" Soderingal exclaimed
with awful jollity.

Hope put one hand to her face. She pulled her companion up into the
middle of the concourse.

"What the *fuck!* We need t' talk, Hope!" Soderingal bellowed. "We've
been to see Humi. She's in a bad way—"

The ex-Maiden wheeled. Her mouth was a thin golden line.

"Oh, Hope," Aneisneida sobbed, "we told her Arity is still alive, and she
spilled the rye liquor—"

"Dog's piss—"

"—on the floor, and we left, and I don't know how she is taking it." It
took a tremendous effort for Aneisneida not to fall to her knees in front of
Hope. She had never seen Humi lose control before—not even when the
entire Ellipse combined to force her to abdicate. Now Hope was all Aneisneida had left to place her trust in. Not because she was a god, but because
of her serenity, her seeming invulnerability to change. She was timeless.
She was an insider everywhere. "I'm sorry, Hope!" For once, it was easy,
not distasteful, to apologize. "I shouldn't have told her—I didn't know what
I was doing—"

"Lords and ladies, may I present Aneisneida and Soderingal
Nearecloud," Hope said acidly, tiredly, "unable to leave well enough alone.
What on earth did you tell her for?"

"She's drunk," Soderingal whispered to Aneisneida. "The gods can hold
barrels of liquor, but *I* can tell . . ."

"We thought she'd be overjoyed," Aneisneida wailed. "We thought—"
The recoup—clearing the air in preparation for the storm—

"Are you stupider than you look? Overjoyed!" Hope snorted unsympa-
thetically. "Your skirt's in the gutter, Aneisneida!"

"It's only cotton." Aneisneida gathered her dress out of the filth. She wiped her nose. Her hand smelled like the sewer. "I can afford a hundred of them. Oh, *Hope*—"

"She'll be all right, I tell you." Hope turned her face away from them. Over the Veretrean's shoulder, she said, "She's resilient. She's recovered from things before."

The Veretrean sailor placed a host of small, sloppy kisses in the hollow of her neck. Her wings quivered as she arched against him. Overhead, a torch flame, caught in the vortex created by the movement of her wings, bent in half and went out. As the darkness swept down, Hope pulled away from the man. "She had to know sometime," she said. "I was putting it off as long as I could. Thank you, I suppose, for relieving me of the responsibility."

"Wait. You *knew* 'e was alive?" Soderingal said. " 'Ow? You weren't there today—"

"Where do you think he's been these past three years? Of course I knew. *And* I knew he had come to Delta City—I saw them arriving myself. I was on a reconnaissance mission in the Old Palace. That was more than a sixday ago. They left again right after that—but now they're back for good." She shrugged. "Far be it from me to guess how Pati has gained such power over him."

Aneisneida bit her knuckles. She had a feeling she knew. The Veretrean lurched in front of Hope, gathered her in, and kissed her mouth. "Let's go," he mumbled with drunken arrogance. "You're comin' back to *Gefiya* with me, my wingy beauty—"

"But does this mean anything's changed?" Soderingal persisted, drowning out the Veretrean's cajolements. "Is Pati gonna change 'is policies? Is Arity gonna be Heir again? Why's he come back, if not? Just to fuck the Divinarch?"

"I think that is quite possible!" Hope called from the darkness. "I doubt anything will ever change! That is the state of affairs we are in, now! But you saw them this afternoon. You can judge—"

"But I thought you were close to Pati," Aneisneida said. "I thought you knew everything!"

Hope laughed. "Well, now you know differently, don't you?"

And the mist-shrouded, barnacled semblance of a world, that hulk of reality of whose slippery hull Aneisneida maintained a precarious foothold, where she had balanced since it capsized two years ago, stood on its beam ends. With a tremor that shook her through and through, it settled deeper into the sands. A mist of uncertainty enveloped her. Hope could not be trusted. Neither could Humi. They were vulnerable—*just like her*—Hope was embracing her lover, but she had forgotten her strength. The Veretrean's back arched the wrong way, and his arms flew out. Just before his spine must shatter, Hope let go, hissing. The man shook his head as if to get rid of water in his ears, and pulled her back to him.

"Fuckin' 'ell," Soderingal exploded, staring at the dark. A purple bright diamond burned there, shrinking to nothing. "Fuck it! Anei—"

"Keep it to ourselves," she whispered. "Soder, we can't—can't let anyone know—"

"What?" He glanced sharply at her. "Are you crazy, Anei? Let anyone know?"

Her teeth chattered. They were alone in the silence of the uneasily sleeping city. The rain grew a little heavier, stippling the waters of the gutter. Far up the street, she could see their porter sitting between the shafts of his sedan, twirling his hat.

The gods are human. The gods are vulnerable. The gods are not.

Years of atheism had not brought it home to her as finally as tonight had.

But Hope had taken her disgusting drunkenness away with her: Aneisneida no longer had to see what she did not want to. After the first shock abated, interpretations slipped into place with the ease of familiar prostheses. It was true after all, it had always been true, it was still true, that the gods could not lose their cool even if they tried. The Veretrean sailor had not been a sign of weakness on Hope's part. He had been a manifestation of her power over the city.

Aneisneida did not feel so alone nor so responsible when she knew that *someone* was watching over her, weighing everything that could possibly happen, choosing each outcome for the best.

She leaned back into Soderingal's arms, pleating the wet cotton of her dress in her fingers. "Don't move, Soder," she said. "Please."

"Well, well." He wrapped his arms around her waist. She heard a smile in his voice, though what he found to smile about, she did not know. "'Aven't 'eard *that* for a while."

"That doesn't mean I am giving you license to take liberties! Hold me. Only hold me still." Reality had just been redeemed from the edge of the quicksands: she needed a few minutes to solidify it in her mind. It was not yet safe to walk on.

Ari.

Humi lay in perpetual darkness. Her fingers crept like dazed mice through her hair. The night mist came in through the aperture in the wall, sewer-scented, kissing her with cold, ethereal lips. It protected her. It would continue to protect her for another couple of hours yet. After that—

Her body did not feel like her own. It was molten: it had no bones or tendons, only heavy, insensate flesh. She could not re-create the chills and glorious climaxes he had sent through it. She could not feel anything at all.

She could not even re-create *him* in her memory. She thought of herself as a moderate to inept blind person, but perhaps she had sunk farther into the darkness than she had realized. She had stopped thinking of people in terms of faces. And on top of that, in fending off the memories of him—*all* the memories, sight and sound and silly little pledges of devotion—for three years, she had reduced them to shadows.

One swam near, suffusing her with a fleeting sense of victory.

He had had purplish-brown hair, soft and loose to his shoulders.

He *still had* purplish-brown hair.

Fresh tears oozed from the corner of one eye. They trickled over her cheekbone to join the crust of dried salt water at her hairline. Her fingers plucked erratically, freeing one strand after another from the tangles produced by her tossing and turning.

But of course there can be nothing between us anymore. He belongs to Pati now. He has always belonged to Pati.

Why couldn't she muster very much grief? Time. Blindness. Numbness. As first-time lovers are wont to, she had loved him without qualification or restraint, scarcely realizing how deep into their union she had sunk until she had given a good half of herself over to him. She had not just loved, but adored him. Until Thani, her misguided little sister, intervened.

And now her devotion had atrophied.

But according to Aneisneida and Soderingal, Thani had never actually accomplished her task. The question gnawed at Humi. If Arity had not been dead, where had he been for three years? In Wind Gully Heaven? Some other Heaven? Then why had he not come to her? Had Pati had him all along?

She wanted to know the logistics of his disappearance—but emotionally, she felt nothing. No longing. No desire. The tears did not bleed from any sort of wound, but from her old friend the hollowness.

Her inability to act. The pointlessness of talking over the recoup with Aneisneida and Soderingal. Emni and Zin's absence. Hope's devoutly and repeatedly pledged loyalty that Humi suspected to be increasingly based on guilt. They emptied her of emotion. The emptiness leaked salt water as regularly as a cracked pipe. She filled her time with rats and seagulls. Had she not been ghosting, she would have been in bed when Anei and Soderingal arrived, and she might have avoided hearing the awful news. She would have had at least another whole day.

But the news was just another wedge in the crack. Just another crack. Whether Arity was alive or not, whether he was still the Ari she had known or not, nothing could ever be the same again between them. The most she could hope for was maybe, one day, to come face to face with him and ask a few questions.

She took a deep breath. She forced herself to think of possible ways around the problem of her blindness in the matter of rallying the masses that were not there.

SOMETHING LIKE NORMAL

Erene derived a sense of accomplishment from weaving that was *fuller*, somehow, and less bittersweet, than any pleasure she had ever got from ghosting. In weaving, one created something from nothing. Ghosting had never given her that feeling. Whenever she used to ghost, she had known in her heart she was reducing a human being to an object of cold, dead permanence. She could not think of it as anything but a process of reduction, now that Tellury Crescent and all the ghosts she and Elicit had made were half a world away, not close enough to chill her with the beauty that had taken shape under her hands. She remembered only the deaths.

But not any more often than she had to.

She sat at the tall floor loom Elicit had made, shuttle nosing from side to side of the warp, gazing out of the window. When spring came, bulbs would sprout from the muddy patch in front of the house. How satisfying it was to struggle for one's daily bread! She and Elicit had the jewels they had brought from Delta City—but they prided themselves that they hadn't yet had to sell them.

The west coast was one of the most underpopulated regions in the continent of Pirady. Here, they had discovered that though they represented themselves as coming from Grussels, they were still mistrusted as foreigners. Thick with hardy forest from which only backbreaking labor could extract arable land, the coast was battered winter and summer by the sea, which stretched to the ends of the world. It was home to widely feared but timid barammoths that left footprints the size of buckets around the house. People huddled in tiny, incestuous clusters. Shikorn town, around whose huts the ground had, over millennia, been plowed into submission, lay three days inland through the forest.

No one lived closer to the Paeans except Shine, in the little hut he and Elicit had built this spring. Erene loved Shine. Yet she often felt a guilty sense of relief that he was not living with them anymore. They had taken him in a year and a half ago, when he stumbled ragged out of the trees, lost and starving in the bountiful forest because he had no idea what was not poisonous. He had hit it off right away with Artle and Xib. But they were *Erene's* babies. Not his. And Elicit assured her that she had not been wrong, as winter storms beat in from the sea and they were cooped up for days on end, to worry that Artle, the elder, was growing to look on Shine, if not as a second father, as a partisan elder brother who gave piggyback rides and played games even when Mama had given strict orders that the house was to be tidied.

But Elicit had not broken the news that Shine would have to move out just to appease Erene's maternal jealousy. Remnants of the piety with which he had been raised still clung to him. Personally, Erene did not understand how *anyone* could believe in the gods after living with Shine for a year, and listening to him make love to Keef by the fire, on the nights when Keef visited from Shulage; but the pious were a mystery to her at the best of times. Even her husband. Elicit had insisted that it would hamper Xib and Artle's development for them to grow up with a god for a brother. In Delta City, they had never lived so close beside the gods—or *auchresh*. He insisted it was unnatural.

Erene knew he was using the children's wellbeing as an excuse to allay his own discomfort. But what of it? Was this strain inevitable between human and *auchresh*—or should Elicit try harder to get over it? They knew little more about Shine now than they had when they first stumbled across him. And the children did not even know that he was different from themselves! Living as they did in the wilderness, neither of them was learning conventional social skills. *That* wasn't Shine's fault.

Still, Elicit said stubbornly, the fur around his mouth twitching as he suppressed his emotions. Better for Shine to maintain some distance.

And Erene had kissed him and assured him that anything he decided was right.

It gave her a thrill to submit to her husband. An ordeal of responsibility such as she had gone through in Delta City did not easily let her forget how onerous it was to have to make decisions.

And every day she gave thanks, to whatever power there might be, that after three years of marriage she and Elicit were still in love with each other. An easy, undemanding love. As parents, they balanced each other perfectly. Erene's natural stiffness—the impulse that told her she had to discipline the children, or they would grow up soft—canceled out Elicit's tendency to overdo everything. His excesses of love, which had helped both of his apprentices turn out disastrously, were carefully monitored by her when it came to Xib and Artle.

But unlike Erene's apprentices, *Elicit's* (according to the last carrier pigeon to arrive from Tellury Crescent) were still alive!

The first Hand who had ever visited Shikorn, two and a half years ago, had stood in the middle of the muddy town square and announced that Erene's apprentice was dead, her short Divine Cycle "terminated" by the god whom Erene had known as the Striver.

Poor Humi. Infected with the ambition that had stretched Erene thin. Distance did not soften Erene's grief, or ease her guilt.

She blinked. Here the children were back.

"Mama!" Artle dashed across the patch of mud in front of the house. Where was Xib? Shine must have him. "Keef here!" Artle stopped outside the door to wipe her shoes. Warmth spread through Erene. Barely three, but she knew her responsibility to help Mama and set an example for the gray fuzzball one-year-old in the arms of the tall god striding out of the trees.

Erene swung around on the weaving stool and held out her arms as the door opened, letting in the cold scent of pines. Her daughter flew across the floor. "Keef ee here! Can we go to the sea? Keef said he—"

"Darling. It's too cold. Keef and Shine have special, hot blood, so they may be able to swim, but *you* can't." Erene lifted Artle onto her lap and rubbed her cheek in the tumble of soft silver hair. "You can help me finish this length of cloth. Mm? And if you're good. I'll let you be taster when I make supper. We'll bake honey buns to honor Keef."

"Wanna," Artle murmured, fumbling with Erene's dress. Erene wondered what was passing through her mind. Was she thinking of the shingle beach at the bottom of the cliffs, where Shine had *teth*"d the children on calm days in summer? Or was she thinking of the promised honey buns? Or had she completely forgotten the conversation when infant memories recurred to her, making her remember that this was where she had sat to nurse? It had been hard on her to cede the breast to Xib. Childrens' minds were even less comprehensible than *auchresh's*. All one could do with either was look after them and hope for the best.

Shine ducked under the lintel, carrying Xib. Tall, winged, pinkish-blue of skin, he gave a beaming smile. "Errie! Guess who's here?"

"I *told* her," Artle squealed, starting up in Erene's lap, at the same moment as a square-bodied, brown-skinned *auchresh* dressed in the uniform of the Hands came in the door. Together he and Shine seemed to fill the room, with their white, glowing teeth and huge cat's eyes tipped nearly on end in their pointy faces. Xib sang a wordless baby song, bouncing in

Shine's grip. Erene stood up, letting Artle slide to the ground. "Welcome," Erene said, smiling, and closed her teeth as Keef took her in his arms and squeezed.

After supper, Keef lit a pipe, put his feet up on the kitchen table, and told them the news from Shulage, the provincial capital. Elicit argued with everything—not for the sake of argument, but in an effort to open a serious debate on theology and politics, such as he often held with Shine. Keef deliberately ignored these gambits, rambling on about cattle markets and apostate flamens, blowing smoke rings.

The fire diminished slowly in the hearth. Candles flickered among the piled dishes on the table. Outside, trees moaned and knocked their branches together in the dark. The sea grumbled softly, far away. Erene stroked Xib's hair where he slept on her lap and watched Elicit get more and more incensed. Keef had a self-important turn of character, but Erene was usually pleased to give him the attention he craved, for he possessed both humor and kindness. Occasionally he was cruel without noticing—that was the effect of spending every day parading around Shulage intimidating people—but she trusted him with the children, as Elicit did not, for she could see him guarding his every word and gesture, like a barammoth tiptoeing around on its huge feet.

Shine's kindness was instinctive; Keef's was studied. But he ought to be congratulated, in Erene's opinion, for studying. Once he had brought a couple of other Hands here. They had refused Erene's offers of drinks and chairs. They had refused Elicit's attempts at conversation. They had stood back to back by the mantelpiece, profoundly uneasy, fingering the crescent knives at their hips. When Artle made a sally at them, wooden doll in hand, they started simultaneously, knocking the mantelpiece off its supports and breaking several ornaments. Artle ran and hid in the bedroom, crying, and Xib crumpled into wails. Keef and his friends left almost immediately.

Yet Keef was always at ease, clean of that dangerous edginess. Erene wondered how he managed it. When Elicit had temporarily talked himself into the ground, she mentioned it.

Keef seemed pleased to have another opportunity to expand. "It has everything to do with one's mental state. Either one absorbs the atmosphere at headquarters—or one doesn't, in which case one can shake it off at will. It gets harder and harder to think my own thoughts instead of my captain's. But I think I'll be all right, as long as I keep coming to see you and Elicit." He chuckled fruitily. "Your family is a palliative! You keep me balanced! That's why Yellow Spruce Heaven welcomes me and Shining Stone whenever we want to go home, not that you ever do, Shine. We're still something like normal. Whereas the fellows from Long Waterfall tell me their *ruthyalim* have chucked them out for joining the Hands."

Shine smiled, holding Artle as casually as a mother might. He sipped from his wineglass, but said nothing. Alcohol generally quieted him—"until," Keef had confided to Erene once, shocking her, "we get into bed. Damn, he's hot! Why d'you think I keep you supplied with the best Riestasis?"

Elicit leaned forward, hands flat on the table. "That's nonsense, Keef. There's got to be another reason your *serbalim* didn't throw you out. How could it have anything to do with us? Erene and I and the children are humans, just as much as the people you and the rest of the Hands herd around in Shulage."

"Ah. Erhmm. You got me." Keef frowned at his pipe, making a to-do out of tamping down a new bowlful of tobacco. "Actually, it doesn't have anything to do with you. I was just flattering you. If you'd been *auchresh,* it would have worked!"

"Enough flattery, then! What's the truth?" Elicit pursued. "How do you and Shine reconcile two different worlds?"

Keef sighed. "The fact is, Elicit, Shine and I come from a very rural Heaven. In larger Heavens, they feel compelled to speak of the earth as 'two different worlds'—as you just did. And they find many different ways of dealing with the dichotomy." Erene stared at him. This serious, intelligent tone was a world away from his usual pompous jesting. The fire and the candles, casting their ruddy gleams one on either side of his face, deepened the lines around his vast jewel-like eyes. "The *serbali* of Long Waterfall Heaven, Weeping Beetle, has been influenced by ideas bigger than his little Heaven needs. As I said, he has prohibited his *firim* from going anywhere near human country, and outcast the ones who defied him. By contrast, our *serbali,* Moss-choked Gully, is wise in his stupidity. He doesn't object to humans at all, because he knows nothing about them except what Weeping Beetle told him. And Beetle is Moss's enemy, so Moss is convinced everything he says must be untrue. It's marvelous!"

"But what did this Beetle tell him?" Elicit asked impatiently.

Keef gestured to Shine.

Shine drew breath. "Did either of you ever hear of Broken Bird and Bronze Water?"

"Oh!" Erene said. The men all looked at her. "We were councillors with them both in Delta City," she explained, suppressing an urge to laugh. "They kept to themselves. Of course, we attributed their reticence to their being gods. But now I think that they were silent because they believed there was no point in arguing anything. They supported the then-

Divinarch, Golden Antelope, who asserted that there was a single fate in store for the *auchresh* no matter what they did. I think I see what you're getting at, Keef! According to Golden Antelope, we mortals were the greatest race, the *auchresh* were not gods, and you had no place in our affairs." Elicit made an incoherent noise. She said, "It's what he told me."

"Yes, and Broken Bird and Bronze Water's views are a derivation of that philosophy!" Keef said. "In their view, you humans are beneath our contempt. *Wrchrethre auchresh* are scarcely any better. The *er-serbalim* tolerate the current Divinarch only because they have to. And Weeping Beetle, like so many others, has embraced their views wholeheartedly! But Moss-choked Gully rejected them simply because he heard them from Weeping Beetle! When Shine and I chose to leave our Heaven, it scandalized Weeping Beetle no end, and Moss was delighted!"

Shine shook his head. "Only out here could he get away with an eccentricity like that. We are a *very* rural Heaven. But there are a great many Heavens like us. The world isn't made up of Divaring Belows and Tearkas and Rimmears. There are thousands of Heavens where Bronze Water and Broken Bird's message has only come by word of mouth, and garbled at that. Before the *er-serbalim* started touring the Heavens, most of us didn't know humans existed; but now tales of humans are reaching every Heaven, either by way of the *er-serbalim* or recruiters for the Hands, and more and more *auchresh* are leaving for one reason or another, and Moss-choked Gully cannot be the only *serbali* in the world who doesn't condemn our departure. Power knows how it will all end."

"Why did *you* leave, though, Shine?" Erene asked. "You're not a Hand. I've always wondered what brought you here. But I never felt quite right about asking."

Shine rocked gently back and forth, holding Artle. "It was Keef, of course." He looked at his lover as if begging permission. Keef nodded. "Keef heard the Divinarch's message through Esult, who was then a recruiter trying to start a troop of Hands in Shulage. Characteristically, Moss-choked Gully welcomed Esult to our Heaven and feted him like a *mainraui.* The glory of the occasion went straight to Keef's mercenary little heart, which had always wanted to shine, and knew it never would, not as one *mainraui* among many *mainrauim* in a backwater Heaven in Fewarauw."

"Ouch!" Keef said. He blew out his cheeks and grinned.

Shine did not so much as look at him. "Several weeks later, Keef walked into Shulage—*walked,* for since no one from our Heaven had ever been to human country, he had no way of knowing where to *teth* "—and presented himself to Esult. Four *mainrauim* from Long Waterfall Heaven had already come, and they told Keef about the reception they had got when they tried to go home—ostracized, deprived of their *mainraui* status. So Keef decided not to risk the humiliation. He never came back.

"But just before he got the idea to be a Hand, he and I had pledged *irissim*. We were young. I decided to walk after him and see what had happened. But once I left the salt, I got hopelessly lost. I wandered for weeks without seeing an *auchresh* or a human being. Eventually, I ended up here. And after a few months, as you remember, I met Keef in Shikorn village."

"And all was right with the world again." Keef grinned. "Oh, Power, oh, Power! Uh-*uh!* Shine, I'll always remember when I realized how much I'd missed you."

Elicit's face was hard as metal in the light of the guttering candles. "It seems to me you've set a dangerous example, Shine."

Shine finished his wine. "To whom? I suppose that's a stupid answer. Well, you can blame Esult, not me."

"Blame Broken Bird and Bronze Water," Keef said. "If it weren't for their influence—even though it was a *reverse* influence—Esult would never have been allowed into our Heaven! And besides, isolationism is so damned unproductive!" He waved his hands. "If it wasn't for the isolationists, all the salt would support the Divinarch!"

Shine frowned. "If it wasn't for the isolationists, all the salt would support the Divinarch!"

Erene shivered.

Elicit persisted, "Esult seems to be like the kind of god who would be happy to jump on the Divine Balance and send any one of us to Hell."

"I have to put in a good word for him," Keef said. "He's my captain, and he's one of the most virtuous *auchresh* I have ever known."

"Virtuous?" Shine said. "You mean fanatic." He turned to Elicit. "*I've* met Esult, too. He's the kind who never seems to show their true colors until they've reached positions of power. His kind would make us a dangerous race, if the isolationists and the Hands could ever reconcile their differences! He's a true son of his forebears."

"Nonsense!" Keef said. "Esult is perfectly sane! He worships the Divinarch like a god!"

"As would you, if you were a proper Hand," Shine said furiously. "You really ought to be sitting on the table while Erene and Elicit sit on the floor. You ought to make them lick your feet clean. And why didn't you force them to cook one of their adorable little children for supper?"

Erene cried out.

"Enough!" Elicit thundered and rose to his feet. "This is my home! You

will have to account for me before you drag my family into your spats! I
demand an apology."

Neither *auchresh* moved. They stared at him, mouths slightly open. *Oh,
Elicit!* Erene thought, her heart aching for her husband. She was perhaps
the only person present, including him, who understood: all evening he
been trying, and failing, to trap the *auchresh* into saying something that
would confirm them as gods in his mind. Now, at last, their petty catfight
over Esult's character, and their drawing him into their argument, had
pushed his understanding of them to the point where he could no longer
bear to participate in the demolishing of the wall between *auchresh* and
mortal.

Xib's crying was the only sound apart from the trees scraping in the wind
outside. Erene remembered herself and held the baby to her breast. He
latched on thirstily.

"Give me my daughter," Elicit demanded, his voice breaking. After a
second's delay, Shine lifted the sleeping child and deposited her in her
father's arms. Elicit looked down at her as if scrutinizing her for signs that
she was god-touched. "I think that you should both go home. This is one of
the least productive arguments I have ever taken part in and it has gone on
long enough. I will not allow you to slander my wife and children as you
did, Shine. If you cannot apologize, you will have to leave."

Incredibly, both *auchresh* rose to their feet.

"Stop!" Erene said. " 'Lici. This isn't going to help you stay pious. How
are you going to worship someone you have bested?"

Keef laughed. "Bested?" he yelped, rather hysterically. "I could teach
you a thing or two, Godsman Paean! I could—"

Elicit shook his head as if trying to clear his mind of a lingering dream.
"Get out." He stood up and carried Artle out through the weaving room,
into the bedroom, leaving Erene alone with their guests.

Shifting Xib into one arm, she opened the back door. A gust of cold black
wind whirled in, bringing droplets of rain.

Keef made a face. "Ugh."

"I think you *had* better go," Erene said. "I was afraid for a moment
there—but the storm has broken. Come back in a couple of days, Shine."
She smiled tiredly. "Everything should have blown over by then. He is too
intelligent not to want ever to see you anymore."

Keef glanced at Shine. "Do you want to *teth*˝? I'm a little drunk: you'll
have to take us."

"No." Shine's eyes were closed, his face tipped to the storm, the globular
lids fluttering. "Winter's here. I should like to walk."

"We'll be drenched!"

Shine opened his eyes. The luminous black pupils reflected Erene and Keef, like little pale statues. "This is why I stayed in human country after I found you, *irissi*. Share it with me."

"Now I know why they say renegades are too strange to live." Keef shook his head. "All right. I can savor life with the best of them." He turned to Erene. "Thank you," he said at the same time as Shine. They laughed at themselves, remembered the gravity of the situation, and gulped it back.

Erene smiled with tears in her eyes. "Oh, you two," she said, almost crying. "Love each other. Don't let—these things—get between you!"

Shine said, "I *hope* you're right that Elicit won't hold it against us, Erene. We argue between ourselves, too. Over the same things. We weren't trying to snipe at him—or anything."

"Yes," Keef said. "Really. You should hear us sometimes. Your friend Shine is secretly a rabid factionalist, Erene! Next thing you know, he'll be bringing *ruthyalim* to tea and forming them into a renegade army!"

The two were outside. The darkness swallowed all of Keef except his eyes, but Shine glimmered like a branch of phosphorus. "See you soon!" he called, blowing a kiss, his hair already wild in the wind.

And Keef's voice, laughing, "As good a night to you as ours is going to be, Erene!"

The whole front of her body was wet from standing on the threshold. Moving clumsily, she shut the door, dropped the latch, and wiped Xib's little gray head with the tail of his wrap. Incredibly, he was still sleeping.

"Come to bed," Elicit said, softly, from the other room.

She woke in the night to find him with his back turned to her, weeping. She raised herself on one elbow and leaned over him, wiping his face with her fingers. "I love you," she whispered.

He did not answer. His silent sobs shook the bed. The children slept peacefully in their cot, and Erene gave thanks for that—nothing is worse for a child than to see its parent cry. Eventually she whispered, "Did you— did you prove something to yourself, tonight?" She did not mean it as a subtle I-told-you-so, but as a you-can-confess-if-you-want, and she knew he would understand that.

But his voice was even more broken than she had anticipated. "Gods . . . ! It's gone! Gone . . . What am I going to do, Errie?"

She bit her lip, caressing him.

"The children—how will they grow—gods! How can I teach them something I don't believe myself?"

A tear trickled out of her eye. His emotions were hers. But now he needed comfort. "Don't worry," she whispered. "They *will* grow up. And that's what matters. They don't need faith. And it would be false to teach it to them if we have none. Everyone around them loves them. What do beliefs matter, if they have love?"

He turned over and grabbed her to him, holding her so tight it hurt. She kissed his tearstained fur and whispered, "Don't worry, don't worry," thinking, *Now I am a mother in body and soul I am not the same anymore. I have fallen into the habit of soothing even him with optimism that I do not feel.*

HOPE'S FOLLY

Hope sat on the edge of the narrow bunk, legs awkwardly splayed, watching the frame of torchlight around the cabin door move up and down. The effect might have been the same if *Gefiya* were rocking in high seas. The ship was lashed close in her berth in the Delta City docks, but Hope herself was rocking, quivering like a door assailed by a battering ram: the Veretrean sailor knelt between her legs, thrusting into her with the vindictive violence that had characterized all his lovemaking of late, whether their trysts were planned, or, like this one, as sudden and inconvenient as assassinations. His fists bundled the tender leather of her wings, holding her in place. In an effort to erode her self-awareness, she let her head flop in circles on her neck. She felt alone and detached up here, with his shaggy black head next to her shoulder, and the onslaught down below having no more effect than a series of not particularly well-placed blows.

"What's wrong with you, eh?" Ders grunted, and Hope murmured, "Oh, *ohhhh* . . ." and stirred herself, moving with his thrusts, trying to find that spontaneous rhythm that visited them on their best nights and transformed ordinary friction into fantasy. But it did not come. He finished and slumped over her, breathing like a beached nightsharque. She supported herself on her hands, gazing at the underside of the top bunk. This was the end of their assignations. Tomorrow morning, *Gefiya* sailed to Port Teligne with her cargo of Chrumecountry fruits. And the thing that troubled Hope was that she could not have cared less.

Humi, she thought. *I should have gone to see Humi.*

"Fuck. Ahhhh." Ders stood up and groped in the clothes sack hanging on the wall. The light coming through the crack of the door illuminated a stripe of sleek brown fur on his back. The cabin smelled of male sweat, and salt, and moldy cheese: six sailors shared it, and Hope had deduced from fragments of overheard ribaldry that they took turns having it to themselves, to be alone with the women they brought back to the ship. Ders did not tell her so, but she was sure she was not the only woman *he* brought here, either. The first time she came, she had got lice from his quilt. The night after that, she had tried taking him to the Folly, but he had glowered with embarrassment at having the social gulf between them pointed up so baldly, and bruised her green and blue in his lovemaking. So they had gone back to dark, cramped trysts on board the ship.

Pulling on a shirt and a pair of clean breeches, he spoke. "You'd better leave."

Hope sighed. "Ders, I'd just like to know . . . what do you feel for me? Anything?"

He wheeled around. "I haven't got time for this kind of talk, milady. Get out of here. And don't get seen, neither. Go in a flash. Some of the boys are pretty pious, and if they saw you, I could be drummed out of me situation."

"Do you love me?" Hope said. "I love you," she added, to encourage him to reply.

"Gods." His face twisted, and as if he could not restrain himself, he spat on the floor. Wiping the back of his hand across his mouth, he started to speak, then shook his head. "How can you ask me that?"

Hope cocked her head on one side. "Do you despise me for letting you have your way?"

He leaned against the wall and folded his arms. "I gotta get my beauty sleep, milady. We're sailing at dawn."

"Do you mean you're just going to end it like this?" She endeavored to put a quaver into her voice, desperately trying to drum up a scene. "Is it because I'm not a good enough lover that you despise me?"

"There ain't nothing wrong with you, Wingy. You're no different from any other woman. 'Ow's *that?*"

"Aha! So that's it!" She bounced to her feet. "No different from any other woman! You were expecting *divine ecstasy,* weren't you? And I disappointed you. So you're punishing me with ending it without so much as a word of affection."

"I never said I was ending nothing!" Ders protested.

A shadow obscured the crack at the bottom of the door. She raised her voice. Whoever was listening might as well get the full benefit. "Well, I'm *not* any different from any other woman! How does that feel? It's all a hoax! The closest anyone can ever come to divine ecstasy is a whorehouse in Heaven!" It wasn't working. Her emotions were still comatose. She felt nothing. However, one did not get angry and then break it off for no reason. "I!" she said, and then realized she had lost her train of thought.

It seemed she had succeeded in one respect, though. Ders took a step toward her, his fists clenched. "You bitch. You fucking *begged* for it. I fucked you once and you begged for more! Crawled on your *knees* for it!"

She retreated, feeling excited.

"I used to be pious, too," he said thickly. "And you fucked *that* up nicely! I'm never gonna be able to look at a god again without remembering what it was like to fuck you! Never mind praying!" He hawked and spat, sloppily, missing her. "And it wasn't even worth it. I've had better whores than you." With a shock, Hope realized he was almost crying. "Better *dog bitches*—"

"Woooooooah." From the passage came the sound of ironic applause. "Finish her *off*, Ders—"

Ders wheeled toward the door, making a superhuman effort not to cry. Hope sobbed.

She lay on her back on the ground, under a rhododendron. The waxy leaves slithered over each other, hiding the stars. It must have rained while she was on board *Gefiya*. The stink of leaf mold filled her nostrils, and her wings flattened it into a concavity under her back. Already her shoulder muscles were jittering with discomfort. This was why she had ordered featherbeds for her Folly into which she could sink like a piece of flotsam. No process of evolution had shaped her to lie on her back. No process of evolution had shaped her at all. Living as an *auchresh* was living with a handicap that nature had intended to kill you, and which you had daily to overcome with grit and will.

Or not.

I was too strong for him. I was a spice that became a poison. I was using him for my own ends. And all the time I was destroying his beliefs, just by being what I am. It's a god's responsibility not to let her subjects get close to her, no matter how foolhardily they flutter to the flame! It's a god's responsibility, for the Power's sake, not to beckon them closer!

If I returned to the salt I would no longer be a god . . .

Arity had stayed in Rimmear for this very reason: so that he would no longer have to endure being the object of the mortals' obsession. But he had come back to Delta City. Not to be Heir, but to be Pati's plaything. He had taken the easy way out, the common cure for the meaninglessness of a life that was the object of no one's obsession.

Hope did not have the hook of love to hold her here. Nor the hook of godhood, for her status as a god was crumbling fast, will-she nill-she, through acts like taking Ders as a lover, and her all-too-visible ineffectuality. All she had was her Folly. But she could not contemplate leaving. Not even for a little while, as Arity had. *We are both* wrchrethrim, she thought. *We can't stay, can't stay away.*

The fatigue of her position ground her into the wet earth. She wasn't wearing anything apart from the shell of her wings. She shivered and twisted on her side.

Visible between the lower branches, the Folly towered in fantastic silhouette against the sky. The grounds occupied all of what had once been Antiprophet Square, and the surrounding mansions' gardens. Pati had razed them as a lesson to the city, but Hope had appropriated the site, and built the Folly using money she made from selling her estates in Divaring Below. She had asserted herself as a power in the city, in those first months when she had been flushed with her conviction that a recoup was inevitable. But she and Humi had let the iron cool—in themselves, and in the hearts of the allies whose support would be necessary in any campaign. Now it seemed that the city was resigned to wearing its new master's yoke. Some people were even starting to believe that Pati *was* the One God, as he insisted. And what Delta City felt, the rest of the world reflected.

The Folly stood like a waterfall frozen before it had leaped to its full height. A shadow bird-netted in wood and steel.

Did Humi know the recoup was never going to happen?

Hope had not visited Lockreed Concourse since she tried to deliver the news of Arity's return, and guilt ate at her for her negligence. Aneisneida and Soderingal, by their own report, had half killed Humi by dropping the news on her out of a clear sky. How had she handled it? Had she survived?

Hope rolled on her face, plunging her fingers into the leaf mold. Worms wriggled around her talons. *Breathe. Stay alive. All you can possibly hope, Hope, to do is . . .*

"I can't bear it," she said aloud.

The night did not answer.

"I can't bear it!"

She hurled herself out from under the rhododendrons, gripping her head with her talons, shaking it back and forth, shrieking softly. *"Do something!"*

Starlight bathed the shrubs. The shadows of the taller trees dappled the grasses. Blood inched down her neck from the burning places on her scalp, down between the roots of her wings.

She clenched her fists. A garbled sound came from her throat. She couldn't stop shaking. She was frightening herself.

She was not completely powerless! There were still a few things she could do. Her own heart might be frostbitten beyond cure, but there were others who could be healed, who could resume their love where it had broken off. And who knew if love might not lead to something more solid!

She, Hope, had merely to do the honors. She still had her secrets, each one a jewel in its own little coffer, and now it was time to start spending them.

CERTAIN ILLUSIONS

Arity had the night shift at the Dog Gate of the Old Palace. Pati had offered to exempt him; but Arity had refused, as he refused every time Pati tried to treat him differently from the other Hands. Pati, it turned out, had wanted Arity to himself tonight. They quarreled. Ordinarily, Arity would have dissolved into shaking ecstasies and flung himself at Pati's feet—but tonight he said, "I'm sorry, I have my duties." He did not know where he got the strength. Pati stared at him. Arity *teth¨d* to the guardhouse, sat down, and accepted a mug of ale from Blue Kestrel.

"Didn't expect to see *you* tonight," Kestrel said by way of a greeting.

Arity took a gulp of ale before answering, "Neither did I."

Perhaps I knew I needed time to myself, he thought, not without conscious irony, as the alcohol warmed his stomach. *In order to maintain an obsession you must leave space between the two of you for delusion. Not reduce it all to bodily contact. Because that has limits, where the other does not.* He wasn't afraid that he might go the way of Melin and the others. But he knew he must be the one to give the flame air, for Pati would not.

After half an hour he was on duty. He went out of the guardhouse and took up his position. Dog Gate opened out of the lowest level of the great courtyard, on a street that had once been bustling and well-to-do. Most of the houses were boarded up now. The silence of an empty beach—stones, darkness, waves silently eating at the sand—hung over the whole palace district. How different from Rimmear. What had it taken to make a human city seem older than an *auchresh* city?

Arity stood loose and relaxed, like Mosquito Ruby on the other side of the gate, flicking his gaze over the street, up the wall towering above him, down to the cobbles. The sentinels were not decorations, but safeguards against attacks from unknown malcontents which Pati still feared, though most of the Hands had long dismissed the likelihood of any resistance to the Divinarchy.

It was bitterly cold. Soon Arity's eyeballs were the only part of him that could still move. The houses across the street were a chiaroscuro in black and white.

Sulfur burned a hole in the night. The smell of an actinic *teth˜tach ching* gusted into Arity's face. Mosquito uttered an oath and drew his crescent knife. Arity was a half second behind, poised to stab or throw.

Hope popped out of the firework, striking the cobbles lightly. She was wearing a lacy dress that reeked of camphor. "Ari!" She grabbed Arity's arm. "You're coming with me! We're going to pay a visit to someone whom you haven't seen in far too long. Hello, there!" she said to Mosquito. "Don't raise the alarm, will you? He'll be back before anyone knows he's gone."

"Who is it?" Arity muttered. "Hope! Who?" He was captivated: he forgot to struggle. He could only think of one person he hadn't seen in far too long, and *that* could not be. He tried to pull away.

"Don't!" she said. "I have to concentrate—"

"I don't know where she *is*," Hope whispered worriedly. They were climbing the stairs that zigzagged upward through the attic of the house in Temeriton. Her talons dug into the back of Arity's hand. "She never leaves the house! It would be dangerous for her to come up here—and she doesn't take risks!"

Arity said nothing. He could do nothing except follow. He did not dare voice his suspicions, in case she laughed at him. The certainty of a horrible anticlimax petrified him. Yet he dared not *teth˜* back to Pati and report Hope's attempt to subvert his loyalty, even though that was what he ought to do, because it *might* be—

It could not be.

But *could* it be? When he saw Hope glowing with this almost treacherous fervor, in her dress with its loops of rotting lace, when she *teth˜d* him to this tumbledown house in the brothel district, he'd seen that she had made some sort of decision, and was determined to carry it out, even if she were forced to resort to underhanded means. He had seen this ashamed yet determined sneakiness in her before, on the occasions when she had resolved to defy Pati.

Dust blossomed from their footfalls.

But it can't be! She's dead!

"Power," Hope gulped as they rounded a worm-eaten partition. The stairs doubled back on themselves, slanting straight up to an open hatch in the roof. A silver sea swirled and lapped at its lip. The dust stirred by their climb, lit by the rectangle of starlight coming in the hatch, resembled foamy, crashing waves. The sky in the hatch, by contrast, was tarry.

"They wouldn't leave it open, not in autumn. This means she's up here." In one leap, Hope was out of the hatch. Her skirt and hair and wings blew out, a tumult of silvery veils. She drew breath—and then froze, beckoning Arity.

He had thought that his courage would fail. But he found himself beside Hope, gazing down a slope of damaged tiles at a gutter as wide as a small river, set on top of the wall that faced the back alley. In the gutter knelt a slim, lithe woman, gazing down into the alley, fair hair tousled in the wind.

Moments of catharsis pass like shocks of pain, with undertones of pleasure. Eagerly sought, or dreaded; dwelt upon before and after the fact with morbid intensity. Yet all Arity remembered feeling at the time was the wind striking through his shirt, chilling him so fiercely that his teeth clattered together.

There could be no doubt that it was her.

No trick of the wind could have duplicated her voice. ("I have never been up here before, you know," she was saying in a pleasant tone, apparently to nobody at all.) No trick of the starlight could have mimicked the grace that almost hid the trembling tension in her poise.

"Our time together has been most pleasurable," she was saying, and Arity believed three years had not passed. "Even if I do not see my way clear to accepting your kind offer—well, I have gained a new spot to idle away my leisure hours! It is nice up here! Also, I think I smell house-monkeys; do you?"

"Yesss, milady." Her companion rose to her feet. Arity gasped. The other woman's robe had let her blend into the night—she could have been a flamen, except that the robe was black. She tossed her head, and her hood fell back to reveal a small, androgynous face. "I smell them. What of it?" Soundlessly, she moved up behind the younger woman, shaking back her voluminous sleeves, flexing her hands.

"I use a variety of small animals in my work," Humi said. "Rats, seagulls, cats—even a dray dog whose master could no longer afford to keep it. But the possibilities of those are limited. A new species to work with is a delightful boon. I do hope I can catch one. Perhaps you could help me!"

The Hangman—it could be no one else—bent from the waist, placing her head a few feet left of Humi's. "If I have granted you sssuch a boon, will you not repay it by accepting my offer?" She straightened up.

Humi turned her face left. Her voice was strained and sad. "I dare not. I am too vulnerable. My allies have all fallen away from me."

Beside Arity, Hope was chewing the tips of her fingers.

"Without more support, I dare not commit myself to a campaign such as you propose. I am sorry."

"I never thought I would hear the Divinarch say *I dare not.*" This time, the Hangman did not bend down to speak. Humi twisted, her hands coming up to shield her face. "Or *I am sorry.*" The Hangman's hands closed on her shoulders.

"I dare!" Hope shrieked. "I dare!" Down in the gutter in a flash, she tossed the Hangman against the roof like a baby. The woman's head cracked against the tiles. Hope pulled Humi to her feet and hugged her. "*Humi!* What is she doing here? I thought we had decided that we wouldn't involve the underworld without agreeing on it together—what did she offer you?"

"Gods! Hope! Well, how do you expect me to get your consent when you don't show up for two months straight? I—" Humi pulled away. She cocked her head as if to listen. She wore a plain dress that hung perfectly on her slim figure, showing her bare shoulders under the tangled cloud of hair. "Who is with you? Who is it?"

Arity stood up. In a voice that came out jerky and strained, he said, "*Irissu,* it's me."

"You thickhead," Hope wailed, "she can't *see* you—"

"I know who it is." Humi's voice turned disconcertingly hard. "What did you bring him here for? He's Pati's plaything. I haven't anything to say to him."

How had she found out? Hope must have told her! Behind him, a housemonkey, maybe two, waked by the noise, jittered in annoyance. He gripped the side of the hatch. Without knowing that he had *teth¨d,* he found himself shaking her violently by the shoulders. *For three years I tried to kill myself to be with you—wherever it is that we can be together without anyone noticing—and you haven't anything to say to me? I'll give you "haven't anything"!* Yet the words that came from his lips were defensive rather than aggressive. "You were alive. And you hid here for three years, and never once thought to let me know you hadn't been killed. You might have spared me that!"

She struggled mechanically, like a hare that has been in a trap for hours. But her face was not in it. Her eyes darted randomly from here to there.

And he knew. He let go of her as if she were red hot, coughing with a helpless nausea. Everything he had meant to say bubbled up and stuck in his throat. *It's the shock. It doesn't make any difference—not really! It's the shock—*

"Sickening, isn't it?" she said. "I must say, yours is the most dramatic reaction I've had yet. But then, no one else was quite as familiar with the old me as you—were they?"

"How—Power! How did you—"

"Gods!" She moved her head impatiently. "You know what happened here! Think!"

Pati. Of course. Part of him rebelled against Pati for concealing the fact that his poison had only blinded her, not killed her. Then he realized that of course, Pati did not know either. "I thought you were dead! Has Hope known all along? Oh, Hope! I thought—" He stopped.

"What difference does it make? I might as *well* be dead. But I *am* glad we've met again. Ari, I want to know"—her voice sharpened—"how could you become his lover? That's one of the things that intrigues me most about the whole business. How could you give yourself to him? You used to be so independent. Was that real? Or was the *auchresh* I knew always an illusion? Did you always love him first and foremost?"

He shook his head. "What do you really want to know?"

"How could you do it?" Did she feel pain? Or was this just the dispassionate needling of an interrogator? "I don't understand."

Two realities warred in Arity's head: one that he saw before him, and one that he had accepted for three years. The conflict between senses' testimony and disbelief made his vision blur and his head ache. A strange exhaustion—the nervous system's response to overstimulation—weighted his limbs down. He fought to think. Humi's face and voice, her very presence, had thrown him back three years into a world of shimmery fabrics and ghosts and bells. His memories of that place were fresh and timeless. He could not deny their existence: not to himself, nor to her, not to her face.

And yet he must be honest—he would be nothing at all if he were not honest—there was Pati. She knew all about it. He could not deny it, and more important did not want to. He floundered. "Before I knew you, I loved him. I suppose . . . I—I suppose it seemed most natural. You know. After you were gone—"

That wasn't true. After he learned Humi was dead, *nothing* had seemed natural, not eating, or breathing, or blinking. But how to explain that the only one who could possibly have replaced her, in any measure, was the one who had already replaced her? In Rimmear, it had made sense in a visceral way. Self-immolation. It still made sense, although less clearly. He had to struggle now to remember how he had felt that night when he and Pati sealed the bargain with kisses.

"I love you." So difficult to explain. "But when you were gone—you don't understand how hard it was—"

"Is it true, Hope?" Humi did not turn her head, only raised her voice. "He says he loved Pati before he loved me. Is that true?"

"That's *not* what I said!" Arity spun around to plead his case with Hope—and fell silent. She crouched in a rain puddle a little way along the gutter, her hands over her ears, beside the unconscious body of the Hangman, shaking.

But Humi could not see that Hope was not listening. Arity cringed as she continued, confidently, as if she were speaking to an attentive audience. "Think back, Hope. When he came to Delta City, twenty years ago, when he discovered Pati had left him for you, how did he act? Before the fall he told me that he realized then that his affair with Pati was only a youthful infatuation. But I always suspected he was lying." She paused. There was no answer. She rubbed her forehead with her hand, an admission of vulnerability. "What am I *saying*, Hope? Why am I wasting my breath trying to resuscitate a dead love affair, when we have political concerns to deal with? Hope . . . Hope?" She turned her head, squinting as if she could see. "Where are you?"

For a moment, with her guard down, she was her old self. Arity stepped forward, meaning to take her in his arms. But before he reached her Pati's face billowed up before him, a cobweb with two burning holes. It clung to his hands and face, stopping him as effectively as if he had waded into quicksand. The left eye, the blue one, smeared itself over his cheek like a streak of luminous paint. When he tried to look straight at the face, it was invisible, a blast of heat roaring out of nowhere. He could not force his way against it.

Humi rubbed the bridge of her nose. "But really, the middle of the night is not the best time to discuss these things."

The wind gusted between them, great downy puffs of cold. Arity did not go to her. He had stopped trying. Excitement heated his blood so that he did not feel the cold. Pati held him spellbound: it was almost as if he had reached out from the Palace and tapped him on the shoulder. He felt like weeping or falling to his knees.

Humi lifted her face, blotched with dark patches in the starlight. "I know you're still here. Go away. I haven't anything else to say to you—and I expect the sentiment is mutual."

Arity drew a deep, shuddering breath. "Humi. Let's be civilized, shall we? Let's remember that love is not the only, or the most important, thing in the world."

She appeared to be listening.

"I'm not your enemy. I might be able to give you more help with whatever it is you're planning than *she* can." He jerked a shoulder at the unconscious Hangman. "Why can't we talk as equals?" Pause. "Allies?"

She gave a tinkling laugh. "Are you mad? You'd betray me."

"All right. You may not trust me. But does that mean we can't be pleasant to each other? I'd thought better of you."

Her face brightened, became a social mask. "Of course I can tell you about the Hangman!"

That had done it. Arity experienced a bitter exultation. Seductive, like sugar in the blood; chilly, smooth.

"It's nothing a man would find particularly interesting! There's *no* political alliance between us. We were friends before the fall. Ever since she told me she was a woman, and she came from Domesdys, we've had a lot in common. Our mutual friends—our mutual goals." She shrugged. "We both have a sense of nostalgia for the city as it used to be. We talk of the past."

"Oh, yes," Arity said. "Well." His mind was working fast. *Nothing political?* Her ambition was so obvious it was in poor taste. She aspired, of course, to regain the Throne.

But that was nothing new. Was it? In Rimmear, recovering from his near-fatal injuries, before he knew she was dead, he had dreamed of a laughing, tawny-haired girl who walked beside him through a salt forest and yielded to his kisses, but who faded before he could taste her, like all dream things. The starlight thinned her to a wisp of mist and she disintegrated. The dreams had threatened him during his waking hours, too, after he learned she was dead, when he sat in the bottom-tier taverns during the day. Laughing at nothing—running away to Veretry for a couple of hours, to pretend there was no such thing as other people—drinking chocolate in her Antiprophet Square apartments as dawn came up over the marshes . . .

But that girl had never existed. She was the invention of a *khath*-inflamed brain.

(Pati whispered to his mind, deadening the nerve ends.)

There had been nothing more than a physical attraction, and now that too was gone. Humi had always been the hard-edged, knife-faced woman she was now. He did not see how he had ever loved her.

He stretched, feeling the chill of the wind once again, calm and collected. It was as if a huge weight had vanished off his shoulders. "Well, we have a great deal to talk about, you and I—but I think we should put it off until another day. Easier than dragging things out tonight." He took care to put a smile in his voice. "Don't you agree?"

She started. She seemed to have fallen into a reverie of her own. "Oh, yes. Have I told you all you wanted to know? My life is rather dull now—there is no other way to put it."

He nodded his head.

"Yes. I suppose—yes. It has been a true delight. Thank you for coming, Ari." She half-smiled. "I see the past in a quite different light now."

"So do I." He saw a possibility of consolidating his victory over her, and himself. "Listen—if there's anything I can do to help—"

"Perhaps there will be. You mean . . . ?" She cocked her head on one side.

"Yes." Arity calculated his hesitation. "Why don't we speak plainly? You want to regain the Throne. Pati wants me to be his Heir. So far I have refused, but I don't know how long I can keep on refusing. I would rather see you become Divinarch than me. So perhaps we can come to an understanding."

"You mean—" She sighed. "Pati."

"Exactly."

"You want me to spare his life, when I regain the Throne. In return for your not telling him about my intentions."

"Yes."

"Well, frankly, I think that's rather premature of you." She touched her cheekbones with the same self-mocking gesture she had used when talking to the Hangman, earlier. "Like this, I cannot see how I shall ever come to have power over him."

Her ambition was a cold flame, then, not a hot one. It made no difference of course, but something prompted him to play with her. "What I meant was that perhaps, with my help, it wouldn't be so remote a possibility. The same thing must have occurred to many people—we'd have to be very careful—but supposing you were to succeed, with my help, we would have to have an agreement along the lines I am suggesting. What I want . . ." *is to have things the way they used to be . . .* Impossible! "What I mean is that if we collaborate, I'm sure we can work things out without anyone's getting hurt. I love Pati—but I think it would be best for everyone if he wasn't Divinarch. All the odds are against him. You do see what I mean."

"You're incurable!" Humi said. "Ari the peacemaker! For starters, I could not trust you that far, and even *if* I ever succeeded, I would—" She stopped. Quick as a viper, she said, "This isn't a ploy to make me speak treason, is it? You're not going to betray me—are you?"

"Do you think I would do that?"

"No," she said mistrustfully.

He smiled. "Then we've already reached an understanding."

Over the whistling of the wind, a sob reached his ears. He turned. Hope curled in the bottom of the gutter, weeping with anger. "No use . . . no use . . ." Her dress floated on the rain puddle. The wind had frozen the wet lace into stiff curves that crackled as she stood. "You *can't* just let everything you used to have slip away! Don't you see how *false* this is, Humi? You know you're just being polite, so as not to make this too painful for both of you. But you *do* love each other! If you would just admit it, Humi, maybe we could win him back. Maybe we could win his *heart* back. But oh, no, you have your *pride*—"

Humi said in a voice stiff as ice, "I do have my pride." Her back formed a razor-straight line. "But I am also honest with myself. And with others."

Hope laughed rather wildly.

"Honest is the last thing you'll ever be, senior ghostier!"

"I am no longer senior ghostier. And I am no longer attached to Charity. He and I understand that the past is the past. Why don't you see that the only way to make *any* future is to stop trying to re-create it?"

"You two were my last hope," Hope sobbed. The Hangman stirred and sat up. Hope wheeled and pointed. "And if you trust this *haugthirre* woman rather than Ari, Humi, you're blinder than I thought you were!"

"I'm going," the Hangman said thickly. She stumbled at the slopes of the roof. Quite dexterously, almost as if she could see, Humi caught her, pulled her close, and whispered. The Hangman sat down heavily.

"Well, don't ask me to do anything more for you and your damned recoup." Hope was crying. "That's all I have to say, Humi! Don't count on me!"

Arity stepped toward Hope and pulled her close. He felt competent now, and hugely successful. "I'll take you home. You're all worked up about this—though I can't see why. Humi and I have behaved with perfect amicability toward one another, considering the circumstances under which we meet."

Hope wept inconsolably. "Listen to you. Just *listen* to you!"

Arity turned to Humi. "We'll talk again, then?"

She smiled thinly. "Can I lay it on you to visit me, not the other way round? I am not able to get out and about with any great efficiency."

By this time his loyalty to Pati had sunk so deep that he had almost forgotten he was going to betray her. She was right, it *had* all been a ploy— a perfectly conscious manipulation of the past that lay between them. But all was fair between lovers, was it not?

"I'm taking you back to the Folly," he said to Hope, meaning to get her out of the way before he returned to Pati to break the news. This might not be an advantageous place to be in the next few hours.

"I'm too tired to *teth*¨," Hope moaned.

He kissed her on the nose. "Then describe it. I've never been there, you know."

Through fitful tears, she did so. The Hangman and Humi stood together—one watching, the other seeming to. The last sight he saw before nothingness was their faces side by side—bony, fair, inscrutable. At that moment they were nearly identical. It shook him. His destination wavered in his mind, and instead of emerging in Hope's second-floor ghost parlor, they slipped down through the floor, and tumbled through thick, scented steam for what seemed like minutes before crashing into Hope's swimming pool.

The water was green, hot, and tasted of incense. They surfaced, gasping. Arity's hair was short now, so it wasn't plastered to his eyes like Hope's. After the initial shock, he realized that the water felt delicious. Succumbing momentarily, he dived, turned a somersault, and came up paddling. It had been too long since he swam. Not since the Divine Guards. He and Humi—

Slam the doors, lock them, ram a chair under the knob! Delicious!

Blue tiles lined the pool. A glass dome, lit from above by torches, could be seen as an opaque, multi-sunned sky overhead. On the walls, murals of salt cats and trulles curvetted through salt forests. "How often do you use this place, Hope?"

"Not very." Her eyes were wide in the steam. "Mostly for relaxing."

"But you keep it heated all the time?"

"I sold my mansion in Divaring." She was swimming with her spread wings. They chopped the water like huge golden paddles. "I have plenty of money!"

Arity knew why she had built this little ocean, hidden away, here whenever she needed it. It was for the same reason there had been a pool in the Divine Guards' quarters—a luxury today's Hands were not afforded—the illusion that it gave. It was the reason all *auchresh* liked to live near water.

"Power, Hope!" Pity suffused him. "You're a worse hypocrite than I am!"

In his and Pati's private suite, there was no water. Only the honesty of nakedness.

He yearned for it.

He breaststroked fast for the side, anticipating what Pati would say when he told him everything that had happened tonight. Humi was nothing to him. And Hope—well, Hope, floating on the undulating sheet of her wings, tears trickling from the corners of her eyes, would just get what was coming to her. That would teach her to interfere.

RED AND SABLE

Night had not yet fallen on the K'Fier wharves. But the light would go soon. Even through his tiredness, Gete felt frantic energy sparking the air, a pressing awareness that the day's business had yet to be completed. The warves bustled with ship's crews and warehousemen, loading and unloading, quarreling and dealing and trading. The noise was unbelievable. It grated on the brain, impossible to relegate to the background.

He lashed *Faith's* painter around a convenient bollard and straightened up, rubbing his back.

The family they had stayed with a sixday ago, the Grimeses of Cithamma, had told him to sail as far down the wharves as possible before tying up. Now he saw why. This small pier was evidently reserved for flamens' boats: the gappy line of two-man craft, scarcely larger than dinghies, clean of fishing nets and the nacreous scales of the lobefish they netted in the Inner Archipelago, told a plain story. But Macul Grimes hadn't mentioned the nerve-racking ordeal of sailing through the shipping, trying not to get crushed by boats the size of small islands which plowed constantly in and out of the calm passages between the stone piers, looming above *Faith's* sails like sudden peninsulas. Eight-foot waves reared on either side of their bows, furrowing the sea into deep troughs. More than once *Faith* had heeled right over.

Gate scowled with indignation, and knelt to help Thani out of the boat. Her cold little paw closed gratefully around his. She did not let go even when he had hoisted her up to the lumpy stone wharf. A stab of familiar anxiety pierced him: sweat glistened on the fur of her brow, even though, here, hundreds of leagues south from the North Reach, the claws of winter had already closed tight and the wind was icy. He had known her a whole season now, early autumn to early winter, and she had never once looked completely well.

"How're ye feeling?" he shouted. The racket behind them disguised the fear in his voice.

"A little tired. I'll be all right once I'm beside a warm hearth. That last hour was grueling, wasn't it?" She smiled.

"I'll say!"

"That family. The Cornwells." Her fingers tightened around his. "Do they live near?"

"Didn't say. But I want to get ye there soon's possible." Macul Grimes had given Gete a string of complex directions, which he was afraid to hold in his head much longer in case they became distorted. "Here, gimme the bag."

This pier, unlike the others, was nearly deserted. A group of scruffy children loitered around the gates that led to the town. Gete paid them no mind, supposing them to be the offspring of wharf-hands, amusing themselves while their parents worked. But as he and Thani approached, they formed an uneven barricade across the gates, and whining voices reached his ears. "Alms . . . please . . . Tuppence for meat, Godsister, o' yer mercy . . . Heal me . . . heal me!" Gete shuddered with distaste. He could not help feeling sorry for them—but gods! "Out of the way. Go home to your mothers!" One boy was naked but for a shirt. "Get some clothes on! Have ye no decency?"

But they paid no attention. As he pulled Thani between them, they actually tugged her robe. "Heal me . . ." pleaded a tiny fellow with one arm strapped to his side. His fur was gray with dirt. "Please, Godsister . . . please . . ."

Accosting a flamen! Why didn't the city governors do something about them? But Thani had stopped dead. *Oh, no*, Gete thought. She tucked the edge of her hood behind her ear—a gesture left over from her days of half-sight—and held up her hand. "What are you doing here?"

An older boy shoved past the little one with the broken arm, his hands cupped as if to catch rain. He smelled terrible—feces and fish. "Alms . . . Godsister, leman, o' yer kindness!"

"*I* been here longest," a girl shrilled, catching Gete's coat. "I ain't eat in two days, waitin' here for a flamen t' show. I'm hungry!"

Gete shook her off, barely controlling revulsion. "Godsister! Come on."

But Thani had stretched out her hands, feeling the children's bare shoulders and ragged heads, and they thrust themselves under her touch like cats eager to be stroked, pitiful hope on their faces. Gete swallowed protests. "Have you no homes to go to?" Thani asked, her voice soft. "Where are your parents? The last time I came through K'Fier, I was not met by a reception like this!"

"Mum and Da been arrested . . ."

"Ain't no livin' for Da no more, this's me little sister Ura, she's hungry . . ."

"Hands took me whole family, Godsister, I got nowhere to go. Nobody'll take us in."

Thani turned to Gete. Her face was stiff with horror. She hissed, "These are *atheists'* children, Regretfulness. What kind of pass has K'Fier come to, that they must beg from *flamens?*"

"I don't know. Maybe the Cornwells can tell us. Let's get out of here." His own feelings were mixed; he could not cope with the scene before him.

But Thani stood still, sweeping the children with her glittering blind gaze. After a moment they fell uncomfortably silent. Quietly, she asked, "Which of you was really here first?"

The silence deepened. Gradually, the children fell away, and the small boy with the broken arm shuffled up to Thani. With a convulsion, he threw his good arm around her legs, butted his head into her stomach, and broke into sobs.

Gete knew what had to come next. He held her shoulders, their foreheads touching, the child's icy little body sandwiched between them. The other children spread into an impromptu circle that stretched across the pier. Thani breathed deeply, gathering her strength, and healed the boy. It took a bare moment. His teeth gleamed, cleansed of filth and decay, as he ripped his splint off, shrieking with delight.

He had time to leap up and down on the hard stone before the other children closed in on Thani again, desperate now, their faces hard and almost cruel, like sharquettes at the sight of blood.

Before Gete finally got her through the gates into K'Fier, Thani had given away all the clothes in their backpack, the backpack itself, the few coins she had on her person, and the remnants of their food supply. Gete shook his head in despair.

Citizens and foreign sailors alike gave them a wide berth of respect as they made their way down the street; men touched their foreheads, women dropped rudimental curtseys. (Kierish folks were apparently, in these days of the new Divinarch, far more pious than they had ever been before.) "Thani, what'm I going to do with you?"

She was trembling with cold, having given away the wrap she wore under her robe. As they sailed south, Gete's smocks and breeches had become inadequate, as had Thani's shift dresses; families they stayed with had supplemented their clothes pack with cozy wool undergarments, and one sheep raiser had even given Gete a shearling coat. But he was shivering nonetheless. Winter lowered yellow and sullen over the peaked slate roofs. "*I'll* have to beg, now, to get clothes for you so you don't die o' cold!"

"They needed it," she said.

"But you couldn't help them all. And there's three more, over there, begging from people who go by. There's a little boy—looks as if he's been beaten. There's a girl, maybe eleven, holding a baby—"

"I won't lie to you, Gete. I have never encountered anything like this. In Delta City, when I was there last, people tried to cheat us, atheistic commoners tried to get Transcendence to change farthings into crowns, men disrespected us in the street without apology. There were paupers on every corner. But never any children! No children without *any* kind of home! The Deltans have that measure of decency, at least!"

Gete prickled. " 'S nothing to do with the Archipelago. We're better than this."

"I didn't mean that." She grasped Gete's hand and pressed it to her cheek. "If K'Fier is like this, what must Delta City have come to? How have people's hearts changed so dreadfully?"

It's because the children are atheists' brats, Gete thought. From the gods who lived on islands near K'Fier, he had heard of the Hands' habit of arresting atheistic families in sudden, swooping raids. Any children who hid, or ran away, would not be worth returning for. And who would help the children of the merchant who had oppressed you every day of his life? You might even get a certain satisfaction out of seeing them starve, as you starved.

But the answer might be more sinister than that. People *were* dropping alms in the children's hands. Nobody ignored them. Some turned their purses upside down to show they had nothing. Was the misery a result of a city's hard-heartedness—or its *poverty*?

Since leaving home, he had learned a lot about poverty. Sarberra had always hovered on the brink of starvation, kept from the edge by backbreaking work and rare miracles. He had thought it normal—now he knew they had been desperately poor. Yet it had been share and share alike, and orphaned children were welcome in a dozen homes. Here, things must be so much worse that people were no longer *able* to help each other.

He did not think, however, that he would have liked the city even in its better days. The messes that the food sellers along the street were cooking up smelled like tanned leather. The stalls that sold jewelry, trinkets, and sundries seemed to be full of trash. Foreign sailors predominated among the customers of every shop. Unsurprisingly, perhaps, Gete saw that the native Kierish demonstrated every sign of deference every time one of these great men hove near, swaggering and blowing smoke from both nostrils; white-furred (but grubby) Archipelagan women hung in doorways, pouting and showing their thighs. For some time, Gete could not figure out why they stood there. When he saw one of them approached and fondled by a sailor, he realized with a shock what they were selling.

Shouldn't—*that*—be kept off the main street of the city? Confined to the night hours?

"A flamen is walking on the other side of the street, Thani. His leman is a boy of about ten. He has seen us. Both of them bow to you." Gete swept a bow, and winked at the little boy, who grinned back across the street, entranced by this sign of fellowship. Thani murmured urgently, as she curtseyed: "Gete. Tell me of his eyes. The flamen's. Am I imagining it, or is there something—"

"Salt crystals," Gete said, puzzled. The Godsbrother looked perfectly ordinary: hurrying about his business, with no time to cross the street and talk.

"No. Something else!" Thani relaxed. "Never mind. They have gone."

It was quite extraordinary how she could tell where other holy beings were in relation to herself. After traveling with her for a season, and seeing her meet various "renegade" gods and a couple of other flamens, any doubts he might have entertained about the authenticity of her "sensing" power had vanished. It was not infallible but it definitely existed. He had almost forgotten the tales of the gods' private lives (true? or not?) that Desti had hysterically spilled out to him on Qalma. And even if he could not *quite* dismiss the feeling that he was missing something, that the gods Thani prayed to and the gods who fished, herded, and played with Archipelagan children were just not the same—the paradox did not demand his attention. He had too much else to think about.

Thani was looking tired, breathing hard. Her salt crystals started out of her eyes like baby teeth. They were passing in front of a low stone wall behind which shrubs and waving grasses partially hid a red-trimmed mansion set back twenty feet from the street—an oasis in the succession of shop fronts and town houses. Bronze catlike beasts supported the portico, and squares of red-dyed glass filled the upstairs windows. This was right, this was a landmark. What came next? He glanced around for a side street on the right, with a blue-roofed building on the corner—and spotted it, with a sinking heart, halfway up the hill. It looked a league off.

"Let's sit down for a bit," he said, making a quick decision. Flamens were not supposed to impose their needs on laity who also had to make their living—but surely this was a fair exception. Across the street he had glimpsed a tea bar, doors closed against the cold, steam and smoke puffing from vents over the windows. "You need some soup, and some meat."

"Gods, Gete. I don't think I could swallow flesh."

"Right. Bread then. I'm not letting you get away without eating today."
She straightened her back. Her posture was so perfect when she wanted.
She seemed like a lady. "You're more than I deserve, Gete. I believe I am
spent for today. If the Cornwells have pressing need of us"—she smiled
painfully—"they will have to wait."

"Indeed!" Gete guided her out into the street at a appropriately stately
pace, forcing a donkey cart and a convoy of wheeled travoises to stop and
allow them past. He pushed open the door of the tea bar. Warmth eclipsed
them. Half an hour later, sitting at a window table with several emptied
dishes between them, he felt comfortable enough to remark on something
that had swum to the top of his mind. "Funny how there don't seem to be
any gods here. And we've scarcely visited an island without one since
Qalma."

She started. She even gave the appearance of glancing around—a sign
she was really perturbed. "Gods, Regretfulness, keep your mouth shut!"

"Nobody's listening," Gete said. *He* was the one who could see. And he
saw that the tea bar was crowded with customers, well-to-do for the most
part, who once they had acknowledged Thani's presence had become absorbed once more in their own conversations. The quiet hum of voices was
pleasant after the racket of the docks and the streets. The scent of mulling
wine pervaded the place. "Lady Tea," as the proprietress called herself, had
offered Thani whatever she wanted, but the woman had class enough not to
dance attendance on them. "Anyhow," Gete said, "the gods don't exactly
keep their existence a secret."

"Not on the islands. But it's high time you learned about cities, Gete.
The difference in population between a city and an island community can
be small, but feelings run differently on streets than they do on mountain
paths. Deception plays a large role. I think"—she paused, and swallowed—
"I have talked to some of the renegades, and I think—well, in cities, you
know, there are Hands. And the Hands do not want to know their country
cousins exist. So in order to keep the peace, our friends oblige them. If
there are renegades living here, they are not walking the streets like you
and me. Red Picarge, whom you will recall we met on Arlanga, said—very
philosophically, I think—that it is a small sacrifice they make, to avoid the
wrath of the Divinarch."

Gete had stopped listening. She had *talked* to the renegades? He
blinked. He had thought—

He muddied with shame. Gods, it had been patronizing, one could not
call it anything else, to think she was only capable of falling to her knees in
front of them! He had underestimated her.

"They're all gods, after all," she said defensively, as if she were aware of his surprise. "All part of the divine entity of which the Divinarch is the living symbol. The Hands and the renegades and the others that we do not see, those who live in the salt. Their affairs are all scripted by the Divine Balance, and in this Divine Cycle they are playing them out here among us to give us an insight into their ways. We are very lucky to live under such a philanthropic Divinarch! A chance to understand the inner workings of the divine! It would be a sin to shut our ears to it!"

Gete felt a rush of love. His Thani was not all flamen yet, not all marble. He seized one of her hands and kissed it. She giggled, pushing at his head. "Stop! Leman, I command you!" He paid no attention, licking her wrist, tasting the salt in her fur. Her laughter turned to hiccups.

Then without warning, she went silent. Gete knew it was not a ploy. He dropped her hand.

"Outside the window," she whispered. "Other side of the street. Describe him to me, leman!" Her face was a mask of longing.

Even before he looked up, Gete knew it was a Hand.

"He's a head taller than the rest of the people," he said slowly. "Their respect for him is great. They circle widely around him. He walks in a bubble of dangerous silence, swaggering like a lord, as if he owns the stones he walks on."

Other people in the bar turned to look out the window. A hush fell.

"His face is"—like something badly carved out of clay—"round and simple. His skin is greenish-black. He gazes into nothing. His back is swollen and rounded, but he carries the deformity carelessly. He wears a loose shirt and breeches—it is like a uniform—"

"It *is* their uniform," someone muttered.

"—of scarlet silk. He has a crescent knife in a sheath on his hip." The figure stopped at the gate in the low stone wall, glanced up at the mansion, then, expressionless, let himself in. Gete let out his breath. "He's gone."

Thani sank back in her seat. "Ahhh," she breathed, as if she had just had a sublime experience. Then her face wrinkled. "Gete, do you see any more of them? In the street?"

The patrons of the tea bar were resuming their conversations. Gete found that he was shaking. "No."

"But there must be. I can *feel* them." Her voice rose a little, slightly hysterical; then she remembered herself, and leaned across the table, hands flat on the rough-chiseled stone. "Maybe they're in the next street, then. Behind those houses." She gestured vaguely. "Four or five of them."

Gete did not know what to say. He knew she was always right about these things. "There's something else coming," he said, trying to distract her. "A carriage. Pulling up at the gate of the large house across the street. Oh, now *this* is beauty, Thani!" The four huge, black dogs that drew the carriage frothed and whined, biting at their harness: beautiful restive beasts, as full of energy as sailboats in a high wind. "Red reins on the dogs, and red trim on the carriage—which is a low, boxy bit with a canopied roof—to match the red trim on the house. And there're little cats holding up the corners of the carriage roof, just like the ones holding up the entry of the mansion!"

"Red, did you say?" Thani said in an oddly constrained voice. "Sables?"

"Cats?"

"Sables. Red and sable are the Salmoney colors. The richest atheist family in K'Fier. Is *that* where we are? Why didn't you tell me? I know this place! Last time I was here, with Transcendence, the Salmoneys' gate boy spat at us. I would never have chosen to rest within view of such a place!"

Gete blinked. "Well. I suppose that's them getting out of the carriage now. There's a girl wearing a red dress . . ." Pretty. A translucent-furred elfin face, and masses of black hair. "And a boy with her, holding her arm. Her brother? No, her betrothed I think. He's not wearing half so many frills. He must be from a poorer family."

"There are not many atheist families left in K'Fier with eligible sons, I should imagine."

"And now her parents are getting out. A plump older lady, with her hair in a pile—a fine figure of a man, with thick white fur—"

"Lord and Lady Salmoney. Gods!" Thani exclaimed. "Oh, gods!"

"What have you felt?" He looked around but could not see anything wrong. "What is it?"

Outside the window, the street was completely empty but for the Salmoneys. Ironic, that even in these days of a forced increase in piety, the Kierish should show more respect for their atheistic lords than the Hands of the Divinarch. The Salmoneys appeared to merit an entire street to themselves. It had been some time, traveling through the Middle Archipelago, since Gete had seen a family as affectionate as this appeared to be: their arms were constantly around each other, and when Lord Salmoney laughed, which was frequently, his voice rang out, coming through the window of the tea bar. The liveried servants did not stand stiffly behind the carriage, as Gete would have expected them to, but lounged around with the family. The fiancé picked a pale green flower from a tree overhanging the wall and offered it to the mother of his sweetheart.

The tea bar had gone uncannily silent. Everyone stared at the Salmoneys. Thani looked as if she were staring, too, but he knew from long experience that she was concentrating. "Describe it to me, Gete," she hissed.

And the Hands appeared out of the air, one after another, like a life-size magic trick, and surrounded the Salmoneys and their servants where they stood, shoving the suitor away from the wall, shouldering all eight or nine humans into a tight, frightened pack. Confusion roiled for a moment as the servants were subdued. The Hands' voices belled out and their knives glimmered in the sullen twilight. "In the name of the Divinarch, I arrest you . . ."

"That's it," someone inside the tea bar muttered, and everyone sagged. Wine and tea was slurped.

"Knew they couldn't last much longer."

"They knew it too. Look at them."

A man near Thani and Gete made a righteous show of spitting on the floor. "But they're scared, aren't they? Scared as sheep."

The Hands postured around the little bunch of prisoners. Six of them, all different in face and form, their variations minimized by the loose, bright uniforms they all wore. The greenish-black-skinned one who had gone into the mansion earlier was rolling off what sounded like a list of charges, knife held high over Lord Salmoney's head, like a statue in a battle-ready pose.

No one inside the tea bar was even trying to hear. They were complaining in low, half-guilty voices about the catastrophic blow that the commandeering of the Salmoney estates would deal to K'Fier's merchants. "Bought half the cloth my man weaves, they did!" said one woman.

"Rab the china shop's gonna have to close up a cause a this, you mark me."

"What about the men in their employ? How many of them d'you think the Hands will take?"

Only Thani was silent, trembling. "*Gete,*" she hissed, plucking at him, "*there are more!*"

Gete twisted in his seat, staring at the arrest. What was she talking about? Nothing had changed.

Then the dull, regular harmony of the Hands' litany was altered, shattered, by voices in a new counterpoint. More gods popped out of nowhere, exclaiming with indignation. From their expensive tasseled and piped clothes, and their outrage, Gete could tell they were on the side of the humans.

The argument was fast and loud. It might have been in another language for all he understood—it probably *was.* He deduced what was happening only by the behavior of the humans. Outside, the Salmoneys had got behind their dog carriage. He glimpsed them furtively helping each other over the wall into the garden. Inside, for the first time the customers of the tea bar were showing real alarm. Many had filtered out the back exit, and the rest cowered against the wall, as far as possible from the windows and the door. Lady Tea crouched behind the counter, only her eyes showing, froglike, emitting helpless little bleats of protest. Belatedly, Gete grabbed Thani and hustled her away with the rest. His voice flowed along smoothly, almost without his help, describing the scene. Thani's brow furrowed as she concentrated on his every word. He was her only link, her lifeline.

All the Salmoneys, men, women, and servants, had vanished into the greenery. None of their captors seemed to have noticed. In ones and twos, more renegade gods stumbled out of the house, clustering behind their leader. There was something dangerous in the air, an uncontrolled aspect to the confrontation, a volatility. *"Gods,"* a man next to Gete breathed. "They're legless, every man jack of them."

That was it. The man chewed his fingers, muttering, "I *told* Ruth he ought not to supply their smokewort for free. Gods or no gods, it's nothing but a temptation to excess. Now look what's happening. I told him. I *told—*"

"Smokewort?" Thani barked.

The man jumped like a startled rabbit. "Local specialty, Godsister! The gods can hold their wort better than any man alive, but even they have limits, may they forgive me for my impertinence." He touched his forehead and added piously, "Divinarch keep them! And forgive my misguided brother!"

"The gods are their own masters, Godsman," Thani said. "Anyone flatters himself who thinks he can corrupt them." She sounded both angry and afraid. The glass in the windows shook as the blue-skinned god shouted with unintelligible passion at the greenish-black-skinned hunchback. When the Hand did not react, the blue-skinned god shoved him in the chest and turned away, spurning the dispute—and behind him, the hunchback slid slowly into his fellows' arms, white blood spreading down his scarlet shirt. The renegade grinned at his fellows, exposing his back to the Hands, quite deliberately Gete thought, in a show of contempt. A wet stiletto gleamed between his fingers. He twirled it, showing it off.

A girl's scream spiraled from the undergrowth, a delayed reaction to the stabbing. As if in response, the renegade raised his eyebrows and opened his mouth. Gracefully, he knelt, dropping his face to the cobblestones. A tooth-tipped crescent knife had filleted him like a fish, laying him open from shoulder to sternum. The dogs whined, tossing their heads.

Gete did not see much of what happened after that. His eyes refused to show him gods fighting and killing each other, any more than his tongue would describe the carnage. All he could tell Thani, rather uselessly, was that although gods on both sides were falling at a horrible rate, the number of combatants seemed to be growing. Soon he saw why. The Salmoneys had emerged from hiding and seized knives from the dead to defend their allies, the renegades. People poured out of the shops and houses on both sides of the street, turning the combat into a free-for-all, crowding to get near the Hands and work out old grievances.

The Hands were fatally outnumbered. Yet as far as Gete could see, only one of them lost courage and *teth¨d.* The rest fought, and died. In a very short time, the remaining renegades stood alone in the street, dripping, their faces twitching with the first twinges of sobriety.

The humans, nobles and commoners alike, were falling away from the edges of the melee, disappearing into doorways and side streets. All the bodies, too, were gone, carried off by relatives or worshippers. The lack of set dressing gave the street a dreamlike feel, as if the massacre had not really happened. The dogs and dog carriage had disappeared too. Kierish were as much opportunists as anyone.

A cold wind blew into the tea bar. The doors swung creaking on their hinges. Except for Lady Tea, gibbering behind her pastries, Gete and Thani were alone: sequestered from the scene, just as they were sequestered from all the lives they passed through. Gete did not feel they were in any danger. The renegades, four of them now, stood empty-handed, looking stunned.

"Forgive them for their sins," Thani said at last. Her voice wavered. "Gods—gods?" She made a noise like laughter. "*Someone* forgive them for what they have done here! I see . . . I see . . ." She gulped. "They have started more than they have ended. Death . . . more death . . . and dis-illusionment—"

"Kierish are going to come looking for you in a minute," Gete said. It seemed to bring her back down to earth. "A good many of them were wounded."

"Well, they will have to look elsewhere." Her salt crystals seemed to glow for a minute, then she sagged against him. Her temples pulsed under the fur. "This is all I can do. I hope they will forgive me."

Outside, thunder growled, and an icy winter rain teemed out of the sky, hissing on the cobbles, slicking down the gods' hair. The blood was soon gone from the street, the gutter cloudy only with dirt as it chuckled down toward the wharves.

She would not allow him to unravel the knots her rain-miracle had embedded in her hair. Late at night, she sat naked on the window seat of the room the Cornwells had given them, alternately picking at her hair and sinking into immobility. Gete could see her attempts were doomed. Her hair had grown longer. He would have to cut some of the tangles off, if she would only let him.

The brazier at the foot of the bed burned like a miniature furnace. A crucible of scented water was attached to the top of its frame: the water steamed constantly, just off the boil. Condensation ran down the slick folds of the curtains and the bed canopies. Outside, the stairs creaked, and whispering voices passed the door in the blackness. The Cornwells were going to bed. "I can't manage," Thani said at last, in a high, strangled voice. "Come here, leman. I need you." Then she jerked her legs up and hid her face in her knees and began to sob.

Looking at her starved, bruised body, with its pale fur sticking up in whorls, Gete felt impatient. Who did she think she was, to command him? *She's your flamen, you son of a turtle!*

But his loyalty was sorely strained. The Kierish who'd been involved in the massacre had sidled up to ask for her help, both men and gods, asking her to heal them—and he had had to refuse for her, over and over. Later, her silence had given way to rudeness directed at the bewildered Cornwells. More than once, during the lavish dinner the family had laid on for their guests, Gete had wanted to apologize for her—or crawl under the table himself. Had she been doing it deliberately, out of evenhandedness? Or just out of blind self-absorption?

He'd never known her so sharp-tongued and edgy. What could be wrong?

Then, suddenly, he *did* know.

Horror froze him. He shivered in the hot room.

You've lost faith, haven't you, Thani? You've lost that deep-down faith you never questioned before, not even when Transcendence died. I felt it coming when you told me you had questioned Red Picarge! I should have understood earlier! Ever since we saw the gods killing each other, you've been wandering on a strange island populated by strange beasts. No wonder you made defensive noises when we tried to approach you.

"Gods!" He darted to her, hugging her, kissing her. What could he do? How could he help her now? "I shouldn't have let you sit through dinner! I should have made excuses! I should have—"

"Gete," she said in a choked voice, "oh, Gete. Help me. Convince me that . . ." Her words were lost in tears. But he heard a difference. The rage was gone from her voice. All that was left was a terrible sadness. The urge to protect her swelled in him, like a lump in the throat all over his body, and he carried her to the bed.

After the first few minutes, she responded with violent passion. It was what she needed.

It felt good to be naked in the hot, damp room. They lay side by side on top of the coverlet. She tucked her head into the hollow between his arm and shoulder. "How are you feeling?" Gete whispered. "Are you more . . . comfortable now?"

She kissed his underarm. "You always make me feel better. You know that."

So another piece of her sight was gone.

"What about the Salmoneys? What d'you think'll become of them?"

"Oh, we need not trouble over that," she said comfortably. "A larger, better destined delegation of Hands will be dispatched to take care of them. The Divinarch will not let them get away with any more insubordination such as we witnessed today." She wriggled against his side. "They are unworthy of our attention."

"Do you remember what *really* happened?" Gete said, rather recklessly. "How the Hands arrested them without provocation, and how they died? Or is there a process in your mind that alters your memories to fit in with your idea of proper, pious behavior?"

For a moment she went quite still. Then she shook herself and said, "Do stop. I'm tired. And we have to get up early tomorrow to find a ship to Delta City."

He said no more. But he felt a sense of victory. He would humor her. The matter had yet to be resolved; perhaps Delta City held the answers. Perhaps there, he would find a god willing to answer the questions he had not asked since he last saw Desti. (Qalma seemed very far off now. Soon it would be even farther.) Delta City. He grimaced with distaste. K'Fier had sickened him. How much more deprived of joy must the world's greatest city be? How much uglier? How much filthier?

And to think he had once rejoiced—so naively—at the thought of going there!

He concentrated on stillness. Don't move a muscle. Don't disturb her.

Gradually, dizzily, he melted into the featherbed, spinning slowly around and around. Thani's body nestled close to his. She was asleep. The condensation coated the insides of his lungs.

BETRAYAL

Arity took a salt grape from the miniature tree on the tray beside him and crossed one ankle over his knee, trying to get comfortable. He hated these jewel-inlaid chairs. The walls of the royal anteroom were lined with ghosts—as if an invisible audience were witnessing every word they spoke. The ghosts of *auchresh*, Pati's previous lovers. Dreadfully morbid.

Pati himself was not sitting on gold and tourmalines. He curled in his special leather armchair, legs tucked under him, like a gangly child. His fingers were steepled before his nose and his different-colored eyes shone. "So where did Hope take you? All Mosquito Ruby told me was that she appeared wearing a dress from the depraved times and commanded you to come." His tone became a mixture of accusation and hurt—"And you went with her voluntarily."

"I went with her because she used to be a friend of ours," Arity said. "But apart from that—" He felt delighted that Pati had worried so much about his whereabouts that he had covered him with kisses instead of demanding to hear his story right away. When his return was announced, the Divinarch had been in an unscheduled Ellipse meeting, but he had dismissed the Hands and flamens who constituted the other twenty twenty-firsts of the Ellipse and swooped on Arity, who was loitering with his heart in his mouth in the royal suite.

"She *teth*'d me to Temeriton." Arity plucked another grape and spit the seeds into his palm. They were exactly the same color as the razor-smooth circles in the hollows of his body that would grow into thorns if he let them. He deposited them in the corner of the tray. "We climbed to the top of a six-story town house. Hope promised me I would thank her for having brought me."

"I confess I'm lost. She didn't steal you just to make me tear my hair out. So why?"

"Well, you'll never guess who I met." Never mind the formalities. Arity had no patience for them. His heart was pounding. "An old enemy of ours."

Pati's smile went as hard and cold as frozen fish. Slowly, his fingers slid together until his hands were locked into one oversized fist. To himself, he murmured, "I should have known she wouldn't die so easily. I do not think she has ever given up a fight in her life."

Arity gaped, deprived of his revelation. Pati obviously knew who they were talking about. But why should he have guessed so readily!

"She's not fighting anymore!" Arity said. "She's blind. Your poison blinded her. She'd be better off dead. I just thought you might find it amusing to hear what she has come to."

The fingers worked. "I find it highly disturbing. I hope you memorized the location of the house. We shall have to surround it. If she's blind, she'll smell any *teth "ing*, so we'll approach on foot. I should think twenty Hands will be enough." He paused. "Hope knew where she was. They're probably all in it together. How far can the rot extend? Humi is blind . . . She drank every drop that was in the glass. Either she has the constitution of a sharque, or it was a miracle. Before she dies, I hope I can extract the name of the Godsbrother or Godsister who did it from her. I will toast them over a furnace. But in any case, it means Hope is the ringleader. I shouldn't have let that cursed *iu* have the run of the city! Dammit!" Pati pounded the arm of the chair—a wildly uncharacteristic gesture that showed Arity just how shaken he was. His wineglass fell off and rolled onto the floor, bleeding maroon into the runnels between the floor slabs. "How am I going to pin them down?" He looked at Arity again. "Tonight the Hands gave me reports of unrest in several foreign cities. I had thought I would concentrate my forces abroad. I've ordered a slew of arrests. Now I find I must turn my attention closer to home!"

Arity did not answer. Pati stopped and peered at him more closely. Then he gave a rather crooked smile. "You see what an impossible task mine is. One day, you will thank me that I groomed you for the Throne."

"When I was younger, I was prepared to take the Throne, even if it wasn't a position I particularly relished," Arity said. "Now things have changed. I've changed." The inevitable consequences of his betraying her—he must have known this would happen—He barked, "Don't kill her!" and his voice sounded to him not desperate but menacing.

Pati peered at him, his eyes hooded and vaguely red. "Are you trying to blackmail me?"

And once Pati had said it, Arity knew that was exactly what had been in the back of his mind. The contorted, terrible faces of the ghosts spun around him like a circle of silently jeering onlookers. They goaded him into speech. "I will not be Heir."

Pati stared at him. "You're not . . . You're in it, too. With her. Did you go to see her because—Was it planned? What trickery is this?"

"Power! That was not, not, *not* what I meant! I wouldn't have anything to do with their sordid little plot if they paid me!"

But Pati had got hold of something now. His beaked face advanced toward Arity, swimming in the dimly candlelit air the way it had rippled in the night on top of the Temeriton town house. "You love her. That's it, isn't it. You'd do things for love that you wouldn't do for status. You weakling."

Arity shrank into his chair. A moment ago he had been ready to stand up to Pati even at the cost of bearing his anger. Now, fear hollowed him out like a cold wind in his belly. His limbs went to quicksalt. Pati's wings buzzed, making rainbows out of the candle flames.

"You've always loved her. You little liar."

"Have sense, Pati! Would I have betrayed her to you if I still cared for her?"

"I don't know what your plan was. But there are certain things I can read as clearly as the look on your face!"

"I don't love her. I have no feelings whatsoever toward her. She's as redundant to me as she is to you."

But the wind blew keen and hollow in him, smelling of salt. He was in the wrong, he was lying, and Pati knew it.

And Pati was all he had now. Humi had thrust him away. *He's Pati's plaything. I have nothing to say to him. And Arity and I understand that the past is the past* . . . The past was the past! The present was Pati! For the same reason he had clung to Pati ever since Rimmear, he had to cling to him now.

"I *love* you." He seized Pati's hands off the armrests of his chair, kissing them. "You're all there is for me!" If he went on in this vein a little longer, ecstasy would come. Even now he could feel himself starting to shake. A branch of the miniature grape tree showed in sharp silhouette on one of the haloed candle flames. "I *love* you—"

"Liar." Pati wrenched his hands away, one thumbnail scoring Arity's upper lip. Arity tasted blood.

Patience. His whole body quivered. "She means nothing to me. I'll prove it. I'll show you the house tonight. We'll *teth* to the roof where I talked to her, and you'll identify the street, and we'll go back in the morning with troops."

Knuckles rattled on the door, and a Hand burst in without waiting to be asked. His step faltered when he saw the overturned wineglass and the blood on Arity's face, but then he blurted, "Lord Divinarch! In K'Fier! Five Hands killed!"

The atmosphere ebbed out of the antechamber like water flowing out of a lock. Arity took a breath.

"Is that anything unprecedented, Vori? Calm down." Arity never ceased to be astonished by Pati's theatrical ability. Pati's face smoothened. His voice was flowing olive oil. "We won't learn who did it. There are never any witnesses. The humans will say the Hands were struck by lightning."

"But lord Divinarch, this time it's different! One of them fled when he saw there was no hope. He *teth*¨*d* back here. *They* did it—the r-r—" The Hand's voice failed him, and he gulped. "The renegades."

In the ensuing pause Arity heard the sea growl, far below, as if it could not abide all the fights and acrimonious accusations it was forced to witness.

Even before Pati's rise to the Throne, Arity had known it would come to this sometime. With the *auchresh* race polarizing into *wrchrethrim* and *salthirre*, it had had to come to this. *Auchresh* killing *auchresh*. Cause for instant execution in any Heaven.

Pati said, "I grant them anonymity and they kill my Hands! Are they trying to force me to respond to their subversive activities? How? They are the *serbalim's* responsibility, not mine. Where is—" He broke off. Too softly for Vori to hear, he whispered, "Where is my liaison with the *serbalim*? Plotting against me." Arity winced. Pati raised his voice. "Where is the *kere* who returned?"

"He—he's wounded. Delirious." Vori hopped up and down with urgency. "Lord Divinarch, with due respect, the Hands ask me to convey a request to you! They want permission to kill the *haugthules!*"

"Fire-bellied young *mainrauim*. Deny them it. Get me Sepia. Get me Glass Mountain. Get Silver Moon. Get Val." Arity cringed. These particular *keres*, the *ex-kervayim*, made him feel weak and ashamed. Their calm authoritarianism masked elitism, and a fiery devotion to Pati. The other Hands were far more tolerant of Arity's status as Pati's lover. *But what am I now? He won't just let it drop.* The invasion of outside concerns seemed annoying, superficial, like a wrong note in a song. *I've never seen him this angry.*

The *kervayim teth*¨*d* into the anteroom, knocking over the side table that held the miniature grape tree. A tumble of silk-clad limbs seemed to bulge out of the room. None of them took seats.

"I beg you, Pati, let us punish them!"

"We've pretended we don't know what's going on in the Archipelago long enough. And it's not just the Archipelago, either," Val said. "Although these K'Fierish fops are the worst of the bunch. If they weren't ready for a nasty surprise a year ago, they really *are* stupid."

"In my view," Glass Mountain rumbled, "it would be as well to crush them before this happens again."

Pati gazed at them in what could have been surprise. "So it is to be a diplomatic embassy, my councillors," he said ironically, and one side of his mouth curled. "I approve."

"Their very existence thumbs its nose at your divinity." Silver Moon watched Pati's face avidly for signs of approval. "And everywhere they go, they spread atheism of a far more subversive stamp than Antiprophet's. They are a threat to your godhead."

"Yes." Pati said. "I am with you there."

"They must die!"

"We will treat them like any other blasphemers!"

"We'll crush them," Val said, shaking back his sleeve, "like this," and he slowly closed his fist. There was laughter.

"Have any of you thought about what you're doing?" Arity said, standing. "*Auchresh* killing *auchresh.*There's no precedent for it. And do you know why?" They were all staring at him. "Because it's *suicide* for our race. Suicide! We can't *afford* to kill each other, when the humans are doing it for us every day!"

"Well, well," Val said. "Loverboy has turned military authority."

The buzz of talk continued as if nothing had been said. Could they let that *pass?*

I was Heir! I was leagues above all of you! Have I sunk so low in your esteem that you insult me as you please?

A voice cut through the noise. Arity's heart leaped, but it was only Coiled Rainbow. "As for a precedent, Arity," he said pityingly, "there is a very clear one. *They* started the killing, late this afternoon."

"Yes," Val said. "They started it. Are you disposed to argue with the facts?"

Pati was talking to Glass Mountain. He did not look at Arity.

The room was loud with plans. A hundred Hands were to go. No, a dozen. No, two hundred. Fists. New recruits. The councillors would go themselves. No, they shouldn't. The Divinarch ought not, with all respects, to go either.

"I shall go," Pati said. "But none of you will. Together, you are as valuable as I am. In the event of my death, you are needed here."

All Arity heard was that the *ex-kervayim* were not going to go, and Pati was. Perhaps he could somehow prove himself to Pati! He raised his voice. "Count me in. I'll go."

Pati swung around. His gaze was like a crack of sky glimpsed from the bottom of a shaft: too bright to bear.

"You. I'd forgotten you were there."

Oh, no, you hadn't. Arity's breath came slowly, painfully, as if the air were sand. He felt himself bending at the knees.

"Sepia." Pati beckoned with one finger, still staring at Arity.

"This . . . traitor." Pati pointed. Arity didn't understand. He felt as though he were drowning. "Take him to Westpoint. Immediately, if you please. I do not want him to escape. I do not want him here when I return from crushing the upstarts."

For one moment their reaction deafened Arity. He nearly blacked out. Then Pati turned furiously on them.

And *lesh kervayim*, that cabal of smoke-stained *wrchrethrim* who had matched their steps with the Striver's on the long march from the salt, taken responsibility for gathering his army of Hands, and now counted themselves privileged to look down their noses at each other: *khath* and *morothe* addicts, as possessive of their gem-encrusted suites in the Palace as they had once been of their lovers: these golden *mainrauim* whom long exposure to each other's company had rendered as alike as deformed fledglings in a lair fell silent at the sight of their Divinarch's face.

Sepia took hold of Arity's arm.

Then he understood.

GOOD-BYE TO THE LAKESTONES

Humi threw her belongings blindly into a bag made of the Hangman's robe. She wrapped her ghosts in her clothes and packed the chinks with the few ornaments and jewels Ziniquel and Ensi had brought her, things from her old life. "Help me with this," she said to the Hangman, and together they dragged the dray dog ghost out from under the bed and stood it on its feet. It filled most of the floor space.

Humi heard the Hangman sucking her fingers to warm them up. "Could *never* of weighed that much when it was alive. My hands're frostbitten! There must be seven ghosts in that bag! You gonna be able to carry it?"

"Of course," Humi whispered, and hefted the knotted robe over her shoulder. She heard the fabric straining and put it down quickly. It was even odds whether her shoulder or the robe would have broken first.

In the end she only took one ghost. The seagull, the last one she had completed. The rest they arranged on the bed, mice and rats and cats and birds all perched on top of each other. "Are they painted?" the Hangman said as they stood back. "No? *Really?* I am something of a connoisseur, milady, but I have not seen this technique before. I am absorbed."

Humi did not intend to show the Hangman how little impact her flattery made. She said, "I'm leaving them for the Lakestones, in partial payment of the debt I owe them. But when I am in a position to make more"—she smiled; the Hangman had moved out into the children's bedroom and Humi lowered her voice so as not to wake Meri and Ensi—"I shall craft you one of my best."

"Ulp," the Hangman said. A second later, Humi felt another presence. From the warmth, and the silence with which he had approached, she knew it was Hem.

"You are leaving us," he stated.

"Hem"—she moved toward him—"I was going to wake you." But she had judged the distance wrong, and she fetched up without warning against his broad warm chest. His heartbeat muffled through his flannel nightshirt. It took a huge effort not to lay her cheek on his chest. She stepped away. "You must eradicate every sign that I was here. The Divinarch will search the house tomorrow. If I were you I'd get the children out on some pretext, just to be quite safe. But if there's nothing to implicate you, you won't need to worry." *Beyond Ari's word.* She swallowed. "I've left some ghosts for you."

"Ghosts?" He seized her shoulders. "Humi, what have you been up to? I thought that you—"

"Hide them under that stack of junk in the cellar. I doubt even the Hands will look there. Then, in a month or so, you can sell them. You ought to get more than enough to cover the costs of anything the Hands may break in their search." The things were probably good enough for that, anyhow.

"One moment, Humi. Why are you leaving? Do you realize what we would have thought if we had woken and found you gone?"

"I told you. I was going to wake you!" For a minute, tears threatened as it all weighed down on her. Arity alive. Arity her enemy. It was all gone, their bond, the one thing in her life that she had thought change could not take from her. Now she no longer had even her memories. He had contaminated them. "I'm sorry," she said, her voice breaking.

"*Gods,*" the Hangman muttered in disgust.

Humi flung her head back. What was she thinking? Nothing had been taken from her but a burden. She was free.

"To cut a long story short," she said, "one of the Hands has found out where I am. He used to be a friend of mine and he tried to convince me that he would not betray me—but he has forgotten how well I know him. I could hear in his voice that he was lying. I played along so that he would not suspect I knew, hoping to earn more time to get away. But I don't know how well I succeeded. They may be here any minute."

Hem was silent for a minute. When he spoke, he asked only: "How did . . . this Hand . . . find out where you were?"

"It was Hope's idea." Humi winced as she remembered the Maiden's tears of anger. It was the first time she had ever heard Hope cry. For *her* sake, she wished the encounter had been a success. "She was here too. I hope she does not suffer on my account."

"I cannot think of anything more foolhardy she could have done," the Hangman said waspishly. "Everyone knows Ar—"

Humi interrupted her before Hem could hear the name. "That is all, I think. The ghosts are there. Give my love to Leasa and the children." Their even breathing came from the beds behind her. It was astonishing how soundly children could sleep. Turning, she made her way to the heads of the beds and dropped light kisses on their hair. "Don't forget to take down the partition," she reminded Hem. She thought he understood without her telling him, that if she ever returned, it would not be in her old capacity as child minder and occasional seamstress. "You don't want even the suggestion that someone lived here."

"Your *room*," Hem said with unexpected feeling. "Ha. *Closet.* Humi, I have leased another room from the Brundels upstairs. One that receives the morning sun. We were going to give it to you for midwinter."

"Oh, Hem." *I'll kill myself if the Hands arrest you,* she thought.

"*Really,* milady!" the Hangman called. She was walking downstairs with deliberate emphasis on each step. "I think we should *leave* before the Hands arrest *us!*"

"I'll put the ghosts in the shop," Hem said. "Where better to hide them? And tomorrow morning, I'll send Meri to Tellury Crescent to warn Ziniquel that they must say they made them, if the Hands make inquiries. Or are *you* going to Tellury Crescent?" His voice was hesitant. She could tell he did not want to know anything dangerous.

"No." Her eyes stung. "I'm not." And she fled downstairs. As she pushed through the jingling door of the shop, her load bumped against her back. The seagull's cold came through its wrappings.

Nothing assailed Humi and the Hangman before they reached Shimorning, except a drizzle. As they made their way through the palace district, the damp stuck their clothes to their fur. Humi did not possess a cloak, or indeed anything heavier than the dress she wore. She had never needed one. This was the first time she had been off Lockreed Concourse in three years.

Yet despite the rain and the silence, and the Hangman's sharp nails digging into her palm, dragging her along to the place she had promised was safer than anywhere else on the island but which she would not describe, she was not afraid.

She felt alive. Alive.

She had forgotten how it felt.

The Hangman did her the favor of telling her when they came to the Folly, before she could become nervous at their deviation from the routes she remembered. "Your lady god friend tore down all five councillors' mansions to build her Folly. You have not seen it."

"No," Humi said. "Describe it to me."

"You are not a flamen, milady . . ."

"But you are at my command," Humi said mildly. "By the terms of the proposal you put to me earlier this evening, you are bound to obey me. Treachery will be punished."

She was gambling. The Hangman had *real* power over her.

"And are we bound by those terms, milady?"

"*You* are."

The Hangman did not answer. Had Humi won? Could the old Divinarch glamour still be working?

Earlier, she had been unnerved at the prospect of throwing in her lot with the Hangman and her scrofulous crowd. But now she could not see why she had hesitated. If the Hangman was not to be trusted—and if Humi could still control her—she would make all the better an ally. The temperamental hound often wins the race.

She knew what the Folly looked like, though Evita had not told her. She saw it floating above her, rising shadowy from the trees, though by now they had surely left it behind. Had Hope ever described it to her? It shimmered in her mind, half concept and half image, like a memory of Wind Gully Heaven. *Her* Folly. The image in her mind was probably very different from the building around whose park they scuttled on damp streets. But that did not matter. For the first time in months, she had imagined something new in terms of a visual image.

It fascinated her, both as a symbol and a solecism, wrenched from the salt to Delta City.

The noise of Shimorning stretched its tentacles out and gathered them in.

The blackness flickered with stars of gray. Humi tripped over her feet as they threaded a complex path along the gutter. Her wet clothes slapped against drunk pedestrians. Everyone seemed to know the Hangman, and hailed her loudly. She replied in a mumble, almost a grunt, as if she feared being caught out in an indiscretion. But no one else was so circumspect. It seemed as if the night freed tongues ordinarily guarded for fear of the Hands. And that made no sense, for the gods' traditional hunting time was the night. The world was upside-down.

People laughed freely here in a way they did not in Temeriton, Delta City's pulsing vein of shame. From the tones of the voices and the smells as Humi brushed past each person, she could tell how he or she had spent his night. She wanted to be out, too, drinking, making love, *doing.* How had she *lived?* She almost dragged at the Hangman's shirt and told her to stop, go into a tavern, accost one of the thousand Shimorningers she seemed to know and ask which dive was buzzing . . . but then Evita plunged down a side street, came to an abrupt halt, and said, "Here we are, milady." She scratched on a plank door with her fingernails.

"Our biggest problem, milady," Gold Dagger said, " 's that the tyrant knows you're alive. If it is as you say. 'Ow much time does that give us? Not much, I betcha. Not enough to get the troops together. We got to find some way to throw 'im off the scent."

"No one saw us coming here," the Hangman said. "I can guarantee that." Even without seeing their expressions, Humi could feel the tension between the crime lords. The Hangman was tense, like a cat walking on her neighbor's territory; Gold Dagger sounded even more jovial than usual. To distract them from each other, Humi made a production out of sipping her brandy. "*Exactly* how much Pati knows is unclear." They had put her in the best chair, but to them the best was the oldest: it was saggy, the jewels on the armrests scratched, and it smelled of mold.

"Everything depends on how strong a hold he has over Arity." Instinctively, she gritted her teeth, but the pain didn't come. She was free of the burden of loving him.

"You mean 'e might not 'ave ratted after all?" Gold Dagger said skeptically.

"Oh, no. I am quite convinced he did. What I mean is that he may not have thought to tell Pati about my incipient alliance with Evita. In which case, Pati will not scent danger beyond my survival, and provided that I can stay out of sight, we have as much time as we need."

"Well"—Gold Dagger cleared his throat skeptically—"I 'ave less faith in the Heir than you, milady. Betcha he told him everything 'e knew. Question is, 'ow much did 'e *hear?*"

"If I remember correctly, when he and Hope arrived, I was refusing Evita's offer." Better to forget that last, confused minute on the edge of the roof. That minute, anyhow, might have been what saved her from the grayish oblivion of the hollowness.

"Did they show themselves right off? Or was they there before?" Gold Dagger challenged the Hangman.

There was a short silence. Finally the Hangman said, "I have no idea."

"You're supposed to be—" Gold Dagger said, starting to froth with indignation, and stopped. A moment passed. Humi wished she could see their faces. Then Gold Dagger cleared his throat. She heard him removing his boots from the table with a precipitous clatter. "You *need* me, Hangman! Without me, you're nothin' but an assassin. It's through *me* you 'ave this chance to hit it big. It's *me* who owns half the men in this city. Not you,

Evita. If I'd gone straight, I could of been an atheist councillor. As it is, I have more power than any other mortal in this city."

Humi felt her blood heating. Without hesitating, for that would have been fatal, she reached for their hands. Gold's was patchy-furred, beringed, meaty; the Hangman's was a furry skeleton. Humi said, "Gold, I think you are in danger of forgetting that *you* need *me*. Without me, you and Evita will both sit quarreling underground until Pati has crushed the city, and you, to death."

Neither of them moved for a minute. Gold was the first to withdraw his hand. "Put us in our places properly, eh, Divinarch?" he said jovially.

The Hangman's fingers jerked, like half-dead things. Humi held on, not tightly, but firmly, so as not to let Gold Dagger see how the Hangman had reacted. *She* was the one who must win this contest. It was the first.

Through her teeth, the Hangman said, "You force me to recognize Gold's strength, Humi. There is no need to force me to recognize your leadership. It is not in question. Much joy I wish you of it."

"Never thought I'd hear it from you, Evvie," Gold Dagger said pleasedly. "After all these years."

Humi knew she could not push the Hangman any farther. Quickly, she took her hands off the table and folded them in her lap. "Now that we have *that* out of the way, let's get down to business. I do not think any of us disagree that what we must create is a war."

"I got the facilities for it," Gold Dagger said.

The air in the cave was ventilated only by the tiny fan in the roof, which drew air from fifty feet above. A child knelt by the wall, working its crank. The fruity scent of the Shimorning gutters wafted in with the air. The caves that constituted the Rats' Den, Gold Dagger had told Humi, immodest with pride, spread for a league under the streets and could be entered through a dozen different safe houses in Shimorning, Marshtown, and Christon. They housed an army of criminals, all nominally loyal to Gold, always in flux, about whom Humi had known nothing in all her time as Ellipse councillor and Divinarch. If she had not been reasonably sure of Gold and the Hangman at this point, she would have been distinctly worried about whatever else they must be concealing.

Evita was a jealous woman, and dangerous. But the understanding between the underworld and the atheists, the agreement that when the conspiracy seized the throne from the Divinarch, it would be the crime lords who provided the necessary muscle and who in return would receive pardons and titles from the new regime, dated back to the days of Erene, Goquisite, and Belstem, and Humi intended to honor it. All that had kept her from seeking Gold Dagger and the Hangman out and convincing them to fulfill their side of the bargain before was fear. They had real power: all they lacked was a guiding hand. In Temeriton (it always seemed years ago) their visits had filled her with repugnance and a dread of illness—physical and otherwise. Now she relished the stink of gutters, and the smell of hot steel. Somebody was working at a forge. The rock walls and plush door curtain of the chamber reduced the sound of hammering to a tinkle, as of water, but Humi was privileged with the blind woman's comprehension of sounds that are just background noise to the sighted. She had that advantage over Gold Dagger and the Hangman, slender though it might be.

As they debated the technicalities of various weapons, and estimated the numbers of troops each crime lord could rely on, the cave took on the feel of a council room, tense and serious.

Someone thumped a steel-butted spear on the rock outside the door. It was so sharp a sound even the fan child squeaked.

"Who the fuck is it?" Gold Dagger thundered in annoyance.

"Get out of my way, gutterspawn," Humi heard, and the curtain swished aside.

She knew that voice. She could not keep from smiling as she shoved her chair back and hurried to the entrance. "Mory!"

Her *imrchu* whom she had thought gone forever. Mory's familiar grip on Humi's wrists sent dizzying thrills of gladness through her. With difficulty, she kept from casting herself into Mory's arms. "Who else is here?"

"I am," Tris said, in a deeper, more confident voice than Humi remembered from the days when the Calvarese boy had been the youngest Ellipse councillor. She exclaimed with delight. He embraced her, kissed her on both cheeks. He smelled of fish scales—a scent belonging to dawn, when the night fishermen returned to Marshtown's jetties with their catch tanks full—and he was taller and better muscled than he had been three years ago.

Mory Carmine and Trisizim Sepal; the least politically active of the ghostiers. Humi had always suspected that the only reason they had been present in Godsbrother Puritanism's parlor when Goquisite and Belstem forced her to resign her throne was because the rest of the ghostiers had all agreed to join the denunciation. Only because Mory and Tris were committed to tradition, determined that the ghostiers should present a unified front to the world, had they been there when Pati and his rabid band of *auchresh* burst in and massacred atheists and flamens alike.

She had always assumed that after that, Mory and Tris had gone underground, out of communication. Ziniquel and Emni had never hinted anything to the contrary.

"What're you doing here?" Gold Dagger said possessively to Mory from behind Humi. She could feel distrust radiating off him. But he did not sound surprised to see Mory and Tris. There was so much Humi did not know!

"And who is *this* you have brought?" the Hangman hissed, apparently in reference to someone else who had come in. "One of your apostate flamen friends, who think that they walk in the light and me and mine walk in the gutter? We are discussing war here, Godsie Carmine! What good will your friends' miracles do when Pati's flamens are prepared to kill and maim for *their* cause?"

It had not been Humi's impression that the apostates were above using their divine powers to kill, but she held her tongue.

"We would not insult our flamen friends by *asking* them to come here with us," Mory said in her prickliest manner. "The Godsbrother *volunteered* to accompany us because he is aware, as you do not seem to be, that we must put aside our personal biases if we are to have any chance against the tyrant." Mory was clearly on her mettle, here in enemy territory. She gave Humi's hand a quick squeeze as she joined it with a stranger's. "Humi, this is Godsbrother Phantasm and his leman Avari, here."

"I am, as Mory has said, the delegate from the apostate brotherhood," the Godsbrother said in a pleasant voice with a refined Deltan accent. "I come to offer the services of all Marshtown apostates to the true Divinarch. We support her bid for the Throne, and conjoin with her in secrecy."

Gold Dagger whistled, and laughed softly. "News travels fast!"

But Humi had no ears for him. Gold was more or less a known quantity; he could wait. In her best diplomatic manner she greeted Godsbrother Phantasm, and exerting all the charm she had at her disposal she thanked him and accepted his offer.

Later, when the council finally broke up, she left the chamber arm in arm with Mory and Tris. Both at once, they offered her bits and pieces of information about their life since the coup. Fleeing, hiding, pondering, and always, always making ghosts. Juniper and sand and metal tanged in Humi's nostrils: a whiff of the desert. It made no sense, since according to Mory and Tris, they had not been back to Calvary, but she knew it. It was the stink of fanaticism. It was quite clear Mory would have liked to be a flamen. Tris had been considering apostate lemanhood before he grew too old. Nowadays, both of them devoted their days to their art, turning out dark propaganda for their new faith, the worship of no gods.

IN THE SEA GARDEN

Morning sunlight soaked into the floor of Hope's dressing room in the Folly. The glass wall had been swung open and the tall herbs on the balcony glowed green. The scent of thyme breezed into the dressing room, carried by the breeze that caressed the roofs of the city. Far off, Hope could hear the first bells of Dividay tinkling. It was one of those rare, perfect winter days like a diamond.

With quick, frustrated movements, she dried herself off. Her eyes hurt from the perfumes in the swimming pool. Her fingers and toes were spongy, like a human's. She flapped her wings and water shot off, making dark pinpricks on the wall drapes.

She had failed to break the weather. But was that surprising? Could one person, even if she was an *auchresh,* call lightning out of an empty sky? She had only generated energy in herself. And it was the energy of frustration.

Together Arity and Humi, the insider and the outsider, could have tied the city in knots. There *could* have been a revolution. Together they had always been radiant, whether they were decried as a scandal or praised as the rising stars in an unstable court. Together, they canceled out each other's tendencies to self-destruction. Apart, neither of them was completely human.

Human?

"Damned *wrchrethru!*" Hope shook her head.

Drawing a deep breath, she dropped the towel. The chill wind rustled the herbs. Goosebumps roughened her limbs. She pulled on her clothes, a ratty pair of breeches and a shirt Ders had given her before she destroyed him. It had a panel of red-and-blue Veretrean embroidery down the front. Picking up her knife belt and her hairbrush, she opened her mouth to call for her servants, but before she could speak, the air at the other end of the room burst into huge blue polka dots. Eight Hands thumped onto her floor.

Two of them looked as though they had been in a fight; the rest appeared to be spoiling for one. The door slammed against the wall and several of her footmen pounded in, yanking gold-trimmed coshes from their belts.

She held up one hand. They fell to a halt, snorting like bulls. In a gesture of pacifism, she dropped her knife belt on the floor, and smiled at the leading Hand. He had been one of the youngest of *lesh kervayim* back when she was Pati's lover. She couldn't remember his name. "What does Pati want of me, my friends? I don't think I've done anything ungodly enough to get myself arrested." She chuckled at her own lie. "Surely he has not quarreled with the *serbalim* again? I won't help him, you know."

"It's worse than that, milady Hope," the Hand said in *auchraug*. She started. They never spoke in *auchraug;* too much of their business was with things for which it had no words. Then she realized it was so her footmen could not understand. She waved them out of the room. The door closed.

"Now," she said in the mortal tongue. "What has happened?"

"We have no time to put it pleasantly," one of the battle-stained Hands said. It was then she noticed one of his rudimentary wings had been sliced completely off. A bandage covered the stump. "We are at war with the renegades. Pati requests your presence in an advisory capacity."

War, she thought. Her mind tumbled over itself with questions. She said only, "You do not mean those silly Foundlings people are talking about who have decided they belong in human country!" *War?* She had never taken them seriously. She'd attributed most of what she heard about them to rumor. Could she really have been so far off the mark?

"Not silly, milady. Not Foundlings." The first Hand held up his arm to stop her interrupting. "Pati demands to see you."

They had spread into a semicircle in front of her. She felt just a little frightened. She was no human, trapped by her surroundings, but perhaps she'd spent too long in human company, for she was keenly aware of the fragile panels of glass behind her and the two-hundred-foot drop. "What is the *er-serbalim's* position?" she asked, to gain time.

"Milady, we do not yet know." They closed in tighter. "Pati demands your presence in the Sea Garden. Your counsel is valuable to him."

"My counsel . . ." Pati had never been short on stratagems. And what did *she* know about war? She did not trust Pati as far as she could fly. This all sounded too outrageous to be true. Impossible that something should have broken at last! She wouldn't put it past him to have invented it just to get her where he wanted her. Suppose—just *suppose* he had found out about last night? She might finally have outlasted her *iu* immunity.

But maybe it *was* true. The Hands were wounded. She did not think even Pati would take set dressing to such extremes. They jostled closer again. They were going to grab her so that she would not be able to *teth¨* without taking one of them with her.

Pati wanted her under guard.

The Power-damned *haugthirre!*

"I may meet with Pati of my own free will. But he is stupider than one perceives if he believes he can *intimidate* me—or trap me." As their talons shot out to grab her arm, she *teth¨d*. The destination locked into her mind, a crystal image, instantaneously re-anchoring her in reality. The Hands would think she had *teth¨d* far away. She would outfox them.

He was sitting on a ledge in the hollowed-out wall of the Sea Garden, waiting for her. They had spoken truth there, anyhow. He did not seem surprised to see her alone. He smiled and beckoned her to sit down. There were too many teeth in his smile. She realized *she* had been outfoxed: he had reasoned one step further ahead than she, banking on her desire to know the truth. "Oh, you misbegotten old *kuiros*, Pati!" she said, going toward him. Both he and the salt trees looked as though they had been painted with frost. He was wounded on the face: the scabbed blood was the same dull white as the salt shrubs in the Garden.

"They could never satisfy me for long," he says. Speaking of himself, his voice is ironic. Waves lap against the cliffs below. The smell of the water is gamy and bracing. Listening to him, Hope thinks she can see all the way out to sea, all the way over the vague blue horizon, past Domesdys, to the ocean that stretches around the world, featureless and populated by strange slow-moving creatures. "I would use them for a little while, and then use Sol Southwind, the ghostier if you remember, to dispose of them. He thinks it is a mark of favor. I wonder if he sees the filth on his hands." He laughs, but it is not quite a real laugh.

"So you sent Arity the way of the others," Hope says softly. "Out of jealousy. Oh, Pati." Under the sententiousness and the self-flagellation there is something deeper. She wants to hug him—his power is such that he has actually made her feel sorry for him—but the scent of the salt enhances her common sense as well as her compassion. Over their heads, the white hyroses whisper in the breeze snaking down between the high rock walls.

"He was just the same as the others. I thought he would be different, but he was the same. Like them, he wanted to hate me. But he couldn't. Maybe that was why I had him killed." His lip twists.

"That's your curse, isn't it? People always care for you. Hate or love, it doesn't really matter. They rip themselves to shreds over you. But I'm not going to do that. Power knows I'm still fascinated with you. I wouldn't have

come, otherwise. But I won't let you destroy me. There needs to be some-
body who refuses to throw herself at your feet."

"I know I need you," Pati says softly. "To protect me from the one other
who won't throw herself down for me. You know who I mean."

The sea makes a glopping splash, as if it is trying to reach them. Hope
experiences a sense of hopelessness. She wants to cry, but not for Arity. That
is too great a blow; it hasn't yet sunk in. She wants to cry for the city, this
dear doomed city poised precariously on an island too small to bear its
weight.

The sun rose high in the sky while they sat in the rock bower. The war
played out fast as a topic of conversation. Pati had been wounded in K'Fier,
it seemed, in an action to destroy the renegades affiliated with a family
called Salmoney, who had killed five Hands the day before. It was all
retaliation, up to that point. But now Pati proposed to turn retaliation into a
full-scale offensive. He had deployed all the Hands he could spare, both out
of the Delta City forces and out of the continental guards, to kill all the
renegades in the world, wherever they could be found. To Hope, this
seemed shortsighted and rash. When did fury ever translate into good
politics? But she knew the hopelessness of trying to talk him out of it. One
thing Pati *never* did was back down. "We must not allow the spread of
atheism," he said—obtusely: weren't they talking about *gods*? "I understand now that I was wrong to concentrate on the cities. It is the country
communities that rest on the edges of our Divinarchy. As such, they are in
the most danger from untoward influences."

"But, Pati," Hope said, feeling that she was banging her head against a
wall, "you're killing *auchresh*. As far as the common people know, these
untoward influences are *gods!* Doesn't destroying them destroy the people's
trust in you?"

"Godhead must be protected at all costs." He shuttered his eyes. "I am
godhead."

Hope stared at him. She could not believe that he meant it. She asked
more and more questions, both uselessly and not so uselessly, for though
she could not get anything out of him regarding his beliefs, she discovered
other things.

Arity had betrayed Humi. She had never suspected him of such duplicity. It seemed almost right that he had died for it.

Glancing at the sun, Pati said that Sol Southwind had already done the
deed; as soon as the results arrived at the Palace, sometime this afternoon,
Pati meant to make a personal raid on the Lakestones' house. Humi, too,
would die.

That electrified Hope. She had to get away. There was still something she could do.

But did Pati suspect her? Had Arity mentioned her involvement? *That* could be why Pati had tricked her into coming here. Not for sympathy, or counsel, but to confirm his suspicions. If she left in time to warn Humi, she would be a rebel. A renegade. If she stayed to see Arity's ghost, and exclaim over its realism and power et cetera, Humi would die.

She shivered. The air off the sea was freezing. Pati was staring out to sea. Suddenly he turned and said, "It was always you."

She knew what he meant. It was in his eyes, on his lips. She laughed. "I've been blessedly free of you for three years. I intend to continue that way."

"It was always you."

"Indeed, it wasn't. It was Arity."

"He's not an *iu.*"

"Neither am I, really."

The sun had risen to the middle of the translucent turquoise sky and it was shining on them, bright but without heat. Their heads were in the shadow of the alcove. He hooked his foot around her ankle and drew her against him. The familiar, poisonous fire raced through her, and she could not keep from kissing him. Conjoined, the furnaces of their bodies created a wavering bubble that protected them from the chilly air of the salt garden.

She pulled back. "I mean it, Pati. I'm not getting mixed up with you again."

"I need you, Hope."

"To help with your holy wars? Or to replace Arity?" She felt ready to cry. Suddenly panicky, she kissed him again, and the fire spread through her, consuming her. His hand inside Ders's shirt squeezed her breast, pinching the nipple, releasing a flood of sensation. Just in time she heard the knife rushing through the air toward her back.

She *teth¨d* aside, the most complicated impromptu *teth¨-tach ching* she had ever done, having to unmake all her own limbs without taking any of Pati's with her. Cold air was a shock as she landed ten feet away. Pati sat poised, his breech strings loose, rather stupidly holding the crescent blade an inch from his own chest.

"What do you think you're doing?"

He was on his feet, his teeth bared. He took one slow step toward her at a time. A small gnolia shrub stood between them. "You betrayed me. You've been betraying me for three years."

She had not dreamed he had brought her here to kill her. To use her,

trick her, but not take her life. She had been so unprepared that she had
teth¨d instead of knocking his knife upward into his throat. Now she had no
time to think, no weapon.

The cold air ventilated her mind. "What about *your* duplicity?" She put
several more bushes between them. "You almost had me! You almost had
me believing you meant it! And all the time you were wrapping me in your
web."

"I did once love you. That was no lie."

"But the rest of it was. You couldn't even be bothered with making me
confess that I helped Humi survive your poison. I hid her. I have been in
constant contact with her. You had no way of knowing that, but you were so
sure you were right that you would have killed me without any thought for
the years we spent together, without any thought for the hundred-odd
years of my life before that." She was backed up against the cliff. She
gripped the rock overhang with a futile desire to somehow fly up, away
from him. She spluttered in a desperate attempt to make him see. "Every
time you kill, it's *time* that is wasted, precious *time* of which this poor
limited world has only so much! Isn't death bad enough on its own? Aren't
we destroying ourselves already? We don't have enough time to live, let
alone die!"

"You're a traitor, Hope," he said mildly, as if her words had been no
more than a fall of tiny stones in his path. He stood before her, one hand on
his hip. She watched the knife hanging in his other hand. "There aren't any
excuses for treachery, no matter how prettily you make them."

"I'm no traitor." She spat noisily at his feet. "I was never your ally! *You*
have been the dupe!"

His face contorted. The knife came at her much faster than she had
expected, and she felt it lodge like a searing coal in her collarbone before
she slapped her hand over his, wrenched it away, and *teth¨d*.

HUMILITY UNDER STONE

Hope found Humi in the council room of the Rats' Den. It was the sixth place she had tried and she was shaking with the expenditure of operative energy. The litter of wine bottles, coffee cups, and empty trays dusted with sugar on the great beechwood table told her that the conspirators staring at her were at least as tired as she. Gold Dagger. The Hangman, sprawling all over the arm of Humi's chair. The apostate ghostiers Mory Carmine and Trisizim Sepal—what were *they* doing here? An unknown flamen and le-man, looking quite at home, and another underworld type with foxy reddish fur. Steadying herself, she bounced Pati's knife in her palm. It was blue steel, with a grip shaped for long, thin *auchresh* hands, and a sapphire embedded in the white-stained blade. The nick on her neck stung. "I have looked all over the city for you!" she said to Humi. "Ari betrayed you. I was sure you were dead. Lockreed Concourse is crawling with Hands."

Humi stiffened in her armchair. When she recognized Hope's voice, her face brightened. She made a movement to rise. "The Lakestones. Are they—"

"As far as I could tell, they are safe. Pati does not know which house you were sheltering in."

"Thank the Power for that, anyway!" Now Humi came toward Hope and embraced her. Hope was taken aback by the confidence with which she moved. She did not blunder into the table; though she stumbled, she caught herself neatly, and you would not have thought she was blind at all.

"I thought you had lost your nerve," Hope said, low.

Humi shuddered. "I had," she whispered, there in front of all the others. "And I might have stayed that way forever, if not for you. Thank you for bringing him. Thank you for showing me what I had become. I guessed he would betray me—that is the first thing I realized when I awakened. That's why I came here." With the urgency of a new convert, she hissed in Hope's ear: "I'm *free!* Hope! Free!"

Hope winced. Tears came to her eyes. "Humi—I have to tell you—I can't let you go on thinking that—Arity. I don't know the intricacies, but Pati's had him ghosted. I'm sorry."

Humi swayed. Then she straightened, and gave a perfect smile. Her hair was a blazing cloud of sand in the light of the candles. "He will die in agony for this." She took Hope by the arm and turned to face the table. "My friends, most of you know Hope. But I may as well do the honors."

Humi gestured carelessly at her new allies as she named them, giving a perfect imitation of a sighted person. The Hangman grinned indolently as Humi pronounced her name. *Evita.* Huh. Hope's hackles stirred. So she was no longer pretending to be a man. All the same, Hope did not trust her as far as she could throw her—not after what she'd witnessed on the roof-top in Temeriton.

"Are you in, Maiden?" the Hangman said.

"I have been *in,* as you put it, since before you were born," Hope said censoriously. "And I should be obliged if you didn't call me Maiden, since we are on a first-name basis."

"My congratulations, milady, on your liberation from the confines of Incarnation worship," the Godsbrother said instantly.

Hope inclined her head. The atmosphere in the room was like a newly painted canvas, stiff enough to stand up on its own.

Gold Dagger, whose head had been resting on his fist, let out a pro-tracted raspberry of a snore.

Almost everyone laughed. In that moment of relieved tension, Humi said quickly, "Now that Hope is here, I think we should all permit ourselves a few hours of rest. We can talk in private," she added to Hope, and her words held a wealth of meaning.

"Why don't you come with me," Hope said. "I know several places, although I can't take you to the Folly. I'm afraid Pati will have it guarded." She envisioned armed Hands in every room, crouched behind the furni-ture, so that if she *teth˙d* in she wouldn't see them before they saw her. The enormity of it overwhelmed her. She could never go back. She was a runaway in her own city. She had broken with Pati: they were open ene-mies now. In memory she saw him gliding toward her like a snake on its tail, knife held high, the jewel the same color as his right eye. She shud-dered. The weapon seemed to burn her thigh.

As the conspirators separated, the Hangman slid up to Hope and Humi. She wrapped Humi's hand in her own pale claw. "The Divinarch is a guest in my home. You, too, are most welcome to share my hospitality, Maiden."

Hope was about to refuse, in high dudgeon, when she realized she did not know where the Hangman's house was. If she did not go, she would be unable to *teth¨* to Humi. Swallowing her pride (anything for you, my heart's own sister!) she accepted.

They were the last to leave the council cavern. From the door, the messy table looked like a child's game left half-done, the candlelit circle puny in the dark recesses of the cave. Their footsteps echoed under the high roof. The foxy henchman, Ferret, swept back the curtain for them. A gust of fresh air rushed into their faces. Looking down, Hope saw that the little boy turning the fan crank had gone to sleep, slumped over his knees, his blistered fingers in his mouth.

INVIOLATE ONE

A featureless roof faced Sol's workshop across the side alley. Individual slates coruscated in the sun, and now and again one struck a splinter of light into his eye, making him toss his head as if to frighten away a wasp.

The labored breathing of the Hand at his feet sounded louder every minute. Outside, in the streets, lemans' bells tinkled, calling worshippers to the Dividay services. Had this been another day, the beautiful, freezing weather would have brought marketers and loafers out en masse—but it was Dividay, and so Westpoint was preternaturally silent. Sol imagined hundreds of dull-faced, cowed people shuffling along Dock Street, on their way to stand pressed together, watched by Hands, to mouth praises of a god whom none of them really respected.

Cling. Ting. Ting.

He looked down at the god and rubbed his chin in frustration. The fellow had come unwillingly, escorted by another Hand. That was a first. Always, before, they had arrived on their own, proud and prepared to die, no matter how frightened they might be. Could this mean the Divinarch's hold over his lovers was weakening? Sol had wondered, as he bowed and smiled and assured the guardian Hand, that the ghost of this young Hand would be not only striking but ready by late afternoon. He (Pati's latest castoff) reminded him of some god he knew, or had once known. Who? He seemed quite mad in a gentle kind of way, wild-eyed, his lips working. Sol, disgusted with the whole business, felt honor bound to get a decent pose out of him. So he had tried to talk him to his senses. Then the god had fainted.

"Hell!" Sol gave the unconscious figure a kick of disgust. His breakfast sat half-eaten on a cross-legged table under the window. "How dare Pati interfere with me this way! Turning me into a monster, a god-killing monster, over and over again." He picked up a roll and bit into it. He had a new ghost, as yet completely unpainted, a teenaged girl the capture of whom in a Shimorning bar yesterday had been an experience to remember. He had been looking foward to working with her.

Ting.

Ting.

Ting.

A male voice solidified out of the faint chorus of bells. Sol knew its words without having to hear them.

"Might as well get to work," he said wearily. He rolled the young Hand over with his foot.

And he choked on his bread, coughing until he had to swig a glass of water to stop his eyes running.

Now the wild, tragic face lay in repose, the features were recognizable. Smooth, bony, yet more human than those of any other god. The eyelashes were the same purplish-brown as the hair, which had been cropped close to the head. That was one reason Sol had not recognized him. But the first reason was the despair that pervaded Arity's sleep, dragging the hairless brows together, crimping the mouth.

Sol's first reaction was an immobilizing exasperation. Then, as he clenched his fists, he was filled with the purest, strongest, most invigorating anger he had felt in years. He wasn't going to be party to a crime of *this* magnitude!

Something had snapped. His sensibilities, admittedly elastic, had stretched too far. Now they sprang back in his face.

You'll have to find yourself another executioner, Pati!

He squatted down and began to shake the unconscious Arity. It had no effect. He got up, fetched two glassfuls of water, and poured them over the god's head. Arity shivered, sat up, and looked at him with bloodstained but lucid eyes. In a voiceless whisper as if of agony, he murmured, "Ghost me."

"Don't be absurd," Sol barked. "I don't know what has happened to you, my Heir, but even in this state, you aren't expendable." He did not have quite the nerve to say, *And even if you weren't Heir, speaking from a purely aesthetic perspective I don't know that your death would be justified.* The other Hands Pati had sent him had at least been compelling, as all gods were compelling; but Arity, the original of the type Pati's lovers all belonged to, looked too human to possess that ethereal intensity. He was neither, nor. Always had been.

How was he *alive?*

Sol had a hundred questions in his mind. But Arity was plainly in no state to answer any of them. Sol remembered him from the old days: self-contained, aloof, loath to fight anyone's battles. Sol had admired his detachment, both personal and political, at the same time as he was irritated by his failure to make the most of the Heir's position.

Now—

Yet *still!*

"I have my limits," he said. "Neither you nor Pati can force me to violate my art." An excuse—it was an excuse. He hated that. It had been a long time since his ghostier's principles rode runner to political exigencies, in-stead of cracking the whip that drove him through the days. "I won't ghost you, no matter what I lose by it. Now get up."

Desperation came into Arity's blood-veined eyes. His hands clenched and unclenched, the talons scraping furrows in the wood floor. He croaked, "It's the only way I can . . . He commanded it! It's the only way I can . . . please him! You can't disobey him! Please! Please! I sound mad, I know, but you are a ghostier, you must have encountered cases like mine before . . . *Please.*"

Just like all the others, Sol thought furiously, his resolve strengthening. *They all do it to please him.*

"How did he bring you to this? You were *Heir!* You were—*dead!*"

Arity's eyes closed and he smiled vaguely, like a man in the grip of a pleasant dream. Then the eyes blinked open. "It doesn't matter. All that matters is that I've lost him now, lost the life he gave me back, all through my own stupidity. You must ghost me: it is what he wishes."

"I have never made a ghost of anyone, man or god, in the depths of despair. I'm not about to start now."

"But you must!" Panic came into Arity's eyes. He clutched at Sol's wrist. Sol jerked away. The talons drew black-welling gashes along his hand.

"I used to like you, Arity." Sol pulled the god stumbling to his feet. "It's for your own sake I am refusing. Come on. I won't have anything to do with it. You can find your own way back to the Palace and tell him to send you to Shimorning, if he wants you killed. They like to catch Hands in dark alleys there. I think they've done three so far. You might even get bumped off on the way through Doxton to the Palace, if you're lucky." He dragged Arity into the other room. Birdcages, pictures frames, and vacant ghost pedestals toppled as they stumbled through the maze of furniture. "Tell him Sol Southwind is not his servant anymore!"

What are you doing? an inner, scandalized voice screeched. *You're jeop-ardizing everything you have! Your ghosts, your reputation, your future, your living, your life!*

He would have to leave these lodgings. That much was obvious. The Divinarch exacted harsh revenges on those (like Arity) who had fallen from his favor. Pushing the god out the door ahead of him, Sol took one last glance around the apartment. It was messy, dusty, and cluttered. It smelled of stale food and pigments. All the chair and table legs, in fact everything remotely edible, was rat-eaten at floor level.

He compressed his lips. A cold draft blew down the stairs from the open skylight. The building was silent. In the quiet, he heard a sound from the street, echoing under the tunnel: *chink, chink, chink,* and a *slllither* as if of cloth on stone.

"Bastards," he whispered.

After an eternity the sound faded.

He drew Arity down the stairs.

As he poked his head out into the tunnel, he glimpsed a Hand disappearing slowly around the corner. The god's heel talons thunked on the cobbles. The body he dragged after him bumped along. It was human: probably the harmless shop boy of one of Westpoint's last major merchants. Pati had enough sense not to kill off all the island's trading class. Delta City did not starve. The Hand would probably go to the Crest and leave his victim strategically positioned as a reminder to other potential blasphemers.

Sol pulled Arity out into the tunnel. The god huddled wretchedly around himself, shivering in the cold air. He was in a bad way. Tears of rage rose in Sol's eyes. "Go on then," he said roughly. "Back to the Palace. And don't forget what I told you to tell the Divinarch! Tell him Sol Southwind sends his regrets but he is no longer his to command. He has taken back his self-respect!"

He stopped as he realized he was shouting.

Arity wavered out into the sunlight. It seemed to confuse him. He tried to rub his eyes, but missed, and rubbed his hair.

Gritting his teeth against the impulse to go and prop him up, Sol strode away in the other direction. He, too, was cold—it had, perhaps, not been wise to leave without any belongings at all! But he would not go back upstairs! And he was not destitute, not in the least. Oh, no. He had his ghostier's talent. And the other, more mundane talents, such as his knack for ingratiating himself. He had not left *everything* in the apartment!

He still had his plans.

He had meant to become senior ghostier by working himself gradually under Pati's skin, until he was indispensable.

Well, what was sauce for the gander might be sauce for the goose.

Emni knew where Humi was hiding. Perhaps she would admire Sol's scruples, when Sol told her how devotion to the onetime Heir had prevented him from ghosting Arity. After all, Humi had been Arity's *amoreuse*, hadn't she? Pity, her throwing herself away like that. A nice-looking girl she had been. She and Sol were almost exactly the same age—twenty-three. He had watched her mature, watched her appear to outdistance him, and not even his hypercritical eye had been able to find anything wrong with the womanly manner she developed. Though of course, unlike most people, unlike even Arity, perhaps, he had always known it was a put-on show.

Of course, she too had probably changed.

He could soon find out if it was for the better or for the worse.

Fanning his long black forelock over his eyes to cut back the glare, he swung along toward Marshtown. He started to whistle. Before long, Arity had faded from his immediate concerns.

AMONG LADIES

That evening at the hour of first glasses, two women and one *auchresh* slipped through the side door of the Peppered Frog and settled at a table at the edge of the barroom. On the stage at the back, five young boys, stripped nearly naked, swayed to and fro. The applause of the enthusiasts below the stage—some male, some female, all loudly drunken—drowned out the pipe music floating from behind the backdrop.

Hope eyed the dirty-fingered crone who plunked her whiskey in front of her with some revulsion. The servers were all ancient. Maybe the idea was to focus attention on the show, or maybe the Frog catered to customers whose tastes ran that way. She pushed the unwashed mug back. "Would it inconvenience your barkeep too much if I requested a clean glass?"

The Hangman looked at her with surprise. Then her mouth twisted. "Maiden, we mortals exist only to please those greater than us. Another whiskey for the lady, Arva."

Hope wore a long robe to conceal her wings, with a hood to shadow her face, and so did Humi. Everyone knew the Hangman, of course; she owned the tavern. Hope's dirty mug vanished and she was offered a shot glass of amber liquid. The whiskey was bad. She made a face. "I suppose your regular customers are easily satisfied."

"You do not find my little entertainment house satisfactory, Maiden?" The Hangman's voice was as soft as oiled fingers sliding up the spine. Her gaze oozed into Hope's hood, and rested there, speculatively. Hope stared back, seething with anger. The Hangman's were the eyes of a lizard. Under the deceptively sleepy gaze, dislike simmered.

Sooner or later they would confront each other. Hope knew the Hangman meant evil toward Humi, and the Hangman knew she knew it.

She said, "I certainly had not suspected you had interests in the tavern business, Hangman. It does not seem consistent with your primary line of work." Was it possible Humi had no clue what was going on? Her hood was up, but her cloak hung open. She wore a gold-trimmed low-cut dress that showed off her figure to advantage. Not too gaudy for the times, yet expensive enough to show she was a lady and could afford whatever she set her eye on. She tapped her fingers in time to the clapping.

The Hangman cracked a smile. "I invested in the Frog for exactly that reason. The assassination business is risky, and one must provide for eventualities."

Humi appeared to return her attention to the table. "Wise," she said with a trill of laughter. "If I had done the same, I would not now have to depend on my friends' generosity."

"Milady, you are not obliged to me. This is my pleasure."

Hope crooked her finger for another whiskey. Drink did not affect her mental faculties, but enough of it, she had discovered, had a calming effect at times like this, when she felt as if she was sparking with excess energy.

"You drink rather copiously, milady, don't you?" the Hangman said, in the tone of one asking whether Hope was really eating rotten fish.

"I smoke copiously, too," Hope snapped. She got out her tobacco pouch and began to fill a pipe.

"It would ease my lot if you two would try to tolerate each other," Humi said sharply. "The air is thick with unpleasantness. Can't you ignore each other, at the very least?"

Hope wondered whether to reveal her suspicions: the reasons she did not dare ignore the Hangman. When she saw the Hangman's mouth open, she spoke fast: "Humi, you're in danger. She means to do you wrong."

The Hangman hissed in outrage.

"You pride yourself on your perceptiveness. Have you really not noticed? I entreat you to break off your relations with her. Deal with Gold Dagger alone, if you must." Humi's face was unreadable. Hope wondered with paralyzing suddeness if she had lost her trust. "I have no motives besides your interest, Humi. Trust me!"

"What a liar," the Hangman said, "what a liar! Sssshe is jealous of me, milady."

"I care only for my Divinarch's safety!"

People turned to stare. Hope lowered her voice to a hiss, training her gaze on the Hangman.

"Power knows what you will do the next time you get Humi alone. I can see it in your eyes, and I will not permit it!"

Humi's mouth was serious. She turned to the Hangman. "If there is the slightest grain of truth in this—"

"It's not *fair*," the Hangman whispered. She clasped her hands around

Humi's arm. "Milady, I offer you my humble allegiance and you will turn it down to let this—this—renegade serve you in my stead. She negates everything we are fighting for! She is the image of decadence! She is a scion of this very regime we strive to overturn! She represents the worst, ugliest degradation of the gods we seek to elevate to their proper places!"

Hope gasped.

"You believe," Humi said in frank astonishment, pulling her arm away. "You are a devotee, Evita! How on earth have you managed to stay faithful in the middle of all this?"

On stage, five girls pranced out and joined the boys. The crowd, which had grown marginally larger, grew much louder. The crooked old servitors scurried from table to table, their cracked voices shrilling jokes and foolery. The Hangman took a long swig of her drink. "For the most part, by keeping it a secret."

Humi gestured around the table. "But then, why are you here? Why aren't you bowing down to Pati's toy flamens?"

The Hangman's pale greenish eyes glowed with passion. "So that the gods can continue to be the gods, without being reduced to squabbling monkeys!"

"Oh, so that's why you hate me?" Hope said. "I have made myself into a squabbling monkey for your sake. For all of your silly little human sakes. And you hate me for it."

The Hangman's lips puckered. Hope ducked in time and the gob of spittle hit the man at the next table. When he rose, his face waxing dark with anger, the Hangman snapped her fingers over her head, and several of the old crones grabbed him and wrestled him toward the door. "You have betrayed your own divinity," the Hangman hissed. "For *her* sake. Thus lowering her to your despicable level."

"Hangman," Humi said warningly.

But the conflict between worship and contempt could not be defused. It was more powerful than a river in flood, for it pulled the woman's bottommost essence up and swirled it about. "*I* am the only one who should follow her," the Hangman spat. "I would praise her with my last breath. *You're* just amusing yourself. And it is below your dignity, below you! Leave us alone! Let us fight your battles for you, as we have done ever since the Conversion Wars!"

"You are making my point," Hope said. The bewilderment had left her, replaced by an icy anger at the Hangman for making her personally responsible for the Hangman's own doubt. "Nothing is beneath my dignity, any more than it is beneath yours. Our races are not so different. They never have been."

The Hangman seemed about to come across the table at her. Humi snatched her arm. "This is beneath *all* of us," she said. "Hangman, we must keep our beliefs out of our dealings with each other. Hope—*please.*"

"You favor her," the Hangman spat. "Favoritism has been the death of many an alliance. Beware!"

"Hope and I have been friends for years—but I value you equally. Can we not reconcile, simply because it is natural for us to do so? We are all women. It would be ludicrous for us to hate each other."

"Don't feed me that pap, milady. Except in bed, I haven't been a woman in ten years!"

You, Humi, are perhaps the only one of us with any femininity left, Hope thought, *and that is because you hold onto it with tooth and claw, the way an aging* serbalu *holds onto her looks.*

But the last thing Hope wanted to do was to agree with the Hangman. The cold anger buzzed inside her. "I think I had better leave."

"I won't allow it. I need you, Hope." Humi still gripped the Hangman's arm. Now she reached out with her other hand and took Hope's. Her slender arms trembling with the effort, she brought their hands together until Hope's scaly golden knuckles pushed against the Hangman's lightly furred paw. "Neither of you will leave without my permission."

Hope had never seen an expression so compelling. Humi's grayish-black eyes seemed to come alive like pools of cold water when the wind stirs them. Hope felt herself sliding toward that brink. The cold took her breath away. The cheering, clapping, and music faded as if she were hurtling at great speed, not down into the water, but out, out, out into the ocean on a fast boat, lashed by icy spray. Her mouth tasted of stale tobacco, foul with the sleepless days.

Humi let go of their wrists. The room brightened, spun, then righted itself. On stage, as the children copulated or stimulated it, the pipe player, a brawny young man with green Deltan fur, tiptoed with exaggerated care among the couples, tootling on his instrument and directing exaggerated nods and winks at the audience. The Westpointers roared with laughter.

"All right, then, Hope." Humi nodded. "You can leave. I am not relinquishing our alliance. And I wouldn't have suggested it if you hadn't. But perhaps—for now—it would be best for everyone."

The Hangman glowed smugly.

Hope knew it. She had to go. Her presence aggravated dangerous tendencies in the humans—atheists, devotees, and believers all: understandably, they felt overshadowed. The Hangman was only one example. They could not cope with the concept of the renegade, as opposed to the god.

Better to leave Humi to the tender mercies of her own kind. If only that didn't mean leaving her in such deadly danger!

At closing time, they were all separated in the confusion. Hope watched Humi snake competently through the crowd. The thought flashed through her: *What am I thinking? She can look after herself! She's not a child!*

When they had been shown to the rooms in the Hangman's Shimorning town house which servants had readied for them, Humi came through the door that connected their bedrooms, floating almost *auchresh*-like over the floor in a wispy silver nightgown. "Here," she said, extending a flimsy piece of parchment to Hope. "Here's where I would like you to go. If you are still intent on going."

"I am."

"Then I hope you didn't expect I was going to ignore the chance to put you to work abroad!" Humi grinned.

"I am *committed* to working on your behalf," Hope said, meaning it. She took the parchment. It was engraved with a line drawing of a house surrounded by trees.

"I am assured the proportions are accurate," Humi said.

In the smoky lamplight, Hope peered at the paper. It gave off a faint scent of human sweat. She guessed that Humi had kept it next to her fur. "I'm supposed to *teth* from this?"

"Can't you?"

"It will require a leap of the imagination, but perhaps I can." Already, her mind was feathering the sketched-in pines with minty needles.

"I want you to work on Erene and Elicit."

"So far as I know, no one has ever died from *teth*"ing with their destination unclear in their minds." She put a smile in her voice. "The barrier between our world and the myriad of others is too strong, too elastic, to be broken by our puny mistakes."

Humi leaned against the bedpost. The filmy gown clung to her breasts. Shadows played in the corners of the bedroom and undulated in the window curtains. "Hope, what really happened between you and Pati? It wasn't just the news about Arity. It was something violent. To tell you the truth, I'm surprised you came back at all . . . You seem—sparkling. I can almost see you."

"I broke with him." A worm of grief twisted in her. Today marked the burial of something that had been dying for years. But neither the length of the bed watch nor the irascibility of the patient had lessened the final pain. "We talked for hours. But I do not believe he said one word that was true."

"He may have let something slip," Humi suggested.

"For a time, we spoke of godhead."

"Yes?"

She shook her head. "We went around in circles. I asked him how he could countenance a war against our fellow *auchresh*. You do know about all that . . . Yes? He insisted it was to preserve his godhead. As you know, he calls himself the One God. Thus far, outrageous as the concept is, it holds together; but you see, there is a contradiction between the way he speaks of himself and the way he lives. He is *wrchrethre*. A humanophile. He is no longer a god in the sense you humans have always meant it. His efforts to maintain the Divinarchy have changed it beyond any hope of returning it to its old self. He *must* see that. But I do not know how he deals with it in his mind. If we knew, perhaps we could guess at the strategy he will use to track us down."

Humi had been listening intently. "The question, it seems to me, is whether he really believes he is a god."

"Or is it, now, nothing more than a desperate struggle to hang onto power? I can't tell. I don't think he confides in anyone."

"Maybe Arity knew," Humi said. A shadow flitted across her face. "Maybe that is why Pati had him killed."

"I don't think so. I think it was to do with you."

"It's always my fault, isn't it?"

"Oh, Power," Hope said, rising to her knees, "that's not what I meant, and you know it." She pressed Humi's head to her breast.

"I'm sorry for *him*," Humi said, muffled. "He deserved a nobler end than that." She wriggled a little in Hope's arms and touched the tender nick on Hope's collarbone. "Did Pati do this?"

Hope nodded.

"It could have been much worse, couldn't it?"

"He was trying to kill me." Hope took a deep breath. "I *was* lucky." She let go of Humi, then pulled her up onto the bed and sat her up with her legs sticking out like a doll's. Humi's lips pooched out childishly, as if Hope's cutting short the embrace had pushed her to the edge of tears.

"Did you"—Hope had to ask—"did you still love him?"

Humi's nose twitched. Her hands dug into the edge of the bed like claws. Finally she said, "Not anymore. He'd changed too much."

"It was his accident that changed him. Ever since then, he's had that look about him—as if he were waiting for the right moment to finish what the leman girl started."

Humi laughed bitterly, leaning her head on her hand, and said not without some irony, "Hope, you are my staff of strength."

"And I'm leaving."

"You'll come back. You must."

"But what'll I have to show for it?" Hope put the picture of the house down on the coverlet. She wore a light nightgown in which she had ripped holes for her wings. Her knees ripped through it, too, as she leaned forward. "There are many other places I could work on your behalf. We don't know anything about the life Erene and Elicit have built for themselves over the last few years. They are sure not to want to be disturbed. Our business is a thing of the cities. I do not think people in the country know anything about the gods' doings! We're in danger of losing our perspective if we don't remember that."

"I think you're wrong," Humi said seriously. The candlelight danced. "This . . . war . . . of Pati's started in human country. K'Fier is a hamlet, next to Delta City. And speaking of that, I want you to investigate the renegades for me."

What could she do? She had agreed to go. And Humi sounded so confident.

"And as for Erene and Elicit, you'll simply have to convince them that they owe us their help in return for four years of peace and quiet. They belong here. They can leave Artle and Xib behind if they are worried for their safety."

Shaking her head in resignation, Hope leaned over and kissed the well-groomed forehead. After all these years she still wasn't quite used to the taste of fur. A good thing Humi was blind, so she could not see her wiping her mouth on the back of her hand. "All right!" she said. "But don't have the revolution without me."

Humi's head came up. "No one will move a finger unless I tell them to."

Gazing at her sharp, elegant profile, Hope thought: *She means it. The fool.*

SOLEMNITY

As Sol came down Tellury Crescent that afternoon, he glimpsed a white face in the window of the Chalice. No Hands guarded the street. That was unusual! Nobody at all was outside, in fact, except for a few children, and a girl brushing her doorstep, who automatically curtseyed to him. He rapped on the door of Albien House, silently cursing his nerves.

Yste opened it, his squinched dark face closed. "She's not here."

"Aren't you glad to see me?" Sol said in a hurt voice, and brushed past. Inside, he breathed deeply. Albien House, the oldest of the *imrchim's* three residences, smelled of perfume, and cookery, and pigments, and overwhelmingly of dust—a musty yet curiously invigorating odor. It was good to know that something, at least, had not changed. "If she's not here, where is she?"

"At the Eftpool." The half-breed boy danced in front of him. "You can follow her there, if you want."

For a moment Sol thought he was telling the truth, and his gut clenched. He could not go to the Eftpool. Not without endangering everything he had once believed in, everything that Emni still believed in.

Then his senses returned, and he saw that the repulsive Yste had sidled around to stand between him and the stairs.

Not *very intelligent of you, Em!*

"Out of my way," he said gently, shoving the boy aside. "Run and tell Ziniquel his wife is closeted with her brother." He shouted, "Run!"

Yste darted into the anteroom. As Sol leaped up the stairs, two at a time, he heard the Chalice door slam.

The third floor of Albien House, which had once been Humi and Erene's workshop and private apartments, now comprised one huge glasshouse. Entering from the hall, Sol experienced a shock of terror as light drifted over him, absorbing him, blurring his sense of self. But again, reason came to his aid. The light was almost granular in its cool brilliance—it was like walking through weak syrup. Not a multicolored sea. Not the Pool. As he advanced, gravity seemed to change from a given effect to a tangible force that one could use as one wanted. Enviously, he thought, *One forgets how well they've got this place up. The ghosts they paint here must be transcendent.*

Some parts of the roof were screened, creating solid blocks of shadow on the floor. Heavy reed mats hung in rolls at the other rafters, ready to be cranked across if the sun got too bright. In a far corner of the room, a pale figure hugged the wall.

"Gods," Sol said sadly. "I'm not going to *hurt* you."

She detached herself from the wall. Slowly, she came toward him. Her long hair fell like strips of shiny black cloth over her shoulders; she wore plain working wools. Her hands were pigment-stained, the nails bitten short, as of old. Sol quelled a desperate urge to seize her in his arms. Deliberately, he looked her up and down. "Where's the baby?"

"Lighte. His name is Enlightenment. I should think you would remember that, since he's the only descendant you're likely to have."

"I have bastards in half the households of Westpoint."

"Liar. I know you, Sol." Her nose went thin. "You'd never even *look* at a woman who wasn't me."

Such arrogance. Such beloved arrogance.

He wished he could taunt her with the possibility of Lighte's being his. But it wasn't chronologically possible. Besides, although the baby had Emni's white fur, it had Zin's green hair and green eyes. "Do you really flatter yourself that that's the reason I'm here?"

"No." She seized her cuffs in her hands, raveling their hems. She was as edgy as he. "There's something more you want out of me. There's always something."

He took a deep breath. "I'm on the run. I need your help."

"On the run? Are you making a fool of me? You're the pet of the Divinarch. He would squash anybody who tried to bag you. Though I don't doubt you've plenty of enemies, being—who you are."

"Em." The room smelled of diamondine: a curiously sharp odor like baking soda. "I tell you, it's *Pati* who wants me. The hunt will be up by tonight. I have to hide."

". . . no. I don't believe it." Emni's lips parted and her brows drew together. "*No.* Sol, don't tell me—*don't* tell me you've gone and allied yourself with Humi—"

"Not yet. But I have to know where she is. She's my only hope." He stepped forward—not too far, not far enough to make her flinch back, just enough to impress his urgency on her. "You know where she is. You've got to tell me, Em."

"Gods! She has a fatal influence over us. I knew I was right not to take the children to see her. First Mory and Tris, now you—is it ever going to be finished?"

Excitement quickened in his chest. "Have Mory and Tris joined her? Where are they?" Maybe *this* was why there were no Hands in the Crescent. Maybe they had all been called to a more urgent posting. "You've given everything away. There's no use in not telling me now."

"Oh—oh gods! Kill yourself along with them if you want, then! It's not as though I care! It was scarcely an hour ago." Her head tossed as if she were being compelled to speak by the blows of an invisible whip. "A courier pigeon came here from Godsbrother Eternity—an apostate. The message said that a flamen of his, with Mory and Tris, who seem to have worked themselves deep into the apostates' trust, have gone as ambassadors to Humi. She is gathering her allies about her. She means to do something horrible. Sol, don't go!"

For a moment he thought she meant to confide in him. Then the door behind him opened. "Em!" Ziniquel exclaimed. "Thank the gods! You're all right!"

Emni brushed past Sol. He smelled her perfume. She leaned against her husband. "Oh, Zin. I told him about Mory and Tris. I couldn't help it—he always drags these things out of me."

Ziniquel's hands nudged aside the heavy locks of hair as he rubbed her back. "How did he get in, love? I told Yste . . ." His eyes met Sol's.

"You would've had to put a good deal more than that child in my way to keep me out," Sol said.

"Yes. I should have met you myself." Zin's eyes were steady, challenging. "It's my duty to protect my ghostiers."

"Turned the senior ghostier properly, haven't you," Sol jeered. "What a comedown!"

"I never wanted anything more than this," Ziniquel said. Sol felt a queer twitch of perception as he thought, *Our desires are exactly the same, aren't they, Zin? Funny. We're so different.* "I never wanted more than to stop the likes of you from hurting the *imrchim.* Now, get out of my house." He jerked his chin toward the door.

It's my house, too, Sol thought. "Not until you tell me where to find Humi."

Emni flung around, her hair flying, and snarled, "Do you mean to break her heart, too?"

Absurdly, Sol's insides leaped. "Did I break your heart? Em, I never knew that."

"No! I mean—"

"It's all *right*." Ziniquel pulled her close. "Sol, she's in Shimorning."

Getting an answer so readily was almost a disappointment. It proved how genuinely, and urgently, they wanted to get rid of him.

"She's at the Rats' Den. Do you know where that is?"

"Sounds like a tavern."

"It's not. We never heard of it, either, until this afternoon. It's Gold Dagger's lair. The vermin are gathering now, and they need somewhere to hide. Go down to Reddew Street . . ." He proceeded to give a string of complex directions. Sol memorized them, nodding.

"I'll be off, then." He bowed to Emni and said sarcastically, "Thanks for your hospitality, darling."

"And good riddance," came a clear voice from the other side of the room. Suret, the Veretrean girl apprentice, stood in the far door with her arm around Yste. Tan hovered behind her, his long limbs in perpetual motion.

"Keep your nose out of things that are none of your business, little girl!" Sol called to her.

"If I had been at the door, you would not have got past the first step!" Tan shouted.

"Not that you didn't do a good job, Yste dear," Suret murmured, hugging the smaller boy close.

A sudden pang went through Sol. There had been a time, impossible as it seemed now, when he and Emni had been those apprentices eavesdropping in the doorway. But those had been halcyon days compared to these. He and Emni had not been taught to hate anyone. They had feared nothing except growing up, though they had feared *that* rightly.

Yet Tan, Suret, and Yste's Crescent was the same as the Crescent of Sol's childhood in one respect: it was the only home they knew. Childhood memories (even if, like Tan, you were already adolescent when you were apprenticed) faded faster than dried flowers, when they were exposed to the bright light of the seasons in Delta City. All Sol had now to comfort him was a Dividay circle on the top of a mountain, and the taste of honeyfish.

"Do you remember," he said suddenly to Emni, "when we were little? On Gelska? How we used to run down to the pier in the morning to see the boats off—"

"I remember nothing," Emni snapped. "Get out!" Her eyes were wild behind the tangled strands of black. Age lines circled them. That made Sol wince. *Are we still identical?* He had not looked in a mirror in a long time. There had been a time when looking at her was like watching himself, only slightly exaggerated. But their changing relations had probably changed their faces correspondingly.

"I shan't tolerate these intrusions any longer, Sol!"

"Don't worry. This will be the last time."

She turned her head away. "I hate you."

"You're afraid of me."

"I despise you!"

Maybe, inside, she was worse mended than he was from the dreadful night he had poisoned her. Was such a thing possible? The clear sunlight showed up the dust on the floor, the dust on the ranks of ghosts standing by one wall, an army contorted by sudden plague, frozen where they stood. How many ghosts had they actually made recently? Tan stepped menacingly into the sunlight, thin arms akimbo. "Out!" he ordered in a poor imitation of a Temeriton bouncer's voice.

Sol laughed at the irony of it, and went.

"And so the *imrchim* are reunited!" Tris said. "We are the *real imrchim*, you know. United by our commitment to our art. I don't honor those spineless fools in the Crescent with the title of ghostier anymore." He stood in the middle of his and Mory's small workshop in Marshtown, looking around. "For the first time since you left us in '57, Humi, I feel we are up to strength again."

Humi objected, "You are only three. I acknowledge your flattery, but"— she laughed self-deridingly—"I do not think I really merit the title of master anymore." Her hand strayed along the smooth thigh of a ghost dressed in the costume of a monstrous bird (every feather diamondine, of course) and Sol saw a sensual tic at the corner of her mouth. "Now, I am reduced to merely appreciating your work."

Mory's and Tris's ghosts were everything Sol had anticipated: startling in the sheer intensity of their emotion, yet more powerful than most other ghosts for that same reason. Many of them wore masquerade costumes. Red and dark green predominated.

"But my dear Humi, even if there are only three of us, we are still more numerous than the Crescent!" Mory objected. "Algia and Eterneli are not masters in any sense at all!" She wore a droopy black robe and boots that added to her height by at least four inches. "I trust you have not forgotten that if they paint one ghost a year between them, they consider themselves productive?"

Humi smiled, acknowledging her point. "However, I daresay the Crescent is cleaner than it has been in centuries."

"Actually," Sol put in, "no matter how much those two sweep and dust and polish, those houses still look as though no one has set foot there in years. I remember while I was living in Thaumagery House by myself, four years ago, the place must have slipped back several centuries in time."

"You have not changed in the least, Sol," Mory said, her eyes resting speculatively on him. With an effort, he stopped himself from flinching.

Humi, too, had matured. He had expected her face to bear a record of the trials she had undergone—but she seemed to have transcended them. Perhaps just coming here had done that for her. Her voice was melodious, and her blindness contributed to her gracefulness rather than detracting from it. Long eyelashes swept like fringes over her eyes, hiding the flat black surfaces. She seemed perfectly sure of herself.

Mory and Tris, like everyone else Sol had met in the Rats' Den, seemed to think it was a given that a battle would soon come, and that Humi would prevail. He saw that if he didn't watch his step, he would find himself getting caught up in their plans. He had already agreed to teach Gold Dagger's men the secret ways of the old Palace: he was the only one of the conspiracy (as they were again calling it) familiar with the renovations Pati had made.

But perhaps Humi *could* win. Perhaps Sol had landed on his feet here.

Wait and see, he told himself, fighting for objectivity. *You haven't yet told them about Arity. Or the ghosts of the Hands. Give it twenty to one that no matter how apostatic they seem to be, they'll hate you for that.*

Flowers of frost bloomed on the windows of the workshop. Outside, moonflower plants swayed, tall green blurs. The workshop was near the Eftpool: another ancient structure in the middle of a block of Marshtown houses, hidden from the streets, and the eyes of patrolling Hands. It had been used as an outhouse by the tenants until Mory and Tris reclaimed it and broke windows in the thick stone walls. Today seemed to have been one long succession of ghosts—from the silent, crystalline Westpoint morning, through the ghost Sol had not made of Arity, to the apprentices hovering like ineffectual shadows in the doorway of Emni and Zin's workshop, to Humi. Humi, back from the dead, beautiful and corrupted, breathing and hot-blooded. Her dress revealed her sandy-furred shoulders. She had dyed her hair auburn. "Hume," he said, "I don't believe for a minute that you're no longer ghosting. You would never be so sleek if you'd been cut off from your art. Are you going to show us your masterpieces now, or later?"

She turned to him, looking cross. "You sound sure of yourself!"

"Did I spoil the surprise? I do apologize."

"Actually"—she glowed—"I *have* been painting ghosts. Not with pigments, but with chisels. I have been playing with texture, using it in some ways I believe are quite original. I only brought one of my pieces with me from Temeriton, and it is at the Hangman's residence in Shimorning, but I should be delighted if you would give me your opinion on it—all of you."

Mory and Tris were unctuous with compliments, expressing their desire to see everything she had done.

"You can go and buy my other pieces from Hem's shop. He would be delighted. If you disguise yourselves, he will think you are foreigners, and it will be even nicer."

"What is the piece you have? A rat?" Sol asked.

"No. A seagull."

He took her hand. Twisting it over, he held the palm to the light, examining the myriad scars. "It clawed you pretty badly. Or are these chisel marks? Whichever it is, your new technique is very hard on the hands."

"*Sol,*" she said, pulling away, and said no more. Mory and Tris filled the conversational gap with news of the people Sol and Humi had known in Marshtown. Inevitably, the subject of apostasy came up. They sat down on the floor, which was scrupulously clean, and wrapped blankets around their shoulders against the cold. "Pati's most powerful weapon will be his flamens," Humi said. "They are more powerful than the quickest soldier. And they have no morals. Or only twisted ones."

"Ha," Mory said. "We can best them any day."

"The Godsbrothers and Godsisters have been practicing," Tris said. "Some of them have refined the use of miracles to an art. They use their will much the same way we do when we make ghosts. It is all the same thing. They are conscious of their technique."

The talk segued into a pleasurably esoteric discussion of craft. Tris poured chilled wine. As it took effect, they began to reminisce. Sol found himself moved by his *imrchim's* unspoken acceptance. He had not experienced anything of the sort for so long . . . They seemed to have forgotten how they had once ostracized him. He was one of them again, just by virtue of having come here, to Humi's side. And if they had once criticized him for his excess of zeal . . . well, now murderousness was a qualification, not a crime.

But they did not know the worst of it. He had to remember that. They did not know the facts, nor the end, of his services to Pati.

He and Humi sat with their backs against a pedestal, scarcely speaking. Her face tipped toward the ceiling as if she were drinking in the purple twilight that filtered in through the frost. It spilled down her throat, bruising the downy fur. She said, "I should like to see some of the ghosts *you* have made these past few years, Sol."

"Most of them have sold abroad."

"I should like to see one in particular. I believe it was commissioned by the Divinarch?"

Gods. She knows. He said, "The Divinarch commissioned more than one ghost from me. I'd say over the years, there were dozens."

She sighed, and seemed to sag. *She believes now that I* did *kill him,* he realized with a pang of guilt.

"You have broken the greatest unwritten law of our calling. Mory and Tris know, too. You have probably sensed that we are all a little in awe of you."

He shrugged. "I'm still alive. That's all that can really be said for it."

She laughed: a low, hoarse giggle. "Sol, I am delighted to have you as an ally. I don't know what to say."

"It's all in the deed, Humi. I had to force my hand every time I did it. The remnants of faith are hard to shake off."

"You are still human, then! That is all!"

"I suppose so . . ."

She trilled with laughter. *Must I tell her?* Sol wondered. *I want her. And if she knows he's still alive . . .* "I didn't kill Arity," he said abruptly. "I sent him back to Pati."

She sat bolt upright. Her face was a dusk-colored mask. She reminded him of Pati, the last time Sol had been summoned to a divine audience, the slim ghost leaning down from the Throne, coruscating with intentness. "I knew. I *knew* that could not be the end of it. I *hoped* . . . but no!" Her hand closed on his shoulder and she bowed her head. She was shuddering. "Why didn't you kill him? Why didn't you? Pati would have been disabled by his loss . . ."

Sol was utterly confused for the space of just one second. Then he lifted her head up by the hair and drove his mouth against hers. Her lips yielded to his tongue with astonishing readiness.

"Quite in awe of you," she murmured. Sol could not determine whether she was jesting or serious, and he didn't like to ask. Instead he kissed her again. Mory and Tris did not appear to have noticed; they sat with their heads together behind a furiously leering ghost in traditional Icelandic costume, discussing politics in soft voices.

They managed to keep from tearing each other's clothes off until they had made their good-byes to Mory and Tris, found their escort of career criminals, and returned by a back route to the Rats' Den. Then, avoiding people who would have accosted Humi, they let themselves into a dark storeroom. They had scarcely spoken a word since leaving the workshop. The air was hardly breathable, the heap of pilfered tapestries an uncomfortable bed, but Humi pulled him close with a fierce passion that aggravated his desire. He plunged into her again and again, thrusting deep as he would have thrust a knife into a living body. Not a word passed between them. Their mouths met with bruising force. She gripped him, increasing the friction until he could not bear it; he gasped as he climaxed. Her fingers grasped his back, slipping. His fur was flat with sweat.

They fell apart, breathing noisily in the bad air.

Outside, far down, steel rang on stone.

A thin rectangle of light limned the door. It was a foot thick, to protect the contents of the storeroom. Humi had a ring of keys Gold Dagger had given her. Sol imagined her and himself as two of the treasures, more precious than the tapestries, the chinaware, or the daggers. He laughed.

"What?" she murmured.

"Nothing." Flinging his arm around her, he pulled her closer, wedging her into the curve of his body, kissing the damp mass of her hair. The flat place below her ribs swelled in and out under his hand.

GOD OF THE CITY AND OF THE HEART

They had reached a crossroads. Gete chewed his lip. Boarded-up storage houses bore metal plates on the doors; not for the first time, he wished he could read. They were probably signs of some sort. The few men and women hurrying along in the street bobbed their heads to Thani, but then scurried past too quickly for Gete to accost them.

And anyhow, he *should* know where he was!

He could not admit to Thani that he was lost. They had said good-bye to their fellow passengers, to whom she had preached several sermons over the course of the voyage, telling them they were going straight to the Divinarch. Then they had disembarked from the *Foam Rider* with their noses in the air and strode off down the docks.

He looked over at her. She had joined her hands in her sleeves against the cold and pulled her cowl down over her eyes. Any minute she would poke him in the ribs and whisper, *Why have we stopped?* For some reason she did not want people to know they were strangers in the city. She jittered quietly, her teeth chattering.

She had had a bad time in Delta City. He knew that much. Something to do with her sister, the woman who had briefly been Divinarch.

She took her hand out of her pocket and thrust it through his arm. He brought her fingers to his lips and kissed them.

Which way?

He chose a direction at random. From the rise of the ground, he guessed that they were moving parallel to the sea, toward the big river. But the streets grew narrower, and twisted and turned at random. Soon he had lost all sense of which way they were going. Now and again, a knot of Hands crossed their path. Instinctively, Gete recognized the almost amorous way in which they jostled close together. It was battle formation. They did not give him and Thani a second glance.

Storage houses gave way to decrepit tenements. Here, at least the city seemed more alive. Not so many Hands. Children dashed across the streets; women fed house pigs by doorsteps. Cooking fumes misted in the air. Gete guided Thani around the splashes of dung. As they progressed through the alleys, every last toddler and ancient stopped what he or she was doing to curtsy or bow to her. But the expressions on their faces were not right. Not love and worship; fear and slyness. They gave him the shivers.

The sun glazed the streets coldly. A glass ceiling seemed to tremble over the roofs of the houses, warping everything on the ground. The Deltans' faces were brilliant green, like cracked lacquer. Features wobbled and spread as Gete stared at them. Lips formed prayers—or curses? The solid black shadows of windows and doors shifted, lifting slightly to let tiny green hands and noses squeeze out from underneath. The hands made rude gestures and clasped in attitudes of mock prayer. Gete could never quite catch them when he swung his head.

"What's *wrong?*" Thani whispered.

Gete stared at the ground. They were halted in the end of a cul-de-sac. Lime-colored faces swam in the windows. The smell of something burning drifted from a door. A hawker wandered past the mouth of the road, shrilly touting meat-pies. "I'm lost."

"No. Oh, *Gete.*"

"Why did you think I knew where I was going? *You're* the one who's been here before!"

"It was five years ago. I was a child. Why don't you ask somebody?"

"They're afraid of us." It came out unintentionally.

"Gods. Perhaps we shouldn't have come. I should have struggled on as best I could—"

"Then why did we come?"

"Gete, I—just couldn't go on!"

"It was what happened in K'Fier. Wasn't it?" Gete was sweating in the cold. "You've lost your faith, and we've come here to find it again."

"No! Oh, no!" She made a noise halfway between a sniffle and a sob and wiped her nose. "How could I lose faith? I am a flamen! My miracles have not weakened! I . . ."

He stood stiffly by her side. The houses seemed to list closer and closer together over their heads. The sun slowly decomposed, crumbling down onto the cobbles.

"It seems so many things have gone wrong," Thani murmured. "There has to be a reason. There has to be. Sometimes I think we are just counters, like the pawns in a game of Conversion—all of us just lemans, just children—and the gods don't care whether we stand or fall . . . but I *know* that isn't true. There's a reason for everything! This war serves to illustrate something which we are ready to comprehend, and I'm too stupid to understand what I'm being shown—"

Gete could not stand to hear her putting herself down! Angrily, he burst out, "Would it be so terrible to believe that there *is* no Balance? The gods are at war! Is that so unbelievable? Maybe the scenes we've been looking at for thousands of years have finally been lifted, and we're seeing the squabbles backstage!"

"You frighten me!" Her teeth chattered. She gripped his arm. "We have lost our way, that is all. We have to find our way—have to ask—the Divinarch—"

At that moment, the last thing Gete wanted to do was to go the Divinarch. The very idea terrified him.

After he had given up trying to understand the world of the gods, Desti's world, he had started trying to *understand* the faith he'd followed all his life, because it was Thani's faith. But what if he had been right in the first place? What if the gods were only a troupe of quarreling play-actors? Worse, what if they were absolutely ordinary—like Desti?

He gazed around helplessly. It was at that moment that he saw the figure curled in the garbage beside a flight of steps.

Thani had not sensed it. What did that mean?

Releasing her with a whispered reassurance, he crossed the cul-de-sac and shook the thin, green-skinned god. The nearly shaved head flopped back. The globular lids were closed. Gete tried again, holding his breath. This time the god's eyes opened and he jumped to his feet.

All around, windows, shutters, doors slammed shut. *Chock chock chock.* Gete retreated across the street.

"Better get out of here," he hissed to Thani. "It's a god. He's mad. Or a renegade—"

"No! A god? How—" She flipped back her cowl. Suddenly, she was all reverent ministry. "Inviolate One!" Her voice carried like a bell. "How can I be of assistance?"

"Not in the Palace," the god muttered. "Thought I got there. Where am I?"

"Doxton," came a sigh from a dozen closed windows. Did Gete detect the gleam of eyes in the cracks of the shutters? No Sarberran would ever be so craven as to leave a flamen to her fate, and *watch!* "Chilte Close," they sighed.

"Miles away!" The god slumped. He seemed to have become suddenly disoriented: as if the substitution of the pungently real Chilte Close for the

phantasmic Palace was too much for him. Perhaps his disillusionment made
him visible to Thani. She moved unerringly to him and put her arm around
his waist. He did not resist. Gete shook himself into action, going to support the god on the other side.

"We can help you to the Palace, Inviolate One," Thani told him. Her
excited breath formed tiny ice crystals that fell like sugar. "Can you show us
the way?"

"I . . ." the god muttered. "I could not believe the insolence of him. He
wouldn't do it. Wouldn't. I pleaded with him . . . threw my pride at his
feet . . . what there was left of it . . . and still."

Gete swallowed.

"Go back the way you came," the windows whispered. "Till you reach
Doxton Concourse. Then turn left."

"Cross Honey Street."

"Cross Immanence Circle."

"Godsister, 'ave pity on us."

"Go past a distillery called Oakyew Brothers."

"Don't punish us."

"Wait," Gete shouted, squinting upward. "Stop!" He was actively hating
the Deltans now, but he had to milk them for what they knew. "Go over it
again! From the beginning—"

It seemed that the voices guided them all the way, a host of tiny, timo-
rous currents wafting them along the river of streets. Before long, Gete had
to clench his fists to keep from hitting out at some innocent passerby. He
wanted badly to hurt someone.

Preferably this Hand. If not for him . . . if not for *him* . . .

Gete and Thani might even now be making their way back to the docks!

The Hand was recovering slowly. His wrists rested on Gete and Thani's
arms; now and again he stumbled against one of them. In the faraway eyes,
Gete saw something that might be madness, or might be dread so great it
came close to approximating peace. What did a god fear that much?

The answer was obvious. Gete found his palms were sweating.

Thani kept up a running flow of talk. It seemed rather pathetic to have to
remind a god of his own divinity, his supremacy, his invulnerability; but the
stream of doctrine seemed to be doing Thani herself some good. Her salt
crystals shot sparks of light and her lips gleamed wetly. Gete's heart
swelled with a helpless urge to protect her.

And maybe, after all, she been working a very minor kind of miracle. As
they entered a very upscale district, where all market activity ceased, and
Thani's voice rang emptily off the walls of the high stone mansions—Gete

observed a change in the god. His face took on an actual expression. It might be amusement.

A bell chimed far off. In the silence that ensued, Gete could hear the sea. He caught a salty whiff of it, too, carried on a freak breeze down countless alleys. Quite suddenly, he felt at home here in the silence, where furtive fingers moved behind lace curtains in the few windows that still held glass.

And the Palace reared up within wood-and-stone walls, a forbidding, yet higgledy-piggledy height; it looked rather rundown. At the top of a long wooden ramp, two Hands stood sentinel under a suspended row of dangerous-looking metal teeth.

One of them let out a shout. "Arity! *Firi! Perich"hi!"* His voice held a curious mixture of amazement and horror.

Thani broke off. "*'Arity,*" she whispered in a dreamlike tone. "No. It is not possible. It can't be." She spun around, shading her salted eyes at the god. They had mounted the ramp and the Hands were closing with them.

The god named Arity shook himself and sighed. "I suppose you'd better take us to Pati." Gete was astonished by the sheer rationality of his tone.

"At once, *perich"hi!*" the Hand exclaimed. What do you think we are? He has been searching for your ghost all of yesterday and today! When the ghostier vanished, we thought he had absconded with it! Just think how happy he will be to see you alive!"

The other Hand pushed him aside. "Let me tell the *perich"hi,* you fool. The Divinarch rescinded the order for your death yesterday, the minute he returned from taking his revenge on the K'Fier renegades."

"I don't believe it," Arity murmured. His murmur was still louder than a human exclamation, giving the comment the tone of a desperate avowal of disbelief. "He never changes his mind!"

"He did this time. He sent a delegation to get you back, but the ghostier had gone, leaving no traces. Sepia, the *kervayi-serbali,* swore he had handed you over to him—but Pati killed him anyway, to be sure." One after the other, the Hands embraced Arity. "He wants to take it out of the ghostier, too. We haven't found the rascal yet, but we're still looking—"

"It would be too bad to kill him," Arity said. "He spared me."

This did not fit with the mood of hapless despair in which Gete and Thani had found him. Gete shook his head, and slipped his fingers around Thani's arm. Perhaps if he could just pull her away—would she stand for it?

But it was too late. More Hands had appeared out of nowhere. Their delight was at once infectious and grotesque. Clustering into a knot, they surrounded Thani and Gete and whisked them across the courtyard, into a pair of doors in the Palace like a hole cut into darkness. Torches flared within, illuminating twisting corridors. After a nightmarish few minutes they attained a hall where a seething queue of Deltans, shifting their feet and muttering, extended as far as Gete could see. The humans fell mutinously silent when they saw the Hands.

"I do hate jumping the queue," Arity murmured.

"Don't be absurd!" One of the strangest-looking Hands, whose face and throat were mostly covered by a splotchy blue patch shaped rather like a bird, punched Arity affectionately. "They ought to thank their stars you're alive! The Divinarch is in such a bad mood he's sentenced every petitioner so far to instant death."

"Gods," Thani whispered, and gulped as if she were about to cry.

For some reason Gete had not credited her with understanding the gods' jabber. He steadied her as the Hands swept them down the length of the hall, past the restless civilians, through another monstrous pair of doors that opened as if by magic.

The Throne Room was dim. The reek of death hung sour in the air. Twelve gods stood on pedestals built into the huge, fantastic throne. But the seat itself was empty.

A pile of bodies lay in the middle of the floor. Black human blood trickled from its base. A slim, pale figure stood beside the gruesome hillock, wiping his fingers on a handkerchief. It was an easy guess that this was the Divinarch of Royalland, Calvary, Veretry, Pirady, Iceland, the sundry isles of the Archipelago, and Domesdys, et al.

When Arity entered the Throne Room at Gete's side, the Divinarch went stiller than any living thing ought to be able to.

Arity swayed toward him, like a sapling in a high wind.

Just before he fell, he caught himself and stood upright.

"Go upstairs," Pati whispered hoarsely. "Wait for me."

"No," Arity said. "Say what you have to say before my friends."

"Shall I? *Oh, Arity*—Perhaps I shall." The Divinarch's voice was soft as falling drops of blood. "I thought you were dead, and I did not have so much as your ghost. I—" His eye fell on Gete, and he stopped. Instinctively, Gete cringed back into the knot of Hands who had brought them. "What is this thing with the fiery head? There is another one? Dispatch them. They have heard too much."

"But, milord Divinarch," one of the Hands on the Throne called out respectfully. He was a small god with parchment-brown skin and a luxuriant mop of hair, "It's a flamen and leman. Should you . . ."

"Oh, very well then, I'll deal with them." The Divinarch flicked a glance at Arity like a slow-uncoiling lash of fire. "It will only take a few minutes."

Arity made a face, and then shrugged.

Gete poked Thani. This was her moment. He had brought her this far by hook or by crook; now she was on her own.

She took a step forward. "Milord Divinarch," she began, "I come in humble suppliance."

"I'm sure you do." The Divinarch's voice was honey. He snapped his fingers. In a sharp-smelling flash, he was up on the Throne, among the Hands, leaning down. "Come here."

Thani took one step. Then another. Swaying, blind, she stumbled to the base of the Throne.

Forever afterward, Gete would curse himself for failing to break the ice of fear off his joints, failing to go to her, to clamp his hands over her budding salt crystals, anything that might have saved her.

Her lord is the whole world.

She can see him in the gray confusion where she lives and moves.

See him whole and entire, sharp enough to make her cry for her sacrificed sight.

See the veins on the backs of his hands.

See his white bangs springing down the middle of his forehead.

See the pupils in the centers of his bicolored eyes.

Hear his voice honey-sweet, louder than her ears can stand. Its purity is spoiled by the buzzing in the bones of her skull. She takes her head in her hands, trying to shake the interference away, but then she understands what he has asked and she forgets the discomfort and falls to her knees on the invisible floor, ready to answer, eager to please.

"Who do you serve?"

"You. You, milord Divinarch!"

"Why did you come to Delta City?"

"To learn the tales and parables my Godsbrother did not teach me." The answers are both rote and heartfelt. "To learn how to worship you better. To learn how to preach your worship in the far corners of the world."

"And what did you find?"

"That—that . . ." With a failing of the heart, she knows she has to tell the real truth. If she does not, he will know, and be angry with her. "The city is under martial rule . . . The teachers are gone . . . The world-renowned flamens of Marshtown turned apostate. The people are afraid of their gods, and their flamens."

"Those who are truly devout have nothing to fear from me. Or you. For not all my flamens have betrayed me. Most, in fact, have stayed in the fold. And this is not martial rule, my darling. I am merely keeping the peace. Believe me, it's harder to keep the peace now than it ever was before! The

forces of Change are at work on the world. I am all that stands between them and you and your people." He jumps to the floor beside her and raises her up. His hot smooth palms completely enclose her hands. "Do not lose faith, little starling."

Do not lose faith! *He* knows. *He* knows *the torture she has been undergoing.*

A marvelous peace enfolds her. After so many months of unfocused yearning, she has found the truth.

It's all a matter of having faith. Why has that been so difficult for her? It is the easiest thing in the world. Faith.

No wonder that when she looked for the old stability, it was gone. The gods are no longer rulers of a well-ordered, cyclical existence. All the cycles have come to an end or been broken. The forces of Change took Godsbrother Transcendence from her; they banished her from Calvary, the land of her dreams. Only the Divinarch stands between her and its further ravages.

It was unfair of me to promise security to Gete the way Transcendence promised it to me. He cannot look to me, nor to the world, to give him a whole, unbroken life. He must look to the Divinarch. The Divinarch is our only hope against the scourge of destiny. He loves his people so much that he is fighting time itself for our sakes. With his Hands he is erecting a dam against the tide.

She trembles. Comprehension ripples like ecstatic sensation through her body. Bells and trumpets pound against the inside of her head. She prays the tremors are not physical. She is so frail.

"Divinarch, I will do whatever you ask." Her voice wavers up and down the scale as if she is not paying attention to what she is saying. But she is, with all her might. "I will keep the faith!"

"My pet. My child. My love."

He embraces her. He could break her in two with his strength. He is so gentle.

She bites the inside of her cheek. Salty blood trickles onto her tongue. "Take me." She smears it with a trembling finger on the back of his hand. "Take my body. Take my soul."

He kisses her forehead, the tip of her nose. His breath smells of her blood. His grip is like a vise on her arms. "Do my will, my own little flamen. Whatever I say. Whatever any of the Hands say. They speak for me."

"Anything! I'll do anything! I—"

But he is gone, leaving her with her arms outstretched, empty. Shining, he strides around behind the Throne, behind the fainter shapes of the lesser gods. She can still see him, but faintly, as if through water. "Thank the Power that's over," he says. "I hate the taste of fur. Now, Ari—"

She falls to her knees, sobbing, crying, pleading with him to come back. Don't leave me!

But the Inviolate Ones grab her arms and she is half-marched, half-dragged out through the great doors into a sea of humans. Darkness. Noise. Where is Gete? She panics.

Gete finds her. He wraps his arms around her. He drags her out of the way of unseen legs and feet.

And little by little she manages to stop weeping. It is then that she senses the light within her. She gasps, puts her hands to her chest, imagines she can feel its heat . . . at the same time as she hears a bugle voice calling, "Chrumecountry . . . first barge," and Gete replies distractedly.

She smiles, conscious of nothing except profound relief, knowing that now, wherever she goes, she is at home. She does not have to doubt any longer. The light will never leave her. She is his, and she will remain his, no one's but his, until the day she dies in his service.

DESTINY BESIEGED

"I was wrong to do it," Pati said. He stood at the glass wall, staring out over the speckled sea. He wore a Kithrilindric bedrobe with spangles that flashed when he moved. "But at the time, I believed I had to. You were making a fool of me, with your human *irissu* and your warped politics!" He turned. "You must see that, Ari. Now you are back, I know there will be no more such incidents."

Contrition. From the warnings of the Hands, this was what Arity had expected. Yet it unnerved him. He could not remember any other time when Pati had acted as he, Arity, expected. And the reason for that, he conjectured, was that he and Pati lived by two entirely different systems— call them the mortal and the *auchresh*, call them what you would. The difference had been there ever since they had come to human country, perhaps all their civilized lives. Pati's path was that of the intellectual, the utterly civilized, unalloyedly rational, and his destiny was where it led: the intertwined mountains and chasms of genius and monstrosity.

Arity had never before seen him speak without thinking, without a plan, without any motive except emotion.

But of course Pati had had a bad scare.

"I regretted it immediately! Didn't the Hands tell you? I reversed my order—"

"And you never, ever reverse orders," Arity said.

"Gods! What has the ghostier done to you?" Pati said. "He's changed you! Has he made you into a ghost after all? No, it can't be! Even a ghost is not as cold as you are!"

"It's not that I don't *feel,*" Arity said, nettled. He lowered himself into a splay-legged chair made from the skeletons of dog lizards, and reached out to the remnants of the supper Pati had ordered. He swiped his finger around the kasha bowl and sucked off the goo. "It's that—well, one has to locate a balance. There is such a thing as giving in to one's feelings. As lack of self-control. I had fallen so far into that trap that I touched bottom— because I *decided*, and kept on consciously deciding to relinquish all self-control."

"That makes no sense," Pati said angrily. The lamplight made him glow against the backdrop of the dark windows. The room smelled of an unfamiliar body perfume. Had Pati had another *ghauthiji* up here while he grieved for Arity? Arity wouldn't put it past him.

"Hear me out," Arity said. "Yesterday, all I could think of to do was die. I had lost you. Without you, I had nothing in the world to live for. But Ghostier Southwind refused to indulge me. And I lack the courage to kill myself. I could not die.

"I suppose it was inevitable that I realized my only alternative was to live." Arity laughed. "It was that girl-flamen you brainwashed this afternoon who gave me the first push. She babbled on and on about our greatness and glory—trying to convince herself of it as much as me, I think, your pets are not as certain of themselves as they were—and I was staggering along between her and her leman, you know, scarcely able to walk in a straight line. I could not keep from laughing at the utter absurdity of the whole thing!"

"Absurdity?" Pati said sharply.

"Yes, absurdity! The gulf of reality between our lives and our pretensions to grandeur." Arity ate a finger of marzipan. "I don't know about you, but I can't continue as I was. The hypocrisy is choking. I feel sick."

"I see that you have changed in a way I cannot quite appreciate. Though I am trying." Pati leaned back against the glass, his robe outlining the bones of his hips. The silk hem pooled over his bare feet. Arity caught himself thinking how elegant Pati was, then mentally reproved himself. The aftertaste of the marzipan was bitter, like straight vanilla. "But this philosophizing is a dangerous new pastime, as well as an irksome one. Perhaps you have forgotten that we have started a war. Every minute we waste is a minute lost to the enemy."

Arity said, "I can't go on subjecting myself to you."

That got his attention. The blue eye and the brown blazed. "I never asked you to make yourself my slave!"

"You did! Think back to Wind Gully Heaven, and you'll see what I mean. But that doesn't really matter. Since I came to the city, the only way I've been able to defy you is by subjecting myself to you still further. Refusing to accept special treatment. It didn't work. In a way, I suppose I'm acknowledging you were right." The bones of the chair were digging into his backside. He did not take his eyes off Pati, whose rigid stance, like that of a predator poised on a clifftop, vividly betrayed the intensity of his emotions. "But you were right for all the wrong reasons. You wanted to confer privileges on me, but you still wanted me to be your slave." He paused. "That's the way it has been between us, ever since you were a *mainraui* and I was a Foundling. And it doesn't work."

"You are so *blind*, Ari!" Pati's cry of pain severed the silk of the argument Arity had woven around himself. "You have completely misunderstood me. I knew that—but that doesn't mean I *wanted* it! *You* wanted to relinquish all responsibility for yourself, to wallow in the mindless pleasure—or misery, how should I know which it was?—of being needed. Of being required by somebody else. I let you do it because I love you. But have you really failed to see that ever since we found each other again, all I have wanted is for you to love me back? I don't want another Hand. I want a companion!"

Arity kept blinking. These impassioned words sounded as if they were flooding from Pati's heart—an organ whose existence he had seriously doubted.

He had forgotten about the vortex of need that fueled Pati's intellect. Need beyond erotic desire or even the longing for companionship. Need for the thing most lacking in the whimsical, merciless court he had created: honesty. The need of the whole *auchresh* race for trust, an emotion none of them was really capable of. A gift none of them could give each other.

(A gift that Humi, with her charm and humanity, had fooled Arity into believing she had given him—)

Gone, long gone—

"Power, Pati, I'm sorry!"

"I'm not everything I pretend to be . . ." Pati's voice broke. If it was not real, it was extremely convincing. "You are the only person who knows that. That is why I . . . need you."

Arity said deliberately, "You're a god." He had to plumb Pati's mind, now he had the chance. He owed it to the whole world. He was the only one in the world who had the faintest hope of finding out what Pati really thought. That was part of why he had returned. "You don't need anybody. Not me. Or anybody. You embody the Divine Entity. You are completely supreme."

Pati laughed. Not insanely. Normally. "You knew me before we engaged in this masquerade, Arity. A god? There is no theory so ungrounded in possibility as the existence of gods. You disappoint me."

Arity nodded, sadly.

The most flawless conceits were, after all, not strong enough to bridge the gaps in reality. Those gaps had to remain mysterious. (Unless one is a flamen, a little voice said inside Arity.) Belief on its own could not span anything.

Yet it was profoundly embarrassing to hear Pati admit it. And even more embarrassing to see him fold up into a dark hump at the foot of the window. Almost unbearable to hear him panting, like an animal that knows it is fatally wounded.

Arity, despite all his intentions to the contrary, went to him and bent down, taking his head on his lap and kissing the vibrant white hair. "I love you," he murmured.

Pati twisted, revealing his face. He was weeping. The muscles at the bases of his folded wings were as hard as stone.

Of course they stumbled into the bedroom. Of course, half against Arity's will and half not, they made love. Sex was after all the mainstay of their relationship—always had been, even when they were not lovers. How could he have thought *that* might change? Pati writhed and sweated and groaned, but Arity enjoyed the pipe of smokewort they shared afterward more than the act. Pati had brought the wort back from the Archipelago. Killing all the renegades in K'Fier had meant ransacking the town. It was potent stuff.

The transparent bowl of the pipe glowed red in the darkness of the bedroom. They lay propped companionably in the high old bed that had belonged to countless Divinarches before them.

I have to clip my thorns, Arity thought. New ones were sprouting, the old bases pushing up from his skin like miniature tablelands. Pati had welcomed the pain of the scratches the razored edges inflicted on him. Arity had known he had a streak that way: its revelation came as no surprise.

"Do you intend to continue as a Hand?" Pati said at length.

"I'll take the title of Lieutenant," Arity said. "Not Heir. Still not Heir." He had thought this out already. "I'll serve as the twentieth councillor, too. I think that's fitting."

"Nothing could please me more. We'll shuffle all the *kervayim* down one. You may have heard that I disposed of Sepia; I would have had to elect a new councillor anyway, and it goes against the grain to promote Hands from the ranks that high."

Arity sucked on the pipe. The smoke slid down his throat like mint ice. Off the top of a lungful, he said, "I have something I want to ask you."

"Anything you like," Pati said.

"Did your patrols find Humi? Or Hope?"

A long pause.

"No."

Pause. Smoke trickled out of Arity's nostrils, thin milky strands, and he released his breath.

"Nor Southwind. Nor the female crime lord. But I doubt," Pati said, "that it will be very long before they all announce their whereabouts."

"You mean . . ."

"They are all in it together. Yes; we would be stupid not to prepare for the worst." The word entered Arity's being, as potent as the smoke.

"Do you really think that's what she intends? I didn't think she had it in her anymore."

"I know she has."

Arity shrugged. "Perhaps you're right. You and she always understood each other in that way. So you intend to defend yourself by attacking?"

"Exactly."

"Two wars at once!" Arity tried to joke. "Just like ancient times, with the Conversion Wars and the quarrels over our role as gods going on simultaneously in the salt—"

"Except that this time we *auchresh* are in control." Pati corrected him. "We know the mortals' capacity for hysteria, and we will try to involve as few of them as possible, on both fronts. And, should we have to crush insurrections here or in the continents, we are not short of recruits. Broken Bird and Bronze Water, the poor misguided *umanurim,* and their obsolete leadership, drive more young *keres* into my arms every day. We even have a few *iuim;* I've made them honorary captains."

"Excellent," Arity said, but the truth was that he did not think it excellent at all. *War.* He wished to the Power he did not have to play a part in it. There seemed not a doubt that neither Pati's ideological crusade against the renegades nor Humi's rebellion could be kept clear of mortal passions, and mortal lives.

Yet he was committed now, and one saw things out to the grim end. One chose one's fate with one's eyes open.

Pati reached for the pipe. His fingers touched Arity's just long enough to convey intimacy, not long enough to be lascivious. The very delicacy of the caress was predictable. But of course Pati's predictability, like that of anything else, depended on nothing but Arity's own predictions. It was he who had changed. After having death snatched from his throat, everything else naturally seemed predictable by comparison. Didn't it?

"Ahhh." The wort glowed as Pati sucked the stem, reddening the concentrated planes of his face. *He is beautiful in the way that any auchresh is beautiful, even more so,* Arity told himself impatiently. *I have a gorgeous lover who happens to be the Divinarch and I have just become the twentieth councillor of the Ellipse. Now why does it feel like I've been here before?*

MURDER IN THE DARK

The killers jimmy the back door with stealthy expertise. They close it behind themselves to cut off the draft, and before you can say "Wait a minute
. . . aren't you . . ." they have slipped upstairs. They do not have to look
for their victims. Do everyone in the house, they were told. So they climb
up to the musty, cavernous attic and work their way down. Another family,
the Brundels, inhabits the top three floors, but the killers don't know that
and it would make no difference if they did. Within three minutes, they've
dispatched Grandfather Brundel, Father Brundel, Mother Brundel,
Maiden-aunt Brundel, and the five children over whose welfare the adults
have spent all evening arguing. The question of whether to send them out
to their relatives in Chrumetown (would the journey be too dangerous?
does the risk of staying in the city justify it?) is moot—at the same time as it
has been definitively answered.

Bruises burst up like tumors through the fur of the Brundels' throats. All
three killers favor the garotte as a means of noiseless, efficient murder. The
sound of breath has stopped: the parents still hold each other but their arms
have been transformed into heavy pieces of meat. The blood no longer
moves through the flesh.

The house dog whines and yips on the landing, sensing something is
wrong, as the trio slithers down the staircase into the Lakestones' apartment.

"Hist," the leader whispers, and with a muttered profanity, the last man
draws his dagger from the sheath in his boot. It whickers through the dark
and pins the little dog to the floor by one eye. The furry beast flops, fishlike,
and is still.

The killers closed all the windows before they started, just in case there
were screams, but all the same, the winter seems to seep down after them
from the upstairs apartment. It is the mute, intangible cold of the absence

of life. The killers breathe easily in it, all their muscles loose. They are not natives of this rarefied, potent atmosphere, but they have been changed by their regular visits to the heights.

The little Lakestone girl and the boy stop breathing without a struggle. The woman, too, slips as quietly out of life as she slipped through its cracks. The man is another story. He is already awake. When the killers enter the room he and his wife share, he is hiding behind the door. When he sees the first man bending over Leasa, he leaps at the killer with a howl, huge hands raking his back. The other two are still behind him, and between them they grab the man and throttle him, one drawing the noose spitefully tight while the other grips his massive limbs until they stop moving.

"Pfuh," says the first killer, dropping the woman on the bed. "Bleeder got me in the kidneys."

"Yer leakin a bit. But you won't die 'fore we get back."

"Fuck it. Less go."

Spitting one after the other, in a ritualistic fashion, on the threshold of the bedroom, they leave through the front door as softly as they came in.

The wounded house stands immobile, crushed between its neighbors, screaming silently for help. Its eaves tilt upward as if it is trying to squeeze out of the narrow space Temeriton has allotted it. One imagines that when it is able to fly, it will wing ungainly off into the stars, flapping its shutters and doors like stiff little wings.

The red lantern of the brothel across the concourse flickers. Night is winding down toward dawn. ~~Delights and~~ Diversions' door swings gently, half-open, scraping along the groove it has worn in the cobbles.

Aneisneida's bodywoman woke her at four in the morning. "Get up! Milady, get up!" She shook Aneisneida roughly through the bedcovers. "Milady, get dressed!"

A shock ran through Aneisneida and she threw the coverlet aside. "What's happened?" Strangely enough, Fiamorina and Soderingal did not spring to her mind. With an uncharacteristic flash of prescience, she saw Humi's face floating in the dark, smiling that faint, bland, superior smile of hers. Petula wrung her hands. Her dress was hooked askew, her petticoat showed, and her hair straggled over her breasts. "It's happened! Milady, they're coming! You must get ready to receive them!"

"*Who* is coming?"

The candle Petula had set on the bed fell over, spilling hot wax onto the embroidery.

Outside the window, the palace district was dark and silent. Aneisneida strained her ears. Nothing.

The bodywoman's hands shook as she struck flint and relighted the candle. "The Inviolate Ones! Oh, milady, you must look your best! Your hair—your clothes—what about your pink gown—the one with the tiered skirts? For them, only the best will do. We must show 'em our importance, or we're lost!"

Aneisneida swung her feet to the floor. She stood rockstill, the coverlet crunched between her hands. Petula forgot herself so far as to tug at her arm.

Aneisneida wrenched away. "Stop it, girl!" She brought her palms together as loudly as she could. A manservant came to the door. Even in the candlelight he looked frightened. "Go rouse Lord Nearecloud!" Aneisneida told him. "And Nurse. Tell her to wrap the little lady up warmly." He did not move. She shouted, "Go!"

When he had gone, Petula begged, "Milady? Milady, are you out of your mind? *Please* dress!"

"It is *you* who are out of your mind! Receive the Hands? They would slaughter us where we stood." Aneisneida knew without having to think about it that Pati had finally decided to exterminate them. The Neareclouds, along with a few other families, were the last seedlings of a palace district vine that had once tried to strangle him. Had she been in Pati's position, she would have assassinated herself a long time ago.

How long did they have? There weren't many families left. Most of them were squatters, practiced at hiding their movements, in case, by some remote chance, the real owners of their houses should come back from Purgatory and punish them. This house lay at the Christon end of the district, within walking distance of Gremlaw Concourse. If the Hands came on foot, as they seemed to do more and more often now, if they swept west from the Palace, if they were keeping Anei and Soder until last, as a child keeps the biggest cherry until the end of the bowl—the Neareclouds might have enough time to get away.

"When they are roused, they are like beasts," she said to Petula. "They do not think. Even if the Divinarch had ordered them to spare us, it would not guarantee our safety."

Petula nodded. Her eyes spilled over and she snatched her gown to her face.

"Get out of my sight." Contemptuously, Aneisneida gave the girl a shove. Smothering sobs, Petula darted out of the bedroom.

Aneisneida picked up the dead candle.

Wax burned her hand. She smelled singed thread.

Cold wind sighed past the gables.

Far away. Gay, delighted shouts.

Fear shivered through her bones.

Calm. Calm.

She stalked to the wardrobe annex and sorted through her pile of dresses. This one had the most jewels on its cuffs. It was not the prettiest. Nor one of those her father had given her. Before putting it on, she slit the hem and weighted it with jewelry out of her boudoir jewel cases. When she was half hooked up, she heard Soderingal come in behind her. He was carrying Fiamorina. "We're leavin," he said. "Get that stuff off of you."

With a contortion that hurt her shoulder muscles, she fastened the last hooks. "Do you really think I'm going to stay here and greet them in my finery? I am not stupid, Soder." She felt no fear now, only a cold determination to enrage Pati, to get away. Like transmogrified terror. Steel.

She shook her wrists at him and the heavy bands of sapphires flapped. "I'll tell you where we are going. We are going to offer our services to Humi. We are going to commit ourselves to the revolution. And thus, we will eventually gain back everything we are going to lose tonight."

"Fuck that. We're goin to join my father in Shimorning," Soder said. "I've 'ad it with bendin my 'ead to Divinarches, no matter what they call themselves!"

"You pampered son of an idle noblewoman." Anger rose in Aneisneida. "What matters is that we have to choose our lord for ourselves. We didn't, before, or only halfheartedly."

A faint, evil orange was flickering in the top panes of the window.

"We're fuckin well not going to throw our lives away. Shut that crap. Humi's a blind beggar, no more, no less. We're going to Shimorning."

Soderingal had never expressed his opinion of Humi so succinctly before. His eyes were like stones.

And Aneisneida felt herself bending, melting—

She *knew* what she had to do! For once in her life she knew what she had to do! And she—

opened her mouth to give in—

And flames rose above the roofs a mere five or six streets away. Aneisneida and Soderingal spun to the suddenly bright window. Fiamorina wailed in her father's arms. The servants hammered on the door. Lord and Lady Nearecloud glanced at each other, and bounded downstairs.

Not even the nurse would accompany them when she heard they were going "to Temeriton . . . to Shimorning!" The servants stood in a tearful gaggle on the front steps, trusting and foolish, ready to throw themselves on the Hands' mercy. Petula begged, "You *can't* leave! All the tap'stries . . . all the silver . . . all yer lovely dresses, milady—"

The loss of her wardrobe did give Aneisneida a pang, but it was a pin-prick compared to the determination the Hands aroused in her. If only she could make Soder see! Throwing themselves on the mercy of a crime lord would be like jumping from the frying pan into the fire.

If the whole city didn't go up in flames.

As they hurried along the broad streets of the palace district, in the biting night air, they argued passionately. Soder seemed to have a childish conviction that her father would be able to protect them from Pati, even if all the Hands stormed the Rats' Den at once. Aneisneida told him over and over that he was wrong. Gold Dagger's army of followers were in it for the profit. Harboring nobility, a practice which had long ago proved fatal, could not exactly be profitable. The Nearoclouds, or at least Anei herself, would be turned over to Pati.

She did not want to be held accountable for her husband's misconceptions! She did not want Fia to be held accountable!

She did not trust Gold Dagger, not as she trusted Humi.

But her feet began to tire, and Fiamorina, passed constantly back and forth between them, grew heavier and heavier, and the prospect of walking all the way to Temeriton no longer seemed so plausible. She was stumbling with tiredness as they entered the alleys that twisted along between the Christon concourses. Her slippers were slowly cutting her feet into bite-sized pieces. And before she realized where Soder was leading her—before she had consented to anything, before she had given in—they were cutting across the corner of Marshtown that lay between Christon and Shimorning.

One of their manservants passed them. The alley they moved in was narrow and dark, but the fellow scuttled past as fast as a spider across a floor too large and bare for its liking. "Hoy!" Soderingal hissed.

The fellow reversed his trajectory and matched his pace to Aneisneida's. His eyes were large and green as toads' heads, bulging from his smoke-stained face. "They burned the mansion, milord! *Burned* it! Everything—the stars gray with smoke. Everything. Few of us got away!"

"Just as I was expecting," Aneisneida said wearily.

The man was drawing ahead again. Soderingal called out, "Raille! One thing more! D'you know how we kin get to the"—he tasted the words carefully before pronouncing them—"the Rats' Den?"

The manservant threw up one hand, clasping his other awkwardly to his side. "You can find it anywhere in Shimorning you look, milord. But you have to know how to look." He laughed breathlessly. "Now good evening, milord, milady! Gods bless!"

And he was gone. Starlight glistened in his wet footprints. He must have been bleeding, Aneisneida realized.

Soderingal shifted Fiamorina to his other arm. "And me 'is *master!*" he ground out, charging along, blind with frustration. Aneisneida understood before long that he had no idea where he was going. But for the haze of tiredness that stilled her mind, she would have been furious.

Windows threw a flickering light on the cobbles. A tavern. The back entrance. She could hear voices and laughter. For the first time since they left their house, the sound did not ring alarm bells in her. "Can we go in?" she begged. "Can we sit down?"

Soderingal glanced at her. "I'll ask directions t' the Rats' Den. We won't stay."

It was a hole-in-the-wall, full of regulars who all knew each other. Aneisneida did not understand any of the remarks they addressed to her; but Soder found himself in his element. Despite his purported good intentions, he did not get around to mentioning the Rats' Den until he had had enough whiskey to weight his tongue and make his lips gleam darkly.

All the Shimorningers exchanged significant glances when they heard "Gold Dagger." But the little green-furred fellow who eventually elected himself as their informant refused to give his name. "Yew don't want t' go down there, milord." He eyed Aneisneida's wrists in a way she did not like. "They be thieves down there. And apostates, now, too. And they do say the Divinarch 'ave hidden there, and tis true there are daggermen at every trapdoor, like as if they 'ad somethin to guard."

The word struck like a sunbeam through the fog in Aneisneida's mind. "The Divinarch?" she gasped. "Not Pati? Humi?"

"They do say it be Lady Garden. But I've 'eard stories like that afore, an I'm not gettin' my 'opes up, not me."

"The Divinarch." Aneisneida looked her husband full in the face. Smoke curled drunkenly between them. All the sounds of the tavern seemed to fade away as she savored her triumph. What an exquisite pleasure to outfox him, and all the sweeter for having done it accidentally! "*Ha,*" she said. "Shall we go, milord? I consent with pleasure. What will you call her now? Even your vaunted father serves her. Is she a blind beggar, or a *queen?*"

Soderingal said nothing. He stared at her with a mixture of emotions she could not read.

And Aneisneida dashed her face into Fiamorina's robe, and as the toddler woke and began to grizzle, she burst into tears, clutching Fia as if the child could compensate for the loss of everything she had ever valued. The Summer name was really gone now. Everything that had been Belstem's was burned to ashes, sprinkled across the city. All that remained was one name.

Humi.

Give me back the past. Or at least make it safe for me to pretend I am there!

Sol lowered his voice as he ushered Aneisneida and Soderingal down the crooked stone stairs. "I ought to warn you. She should be sleeping. We can only spare her for a few hours at a time. But she just found out that some friends of hers have been killed, so she has come down here to be alone."

"You did not tell us this!" Aneisneida whispered. "Should we come back later?"

"No. She wants to see you." Sol's mouth pulled downward at the corners. "Just be aware what she has passed through. You would never know to look at her that an hour ago she was raging and weeping in my arms."

So the two were lovers? That was all right. Both of them were ghostiers, so the involvement was almost proper—far less scandalous, anyhow, than Humi's most publicized liaison, Aneisneida thought hopefully.

The green moss and lichen on the roof glowed over Sol's torch as he led them around the last corner. He stepped aside. Anei and Soder found themselves in a monstrous cavern. A table stood some way into the space, and on it was a ring of candles, flickering in a weary little breeze that must have found its way down from miles above and could not get back out. The small circle of light only emphasized the size of the place. Shadows crouched in the roughnesses of the floor like furry beasts. Water dripped down a distant wall. Aneisneida heard clawed feet in a corner.

She clung to Soderingal's arm. Uncharacteristically, he did not shake her off. They had come down through a complicated maze of stairways and tunnels, a labyrinth whose existence Aneisneida had never guessed: it was humbling to realize you were lady of so much less and so much more than you had thought. She guessed that Soderingal, like herself, felt less confident than usual.

Humi sat at the table, quite composed, with something long and scaly crawling over her arms.

"So it has started." She caressed the creature. It sat on her left hand, its long scarlet tongue leaping. "They have taken the palace district. I expect everything is confusion?"

Sol nodded. "They're jumping like fish on dry land. Two knife gangs are scheduled to mobilize within the hour. We're going to take advantage of the element of surprise and try to pick off as many Hands as possible, while keeping our real strength hidden."

"Have we received any word from Hope?"

"No," Sol said. "Not a thing."

Humi sighed enormously. "Well, I suppose I shall be needed upstairs.

But we have a few minutes. Lord Nearecloud—Lady Summer." She nodded. "Will you sit on the table? I should not like to make you stand. You will be doing too much of that in the next few days." When neither of them moved, she said with a hint of irritation, "I mean no insult to your dignity. We have had to put etiquette temporarily in abeyance, here."

Rather awkwardly, Aneisneida hitched herself up on the table, arranging her skirts. Soderingal stood quite still.

"Sol, you'd better stay," Humi said. "I think it best if we have a witness to this little meeting."

Soder's mouth opened in indignation. Aneisneida thought, *Oh no, please be quiet!*

But he had not yet got beyond the first blow Humi had delivered to his pride. "Wotcha mean calling my wife Summer? She's been Nearecloud for close on five years!"

"Oh." Humi sighed. "I am not implying that your marriage is invalid. Only that if you plan to remain here, on my side, it will be necessary for Aneisneida to reclaim her maiden name. If you conferred it on your daughter, too, that would be even better."

"No child of *mine*—" Soder spluttered.

"Have you ever seen a sword lizard?" Humi asked in a louder-than-necessary voice, drowning his objections. "They live down in these caverns. Historians think them to have been extinct ever since the city covered the island, for Delta Island is the only place in Royalland they ever lived, apart from a few other marshlands. But they did not die. They moved underground. They have gone pale through lack of sun."

The creature she fondled was as white as a ghost coated with base paint. Apart from the slap-slap-slap of its tail on her forearm, silence filled the cavern.

"And they are quite blind. Look at its eyes—aren't they beautiful? Purple. But it can't see—"

Roughly, Soderingal interrupted, "Milady, we didn't come to meet your pets. My father sent us down 'ere for some reason I have yet to comprehend. Apparently not even 'is own *son*—not even the last real lord left in the city—can stay 'ere without yer say-so. Not even in the middle of a war. I need yer *permission*—"

"I think it would be more correct to say *especially* Gold Dagger's son," Humi murmured. "*Especially* the last lord in the city. You have been known, both of you, to provide intelligence to the tyrant."

"Gods' blood! All I want is yer *gracious permission* to stay 'ere an' fight on your *side!*" In Soder's sneer, Aneisneida could hear the pain of Gold Dagger's less-than-wholehearted welcome. "Is that too much t' ask? I can

'elp you get recruits—I have contacts—I'm not exactly penniless, an' nor is
my wife—"

"All my followers carry weapons." Humi stroked the sword lizard's skull.
"Even the blind ones. Even the flamens and lemans. Even the rich. Are
you ready to fight, Soder?"

Aneisneida smothered a gasp. Without trying it seemed, Humi had hit
Soderingal's weakest point. The thing for which he had had his bodyguards
knock men down. The thing for which she herself could not help despising
him.

"What are you accusin' me of? *Cowardice?*"

In the corner of her eye, Anei saw Sol drift closer to the table.

"I merely asked whether you are prepared to fulfill *your* half of the
bargain implicit in your arrival. Your offer of recruits is very generous—and
I shall take advantage of it—but just because you are noble does not mean
you are exempted from other obligations. Please do not feel singled out.
This is the means by which I ensure the loyalty of all my followers. A knife
in the hand is the greatest temptation, after all, is it not?"

Soder had gone the color of mud. Aneisneida could smell his sweat. She
wondered what vague plans he had been harboring. Nothing that involved
personal risk, she knew that!

"Let me put it another way," Humi said. "You and Lady Summer are a
serious threat to our secrecy. If I take you in, you must assure me that you
are not only committed to *your* safety, but to *mine.*"

"But we had nowhere else to go!" Anei pleaded. "Why would we betray
you? We would be betraying ourselves!" She and Humi were old friends!
They had come to see her in her isolation, when even the ghostiers had
shunned her! How ungrateful she was! And when had her voice grown so
brittle?

"Aneisneida, I have turned hundreds of men away from my service.
Atheists, devotees, apostates. They were, to put it bluntly, out for number
one. When we are enthroned once more, we will have the latitude to
tolerate self-interest." Her voice hardened. "But for now, all my followers
must be fanatics, for that is the only way we can combat the fanaticism of
the Hands."

Something stirred in Aneisneida, nudging up through her fear.

The need to trust someone.

"I believe in you, Humi," she whispered, almost meaning it. She looked
into the tranquil, tawny face. "I'll carry your knife. And I vouch for my
husband." She elbowed Soderingal hard as he was about to speak.

Water dripped, splashing thinly on stone.

In the silence, she heard all of their lungs propelling the bad air in and out, in and out.

The sword lizard moved its razor-edged tail smoothly up and down, narrowly missing Humi's face. A few strands of frizzy hair floated free.

"Thank you, Aneisneida," Humi said. She nodded. She might have been embarrassed by Aneisneida's confession—or she might just have been miles away. "We acknowledge your pledge."

Soderingal puffed out his breath. "What do you want from me, then?" he said with bad grace. "Can't leave. You wouldn't let me, now. A fuckin' signed an' sealed declaration?"

Humi shook her head. She held out her hand. "A brush of the lips. One can tell a great deal about a man from the way he kisses."

Aneisneida felt slightly shocked.

"For Anei and Fia, mind!" Soderingal grumbled. "Wouldn't accept such an insult to m' honor for anythin' less!"

He kissed Humi's hand. Despite everything that had passed, Aneisneida noticed he lingered longer than necessary over it.

"Your father did this for me," Humi said, wiping her hand on her skirt.

"Did 'e," Soderingal said. "You brainwashed 'im into it."

Sol grabbed Soderingal by the neck. He dragged him away from the table and Aneisneida screamed. The knife licked Soderingal's throat, shaving off tufts of green fur, and Sol hissed, "Never a word of that. *Think* before you bandy about terms more appropriate to an audience in the Palace! Here, we fight for *freedom.*" With a shove, he released Soder. "Freedom!" The sword lizard jumped off the table and scuttled into the shadows. Soderingal rubbed his throat.

Aneisneida cringed, fully expecting an explosion.

"You're gonna teach me 'ow to do that," Soder said thoughtfully.

She thought Sol would refuse. But Humi said, "Yes. Teach him. That would be good for both of you." She was half standing up now, both her hands pressed into the table. "I am going upstairs, so they will be able to spare *you* for a while, Sol. Conduct Lord Nearecloud to the bouting rooms. Work out your distrust with wooden blades. You might as well get it over with. We will have little time, once battle is engaged."

Neither of the men noticed when she gasped as if she were about to fall. Without thinking, Aneisneida slid off the table and slid her arm around the other woman. Humi's heart was beating furiously. Her palms were wet.

She stiffened. Aneisneida understood. Abashed, she took her arm away.

"No," Humi whispered, clumsily clutching Aneisneida's shoulder. "It's just that I cannot forget." Her voice was urgent, furtive. "I keep trying to forget. And then remembering—all at once, like that. It was my fault, you know. My fault, for not protecting them better from—from Pati—"

Aneisneida gaped. Shock stopped her from replying. And in that minute of hesitation, she lost Humi's confidence. The Divinarch pulled away and smiled with that artificial blandness which always soured Aneisneida's mouth. "*You*, my dear, look positively exhausted. You and Fia shall stay in the Hangman's house. You may have the room I used to have. The hand-maid who served me is quite sweet, and efficient, though she is only two years out of Veretry. I suggest you take an escort there soon. The Rats' Den is no place for a woman, and especially not at night."

She blew out the candles, accurately.

GALLOWSBIRDS

Hope had been in Pirady two sixdays, succumbing to the rhythm of Erene and Elicit's life. Her hope of persuading them to return to Delta City was diminishing. They said that of course they were in favor of ending the tyranny. But they would not commit themselves to the war effort. Furthermore, they insisted that before Hope, or Humi, embarked on any course of action, they must speak with the renegades. What they had in mind was for Hope to meet two *auchresh* friends of theirs, Shine and Keef. It all seemed a little ambiguous to Hope: wasn't *she* an *auchresh*, so wasn't *she* a renegade?

Erene and Elicit seemed to hold her exempt from all such classifications. And they looked at her with kindness that made her want to melt, even as she hardened, and said of course she was different.

She was a trifle surprised that they had *auchresh* friends at all. Elicit, at least, had once been so pious.

But the two renegades did not show up, and did not show up, and Hope decided that whoever they were, they hadn't *really* been Erene and Elicit's friends, they had just been playing with them. It was still Hope's opinion that the whole "renegade" rumor was nonsense. In the country, even in a household headed by two émigrés from the capital, nothing had really changed since a thousand years ago. The goings-on in Delta City were of no more interest to people here than news of a hurricane in Veretry. Nothing ever changed. Hands, taxes, visitors from the past—all passed, and all were insignificant in the context of a Piradean winter that enfolded most of the day in darkness, and had even Hope shivering constantly.

On the first bright day of Hope's visit, about noon, when the sun peeped coyly over the trees and made the snow on the pines gleam white, and Hope was gathering the two children and their coats to go play outside, Elicit said to her: "I'm worried, Hope."

"About who? What?"

"Shine and Keef, of course! I think we should go to Shulage to—to see if they're there."

Ungraciously, she capitulated. It could not hurt to humor him, she supposed, as long as she did not let herself be seen by the Hands. She had already visited Shulage, and decided there was no anti-Divinarchical activity going on there or anywhere else. The incident of the "renegades" in K'Fier had been a freak thing, and Pati, the craven paranoid, was going to scatter his troops to the corners of the world to flail at shadows! In Shulage, as everywhere else, there were only the familiar scenes of Hands bullying and tormenting human townspeople who were too much in awe of them to do anything except take it.

Tomorrow Hope would go home and tell Humi to concentrate every particle of her forces on winning Delta City.

But when she and Elicit arrived by *teth˝tach ching* in Shulage, she realized just how wrong she would have been to do that.

They stood in the shadow of one of the funny, squat wooden houses that lined the market square of Shulage. Elicit, beside her, quivered with wrath. Occasionally their trembling brought them into jolting contact. Hope thought over and over, *I will kill Pati with my bare hands for this.*

In the square with its market stalls, people shopped and gossiped and children played games. A water pump squeaked and splooshed. But the winter sunlight seemed false, with blackness in the brightness—as if the sun were only a huge candle shining in the nothingness of the sky, guttering before it went out. Hope felt light-headed. It seemed that the world had wobbled a little on its path, changed its course slightly to accommodate a new heaviness.

A gibbet of raw tree trunks stood to one side of the square, between a costermonger's stall and a beer seller. Six Hands hung from it, their uniforms flapping in the breeze. Chains looped their bodies. They had been hung while they were still alive. The chains were to keep them from using their strength to break away from their captors. Their faces had decayed quite badly. They must have been hanging for at least a sixday.

Hope leaned against the side of the house. She buried her face in her arms, gasping in the scent of pine logs.

By her side, Elicit was being weakly courteous to a human with a thick Piradean accent. "I'm glad I didn't permit Erene to come into town," he was saying. "She wanted to. It had been a long time since we'd seen Shine or Keef, and we were getting nervous. Rightly so, as it seems . . . ! Can you tell me something of what *happened?* Is Shine—is Keef—"

"No, it would not have done for the lady Paean to come into town, it would not! Hardly a sight for the women and children, though they do enjoy it, 'tis not right," the Piradean said lugubriously. "It's the *auchresh* themselves who are wanting us to take the gallows down. Did you ever hear such strangeness?"

"Which *auchresh*?" Elicit said sharply. "Do you mean there are any left alive?"

" 'Course there are, Godsman Paean! The new ones! Like your Shine! He's somewhere about . . . I can find him for you . . ."

Elicit made a distressed noise. "In a moment, Godsman. I must know what happened."

"Ah, well, to cut a long story short. Twas the Hands that started it. Going about saying they were at war with all other *auchresh*. Well, our Kingfisher, who's been living with the Redforests out of town for a good year now—surprises me you haven't heard—he feels the barammoth at his back, doesn't he? Word came he was organizing a rumble, and our young men was to show up at this-and-that place on thus-and-so day, and Kingfisher turns up with your Shine and a score of other gods none of us ever saw before. Fresh out of the salt, we find out later. And wild!" The Piradean grinned. "We did the Hands right. Got my knife into one of them meself. I just thought about all the times he'd made me crawl through the muck when he walked past—and him dressed in me own hard-earned furs like as not . . . Felt good, that did. Anyhow, the new *auchresh* haven't gone home yet, and I can't say as they've outstayed their welcome at all. Hellish strong lads, and friendly, for all they can't quite speak right."

Hope turned around, wiping her eyes. "Where are they?" The Piradean was a plump, dark man in the dress of a merchant.

"Ay, milady *iu*, my respects! You must be new here, too! Friend of Godsman Paean's, are you?"

Hope nodded.

The Piradean relaxed. "Then I'll point out our boys for you." He jabbed a charcoal-furred thumb in the direction of the eddying mass of dull color in the square. "That's Rippling Pool. And Red Arrow. And Kingfisher, with Godsie Redforest, in the yellow dress."

Finally she managed to make some of them out. They wore the garb of rural Pirady, accessorized here and there by a garment from the salt. Most of them wore their hair long—perhaps to emphasize the difference between them and the Hands swinging silently overhead. They played with children, talked shop with foresters, haggled over a cut of meat with the butcher. One was even behind the counter of the beer stall, handing out foaming mugs.

It made Hope's head spin.

So *these* were the much-bruited renegades! They existed, all right—and they were hot-blooded, impetuous country *firim,* most of them probably low-status at home, and so selfish-spirited. Dangerous!

She felt that if she did not keep her eyes on them, they would slither like eddies of colored water into the mud.

She could see that within the space of a few days, they had become *units,* members of the community, in a way that was never possible in the salt. Yet at the same time, they were treasured and looked up to as they had never been at home. The mortals hung on them adoringly.

What a seductive prospect!

"There's Shine, Godsman Paean," the Piradean said. "Go get him, shall I?" Hope saw that he was rather shy of Elicit, in a grudging way, but that at the same time he wanted to impress him. The foreigner. The "man from Grussels."

Elicit started. "Yes. Yes, if you will, Godsman Frotto." When he was gone, Elicit turned to Hope. "I cannot believe it." His eyes were slightly wild.

"The killing. Power." She swallowed, and her eyes went again to the small figures on the gallows, unable to resist their ghastly allure.

Ruthyali against *ruthyali.* Lover against lover. The humans committed sins like this every day, of course, on a lesser scale. But in the context of Hope's cool, philosophical race, the reality of it was insupportable.

"Gods . . ." Elicit's gray fur looked muddy. "It is my curse, Hope, to be just a little bit more intelligent than the people here. Intelligent enough to understand the impossiblity of living with the gods and still worshipping them—but not intelligent enough to resolve the paradox. Did you hear what Frotto told me? It is unbelievable. Some of the Shulage merchants are sending their sons into the salt, to the Heavens where these *auchresh* come from. It's a kind of exchange. A goodwill gesture. Of victory."

"And here we stand uncomprehending, an *auchresh* and a human," she said.

"No need to impress it on me!"

But she knew she could never really understand his horror, because for her, the taboo of the sacred did not exist.

Only one injunction beat at her brain, and it was like a gale.

Let them do whatever they want to do. Only let there be no more killing.

She had to get home to Delta City. The provinces were vitally important, she knew that now, and Humi must know too. *Let there be no more killing . . . !*

But by all accounts the Hands had been murderers. Had it been *necessary* for the renegades to kill, that the cruelty might end?

The gibbet flickered against the pale blue sky, its row of corpses like gap teeth in the maw of a skull. She lost her balance and put out her hand to the side of the house, steadying herself. Mud glopped around her feet.

"All of these *auchresh* will be killed," she said in a low voice to Elicit, while the chatter and clatter of market day eddied around them. "Pati will descend in full force to punish them for this. Like he did at K'Fier. And there isn't a damned thing I can do. How can I tell Humi to send what few men she has here when the same thing is probably happening in a hundred other towns? I can't even warn them. It wouldn't do any good!"

"I know." He gazed down at her. The corners of his eyes were red.

Godsman Frotto strutted up, puffing, with a young *kere* in tow. It seemed increasingly unlikely to Hope that the merchant had actually stuck a knife into one of the Hands, unless the Hand in question had been dead already. He did not seem very healthy. Neither did the *auchresh*. Dressed entirely in human garb, he was tall and fair-skinned. Bruises of sleeplessness hollowed his eye sockets. His hands knotted together in a nervous yet listless tic.

The merchant looked at him worriedly.

"I'm all right, Frotto," the *kere* said in fluent mortal. "You can leave me with Elicit." He flapped one hand. "I know you have a lot to get on with."

Reluctantly, Frotto backed away, mumbling something to Elicit about riding out to see the family one of these days.

A bubble of silence seemed to burgeon about the three of them.

Elicit said, "You look absolutely terrible."

"Yes. I have a bit of a headache. I forgot you didn't know what had happened." The *kere* seemed to see Hope for the first time. "Forgive me, *iu serbalu!*"

"None of that!" Hope snapped.

He looked surprised. Then understanding came over his face. "You must be Hope. It is my honor."

"And you are—" She had forgotten the names. Shine? What was the other? Which had been the Hand? "Keef! You are Keef."

Elicit hissed between his teeth.

The *kere* gave a humorless smile and jerked a thumb over his shoulder. "*That's* Keef. I'm Shining Stone."

"Shine, where have you been sleeping?" Elicit said. "What have you been doing all this time?" He interrupted himself. "Never mind. I know Erene will have it out of you and I would not make you tell it twice."

"I cannot," Shine said.

"Then I will, my lad," Hope said with a firmness she was far from feeling. She could see this young *firi*—bereft of the one who had, according to

Elicit, been his *irissi*—was in dire need of firmness. Steeling herself, she looped her arms around Shine's and Elicit's necks. Shine's skin had the texture of porcelain. His breath was slow, as if he could not be bothered with filling and emptying his lungs. Elicit's grip was powerful, his fur as soft as moss, and she thought she would rather have hugged him any day. Touching him reminded her of Ders, but the sights she had witnessed today had bled that painful episode of its sting, replacing it with broader implications.

Erene stood in the front door wanting desperately to hold Shine, to kiss away his despair as she would have kissed away one of her babies' tantrums. She knew the urge to be only the mother instinct that told her she could make everything all right with enough love, that dangerous instinct that makes so many women ineffectual; she did not give in to it. She did not want to lose Shine. She had not forgotten losing Hem, or Humi. She might not like Shine unreservedly, but he was part of their life here in Pirady, this costly fragile life. Losing him would be like coming home one day to find that someone had emptied the house of everything that made it hers.

But she could not say that. And there did not seem to be anything else to say. He had sat down on the bench against the front wall, his cheeks in his hands. Elicit slouched at the other end of the bench, dragging at his pipe. Hope squatted on the frozen mud, playing with Xib and Artle. Her wings floated over her, tips raised above the dirt. She looked like a young girl, the golden skin of her face still unlined after years of alcohol and tobacco and Pati. Erene could not suppress a pang of envy. She herself had started getting fat.

Hope loved the children. When Erene hugged them, fed them, played with them, scolded them, she would sometimes glance up and see Hope watching with an almost greedy look on her face. Erene guessed Hope had those powerful mothering instincts, too, and they were part of what made her so eager to leave Shulage province. That slim, girlish body would never bear a child—even if she were human.

Sorry for her. I'm sorry for her.

And poor, poor Shine!

They are all tortured by needs they cannot fulfill, she thought. *None of them that I have known are able to take any kind of affection for granted, and so each friend is a gift whose snatching away is all the more painful for having been dreaded so vigorously.*

Poor Shine!

A queenbird tooted in the pines. Erene smelled the smoke from Elicit's pipe, spreading in the chilly air.

"Hope?" Shine said.

Hope twisted around, letting go of Xib, who tottered a few steps and then fell. Erene moved outside to scoop him up.

Shine squinted at Hope. "I think I should like to come back to Delta City with you."

"Oh, no, no," Hope said. "Not possible. You would be out of your depth, my friend."

"There's nothing for me here. Don't you need all the help you can get?"

Erene interrupted, "Shine, that's absurd! You don't have to leave! You know we would love to have you here. You have your cabin—you wouldn't want to waste all the work you put into it—"

"Keef worked just as hard on it as I did. *He's* not here to enjoy it."

Erene winced. She went on, "And the children would miss you—"

"It wouldn't be forever."

Hope said, "Well. Well . . . Shine. Have you—are you—do you know the other *auchresh* who have come to Shulage?"

He pulled a face. "They are mostly my *ruthyalim*. We speak."

"Are you—are you permitted to return to Heaven? Are they? Or would you be . . ."

"Reviled? No. The *er-serbalim* don't have much influence around here, *iu*. I could go back"—his face darkened—"if I wanted. But I don't. The war is in Delta City." Plainly, he was eager to put Pirady behind him. Erene understood that. But she did not think Shine understood that he couldn't leave Keef behind in Shulage.

"That is where you're wrong." Hope was shaking her head. "Since seeing the town today I no longer believe the war is in Delta City."

"But, Hope!" Erene objected. "Your war is different from ours. Humi's struggle for the Throne has nothing to do with the renegades. She's fighting for power; they are fighting for freedom—"

"Against a common enemy," Hope said.

Erene closed her eyes.

"Against oppression. Against the rule of the gods."

"I see what you're getting at!" There was a note of enthusiasm in Shine's voice. "If other renegades did . . . what we did here . . . if enough of them could be coaxed into sticking their necks out . . . the Divinarch would have a real imbroglio on his hands! He would be besieged on both sides!"

"Shine," Elicit said. His eyes were closed. His face looked tormented. "Why did you join in? I have attempted to understand." He opened his eyes. "I cannot."

The fair-skinned *auchresh* winced, and shivered.

"You don't have to say anything, Shine," Erene said quickly, but no one noticed.

"I would have stopped it by any means possible if I had known what was going to happen!" Shine's eyes were bloodshot. "I didn't know about the Divinarch's war on us. Kingfisher always has his ear to the ground. He gathered the *ruthyalim*. I tagged along hoping to get to warn Keef. We fell on them in the middle of the afternoon, when they were sleepiest. It turned out that Kingfisher had arranged for the humans to join in, too. It was a massacre." He stopped.

"Why? What did you hope to gain?"

"Just what you saw today, Elicit," Hope said, softly.

"I understand that you wanted to save Keef. But if you had lain low, he would never have been killed!"

Shine shrugged: a jerky movement, like a Piradean glass sculpture breaking. "I told you, it wasn't me, it was my *firim!* Esult had publicly vowed to hang each and every nonaffiliated *auchresh* he found in human country from the gallows. My *ruthyalim* in Yellow Spruce Heaven hadn't seen the Hands in too long. They'd almost forgotten they were their *ruthyalim*. Anyhow, they were concentrating on Esult. He was the outsider. The Kithrilindic. They did horrible things to him before they hanged him."

Erene coughed, tried to find her voice, tried again. "Who killed . . ."

"Keef? I don't know. The townsfolk. I don't know which one actually pulled the step out from under him. I wasn't watching."

Erene cursed herself, cursed her whole race for having made this boy's world turn so gray.

"I wasn't watching."

"There's so much hatred," Elicit said bitterly. "Pati doesn't know what a graveful of maggots he has nurtured here. He can't."

"But we can turn them against him," Hope said. "We can give them teeth." She bounced to her feet. "It'll be so easy. All they have to do is cry Humi's name before they attack. I couldn't have thought of a better way of frightening Pati witless if I tried! After this it will be child's play—"

Artle paused in her steady consumption of mud to ask, "Who's Pati, Mama?"

Erene bent to ruffle her hair. Staring straight at Hope, she said, "Someone you don't know, darling."

After several more hours of impassioned discussion, Hope and Shine departed for Loge, the town closest to Shulage to the south, where Shine said he had a friend. The subject of Erene and Elicit's accompanying them was not raised again. Maybe Hope did not want to push her luck. Erene scolded herself for attributing such a calculating mind to the *iu*. Before they left, she had been bubbly and excited, kissing each member of the family half a dozen times more than was necessary.

And Shine seemed, incredibly, to have come back to himself. He was reserved, humorous, now and then gracing the dinner table with one of his beautiful smiles. After they finished eating, he slipped away into the forest at the back of the house.

Erene followed him, skidding and cursing on the slimy slopes, wondering why she was going after him when he clearly wanted solitude. When Shine passed through the fringe of the trees she stopped, peering around a flaky trunk. Shine had come to the cliff. The sea breeze ruffled his fine hair as he advanced across the frosty grass to the edge of the precipice.

From here, she could not tell whether he was contemplating the sunset, which bled spectacularly gilt and mauve across the sky, or suicide. Perhaps he was remembering when he and Keef had *teth¨d* Xib and Artle to the bottom of the cliff, to swim off the scrap of stony beach. Or he was thinking about stepping into nothingness.

Would that be possible? she wondered. Or would instinct take over, would his natural abilities land him on his feet at the bottom?

Maybe he'd have to use more direct methods. He had no knife. Hope did, and she was sure to equip him with one, too, but maybe by then the danger would have passed. Maybe.

Deliberately, he turned. Erene saw the sunset sparkling in the tears of his face.

"You can come out now."

Though he flinched back at first, she hugged him, aware of her dowdiness in her spindlespun gown, a painful contrast to the figure of pink light and air with his transparent wings: all her talents forgotten except the talent for love, which she found herself getting better and better at now she had all her days to practice it. She gave him the comfort she had wanted to give earlier, holding him close. "There's something more, isn't there?" she murmured. "Are you telling us everything? You don't have to . . . but you can. If you want."

He stayed silent, as if he were really somewhere out there in the sunset, not with her at all.

"I know I have to let you leave. But not like this. Please, not like this, with secrets between us." She smiled weakly up at him. "There were never secrets between us."

"There were always secrets."

She winced.

"But everything has to . . ." His voice broke. "Erene, I joined in. I lied when I said I had nothing to do with it. I wanted to end the injustice. I thought Keef would get out in time. I thought he would *teth*¨. And later we would meet and celebrate the end of his bondage.

"But I saw him fighting. I was in the thick of it, shoving to get closer to the place where a Hand from Yellow Spruce Heaven was being chained up, and I saw Keef using his knife on the humans, trying to kill as many of them as possible before he went under. Shulage lost ten men and half as many women, and I daresay Keef did his share. I saw him. Our eyes met. But I didn't drop my cudgel. I didn't go to him." Gently, his head came to rest on her shoulder.

She squeezed him, stroking his hair with rough fingers, muttering, "It's all right, it's all right, you couldn't have saved him . . ."

But he twisted and moaned at the onslaught of untruths. She stopped. On the horizon, the crimson sun melted into the sea. It was not a moment for silence; it was a moment pregnant with things that needed to be said. But they had reached another crescendo of guilt and shame and mistrust in their mutual history, and Erene could not find any words that were keen enough to express her sympathy, yet gentle enough not to draw blood.

RECRUIT

"Hi! There! Get on!" Merce shouted. "Night's coming, you stupid beasts! Get on!" He brought his stick down with a *thwock* on the nearest sheep. "In!"

The flock danced into the barn, throwing him slanted glances out of their orange eyes. He'd had the gods' own task getting them rounded up off the mountain—they were even more willful than usual, it must be something in the wind. Now that he was worn out and ready to slit their woolly throats, they obeyed him as blithely as might be. "Get!" He landed a boot on the last shit-caked rump, and pushed the woven-stick doors to. He jammed the bars through their loops and wiped the sweat off his face before the wind could freeze it.

Merce hated sheep with every particle of his being. He couldn't wait until his little sister Asure and Cousin Rety were old enough to take over the task of shepherding. Two could work faster than one, no matter how young and silly they were. Or if only Sion had been here to help him! With his trick of disappearing and reappearing, the god could set sheep's sly stupid brains spinning.

There was something odd in the wind. Merce sniffed. Burning? It blew steadily from the direction of Nece, for which Cousins Brit and Emper had set off yesterday with a load of tubers. Butterfly Cote was probably burning dung.

The dun-colored ridge behind him was barren of everything except the furze that left hundreds of tiny bleeding scratches on one's legs, no matter how thick one's breeches were. A twist of smoke rose from the fire pit in Beaulieu's courtyard below. They were all in the fields. Everyone from Cand, Merce's oldest uncle, to his littlest second cousin Ality, was down the other end of the valley, digging more of the hamlet's precious tubers. The yield was poor this year: not yet Midwinters, and they had had to start turning the third field. What gods had decreed that one had to do the most backbreaking work of the year in winter, when the cold chapped your fingers and turned your eyes red and gave you the sniffles? Merce hated shepherding—but he had an inkling that it was the rest of his family who really had the short end of the stick. If he went down there they'd put him to work, too.

Well, he wouldn't go down! A boy deserved *some* free time! Didn't he?

Squinting up at the sky, he thought, *Still an hour of light. Good enough, Sion'ull bring me home. And everyone'll be happy to see him, so they won't care I got back late.* He started to tramp uphill, the wind buffeting his back. *More'n two sixdays since he was here. Wonder if that fellow from Pirady's come back? I hope so. I wanna hear about the war. I mean,* Pirady! *That's the other side of the world!*

Merce joined his hands under his smock to warm them. The fur on his belly was sticky with dirt—it had been months since he had a bath, and he liked it that way. Reaching the top of the ridge, he scrambled down into the next forage valley, where tufts of wool decorated the furze and the few stunted trees; then up another ridge, north a bit, and an arm of the salt glowed in the valley below him. The slippery whispering of leaves on leaves came faintly to his ears. The vegetation that was so much denser than the scrub of the saltside undulated under the wind like the waters of the sea.

He shook his head firmly. You didn't walk through the salt if you didn't have to—that was just plain stupid. He circled the head of the inlet, pelted over the slippery brown slopes of the last ridge, and halted, breathing hard, on the sloping skirt of grass where hummocks of salt popped up through the ground. The salt merged into the soil gradually, as if it had been scattered on the ground like sugar on a table. The first few salt trees were as stunted as any in human country, and nothing moved in their branches.

Grinning, he plunged in.

The clouds overhead were thicker than wool. He didn't need the eye band he kept in his pocket. He followed the way markers he and Sion had left, heading for Heaven. He'd give Sion a grand old surprise. A bluish scrap meant northeast. Off-white, north. In a hollow, a black strip tied to a bush was being industriously nibbled by a salt squirramunk: west. *Sheepshit!* He hoped no more of them had been eaten. Neither he nor Sion had thought of *that.*

But the next marker, which should have been red, wasn't anywhere to be seen. And twilight was dropping heavy from the clouds. Merce felt frightened.

Spitting on his hands, he shinnied up a stone-colored tree. Smears of blood trailed him up the trunk—when salt bark flaked, it was *sharp*. But he didn't care. He was terrified of being stranded here for the night. Too dark now to get all the way back before the predators came out of their lairs. And even if he escaped the predators' claws, and got home safely, *Mother* would kill him for disobeying! Joy liked Sion—but she said she would not have Merce going near Oakbranch Heaven. Of course, that had never stopped him.

The top of the tree nodded under his weight. The wind whipped his hair into his face. But he could see—with a sudden rush of relief—that he was in a hollow halfway up the white slope on whose peak Oakbranch Heaven flared like a frozen fire.

He gripped the tree, balancing, drinking in the sight. "Stupid," he said aloud. "Young fool." That was what his father called him. "Whatcha get so skeeted for?"

Heaven stood boldly on the crest of the hill, its strong walls raised like a finger in the face of weather and predators and enemies. In his mind, he compared it to Beaulieu, those low frost-eaten sheds crowding together in the deepest valley of the saltside. "Halloo! *Tith˝ahim!*" he shouted at the top of his lungs. "It's me! Merce! Somebody come get me!"

No human could have heard him, not from halfway down the hill with the wind blowing, but the *auchresh* of Oakbranch Heaven were better than humans. They had special abilities, some of which—like the vanishing trick—Merce was determined to learn. If Sion hadn't told him they were not gods, not really, Merce would most certainly have been fooled.

He yelled again. Several heads popped out of windows, dark blots on the creamy walls. Merce waved vigorously. His fingers were getting numb. But before they let go of their own accord, one of Sion's friends, a *mainraui* named Sedge Runner, popped out of the air at his ear. Grabbing the tree with one hand, so that it dipped heavily toward the ground, he fastened Merce in his arms. His grip felt wonderfully warm. He had probably been asleep. "Sorry!" Merce shouted contritely over the wind. It was difficult to remember that the *auchresh*, when they were at home, slept during the day. While Sion was in Beaulieu, he kept scrupulously to the Gardens' schedule.

The sulfur got into Merce's nose. He sneezed.

And the tree vanished out of his hands. There was that moment of panic. Then his feet hit the floor of Sedge Runner's room in the topmost pinnacle of Heaven.

The window was only a slit—in Heaven having a window at all was, he had learned, a great privilege—but Merce was unused to windows in any case, and he was glad it was no larger, for he liked the feeling of shut-in coziness. The walls were coated with layers of soft tapestry decorated with pictures of *auchresh* hunting, harvesting, wrestling, caring for Foundlings. A fire burned under the hood in the middle of the floor. On the small table was a metal pot. Merce recognized the tannin scent of the drink the Carelastrians called "Tearka sludge."

Sion was sitting cross-legged on the bed. Merce grinned happily when he saw Gamefly was sitting there too. *Officer* Gamefly, the *auchresh* from Pirady, or Fewarauw as they called it. He was older than Sion, or he looked it, with his heavy head like a big dog and no wings. They were both staring at Merce. "What are *you* doing here?" Sion asked at last.

Merce shifted, somewhat taken aback. "Felt like coming." With sudden inspiration, he added, "Wanted to get off tater-digging."

Sion smiled with relief. "Slyboots! Merce, you are the laziest boy I ever knew! When you are a man, I think you will live in abject poverty!"

"When I'm a man," Merce said, "my kids 'ull do all the work for me." He relaxed. "Can I have some?" He pointed at the sludge pot.

Gamefly coughed. "Heat it up, Sedge," he said. "I did not know your human friends visited you in Heaven! Surely Fretseeker does not approve? He is a follower of the *erserbalim,* is he not?"

"Yes. But he doesn't—ah—well, to be honest, Gamefly, he is not in the best of health. *O-serbali* Sivene is running Heaven—and he is one of us younger ones. He has spoken of our making ourselves known in Nece. That's the nearest human town. The Hands have an outpost there."

"Soon all the old ones will die off," Gamefly said rhetorically. "Even the *er-serbalim* will die, eventually. Then we shall run our Heavens just as we please. Humans and *auchresh* Foundlings will play side by side."

"I'm not a Foundling," Merce said, stung. "I'm twelve. Foundlings are stupid. My father calls me a fool, but at least I can *talk*—not like those silly bits."

The stranger opened his mouth and an avalanche of laughter roared out. Merce put his hands over his ears. He removed them just in time to hear the *kere* say "—approve! I approve highly!"

Sion beckoned Merce to his side. He whispered, "It's all right for you to stay, I think. Here. Sit down."

But why shouldn't it be all right? Merce wondered, as Sion made room for him on the bed. Something was wrong. Why was Sion so tense?

Sedge Runner squatted by the fire and settled the sludge pot on its tripod with a clank. Then he plunked himself down cross-legged on the floor and wedged his chin into his hands. Something was wrong with him, too. Why had he done a servant's task? Merce was a little afraid of all the *mainrauim*—Sedge Runner counted it his right to have Sion (and Merce,

when available—he was not particular) wait on him hand and foot—so why
was he obeying Gamefly? That time Sedge Runner, Sion, and Gamefly had
come to Beaulieu, all of them had pitched in (much to Merce's disgust) and
helped the women repair the roofs of the fowl house.

Maybe it was something to do with the war, and Gamefly's being an
officer.

Merce said, "Gamefly, godsman, you've just come here from Pirady,
haven't you? Is there fighting, there? Is there eeroics?"

Gamefly gave him a surprised look. "There haven't been, yet. The war is
in its early stages. The battle at Grussels will be the first real test of our
mettle. We will be hard put to it, I can tell you! The Hands, of whom there
are thousands, are far better trained than our mixed human and *auchresh*
troops." His head swung, his gaze sweeping Sion, lingering on Sedge Runner. "That is why we need every *mainraui* we can get."

"I won't have anything to do with it," Sedge Runner said.

"You were Found to be a soldier. So were all *mainrauim,* did they but
know it. Our traditions date from a time eons past when we were less
civilized than we are today."

A war, Merce thought, dazzled. *A real war. It's going on right now.*
Visions of challenges and duels, like vastly enlarged versions of the games
he played with his sister and cousins, flickered across his vision. Suddenly,
he wanted more than anything to be there. The prospect of going back to
Beaulieu seemed unbearably empty and gloomy. He felt like a fish that has
been kept in a tank for its whole life, and then one day the sides become
transparent, and the fish sees the sea lapping on the outside of the glass.

The air in the room had the ill-oxygenated tang of tension.

"Time is different in Fewarauw, Sedge Runner," Gamefly was saying.
"We are closer to the sun than you are in Carelastre. When I returned
there, I thought I had somehow *teth¨d* into tomorrow. It was morning, and
I had left in late afternoon. The tents cover the meadows around Grussels
city like foam on the sea. The spears are as thick as wheat at harvest time.
Everywhere, the name of the Divinarch is whispered, praised, and sung.
Humility Garden. She is our Maiden General's idol: she is the one in whose
name we fight. Her victory will be the *final* triumph of the new over the
old."

"Many recruits?" Sedge Runner said skeptically.

"More every day. When I joined up, in Ekmar Province, the army was a
hundredth the size it is now. I am merely one of a thousand recruiters.
Humans as well as *auchresh.*"

"You oughta try and recruit saltsiders," Merce said, finding his voice.
"Divinarch taxes us, too. Hands bleed us of a third of our tears and sweat

and toil. We hate 'em." After the Hands left the last time, in the summer, Merce's uncles had shouted at each other. His skin prickled all over again as he sensed their frustrated fury, only dimly understanding it. He had taken the babies inside to stop them from crying while Joy, Mercy, Reedo, and Indine tried to calm down their menfolk.

He became aware that the moment was stretching out and out.

"Perhaps . . ." Sion said. "Perhaps . . . we should take Merce!"

It was then that Sedge Runner spoke. "Oh, no you don't, Sion. Gamefly has manipulated you into this, and I'm throwing my life after yours—because I love you. But you aren't getting the Foundling. I put my foot down."

"Temperament!" Gamefly murmured.

On the fire, the sludge pot boiled over. Sedge cursed in the *auchraug* language and pulled it off with his bare hands. Merce, his mind bubbling with dim possibilities, smelled burning flesh. The scent was oddly familiar.

Sedge's lean, flat-cheeked face showed no emotion. But the tiny wings on the tops of his shoulders fluttered.

There came a knock on the door. "*Mainraui? Firi?* May I be of assistance? I heard something fall—"

"Damn," Sion whispered.

"You must not tell them!" Gamefly hissed. "Not let them know I am in here! It would delay your departure!"

It was Sedge who wrangled his voice into some semblance of normality. "No, thank you, old one. Go away. We'll be in the great hall before long."

After a moment, a snort came from outside the door, and footsteps shuffled off down the hall.

Sweat stood on Gamefly's furrowed forehead. The room seemed to have gotten hotter. It reeked of burned sludge. "We must be off. Quickly, before anything else happens."

"What about me?" Merce squeaked.

Sedge said quickly, "Don't worry, Merce. We'll drop you off at Beaulieu."

"No, I mean, I want to come!" He directed his plea to Gamefly, aware that all decisions were ultimately up to the officer. Maybe *that* was what made Sedge so irritable. "I'd be more use to you than ten *auchresh!* I know how to fight, I practice a lot—*please!*" His heart was pounding.

"Don't be absurd, Merce," Sedge said. "Even if you are not a Foundling, you are a child."

"Wait," said Gamefly. The heavy red gaze rested on Merce, considering him. "Not so hasty, my friend. The boy could be of use."

Sion dropped to his knees and seized Merce's hands. "How'd you like that, Merce! How'd you like to be a spearman! Damn, your family'd be so *proud*—"

"*No,*" Sedge said harshly. He stood in front of the bed, a knotted blanket over one shoulder, his face as flat as a slab of rock. His lips scarcely moved; his voice seemed to emanate from the air. "Hear me on this, my flighty young *irissi.* The boy stays. What *possible* help could he give us that would outweigh his loss to his family? He stays. It is not his war, whatever you say."

Merce's eyes flowed with boiling tears of embarrassment and disappointment. He tried desperately to swallow them. They must not think him a child. He was as able as—as—well, not as a *mainraui,* but he was *almost* as strong as Sion. "I want to know what it's like," he pleaded. "I have to see! I want to help!" He produced his trump card. He never even let himself remember this unless the situation was desperate. "The Divinarch, Humi I mean, Humility Garden, is my cousin! Did you know that, Sion? I never knew she was alive, my family are shamed of her so they never tell no one she came from us. But I bet she'd like to see me! I could tell you about the way she is! I could—"

Gamefly's eyes flickered. "The *same* Gardens? Can it be?"

"You young idiot," Sedge said. He came forward and his hands closed on Merce's upper arms.

Then the fire flared in Beaulieu's courtyard, lashed by the wind, and a tumult of voices sent Merce staggering against a bench.

The whole family was gathered in the courtyard. The trestle tables still stood against the walls: nobody had cooked the least slop of dinner. That, to Merce's mind, was unthinkable. It meant either famine or domestic disaster.

Brit and Emper were the center of the disturbance. They were telling a story at the tops of their lungs, even more hoarsely than usual. Merce pushed himself up off the bench and shoved into the crowd. His mother took hold of him and said distractedly, "Oh, Merce. Thank the gods you're home. I was afraid the sheep were lost and you'd gone chasing after . . ."

From beyond Grand-uncle Cand and Grand-aunt Prudence, Merce heard the word "dead."

"You smell funny," squealed Asure. "Ave you been in the salt?"

Merce clipped her on the ear to shut her up. He wished he'd never told her about his visits to Oakbranch Heaven—she was too little to keep a secret! "What happened to Brit and Emper?" he asked, stooping.

"They went to Nece!" she squeaked.

"I know that!"

"There was a fire!"

From a couple of relations away, Uth, Merce's father, shot out an arm and pulled Merce to his side. He tipped Merce's face upward and said quietly, "Son, there's been a disturbance in Nece. People turned on the Hands—burned their guard station. People were killed. The town is in chaos, people stealing from each other, neighbors arguing and killing each other over it. Port Taite'll be down on the whole region. There was a god involved. Not a Hand. It would have been better if Sion was here, then we could have vouched for him, I am afraid we'll lose his help—"

"It wasn't him!" Merce said with relief. "I was with him!"

"That's something." Uth's grip relaxed a little.

"And they *won't* come down on us!" Merce was bursting with his news. "You don't know this but the Divinarch 'as declared war on the other gods! The Hands won't have time for *us* cause they're all in Pirady fighting the Maiden General!"

"The war, yes," Uth said. "They knew in Nece already. Brit and Emper just found out."

Merce gulped. It was his cousin's war. Did Father realize that, or had he blocked Cousin Humi completely out of his memory? Humi's war—it was Merce's war!

Brit's and Emper's clothes were blackened with soot. Emper had a great gash on his arm, which his wife Indine was futilely trying to bandage. "Would that we could stamp out every last one of them!" Emper was shouting. "Would that we were our own men again, as we were in the days of the old Divinarch!"

Over the scent of unwashed bodies and soot came a stink of sulfur. Gamefly appeared by the fire. Merce could just see him. He was flanked by Sion, and Sedge Runner, who after dropping Merce off must have worked his way unseen around the walls of the courtyard.

"I am Gamefly of Durenesse hamlet in Ekmar Province, Pirady," he said by way of introduction. "A friend of Sion's. Godsman Garden, your desire to pay the Hands back for the injustices they have done you is heard and understood. It is shared by thousands. In Pirady, an army of humans and gods is preparing to take Grussels from the Divinarch. Our strategists say battle will be engaged next sixday."

Emper shook Indine off. "Inviolate One, are you by any chance here to find volunteers?"

"If so, you've got yourself two!" Brit said.

Merce's other uncle, Gent, stepped out of the crowd, his face muddy. "Three!" The men faced the *auchresh* across the flaring fire pit. Red light glowed on scaly skin and fur alike, giving them all a terrifying aspect.

Merce gripped his father's arm. Uth quivered; Merce knew he was debating whether to step forward, too. *No, Father!* he thought. *Don't! It's* me *they're taking!*

"We welcome you with joy," Gamefly said in a sonorous voice that made Merce's bones vibrate.

Grand-uncle Cand coughed. "No. My grandsons, I cannot permit it. We need you here. This is madness."

"Thank you, Godsman," Sedge Runner said quietly. "Godsmen, stay here. This is not your war."

"Yes, it is, friend *auchresh*," Emper said. He narrowed his eyes at Sedge Runner. Merce could not believe they were all on the same side. This felt too much like a confrontation, where justice and reason bowed low before strength. Passion trembled in Emper's voice. "They burned our town. Our granary. For all we know, they have burned every town in Domesdys."

Uncle Reng, Cand's brother, spoke for the first time. He was younger than Cand but he wielded more authority over the hamlet. He must have deliberated calmly for his voice was still and carrying. "The god is right—you must stay, nephews. We can't survive without you."

"Every hamlet needs its young men," Gamefly said: a simple statement of fact.

In the moment of silence that followed, Merce wrenched away from his father and pushed his way to the *auchresh* side of the fire pit. "You don't need *me. I'm* going."

"Nonsense," Reng said.

Reng's wife, Faith, laughed.

Merce's cheeks muddied, but he knew the firelight would disguise the color. He stood firm.

Gamefly opened his mouth, paused a minute, and then closed his hand on Merce's shoulder. He said to Cand, "But, Godsman, how can you disallow *this* volunteer? A twelve-year-old boy is not essential to the well-being of the hamlet. But he could be of infinite use to us!" His voice thickened, betraying real fervor. "Is it right for Humility Garden's family not to send a single representative to the Divinarch's banner? Can you permit *that?*"

There was a brief, shocked pause.

"Humi," Merce's aunt Faith croaked, "my *daughter.*"

Her wrecked, beautiful face hung at Reng's shoulder. Her nails dimpled Reng's smock. Merce was a little afraid of her. Her face was haggard, her throat loose, but her fur and hair were a rich ruddy chestnut.

"Humi is in the best of health," Gamefly said to Faith. "And preparing to take back her throne. You are to be congratulated on the excellence of your bloodline, Godsie."

"Humi. Gods. Humi." Faith launched herself forward. "I must see her! I must tell her—that I was wrong—"

Reng seized the back of her dress. He held her at arm's length, an expression of disgust on his face. Merce had heard from his older cousins that Reng and Faith had not lived as husband and wife since Faith allowed their daughter Humi to go to Delta City—worse, that they hated each other. Faith did not struggle in her husband's grasp. She began to cry softly.

"Humi is in Delta City, Godsie," Sion said gently. "But we will remember you to the Maiden General. And Hope is in constant communication with your daughter. Merce will convey the message himself, that Humi's family still cherishes her, and looks forward to her reinstatement on the Throne."

"I don't believe you," Faith cried quietly. She brought her ruined face up. "I don't believe you will let Merce near your precious Maiden General. In fact, I think it would be better he didn't go to Pirady. Do you hear me, Reng?" She turned to her husband. "I made that mistake once, but I shall not let it be made again. We will not lose another of our eldest children."

Reng's face twisted. With a kind of delighted dread, Merce saw what was coming. Reng would do *anything* if he thought it would hurt his wife. "On the contrary. Merce can go wherever he wants. You have no authority over him." Reng watched her reaction with detached sadism.

"As you say, my brother," Cand wheezed. Merce saw he was half-sitting against Prudence. "As long as—my sons—stay where they belong—"

"No!" Joy cried, a high predatorial shriek. "Nooo! Reng, you're abusing your authority! *Please,* Cand, don't let him!"

Oh, gods, Merce thought, *oh, gods!*

But it was too late for his mother to intervene. Gamefly evidently considered it fair and aboveboard to make his getaway now. Beaulieu vanished, and in the place of soot the wet green reek of bruised sphagnum filled Merce's nostrils, and it was morning.

"Now here you are." Preoccupiedly, Sion stuffed bundles into Merce's arms. "Your blanket, your kit. Your weapon."

Merce hitched the armful on his hip and tested the weight of the knife. He'd never had one before. It was long and curved like a Hand's blade—unwieldy for a boy his size, but so sharp. So cruel. He imagined it cutting through armor and flesh, and shivered and grinned.

"And these, I think, are the scouts?" Sion pulled a face. "I think so. I really have to get along. Merce—the Seventh Younger Cabal. Mode is the captain, so Gamefly says."

Mode was a friendly-seeming boy of sixteen or so, with gray Piradean fur and a catlike smoothness to his movements. He clasped Merce's forearms for a moment. "Welcome." He shot a glance in Sion's direction.

But the *auchresh* was gone. A puff of purple dispersed in the air.

He must really've *been in a hurry,* Merce thought. He had already noticed that as a rule, here, *auchresh* did not *teth¨*. Perhaps it was in order to conserve their extranatural energy for the coming battle.

The camp crouched still and low on the meadows. Mode laughed. "Dumped *you* quick, didn't he, Domesdean? How good are you with a knife?"

The billowing tents, raised out of the mud on wooden platforms, were novelties to Merce. Some of the soldiers dragged travois laden with wood or water; some carried game slung across their shoulders; some just wandered along, whetting their blades, carving arrows, batting short bursts of conversation from one to another. Voices echoed through the morning, sharp and loud. The air felt taut, as though the whole camp were being held like a bubble inside some huge creature's lungs. The air was colder, and calmer, than Merce had ever felt. He could feel the hum of the camp in his bones. *Auchresh* voices made up most of it.

He had never seen so many gods in one place. Gamefly's talk of thousands made sense now.

Gamefly, it proved, was the Maiden General's officer in charge of human recruits. When he had persuaded Merce to come, he was just doing his job. It had been a bit of a blow to find out that no one cared two farthings whose cousin Merce was. But all the same, now he'd got here, to this green, cold clime, he was *glad.* He might be the lowest of the low, nothing more than a go-see boy. But better a scout here than a shepherd at home!

The members of the Seventh Younger Cabal were all staring at him.

He would not look down.

"Not such good ground for a camp, is it?" Mode said. "It's all bog here. There's standing water in the hollows. See the sphagnum round the edges of the tents? See the logs, how they're raised up out of the wet?"

"Why did the Maiden General camp here then?" Merce asked.

"We had to surround the city. Like this, we've got the Inviolate Ones penned in. They leave, and turn Grussels over to us, or they fight. We've got 'em!"

Merce shuddered. It was the cold.

"Hey." Mode was smiling. His eyes were kind, though so dark—all the boys were dauntingly foreign, not another Domesdean among them, mostly Piradeans with a few Veretreans, Calvarese, and Royallandics thrown in. "When it comes down to it, you won't have *time* to be scared. I know. I was in the fighting in Whitecliff last sixday." Mode turned Merce around and pushed him a couple of steps to the left. "Look through that gap. No, toward the forest. See that tent?"

"The one with the yellow flag on top?" Merce guessed.

"That's the Divinarch's banner. And *that's* the Maiden General's tent." His voice quivered with an unwonted tremor. "We can't go look now—we've gotta relieve the Fourth on fringe patrol—but I'll show you where to hide next time she reviews the spearmen. Then you'll see her. She's *beautiful.*"

GROUNDSWELL

Hope pushed the parchments away from her until they fluttered off the other side of the camp desk. She sank forward until her head touched the wood, her arms stretched out before her, and breathed long, shallow breaths. The roof of the tent shivered above her. Outside, she could hear the sentinels chatting. Recently, whenever she tried to sleep, her tiredness evaporated as soon as her head touched the pillow, to be replaced by a kind of edgy supersensitivity. She found herself clenching her fists at small noises and irritations that had never used to be irritating. Because of this she was almost glad she was too valuable to lose, and therefore would not be fighting in the coming battle.

And at the same time that she despised her own cowardice, she was sneakily glad. She was an *iu*. Her place was not in the field.

Instead she sat here, the Maiden General, her presence and her dedication to Humi keeping the cause from being diluted with a thousand petty grievances. She had made the decision early on to sacrifice fanaticism for numbers. She knew it would mean a higher proportion of losses. But the recruits were coming in at such a rate she did not think it mattered. In Delta City, Humi had made the opposite choice: one of her dispatches had said, with the merest trace of self-satisfaction, "From Gold Dagger himself down to the youngest renegade, everyone in the Rats' Den is mine, body and soul." Hope feared she was not flattering herself when she went out on inspections and saw the same thing in the faces of her own followers.

It was like having a pot of water come to the boil while she held it in her bare fingers. All she could do was to try to keep them focused while they waited for the Hands in Grussels to break.

The same thing went for the other continents. To that end, she wrote countless letters and dispatches to her lieutenants in Domesdys, Calvary, and the Archipelago—Shine, Truth, and Whitenail, all of whom had started amassing their own armies. In her name. In Humi's.

They would be visiting the camp today. The *er-serbalim.* She had to prepare herself.

Their consent to give her an audience was perhaps the most significant thing she had achieved yet; after Divaring Below, she'd thought she had lost their confidence forever. She should not receive them when she was this tired!

Her nails dug into the parchments, splitting them. She got up. Her booted feet thudded with an unfamiliar noise on the planks as she crossed the tent. She sank down into one of the expensive armchairs she had had imported from Delta City and began to fill a pipe. It was thus they found her.

The tang of sulfur filled the tent. The space filled with overheated *auchresh* bodies. Hope stood up, mentally congratulating herself for having been found at her ease, and embraced Broken Bird and Bronze Water. "*Perich* "him!" she exclaimed. Inside her head, something screamed, *Old . . . they are so old . . . look how heavy Bronze has let himself get . . .* "My quarters are not large. Would it be too great an inconvenience for you to send your guards outside? I assure you, you are safe!"

She grinned at them.

"My dear, we did not mean to imply that we do not trust you!" Bronze rumbled. "Out!" He snapped fleshy fingers. "Disperse! Gather information! Report back!"

He winked at Hope.

She suppressed a sigh of relief.

When the *keres* were gone, Broken Bird sank into a chair and said, "We only brought them because . . . well, let us say that *they* brought *us*. We have too many demands on our energy, now, to waste it *teth*"ing around the continents."

"I summoned you from Iceland!" Hope said. "I apologize."

"Think nothing of it." Bronze Water lowered himself with an exhalation into the largest armchair. Hope held her breath and wondered whether the springs would hold. It looked as though they would . . . just.

They all smiled guardedly at each other. Hope felt the atmosphere was one of goodwill, and she experienced a surge of confidence.

"Beautiful work." Bronze traced the labyrinthine red swirl on the arms with a fat finger. "Must be human crafted."

"There are some extremely talented upholsterers in Leadentown," Hope agreed. "If you had come by sea, Leadentown is the port you would have landed at."

Broken Bird had wedged herself into a corner of her chair, knees drawn up to her chest. Her *urthriccim* covered her like a raveled blanket. She looked like a wizened child. "Well, Hope," she said in a suddenly brittle voice, "enough of this false informality. What do you want of us?"

Hope gasped. *The haugthirres,* she thought. "Ah . . . it . . . has been . . . too long. I thought we would renew our friendship at our leisure—"

"Nonsense," Bird said. "Bronze, pour me some of that slop, will you? Hope, your agents have been reporting our movements to you for at least eighteen days. We've seen them. They find it difficult to hide in the Icelandic Heavens. Three sixdays is quite long enough for you to have formed a detailed picture of our life. Nothing has changed since you saw us in Divaring Below, almost a year ago, except that we do not move from Heaven to Heaven as fast as we did. Nothing has changed."

What did she mean? Was this genuine hostility, or just intimidation tactics?

"Yellow Riestasis." Bronze placed a cup in Bird's hand. Then he turned to Hope. "We would have come to you before long, even had you not invited us. But this is better. Now we know that we all have a concurrence of purpose. And this little layout"—he waved a hand at the tea table and silverware, the small red glass lamp burning in the center of the table— "the milieu you have prepared to receive us in—tells us more about you than we could have learned if we came on you unawares."

Hope leaned forward and poured wine for Bronze Water and herself. She did not have the faintest idea what they really wanted. She had lost control already. She must not let it show. *Concurrence of purpose?*

That seemed impossible, too easy. Such neat circles of intentions were created only by slipping through the loopholes that destiny left—by outguessing the game a dozen moves ahead. Neither she, nor Broken Bird, nor Bronze Water, was *that* clever.

She had to reassert her primacy. *That* could very easily be what they were trying to put over on her: that, and no more. For them, it would be a diversion.

"I make no threats," she said. "No offers. No promises, beyond that of my lasting friendship. This, with my most humble respects, is what I suggest to you. Your ideology, your method, are failures." She paused, neither of them blinked. "You *must* be aware that nothing has changed since you began preaching isolationism—except that more *auchresh* have left the salt, to join Pati or more recently, to join us. *War*—the one thing the salt cannot offer—is drawing them out. What have you got to hold against that? Theories."

She stopped. A drizzle was falling on the tent roof. *Plip plip plip* on the waterproofed spindlespun. A shadow had slipped over the afternoon; Broken Bird's and Bronze Water's cheeks appeared to sink even as their features pushed out from their skulls, until they looked as exaggeratedly *auchresh* as an effigy-maker's apprentice's practice pieces.

"Well," Bronze said testily, "it seems your spies are doing a good job. But there is one place they have not been able to see, and that is Broken Bird's and my hearts."

Broken Bird steepled her fingers. "Hope, we are aware of our failure. We have been aware of it for longer than we care to think. Isolationism is dead and buried. It was only ever useful as an antidote to Pati. I remain convinced that in the early days of his rule, our influence was the only thing that kept the tyranny from spinning utterly out of control. But now our medicine is no longer strong enough. The time for stagnancy has passed. We are waiting for you to provide an alternative ideology. So far we have seen no sign of one." She drank deeply of her wine. "We have come here to spy on *your* heart, Hope. We will weigh everything you say fairly."

"What a challenge!" Hope said. *And what an unsurpassed chance to win them over! I can't blow it!* "But you really need to talk to Humi. She's the one with the grand theories."

"But she is not *auchresh*." Bronze Water pointed out.

"That means nothing now. *There's* my ideology, if you want. I believe in the equality of the races. The fact that I am an *iu*, not a woman, is only a disappointment to me." She looked straight at Broken Bird. "*You* understand."

Broken Bird nodded imperceptibly. Hope's heart lifted.

"You will see I have taken to wearing boots." She lifted one of her feet. "It is a poor example. But I am ready to subordinate—or make use of—my *auchresh* nature in any way necessary. I do not discriminate." The words were flowing more freely now. "All I care for is Humi's cause."

"That troubles us," Bronze said gently. "You care so deeply for Humi's 'cause.' But we have been doing our own spying, and some of your followers feel that this war ought not be a *cause*. They fight only for their own freedom. To you, *wrchrethru*, and to others steeped in the history of the Conversion, a war without a cause may sound like a paradox—but think of it in practical terms. Many of the older renegades are worried by your commitment to a mortal woman they have never seen. This commitment seems divorced from the concern you profess for their freedom."

"Why must the two things exclude each other?" Hope said impatiently. "We are all fighting Pati. *And* you would do well to remember that this is *my* army, not yours."

"No threats, mm?" Bronze hummed ruminatively.

"You have never given me anything. Why should I now start to accept your advice? Simply because you are my *elders*?"

There was a short, ringing silence. Then Bronze Water laughed. It sounded as if saucepans were banging together in his belly, as loud and sad as a gong. "There was a time"—he hiccuped—"There was a time—"

Broken Bird put her hand on his arm to quiet him. "But we are no longer idealistic enough to be driven away from the honey tree by our ideological differences with the bees, Hope."

Hope inclined her head graciously. Her insides were churning. Did this mean she had *won*? Did winning, in fact, mean she had now to make concessions? She knew she would never get any less abstruse an admission of defeat out of her *perich¨him*. She had to seize the moment, had to gamble, pray she was right.

She shivered. Injecting as much fluty sweetness into her voice as she could, she called, "Blackash! A fire! It grows late!"

A human orderly scuttled in, head down, and started a fire in the metal brazier in the center of the tent. When he left, Hope settled herself more comfortably, and turning her unlit pipe between her fingers, stated (flatly, to hide her nerves): "As I said before, I offer no terms. Only opportunities."

Bronze Water sniffed the singeing pine logs. "There are some sensory experiences which only human country can offer. Of course, those are acquired pleasures—but then, human babies are not born with developed palates or discriminatory sensual tastes, either."

"At the moment, I cannot offer you riches or possessions," Hope said. "And anyhow I hardly think you want them."

"No," Bronze Water said. "We cannot slough our years."

"Then perhaps you will deign to accept some of my young humans into your retinue." She paused. So far, no explosions. "I know this may not seem appealing. But what I should also like you to do is to mention Humi's name in your speeches. I need you to speak of the—the cause. I need you to be inflammatory." She held her breath. If they promised, she could trust them.

Bronze Water shrugged. "We cannot adjust our rhetorical style. As I said—we are too old. The other seems easy enough. There is no need to be sincere, I hope. As for your young men, they are welcome, as long as they can adjust to *teth¨tach ching* and keep out of fights."

"But there is something I must know." Broken Bird was suddenly, disconcertingly forthright. "Hope, are you really doing this for Humi? What are your own ambitions?"

Hope gasped, caught off guard. Astonishment washed hotly through her. How could they doubt the sincerity of her allegiance to Humi? It was the one thing she was sure of in a troubled world. The one expression of her beliefs that was not ambiguous. "I have no ambitions." Her face was burning. "Do the honeycats not love honey? They have no need to cut down the tree!"

Broken Bird smiled with a mouthful of pointed, feral teeth. "Just making sure."

"We should not want the bees to swarm without warning," Bronze explained ponderously.

The audience seemed to have come to a standstill. The fire crackled happily. Hope swallowed. She was no longer sure who was interrogating who. "Your metaphors are confused. I still do not understand—"

"Why we are here? For *you.*" Broken Bird's lips scarcely moved. "For you, Hope."

She blinked.

"And perhaps for Arity. We used to like him, you know. Pati has ruined him. All one can do is dismiss it as a bad job—but one cannot help wanting to redress the evil. And we recognize now this is only possible at a personal level."

They stood up, and Hope followed suit, like a sleepwalker. One after another, they pressed her in their arms.

She had hardly extricated herself from their hugs when their Icelandic *auchresh* clattered into the tent. The *keres* studiedly did not look at her as they took their leave. She was left standing alone by the fire, coughing, her eyes running with the smoke of a dozen simultaenous *teth˝tach chings.*

She had to believe in herself. Rightly or wrongly, she *had* to believe it was she who had put one over on them. She had to believe in her ability to keep track of all the strands of the vast, tangledy net she found herself knotting with both hands.

And she had to believe in Humi. Humi was her groundswell.

Her head had started to ache. She picked up her neglected pipe. It was a means of comfort, a reflex, like a swallow of chocolate before bed—a habit of her youth she had never grown out of.

She put it down. Going to the camp table, she called for her orderly. "Blackash! Come here!"

He entered at a run, his dark, furry face set with devotion. She smiled at him and was rewarded with a frenzied leap that lifted him several inches off the floor and brought him down with a thud. He loved her insanely, considering she had never spoken a personal word to him.

"Set up my bed, please. Then you can go fetch Scribe Dryburn." For the benefit of the rumor mill, she said, "I am going to dictate a dispatch to Humi."

THE WALL OF THE CHRUMETOWN GRANARY

When the fighting rang out in Curentise Street, not two streets away, Gete realized they were backed into a dead end. Pressed against the heavy stone wall of a granary, with equally impenetrable walls on either side, in the hot clinch of a weeping, praying, cursing crowd of Chrumetowners, he tried to assess his chances rationally.

If he and Thani did not escape, they would die. Being on the wrong side of Chrumetown when the violence bubbled over this morning had marked them as devotees—whereas had they been a half-league to the south, they could have passed as atheists or apostates, friendly with the south-towners who had sheltered the renegades. As it was, when they fled the square where blood had first been spilled, they had run north, downhill, riverward. A renegade had yelled in his god's voice, "Hands' sheep! Devotees!" and hurled a knife that whickered past Gete's shoulder.

He had been right as it happened. Thani was as staunch a loyalist as anyone could imagine. But on the whole the killing was horrifyingly non-sectarian, while it pretended to be directed by ideology. Apostates, loyal flamens, foreigners, Deltans, and outcountry folk, some of them looking askance at each other, some openly hostile, were all crushed about Gete so close that he could taste their breath. There had been two stabbings. The dead men were held upright in a ghoulish semblance of life. But when the porous line of Hands—their ad hoc defenders—in Curentise Street gave way, *all* of them would die.

Predators, Gete thought, his fury and fear compounded by a sense of unfairness: the renegades should have recognized him, if anyone, as a sym-pathizer! They were slaughtering everyone they uncovered in their surge toward the river. With the blood lust in their veins, they seemed scarcely to distinguish between gods and men.

In the short sixdays since Gete and Thani reached Chrumetown, he had seen a few of them about. They had worn hoods to disguise their *auchresh* features; but that was only wise, in a town in the heart of human country heavily policed by Hands. One would *never* have guessed *this* was brewing.

Fear smelled sour, like turned milk.

Babies wailed. So did grown-ups.

Gete could hear the Hands' and rebels' war cries over the racket of the terrified crowd. A wonder they had any breath left to kill each other. But they did. Gete's boots were stained piebald with divine blood. There was some agent in the white stuff that took the tan out of leather.

Thani had a child in each arm which she was trying to soothe. People were looking at Gete with a kind of wild hope in their faces. He was a leman: he had to do something. Escape to the river was impossible, unless they could get *through* the granary . . . He wriggled, scanning as much of the wall as he could see. No door. No opening. Thani had done so much already—could he ask her to break a hole in the granary wall? She would do it, of course, if he said she had to, but it might kill her. As a loyalist, almost all her miracles were worked on people, and she had told him that inanimate objects were far more difficult to "heal," let alone "injure." He would not ask her unless he had no choice.

But it was beginning to look as if he did not.

The Hands had been outnumbered from the beginning. A good many of them had left Chrumetown three days ago. Maybe Gete should have guessed then trouble was brewing. But Thani wouldn't have left anyhow . . . Rumor screamed silently that there was fighting in the capital. Since the departure of the Hands, Chrumetowners had gone about looking lost in their familiar streets. Thani had healed a rash of sudden, severe illnesses.

A big old man with turquoise fur, near Gete, was fighting to get out of the crowd. "Let me through! Let me out! I am an apostate! I can help the Hands!"

The world is turned upside-down.

"Godsbrother!" Gete shouted. It was necessary to shout. He caught the apostate's red old eye. "Listen a moment! Can you use your powers to break through this wall?"

"Why?" the apostate shouted.

With dismay, Gete realized the old man was in the claws of his own, obscure killing lust.

Am I the only person here who is even trying to keep his head? "We have to break down the wall! Then even if we can't escape, we won't trample ourselves to death!"

"Save us, Godsbrother!" a woman screamed. Others took up the cry. Though it did not seem possible, they squashed closer together, creating a little space around the apostate.

He clenched his aqua-furred fists. Then the rage that had seemed in danger of spilling over onto the Chrumetowners evaporated. He dropped his chin to his chest as if he were nodding off.

Gete dived under peoples' arms, pushed an old woman out of his way, and caught the apostate as he began to crumple.

He had expected to fetch up against the wall. But the wall was gone. Before he apprehended this, the world whirled sideways and he landed with the unconscious Godsbrother on a pile of rubble. The sky glowed at his feet. Bodies blotted out its blueness. Instinctively he curled around the apostate, trying to shield both their heads. Boots hammered his hands, his arms, his legs. A corner of stone dug into his kidneys. People were stampeding over them, fleeing like sheep before the slaughtermen's knives.

After an eternity, the pounding ceased. Footsteps rang on wooden stairs. Thani knelt over him, shaking him. "Gods! gods, you're bleeding . . . your face . . . oh, gods' breath, please wake up, Gete!"

He sat up, hugged her briefly. Then he felt his nose. The fur of his face was sticky with blood. The apostate did not look in very good shape either. He was breathing, but not moving.

Gete suddenly realized that he had failed to think of the most important thing of all. "Thani!" he said urgently. "Close the hole!"

"What hole?" She stood up, patting the air. She sniffed the breeze and made a face at the scent of bloodshed.

She thought she owed him anything he wanted, for taking care of her, when in fact it was he who owed her everything. He owed her the life she had given him that night on Qalma, when she woke him from the sleep that had been his life on Sarberra.

He guided her hands around the ragged edges of the stonework. The gap was slightly higher than he was tall, and as wide. The cobbles of the dead end shone with a scuffed patina of blood and dirt. Three bodies and some dropped possessions were the only things left in the dead end. He could not see how the crowd had fit in such a small space.

From the noise, the Hands must have been pressed back into the next alley. They had seconds, at most. He tried not to let urgency into his voice. "We're inside a building now. We have to seal this wall. When the renegades get here, they mustn't know where we went. If they can't see us they won't bother to look. The lust is on them. Use a miracle the way the apostate do. I know you never did it before, but it's our lives, Thani," and he was begging. "You *must* have it in you! I know you do!"

"To foil the enemies of the Divinarch," she whispered, and grabbing his hand, she screwed up her little blond face and stood as still as a column swathed in drab homespun, her feet planted firmly on the rubble beside the unconscious apostate.

He held her as she lurched, held her through the blue disorientation, the trembling strain that felt as though every muscle in the body were being pulled, the certainty that it was impossible—that this time, she would fall into the void instead of bridging it—

and the *twitch*.

In the days before her audience with the Divinarch, when she had told him everything, she had wept hours afterward with the remembered pain of healings. Nothing could make her cry except his sympathy.

The air felt different on his face. Stonework swept from the vaulted ceiling to the floor of the granary. The pile of rubble had changed shape to accommodate the new wall, but it had not diminished.

They were alone in the vast, empty space. Stairs zigzagged up one wall. The wooden banisters showed yellow where they had recently been snapped by the herds of Chrumetowners. Kerneled wheat lay drifted in a corner. The air smelled musty. Gete bent to shake the apostate.

Above him, Thani smiled carefully. "We're safe now, aren't we?" Her lips cracked, dribbling dark blood down her chin.

When the noise of the fighting finally diminished toward the river, the Chrumetowners breathed again. Several times during the afternoon that ensued, renegades' footsteps rang below in the granary. Every man, woman, and child froze, aware that one creak, one cry . . . or if the renegades saw the broken banister . . .

There had not been a sound for several hours.

But no one in the attic moved. Families huddled together. Those who had been caught alone slumped in groups scattered through the vast, dusty crawl space, Deltans with Deltans, Veretreans with Veretreans, and so on. Gete supposed they drew some measure of succor from the default bond of ethnicity.

A man could not stand upright even in the middle of the attic. Piles and piles of ledgers (etched, in the old-fashioned way, on large wooden tablets) blocked Gete's view. He sat with the apostate Godsbrother's leman, a sly-looking Calvarese boy of ten or eleven, and Thani, and the old apostate himself. Two flamens, two winged souls encased in depleted, infirm bodies.

Gete had refused requests for Thani to heal that child's cut, this one's fever, examine that little girl who had not spoken since her mother was killed. "The Godsister has saved you once already today. Let her sleep. Please."

Perhaps because they knew that if Thani had been awake, she would have tended them all, squeezing the last drop of strength from her soul, they nodded and tiptoed away.

And Thani did sleep. Gete wrapped her in his cloak without waking her. The infinitesimal disturbances of dreams made her dirty face twitch; insect-sized motes of dust settled on her hair. As day faltered, stopped, and relinquished the field to night, they became invisible.

Gete was cold in his shirt sleeves, but in a way he enjoyed shivering, after all the horrors of the day. Enjoyed controlling it. The old apostate was "watching" him in that way Thani had—fingering him with all his senses. His leman slept, curled doglike around the apostate's legs, all the precocious stealth drained from his face by exhaustion. His dark-furred cheeks were as round as a baby's.

Periods of drifting marked that long night, when Gete felt as though his mind had come loose from his body and floated into the rafters. In one of the intervals between these delusions, the apostate started talking.

"My name is Godsbrother Quest." He touched the sleeping boy's head. "This is Avi. You are Gete? Let me guess. Your name is Regretfulness."

He asked about Gete's relationship with Thani, their history, how long they had traveled together, where they planned to go next.

"The Divinarch posted us here. I suppose we'll stay until he sends us somewhere else." Gete could not keep the bitterness out of his voice.

"Do you think he will remember to call for you in the middle of *this?*" The apostate gestured around the attic. "Mark me, Archipelagan, he has forgotten he ever saw you or your flamen. You should have stayed in the Archipelago! He has more urgent matters to deal with now. The Divinarchy is eroding out from under him faster than a sandbank in a flood. Have you heard about Pirady? Domesdys? Veretry?"

Gete shook his head.

"They are all in the hands of the rebels. The Divinarch will have to fight merely to hold on to what he still has. And anyhow, in my opinion, the flamens were never more than a pastime for him." Gete opened his mouth in outrage. "No. Perhaps that is not quite fair. You were part of a test he subjected himself to, to prove he still possessed whatever ability it is that he has."

"He brainwashed Thani!" It felt good to come out with it. For Gete to admit that he resented, no, *hated,* the Divinarch for the huge open spaces he had installed in Thani's soul.

"*That* is a mystery. Some of my own faith speculate, because of his unusual powers, that the traditional belief that we flamens draw our powers from the gods—is not altogether unfounded. But then—there are humans rumored to have this ability, too . . ."

"Who do you mean?"

"Humility Garden . . ."

"That's my flamen's sister." *Perhaps I shouldn't have told him that!* The apostate seemed to invite confidences. Gete bit his lip.

But all the apostate said was, "Really? I have never seen her, but I heard from a friend, an apostate in Delta City, one Godsbrother Phantasm, that she does have unusual powers. Phantasm was sent to offer the apostates' allegiance to her, back when we were still questioning where our political loyalty lay. He described her as 'coruscating.' Do you know what that means, Archipelagan?"

"That's how Thani talks about seeing gods."

"Precisely. I confess I felt a slight trepidation when Avi read Phantasm's letter. My brother flamen was shaken by his experience, which at the time was very recent—too shaken to have been impressed either favorably or unfavorably by the Divinarch. But I hazard a guess that that visit had a great deal to do with his subsequent suggestion that we all offer our allegiance to her."

"What is it?" Gete asked. "This 'seeing'?" Starlight came through a crack in the roof, painting a white streak across both their laps. Godsbrother Quest's hands lay interlaced, calm. With a conscious effort Gete stopped fidgeting with the frayed cuff of his breeches. He said, "I've talked to—I've talked to gods—who say that it is all nonsense. That they have no divine blood in their veins."

"Rebels, I suppose. But they are not flamens," Quest said crisply.

"That's blasphemy!"

"Inasmuch as?"

Gete rubbed the bridge of his nose. "You're—you're saying you and Thani have powers gods don't!"

"Exactly. Boy . . . boy. Power has nothing to do with superiority. What do you think the prime doctrine of the apostate creed is? Do you know *nothing* about us?" Godsbrother Quest smiled. Perhaps it was meant to be reassuring, but his eyeteeth caught the starlight and his salt crystals glowed over them like a pair of white flames, and for a moment all Gete could see was the hollow, carved head of a god standing on his mother's table in the middle of the winter when the sun only rose for an hour. A head with a candle inside it. Flat planes and raw edges of stone.

"You think you are all-powerful," he said fearfully.

"Not in the *least.*" The Godsbrother unlaced his hands and shaped the air emphatically with them as he talked. "We do not believe the gods are divine. We believe they are merely another race, whose oddities and weaknesses we have yet to discover. The renegade gods are working toward an acceptance of their own ordinariness; but the majority of them still, in their hearts, believe they are superior to us. The only way we can achieve equality is through years and years and years of the intermingling the renegades have started. And it is bound not to be so easy as it has been thus far. It may look to us, *now,* as though the numbers of gods in human country can increase illimitably, and mortals will only be pleased and flattered—but eventually the common saltsider will realize that his 'divine' guest is really no different from his own cousin. The fact that the god can do the work of ten men will certainly sweeten the cup—but eventually, there must be a backlash. I do not know if we will ever really live in peace." He leaned forward. "But to apostates the question is more or less irrelevant."

"What do you mean?" Gete frowned, mentally struggling to understand. "What difference does it make where the gods live?"

"No difference. That is what I say. The gods have nothing to do with miracles."

Gete laughed.

"And the power does not spring from within ourselves, Archipelagan! If it did, *you* would work miracles. Every street urchin would keep himself clothed and fed. *We* would be gods.

"It seems safe to say that the power comes from the salt pilgrimage. Perhaps miracles' source lies in the salt, in some deep locus of brilliance. Perhaps it is in the air, in the salt winds themselves, in a chemical reaction of that sodium with our vital fluids." Quest shifted, tilting his slablike chin, and the starlight died in his crystals. "If so, the gods know no more about it than we do."

"Then you aren't any cleverer than Thani," Gete said disgustedly. "You don't know what you're talking about, either. The only difference is that you *know* you don't know."

"You have hit upon it!" For the first time, the apostate laughed. "We are mystics, Gete. That is our creed." Merriment rolled out of him like hands hitting a bass drum. Unwillingly, Gete smiled. The other leman raised his head, blind with sleep, and felt clumsily for his knife.

The Godsbrother stopped laughing. "It's all right, Avi."

The boy nodded. Quite clearly, he said, "Good." Wrapping his arms securely around Quest's foot, he curled up in a ball. In minutes he was breathing regularly again.

Uncontrollable shivering, the kind that relieves excessive tension, was making Gete's teeth chatter. He shoved his knuckles into his mouth. Around his fist, he said, "What do you believe in, then, Godsbrother?"

"We give it a name." It was almost as if Quest had been waiting for this question. Quite suddenly, Gete realized that the purpose of this little disquisition was to try to convert him. He felt an overpowering, but brief, desire to laugh as the Godsbrother had done. "The Power. A translation of the word *Rigethe,* from the language of the gods. They use it like the name of a deity in their speech, but we cannot make out from the renegades, who are mostly antireligious, to what extent they actually worship it. To us, it is not something one prays to, anyhow. Reverence toward it signifies our belief in something greater, something beyond—something whose existence must be acknowledged, and which must be feared, as one fears the unknown, as one fears destiny."

Gete did not want to give these crazy ideas time to sink in. But he could not think of anything else to object to.

"The Power is a source. A reason. The future."

In the morning, this will all seem like nonsense. "Well—but—what—" The minute Gete spoke, he knew it was absurdly irrelevant. "What does this all have to do with what we were talking about? The Divinarch's powers?"

Godsbrother Quest laughed again, more softly this time. "Aaah. We come full circle. It has *everything* to do with it—it is the *proof* of all I have told you. In that it is nothing. Gete, my dear boy, Pati's power is nothing more than an excess of charisma. Such a human trait, to mistake imbalanced souls for geniuses—or divine entities."

Outside, far off, a cheer went up. *Auchresh* voices, laughing and shouting with pure abandon. Gete did not smile in response. He was too afraid. He scrambled to his knees, twisting his head sideways, and screwed his eyes into the crack of the roof.

Yellow light showed over the roofs at the top of the town. Rivers of fire flowed down one street, then another. The topmost streets were glowing steadily now.

Arson.

"It's burning," he gulped, "they're burning the town, oh, gods—"

Abruptly he stopped. The light did not leap with the ravenous lack of inhibition that characterizes house fires. There were no flames at all.

He could smell the river, which flung its muddy mists over the whole town as it rolled by, leaving a dusty residue of algae on stones and windows, sliming the streets when it rained. He could not smell fire.

In Curentise Street, below one side of the granary, flame leaped. And steadied. Gete saw the huge squares of light swaying on walls, which meant lanterns.

Footsteps rang on cobbles, fading eastward.

The Hands were lighting the street lanterns, which had been neglected all winter to save fuel, in celebration of their victory. On the hill the cheering swelled, louder than ever.

Gete sank back, disappointed.

CITY OF CHARITY

There was no traffic on the Chrume. The devotees who had recovered enough from their ordeal in Chrumetown to notice such things muttered that they had never seen anything like it. For ten days, the barge swished down the river in a padded cell of fog. Only the cry of a heron, or the complaint of a hungry child, broke the silence. "Don't fret," mothers murmured distractedly. "When we get to the city there'll be food. Plenty of it. Hush. Hush."

After a four-hour shift, the blue-furred Veretrean sailor, Godsman Reedbloom, relieved Gete at the *Sunflower*'s wheel. Gete sought out Thani. She perched on the prow of the barge, wrapped in woolen robes. "Regretfulness," she said dully.

He cast a worried eye over her. Her fur looked clumpy. The damp air on the river was doing nobody any good—but she had been squeezing far too many miracles out of herself these past few days, healing burn victims, stab victims, and those who had simply refused to move or speak after escaping Chrumetown.

"Ye're not all right."

"Yes, I am." She clutched her robe closer, her pale fingers like buckles on its folds. "Gete, they're all depending on me. I should never have brought them onto the river. I'm so afraid this is horribly wrong . . ."

He could not believe she had actually admitted her doubts. He had not known for so long what she was thinking. Only what she had decided to do. And for her, the decision-making had always been the most tortuous part. "Don't be a goose!" he said robustly. "We couldn't've stayed in Chrumetown. Renegades would've killed us all for some reason or other." Almost all the refugees on the barge were devotees who had risen to affluence under Pati's rule; they could adequately have been described as "Hands' sheep." "Ye *know* that. That's why we left."

"But would they have killed them? The sentinels on the docks didn't stop us casting off. Perhaps they really didn't care one way or the other what faith people professed. Perhaps theirs is a new creed we are incapable of understanding."

Gete had sometimes wondered what happened to Godsbrother Quest, the old apostate with whom he talked all night in the granary attic when they were hiding from the Hands. Those crackling, brilliant ideas had looked so faint when day came and Thani needed him again. Out of politeness, Gete had offered the Godsbrother a place on the *Sunflower;* but Quest had gently reminded Gete that *he* was not a devotee, that he was in fact well known for his apostasy, and thus was in no more danger, now that the killing was over.

Were the renegades apostates, then?

It was all too confusing. But perhaps Thani would not have been in danger any more than Quest was. Gete remembered the renegade sentinels' hollow eyes, their gratitude when people sidled nervously out of their houses and offered them chairs to sit on. "They were *exhausted,* Thani," he said now. "That's why they let us take the barge. If we'd given them so much as one day to recover from the battle, they would've cracked down. We'd never've gotten away."

"It would be wonderful to believe you, Gete. But I *cannot* stop wondering what might have happened if we had not fled." She gestured behind him at the barge, the masts with their enormous, limp bundles of sails, the grilled hatches that opened into the hold. "They are all in my care! What if I have misled them?"

"Look"—he put a smile into his voice—"right now, they're all in Godsman Reedbloom's care. If he falls asleep at the tiller, in this fog we would plow right into the bank before anyone notices we've lost course."

She grinned thankfully, and for a moment she was the old Thani, the Thani he had known before their audience with the Divinarch. "You are right! I accord myself too much significance! That way lies vanity. They aren't my responsibility."

"*There's* the spirit!" Gete said pleasedly.

"They're the Divinarch's."

Gete closed his mouth.

"He *can't* turn them away! They are his people. His Hands died defending them. And I'm his flamen. *There's* my responsibility, if you like, Gete. Even if there were too many supplicants in Delta City for Pati to help our little flock, *I* could get them a hearing! He knows me. He loves me . . ."

Gete stepped forward and took her in his arms, pulling her down off the rail. The veils of fog twined around them, drifting back along the barge, striping the white sails gray. There was a smell of mud. A seagull hooted. Gete held her close, pressing her face into his shoulder. They were almost to Delta City.

A pack of children materialized out of the jumbled riverfront and helped the refugees tie the *Sunflower* up at one of the jetties that jutted into the Chrume. In six dozen berths, there was not one other barge. Gete bit his lip. He remembered rumors of fighting in the capital. But perhaps everyone was just hiding in their houses—perhaps the rumors were exaggerated, and people were only frightened, not dead.

Or perhaps it was Dividay. The day of rest. He had lost track of the sixdays.

As the refugees clambered unsteadily up onto the jetty, the Deltan children jumped, froglike, around them, hissing demands for money. "Or sump'n t' eat! Give us sump'n nice, Godsmen, an' we'll let you go!"

By this time the refugees had barely enough provisions to make themselves one more meal. Some of the men cursed the children and told them to take themselves off. Thani protested, but the men ignored her, and drew their daggers.

The urchins broke their mandate of whispering and fled, screaming.

Each Chrumetowner family had knotted together, arms around waists, heads on shoulders. The journey from Chrumetown had started in a delirium of terror, and concluded in a near-coma—not a relief, but a distillation of that terror, induced by the silence, the fog, and the paucity of food. Delta City's silence seemed to have infected the Chrumetown children: not one was making a sound, not even the babies. Their eyes were wide, their fur stretched sparse over their delicate skulls. The little ones clutched big brothers' or sisters' hands. Quite unexpectedly, the sight rent Gete's heart: for the first time in months, he missed his own little sisters.

Godsman Reedbloom, the Veretrean sailor, rolled up to them. "What now, Godsister?"

Thani shook herself. "The Palace, I suppose. Gete and I have been there before. He remembers where it is. He can lead us there . . ."

Gete shook his head in helpless anguish. "No," he mouthed silently to the sailor. "No." Over Thani's shoulder, he could see something truly dreadful. Without looking at the flamen, without looking up from the ground, the Chrumetown families were slipping away. One by one, they sidled out of view between the shuttered houses.

Godsman Reedbloom's throat jumped. He glanced at Thani, then over his shoulder at the departing Chrumetowners. Finally, with obvious dis-

comfort, he said, "Godsister . . . will you excuse me? I see Widow
Sevenna is alone. The city may be dangerous, is it? She may need—"

Gete answered quickly for Thani. "Yes. Go." He held up his fingers and
moved them to and fro as if for a blessing. "Gods be with you, Kines."

Quickly, shocking Gete a little, Kines Reedbloom turned his head and
spat on the boards of the jetty. Then he mumbled a courtesy to Thani and
strode off. Gete watched him catch up with the widow and her little son
and place his big hand on her shoulder. Together, they vanished into an
alley.

Thani let out a long sigh. "Well," she said hopelessly. And again: "Well.
They are gone, aren't they? They didn't trust us."

Gete certainly did not trust himself to say anything forgiving about the
Chrumetowners. White flocks of seagulls pitched and tossed overhead. The
Chrume churned around the piers of the jetty, sheeny brown, roiling seaward. A curtain of gray fog cut down after twenty feet, hiding the sea,
hiding even the last jetties. Thani stood like a badly constructed scarecrow,
unmoving, head tipped, no more intelligent than a machine in repose, and
seemingly as incapable of thinking for herself. Their knapsack of possessions sat lopsided at their feet.

"You and I must go to the Divinarch, anyhow," she said. She pulled
herself upright. "We must tell him that we are here, and will serve him. It
is obvious *something* is wrong: the city is far too quiet. We must help in any
way we can."

But what kind of machine?

Regardless of the months they had spent together, regardless of the ever-
increasing esteem in which he held her, not until that moment did Gete
fully appreciate her strength.

One thing of which there was no shortage in the capital was corpses.
They lay undisturbed in corners, intersections, doorways, human and divine bodies both. Nearly all of them wore some kind of emblem. The
Hands had bright silky uniforms rucked around their immobile limbs, and
the rest, men and renegades, sported the white-and-gray patches Gete had
come to recognize as the badge of Humility Garden's followers. Some of
the Chrumetown renegades had had those, some not. They gave even
corpses a dreadful air of officiousness. Gete shuddered. This was all becoming so organized!

So many bodies. Few of them showed signs of having been looted. The
Deltans must be afraid.

But the common people of the city scurried along the streets as briskly as
they had the last time Gete was here. In some places they had spilled stone

dust over the bloodstains. They looked behind them more often than rabbits on an open hillside, but at least they had not all disappeared into thin air. The shop doors stood open, though few people carried any purchases. The relative liveliness of the city surprised Gete. But then he thought, *How else could it be? These people have nowhere else to go. They're already in what we thought was a refuge.*

He did not shrink from describing the carnage to Thani, but he left out the badges. She did not want to hear of anything connected with her sister, although that was growing increasingly more difficult to manage.

Some of the sprawled dead were flamens. If the faces were hidden, or the salt crystals gone, he knew them anyway from the way little and big corpses clung together, faithful to the last. Would that be required of *him?* No pilgrimages for these children. Would the world feel their loss? After this was over (and he knew in his bones it must end soon, it could not go on, could not, this silent scream which was the city), how many flamens would be left?

Death was a loud, rich note in the air.

Everyone avoided Thani as industriously as if she were six feet tall and wielding a fiery knife. He knew she sensed it: an expression of pain grew on her face as they passed along the broad concourses, so that he was relieved when they reached the palace district and there was no one to stare at them and run. Here, many houses were blackened shells. In some places the sides of mansions lay in rubble all over the streets, as if they had been demolished by battering rams. A little way to the east, Gete heard shouts and cries. He quickened his pace, wondering how to avoid the confrontation.

A knife whizzed by his head, seemingly out of nowhere. "Gods!"

A few paces in front of them, a Hand appeared in a puff of brimstone. Gete staggered back. "Where are you going?" the Hand shouted. "Where are your colors? Quick!"

"We come to serve," Thani said simply, while Gete retrieved the Hand's knife.

"Who?" The Hand took the proffered knife in a way that was almost an insult.

"The Divinarch!"

"Thought you were creeping up on our flank, and making a damn poor job of it at that." He eyed Thani scornfully. "But I can see you're upcountry. Good, that's good. We need you. Right over there, in fact. Wait—" He raised his sleeve to his mouth and ripped the silk with his fangs. It shrieked thinly as it parted. Glancing thoughtfully toward the noise of the battle, he came forward and handed Gete two burnt-orange strips. "Tie this around your arm. And have her wear it somewhere it's visible." He shook his head tiredly. "You wouldn't believe how many of the deaths—on *both* sides— have been caused by overzealousness."

Overzealousness! Gete thought. *That's what killed half of Chrumetown.*

"Now get moving!" the Hand shouted. "Go on! Get over there!"

When Thani did not move, he cursed impatiently, and pulled her toward him.

She let out a squeak of fear. Gete made a grab for her, alarms clanging in his mind, but he caught an armful of nothing.

Sulfur shimmered in his eyes. He reeled back, tears wetting his cheek fur. He was alone.

Gods' blood. Damn!

The worst possible eventuality, the thing every leman feared. In all his months with Thani this had not happened.

Without pausing to get his bearings, he flung himself down a side street, toward the noise of the fighting.

But it was farther away by foot than by *teth¨*. The streets of the palace district lay treacherously coiled one upon the other, linked by alleys that looked like service doors, rife with dead ends. To one whose sense of direction was already blunted by desperation, the maze was impenetrable. Gete was beside himself, a stitch biting into his side, by the time he located the battle.

And by then, it was over. Cold air rang with the note of death. Gete could smell the sea. The wounded and the dead—all *auchresh* except for one flamen and leman—sprawled in the windows of a mansion with a good-sized front garden, which must have looked very fine before it was burned to soot-streaked stone. A strip of bright blue silk twisted from a chimney pot. Rivulets of lurid crimson trickled in the gutter. After a minute of incomprehension, Gete realized the strange color resulted from the mingling of human and divine blood.

The Divinarch's forces had apparently taken the day. The Hands glanced up to see who had arrived, and then paid no attention to Gete. *Where was she?* The Hands were winding their way among the casualties, cold-bloodedly slitting the throats of wounded enemies, doing the same for their friends if they were beyond help, *teth¨ing* away with the wounded *auchresh* if there seemed to be any hope at all. They paid no attention whatsoever to Gete's wild inquiries, speaking when necessary to their fellows in weary undertones which ill matched their quick, graceful movements.

A little way off, several ragged flamens and lemans stood in a dejected group. They were *not* prisoners, but the Hands' allies. And there—*there* she was! Not standing with the rest, but slumped on the cobbles, her back against a wall.

Dead.

He dashed to her side and chafed her hands, kissed her face, whispered into her hair.

She stirred. Light moved in the depths of her salt crystals.

"First fight?" said the girl leman, a Piradean of about fifteen.

Gete nodded.

"Thought so. She was blooming terrified."

"What'd she have to do?"

"Only what my Godsbrother does. What they all do. Miracle spears. Fire in the eyes. Fire in the guts. Twist the guts. Things like that."

"Did she? Did she kill anyone?" He felt like a cad, going behind Thani's back. She hadn't returned to full consciousness yet. "Or is she no good at this? Should I take her away?"

"No, no! We can use her!" A tall Piradean man—the girl's Godsbrother?—took an interest for the first time, swinging his head with its heavy crystals toward Gete. "At first she was too frightened to move. I had to show her what to do, so that she did not hurt herself. But she understood quite quickly. Before it was over, I would guess she dispatched half a dozen of them. I could hardly believe she had not fought before."

"At least ten," his leman said admiringly.

"We faced no apostates today." The Piradean flamen was silent a moment. "Lucky for her we did not. She knows nothing of self-defense. That is more difficult. But if she can master it, I daresay she will be a great asset to us. She is not afraid to use her strength."

Oh, gods, Gete thought. *Poor Thani.* "But she's exhausted, Godsbrother. She won't be any use if she doesn't get some rest." It irked him to appeal to these loyalists. "She needs a bed, and good food, and a fire—" But if Thani had to fight again . . . *gods, gods* . . . maybe these flamens could help him keep her alive. Maybe they knew tricks. He would take the brunt of the fighting himself, if that would do any good. "We just got here today, from Chrumetown," he said desperately. "I don't think—"

"Ah. I heard that Chrumetown was burned."

Rumor travels fast! "No, it wasn't. But the renegades have it."

The Piradean flamen shook his head in pious disapproval. For a moment he looked ludicrously refined: far too gentrified to be standing out on a gray winter's day with no cloak, and soot stains on his face, and obscenely red blood trickling past his feet.

"The renegades have Domesdys and Calvary too," the other leman murmured in Gete's ear. "And Pirady. Me and my Godsbrother can't ever go home again. Unless the Divinarch wins it back."

"I will show you myself where you are to stay," the Piradean flamen said abruptly, almost as if he did not want to hear what his leman had said. "The Inviolate Ones have no need of us at the moment. The Divinarch has offered his hospitality to all whom the city has refused it to. The soup is hot, and there is a floor to sleep on; a flamen needs no more."

Gete winced. He knew it was a gentle reproof for begging luxuries for Thani.

In her slumped position, she shifted. She said in a clear, dignified voice: "Thank you very much, Tranquillity, for your kind offer. We are pleased to accept. Now, Gete, if you will assist me to my feet . . ."

The Hands barely looked up as their allies straggled off. The chilly air had a bite to it that took the smell of blood to Gete's nostrils. His feet remembered the turnings that led to the Palace. Before long, he found himself leading the motley band.

Loyalty is the blindest so-called virtue on the face of this earth.

He had got a bad scare. Losing Thani . . . ! He gripped her arm tighter. Her flesh was cold through her robe. It was then he knew for the first time that they were both going to die, and that there was nothing he could do to stop it, and that he was terrified.

The air seemed to tingle. A vast, shimmering maw hung overhead, greedy to swallow the roofs of the houses, to consume them until its heavy swollen grayness sunk to the earth and nothing was left but a few inches of air between the dirt and the sky.

Is this what we know as prophecy?

No symptoms. He kept walking. He might even have been talking to the Piradean leman; he wasn't sure. No shaking, or foaming at the mouth, or loss of control over his limbs. But he could think of nothing except death. Her death, and his own. He had not known he was such a coward.

The energy of fear galvanized his step.

This is for you, he thought, looking sideways at the girlish, set face of the Piradean leman. *This is for everyone in Chrumetown, for everyone in this hateful city. I don't think I ever did anything really disinterested before. So this is for all the times I failed in my duty to humankind. All the times I acted out of love for myself. Or love for her. Atonement.*

I understand now.

That had probably been his worst crime. Loving her.

That, at any rate, was what that made it hardest to reconcile himself to a swift, ugly end to everything.

CONQUERING PASSION

Arity and Pati balanced on the ancient Ellipse chamber chairs, one at either end of the council table. It had been a sixday since either of them had a full night's sleep. Deep within the Palace, they couldn't hear the noise of the fighting that drew constantly closer to the fortress. But they were not safe even here. Right now, guards stood three-deep outside the Ellipse door. On one occasion a scruffy little assassin trying to earn glory had burst in while they sat in session. That was when *lesh kervayim-serbalim* had still been here. He had been crucified on the east turret.

Pati played with the old voting stones, spinning them like dice. Sacrilege, none of the stones was ever supposed to "meet" each other. Arity sat bolt upright, concealing his restlessness.

All the *ex-kervayim* had gone to the continents to conduct campaigns against Humi's lieutenants. Some of them were dead. Glass Mountain. Crooked Moon. Unani. Pati's coup had not dissolved *lesh kervayim*, but the war seemed likely to put an end to them once and for all.

"Why are you unwilling?" Pati said. "Because we have not got a full council to vote on the motion?"

"Well, it *is* technically illicit."

Pati sneered, "Don't be absurd. This is war."

"I know."

"Some things are necessary evils! With its head cut off, the beast of rebellion must die—or at least sicken. We have to roust her out before the damage spreads any further!"

He was right about one thing, Arity thought. This ploy would bring Humi out of hiding, if anything could. They were pretty sure she was in Shimorning; but since the whole district was tacitly on the renegades' side, not even *auchresh* willing to die for their Divinarch could find out where the rebel headquarters were. Or if they could, they were invariably silenced before they could pass the information back. Humi had some method of spotting traitors which was extremely effective. Every agent Pati sent to try to infiltrate the Shimorning network was returned to him, dripping, in a little gold lamé bag. Suicidal attacks had been no more successful.

At last, even Pati's tolerance for needless death was strained. That was when he had come up with the idea of using the ghostiers—not to find out where Humi was hiding, but to bring her out.

"It's destroying the Crescent I am averse to." Arity steepled his fingers, aware he was stalling. "The ghostiers are one of the most valuable bargaining chips we have."

"And at any moment they may decide to flee overseas."

"I hardly think they will do *that* . . . they are too strongly bound to the city. And Delta City would not be Delta City without them. Aren't you sacrificing them too readily?"

"I would not sacrifice them at all, had I the choice! But if you think you can manage to spare them while preserving the verisimilitude of the ambush . . . you have my blessing!"

Humi was cleverer than that, Arity knew. She would not come near the Crescent if she smelled the least whiff of trickery. Reluctantly, he realized he would have to go through with it.

Better that than give Pati cause to doubt him. False though such doubts would be, they could prove fatal. Arity was painfully aware he was not immune to Pati's suspicious rages. Poor blameless Val had died in one such. He sighed.

"How many Hands do you think it wise for me to take?"

"By all means take as many as you can without making yourselves a target. Marshtown is not neutral territory! *Don't* take any unnecessary chances. I cannot afford to throw *you* away."

Pati met Arity's eyes. His mouth shaped other words. Arity closed his eyes. Heat spread from his ears to his cheeks. Thank the Power they were alone!

There was a sudden stink of *teth "tach ching.* His eyes flew open. Pati's face pressed close to his; steel pricked his throat. He overbalanced, and his chair crashed to the floor. By windmilling his arms he managed to keep his feet. "Power! Don't *do* that!"

"Every now and then, I have to make sure you *really* trust me," Pati said. He jammed his knife into its sheath. His eyes were stars.

"Power! I'm going to murder the *ghostiers* for you! How can you suppose I don't trust you?"

"Perhaps you merely agreed so that you could get a chance to see . . . *her.*"

Arity was angry now. *Let* Pati think that if he wanted. It was untrue! All he wanted was to get the abominable task over, so that he would never have to see her or think of her again.

He slapped his hip knife. "I'm off. Anon."

Pati let him walk a few paces toward the door. Then he *teth˚d* again— wasting precious energy, when so many were starving!—and clamped his hand down on Arity's shoulder.

Arity stood stock-still, staring at the intricate fruit-and-vine carvings on the door of the Chamber.

"Don't get killed," Pati hissed in his ear. "Why do you think I sent all the others to the continents rather than send you? Some would call if favoritism: they would be right." Hot breath on Arity's ear, and for an instant teeth nipped the lobe. "I *love* you."

Arity let out an angry sigh. Why did those three words always make him so impatient to be free of him? It was unbecoming. Unbecoming. He wrenched away and walked to the door.

"When next I see you," he said, "I'll have her head in one of those little gold bags she favors. Perhaps you'll trust me then? Mmm. I always have valued trust over love. Couldn't tell you why, but I believe it has something to do with being *auchresh.*"

The door thumped shut behind him, and the faces of the guards swam in his vision. Pale, tan, black, country-boy flowers, with strange mutated petals. *Wrchrethrim* all, loyal unto death, most of them both stupid and immature. Arity straightened his back. It was not difficult to feel taller than them, though several were over six feet. *Take the stupidest ones.* "You," he said, pointing, "I want *you* on detail right now, for a strike. And you. And you."

While the Hands outfitted themselves, Arity paid a visit to the human quarter of the Palace, where fanatical devotees willing to carry out suicide missions could always be found. He picked a starved-looking adolescent and told him to run to Shimorning and spread the word that the Hands were planning an attack on Tellury Crescent. The boy was not to try to convey this intelligence to Humi herself; that would be risky. She might smell a rat, and torture the boy until he squealed. He was merely to drop significant phrases in certain taverns known as hotbeds of rebellion. "That way," Arity said kindly, placing his hand on the boy's neck, ruffling the fur, "you'll live to serve us another day."

Shuddering with joy, overwhelmed to be chosen, the boy seized Arity's hand and planted a kiss on it. Then he ran off.

The squad made their way quickly through the palace district, circling the Folly (empty now and staffed by Hands), and concealed themselves in a dead end just outside Tellury Crescent, wrapped in drab rags, like a band of immigrants with nowhere to go. Two of them strolled openly down the street, masquerading as an ordinary patrol. The locals scurried out of their way. At the end of the street, they faced about and returned to Arity. In whispers they reported that they had glanced in the windows of the Chalice and seen the ghostiers relaxing after their midday meal.

"What luck!" said Arity cheerfully.

The sky hung low and fleecy, like a sheep's belly, over the city. A mean wind was screeching higher and higher. Scraps of cloud tore off and blew underneath the mass, pale on dark gray, fleeing landward.

With a gloved hand Arity secured his cap more firmly on his head. "All right. On my word."

The squad stormed the Chalice with all the hullaballoo they had been careful to avoid as they slid through the palace district. Arity ordered the ground floor torched immediately. Flattening himself against the wall of the anteroom (where so often he had listened with Humi while the ghostiers talked of him and her) he heard screams from the street, and running footsteps. Within minutes, Tellury Crescent would be empty of men, beasts, and valuables. That did not matter. The ghostiers couldn't escape. Hands ringed the Chalice and Albien House, up the stairs of which the ghostiers had been seen hurrying when the first windowpane shattered on the ground floor. Hands combed each floor, covering all possible bolt holes. The ghostiers would be caught on the top floor, in Humi and Erene's old apartments.

Wiping smoke out of his eyes, a single guard at his side, Arity waited for her. The wave of fleeing civilians would convince her that the strike was for real, even if the informant had not succeeded.

She had better come! How despicable this strike would be if it had been all for nothing!

Fire giggled inhumanly on the other side of the wall.

Airty dug his elbow into the guard. The Carelastrian jumped to attention. "Upstairs!" Arity shouted over the sound of the flames. "Tell Night Dog not to kill the ghostiers—not yet! Take them prisoner! Wait—until she comes!" He yelled out the message again to make sure the Hand had it. The little yellow Carelastrian nodded, and *teth¨d*. The sulfur of his departure was no fouler than the smoke bulging around the ill-fitting Chalice door.

What could be burning in there? Paintings? Silverware? Arity knew better than to open the door. He moved away from the wall. It was getting hot.

The Chalice was all stone, but for its roof, floorboards, and furnishings. But Albien House was of antique wood—and so was part of the connecting wall. If they weren't careful, the conflagration might spread, and the Hands would die along with their victims.

He yelled at the top of his lungs for his sergeant, Night Dog. When the tall, black-skinned fellow appeared, Arity ordered, his voice cracking, "Have six men draw water from the kitchen and stand by to douse the fire when it's done its work! See it doesn't spread to the roofs!"

"The fire is in the kitchen, *perich¨hi*," Night Dog volunteered.

Power! He should have thought of that. "Have them draw the water anyway! Fire be damned! They can cover their faces with wet cloths."

He knew that the Hands considered him soft. It pleased him to watch Night Dog's esteem for him rising visibly. "Yes, *perich¨hi!*" The sergeant executed a minimal bow, stamped his booted feet (all the Hands, in their fight against a movement composed largely of humans, had taken to wearing hobnailed boots; they gave better purchase), and *teth¨d*.

Arity stood, listening. The flames crackled closer to the wooden wall.

Sweat ran in rivulets down his face, down inside his uniform. The smoky air was nearly unbreathable. By sheer strength of will, he held himself still.

Then, almost simultaneously, he heard a ripping, splintering discord from overhead, and something hit the floor of the Chalice, shaking Albien House like a battering ram.

With unbelievable speed, the smoke was sucked back around the door. Arity pulled off one glove, wrapped it around his other hand, and used that hand to throw open the door.

The whole section of wall surrounding the door gave way and tumbled into the Chalice.

Roiling billows of smoke showed him: glimpses of blackened rafters fallen in crazy configurations, some of them reaching from floor to ceiling, making a dead jungle out of the hall; Hands popping in and out of sight, rags wrapped around their heads; glittering sloshes of water heeling through the air. A sour stink rose from the remaining section of the wall. The Hands nodded to him and kept on sloshing, except for one who ceased his duties in order to beat out the flames that had caught the shoulders of another.

He yelled to get their attention. When they had all solidified where they were, he said, "Enough. Get upstairs! The ghostiers are more subtle than you think!"

"Yes, *perich¨hi!*"

"I'll cover the ground floor. Listen for my summons."

Some of them shot him uncertain looks. But they all vanished.

Alone, Arity coughed and spat phlegm. Almost all the flames were out. The walls of the kitchen and library were stone; they still stood, though unquestionably all the books and tablets (thousands of years old, some of them in *auchraug*) were ash. Little puffs of smoke curled around the fallen rafters, giving the scene a look of steaming completion, like the frame of a second, inner building designed by an eccentric architect. Outside the shattered windows, nothing moved. Even the larks that usually flocked around the eaves of the Crescent (as he remembered from days of another life, memories of another self) had decamped. Somewhere, a woman was sobbing. How much longer could he keep from going up there and having Night Dog replace him on lookout? He ought to be there. The execution was his assigned task. *Must* the ghostiers be executed? If she wasn't coming—

If he did not go upstairs, the Hands' blood lust, which surely must be lapping at the backs of their throats, after all this destruction—would cause them to kill the ghostiers regardless.

At the library door, somebody stepped on a red-hot ember and said, "Damn."

Arity went rigid. Without breathing, carefully he turned.

She was alone.

In all his hastily dismissed dreams of this moment, he had never dared to hope she would come *alone*.

She wore an old-fashioned, beautifully embroidered dress of green silk, cut on the bias so that it lapped the curves of her hips. She wore tiny green slippers. Soot already blackened their toes and streaked the dress. Her hair fanned electrically about her face. She advanced with halting steps, hands patting the air ahead of her. When one hand encountered a rafter, she brushed her fingertips along the wood, then raised them to her mouth. She grimaced as she tasted the soot. "Too late," she said aloud. "Too late. Gods!"

No time to think (*don't think*) no time to plan (*don't plan*) just *do* it.

He *teth¨d* behind her and jammed his arm under her chin, forcing her head back, pinning her arms, drawing his knife from the sheath slowly, so that she could hear the rasp of leather. "Don't struggle," he whispered. "You'll only make it worse. It'll be over in a moment."

Actually, he doubted his ability to finish it quickly *or* slowly. But then he could not get enough breath to shout for the others. She was struggling, of course; how stupid to imagine she would not struggle just because he told her not to. Only she'd never been a match for him.

Power, enable me to get this over with.

"It's me. I wouldn't have let anyone else do this. That's scanty comfort but—I want you to know I still hold you in the highest esteem."

"You have become like Pati," she breathed. "Trickster. Heartless trickster. You sacrificed Emni and Zin and the rest of them, all to get at me. I did not believe it could be true. I was sure it was a double blind."

His voice would not come. His hands would not obey him. Touching her, protecting her from the chilly wind (for her bodice left most of her beautiful breasts bare), tasting her hair in his mouth, he found it difficult to remember exactly how they had both come to be here. All he knew was that it was wrong. The configuration was all skewed, the knife was in the wrong place, the wrong hand, its blue-black sway razoring the air as if it were silk, carving a distinction between the reality that was and the reality that would have been had he not drawn it; that distinction finer, ever finer.

Indifference was the real trickster. Indifference blunted the blade, numbed the agony of bifurcation, that splitting of the soul which Pati prompted in all his creatures. Indifference had corroded Arity faster than anything that preceded it. He had done more atrocities as a lieutenant than he had in all his months as an ordinary Hand.

Now there was no other option for him but to turn. Turn away. Open his eyes to this changed Humi of the arrogant, halting carriage, the dead eyes, the vicious whisper. Place himself on one side of the blade.

"You always had that gift"—he whispered to her—"of making one see oneself more clearly. I know it sounds ironic to say that to you now. But I can't . . . I can't—" With the thumb of his knife hand, he touched the poor useless eyelids.

She shuddered, shook, and started to whisper abuse at him. A continuous stream of highly charged obscenities. Her voice sounded more and more like crying every minute. But at least she was not indifferent to him. At least she wasn't laughing!

"I wish I knew what to do," he told the swearing girl helplessly. "But you see, I have been a hypocrite for so long now—"

"And you still are!" she hissed, practically in tears. Then she sidestepped quickly, neatly, and wrenched away. He had not been ready. Belatedly, he cursed himself for watching her face instead of her feet. But then as she edged rapidly away, the end of a charred beam caught her in the lower back and bent her double.

Arity was terrified of approaching her again. She straightened up, coughing, with tears running down her face. One of her false-ribs, cracked, protruded whitely through her bodice. "Do you know what's changed, Arity, why you are going to kill me now? We have become conscious of ourselves. We know ourselves. And when you know yourself you know the unreality, the lethal transcience of faith. In *anyone.*"

Her nose was running. She wiped it with her sleeve, a gesture that made him want to sweep her into his arms.

He must have made some small noise. She stiffened, and on her face was masterfully controlled fear. "Do you still love me, Ari? Drop that knife, then! Drop it!"

He let it fall. It bounced, ringing dully on the flags.

"Oh, hell," she whispered wretchedly.

And warned by some instinct passed down to him by his predator parents, Arity realized what was happening. Just as he spun around, someone snarled a mad-cat noise behind him and slammed a powerful arm across his neck.

Caught, just the way he had caught Humi!

And now *genuinely* unable to call out. A blade traced spider tracks under his jaw. White blood coursed down his captor's arm.

"Got him!" the man breathed.

Upstairs, all was silent. Or perhaps Arity just couldn't hear over the blood in his ears. What were they *doing* up there? *(The treacherous daughter of a predator.)*

"Hume," the man said, "are they—Emni—Zin—"

"I expect so," Humi said. "I didn't think they really would massacre them, Sol. I'm sorry."

It was Sol. Sol Southwind, the ghostier who had refused to make Arity into a ghost, a lifetime ago, in the nightmarish days before he learned the secret.

"I was wrong."

Sol gave a great gasp, and clamped Arity's neck until Arity could not breathe. Did Sol remember him? "So what now?" he said roughly. "Have you thought through to this eventuality? Or were you so sure it wasn't true—"

"Of course I have thought it through!" Humi said. She slumped against the rafter, smiling, soot staining her sleeves. "I always think things out, don't I. But Ari says—he says he will turn. Much good that it does now . . . The bastard!" She laughed hoarsely. "Anyhow, I don't believe it. He betrayed me once before, and he will do so again . . . he has already done so . . . he is a hypocrite of the yellowest dye. Unless I mistake myself, killing him is the order of the day. It will end this war. The Hands will be thrown into disarray. Pati will be devastated." She flapped one hand, as if to say, Go ahead.

Sol's arm tensed. His breath quickened. Arity could tell through the bloody throbbing in his brain that demoralized though he might be, the ghostier did not want to do it. Whatever principles he had, they forbade him to kill a god without the justification of making a ghost.

But though Sol had rebelled against Pati rather than kill Arity for him, he would do it for Humi.

She had always had that knack, too: the knack of getting men to do what she wanted.

"Get on with it," she said. Her voice was almost a sneer. What were the relations between these two? Why was Arity wondering that now? "What are you waiting for? You don't suppose he's here *alone*, do you? I tell you, that boy we captured wasn't exaggerating when he babbled about death squads. The Hands never do things by halves. Perhaps we should learn their lesson."

"Humi, for the gods' sake," Sol said. "If you're doing this for *love*, you'll be sorry—*I* know—"

"He's *Arity*, isn't he! First Lieutenant to the Divinarch! Do it!"

And a piercing *auchraug* call split the air. Sol's body vibrated. Arity staggered free and sprawled on his hands and knees, retching. Blood from his throat dripped on his hands. When Sol was hit from behind, the knife had gone in deep. Sweat stung in the cut.

Then hands took hold of him, strong Hands, friendly Hands, helping him up. "Master! *Perich¨hi!* What happened? Are you—"

Later he would discover that—just as he had feared—the Hands' impatience had been too much for them. To pass the time while they waited for the ambush to be sprung, they had slaughtered all the ghostiers in various, intriguing ways, first jamming rags into their throats so that they should not scream. It was a source of hilarity among the Hands how easily and involuntarily mortals gave way to pain.

Only when that amusement was no more, they took it into their heads to wonder what had become of Arity. Having heard no noise, they presumed there had been no developments, but nonetheless Night Dog took every caution as he slunk downstairs to investigate. He saw what looked like his lieutenant in danger of his life. Luckily for Arity, he did not stop to wonder if the situation was what it seemed. He just *teth¨d* into the air, letting out an ululating yell, and brought both hobnailed boots down on Sol's head.

But after that, his concern was all for Arity's life. In the minutes it took for the other Hands to hear his shouts, and straggle down from the scene of their carnage—which they had arranged as artistically as any of the dead ghostiers could have, and in which they took as much pride as a child takes in his pickled frog collection—Sol had recovered and fled with Humi out into the street. The two of them were alone, and they knew Marshtown inside-out and upside-down. There was no trail to follow. But Night Dog assured Arity they could not get far. The whole city was still the

Divinarch's territory; they could not *teth*"; the whole pack of Hands had set off in pursuit.

For maybe one minute Arity gave in to despair, dropping his face into his hands. Then he ordered Night Dog to report back to the Palace while he, Arity, organized a citywide hunt for her.

THE FACE OF TREACHERY

Emni.
   Ziniquel.
   Tan.
   Suret.
   Yste.
   Lighte.
   Algia.
   Eternelipizaran.
   He was not able to keep from her the fact that they are dead. Add them to the roster, *she thinks as Sol drags her through the darkness that conceals the Marshtown alleys, stumbling wet palm in wet palm, turning, starting to jog. Several times he curses and wishes they were in Christon, where they could lose themselves in the maze of the roof roads. He wants to bang on a door and beg for shelter, but she keeps saying,* No, No, No. *Any door would open to them here, but it would mean death for their hosts. The Hands would discover the work of a few minutes and a seditious heart, and would string the hapless family (father, mother, and even the baby) from the Palace's turrets, new beads for the grisly necklace it already wears.*
   She hisses again at him. "Our only hope is to get back to Shimorning!"

   Throw their bodies on top of Hem's and Leasa's, on top of the little corpses of Meri and Ensi, the children. I am amassing quite a heap here in my heart, aren't I? They are rotting, too. How will I feel when I have managed to clamber onto the top of it? Revenged. Satiated, I hope.
   Victorious. Content.
   Maybe Hope could tell me how to rescue someone in time, before rescue is useless, before there is nothing to do except revenge. She rescued me, four years ago, though I'm not so sure her actions were for the best. Why didn't I

*realize she was my dearest friend until I sent her away? Hope. I miss her
sweet and oh so obvious flattery. I miss the spicy warmth of her embraces.*

*I hear she is fighting in the front lines now, with her troop in Calvary. If
she falls, too, I think I shall destroy myself, as a service to my friends.*

*Or perhaps I'll just turn myself over to Ari. We can make love once more,
for old times' sake, and then I'm sure he will hand me to Pati.*

*But that would mean giving the world also to Pati in a gold napkin, the
way the Hangman packages their spies (I hate it that I have become so
indispensable; my having let it happen reveals my own weakness). Giving
the world to Pati, its corners all tied up with the old, strong thread.*

*She cannot forget that when he embraced her, a fearful passion flared up
inside her. She was afraid she would crumble and cave in like the burned
Chalice. Nothing mattered in that moment. Not the loss of her imrchim. Not
death. For if he killed her, she knew she held onto his heart so tightly they
would both perish. His arms around her made her forget all the hard bar-
gains and points of honor and boredom she cherished as ammunition against
him and Pati. His arms came very close to making it all worthwhile.*

But there was a knife in his hand and everything was wrong.

*Conquering that passion is something she believes she will count, in the
future, among her greatest achievements.*

*(That is, if she can truly be said to have achieved anything; if the very
notion of achievement must not now be classified as an irony with this rank
of murdered friends behind her, this mute army of watchers following her
with lidless eyes—and how is it that with death those who in life were just
flawed mortals grow into giants, withering the significance out of all our
deeds with their dark breath, their complacent possession of the Answer
before which all of us can only flinch?)*

*She hardly hears Sol whisper: "It's no use. They've got ahead of us. We
shall have to hide, and pray. We have no choice."*

The breath rips painfully through her lungs as she sinks down.

She felt as if she were flattened into a corner. Dampness touched her
through her dress. She smelled mold. The Hands' voices echoed through
the streets, circling, closing in. She smelled a faint waft of sulfur.

Sol wrapped his arm around her, caressing her shoulder. His touch was
absent, repetitive. Although she was too numb to be afraid, she felt the
familiar, rote apprehension that a reader feels, flipping the limp pages of a
book toward the denouement.

She could no longer lean heavily on him. She prayed they got out of this
before she had to make any more demands on his loyalty. They *should* have

taken shelter! The sacrifice of one Marshtown family would not have weighed so heavily in the Balance—so many more would die, if she died . . . That rankled, like an imposition of her freedom. Too hard that she must try her utmost to live, when the odds were stacked against her!

But she must try. And without Sol's help. The attack on Arity had exhausted the limits of what Sol would do for her. He had just lost a sister—no, more than a sister, a twin, a lover, a friend, for whatever Emni had been to Humi, she had been a thousand times more to him—and that not unjustly, he blamed it on Humi.

And grief did strange things to people. She remembered how she herself had wept when Erene eloped with Elicit—as if she'd been genuinely bereft. The only thing that eased the pain had been taking control of her new position as senior ghostier.

Likewise, while Sol mourned Emni's death, other things might swell large to fill the place she had occupied in his hopes and dreams.

What possibilities might he see on a Conversion board suddenly swept clean of half its major pieces?

His touch on her arm grew intensely irritating. She brushed him away. Booted footsteps rang almost over their heads.

"Where are we?" she breathed.

"Storage bin. Underground. Behind a bakery." His body was rigid with tension. "*Shush.*"

Twice, at least, now, she had made the mistake of interpreting ambition, disguised with a superficial affection for herself, as loyalty. Self-interest was in Sol's very character: he could almost be forgiven for the crime he had not yet committed. At a stretch, it was even possible to think of him as innocent.

The Hangman was the other one, Humi knew now, who had betrayed her. Evita: sly, calculating, cold-blooded. The knowledge. Evita was a traitor: she had had the Lakestones killed in order to bind Humi, who believed Pati had done the murders, closer to her, and incense her more thoroughly against Pati (as if that were necessary!). Humi's lingering softness had refused to accept that possibility then. But now she had done away with softness. Now she knew that Evita was a snake in the grass. And the snake would be extirpated.

In order to do *that*, at least, she must escape. She must go on living.

Her fur stood on end. She prepared for Sol's shout. "Here! She's here! Take her—but let me go free! I was always faithful to your master!"

She smelled Sol's human sweat, and her own. The tiny cut Arity had opened in her neck ached. The wall of the storage bin pressed grittily into her back. *Auchresh* voices resounded through her bones, seemingly in the very pit where they crouched.

It came as a rude, painful surprise when, although Sol had not made a sound, iron slammed back along its grooves and a loud cry split her ears. She felt herself grabbed and yanked up out of the bin, thrown face first against a wall. The impact brought tears to her eyes. Blood streamed from her nose.

She straightened up, lifting her head, holding her sleeve to her face. Her ears tintinnabulated. Somewhere in front of her, a fight was going on. At first she did not understand; then it hit her like a blast of cold wind through a door.

Sol was fighting to get near her.

To save her?

Wrong? Could she have been *wrong?*

Fists connected with flesh. The Hands chattered in *auchraug,* congratulating themselves. Sol hit the wall beside her. He slumped against her side. His breath whuffled.

She could not forgive him his loyalty, could not feel any gratitude. She wanted to jerk away and let him slide to the dirt. She hated him for deceiving her.

Pure, unthinking loathing suffused her. She lifted her head. "Kill us then! You have us where you want us! Do it!"

"Oh, no, milady. Beloved Superior has more things than a few to say to you. You cannot remove yourself from our inflicting of punishment," one of the Hands said happily.

"Speak *auchraug!*" she said in that language. "I would understand you better."

They jostled and muttered. "How does the lady come to know our tongue?" a different Hand asked.

"I have been a frequent visitor at the Heavens."

"Might this humble servant ask which ones?"

She sighed. "Mostly Wind Gully Heaven, in Kithrilindu, by the side of the *Writh aes Haraules* . . ."

"I'm from Red-tongued Bird Heaven!" another Hand said delightedly. "Did you ever—"

"Yes. The *mainrauim* and I visited the Red Tongue frequently. We always walked instead of *teth˜ing.* Those are pleasant hills." A knife of memory pierced her. Silky salt grass swishing about her legs, trees low and pale in the distance, the vast purple arc of the twight sky. *Sight.* Early morning, for the *auchresh.* Arity's arm about her shoulders—

"Oh, they are!" the Hand agreed. "We used to—"

"Enough!" snarled another Hand. "Silver Eye, I shall have you disciplined for insubordination. You too, Ordi!"

"Oh, no, you won't!" Humi straightened her back. The wind was drying the blood on her face.

Emni. Zin. Hem. Lease. Lighte. Algia. Suret. Yste. Meri. Ensi. Eterneli. Tan. Sol. Ari. Evita.

She put them all aside, to be finished at her leisure. Took a deep breath. Putting more into her words than she had ever done before, she started to speak.

Not until he was moving fast through Marshtown, jostling close beside Humi in the knot of Hands, his wrists untied, his face wiped clean of blood, did Sol realize exactly what had happened. The Hands behaved as if they had just awakened from a dream. They were looking forward to meeting old friends in the rebel stronghold. All eighteen were boisterous, joyful, forgetting again and again to modulate their voices, until Humi had to remind them they were no longer in friendly streets.

Everyone gawked as the party filed down into the Rats' Den. The Hands held their heads high. Sol could see the pride gleaming off them, as if they had just been polished.

Humi dismissed them to Gold Dagger's underground apartments, to receive badges and destroy their loyalist uniforms. Then she beckoned an errand girl. "Bring me the Hangman."

"Yes, milady!" squeaked the cringing child.

"In manacles."

The child's eyes popped. "Yes, milady!"

When the Hangman was escorted into Humi's presence, in the little cave that served as a temporary audience chamber, she was bound only with ropes. Sol supposed they hadn't dared to manacle her, on the off chance that the errand girl had been wrong. She wasn't. Neither was Humi. And Sol had a pretty good idea what Humi was doing: she had finally realized the truth about Evita, realized the woman's obsessive near insanity, and she was losing no time in acting on it.

Humi's jaw was locked, her fingers steady on the reed-bundle arms of her makeshift throne. Difficult to remember that she had just had as devastating a loss as he had. But maybe that was what had brought this on. The massacre of the *imrchim* had caused her to see her own actions anew, perhaps; had scrubbed the glory off the war.

The Hangman's mousy head rose proudly out of her cowl. Sol found it hard now to see how anyone had ever mistaken her for a man.

Humi seemed to stare at her for a long moment. "I accuse you of mur-

dering the family of Hem Lakestone, Evita," she said finally. "Four crimes
against innocents, and *allies*. Treachery."

"I did not," Evita said steadily.

"You had a motive. Political. Self-ingratiation by elimination of rivals.
Rivals who didn't even know you existed." Humi took a deep breath. "And
it *worked*. Oh, yes, you are *richly* deserving of punishment."

Sol looked down at his feet. He stood with his back to the wall in a
corner of the audience room. Poor-quality reed torches flared dimly around
the walls, dying and being replaced by servants. Flames flickered as fast as
Emni had died. As she would be replaced.

He would be the one to replace her. When the time came, whether Humi
fell, despite her visibly mushrooming abilities as commandante, or she tri-
umphed, the victor in this war would still ordain Sol as senior ghostier. He
was the only candidate. Mory and Tries were too far gone into rhapsodies of
pain, too far off the normal aesthetic map. They didn't know the things
about popular appeal that he did. And no matter what it cost, he would take
the post that would allow him to use that knowledge—to do the only job he
was really trained for. This business of war was not only grueling and
painful, but *boring*. He missed his art. Missed ghosting. As soon as this was
over—no matter how it turned out—he would sever the links that tied him
to the new regime, chaining himself into the antiquated set of rules he
knew so well, that hierarchy custom-fitted to a system of government as
dead as she was. He had wanted command of Tellury Crescent for as long
as he could remember.

But strangely enough, the prospect gave him little joy. His resolve sat
bitterly in his mouth, like a pellet he could not swallow.

Emni. Sister. Lover. Enemy. His reason for living.

Smeary light, smeary soot stains on the rock walls, smeared vision.

The Hangman stared at Humi. At last, Humi sighed and said shortly,
"You're executed for treachery. Take her away."

That jolted the Hangman into speech. She railed at Humi, first denying
that she had ever betrayed her, and then cursing her for a bloodless bitch
and avowing she would have killed twice as many if she could once have
seen Humi weep.

"For your insolence," Humi said, "burial in the marshes. And there will
be no flamen to consecrate your body to the gods."

The Hangman's face muddied in horror. Sol remembered she was pious:
an unconsecrated burial, for her, was probably more frightening than death
itself.

The guards dragged her backwards out of the room. She fought grimly against their strength until one of them drove his knuckles together under her ears. Then her head flopped.

Her thin, pale, foxy face was vacant. But Sol knew she was not dead. They wouldn't kill her for several days. Execution for treachery took an especially ugly form here in Shimorning. It was the only type of execution Humi sanctioned that was not merciful.

Later, in bed, he said, "Why did you execute her? You realize what this means to Gold. He'll be chortling. You may actually have endangered your authority."

She lay on her back beside him, hands folded behind her head. Their underground chamber was tiny, only a cubbyhole, but out of reach of the noise of the forges and the newly excavated barracks. And it enjoyed access to all the major escape routes.

They had burned candles earlier while they made love. The scent of lavender still lingered in the darkness.

"She was a traitor," Humi said. "I don't have to justify my decisions to you, or anyone."

"Do you mean she *did* kill the Lakestones?"

She started. "Did you think I executed her out of paranoia?"

"I thought you did it because you'd come to see who she was."

"I *liked* her, Sol!"

"I know you did. Too much. Mory and Tris and I thought she might have done it, for the very reason you said. Even Aneisneida had an inkling. But we didn't suggest the possibility to you because we didn't think you would believe us."

"I would at least have considered it."

Sol swallowed. "Perhaps we didn't want you to." He remembered those conversations, most of them held in the apostate ghostiers' workshop. The comforting safety of bitchery about other *imrchim*—safe because it was based on unshakeable affection. "We found it sweet that you refused to see. That you still needed to place absolute trust in *someone*." He smiled. "At heart, you were still our little Humi who loved Erene so deeply and absolutely."

Her voice went chilly. "I placed absolute trust in too many people. Now I know that you and Mory and Tris were among them. What if she had killed me? What would you have said then? Keeping your suspicions to yourselves was indirect treachery!" Her voice shook. "Trust is the most misbegotten of emotions!"

"What absolute crap," Sol said. "That's rotten fish guts."

She turned on her side. Cool air rushed down the gap between them, under the bedclothes. "I realize that you are not everything I thought you were."

"Because my sister was murdered? Because I was half mad with anguish and I couldn't manage to hide it?"

"No," she said sadly. "No. That's not it at all."

She curled up, pulling the covers around her like a little girl. Sol flopped back on the mattress, stiff with fury, waiting for her to qualify her rejection, to apologize. He was aware that his limbs were relaxing. Waves of tiredness washed over him: tiredness like an abnegation of the world, the inevitable result of extreme grief. *I have to . . . have to . . . she'll come around, I know she will, she's only a girl . . .*

At last he could stay awake no longer.

SWORD-LIZARD-WINTER

The war in the city had been going on for almost a season. Guerilla attacks and bloody ambushes had worn down both forces. But the rebels and the loyalists had not yet met in a full, pitched battle: an event that Humi held would end the excruciation of the city once and for all. Hope's dispatches, written in a hand that grew less hurried and more fluid every day, said that her lieutenants, renegades every one, now controlled all the continents except Calvary. In reply, Humi dictated instructions to the lieutenants as to how their new possessions were to be managed. Hope herself was still in the northernmost land. Pati had consolidated the remnants of all his defeated armies in Samaal—determined, Sol thought, to hold onto "the land of the pious" both out of pride and because, should the war drag out much longer, Calvary was home to the metal mines.

He sat beside Humi, watching the faces of the people he sometimes, jokingly, called his new *imrchim* while the renegade who had brought the latest dispatch read it out. The messenger was still sweaty from the northern sun. Hope had amassed her forces outside Samaal; they planned to attack within the sixday.

"Excellent!" Gold Dagger chuckled when the *auchresh* finished. "Victory is ours, eh? Eh, Hume?"

He seemed to have gained weight every day of the war. Mory had said, cattily, that his gold-plated waistcoat showed signs of having been let out. She noticed things like that. Sol didn't. But he took a particular interest in Gold Dagger. It was his self-claimed duty to guard Humi's back. And Gold was the most obvious threat to that tawny pelt. He stared at the fat Deltan, and kept staring, his face blank. That had always worked on the ghostiers. Sure enough, it silenced Gold Dagger's laughter. "We 'ave to make a move," he grumbled. "We've been sittin' on our arses too long. Gotta finish it. Men are gettin' tired. Impatient."

Humi blinked, lizardlike. "Yes," she said. "I know this: without Delta City, we are not victorious. And the danger that we will be burned in our beds increases the longer we stay here. Pati knows where we are. Somehow, he has found out."

Nobody mentioned the possibility that it had been the Hangman's vigilant eye for spies which had kept the location of the Rats' Den a secret for so long. Nobody looked at the chair beside Humi's—still empty after months. Gold Dagger muttered something in a voice too low for anyone to hear, and his eyebrows met and shook hands, ominously.

"But there is a reason why he hasn't attacked us," Mory said, and supplied it, looking pleased with herself. "He is afraid."

"His forces are inferior," Tris said. "He doesn't want to fight in Shimorning, where the people are on our side. He thinks to force us to carry the battle to him."

"Then perhaps we ought to do just that," Sol said.

"Nope," Gold Dagger said. " 'Be a bad move. I've *heard*—never mind *ow*—that 'e's been callin' more and more Hands back from Calvary to bulk up the forces in the Palace. We'd be squashed like soggy lentils. Gotta wait till 'e's off his guard."

The rumor about the Hands, at least, Sol knew to be true. For the past few days, when the wind was right, the smell of sulfur had blown steadily from the Palace, a foul exhalation. For many Deltans who had remained stoic in the face of civil war and the ravaging of their homes, this was the last straw. They knew it for the demons' wind, the devil's breath, the yawning of the gates of purgatory, where all the atheists who had been arrested in the early years of the tyranny hung screaming. The core population of the city had started to break down. Bargeloads of Deltans sailed for the mainland every night—until the Chrumecountry folk, weary of the uninvited burden on their hospitality, started forcing them back across the river with arrows. Devotees who came to Delta City from farther up the river, supposing it a last haven of safety, found themselves mired in suspicion, hostility, and petty crime. Food supplies having been almost completely cut off, the islanders were killing each other for bread and pork.

As a result, a counterrevolutionary swell had begun to rise under the poorest districts of the city. Pati had started offering food and lodgings to any human who would fight for him; previously, only Hands had been allowed into patrols and battle squadrons. A thin, but not insignificant, trickle of Deltans was flowing daily into the palace district. The edge that Humi would have enjoyed in a pitched battle there—the advantage of not having to worry about injuring human civilians—was disappearing.

The apostates were no help. Never better than provisionally allied with Humi, they had started to preach against all Divinarches, all uprisings, and all gods, be they Hands or renegades. Mory and Tris tried to apologize for them; so did the harried Godsbrother Phantasm, who, having fallen absolutely under Humi's spell, was a pathetically divided man. Humi could not stand their moral double-dealing, and often said so in Phantasm's presence. But Phantasm's fellow flamens seemed not to see anything wrong with working dark miracles against the Hands one day, and preaching Humi's redundancy in the Marshtown streets the next. Their audiences were motley, and fervent.

The conspirators, as happened so often, had got themselves mired in arguments and counterarguments. Sol had not been listening. He interrupted brusquely. "*I* think Gold Dagger is both right and wrong. We have to finish this war before it's too late. But in order to do that, we *have* to carry the battle to Pati. There's just no other way."

He sat back.

"Thank you, Sol," Humi said. "I have been trying to make these people agree to that for the last fifteen minutes. But I don't blame you for rationing your attention. There is nothing less interesting than listening to five intelligent men and women try not to look like cowards."

"But *I'm* for it," Mory said hastily. "With the apostates in our front lines, we can hardly lose, no matter where we fight!"

Tris pursed his dark lips.

Soderingal glanced at his wife. Aneisneida gave a tiny nod. "If the Divinarch is for it, so are we," Soderingal said reluctantly.

"It seems we have a majority, then! Are you with us, Gold?" Humi's voice carried a hint of menace.

Gold Dagger beamed. He had evidently decided to make the best of being outnumbered. His cheeks bulged like green plums. Sol marveled at how innocuous he seemed. You would never think, to look at him, that here was the most dangerous man in Delta City. He was an amazing dissembler, better than any of them, even than Humi. Soderingal remained a pale copy of him, brooding, vicious, cowardly.

Aneisneida, on the other hand, resembled *her* father more markedly every day—except that she remained slender, as Belstem Summer had never been. Recently Sol had found himself looking at her with new eyes, marveling at the ingenuous, instinctive, not quite conscious artistry with which she played her husband on a string.

"Of course I'm with yer!" Gold Dagger boomed. He slapped his hands

flat on the table and, slavering, did a realistic imitation of a wild dog about
to attack. Then he let loose a boom of laughter.

Tris flinched backward, then made a face of disgust. *That boy's really
been spoiled by piety,* Sol thought. *He used to be up for a laugh anytime,
though he was so shy—and you could depend on him.*

Aneisneida giggled.

"What else 'ave I been waiting fer you pigheads to agree on?" Gold
Dagger heaved himself to his feet and offered Humi his arm. She accepted
it, beckoning behind her back for Sol to lead the way. He resented the way
she ordered him about, but he knew she was grateful for his protection; it
was only that she would not admit to it herself. "Come, milady Divinarch,
soon ta be enthroned!" Gold Dagger bellowed.

Sol was intimately familiar with the Rats' Den barracks, but he did not
like them. To his fine-tuned ghostier's sensibilities, they were impossibly
wretched. Dirty, steamy tunnels, newly hollowed out; some sections dug in
antiquity, but unused for generations, for a good reason—they were
cramped and labyrinthine. Several times he lost his sense of direction, and
had to fight to remember if they should climb up or down the next flight of
slimy, twisting stone stairs. He was supposed to be leader, and if he had
deserted the others, they would have had to apply to the soldiers themselves to be let out. That would have been an unthinkable humiliation. As
Gold Dagger and Humi progressed from squad room to squad room, announcing that the end was approaching, cheers followed them, echoing off
the walls of the maze.

The Rats' Den had never in its history been so crowded. Only tallow
candles lit the tunnels. The smell of frying hung heavy in the air. Only the
inadequate fans, which shifts of skivvy children cranked day and night,
ventilated the low-ceilinged squad rooms. These same rooms were used for
sleeping, relaxation, some drilling, elimination, and food preparation. How
did the human soldiers bear it? *Auchresh* were naturally hardier, but even
they had soot-blackened faces, and looked weary and underfed. There was
not the least sign of organization in the whole giant honeycomb. The thing
that held them all here was no longer their love for Humi and her cause but
the fact they had burned their bridges behind them when they came.

Gods and mortals mingled indiscriminately here, as they did everywhere
in the Den. Sol and the rest came on most of them in the act of honing or
testing their weapons. They leaped to their feet and fell instantly silent,
bowing to the ground. But they never sheathed their blades. As soon as
Gold Dagger steered Humi out again, Sol would hear the bubble of silence
pop, and the buzz of talk jump to a feverish pitch.

That was how they bore it, he supposed. Dreams of blood. Pathetic.

But then, *he* hadn't had enough contact with foulness in his life to know what it was really like, had he? His sunny, pristine Archipelagan childhood. His years as an apprentice, a ghostier, a councillor, cloistered—*in* Marshtown but never of it. And in Westpoint, he had commonly passed whole weeks without speaking to a soul except the woman from whom he bought his bread and the landlord who took his rent.

Foulness took many forms, though!

In one squad room, they came on an able-bodied Deltan soldier and a Carelastrian *auchresh* making the beast on the floor, while the rest of the squad cheered them on. When Humi stepped through the doorway and stood silent, waiting, the whole crew bounced to attention, their faces muddy or dark with shame; they made more fervent obeisances than any others had done before them. But after the party moved back out into the corridor, Sol heard the fun start up again, more quietly.

Aneisneida asked in a small voice, "Humi, is it really necessary for us to do this ourselves? Your lieutenants—"

"I have to reassure them that I have faith in them," Humi said. "That I am depending on them. That I need them. I have to do this in person, or it would be pointless." She turned as if to look over her shoulder at Aneisneida. "*You* can go, if you want."

Aneisneida shuddered, and clenched her teeth. Gamely, she said, "No. I suppose I shall have to get used to—this. When we are victorious, I shall have responsibilities. My father was never afraid to walk the streets where he grew up. I will not be, either."

Humi sounded surprised as she said, "Excellent! Anei, I am proud of you!"

By the time they reached the lowest levels of the barracks, the news of their advent had traveled ahead of them. Communication between the squad rooms, beth *teth*˙*tach ching* and ordinary, never ceased. In the great mess hall (where the sword lizards had first been discovered, before they were chased lower yet, to Humi's private cavern) a sea of men and gods waited for them. Sol boosted Humi up on a table and climbed after her. Gold Dagger heaved himself up and stood on Humi's other side, flanking her.

Erect and beautiful in her simple gown, she bathed in the noise of adulation. Sol felt her hand clenching into a fist. He was slightly shocked to see tears sparkling on her cheek fur. Her artifice extended even to details no one except he and Gold Dagger could see. Or was it artifice? Did she really believe they all still loved her? She couldn't see, but surely she heard the sour notes in the hullabaloo?

"You ought to be cheering for yourselves!" Sol heard her whisper. She sounded unutterably miserable. "Not for me!"

He shot an appalled glance her way. The tears were *real*.

She cleared her throat. She shouted, "Thank you!"

THE RED HAZE

Arity stopped the messenger *kere* at the door of the royal bedroom and put his finger to his lips. Pati was sleeping for the first time in many nights.

Closing the door behind the uniformed *kere,* Arity rubbed his nose thoughtfully.

The cold tile floor and glass and bone furniture of the royal bedroom took on a soft, misty aspect in the gray light rising off the starlit sea.

The prospect of waking Pati up with *this* news had a certain masochistic appeal.

But not yet!

He had no patience. He *teth¨d* from the floor where he stood to the foot of the great bed. Golden Antelope had always had it in the middle of the room, but Pati and Arity had shoved it against one wall. Late in Golden Antelope's life, when he spent all his time in bed, he had often had himself wheeled out onto the balcony. The Old One had, Arity thought, enjoyed being afraid. Of attack, of oblivion, of the five-hundred foot drop to the gnashing sea.

He sat on the footboard of the bed with his elbows on his knees and watched Pati sleeping. The sight had never ceased to entrance him. Only when Pati slept could you see how young that wolfish, delicate face still was. Responsibility had left no physical marks on him. His nacreous hair spread like fine straw across the pillow.

Did he feel Arity's stare?

Did he dream?

I could do it right now. This moment . . .

Panic took hold of Arity, freezing him in its iron-clawed grip. The ability to imagine more than one possible course of action was surely the worst feature of intelligence! Unable to bear it, he *teth¨d* again, outside to the sea

balcony. An unexpectedly freezing wind greeted him: in seconds, his body
was the same temperature as the air, and as liquid. Salt water. *The wind—*

Below the sea, a haze of freezing spray misted the waves that lapped
grayly to the horizon. Strange bright quality to the night. Almost like it was
in the salt just before a blizzard. Perhaps it was going to snow.

He knew what he had to do.

But whenever he thought about *doing* it, the indifference that carried
him so smoothly without trouble day and night quailed and trickled out of
his brain. The trouble was that he could envision the act so well! And that
picture cast a red haze over everything that might possibly occur afterward,
so that he had no way of guessing which course of action was best.

And according to the messenger, it would soon be too late to choose
either one.

The cold iron railing pressed into his forehead. He straightened up. The
trench in his skin burned as he went inside. Getting Pati awake was a task
for a predator. He flailed and groaned, and finally Arity lost patience and
slapped him.

Huge eyes, one brown, one blue, blinked up from the snow-colored
drained mask. Power, he was beautiful. That look would have melted anyone's soul. Arity bent down and kissed him. "Get up," he murmured. "It's
started."

The Folly stood like a rock in a river of blood, parting the sweep of the
devastated gardens. Gete had backed up against one of the wrought-iron
perimeter fences. His feet slipped on bloody swathes of chopped-down
greenery. The sword slice in his leg kept trying to intrude on his attention,
but he had to concentrate on keeping Thani safe in the circle of his left arm,
and moving, wielding his knife, weaving a net of clear space in front of
them. Aeons ago, when the whole company waited tense and silent beneath
the base of the Folly, he had felt so keenly the weight of the blocky, refractive mass hanging over them that he thought he must move out from under
it. Move, move, move, *move,* or the breath would be driven out of him by
the weight of it. Poised there it compressed the air into something liquid.
Sublime. Leather-clad loyalists shifted and fingered their weapons in three
painful dimensions. The smells of fresh-forged metal and unwashed flesh
scorched his nostrils. Smiles glinted like stars. The crushed grass beneath
the Divinarch's army's feet was a carpet of razor-edged oxidized knives.

Flamens stood motionless, heads tilted to catch the whispering of the
lemans at their sides. Loyalist girls and boys too young to be here rolled
their eyes, more frightened than they would admit, and made dirty jokes.
Grown men stared into space, caressing the knobs of their hilts. Only the

Hands seemed perfectly at their ease: smiling, feet planted wide, rocking slightly back and forth. Blood lust crackled tangibly around them. Within the tight squad formations, the mortals gave them as much space as possible.

Gete and Thani's squad comprised both Hands and civilians. Thani herself was supposedly its prime weapon. Gete had taken up a position in the front center of the wedge: she would not take the brunt of the attack, but he could see enemies, pick them out for her.

And she had proved her virtuosity. Oh, she had. She killed neatly, by reaching within her enemies' bodies and stopping their hearts. Unlike the apostates on the other side, she did not mangle her victims, nor make them drown in their blood, or claw at the entrails wrapping around their throats. Some of the human soldiers bawled hysterically, "She's not doin' nothin'! Make her use her powers, leman!"

"She is!" Gete yelled back. " 'Tweren't for her ye'd be dead already!"

Gete himself wasn't a killer. He was a fisherman, a sailor, crofter, leman. Yet now that the necessity presented itself, he found himself quite capable of hacking necks and limbs, stabbing eyes, slicing faces into bloody messes. It had surprised him a little that he was not desperately outclassed.

But he quickly realized nobody on this battlefield except the Hands, and some of the criminals, knew how to do what they were doing. They had only the weapons and the instinct, like tame beasts who have never had to fight for survival. And like animals, they killed without regard for the suffering of others. Gete had never before realized just how much pain people were capable of. The dead and the dying fell like snow on the gardens: they hindered the feet of those who fought, sometimes maliciously, with their last gasp of strength, and sometimes insentiently, like briars. He stepped on still-living bodies as the squad retreated by painful inches to the fence.

Thani, like precious few other flamens, operated in a more humanistic style. Her way took more finesse. But she was determined to keep to her standards as long as she could. She inflicted mercy, not pain.

Though they had retreated as far as possible, she kept on destroying targets with mechanical economy, barely killing one victim before moving to the next. No more than a quarter of their squad remained alive for her to defend. The battle had degenerated into a panting struggle for life. Blood and mud misted Gete's vision. Everything seemed to have gone dull, devoid of reality, as if the gray sky had slumped down onto the battle and enveloped it, like the roof of a tent collapsing. The only color was the wet magenta haze hanging in the air, the reaction of human and divine blood. Its fetid, chemical smell filled his nostrils. Its redness was both the mark of death and the stamp of unreality.

"They're 'xhausted," panted Godsman Freebird, on Thani's left, leaning on his sword.

Bodies lay in drifts around the few trees that Pati had not had cut down. Each heap was soaked with that unholy crimson—as if the bodies were gradually coming apart, disintegrating into each other, like bread soaked in milk. *If only we could all melt into the ground,* Gete thought with sudden, maniacal sentimentality. And the sky would come down and cover the earth like a blanket, and there'd be no more scurrying and sticking pins.

Oh Thani Thani.

He rememered making love to her, in the days before K'Fier. An obscenely malapropos gust of sweetness.

melting.

"They're comin' on again!" Godsman Freebird cried.

And indeed, there seemed no end to the stars flashing in the magenta dusk. Fresh forces? Could it be? No. It was the onslaught. Gete felt the remains of the squad gather about him. A physical drawing up. A tightening as of the strings of a little bag. He and Thani were the jewel. He felt an exquisite gratitude. Cowardice: that was what it was; a craven hope that the deaths of the rest of the squad could keep him from dying. But cowardice would do him no good. Retreat was not an option. They had nowhere to go. The squads stationed behind them, in the palace district, had orders not to move, but to slay any deserters from the front lines. Each division of squads was another wall of defense around the Palace. The Divinarch's plan, as far as Gete understood it, was that somewhere between that first clash on the borders of Christon, and the Palace, the rebels would exhaust their forces. They would die on the spiked wall of the loyalists who had not yet fought, who were fresh, and dying for blood.

But who knew how large the rebel army had been to start out with, how far back into Christon it had extended? The squads who took the brunt of the first attack had known they would be crushed. That was why the first division had consisted solely of Hands, who could *teth* away when they were wounded, before they were annihilated. The burning question was, how much farther could the rebels press before they exhausted themselves?

The lines on the far side of the Folly must have disintegrated, letting the rebels flow over them *en masse.* It was now Gete's and Thani's turn to try to stem the momentum of the slavering atheists and apostates.

Gete's sergeant, Chequered Moon, gave a hoarse yell. The attack was upon them.

"Here, Godsister, in front of us!"

"Ten paces before you, in front of Moon, Godsister!"

It was necessary to sustain two levels of consciousness at once—the bodyguard and the leman, the knife hand and the tongue.

Flash, stab, hack.

Chequered Moon went down in front of them, the top of his skull gouting blood. Gete brought his knife across, parrying the blow of a faceless, hurtling assailant. The god's superior strength and speed were his undoing: he knocked Gete's blow so far aside, and his lunge carried him so far into Gete's reach, that it was a simple matter to slash sideways and open his guts. He wore no armor. None of the gods did. They were too proud.

Thani finished one rebel. Then another. And another.

Gete defended her desperately.

Then he heard Godsman Freebird's death rattle. Emptiness blew cold on his left arm.

He felt Thani quiver, and become a dead weight, dragging on his shoulder.

Gods no! He lost his balance. His left foot skidded out from under him, and his knees buckled. A star flashed in his right eye. For a moment he saw the battlefield starkly *reversed*, white on black, the whole thing canted, so that people were fighting at an angle, like dolls with their feet nailed to a board. Simultaneously, he experienced a powerful physical memory. He was on board a sailboat. Not an intercontinental clipper like the *Foam Rider*, but one of the little fishing boats he had grown up in. He must be very small, for he wasn't holding the shrouds but sprawling in the prow, his chin on the bulwark, gripping the sun-warmed wood, tasting the spray. When the boat listed, he listed with it, so that the shore became a black silhouette as the sun exploded behind Sarberra peak.

Bright, incredibly bright, darkening everything that had happened to Gete to mere cloudy memories, nightmares for which there was no room anymore. The sun hurt his head as it expanded, bulging out and out and out, losing its sharp snowflake edges, until it grew bigger than his head could hold and it burst free.

Reality's needled jaws closed on him, and would not let him go back to sleep.

Far across the field, broken edges of windows glimmered in the lower stories of the Folly. All about that great black shape, stars peeped guiltily through the clouds. Trees slumped haplessly, branches half severed. Most of the fences had been rooted up and cast down.

The smell of death hung in the air.

All the living had gone, leaving behind them a terrible silence. In their battle lust, they had rolled over their refuse like the sea churning over rocks. He knew they were pressing on to the Palace, inexorably to the Palace. But he had not breath to worry about what was happening anywhere except right here. The dusk took the color out of everything. Thank the gods for that. He felt as if he would not be able to look at anything red ever again.

Don't thank the gods! They are lying flat all around, pitiful dead things like I nearly was, like Thani! Thank the Power it's dark and I can't see her! "Thank the Power for night," he whispered aloud.

Vague, ambiguous. Good enough.

The power of night.

Good enough.

He raised himself up on one elbow. He could just see her beside him. Her lips, normally thin, were swollen with blood. Her robe was torn. The sharp edges had been broken off her salt crystals, leaving a grainy mess in one eye socket and a clot of blood in the other.

But her chest rose and fell ever so slightly—

He let out a hoarse, desperate cry of thanks and gathered her to him. Never mind the pain, never mind the dizziness, kneel upright, cradle her, *tenderly!* The wound was in her back and shoulder, a hideous wet gash. Oh, Power. It must almost have bled her dry before her blood clotted. *Remember all you know about healing, don't reopen it, moving her might finish it—* "Thani!" he whispered urgently. "It's me! Are you all right?"

Did she hear?

She moved her head, infinitesimally.

Grief crashed down on him like a weight of water, knocking his breath out of his lungs.

She would know if she was all right!

A chilly wind fingered his hair, tossed a filthy lock into his face. It stung. His eyes filled with tears.

His red hair. She had chosen him for it. Because of it he had come halfway across the world with her, only to watch her die.

He was crying on her neck. *Oh, Power, no, wipe her fur—*

She reached up and touched his lips. Her hand fell back on her chest. Her mouth formed slurred words, but no sound came out. He had to bend close to catch even the ghostliest whisper. "Gete: love . . . you."

"And I you! Oh, Godsister—"

"Gete . . . there is something you do not know." The facial expression was hardly anything at all, a mere twitch of the lips, but his familiarity with her face showed him a self-mocking smile. No humor in it. None at all. She breathed: "Do not . . . grieve. I am not worthy of it. I was born . . . evil. So that I could fulfill . . . the task . . . which I prophesied. I had to kill a god. A . . . renegade . . . but still a god . . . someone utterly evil was needed to destroy him. So that no one's soul should be contaminated. That was my task. After that . . . we came to the Archipelago. And every minute I lived . . . was a gift from the gods. From *him.*"

Her hand was cold in his. It exerted no pressure. A night wind blew through the garden, rattling the remaining twigs of the trees, stripping the last vestiges of warmth from the limbs of the corpses.

"I was steeped in evil . . . Gete . . . when we met. But you did not know . . . it was not a girl . . . who you seduced with your red hair. It was evil . . . in human form. Evil. And *he* . . . he is evil, too. *He* made me what I am. The gods cause all of us to exist . . . if they caused evil, then they must be evil. Do not look at them for succor . . . Gete."

"You can't believe this! Thani! No!" He did not know what to say. In the deserted battlefield it was hard to have faith that she was deluded. She could be visionary.

She turned her head to one side, as if to refuse argument.

He did not doubt the truth of the first part—that she had killed a god. Unbelievable though it sounded, she was in no state to lie. That meant— that the rest of it—

Unbelievable. Could pain alone have brought this on? There was already so much pain in her day-to-day life. And as blindly as a child trusting in its mother's goodness, he had thought it could never taint her compassion, her belief in human and divine goodness. She forgave flaws in others and in herself, even as she aimed for perfection.

Apparently this battle had managed what nothing else had been able to. Was it the battle? Or was it that she was *dying?*

Could dying confer a clear-sightedness life, with its cares, never had? She *wasn't* dying! She could live!

"You mustn't!" he hissed at her. "D'you hear me? You mustn't talk this way! It's a sacrilege! The—the—the Divinarch wouldn't want you to say these things!"

As if she had merely been gathering her strength, she resumed.

"But I failed to kill the god. And my evil . . . was consolidated. Evil thwarted . . . feeds on itself. I did not know I had failed until . . . I met the dark one face to face. Face . . . to face . . . when you and I returned to Delta City. Do you . . . remember? I spoke kind words to him. The renegade. *I did not know him!*"

She hissed this so loudly that Gete flinched.

"*You* . . . you are good all the way through. You must not . . ."

She paused, blindly gulping air.

"Evil . . . is useless. Violence focused . . . toward no goal. I am the tool . . . the gods are the sources . . . renegades or no, they are the sources . . ."

"You don't have to explain *evil* away! The gods aren't evil! Neither are you! Do you think you can cleanse the world by *dying?*" Tears boiled in his eyes. "You're kind. You're generous. Compassionate. Selfless. You're *good!*" He was shouting into her face. "You're the goodest person I ever *knew!*"

She made no reply. Perhaps she did not hear. The wind whistled. In his anguish he must have gripped her too tightly: the wound reopened, and wetness trickled over his arm. The pain must have momentarily restored her faculties. She jerked as if she had been hit. Her free arm lifted, and her hand, hitting his, seized it with remarkable strength.

Half out of his mind with grief, he shouted, "You were always good! Do you remember those children? Do you remember—I could tell you a thousand stories about your goodness! You're compassion *itself!*"

The clots of blood in her eye sockets had begun to trickle darkly again. The wild jerking ceased. He heard her whisper, hoarsely, quickly, as if she were trying not to let her pain overhear her, "What was that? Good? D'you think so? Really?"

"With all my heart! Oh, *Power,* Godsister—"

"Heh. You'll learn, Gete. You'll learn." She smiled almost kindly. The old Thani's smile. And she snuggled impatiently into his embrace, tugging at his clothing like an infant hungry for its mother's milk.

But no matter how close he held her, he could not protect her from the cold wind. Could not prevent the blood from flowing out of her, soaking his knees. And all at once she shivered, a violent shiver that made her spine arch and her neck twist, as if she were trying to see something behind her.

SLOW TIME IN THE EYE OF THE TIGER

Nobody had ever seen the Old Palace as a fortress. But a fortress it had become. The wooden ramp was winched up; it fitted into the cavernous gateway that had led into the calm, tree-scattered courtyard. The dirt and rot of thousands of years, clinging darkly to its underside, contrasted with the smoothly weathered walls. "But no less solid for that," Soderingal muttered.

A day and night had passed since the battle started. Aneisneida and Soder were standing in the sixth-floor window of a town house which, in the days of the atheist court, had been unfashionable because of its proximity to the Old Palace. They could see the army seething outside the gate of the fortress. Humi had invited the Nearclouds to the front with none of her usual ambiguity; through her *auchresh* messenger, she had assured them that her men had scoured the town house for lurking loyalists, that there were decayed but luxurious armchairs for them to sit in, and chilled wine to refresh them. For some reason, right in the middle of a battle which looked like being decisive, she had started to treat them like the nobility they were. It gave Aneisneida a comfortable feeling of safety. Fia was back in Shimorning with her nurses: out of sight, out of mind. Six *auchresh* guards stood in a row at the back of the room, ready to *teth* her and Soder away, should an unexpected reversal sweep the army back. But that hardly seemed likely.

When they first arrived, Aneisneida had stepped right up to the window. Before Soderingal yanked her back, she had glimpsed the topmost turrets of the Palace, sparkling with the metal shields that had been slid across the windows. On three sides the keep was deeply ensconced within the courtyard; on the fourth, it rose sheer from the sea. Humi had no way of assailing it save by taking the courtyard. Fire had been ruled out. Her consideration there, Anei thought, had been not so much a reluctance to sink to the level of the Hands, as an unwillingness to gamble with the seat of her future majesty.

Majestic the Palace certainly was, like an old man taking up his sword in time of duress. No one can deny the razor-edge of the sword he has kept sharp for decades. Flattened mansard roofs topped the outer walls of the courtyard; the shadows under their eaves sparkled with blades. Now and then, a crossbow bolt darted out of the darkness, down into the seething mass of the army. Roars arose where these arrows fell, and flocks of bolts lofted back into the air, almost slowly it seemed, like pigeons. Some crested the walls and descended out of sight; some stuck quivering in the mansard roofs. The window at which Aneisneida and Soderingal stood was on a level with the shadows under the eaves. The distance across the street was no more than twenty yards. That the two sides of a street could belong to opposing armies—the very idea was fantastic! Aneisneida knew she was safe. She could not discern the Hands themselves, and therefore, they could not discern her. Here and there metal caught the daylight, or a flame glowed as a Hand lit a pipe. It had become something of a waiting game.

And Aneisneida could see into the enemy's territory! It terrified and exhilarated her.

Soderingal's arm around her waist was a fleshy rope. She wanted to shake him off and soar out the window, as free as a crossbow bolt, as impossible to harm.

Her legs quivered. She wanted to step closer to the window. But there was her father's memory. Belstem would not have stepped closer to the window. *You could be* killed! And there was Fiamorina. And there were her responsibilities as a Summer.

This morning she had been afraid to go right down into the battle. But she had admitted it. She had said, "I'll stay behind. I'll follow at a safe distance."

Humi had nodded, preoccupied. "But someone must guard you. You make an excellent target for an assassin, you know."

With alacrity, Soderingal had volunteered to stay. He was afraid to go into the battle *and* afraid to admit it. Aneisneida felt glad Fia was safe in the Hangman's old residence, which Humi had given them when Evita was executed; the child's new nurses would take care of her. Anei did not even trust Soder to care for their baby! *That* was how much she despised him!

From below, she heard a monstrous sound, halfway between a cheer and a roar. A mortal woman's voice lifted above it, ragged but piercing. Aneisneida could not make out the words. She quivered violently, poised on her tiptoes, desperate to run to the window, terrified of feeling the bolt bite into her breast. She whirled to the *auchresh*. "What did Humi say? Did you hear her?"

The renegades were shifting in place, plainly cursing their lot. Impassivity was not the forte of those gods who chose to march under Humi's banner; on their faces, Aneisneida saw clearly that they wanted to go down and join in. Well, that was too bad. A Summer's wish must be obeyed, and Aneisneida wished for more protection, here, than her beloved husband would or could give her. "What did she *say?*"

"We are storming the courtyard, milady," one of the guards said. "We are going to break down the gate."

But at that point it was hardly necessary to explain. The first *thump* went through Aneisneida's very skeleton.

The army kept growling, a liquid, ugly, low-pitched, incessant noise.

Shaking Soderingal off, Aneisneida ran to the window and pressed herself against the wall beside it. Rolling her eyes sideways, she saw the packed flesh surge in waves, as if Humi had told her soldiers to hurl their very bodies against the barricade. The actual ram was invisible. Where had they got it?

Something *wheeted* past her face. For a minute, she was so caught up in the spectacle below that she did not see the crossbow bolt trembling in the floorboards. Then she gasped, "Gods!" she flattened herself against the wall.

It was black and crude and unexpectedly tiny. It had shot in through the glassless windowpanes without touching the lead.

"They don't know we're here!" one of the guards was saying urgently to Soderingal. "It's a stray bolt, milord! Please be calm!"

Aneisneida felt herself shaking. Her whole body vibrated, like the bolt quivering in the floor.

Life can be no sweeter than this.

Had Humi ever experienced this exhilaration? Anei was inclined to think not. Her voice was always cold with irony—she was like a fisherman, ripping the pride out of everyone she talked to with words like gutting knives. No matter how kindhearted they were, she could put it in their heads to do murder, on the off chance that it might please her. Sometimes Aneisneida looked at her and thought with a curious sentiment that was almost pity: *She has started retching up the wine she brewed. She is gritting her teeth, trying to hold on until the end.*

How I pity her!

Aneisneida, for her part, never wanted it to end. The terror, the giddiness. *This* was being *alive!* Hate for the Hands on the other side of the

street (new, but not unpleasant) bulged inside her like a new muscle. She
felt like a Veretrean tree cat. She stretched her claws.

The logic of it was simple.

Arity sighted along the stock of his crossbow and released. The shock
vibrated down his arms.

Outside noises: that was an *auchresh* dying. That was a battle yell. That
was the battering ram hitting the gate. How long would it take the timbers
to give way? From the west turret, he and his cabal had a stunning view of
Humi's army surging around the gate. Due to the shields that left only slits
of the windows open, the rebels did not have a stunning view of the cabal.
The square walkway that ran all around the rooms inside the tower echoed
with the eerie music of bows being loaded, wound back, and fired. Yells of
fear and delight. Arity wondered if they realized how lucky they were that
the rebels had bowed to pressure and initiated battle sooner rather than
later: as it was, defector Hands constituted only a tiny percentage of Humi's
army, but in a couple of sixdays there would have been more—and *they*
would have been able to *teth* into the Palace. A few renegades had tried,
presumably from pictures, but Arity had taken the precautions of having
human workers knock down some walls, and build others in unexpected
places, and then the infiltrators died instantly, their bodies in neat pieces.

He shouted an order, then stepped back to let another Hand into his
place. He was thinking about dying. Did it enter the minds of the others?
He doubted it. They were good soldiers, unlike him! Their minds were
focused upon the single slice of the world that included crossbow and
target.

What would the consequences be?

In the salt, *auchresh* could and did *teth* away from natural dangers and
overwhelming odds. But fights, showdowns, duels, were a different matter.
When faced with an inferior enemy (as the *auchresh*, with their traditional
arrogance, judged all enemies) *teth*ing dealt a crippling blow to the pride.
Not to mention the loss of status it provoked. One's *ghauthijim* would cast
one off, one's *breideim* would be disappointed, one would set a terrible
example for one's Foundlings. The same went for any fight conducted in
human country. In the dense, subtly warped world of the Hands, the respect of one's grand set of *kervayim* was even more fragile and desirable
than life.

Arity picked up the water-skin lying dribbling on the wooden floor and
took a swig. "Pathetic," he muttered.

What it came down to was this: like the rest of the *auchresh*, once confronted with a challenge, he just could not back down.

* * *

The extent to which he despised his own race amazed him. It was nothing new. He had felt it to one degree or another, consciously or unconsciously, all his civilized life. He even remembered (dimly, as in a series of faded tableaux) the time before he was Found, when the childish uncouth beast he had been scarcely knew it could think, let alone talk. In his shambling roamings through the salt forest, he had once come on another of his kind. The first *auchresh* he ever saw. An *iu*, a pale night spirit grubbing for termites in the ground, slurping them off her twisted fingernails.

The young mutant Arity had attacked her, mindlessly flying at her with fangs and talons. He had driven her away crying.

It had not even been his termite patch. He had hated her instinctively, desperately. Deep down in his being he had understood that they were the same, and denied that he could be like *that*.

In later life the incident had swum up from the mists of forgetfulness. And he had realized with wonder that if he met that *iu* now, he would be struck by her beauty.

An emaciated being with a form like a woman's and a face like a predator's, and no wings! Absolutely breathtaking!

(The whir and scream of arrow music; the grind of death below; the sulky thump of the ram. A Hand fell frothing on Arity's feet and his bow skittered across the walkway as if it were light as a feather.)

Time to find Pati!

The corridors were empty and dark. The smell of stale brimstone hung in the air. They hadn't torches to spare to light the inside of the Palace. Not anymore. Pati's habit of keeping the upstairs corridors as bright as day, as previous Divinarches had done, had been just that—a habit—and a feeling, Arity thought, of obligation: if he skimped on any tradition, he was not living up to the title he claimed.

The few Hands Arity encountered had not the temerity to look at Arity with reproach. They'd probably been hearing stories about his marvelous exploits with the crossbow. But he did hear notes of surprise in their voices as they murmured, *"Perich ˝hi,* Arity." Why wasn't he on the walls where he belonged?

He ran up the spiral stairs in the eastern turret, the one that topped the facade over the great doors.

The heartbeats of the battering ram had slowed down. A sense of urgency began to prickle under his skin.

The tower culminated in a large unfurnished room like a pagoda, with weathered wood-paneled walls and octagonal cutout windows. It always

put Arity in mind of the inside of a tiger's-eye gemstone. Pati sat alone on
the window seat, staring out. When Arity climbed through the central trapdoor, his face lit up. He swung his legs off the window ledge and came
toward Arity, hands out. "I'm so glad you're here! I was going to send for
you. We have to make some strategic decisions." The words were delivered
with no hint of urgency: no awareness that his Divinarchy was in immediate danger of destruction. He was clearly far gone. He kissed Arity on the
mouth: a brisk kiss of greeting, which lingered just long enough to intimate
that he would have liked to do more.

For just a second Arity felt the old weakness. A numbness in his fingertips, a blurring of his vision. Pati exercised his power even when he did not
mean to.

But Arity was no longer susceptible. Pati had made him kill the ghostiers.
He had put that blood on Arity's hands. He had corrupted Humi, the only
person Arity ever truly cared about: Arity had seen the result of that corruption firsthand. And the months stretched back, dim with clouds, shot
through with lightning, and Arity could not even count the numbers of
other times Pati had compelled him to his will.

And these were his offenses against one person only! The world teemed
with mortals and *auchresh* who, in Arity's place, would lose no time in
seizing their chance.

That was why he had to do it.

And in some twisted way he did not understand, it was also for *her.*

"Selflessness is the province of the emotionally destitute," he said to Pati.
"Don't you think? Sacrificing oneself—surely that is the last pleasure of
all?"

Outside, the screams and cries of the battle rose louder. "Hmm." Pati
leaned against the wall, brows furrowed in thought. Arity himself knew
what he had meant; he was rather shocked how obvious he had made it.
Was some part of him trying to *warn* Pati? *Imbecile!* he told himself. *Seize
every advantage!*

The wind blowing through the windows smelled of snow. It rushed over
the roof with a sound like the grass on the Veretrean plains. The day
outside was bright gray, as if the sun had dissolved, saturating the sky.
Thousands of loyalists and rebels lay dead in the forsaken districts of Christon and Marshtown.

"I'm not sure you're right," Pati said. "I've always tended to think selflessness is a deficiency of self-awareness. An inability to see what's important. Of course, for all sentient beings, that *is* the self."

"But true selflessness comes after one's illusions are gone," Arity said with some annoyance. "And that includes the illusion that one's self is at *all* important."

"My dear Ari"—Pati shook his head indulgently—"there is no such thing as true selflessness. It's always a pose of one kind or another. The most common pose being that of the mortal who believes that giving things to people for free will force them to see how magnanimous and brilliant he is, when in fact it makes them resent him."

Disgust warmed Arity to the fingertips, welcome as a hot mug to clasp his hands around. "Is that why you never fell prey to the vice of benevolence?" he asked scornfully.

Either Pati had not heard his sarcasm, or he chose to ignore it. "The masses' perception of me has never affected my policies. The wheels and pulleys of the world are set in place, and they are as solid as diamondine."

"There was a time when you would have told me you carved those wheels yourself," Arity said.

Pati looked at him with unreadable eyes. "Why are you baiting me?"

For a minute Arity could not speak. Finally he said: "Look out the window and maybe you'll understand."

Pati glanced out. "They have penetrated the courtyard."

"It's insupportable! I may have stood behind you this far, but now I cannot but condemn your—*strategy*. Do you know how many of your Hands are dying down there? Not to mention the mortals?"

"I think I pity those with the illusion that they're going to Heaven more than the others." Leaning against the wall, Pati spoke to a point somewhere outside the window. "At times like this one *has* to pity them. Born so ignorant, into a society that can do nothing to redeem their ignorance. To be shoveled into the machine." His voice hardened. "But then there are the others. The apostates. Who are not to be pitied at all. Wanton blasphemers! And the so-called gods who have corrupted them—*haugthirres* of the blackest dye! I would sacrifice the whole human population of Delta City if I could wipe *them* off the face of the earth!"

He shook his head. His eyes were big and shocked. His pale curls danced, turned to flames in the daylight.

"I think you've gone completely blind," Arity said hard. "Those powers of yours go on at full strength to try and subdue me, and you still refuse to admit to yourself that I am a danger to you. You really are remarkable."

The roar of the fight swelled. He spoke louder. "Do you realize what you've done? You've singlehandedly destroyed the Divinarchy. And you've destroyed—or irreversibly altered—a whole generation of our race."

"I suppose I have." Pati nodded. "Of course, I had a great many helpers. You haven't done so badly yourself."

Arity stared at him. "You know—don't you? You *must* . . . I've given you enough clues . . ."

His voice trailed off. There seemed nothing more to say. He drew his knife and sprang forward, knocking Pati back onto the floorboards, and slit his throat. Not deep enough to sever the jugular, but the white blood flowed, flowed like milk, almost as profusely as it had on that day when the leman from Calvary half killed Ari. The curve of Pati's white neck fit the curve of the blade perfectly. It was a standard Hand's knife, but it might have been forged for the job. Arity upbraided himself for not fitting the puzzle together sooner.

Pati did not speak. The bicolored eyes glowered up at Arity, brilliant with rage and fear. The dust and silt of the tower room tarnished the silver-white hair. Arity's heart was thudding. He took a deep breath. It did not help.

"Your only mistake," he told Pati, "was when you admitted to me that you didn't believe you were a god. Until then, I was still guessing, so I respected you, I feared you, just like everyone else. But you didn't want me to respect you. You wanted something else. So you told me your secret. You should never have told it to anyone. Because maybe there's something in your theory of not giving people things for free, because I hated you for doing it."

He heard the contempt in his own voice. "You're not flawless. You're not self-sufficient. You're just a near-perfect example of an *auchresh!* And just like the rest of us, you're terrified of being alone! We are a race with a dread of primitive things, and a craving for them, a craving we are so embarrassed by we hide it behind stone walls! And the most horrible part of it is that to us *love* is a primitive thing! In Rimmear it carries a taint of absurdity. My *elpechim* considered it laughably quaint. You saw what lone-liness had done to Golden Antelope, and you thought I could save you from that. But the sordidity of the thing ruined it."

Pati jerked urgently.

He deserved to speak. He deserved that. Arity lifted the knife blade out of the blood-spiderwebbed skin.

Pati coughed and coughed, his eyes running, his throat pumping blood into a little pool under his head. Arity watched. After a while, he wiped Pati's eyes with the corner of his sleeve.

"You thought . . . I wanted to be saved . . . ?" Pati whispered. "You are wrong. I didn't need saving. *You* did. Maybe it was vulgar of me . . . but I was content living alone in what you're pleased to call"—one corner of his mouth twitched—"my overcivilized world."

He knows he is trapped. He thinks he has a hope if he comes clean—or pretends to. Arity thought, *I will not be touched. I will not be deterred.*

Pati continued in the same rather abashed explanatory tone:

"Golden Antelope was alone, too. He had his schemes, his philosophies, his mad theories. He was his own companion. He wasn't lonely. He lasted so long, the dear scrawny old *haugthule,* because he cared so passionately about living. Likewise, I was always driven by passion! My love for you, through those years when we were apart, was a reward in and of itself. I didn't *want* to consummate it. Like Golden Antelope, I was full of other things to do, I had plans and projects that consumed my energy. And I had my *ghauthijim.* They satisfied me."

He sighed, and abruptly his face darkened. "But I felt sorry for you. In fact, I couldn't stop thinking about you. You were alone in Rimmear, ripping yourself to pieces, with only your ghosts for company. I wanted to save you."

Arity swallowed. He shifted off Pati, knelt on the floor, and jammed his knife back into its scabbard without bothering to wipe it.

"Oh, don't give up *now!*" Pati said. "I thought you were really going to . . . You disappoint me." He rolled over, slowly, painfully, clutching his throat, and sat up. "I think now that when I went to find you, I was setting foot on a ship I had been harboring for a long time." Eyes like suns. "Bring it into port, Ari. We've traveled all the way around the world. Bring it into port."

Arity shook his head wordlessly. This was not the larger-than-life Pati of the Throne Room, nor the urbane, rapidly disintegrating Pati whose madness Arity had condemned out of hand. This was a Pati he had never seen clearly before, though he had always sensed he was there.

Pati laughed. "You won't, will you! Your idea of civilized conduct is more human than you realize!"

We are keres, *not men,* Arity thought through the snow of confusion in his head. Had they been mortals, they would never have been lovers, and everything might be different. But they were *keres:* by human standards, *keres* were both pompously, exaggeratedly male and effeminate. And therefore their friendship had become love, and their love had had to be a uniquely *auchresh* compound of feminine sentiment and masculine power play—saturated with sexual tension, violently combustible.

But *love?* It could never have been love unless—

"*You* are *wrchrethre,*" he said to Pati. As if that was a revelation. "More than any other *auchresh* I know, you are *wrchrethre.* Do you know how much"—he stopped, and let out a small, mirthless gasp—"do you know how much you are *like her?*"

"There you have it. The whole, sordid tragedy of this story. You made me like this," Pati told him softly. "You enabled me to see the hollowness of my claim to godhead."

"What on earth do you mean?"

The wind blew keenly through the tower room. Time had slowed and almost stopped. Minutes dripped by as slowly as bubbles moving in oil.

Pati pushed himself into a half-sitting position. He massaged his throat gingerly, the long knuckly fingers splayed down one side of his neck. His wings awkwardly open behind him, crushed against the wall, made him look like an injured seagull. "Before you and I were reunited, I believed completely, wholeheartedly in myself. After we were reunited"—he smiled crookedly—"less so."

"Don't blame me for your failure," Arity said. "It's not worthy of you."

"I am not blaming you. Not in the least. My *fascination* with you is the intangible villain in this drama. Gradually I found it overcoming me. I could no longer exert myself singlemindedly in the cause of the Divinarchy." He shifted, and looked sidelong at Arity. "I should have killed you then. But you were a project to me, too, no less important than any of the others. I was interested in you. I came to be obsessed by you. At first there was a balance. Then the balance tipped."

Arity hitched himself back against the wall. The weight descended like a yoke on his shoulders. Of course, it was his fault; it was both their faults! Carrying the weight of it had worn Pati down to this nubbin.

Weathered. Wise.

But still Pati.

Still capable of deceit, to save his own skin.

"You're spinning stories!" Arity broke out. "You're convincing! You almost had me! But it won't do any good."

He shifted, sliding one hand under him, feeling for his knife. The belt had got twisted in the scuffle.

Pati smiled. A sweet, heart-stoppingly immediate smile. "And bring the boat into port."

Arity froze, his hand on the hilt.

"I don't like calling it love. We are *keres*, after all. But I can't think of a better word for it. It is an evil thing, and it is everything."

"Obsession," Arity said, and readied himself to spring.

"No. More than that. Much more. And you didn't have very much to do with it, strange as that may seem. You only had to be your sweet, indecisive self. You were the instrument—as you are the instrument now.

"Arity. If we spend our meager hoard of days in the pursuit of intellectual triumph, like Golden Antelope, we crumble to dust and are laughed at by posterity. If we throw ourselves against the walls that surround us—not metaphorical walls, but real walls, the boundaries of the world: the Chrume, the edge of the salt, the sea that stretches to the end of the world, the boundary between the races—if we hurl ourselves at them, thinking to break them with faith, then when we die we have accomplished no more than our *breideim* before us.

"But if we climb those walls!" Pati half smiled. "*That*, my *irissi*, is the true quest. That is the only noble way to spend a life, to waste a life, or give a life. I did all three."

Arity blinked.

And rubbed his palm across the hilt of his knife, to keep himself anchored in the real world.

"You are not noble," he insisted. "Evil! You're evil!"

Pati's powers were many. And he was so subtle . . .

And yet he had loved Arity. Despite his predisposition to violence, he had not killed him, as he had killed those other *keres* when they threatened his singlemindedness.

Instead, he had confronted that (oh so human!) love, and accepted it. He had smashed all the bonds with which tradition bound the *auchresh* race, and saved Arity's life.

Saved his life. That job had not been completed until this moment, at the top of this tower, with the battle snarling below.

The degree of *selflessness* required in doing what you know is bad for you, the right thing, the only thing you can do . . .

Nothing had been an illusion. Not a moment of the past two seasons had been an illusion. It had all been real.

Now it was over.

And the tragedy was that even though Arity understood now, no other course of action lay open to him besides the one he had already decided on.

"We've reached the top of the walls, haven't we?" he said. "We can't climb any higher."

"Want to jump off with me?" Pati smiled. "I never expected we would conclude our little drama against such a melodramatic backdrop. Did you? But I suppose it happens to the best of us. No, don't jump, Ari. That would make all of this a waste."

An earthquake shook the Palace. The battering ram must be at the great doors. The shouts and the ring of metal crashed into Arity's ears.

He stood up and brushed off his hands.

A crossbow bolt whizzed past his head. He dropped to the floor. "Damn!"

Pati's face was very close to his. It looked angelic. From the slim, well-defined lips came calm words. "I'm going to die, Ari. They're battering down the doors. But if you do it now, *you* don't have to die." His wings, tightly thrumming, scraped over the unpolished wooden wall with a sound like sheets of parchment being crumpled. "Do it!"

Arity moved his hand to his dagger. But Pati did not see. His voice rose. "Do you imagine I don't know how she will *kill* me? I have my pride! I know when it is time to bow out, and I mean to do it gracefully!"

A flash of the old Pati, gone as quickly as it came. Fear sharpened the smoothest tongues. And Arity felt Pati's fear as if it were his own. If Pati were captured, he would be chained to a choice of slow death by their tortures, or slower death somewhere in exile, through the festering of his own mortally injured pride.

Auchresh did not commit suicide. It was beneath their pride. It was too easy.

Twilight drifted across the sky huge and blue and gray like monstrous wings.

The cacophony of human noises from the battle, which seemed almost tasteful now, jumped from key to key, punctuated by the drumbeats of the battering ram.

Arity sighed, and squatted up on his heels, careful to keep his head down. He could not keep a corner of his mouth from quirking as he pulled out his knife. Here a bit of flash, there a bit of flair! All Hands were showmen.

Something zinged loudly off the blade as he tossed it in midair. When the hilt thunked into his palm again, the steel bore a dent the length of his thumb.

Pati squinted up at him, laughing silently. The bright, still quality of his eyes seemed to prevent him from seeing Arity. But it was not tears. It was something else altogether. "Take care how you cut now!" His voice was light, bantering. "Whatever you do, don't make me jangle like a mortal! I want to look my best when she hangs me on the gates." He shook his hair back, baring his throat.

SWORDFISH

Sol threw his weight into the blow, felt steel grind bone as his sword sank through the old Deltan woman's heart and out of her back. The woman, who had not known how to defend herself, crumpled to the flagstones. Black blood spurted out along Sol's blade. *Nineteen.* He was keeping count, in a rather delirious way. He kicked the corpse away and whirled, staggering slightly.

Someone grabbed him from behind, shaking him with *auchresh* strength. He flinched, spun, and stabbed at air. The enemy had got behind him again. *Gods—gods—*

"It's over!" a voice shouted deafeningly in his ear. "Look up! Look *up,* man!"

The voice did not belong to an enemy.

There were no more enemies in the vicinity.

This fact took some time to seep into his consciousness. In the meantime, he swayed away from a blow that was not there, blinked, and lunged rather halfheartedly at a shadow. He felt as weak as if he had vomited. His muscles twitched, urging him to lash out at the figures around him, although they had mostly stopped moving and he sensed they were his friends. After an interminable delay, the real world, the world made of sights and sounds and people who had fallen still, coagulated about him. Twilight was gathering. He could not hear the sea, or the wind, much less any birds, but that could be the ringing in his ears. For hours he had been an unthinking fragment of the bloody chiaroscuro of the battle, as a bird is part of a formation winging across the sky, constantly changing place with other fragments, blocking, parrying and stabbing, communicating (when there was time to communicate) in the terse, expletive-laden language of necessity.

It all seemed to dissolve very quickly.

Someone close to him let off a crossbow bolt. It whirred into the sky, and a ragged shout went up from the rebels all over the courtyard. "Stop him!" "Cease fire!" "Stick the bastard!"

Men and *auchresh* were craning their necks, peering up into the bluish-gray dusk. The sky was soft, near, the color of a pigeon's neck. Sol tried to make out what the misguided crossbowman had been aiming at.

On the battlements of the turret that reared above the splintered wreck of the great doors, a lone figure stood. An *auchresh*, from his fearless stance on the parapet. Unharmed. The marksman had missed.

His voice floated faintly, but distinctly, down into the courtyard.

"Listen to me! I am on your side! Put down your weapons! I—say—throw down your blades! The Divinarch is dead! The Palace surrenders!"

Wasn't the voice familiar somehow? Sol could not conjure up the memory from his leaking mind.

Then he realized what the fellow had said.

Whispers darted like fish through the disarrayed army.

"*What* did 'e say?"

"Oo is it?"

Not even *auchresh* lungs could make themselves heard perfectly down a drop of two hundred windy feet.

"We've won," Sol said. "And I know who that is."

"Won, 'ave we? Wivout even stickin' all of 'em? Ho well, I like *that!*"

Humi had done her job well before the battle. The speaker sounded disappointed, angry even, at the prospect of not getting to plant a banner in a bloody heap of Hands' bodies on the highest tower of the Palace.

In the shadow of the ruined doors of the Palace, the remnants of the loyalist army clustered, looking lost. They had not dropped their weapons, but they had dropped their guard. Sol watched without pity or hate as they turned to each other, blankly questioning. It was as if the possibility of their Divinarch's betrayal had driven everything else from their heads.

"It's the Heir!"

"Arity!"

" 'E's turned 'is coat!"

The figure on the turret stood silhouetted against the dusk. Some of the whisperers condemned him for his treachery; some praised him for his integrity.

"But there was no *point*," Sol said aloud.

The Hands were nearly all dead. He doubted there was one Deltan loyalist in ten left alive. Half an hour ago, perhaps, surrendering might have done some good.

Bitterness filled his throat. His sword shone with wet blood. It dragged at his hand, like a lead ball. He had gripped it for so long that he could not make his fingers uncurl.

Arity hasn't changed, he thought, staring at the small, slim figure with disgust. *He still makes an effect by being ineffectual.*

The renegades, apostates, and Shimorningers did not move. They stood leaning on their swords, whispering uneasily. Sol fought the force that drew his eyes again and again toward the bemused loyalists in the ruined doors.

A flock of cold wind birds swooped into the courtyard, invisible predators grabbing the souls of the dead in their claws. The sea roared, as if it were rising up over the island, a hallucinatory deluge of black that drenched Sol's eyes and ears with momentary blindness and deafness as night usurped twilight's throne on the peak of the sky. It came to him that somehow, in one of those cracks of his perception, Humi had entered the Palace with her bodyguards. Perhaps the wind had carried her in. That was what they were all waiting for. Waiting for her to replace the Heir on the parapet, signaling a *real* victory. Waiting for that white and gray flag to flap out, so that they could toss their helmets in the air and hear their own yells rain comfortably down on them.

VICTORY

Humi had told Hope she would find Arity outside. She left the Palace through the ragged maw that had been the great doors. The sheer amount of damage that had been done to Delta City while she was fighting overseas still shocked her; and the Palace had not been spared. The ramp into the courtyard was a mass of twisted timbers. People had to clamber over it, as if up a giant stairway. Crossbow bolts bristled in the eaves of the roofs that topped the outside walls.

Her dagger banged gently against her thigh as she walked. She was aware of the smooth play of muscles from her toes to her shoulders. The soldier's walk. I have a soldier's body. Not a lady's, not an *iu's*. Try that one on for size.

She had got quite used to fighting in the lines; even started enjoying it, in a terrified way.

The winter sun flooded over her. It wasn't as bright as it had been in Calvary. But the light had a freezing clarity. No one was left to light fires in Delta City; no smoke sullied the air. They were returning: Humi had told her of the barges ferrying refugees back to the Marshtown jetties. Mothers and fathers and children and craftsmen and immigrants, fearfully venturing throughout the city, returning to plundered, scorched houses. Law and order, supposedly, had been reestablished. But privately, Humi had said she anticipated a good many skirmishes and petty vengeance killings before the city settled back into any semblance of normality.

Then she had said, *But that will be for Aneisneida and Gold Dagger to worry about.*

It had taken Hope a while to understand. In the end, Humi had had to tell her straight out. She had presented it clearly, sanely, and in the end Hope had not been able to deny that she was right. That it was everyone's fault, and no one's. Hope's fault, for being so desperately loved by her soldiers. Humi's fault for being blind, for not being able to *teth*¨, for being tied to Delta City. Shine's fault. Whitenail's. Truth's.

Hope stepped aside to let a family of nervous Deltans shuffle past her. A woman and an old man, with three small children. They gazed aimlessly about; eventually they attached themselves to the end of a queue that snaked around the courtyard, spiraling in toward the spot where Aneisneida, along with several women volunteers she had rooted up from the remnants of the merchant class, was serving hot stew and bread.

Hope had forgotten to ask Humi where Aneisneida found the food. Even as she wondered how the Summer girl had managed it, in a starving city, the conundrum solved itself. A delicious whiff of new-baked bread blew into her nostrils. She jumped out of the way just in time to avoid a crew of *keres* hurrying out of the dark Palace. They bore trays of new-baked loaves on their shoulders. Their faces glistened with useful sweat.

So she had *auchresh* importing food from the provinces. An absurdly labor-intensive enterprise. Nobody would dream of going to such extremes, except a woman like Aneisneida, who had no conception of what *teth*¨*ing* really was. And even *she,* Hope thought, giving her the benefit of the doubt, would have to have been convinced this was really an emergency.

Things had changed. The Palace's great underground kitchens had been put back into operation. Had the first Divinarch, their architect, ever envisaged their use for such a project? That ancient *er-serbali's* shade must be restless.

Laudable of Aneisneida. Laudable. Of course it is. Power—how that girl has improved.

Hope's mouth watered as the breeze wafted the scent her way. How long since she had eaten? Not since returning from Calvary yesterday. She had been too sick at heart, choked with the duty of telling Humi that a cousin of hers had been scouting in the army since before the first battle for Grussels, and that he had died after the battle for Samaal. Hope had apparently been supposed to find out about him, but someone had forgotten to inform her, and the boy had had too much pride (or been too intimidated) to come to her. At times like that she hated the power she wielded—will-she, nill-she—over her followers. It was too much like Pati's power over the Hands! It was during the mop-up of Samaal that a scout of one of the Younger Cabals had approached her, hop-skipping sideways, paralyzed by bashfulness. In tones of terror, he squeaked something at her about a child named Merce—Humi's cousin, and almost dead.

With her bodyguards, Hope had followed him to the rocks of the Eastern Rim, where the other survivors of the cabal had carried the boy. The dust kicked up by the battle thickened the air into a solid substance, through which the boys moved as awkwardly and agilely as salt herons in the morning mist. The sun was going down in a blaze on the desert. Hope was still in full battle gear; her metal-reinforced shirt clinked as she knelt by the boy's side. "Are you our true Divinarch's cousin?" she asked him gently.

He didn't look twelve. He looked a stunted twenty-five, what with the lines on his face and the scars on his thin forearms and the tobacco stains on his teeth when his lips parted. If he had been anything like Humi was when she first came to Delta City, three months in the army had changed him a good deal. "I . . . my name . . . Merce Garden."

She could hear the Domesdean accent even in those few words. The wound in his thigh was killing him fast. The black arterial blood seeped through the bandages, redolent of hot metal. There were no flamens left alive who could have helped him.

"Then why didn't you come to me?" she asked. "I would have made sure this didn't happen! I would have sent you to Humi in the city—you would have been safe with her, and having you by her side would certainly have made a difference to her!"

"It . . . doesn't matter . . . what you would of . . . milady Maiden . . ." he whispered. "I couldn't . . . of left the Seventh!" He threw up an arm, as if begging his friends to agree. One of them seized the chapped fingertips and held them. The rest of them hovered around: children with patchy fur, gangly and scarred, the very flesh of Hope's army.

"I wish my little sister . . ." Merce turned to the boy who was holding his hand. "Tell her . . . tell her I asked for her . . . not for Humi . . . tell her . . ."

With a quiver, he died.

Hope clenched her fists.

"Bury him," she said coldly to the Seventh Younger Cabal. "Don't leave him for the hyenas. That is beneath the standards of this army."

When she told Humi the little tale, she had left out the most painful details. The tattoo on Merce's arm, in a patch of burned off fur, which matched those on the other boys' arms. The impossible loneliness of the sunset, the silence of that place above the cauldron of life and slaughter. What she, Hope, had thought that night, tossing on her camp bed, when she could not get the child out of her mind, and she felt cold sweat on her back and her forehead, and she knew that—even had it not officially been over—it was over for her.

The news of the cousin's death had shaken Humi. That surprised Hope. Muddy-faced, looking quite unlike the serene conqueror into whose presence Hope had been ushered, she clutched the arms of the Throne.

Hope had muttered something in an unmodulated voice and fled out into the sunlight.

She looked around the courtyard. There was Arity, unobserved and unobserving in a corner, his face shaded by the hood of an *auchresh* tunic too big for him. His head was tipped back; the sunlight shone on the apple-green skin of his throat.

She *teth˙* up to him. He started upright, fumbling at his side for a knife that was not there. She stepped back.

"Hope!" He moved to embrace her. She slid aside. Hurt, he stopped. She stared at him, trying to see *through* him.

How was he different? How had he changed? She would not have it that he had not changed at all.

"*Is* it you, Ari? Is it really you?"

He leaned back against the wall, picking at a splinter. The weathered, perfectly fitted planks, undamaged but for a few blade marks, soared twenty feet over his head. "Forever picking at half-healed scabs," he said sadly. "You are a true *auchresh*, Hopie."

"You know what I mean," she said.

"I suppose I do. I had hoped that you, of all people, wouldn't harp on it."

"Have other people?"

"No." His mouth quirked. A smile, almost. "That's what makes it worst of all! No one has mentioned it, although I half expected to be executed. No one except Humi, who *had* to. And she just offered a few cut-and-dried words of thanks."

Hope drew a deep breath. "Don't take this the wrong way, Ari. But I didn't think you were capable of it."

He sighed. He tugged his hood down, revealing that same vulnerably handsome face that had always tugged at her heart strings. A small cluster of brown circles shone on his neck, in the shade of the hood. He was still clipping his thorns. He was not going to revert to the state in which she had left him in Rimmear.

His expression was philosophical; he looked tired. "When you last met me, I wouldn't have been capable of it. But while you were away—a lot happened . . ." He smiled wearily. "I think Pati knew all along, deep inside, that I was dangerous to him. Maybe he even knew I would be his death. So he tried to control me. And by trying, he made me able to break free."

"Which came first," Hope said, "the flower or the seedpod?"

Arity's nose wrinkled. "I'm through with paradoxes now."

"So am I." She shifted. "We are equals now, Ari: I think. We both stood up to him, each in our own way."

His eyes sparkled, but he did not respond. She felt slightly disappointed. In her interactions with other *auchresh*, she seldom admitted equals. That was not the *iu* way.

But then, both of them had left such finicky, obsolete standards behind in the old world. She said, "Of course, your gesture was far more dramatic."

He flung his arms out. "I am Drama!" Then he dropped his hands, and swept his eyes up and down her. "But I don't know! You have become rather dramatic yourself—everything from the way you smile to the way you stand! That's what soldiering does to you, isn't it? It makes you feel that the world is a dramatic place, worth giving yourself to, body and heart." He sobered. "And you gave yourself to it. I did too. *That* was the thing, wasn't it?"

"Yes." Hope thought of splitting Calvarese teenagers on the end of her sword, of sleeping with a human soldier twice her size whose passion had briefly been able to overcome his urge to worship her. She thought of Humi's cousin dying at her touch on Samaal's Eastern Rim. "That was the thing."

He nodded. "You *do* understand. You are the only one. Perhaps there's something in this business of blood."

"Doesn't Humi understand?" She had to ask. It was all over now. Nothing more stood between the two of them. Surely . . . surely . . .

"She is blind," Arity said with unexpected vehemence. "She didn't *see* the battle. In just the way that Pati, in his turret, didn't see the suffering. She did not see. She still does not see."

"Give her credit where credit is due, Arity! She's changed, too!"

"Fig juice! She still believes all this is *glorious*."

Hope did not know what to say. Behind them, the queue of Deltans shuffled slowly around and around the courtyard. More supplicants came all the time, even while those who had completed their circular pilgrimage shouldered out through the queue and plopped themselves down by the walls, wolfing their bowls of stew. They spoke in whispers, as if they had not yet realized that it was safe to raise their voices. Aneisneida's recognizable treble rang out in laughter for a moment. *There* was a woman whose energy had scarcely been tapped. *She*, Hope was willing to bet, still saw a possibility of deriving glory from this mess.

Humi was beyond that. Hope knew she was.

"It's absurd that *I* have to defend her when *you* were here," Hope said. "But I can see you're biased. So I'll do it."

She had to remind him, although she herself did not like to remember. The wound was still raw.

"I have talked to her. It was the assassination of the ghostiers, I think, which convinced her once and for all that there is no glory in this war."

"Do you know what part I had in that?"

She nodded. "But that hardly matters now, does it? Not after—what you did. I meant that she has lost as many friends as anyone else. She is to be pitied."

Arity was staring at the soup queue. "And if she has not had her fair share of suffering," he said viciously, "she will."

"Not here, though. This act is over. For her." Hope took a deep breath. "She is abdicating."

"*What?*"

"She hasn't announced it yet. But she is quite set on her plan."

"She—she *what?* She *can't!*"

"She is Divinarch. She sits on the Throne. Or haven't you realized that yet? She can do whatever she wants to."

Arity stiffened. He looked searchingly into her eyes. Puzzled, she didn't respond. Finally, he relaxed. "Thank the Power! For a moment, there, I was afraid you—had suggested it to her!"

"No," Hope said ruffled. "I have no ambitions of that sort. All I meant was that it is completely within her scope, if she wants to. She is supreme."

Arity's face softened, green wax in the sun. He smiled broadly, and then he hugged her. "I love you," he said into her ear. "You understand everybody. Power . . . ! Saying that makes me feel like a Foundling again! But I mean it."

"Oh, Ari." Overcoming astonishment, she extracted her arms from the cinch and hugged him back. They stood pressed together for a long moment. She closed her eyes. His clothes were warm from his body heat. His breath thawed the chilly point of her ear. He smelled faintly of salt mangoes: she guessed he had been for a visit to Wind Gully Heaven. It was a comforting smell of Heaven, of home, of long-ago Foundlinghood. But he had come back here again, to the city.

"I love you, too, Ari," she whispered. "I always have. But now . . . now I can depend on you."

"Whatever is within my power, Hope."

"I only ask one thing of you. Survive, and keep on surviving."

"That's a lot to ask."

"I ask it anyway. You will do it. For me."

He let out a deep breath. After a moment, he said in *auchraug,* with a smile in his voice, "All right! All right, female one, you have your way!" In *auchraug, female* meant *powerful* and *manipulative,* and at the same time "weak in a way which makes one want to aid her." Hope in her turn felt small and young and loved. He gave her a last squeeze and then let go. "Now I had better go speak to Humi. This decision of hers changes things."

Oh! Oh . . . but Ari, don't be a fool! She won't thank you for coming to her when she is at her weakest! She closed her mouth on the words. *Perhaps what she needs is foolishness.* "What are you going to say?"

"I don't know."

"You'll probably do more harm than good."

"I know that."

His eyes were narrow. He was no longer smiling. He drove his hands decisively into the pockets of his tunic.

"Go then," she said, and moved to the wall and leaned against it as he started toward the doors. She was no longer the Maiden General, whose followers, after the battle of Samaal, when she officially disbanded the army, when she expected them to throw stones, had shocked her by opening their throats and letting out a yell of adoration that would ring in her ears forever. For love of her, they had died. For love of her, the rest of their lives would be pale. Her authority sickened her; she had not been sorry to cast it off. She was no longer the Maiden General, or a maiden, or even, she thought, possessed of any qualities one might term general. No virtues. Only tiredness. *Cold wood hold me, hold me up.*

Humi had taken up residence in a suite high up in the Palace. Ari had been told she wished to emphasize her break with the old regime. He understood that—especially if her resolution were only tentative, and she feared that the shades in the royal suite might whisper in her ears and convince her she was really meant to be Divinarch, after all. He nodded to the *auchresh* sentinels who stood on either side of the heavy blue-glass door, jaws jutting at the ceiling. They studied him from the corners of their eyes.

From inside, he heard voices. A human woman and a human man. In another minute he indentified them as Humi and Sol.

"What is the layout of the suite?" he asked the sentinels softly.

"Lieutenant?" one questioned, finally. The fellow must be an ex-Hand. None of the renegades conceded any title to Arity except *perich"hi*—and that grudgingly.

"Is there an anteroom, or does this door open directly into the reception room?"

"Oh," the ex-Hand said. "Yes, there is an anteroom!" He grinned. This kind of thing was, of course, familiar to him from the days when the *kervayim*-councillors plotted and schemed against each other. Arity remembered those night and days of eavesdropping with a flush of shame. "It has heavy drapes, Lieutenant! And this door makes no noise!"

"If I were still Pati's lieutenant," Arity said as he pushed the door open and slid through, "I would have you executed for that." The slab of opaque glass closed behind him. It was a small room, and it felt as if it were underwater. Heavy blue velvet curtains hooked back to reveal aquarelles, and a blue frescoed ceiling gave an impression of the surface of the pond. Flaking, ancient ghosts, most of them Deltan or Veretrean (in accordance with the color scheme) struck old-fashioned poses.

He stepped to the far door and pressed his eye to the crack.

Diffused sunlight filled the reception room beyond, rippling on the ceiling, bouncing off various refractive *objets*. Piradean glass sculptures, a silver incense burner, a glass table. One wall of this room, like the royal bedroom several stories below, was completely glass, offering a panoramic view of the sea. Humi sat in a hard chair with a solid back that had probably been crafted for someone three times her size. She faced the sea and her back was to the door. Her feet rested flat on the floor, her hands rested flat on the claw arms of the chair. Her mint-colored dress lapped over the green handkerchief points of the seat drape, blending with it, as if she were sewn in place. "I tell you, my mind is made up," she said flatly. "You might as well leave. Do you understand? I am speaking the truth."

Sol paced up and down behind her chair. His skin showed dark and muddy through his white fur; his mouth twisted. "I do not think you have *ever* told me the truth," he said in a controlled tone. "Not in all our years as *imrchim*, and not afterward. I see no reason for you to have straightened your tongue now."

"But I have changed."

"Yes! You *have* changed! You've become *weak!*" Sol swung to face the armchair, gesturing—pointlessly, of course, for all Humi's victories had not given her back her sight. "How can you give up the Divinarchy, now that you have it in your very *hands?* How can you have lost your ambition? You used to glitter with intent! We loved you for your energy! It was like—like drinking wine!"

"I *told* you. I have *changed!*" She laughed mirthlessly. "Sometimes I think Emni's death affected me more deeply than it did you. Do you understand? Are you listening to me?"

"You certainly weren't listening to *me* the day she died," Sol muttered, too low for Humi to hear; but Arity's sharp ears picked it up.

"And my—loss of ambition, as you call it—is compounded by the state in which I find the world." Humi sighed exhaustedly. "I've already explained this once today, to Hope, but I'll do it again. Think, Sol. Really, I have already lost the Divinarchy. Despite all our efforts, we did not make the war cohesive enough. It was too ragged. How did we put it? 'Sacrificing dedication for numbers.' Well, we might not have won if we had done otherwise. Our losses were staggering, even though our armies were ten times the size of Pati's. But from the point of view of keeping the Divinarchy unified, it was a terrible mistake."

"I don't follow," Sol said angrily.

"Each continent was freed by one of my *auchresh* lieutenants, through the exertions of soldiers who adored that lieutenant. Each continent *freed itself from Pati*. It did not *deliver itself to me*. My name was no more than a symbol for freedom. My goal was to end Pati's tyranny. It seems I succeeded too well.

"In four short years, Pati created a miracle. By taking the flamens for his own, and spreading his Hands throughout the world, he made the structure of local and continental government so thoroughly *his* that the only way to take it back was to destroy the structure. And so we did. And now the continents are all spinning off in different directions. Domesdys follows Shine. Iceland follows Whitenail. Veretry follows Truth. The Archipelago is sliding into quiet anarchy. And Power knows what will happen to the continents Hope won by herself, because unlike the other lieutenants, she has absolutely no wish to govern. Other renegades may try to fill her shoes. But more likely, quarreling human upstarts will shove them out, and there will be civil war again. Pirady and Calvary may even split into separately governed countries."

Sol had stood still through this monologue. Finally, as Humi halted for breath, he interrupted. "And like Hope, you have *absolutely no wish* to try to stop this projection of yours from coming true? What about *duty*? Don't you consider it your *duty* to hold the Divinarchy together—"

"Honestly, Sol, even leaving my personal indisposition to ruling out of it, looking at the situation objectively, there is no hope. Holding the Divinarchy together for five more years, or ten, would simply make things worse when it finally breaks up." She paused—"Or else—and this is a possibility I'm afraid even to speak of—I would turn into another tyrant. Then it would break up at my death."

"You think you have the ability to be like Pati? After all you've said about your lack of ambition, and so forth, and what I remember from your first reign—your indecisiveness, your *chronic* indecisiveness that forced us finally to ask you to step down—you expect me to believe that you fear becoming a *tyrant*?"

"Yes."

On the other side of the door, Arity understood. Intuitively, like a flash of pain.

Sol evidently did not. He let out an exasperated puff of breath. He began to pace again, three steps and whirl, three steps, whirl. "But you can't give up the Divinarchy because you think you would make a bad Divinarch! That is pure cowardice."

"Haven't I made myself clear by now? I do not think there *can be* another Divinarch."

"Delta City is yours! You can't argue with that! Royalland is yours! And Delta City *is* the Divinarchy!"

Humi let out a mirthless little noise. "*Was*. Royalland was damaged too badly in the war for it to worry about anything now except getting back on its feet. And the city. What is it now? A tiny island awash in starving refugees, whose oldest and most beautiful districts have been burned out. The intercontinental ships have stopped coming here. The city can recuperate. But I would hinder its recovery, rather than help it."

"Who will have the city, then? You haven't thought about *that!*"

"Do you want to have it?" Arity could not hear a glimmer of humor in her voice, yet this time, he could not believe she meant what she was saying. "You can, if you do. And Royalland, as far as I am able to give it to you. I was planning to hand the reins to Gold Dagger, Soderingal, and Aneisneida—I like the idea of creating a new Royallandic dynasty, only human this time—but the strongest contender will come out on top, no matter what I dictate. And you're stronger than two, anyway, out of those three, so I might as well forestall the infighting by giving it to you."

"No," Sol said in a strangled voice. "I have no ambitions in that direction." Arity heard Hope, in his head, echoing those words almost exactly: her voice which had been like a length of silk hoarsened to burlap by years of tobacco and months of open air. He blinked. For the first time, he felt the pinch of his scruples. This was an intensely private scene he was witnessing: was it the breakdown of an old understanding—or the start of a new one? The cause he had come here to plead, continents and monarchs regardless, could pivot on the next few moments.

He couldn't *not* watch. He glued his eye to the crack again. The incense burner in the other room exhaled a musky twist of smoke, marbling the air.

"There is only one thing you could give me that I would care for," Sol said in a careful voice, higher pitched than usual. "Tellury Crescent."

Humi's hand jerked. It was the first movement he had seen from her since he began to watch. "Tellury Crescent? Sol, are you *mad!* Nothing in the world could make me go back there! The Chalice is a shell! Soot and rain puddles! Nobody has—nobody has removed the bodies—"

Arity gritted his teeth, closed his eyes.

Sol said, "But *imrchu, I* would go back. *I* would rebuild the ruin."

"Take it, then!" The arm resting on the chair vanished; Arity guessed she had muffled her face in her hands. "Take it. Make the ghostiers a power again. Be senior ghostier. Enlist Mory and Tris to help you. What a different institution it will be when *they* have a hand in its shaping!" She yelped laughter, unstably. "You *do* have a nose for the unworthiest of all our unworthy problems!"

"What have I done?" Sol said. "Is it a crime now to yearn for beauty?"

"It—Sol, have you *forgotten?* I am no longer a ghostier! I am *blind!*"

"But *I* am a ghostier! You are so incurably self-absorbed! I sometimes think your heart was never in ghosting at all. But me—it's in me. I always have been a ghostier. I was born yearning for beauty."

Her voice was small, not like Humi's voice at all. "I think you are stronger than I am."

"But I'm a very simple man, really." Sol clasped his hands behind him. His back was to the door, his face to the sun's glare and the sparkling black sea. Arity wanted to look away. "I need something on which to fix myself. Then I circle around that center, snapping. Like a dog on a lead."

"Emni!" Humi breathed.

"You," Sol said brutally.

"Did you ever . . . I have to know, Sol. Did you ever think about betraying me?"

"I wish I could say I never thought about it. But that isn't . . . isn't my nature. I thought about it many times. But I couldn't betray you. In the end, I didn't want to." He paused. "I didn't know that *you* would betray *me.*"

"Gods . . . !" Humi was, Arity thought, close to tears. The idea shook him strangely; made his stomach churn.

"You've let a great many people down," Sol said. "But to me, personally, you have made everything up. Giving me Tellury Crescent has erased any debt there ever was between us!" His voice was brisk now, businesslike. He walked to the door, saying over his shoulder, "Come visit me there before you leave. If you can overcome your horror of the place."

"How—how did you know I was leaving?"

Arity hastily scrabbled his mind into order for *teth˜tach ching.* Sol stopped with his hand almost literally on the doorknob. "Doesn't everybody know? You're going with *him.*"

Arity's mind reeled. He did not manage to *teth˜* until Sol strode out of the room. But Sol did not see him. The Archipelagan was walking fast toward the door, gripping some kind of a glass ornament, twisting it in both hands. Purplish blood ran down his wrist. His jaw was set. Just as Arity finally *teth¨d,* and the other whirled toward the shrinking light, Arity saw the tears spill out of Sol's eyes.

By some meaningless quirk of image memory he found himself in the Sea Garden, in the cliff below the Palace. Winter gave it a bluish-white beauty: the salt shrubs, leafless and stark, looked their best. The sea threw sequins of light up into the watery shadows of the rock grotto. Somehow his *teth¨* had gone slightly wrong and he had got sulfur in his throat. He slumped against the side wall, coughing. He was exhausted; he had not been able to sleep in over two sixdays. Not, in fact, since that twilit evening.

The smell of salt rejuvenated him like a quick glass of *morothe.* For five minutes he let himself dwell on the memory of those last, terrible moments.

Then he gathered himself and *teth¨d* back to Humi's subaqueous reception room, where he found her sitting in the same place Sol had left her, weeping softly. She was beautiful; she was blind; she was twenty-three; she was tall, and too thin; she was the Divinarch. Her cheeks were rumpled and wet.

DECENT BONES

"It's me." He squatted at her feet and took her hands in his. "I heard everything."

She did not resist his grip. "Heh. I should have guessed." She appeared to be staring out over his head, at the sea.

Didn't she feel the tension in the air? Didn't she remember everything that lay between them? Did she plan *ever* to let down her mask? Could she?

At last she said, "I know now why Sol is more of a ghostier than I ever was."

"Why is that?"

"Historically we—they—have taken murder lightly. It is a requirement of being a ghostier. And Sol still does. Being a ghostier made him immune even to his own twin sister's death, I think. I—I have always been different. I killed ghosts with a clean conscience—"

"Not your first. I was there. Don't you remember?"

"Ari." Her voice was raw—as though the reminder had peeled away a protective rind. "I'm trying to *confess!* Aren't you going to listen?"

He squeezed her hands. "Go on," he murmured, modulating his voice.

"I never entered all the way into the *imrchim* bond. I never killed another ghostier. I always held back, living half the time in Tellury Crescent and half the time in Antiprophet Square. Sol, on the other hand, has been *imrchi* right to the bone for years. He killed Beisa. And that's what's keeping him going. That strength."

She paused.

"Emni was his only weak point. Now she's gone, and he is invulnerable."

Arity thought of Sol striding out of the reception room with tears spilling from his eyes. But he didn't mention that. Instead, he argued: "You're equating strength with the ability to do murder!"

"Oh, you mistake me! I mean the ability to *recover* from the death of your loved ones. Whether you caused it, or someone else did, death is fair, no matter how unjust it seems, and one person is essentially like another. And there are always others to love." She stopped, and finished in a half whisper. "I think at the end, Sol was glad to be free of her. I, on the other hand, have always been unnaturally afraid of losing the people who make me weak."

Oh, Power. Arity's restraint almost crumbled. He wanted to take her in his arms and tell her that in his eyes, her weakness made her beautiful. But he could not bridge the gap. The incense smoke stung his skin. He said, "I think you are wrong. I believe that real strength is the ability to not lose people. To hold onto them. Even if they made you weak."

"Ari, Ari, Ari!" She smiled faintly, shook her head. "You were always so marvelously impractical. It's nice to know *somebody* hasn't changed."

He bowed his head. With that one remark of hers, the gulf between them had widened, yawning.

For a moment there, we were close . . . !

But it was an illusion. She doesn't, can't understand where I have come back from!

His thighs were starting to quiver. His head spun. He knelt down on the floor, still holding her hands, and leaned carefully against her knee. Touching her, even through the folds of green satin, soothed his body, soothed his nerves.

"What are you—I can't see! Ari, get away from me!"

He shifted away, clamped his palms onto his cheeks, rested his elbows on his knees.

She breathed harshly. A wind was getting up. Far below, far away, white horses the size of cats frolicked on the tops of the waves.

All around him, the abyss whistled.

And Pati stood in the abyss, barefoot, his toes mucky with the slime at its bottom, looking at Arity with mournful inscrutability. A hollow-eyed enigma.

Sadness gripped Arity like a rage.

"There have been moments," he said, "when I think you and I can be again as we were. Companions in weakness. Trusting. *Loving.* And at those moments, it seems to me that this ghastly deluge of racial enmity, the toppling of false gods, the arising of real ones, the destruction of the Divinarchy, your abdication, my—my killing Pati—*everything*—has all been organized by I don't know what—*Rigethe*, perhaps! to lead to one thing: our better understanding of each other."

"What appalling arrogance," Humi said.

Of course I don't really believe that is the truth!—The cold wind. Withering all arguments, withering all impulses.

"You are as arrogant as every other *auchresh*," she said. "You think the world turns around you. I used to think the same—but I've been cured of it."

"And this is one of those other moments," he said loudly, "when I know you no longer understand me at all. And I no longer understand you. I think I never did."

The sides of the abyss creaked farther apart. The wind gathered speed, a lightless wind from nowhere, howling. In the darkness Pati laughed self-deprecatingly. Arity squeezed his head in his hands and shook it in a vain attempt to dislodge the sound. With the progression of the afternoon, the sun had ceased to come into the room: all the little reflective *objets* were dulled. Humi's fur held none of the reddish glints the sun habitually gave it. Her dress didn't flatter her. That was one of the most crippling blows she had ever taken, he thought. The loss of her fashion sense. And she didn't even know about it.

"Love is a sideshow," she said harshly. "The war was ugly, but it was necessary, and for a long time it was everything. We were all caught up in it. You and I weren't the only ones whose sideshow got trampled."

It sounded as if she might be making an effort to explain. Arity put his fingers to his temples again, pressing, as if he could press out the other voices in his head.

"And now it's finished with us. It isn't over. It won't be over until everyone alive now is dead, and new babies have grown up—and probably not even then. But it's finished with *us*. We can go."

"You're trying to avoid responsibility for the part you played in it! That's not worthy of you!"

"Everyone keeps telling me that this or that or the other isn't *worthy* of me!" Anger flared. It made her momentarily beautiful. Arity wished he could appreciate it with all his being. "All I can say is what Erene said once to me. *Nothing is unworthy of me.*" She stopped, and chuckled morosely. "Make sure they write that in the histories. If there are any more histories."

"Why don't you write it in them yourself?"

"I shan't be here. I am going to visit Erene and Elicit, in Pirady. Did you know that was where they are living now? Hope is coming with me." She bowed her head.

She was so sad. So young. And completely hollowed out. He wondered if there were anything left inside her apart from theories and enmities and justifications rattling around loosely. Did she *ever* dwell on her memories?

If you have pulled a plant up and shaken it bone-clean, scraped the last traces of dirt from the crack where it grew off its roots . . .

The cruel, the terrible thing was that he, Arity, was no better than that himself. When he killed Pati, he had killed so much of himself that he could not even sum it up yet.

The gulf closed. Its vanishing left the room bright and quiet and still.

He sighed. Getting up, he sat on the arm of her chair. He slipped an arm companionably around her shoulders. "Skin and bones. You're just a satin bag of bones."

"I know I haven't—haven't been eating."

"I'm coming with you to Pirady, you know. We'll fatten you up—Erene and I between us. She's a mother now, after all."

If it had been a different kind of moment, they might both have started crying. As it was, she just rested her head against his hip. She sighed, tremblingly. "*You're* skinny, too," she said, tracing the protruding bone of his hip. "I never liked skinny men."

"Doesn't matter. I have decent bones."

She smiled: a hopeless little twitch of the lip. "If you really want to come. I don't care."

Outside and far below, afternoon was expiring gently. White horses glowed in the half light. Night seemed to sink to touch the sea, not so much a curtain as a mist: the world's thankful retreat into amnesia.

SIDESHOW

Watching Humi say her farewells, Arity thought her manner unnecessarily regal. This, after all, was not a formal abdication; *that* had gone past half a sixday ago, in a blur of wine and improvised finery.

Humi stooped and kissed Fiamonina's little furry cheek. She straightened up and moved her hand across the air like a benediction. "Power be with you," she said to the group assembled on the newly built stairs into the Palace courtyard.

From now on, Aneisneida had said to Arity as they watched the workers hammer pegs into the joists of the steps, *the sedans will have to enter the stables through the Hare Gate. I will construct an arched walkway from the stables to the Palace doors, so my ladies don't get their hair wet if they arrive when it is raining. But the courtyard itself will be a plaza with a fountain and a performing space for public use.* Her face shone.

She doesn't understand, Arity thought. *Her business won't be with building fountains. It will be winning more of the people than her husband or her father-in-law can. It'll be about promising the people the good things they used to take for granted, and slithering out of the promises when the ships don't come.*

But maybe his guesses were too dark. Maybe there would be no infighting. One could not forget Sol, stewing away in the Crescent with Mory and Tris; already there were rumors of rebuilding the Chalice, and screams in the dead of night. But these things had been run of the mill for the old Crescent. And Arity had never found Sol as objectionable as other people seemed to. Especially now there was that double link between them. A life spared, a woman shared. They had never spoken plainly of it, and they probably never would. But the point was that Arity knew Sol had scruples. It was quite possible that that *look* of his, the look that could chill the blood in your veins, was merely technique.

So Arity hoped. And a few huge flakes of snow sparkled in the sunlight as they tumbled out of the sky. One landed on Fiamorina's head. She giggled and patted at it.

Aneisneida came down from the steps, bringing her child with her. While Fia squatted, one arm stretched over her head, and scraped industriously at the cobbles, Aneisneida talked to Humi. Her teeth glowed, offset by her light green fur. On the steps, Hope was speaking with Gold Dagger, Soderingal, and a newly washed trio of young Deltans—Gold Dagger's henchmen. By Aneisneida's grace, the crime lord had been made a *real* lord. Lord Dagger! It sounded like a tavern singer's stage name.

Hope still wore *kere* clothes, and like Arity, she still carried her knife. She leaned back and stuck her hands in her pockets as Soderingal expressed himself eloquently into her face. Wrinkling her nose, she dragged one hand out of her pocket and indicated the cobblestones. She was modulating her voice well, so that Arity couldn't hear what she was saying; but from the way Gold Dagger mimed scrubbing a window, he guessed they were talking about getting the bloodstains off the street.

This was where the second biggest clash of the battle had taken place, of course. Was there anything in the *breideiim* tale which said that where blood had been spilled nothing would grow for a hundred years? The blood still blackened the cracks between the cobbles, and stained the dented walls of the courtyard. The sprigs of grass around the bases of the walls were brown. But then, it had not rained. Winter, and no rain. Was that usual? He could not remember.

He turned to survey the mansions on the other side of the street. Somebody had hung brocade curtains in a downstairs window. Could it be Aneisneida's ladies?

Humi could feel Anei's closeness like the heat from a bonfire. Somewhere along the road, she had become as sensitive to humans as if they were *auchresh*. She fought the urge to lean back.

"I feel so *free,*" Aneisneida was saying intensely.

"What do you mean?" Humi put everything she had into her smile.

"I don't know!" Aneisneida laughed. "No, Fia, don't eat that! Stand up straight! Gods, Humi, this child. A fine Divinarch she'll make if she can't keep her hands to herself!"

Humi laughed. "Don't worry about Fia! She's both precocious and well-mannered—and that's rare in a child so young!"

"Do you really think so?" In Anei's voice, Humi heard a mother's pride—and fear that her pride might stop her from seeing her child clearly. Silently, Humi congratulated her for understanding her own instincts.

"I do. But please school her well. An all-around education is so important."

"Ah." Humi could almost hear Anei's false-ribs squeaking as she swelled
up like an excited cat. "Do you know what I have arranged, Humi? We
finalized it just this morning. I am going to apprentice her to Sol. She'll live
at home, but she will be trained as a ghostier. I remember existing in the
shadow of the ghostiers, when I was a councillor . . . gods, I was miserable! And thoroughly aware of my own incompetence. I am convinced now
that there is no better school for a diplomat than Tellury Crescent. It will
cement the ties between Marshtown and the Palace—which your lovely
Erene, gods rest her soul, instituted—and Fia will avoid potential enemies
by growing up alongside the future ghostiers. What did Sol say they would
be? There is a word for it . . ."

"*Imrchim,*" Humi murmured.

"Yes, that was it! Sol and Lady Glissade and Lord Sepal and I spoke
frankly about these things! None of us want to destroy the little that we
have left through . . . misunderstandings."

Humi felt a smile cracking her impassive mask. She had almost forgotten
what it felt like, having someone out think her. "Anei, you're a marvel. It's a
masterstroke. I would never have thought of it."

"Oooh," Aneisneida said. She embraced Humi tightly. Fia didn't make a
sound. Humi guessed she was eating dirt. Her mother smelled overpower-
ingly of old perfume—probably the last she had been able to dig out from
the last old trinket box in the city. "I *shall* miss you, Humi!" she sputtered.
"Isn't it odd how we never used to be friends?"

A snowflake fell on Humi's exposed nape, below the knob of her pulled-
back hair. No colder than her skin, no drier than her eyeballs. "Terribly
strange!" she said. "But I'm sure we had our reasons at the time—"

The apostate flamen spoke eloquently. Hope had heard all his sentiments
before, and so probably had the ragged audience but they were hanging on
every word. Hope stood beside Ari and Humi at the back of the little
crowd, in the shade of a mansion with high, broken cornices. The apostate
had set up his podium in the open, at a crossroads of the palace district
streets. A month ago, he would not have lasted ten minutes here. His voice
had been faintly audible as they walked away from the Palace. They had
wandered over to hear what kind of thing an apostate would say in public—
whether it would be inflammatory, or at the very least thought-provoking.
The patchwork beast of the crowd swayed and writhed. Whenever the
flamen paused to make a dramatic point, they hummed:

"Speak aright, Godsbrother."

"In the name of the Power."

The Godsbrother smote the air constantly with his heavy hands as he spoke. His words were unpolished, unpremeditated, and occasionally embarrassing; but they carried a certain heartfelt conviction.

"All given to melodrama, these apostates," Hope muttered.

"And trusting in the ineffable correctness of the Power! We may forgive our old masters for their atrocities against us. We may open our hearts to our new masters, and fairly . . . *fairly* . . . *!* reward their benevolence toward us with trust or punish their hubris with uprising. For now that the rule of the *serbalim* is over—"

"*Serbalim?*" Arity hissed, advancing his lips to her ear. "How does he know . . . ?"

Hope shook her head. "An ex-Hand. A renegade. Anyone. I don't doubt that one thing we *will* have to resign ourselves to, now, is the loss of *auchraug* as a private language."

"Maybe we can come up with a new one."

The flamen was in full spate. ". . . I say, now that the rules of the *auchresh* is over, it will be possible to divide the rule of the body from the rule of the spirit. The task of governing belongs to those who lust after *secular* power. Be they *auchresh* or mortal! And this is all it has *ever* been. But the rule of the spirit belongs to the Power. And *the Power is unknowable.*"

"Say on, Godsbrother."

"All we can know is its attributes. It creates the Balance anew every day. And the Balance will *ever* weigh down on the side of benevolence, goodness, sympathy, and renewal. Yea! And death!"

"Yea," murmured the crowd. "And death."

Most of them had sunk into a kind of exalted reverie, stilled by the flamen's words. Just like every generation of Hands' sheep since the Wanderer, Hope thought. For them, the apostate's theology, though it might subvert every precept of religion—falsely or enduringly, who could tell?—need do no more than justify the immense changes in their lives. All they wanted was to be assured that the deaths of their loved ones had not been meaningless. They *wanted* to be dragged from the side of the grave of "If only." They wanted to be exhorted not to give in to apathy, now that the streets were rusty with blood and parched grass straggled along the doorsteps of the palace district where maids had once scrubbed twice a day.

And no traditional flamens, with their insistence on gods who had proved undependable, could have met their need. Only the apostates would be listened to now. This man altered old formulas enough that his listeners did not intellectually recognize them; yet his concepts were not in fact provocative. He dared not leave out the Balance. *That* was essential even to Hope's conception of existence. Without the necessity not just of momentous actions but of slight ones, what point was there to *anything?* The people needed desperately to be reassured of that necessity.

Taking that into account, Hope knew she would have been churlish to criticize apostasy. But she *felt* churlish. Ghastly images drifted just under the surface of the day. Blood was seeping from the old sword slice on her ribs: she could feel it trickling down her side. Her stomach felt sour with cynicism.

The trouble was that once the flamen admitted divine justice—even if he called it something else—his doctrine was the same as that with which everyone here had grown up. Only its focus was altered, from the *auchresh* to the Power. And after all, most *auchresh* had always denied they were the judges in the divine court. At most, its watchdogs.

"*Rigethe,*" she said to Arity. "Do you think it can satisfy them for long?"

"The mortals?"

"I don't think they are disaffected enough to keep from trying to embrace it. And of course you can't embrace *Rigethe.* It slips away. You have to hate and distrust and revere it—the idea of it—all at once. And I don't think they will be able to keep their distance from it, the way we can. They need a headier belief."

Arity rubbed his chin. "But hatred, distrust, reverence . . . isn't that what they used to feel for us?"

"Mmm . . ." She hadn't thought of it that way. "The more *awake* mortals, perhaps. The nobles. The councillors. But not these!" She gestured at the backs of the crowd. Most of them looked like refugees. A few wore soldier's garb. Some wore the more countrified dress of Marshtown. "They *loved* us! That's why they need this playacting Godsbrother so badly now."

"Well then, perhaps the pursuit of apostasy will force every last mortal to wake up," Arity said. His mouth quirked, but his eyes were tired. "Awareness. Investigation and comprehension of the impulses. That would be a noble goal for any religion, wouldn't it? As a matter of fact I could do with some of that comprehension right now."

She looked more closely at him, and modulated her voice until her lips scarcely moved. "Do you mean—" She jerked her chin toward Humi.

Ari nodded, and grimaced. "Do you see? I think that if one completely understands one's impulses, one ceases to feel them."

"Power, Ari."

Whetted beams of sunlight drove down the street. Blood trickled from windows, dripping off the sills onto the Deltans' heads. Blood everywhere. Hope's eyes hurt.

"And let us keep this in mind"—the Godsbrother brayed suddenly, at top volume—"as we turn and go forth to rebuild our city! To the delight of the Power and the appeasement of the Balance!"

The crowd had been growing more and more restless. When he finally released them, throwing up his arms and then dropping them by his sides, bowing his head (a marvelous bit of stage business, Hope noted), the moans of approval swelled to a crescendo, then broke in a cheer.

"Praise the Power!" the Godsbrother shouted. "No mortal is worthy of your adulation—least of all, your ignorant servant! Praise the Power!"

Arity's hand rested protectively on Humi's neck. She slumped loosely against him. Throughout the sermon, Hope had noticed she was as still as a stone, and that her eyes gleamed. Tears of rage, or real feeling? Or just artifice, triggered by years of crying at the proper events?

She leaned over and touched the girl's arm. Ari seemed ambivalent about their reconciliation—but her own reaction to the news had astonished her. She was saddened just as much as she was overjoyed. And in the black depths of that sadness, she sensed selfish, wrong emotions, not to be touched even with the tip of a finger.

"Shall we go?" she said. "You wanted to come and listen, but I think we've heard all there is to hear. There are clouds coming up."

Humi shook herself. "I would like to talk to the Godsbrother," she said clearly.

"*Hume*—" Arity expostulated irritatedly, then cut himself short.

"Would you lead me, Hopie?" Humi placed one hand on Hope's arm and walked fearlessly out of the shadow of the building where they had stood. Hope, skipping to get ahead of her, tried not to flinch in the sunlight. The crowd had dispersed, but the ripe stench generated by the gathering of Deltans still hung in the air. She and Humi attached themselves to a short queue of men and women. People stared at her full-size wings, their golden tips brushing her boots. She had sickened of cloaks, so today she let her wings poke through slits in her tunic. Already she wished she hadn't. Though there had been a couple of renegades in the crowd, none of them looked as obviously *auchresh* as she.

Finally their turn came to speak. The flamen sat on the edge of the overturned fish crate that had served as a podium. Close up, he was not a large man. His jowls rested meatily on his collarbone, and his arms were eel-like—all muscle and no bone. His face hung down from his salt crystals, vertically creased with tiredness. He had pale blue fur. He could have been Veretrean, Icelandic, or even Piradean. The leman holding a metal cup of water to his hand, waiting patiently for him to take hold of it, was unusually mature—a young man of at least twenty-two or -three, with arms like a sailor's.

A strange pair!

The flamen smiled up at Humi. He appeared not to *sense* Hope; or at least, not to *sense* her as anything more than mortal. "Why didn't you have them gather in a circle?" Humi said bluntly.

The flamen's face registered surprise; then he laughed. "There wasn't room. I do agree it's more communal. And more traditional. Next time. Any more questions, my dear?"

Hope's heart hurt when she saw how Humi softened—like stale bread under a drop of water. Then Humi shook herself. "No," she said in the same hard, jagged voice, "I liked your sermon. That is what I wanted to tell you."

"Any merit my words may have is that which they produce in your heart. But remember the rule, child: No living thing, be it mortal, *auchresh*, or flamen, is infallible. Everything I've told you today may be wrong. But this is how the Power chooses to inspire me. And *that* is all that matters." The flamen shrugged engagingly. "If you are inspired too, then speak accordingly. There is nothing that separates us, you and I, except the miracles. And *those* I will only employ insofar as they benefit you."

"A well-rehearsed disclaimer," Humi said. "You cover all eventualities."

The flamen gave a puzzled smile. Somehow Humi's tone of voice had made the observation into a compliment. But he was too clever not to see that it was really an insult.

The leman stared at Hope. His honest, snubby features were covered with white Archipelagun fur, but he had blazing red hair such as Hope had never seen, not on the battlefields nor in the cities. She shifted under his scrutiny.

"I am Godsbrother Quest, my children," the Godsbrother said. "And who are you, that I may address you by your names when we meet next?"

"We won't—" Humi was replying stiffly, when Hope interrupted. Giving Humi a little shove, she said:

"I am the erstwhile Maiden, Godsbrother. And this is the erstwhile Divinarch."

Humi muddied painfully. Hope almost wished she could allow the girl to hide her identity. But that wouldn't be good for her—not in the long run.

"Humility Garden."

"Ohhhh!" the leman exclaimed. With a quick, careful movement he put down the cup of water and sprang upright. Hope felt his hostility. She yanked Humi backwards, keeping a mask of pleasantness in place. The leman stopped at the sight of her divine inscrutability. Grudgingly, he bowed. "My flamen . . ." he said. "My *last* flamen was her sister."

"Oh, Power," Humi said. "It's not true. It's not. Tell me what her name was!" Her hand seemed to press into Hope's elbow like a brand. "Describe her to me!"

The young man narrowed his eyes at Humi. "I don't think you *want* to believe me, Divinarch. But it's true. You killed her, indirectly. So you ought to know the truth. Then you can choose whether to believe me, or not. Her name was Thankfulness. I called her Thani. She was the devoutest loyalist you could ever hope to see. I loved her for it. I loved her for her strength."

He could have been any commoner with a grudge against Humi, some scraps of inside information, and a flair for cruelty. But Hope understood in a flash that the brittleness of his voice was not designed to hurt Humi, but to stop his own pain from breaking him open. This *Thani* . . . she was real. She was that sister of Humi's who—how cruel the Balance could be!— had tried to kill Arity five years ago. Humi had helped her to escape, then.

"Describe her," Humi rattled. Brimstone swelled into the air, melting the falling snowflakes, so that for a second it appeared to be raining, and Arity materialized at her other side, taking her arm as if to hold her. She shook him off. "Describe her, I say, Archipelagan!"

"She . . ." The boy closed his eyes. He was not as old as he looked, Hope saw. Probably only seventeen or eighteen. His Archipelagan accent was muted, but still recognizable. "She had very light hair. Sunbleached, not natural. And blond fur that looked so rich, when she was healthy, because of its dark roots."

Humi pushed her fingers into the thick fur on her neck. The ends were tawny, like the backs of her fingers, the roots were darker.

"I can't remember her eyes. I saw them just once before her salt pilgrimage. But I think they were gray. Maybe black. Like yours, blind woman." He sighed. "She was generous, and loving. More than her calling asked, I mean. She was as thin as a thread. She pushed herself and pushed herself until she didn't even have the strength to eat. Then she would get ill and not eat anyhow. Gods." He shook his red-tousled head angrily. "The struggles I used to go through to get a little food down her—"

"She was always a stocky child," Humi said.

"You haven't *known* her since she was a child!" The boy shook his head. "I don't even know why I am telling you this! I shouldn't have started!"

"You are speaking aright, Gete," the apostate Godsbrother Quest murmured. "You are evening the Balance. No need to stop."

"Yes, *indeed* I thank you!" Humi said. "You will never know how much it means to me to know—"

The Archipelegan turned on them, red hair blazing. "To know *what?* That she is *dead?*"

Hope flinched from the full frontal blaze of his grief. Arity flinched too— she saw him physically pull back, as if he were going to be attacked.

Such unwieldy, devastating emotions mortals fermented in their hearts! Razors of passion, cutting them apart inside.

One could only profess flippant incomprehension.

Because the other possibility was to envy them.

Humi spoke in a measured voice. "To know that my last hope of even a little good surviving this year's inferno was an illusion. For that, I can only thank you."

"*Power,* Humi," Arity wailed softly. He tried again to pull her against him, but she resisted. Godsbrother Quest got to his feet. He was the most obvious figure of authority in this muddle, from the spectacle of which the Deltans had fled, like servants slipping out of the room when milord and milady have a tiff. Hope noted that the flamen kept clear of his trembling leman as he reminded them, "Humility, remember . . . the Balance. The good which survives the 'inferno,' as you called it, the good which *stems* from it, doesn't have to be restricted to you. Thani's death fulfilled some other necessity."

Humi said, not to him in particular. "Fuck off. My sister is *dead.*"

"She died in my arms," the leman said. If Hope had not been able to see otherwise, she would have been convinced he was trying to hurt Humi as much as possible. "In the battle for the Folly. At the end, she recanted everything. Everything. Though I can't be sure"—he bared his teeth—"I couldn't even keep her alive long enough . . . long enough—"

"She saw the truth," Humi whispered.

"I couldn't even convince her that I *loved* her!" For a moment he looked a great deal like Godsbrother Quest as he rocked on the balls of his feet. "There has to be something beyond. That was when I went to look for Godsbrother Quest. I had met him before. He had a leman then. Avi was killed in Chrumetown."

"You," Humi hissed. "My sister's leman. An apostate."

"I plan to go home to the Archipelago to make my pilgrimage. I have a friend there who will care for me, and he may even want to join me on my travels. Though not as a leman." His eyes rested on Arity. Then he looked at Hope, with the same air of seeing *past* her—as if the very core of her being was not enough to distract his attention from the distance. His fury was concentrated, contained. She felt her heart stop as she saw the future in his eyes. Bluer than the sky.

Humi was shaking, leaning heavily on Hope and Arity. "Did she speak of me at all?" Her voice was hoarse. "Did she hate me?"

"I could never tell. I know she thought of you. You were one of the burdens she could never shake off. The other—the other was her conviction that she was responsible for her Godsbrother's death."

Humi moaned. Arity snapped at the leman. "You could have spared her *that*."

The leman turned and looked at him. His clear blue eyes held all the anger in the world, compressed into two points.

Hope had to take control of the situation. She had to stop this. It was turning into torture. "I agree with Ari. That's enough! When we stopped to listen to your sermon we were on our way . . . on our way! It would have been better if we'd never come!"

Humi lifted her face. Tears were coursing down her cheeks. Hope was frankly appalled at how completely she seemed to have lost control of herself. Arity hissed through his fangs. "Sister or no sister, we have to get her away, or the tales will never stop circulating."

Distancing oneself from them was the only way

The only way

"What's your name?" she asked the leman.

"Gete," he allowed.

"And you can call me Hope, and this is Arity." She turned on her heel, pulling the others around with her. "Good-bye."

Humi twisted her face over her shoulder. "Don't ever go near the Crescent without your flamen, redhead!" She smiled horribly. "My friend Sol would make a ghost out of you . . . just as quick as *that!*" She snapped her fingers. "So would Mory . . . so would Tris . . ."

"On the count of three," Arity whispered, rather desperately. "Around the corner. Anywhere. The Folly! Just outside the gate—"

Only as they *teth¨d*, in the instant of nothingness, did it occur to Hope to wonder how Humi had guessed Gete had such red, red hair. Humi was no ordinary blind woman; Hope had known that for a long time; but what had made the boy visible to her extrasensual perception?

ELPECHIM

They ended up, by some fluke of Hope's imaging, just outside the fences of the Folly's grounds. Beyond the twisted fences, the gardens rolled downhill, denuded humps and hillocks. In many places island rock showed through the soil. The barrenness of it insulted the senses. Every time Arity thought he had gotten used to it, it slapped him in the eyes again, forcing him to look.

"Let's get out of here," Hope said abruptly.

"No," Humi said. "Are we near the Folly? Good. I want . . ." She shivered, and brought her head up proudly. "I want to walk in the gardens."

Hope looked at Arity. He shrugged. They counted to each other and *teth˝d* over the flattened fence, into the devastation.

The snow fluttered silently onto the brown earth. The sky was clouding over. Arity envisioned the thin, huge, icy-lipped maw of winter sinking its fangs into the ground. Icelandic weather in Royalland.

But Pati had chopped down all the trees. And maybe the *breideim* tale about the spilling of blood accounted for the parching and withering of what scraps of greenery were left.

Scraps of cloth fluttered from the twigs of the broken saplings. The Folly loomed silently. The huge windows of the lower stories gaped with broken glass. Many of the upper windows had been broken, too.

"Looters," Hope said.

From outside, the broken windows gave the Folly an appearance of having succumbed to some dreadful pock-marking disease which had crept upward from the ground. Hope walked with her hand through Humi's arm, lips pursed, holding her wings at a fastidious angle above the ground. This must be worse for her, Arity thought, than for him or Humi. Humi was walking with her eyes half closed and a look of intense concentration on her face. Arity attempted not to glance at her every other moment. He knew she could feel it.

He stepped over a fallen log and his foot sank into a partially decayed *auchresh* corpse. It lay curled in a fetal position. Since he had stepped on its face, it was no longer grinning. He just managed not to yell. "Damn it," he said softly, and pulled away from the females, trying to wipe the foul stuff off his boot on the earth.

"What a revolting smell," Hope said, wrinkling her nose.

Humi sniffed. "Why don't you just take your boots off? Leave them here. It's not as though you need them."

She was right. A short distance away, a wooden half tub stood bottom up. Must have held water for Humi's troops. How had she managed the frentic planning, the ability to think of a dozen things at once, all that was necessary to organize a war more or less singlehanded? He sat down on the tub to unbuckle his clumsy footgear. "Just as long as I don't step in anything else," he joked. The gesture seemed all too significant.

The dusty-damp earth, with its tiny cold wet patches, felt uncommonly good under his toes. Resilient. His heel talons dug in, providing a satisfying *connection* with the ground. The cold traveled up through his body, clearing his head.

A little later, without a word, Hope took her boots off and left them standing.

They circumabulated the Folly.

Nothing moved except a few stray blades of grass. The snowflakes fell a long way apart, slowly.

"I went to such expense to have those windows put in," Hope said regretfully. "A Power-damned expense."

"I never even went inside," Humi said. "After all the times you said we'd go."

"Do you want me to show you around?" Hope brightened. "It's probably been looted more thoroughly than any other building in the city! But the structure of the place is really the thing. Some of the inner chambers—"

"No," Humi said. "Thank you, but I don't think I could appreciate it as you meant it to be appreciated."

"I didn't forget you were *blind,*" Hope said. "I meant you could touch the walls, feel the ghosts and the furnishings and ornaments! If there are any left—"

"I know!" Humi faced her across Arity. There was something unnerving in the way her eyes remained wide and blank. Unhuman, un*auchresh*, in fact rather animal. "I meant that the *circumstances* under which I would have to *enter* your monument to the old days, namely my sister's being *dead*, and my having failed in what I tried to do, would keep me from concentrating on the architectural merits of the edifice! Am I not allowed to *mean* what I *say?*"

No, Arity thought. *Not anymore.*

"The privilege of unpleasant memories is not yours alone!" Hope said angrily. "Why did you want to come here, then? Why are you putting us all through this?"

Humi wrenched her hands out of Arity's and Hope's arms and hugged herself. "If you must know, I was hoping to find my sister's body!"

"Morbidity doesn't help anyone!" Arity interrupted.

"Oh, Humi," Hope said. She pulled Humi across Arity, and wrapped her arms around her.

They swayed to and fro in the middle of the empty battlefield, and Humi started crying.

"She was my responsibility," Arity heard her sob into Hope's shoulder. "She was my baby sister. I wish I had cared for her better—then she might have married and had children! She might have been allowed to stay at home! I know that damned man Transcendence chose her because he thought she looked as though she wasn't loved! Power, Hope, do you realize how *badly* all of us Gardens who dared to venture out of the saltside have ended up? Our story could be the stuff of a bad joke! A punch line! A ghost . . . a slain soldier . . . a dead flamen . . . and a broken-down diplomat!"

"Don't sell yourself so short," Arity said in irritation, but neither of them listened.

"My mother must have learned I was still alive. I can't hope *that* kind of news failed to reach Westshine. But there's a real chance she'll never know Thani died. I pray she never finds out. Oh, Power!" Tears drowned her voice.

Arity had seldom heard her speak of her mother. It put his mind at rest on one thing, anyhow: she did not contemplate going home to Domesdys.

Where *did* she contemplate going?

Did she have any idea?

It looked increasingly as if *he* would have to make that decision.

Hope patted Humi's back and whispered endearments. The golden fringes of the *iu's* lashes were wet.

Arity folded his arms. The snow was falling more thickly now. He gazed up at the top of the Folly, where it opened into the sky like a flower. The ridiculous little cupola was invisible from here. This huge building wasn't going to last forever: Hope had built for effect, not endurance. He could see the early signs of deterioration in the way the overhanging floors of the topmost stories bellied downward.

THE RETURN OF THE GOOD THINGS

"The balls at Divaring Below have been delightful," Broken Bird said. "Sugar Bird's Foundling Uali has returned from human country and set up house. He has brought a most eclectic entourage with him, and he seems likely to be a natural host."

The last time Arity had seen Broken Bird, at Rose Eye's estate in Rimmear, with Pati, she had seemed tired of existence itself. Now the very wrinkles in her shriveled blue face danced with animation. She sat on Bronze Water's lap, her little legs swinging as she turned her benevolent regard on one member of the party after another. "You really should consider coming to Divaring with us, Hope! You would be quite a celebrity. Arity—well, perhaps it would not be so advisable for you to return! Not just yet. There is a little ill will fomenting around your name—at the best houses you would be, if not *endangered*, certainly not an honored guest."

"*Someone* has to be blamed for everything," Arity said without rancor. "And after all, I did kill him!" He laughed, turning the stark statement into an outrageous sally. "No, I don't contemplate returning to Divaring—or to the salt at all—anytime soon."

Bronze Water stroked Broken Bird's thigh indulgently. "Just as well. If you were assassinated, you would upstage us all!" He turned to Hope. His demeanor was genial, but he was evidently getting down to brass tacks. "What about it, Maiden?"

Hope sat in the corner of the hearth, holding Erene and Elicit's little daughter Artle. The fire's red glow danced over her. Since Broken Bird and Bronze Water arrived that afternoon, somehow having learned where Hope, Arity, and Humi had hidden, the *iu* had been unusually reserved. Arity hoped she knew she did not have to respond. The atmosphere was social, not political.

But she did answer. "Bird, I'm sorry. Humi and I appreciate the work

you did on our behalf during the war." ("We do," Humi murmured from
her seat in the shadows.) "I *should* oblige you. I know. But I can't."

"Can't—*why?*" Bronze Water said. "Are you afraid of finding Heaven
changed, my dear? It *has* changed, with the return of so many Hands, and
the influx of young men and women from human country—but this has all
led to a sort of *reawakening,* which means Divaring is more itself than ever
before! Old Divaring Peak glitters at night like a girl in a new set of jewels.
Heterogeneity is the craze; you'll hardly see a couple on the lakeshore who
aren't of different races."

"And if the rebels are so celebrated now—aren't you two rather on the
outs for misleading your people before the war?" Elicit asked.

Elicit did not comprehend the issue of status among the *auchresh,* Arity
thought. He did not understand how the title of *er-serbalim* protected Broken Bird and Bronze Water from anything that might befall them. Even
from ridicule. The ex-ghostier sat beside Erene on the floor, in the shadows, holding their son Xib on his lap. Erene had one arm around him and
one around Humi. A slack-furred woman with a discernible belly, well into
middle age, she might easily have been the mother of the lanky girl leaning
against her side.

It had been about six years since Arity last saw Erene, but motherhood
seemed to have aged her twenty. The beautiful, forcefully urbane senior
ghostier of Golden Antelope's court could have been a different woman. Yet
she evidently felt at ease with herself. She had exhibited more kindness in a
sixday than in all the years Arity had sparred with her in Ellipse. When the
trio arrived in the clearing in the woods, tired and wet with snow, even
before Erene greeted Humi she had thrown her arms around Arity, whispering, "I thought we would never see you again, dearheart."

He had almost wept. Shocking.

And the children were adorable, of course. Like all children. Hope was
hardly able to keep her hands off them, hugging, petting, spoiling them
with games and indulgences. They melted her. Erene said she would make
herself indispensable if she didn't watch out. In the last sixday, Erene
herself had got three times as much weaving done as usual; she said she
had time to make things instead of just mending them.

Make what?

Arity observed her covertly. Pine-needle baskets. Festival clothes. Little,
pretty, useless *objets* of yarn and wood. There was not a ghost in the house.
Except, of course, the ghost Humi had brought, that white seagull with its
charge of murky emotion that could knock you down at a touch. Erene had
said she could not keep it in the house because it would chill the rooms too
much. Elicit ignored her, installing it high over the head of the big bed in

the third room. Arity had made a point of going to him afterward and
thanking him.

Resin-flavored smoke bulged into the room as a puff of wind came down
the chimney. Bronze Water was considering Elicit's question, but not seriously. Smiling, he rubbed his jowls. "No one can accuse us of hypocrisy,
Elicit! We do not think we were wrong to promote isolationism. We only
changed sides for the sake of political expediency."

"Oh," Hope whispered.

"Let us just say, events have not yet proved that those who disagreed
with us were right. We stand by our theories."

"And I think that our steadfastness earns us admiration, rather than disapproval," Broken Bird said immodestly. "We maintain that isolation would
also have been a viable alternative. And at the same time, we accept defeat
with grace, and maintain a perfectly—perfectly! courteous demeanor toward the humans who have moved to Divaring." She expected her explanation to be taken in good faith, Arity saw. It was only now that she introduced a note of humor. "Why, some of those boys are quite delicious. Even
the older ones . . . mmm! Don't you agree with me, Bronze? And once
we have taught them how to dress properly . . ."

"But you're lying," Hope said. She sounded really upset. Why oh why
now, Hopie? Arity thought wearily. "You did not flip-flop for the sake of
political expediency! You knew your beliefs were wrong! You affect unpopu-
lar attitudes now, because your status protects you, and you think it gives
you an interesting reputation! You will do anything not to get left behind by
the quickly moving chariot of society!"

Everyone, including the three humans, turned shocked stares on her.
Hope put her hand to her face. The little girl, Artle, reached up and tried to
pull it down.

"Well, I'm sorry if I told the truth!" Hope said.

Humi said, "But aren't you going back to Divaring Below, Hope? And
won't you, too, be just as much of a social hypocrite?"

"No. I'm not going back. I'm sick of glitter and games." Hope pulled
Artle fiercely to her. The little girl wriggled. But she must have felt the
tension in the air, for she didn't make a sound.

"I'm staying with Erene and Elicit. For the time being. Since Shine is
quite firmly entrenched in Domesdys . . . and they will need help . . .
when spring comes . . ."

Artle looked around the gathering. "I'm glad," she squeaked.

Bronze Water laughed, then stopped when he saw no one else was.

Arity caught a movement in the shadows. Elicit disengaged himself from
Erene. He brushed past Arity's chair, his coattails releasing a waft of the

scent of the dried flowers Erene kept in the clothes chest, and gently put
his daughter aside. He lifted Hope to her feet. She was more than three
times Elicit's age in years, but with her smooth face and slender form she
could have been his daughter as easily as Humi could have been. Gold
shadows rippled in the folds of her wings. Elicit said, ostensibly to her, but
really to the whole gathering: "I asked you to stay, and I'll stand by it.
Erene agrees with me. When you came, we realized how empty our house
has been since our gods left us. Of the two who used to live here, Keef is
dead, and Shine is the governor of Domesdys. *You*, on the other hand, are
alive. You are a reminder of everything we did not remember we had lost."

Broken Bird resettled herself in Bronze's arms. "Well, *elpechu*, I do hope
you will reconsider," she said in *auchraug*. She sounded ruffled. "It may be
congenial here, but nobody can make such beautiful gowns as they do in
Fewarauw! I should be surprised if there is even a decent beautician within
a hundred leagues!" Her voice took on a vicious edge. "Soon you will look
like a perfect *salthirre*."

Arity and Humi walked through the trickling woods. The evergreens
fluttered in the darkness. Birds hummed fragments of melodies which, had
they been completed, would have shattered the world like glass.

Arity was barefoot. His breeches were soaked to the knees. Water
dripped down his neck. Humi's shoulders were cold under his arm. He had
asked her to come walking with specific things in mind, but he could not
broach the subject.

They climbed another of the many slopes that comprised the forest.
Above, a faint light slipped through the trees.

"Surely it can't be dawn already?" Arity said.

"We're coming to a cliff. I can feel it in the air. Look out," Humi said
sharply.

And indeed, the trees fell away, and they found themselves on the top of
a precipice.

Arity took a deep breath, then guided her slowly to the grassy edge.

Impossible to tell how far down the sea was. Little white curls broke in
stately motion on a scrap of beach. The dawn would come, eventually, from
behind the trees; but the sky was paler over the sea than anywhere else.
Starlight shone through the thin cloud cover, down onto the water. Humi's
face looked ghostly and stiff, like the stretched mask of a dead animal.

He turned from her to gaze out at the ocean. Thousands of leagues of it.
Royalland did not extend this far south. The closest land in this direction
was the South Reach of the Archipelago. "Where are we going to go?"

She let out a long sigh, as if she had been waiting for him to ask. "I have given it some thought. But I don't know. I can't seem to imagine any farther ahead than this."

"We can't stay here. Not now that Hope has declared she's going to. It would look mean for us to try to share Erene and Elicit's hospitality—and their lives—when it's her who has claimed them!"

"I know. I know. And it will be best if we go soon. Erene and I love each other—but it'd be fatal for us to try to live together. We have discovered that very quickly. In no time, it would be Tellury Crescent all over again."

"Well, then"—he sliced the grass with his toe talons—"there are other places we'd be welcome."

"I can't go—"

"Back to the city? I didn't ask you to. At least, not now." He nudged her, trying to make her smile.

"Not ever!"

"What about the salt?" He dropped into *auchraug* without thinking about it. "I know that in most Heavens I would be an outcast. It'd be a miserable existence. But I shouldn't mind going back to Wind Gully. I'm pretty sure Cheris and Oak would take us in. Pati wasn't really popular there, the *ruthyalim* envied him too much—and they have longer memories there than they do in Rimmear, or Tearka, or Divaring—"

"No! I couldn't bear that!" The gutturals and trills of *auchraug*, on her lips, sent unexpected shivers down his back. "I used so much to love the ghostly way the salt forest looks at night. And the storms boiling up the gully. And your *ruthyalim* themselves, with their horns and wings and tattery clothes. Wind Gully Heaven *was* heaven for me, Ari, did you never notice that? An escape from reality into strangeness so . . . so complete . . . I could understand nothing about it except that it was beautiful. I don't want to ruin those memories. If I go back, *blind*—"

"Your last illusions would crumble." *You would have to learn the hard way that there is very little underneath the beauty. That* auchresh *treat profundity like a dead enemy—a corpse to be shredded and then laughed at. Is that why I want to go back?*

The very idea chilled him.

"But you must go!" she said in a cold little voice, still speaking *auchraug*. "I shan't have you sacrificing yourself for me."

Rain began to fall, fat droplets oozing from the clouds, tumbling down and splatting on the ground, on their faces.

Arity squeezed her tigher.

"*Irissu,*" he said quietly, "if I went without you, I would be miserable. And if I went with you, I would lose you. The salt isn't part of me anymore, and I can't get it back. Let's not speak of it again."

"Oh, Power," she muttered. The rain plastered her fur to her skull. She stared straight ahead, blindly. "Why do you love me? Why, why, why?"

A soft, pervasive, susurrating roar identified itself as the sound of the rain on the sea. The ground exuded a wet, earthwormy smell.

"I want to know. I fail to—to understand it."

"Do you understand *me*?"

"N-no. And I don't think I ever will. But I'm *trying*—I'm *trying*—" She was close to tears.

At one time an admission like that would have sent him wheeling away from her. But that had been too soon after Pati. He had rocked for a long time in the waves of that passion which had grown all the more terrible as it atrophied. Now, despair just shivered briefly through him and vanished. He kissed her on the mouth. It was the first time he had touched her since their reunion. Her lips were soft and icy. "You have to stop trying to understand. Give up. That's my conclusion, my dear. Just stop understanding."

"Ohhh. Oh, Power!" She shuddered as if it did not bear thinking about. Quickly, she said in a caressing voice: "Do you remember how we used to *teth*˜ to Veretry, to have some time to ourselves, and it would always be raining? I came to love the rain. It meant something like Wind Gully Heaven meant to me. This rain is different—but it brings those days back. I remember . . ."

He kissed her again. This time she kissed him back, hesitantly. They moved closer together and she shut her eyes, pressing herself against him. Momentarily she drew back. "Gods, Ari, you're all covered in scars."

"So are you." He pulled her close again. Either through heat transferral or excitement, her flesh was warming up.

She giggled. She actually giggled. "But yours are on the outside."

"Wait till you see me naked." He cursed. "Damn! I didn't mean that!"

"I know you didn't," she said. "Anyhow, I'm used to it. It just means you aren't guarding your tongue around me—which is a measure of trust I don't get from many other people."

Her movements as she rubbed against him became languid. After a minute, in a half-wondering voice, she said, "I shouldn't mind going back *there*."

"Where?"

"Veretry."

"*Veretry?*"

"Can you take us there?"

"Not now." He kissed her eyelashes, her cheeks, tasting the salt on her fur.

"Yes, now!" She pulled away, keeping hold of his tunic. "It's important. It's raining, Ari. We can come back later for our things. *Please—*"

The rain had thudded so loudly on those vast expanses of grass. You could see nothing in those storms. You could hardly breathe. It was like a warm perforated sea.

And there were the jungles. Arity had never been there, but he had heard countless accounts of them, as everyone in the civilized lands had. Steamy green labyrinths that never turned brown, even in the depths of winter. Crystalline streams trickling by knotted tree roots, and moss monkeys kneeling on their banks, chattering. The tree cats never came down from the tree cover. They drank from the hollows high up, where the rain collected.

Humi launched herself forward again and wrapped around Arity like a skinny little beast. She was almost warm all over now, except for the ends of her fingers and her knees. "It's coming back, Ari. I don't know exactly what it is, but I think maybe it's what I felt, all those awful nights in Hem's house in Temeriton—before the war got in the way—the stuff of my dreams of you. But it's so—so tenuous—I don't want to lose it—I think—I think if we go *now*, I might be able to love you again—"

I might be able to love you again.

"Hold on," he said. He wrapped his arms securely around her and stepped off the edge of the cliff.

The air screams past their ears. They tumble with their fingers locked in each other's clothing, curving farther and farther from the gray rock. Her mouth stretches in a soundless scream. Their wet clothes clap loudly.

Falling

Into the red blackness where there are no heartbeats, no noise, no air, where it is like being underwater in a sea the consistency of sand.

IN HUMAN COUNTRY

Humi wore the heat like a second coat of fur now. The damp tepid air; the daily rainstorms; the rare, freezing winds that blew at high speed through the forest, tearing leaves and branches and small animals from the trees, leaving great gaps in the tree cover, disarranging, destroying, *cleansing*. She loved them. The currents in the air, the wafts of sweet and sharp and disgusting scents, the prickle of dead twigs and the squish of ground-runner liana under her feet as she walked. These were her world.

But it had taken her much longer than she had anticipated to get used to them. For at least a month, she and Arity had been absolutely miserable. They had caught a southern chill and spent days stretched coughing by the side of a stream. Finally they had realized that the atmosphere in the forest was too strong for them. That was why nobody lived here. One day in twelve, on the average, they had to breathe fresh air. So they *teth¨d* to the pampas plains, where no mortal ever went except for the bands of blue-furred nomads. And field mice as big as her fist. Their flesh was tough but it had a subtle smoky flavor. Ari spitted them, and she cooked them over a fire, basting them with pijreed juice. They had to clear their blackened fire circle anew each visit, the grass invaded so fast. It was manual labor of a sheer relentlessness she had not experienced since the long-gone days in Beaulieu.

The wind blew constantly on the pampas, fresh and sweet. At night they had to cuddle together for warmth. Not that they wouldn't have slept curled together, anyhow. "But it *would* be nice to live like people instead of animals," Arity said wistfully.

In the vine-hung clearing which they had chosen for their own, deep in the forest, stood a one-room cabin they had built with their own four hands. They began to consider setting up a tent on the pampas, too, with materials they could obtain from the nomads.

Barter capital would not pose a problem. They could *teth* ˜ to any one of a number of places—Shulage province, Delta City, even Wind Gully Heaven—and whatever they wanted would be given to them.

But so far they had not gone back. Not even to get their things from Erene and Elicit's house.

No one knew they were here. Power knew what people thought.

Humi did not care.

It had been almost two years.

They lived on an *auchresh* schedule now, like the forest animals. To Humi, it made no difference: her ruined corneas perceived only a slightly redder darkness during the day than they did at night. And *wrchrethre* or not, Ari tangibly gained energy when the jungle was cool and the screams of the night monkeys echoed from tree to tree. So she was happy to go along with his wishes. She found it more difficult to get to sleep, true, when birds were singing outside the cabin and the sun fell on her back—in the clearing, the trees couldn't obstruct it, and she *felt* the rough-cut shape of the window Arity had chopped in the wall, hot on her fur—but she never told him. She liked to lie beside him when he was sleeping, anyhow. Times like this, right now. Honey bubbles of euphoria. Heaven in human country.

She curled inside a warm, gently pulsating envelope. The sun warmed her back and the heat that radiated off Arity's poor, scarred body warmed her breasts and stomach. She turned her face to him. With one finger she touched a budding thorn at his hairline. His thorns were so sensitive; she teased him about it!

He shuddered. She let her hand fall, and wriggled closer until their noses touched. He smelled of sweat and woodshavings. Covertly she shared his breath.

They shared everything. More often than not, she did not need to speak more than one word for him to know what she meant, and the same went for him.

Not that they no longer talked. Almost every night after supper, as dawn drew near and the forest quieted, they held long, rambling conversations. They talked of grudges and murders and pederasty and poisonings. Dark and unpleasant, but comfortingly familiar. If they were in the pampas, Humi felt glad she could not *see* the vast, rustling darkness outside the circle of their fire. Ari could keep watch for both of them.

But of course, to him, night was not dark. The pampas was a rippling, endlessly shaded chiaroscuro of starlight. Once, he had described to her how he could *see* the breeze sweeping across the grass, the glider bats riding on the breast of the wind like gulls riding the sea. It had made her want to claw her useless eyes out of her head.

Quite often, now, she grew frustrated enough with her own particular darkness to weep. It usually happened on her rare escapades into day-light—her indulgences in mortality. When she was with Ari they were not woman and *auchresh*, but differently evolved beings, the only two of a race of their own: forest dwellers, hunters, gatherers; Charity and Humility. But sometimes she needed to be alone. And then, when she sat by the side of a brook in broad day with her tiger spear beside her, her toes in the warm water, or when she roosted in the crutch of a tree, the bark dust tickling her nostrils, the tears came. She had no more control over them than she did over the running brook. She was reminded of those nights in Hem's house when she cried uncontrollably, confused by a weakness she had not sus-pected in herself.

Then, she had thought she was crying for Ari. Now—

Thani was dead. Pati was dead. Hope was presumably far gone on her quest for humanity. Sol, Humi only remembered in the same vague night-marish way one remembers a fever. There would not be another end to her and Arity's togetherness.

Then what was she crying for?

Ari always knew after it happened, and he took special care to make absurd jokes, or tickle her, or surprise her—anything to get her laughing. That was when she loved him most of all. No. Most of all were the times *she* found *him* alone, when he said he was going hunting, or woodcutting, and she (sitting outside the cabin plaiting lianas, or pounding leaves for cloth) lifted her head with a sudden knowledge that he was just standing there, somewhere deep in the forest, gazing into the greenness. She had not his self-control. She would drop whatever she was doing and run to find him, and seize both his hands and kiss that strange, dazed expression off his face. That look . . . ! She could picture it so clearly it was almost as if she had *seen* it.

She still thought in terms of images. Even though she had not made a ghost in well over a year, that tendency of the visual artist was embedded in her. But at least she was no longer stuck in a world she could not see. She had developed a sort of sixth sense, a forest sense that let her walk through the undergrowth at a normal pace, putting a hand up to ward off branches just before they caught her in the face. When she heard a wild pig in the brush, she could spit it cleanly through the eye with her tiger spear before it even attacked.

Nostalgia, crying fits, fresh tropical fruit, the best water she had ever tasted, long lazy days making love and dozing.

Was this what she had yearned for, all those dark days in Temeriton?

* * *

She thought of the last, miserable days at Erene and Elicit's when everyone had been so kind to her. She had not really wanted anything at all, then. So cloyingly kind they had been. Tiptoeing around her with soft-shod feet, touching her with careful hands, trying to make her feel at home with "*imrchu*" and "my little Humi"! And it was all wrong. She had scarcely been able to think for disappointment. But she had known it wasn't what she wanted.

They were still *afraid* of her.

All she wanted was to be with *him*, to talk with him, to sleep curled up with him, to char to ashes with him if that was what it came down to.

In that last half a minute, she had been pretty sure that was what it *had* come down to. On the top of the cliff in Pirady, as it started to rain, she had forced herself to say what she meant. She had torn down the walls of stone around herself by force, and clutched him with her bleeding hands. And it had somehow been too much. He meant to kill them both. She had pushed him quite literally over the edge.

There was nothing she could do about it, and she didn't care. As they hurtled downward, doubling their speed by the split second, and the air whistled around them, cold and hard as a stone tube, they were *together*. The whistling vacuum stre-e-e-etched into a long, freezing silence and she heard her scream die away.

She had time to think, exultantly: *How superb that it should end like this! It is like a flamen's precautionary tale: the wanton lovers, offenders against rectitude, falling to their deaths in each other's arms!*

The waves roared louder and louder. She was falling facedown. Tears streamed up over her temples. The surf breaking on the beach was much stormier than it had sounded from up above. Hungry, violent waves. She wouldn't have been surprised if they were twenty feet high.

And

then

———

Damp grass under her palms, and warmth. And heavy scented air filling her lungs like water.

"We can't stay here forever, you know," Arity said.

They were perched on their log-stump stools, warming their feet at a fire they didn't really need. In a baza tree at the edge of the clearing, a dawn-flute sang his piercing good-morning song. But for Arity and Humi, it was the end of a sweetly tiring night. They had decided to build their tent in the pampas without approaching the nomads; they had spent the day transporting piles of the huge, fibrous kibre leaves they used to make cloth to the campsite. Ari had had to do all the *tech¨tach ching;* Humi had only done the fetching and carrying. He was weary to the bone. *That* was why he had said something so unexpected.

But was it really unexpected? That strange little frown she sensed more and more often in his voice—

"We can't go on, and on, and on like this."

She moved to him and put her arm around his shoulders, stroking the packed muscle on his chest. "Of course we can't. But do we have to talk about it? I'd rather not."

He sighed, and shook his head. "Power," he said, admiringly, "you moved like a sighted person just then."

She knew her "forest sense" worked best when she wasn't concentrating on it. But she was flattered all the same. She smiled. "I can fake it well enough to fool everyone except myself!"

"And me."

"Mmm?"

"Everyone except me. You still wear the sapphire necklace with the ruby earrings."

"They feel the same!" She laughed. "And does it really matter what color they are, when I'm wearing them both with dresses made of *leaves?*"

"They're very nice leaf dresses. Especially the patchwork one. Our *er-serbalu* would be envious. I wish you'd make me a tunic like that."

"Make it yourself!" She nudged him.

He pretended to think about it. "Only if you kill that tiger that's been leaving tracks over by the Chrume"—this was the title they had bestowed on the largest of the local trickles—"for me."

"Oh, you!" In fact it was quite possible that he would take it inot his head to make a tunic. He was nearly as proficient with a needle as she. It had rather surprised her when she first found out: he said he had had to learn, in Rimmear. After she discovered *why* he had had to learn, she had worked extra hard at acquiring the *mainraui* skill of the spear, as a kind of compensation for the horrors he had put himself through in that shadowy *auchresh* city.

It had all been for her sake. If she ever felt herself getting annoyed with him, she convinced herself of that all over again.

He shifted in her arm, and she felt him grow serious. "But doesn't it make you want to find out if you really *could* fool someone who doesn't know you? Doesn't it make you want to go back to Delta City and try out your skills on the court? I'm sure Aneisneida has a fine new flock of courtiers and nobles scuttling around the palace district by now, plump and ready to be skewered."

"You aren't really suggesting it!"

He shrugged. "Am I?"

"You're assuming Delta City has grown soft in our absence," she pointed out. "I think that if those fat nobles exist, they probably have fangs that even you should take into account. Humans have learned two lessons they won't forget in a hurry."

"What are those, then?"

"Never trust an *auchresh*." She was warming to her subject. It was not exactly an unfamiliar one, although neither she nor Ari had ever placed themselves in the hypothetical picture before. "Of course, that doesn't mean there aren't any *auchresh* in positions of power. I should guess that whoever is left of the *ex-kervayim* has worked his way to the top, or close to it."

"And what's the other lesson?"

"Believe in *nothing*. In other words—never let your guard down."

He pulled her down beside him. She knelt up on the ground. The gathering dew soaked into the knees of her skirt—the old, tattered one she had brought from Pirady, her "work clothes." "We *auchresh* used to secretly worship your people for your ability to trust others. I shouldn't think even Lady Summer, Lord Nearecloud, and Lord Dagger can entirely purge themselves of that ability! There are some people who will be simply beyond suspicion—who will have been transformed into legend. And I'm not talking about the flamens, either. Or the apostates. I suspect *they* play a very active role in the court."

"Then who *are* you talking about?" she said, although she thought she knew.

"Us," he said, his mouth close to her ear, his voice intense. "They wouldn't be prepared for us."

"Ari!" She pulled away. "What are you thinking?" But the pictures had flashed through her mind, of course. The possibilities. The flattery and the delightful hypocrisy of politeness to a mortal enemy, and the far more visceral sense of triumph when someone creeps up behind you intending to stab you (it had happened to her twice during the war) and you let him get close, secretly tensing your muscles, and then whirl around and get him with the pearl-handled stiletto you keep in your bodice as a brooch before he gets you. Straight in through the eye. Spurt.

"Never," she said. "Never!"

"You've thought about it, though. Haven't you? I know you, my love."

She kissed him and pulled him to his feet. "You know me too well. You're really tired. We need to damp this fire and get to bed. And we should spend tomorrow on the pampas. We can work on the tent. Today was the first time in a couple of sixdays we've been out of the forest; I think it's getting to you."

"Do you still keep track of the sixdays?" he asked, slinging his arm around her waist. They padded barefoot toward the cabin. The grass licked her legs, a thousand sharp, wet little tongues. No matter how much they walked over it, it sprang back up every day.

"More or less."

"I have been, too, recently."

"Oh, don't say that. Stop it!" She spun around and threw herself against him. She clasped her hand over the back of his skull, burying her fingers in the soft curls. Their lips met. His hands worked down over her hips, squeezing her buttocks, and she slid her other hand inside his shirt, fingering the closed mouths of the scars on his back. Some of those were erogenous. What a bizarre and wonderful beast her lover was! She delighted in the streamlined shapes of his shoulder blades: she imagined baby wings folded wetly inside, stillborn.

His breathing quickened. His body heat increased. She felt her heart responding to the excitement, too, thud a *thud,* thud a *thud.* He probed her mouth rhythmically with his tongue. Pride in her new flesh, her repossessed curves, flickered through her. Power, how she loved satisfying him. She writhed against him, pushing her hips against the lump of his erection. They were exactly the same height. She had always liked that.

"*Irissu,*" he growled. "*Power—*" The flowers of human country scented his breath. Lilies of the valley, honeysuckle, roses. It was the scent of predators, of every last saltborn creature, no matter how mean or foul. It exuded through his very pores when he was most aroused. "Love. You," he whispered. "Love. You. Love. You."

Her lips were seared when he took his away. His hands left branded marks on her hips. The dawn air flowed down her throat like some freezing acid drink. "Come on!" He took her hand and pulled her across the clearing at a run.

CAST OF CHARACTERS

The Mortals

Humility "Humi" Garden	
Beauty "Beau" Garden	Her cousin
Faith Garden	Her Mother
Strength "Reng" Garden	Her father
Godsbrother Sensuality	A flamen
Mitigation "Miti"	His leman
Godsister Decisiveness	A flamen
Correction "Cor"	Her leman
Cheerfulness "Cheer" Larch	A beautician
Ministration "Ministra" Bareed	A couturier
Godsbrother Puritanism	A flamen councillor
Auspice "Auspi"	His leman
Godsbrother Joyfulness	A flamen councillor
Flexibility "Lexi"	His leman
Belstem Summer	A lord councillor
Aneisneida Summer	His daughter, also a councillor
Goquisite Ankh	A lady councillor
Marasthizinith Crane	A lady councillor

Pietimazar Seaade	A lord councillor
Serenity "Erene" Gentle	Senior ghostier and councillor
Fragility "Fra" Canyonade	Master ghostier and councillor
Felicitous "Elicit" Paean	Master ghostier and councillor
Nostalgia "Algia" Cattail	His older apprentice
Eternelpizaran "Eterni"	His younger apprentice
Memory "Mory" Carmine	Master ghostier and councillor
Trisizim Sepal	her apprentice
Obeisance "Beisa" Thunder	Master ghostier and councillor
Solemnity "Sol" Southwind	Her apprentice
Solemnity "Emmi" Southwind	Her other apprentice
Ziniquel Sevenash	Master ghostier and councillor
Purtiansim "Rita" Porphyry	Master ghostier and councillor
Owen Phyllose	Her apprentice
Afet Merisand	A porter
Mell	Of Djanneh, Calvary
Soulfulness "Soulf"	Of Marshtown
Exhilaration "Xhil"	Her husband
Hem Lakestone	A shopkeeper
Pleasantry "Leasa" Lakestone	His wife
Sensitivity "Ensi"	Their daughter
Merit "Meri"	Their son
Godsbrother Transcendence	A flamen
Thankfulness "Thani" Garden	His leman

The Gods

Golden Antelope	The Divinarch
Charity "Arity"	The Heir
Hope	The Maiden
Broken Bird	The Mother
Patience "Pati"	The Striver
Bronze Water	The Sage

Valor "Val"	A Divine Guard
Glass Mountain	A Divine Guard
Sepai	A Divine Guard

Sweet Mouse-eater	*Serbalu* of Wind Gully Heaven
Wrought Leaf	*O-serbalu* of Wind Gully Heaven
Flowering Crevice	Of Wind Gully Heaven

Sundry family members, ghosts, servants and gods

AUCHRAUG
The Language of the Gods
A Brief Glossary

ae(s) of (pl.)

auchresh sing. or pl.: intelligent beings born in the salt, colloquially known as "gods"

auchraug the language of the *auchresh*

be¨leth drum traditionally used or dance rhythms

breideim older siblings (connotes respect)

cujali any *auchresh* (a Foundling, *irissi, ghauthiji*, etc.) attached to the *auchresh* in question

denear money (sing. or pl.)

Eithilindre Iceland

elpechim close friends—lovers or not

er- prefix: supreme, over

escorets deer-like salt beasts

fashir v., to force, to compel, to order

Fewarauw Pirady

firchresi younger brother (term of endearment)

firi younger brother (impersonal)

ghauthijim casual lovers

ghauthi kere prostitute (always male in the Heavens)

gherry traditional Kithrilindic drink of a red color and bitter flavor, served hot

graumir v., to go, to leave

haugthirre adj., throwback
haugthule predator
hymanni adj., mortal
hymannim mortals
imrchim ghostiers (occasionally applied to *auchresh* with living arrange-
    ment similar to those at Tellury Crescent)
irissim two bound together as closely as possible, almost always lovers
iu n., female (also connotes high status
iye no
kere n., male (pl. = *keres*)
kervayim, lesh the cabal
khath clear Uarechi alcoholic drink
kiru iu n. lesbian
Kithrilindu Royalland
kuiros strong-man, criminal (pl. = *kuirim*)
le(sh) the (pl.)
mainrauim hunters, gatherers, suppliers
nem us
o- prefix:– below, nearly
perich¨hi term of respect used toward an *auchresh* of higher status
Rimmear largest Heaven in Uarech
ruthyalim people of one's own Heaven
saduim business partners
serbalim leaders, usually of a Heaven
skri Fewarauwan alcoholic drink
teth¨tach ching instantaneous travel
tith¨ahim one not personally known to the speaker, of a different Heaven
triccilim menial servants
Uarech Calvary
urthriccim slender tentacles that look like hair
wrchrethrim the corrupted ones
wrchrethre adj., corrupted
wrillim earrings
Writh aes Haraules Sea of Storms